PRAISE FOR MARK OF THE LEAST

"A wildly original and magical twist on the Robin Hood narrative, Kendra Merritt's *By Wingéd Chair* is packed to the spokes with complex characters, wry humor, and flawless world building."

-Darby Karchut, best-selling author of DEL TORO MOON and FINN FINNEGAN

"With a wonderfully crafted blend of swords and sorcery and characters based on Robin Hood, Merritt tops this story off with the lead character readers need nowadays; a strong, independent, powerful female mage who also happens to be in a wheelchair. Readers will be constantly turning pages to see what happens next to this fun group of characters through the twists and turns they won't see coming."

-The Booklife Prize

"Kendra Merritt's prose is fresh, with one-line descriptions that crack like a whip, and she doesn't miss an opportunity to surprise the reader. From the first line to the last, I was enchanted with *By Wingéd Chair*."

-Todd Fahnestock, best-selling author of FAIRMIST and THE WISHING WORLD

ALSO BY KM MERRITT

Mishap's Heroes Series

Magic and Misrule

Death and Devotion

Trust and Treason

Illusions and Infamy

Sparks and Scales

Wastelands and War

Creation and Calamity

Mark of the Least Series

By Wingéd Chair

Skin Deep

Catching Cinders

Shroud for a Bride

A Matter of Blood

After the Darkness

The King in the Tower Collection

Unmasked

Daybreak Colony Duology

Surviving Daybreak

Daybreak Sentinel

Eldros Legacy

The Pain Bearer

The Truth Stealer

MISHAP'S HEROES

4

Illusions and Infamy

Whoever said you can't
go home again?

KM MERRITT

MISHAP'S HEROES

4

Illusions and Infamy

KM MERRITT

BLUE FYRE PRESS

For Kevin, Arielle, Lauren, and Dave. Thanks for the Restoration.

ONE

Vola was hip-deep in shit. Again. When all this was done, she'd be able to navigate Glenhaven's sewer system in her sleep. Although hopefully, the nightmares full of tight tunnels and muck-smeared walls would eventually fade.

"Vola," Lillie's lyrical voice said in Vola's ear even though she knew the wizard was several pipes over and well out of ear shot. "It's headed your way." The magic tickled and made the hair along the back of her neck stand up.

Vola resisted the urge to scratch. Not a good idea, considering the slick gunk between her fingers. "Thanks," she said.

"You're welcome," Lillie answered, perpetually polite, even in the middle of a sewer.

"You know we could just let it stay here," Sorrel's voice chimed in. "It couldn't have picked a better home for itself."

Lillie had managed to connect them all through the spell, making Vola feel pleasantly crowded even though she stood alone.

"It's terrorizing the people of Glenhaven," Talon grated from her place at the end of the trap. "And it's sort of our fault it's down here in the first place."

"Yeah," Vola added. "Only leave out the sort of, and you've got it right. Besides, Rilla wants this done."

And when your employer said get it done, you got it done. Especially when said employer was the princess of the Dagger Throne.

Vola ducked so she had enough room to draw her sword and shield in the tight space of the tunnel, and she planted her feet. She braced herself, head cocked, listening for the scrape of broad, blunt claws on tile. That was another sound she was likely to hear in her dreams for months to come.

There. A swish and a scrape. Then a blast echoed down the tunnel as the monster encountered Lillie's trap, and a wash of hot air made Vola hold her breath. Shit didn't smell good in the first place. Lighting it on fire didn't make anything better.

The creature they hunted screamed, its rage bouncing down the tiles, and suddenly the sounds of splashing came toward Vola.

Her grip tightened on the hilt of her sword, her sweaty palms creaking against the wrapped leather.

At the end of the tunnel, a squealing, rushing whirlwind of scales and spit and spite appeared and careened down the tile. The creature's evil eyes narrowed when it saw Vola.

"Not this way, beast," Vola muttered and swung her sword to deter the swamp monster from charging through her into the rest of the sewer system where it would disappear like soap in water. It had done it multiple times in the last two weeks.

The swamp monster had learned some new tricks in its time underground, though, and instead of trying to charge through a fully armed and armored paladin, it sped up the side of the tunnel and used its speed and claws to scrabble along the ceiling.

"Uh oh," Vola muttered. "I didn't know it could do that."

"What? What can it do?" Sorrel's voice asked anxiously in her ear. Apparently, the spell connecting them all was still active.

Vola swung at the monster as it sped past her, but it spat greenish mucus at her, making her duck. The wad of spit hissed where it landed.

"Vola?" Lillie's voice asked. "Vola, please check in. What's going on?"

Vola growled and stepped back to sling her shield toward the monster, who squealed with glee as it escaped down the wrong tunnel.

Her shield flew true down the pipe and struck the beast hard enough to knock it from the ceiling.

Vola leaped on it, arms splayed, and wrestled the creature around, twisting to avoid the razored teeth that tried to snatch at her limbs. Its slimy crest trembled, and its nostrils flares as its jaw snapped just inches from Vola's face.

Red crept into the edges of Vola's vision, and a surge of heat rose in her chest.

No. No, she refused to lose control here in a sewer. She was more likely to beat this foul creature into a nasty red paste than actually capture it that way. And they needed to get this done right. If only to earn Rilla's goodwill again. The princess of the Dagger Throne was still unhappy about the mistakes they'd made during the palace coup three weeks before. And Vola didn't blame her. One of the princess's people had died, and Vola was indirectly responsible.

But the only thing she could do about that was prove to Rilla that they were still competent. Still the best at their jobs. And that Vola wasn't going to be caught unprepared again.

With a mental shrug, she thrust away the rage swelling inside her and yanked the swamp beast around, then released it back down the tunnel the way it had come.

It scrambled away from Vola, but before it could escape deeper into the sewers, a figure appeared and wove a net of green light across the main tunnel.

The swamp beast hissed and ducked down the only way left to it, the side passage Vola had been stationed to herd it into in the first place.

"Great timing," Vola said as Rilla strode down the tunnel.

The muck didn't dare cling to the princess's dark clothes, and she was short enough she didn't have to stoop to keep her curly hair from brushing the ceiling. She managed to look sleek and perfect even in the bowels of the city.

The princess didn't answer, only extended a hand with a frown.

Vola winced and used the hand to help herself up out of the shit. "Talon," Vola said, knowing the others were still listening. "The plan's working. It's headed your way. Costa, we're ready."

"Ready for a shit storm?" a gleeful voice rang in Vola's ear. "No one's ever ready for a shit storm. Hold on for your lives."

Vola and Rilla stepped back from the opening as a foul-smelling whoosh rushed down the passage where the swamp monster had disappeared. A wave of sewage blasted past their opening, carrying an angry scaled creature with it. The noise drowned out its scream

Vola and Rilla pressed themselves against the wall and turned their faces away, waiting for a count of twenty before the roar gradually decreased to a rush and then a trickle.

As the unholy flood subsided, Vola ducked to retrieve her sword and double-checked her shield for damage. The round buckler was as dented and scarred as always but she was pretty sure those had all been there before. The vicious slash mark where Henri had defended them against an acid-throwing swamp flower had faded some, but the metal around it was still bright.

"Let's move," Rilla said. "Make sure it ended up where it was supposed to."

Vola settled her sword and shield on her back again as Rilla took point, slinking down the tunnel, her knives drawn. There wasn't anything to fight anymore, though. Costa's sewage tidal wave had swept everything downstream.

They'd picked this particular pipe for a reason. It wasn't very long, and it ended abruptly in an opening that dumped out into Costa's home turf.

Rilla and Vola stepped out into the light at the edge of the pipe and squinted at the scene. The afternoon sun glinted from three large tanks angled directly underneath them. The closest was filled to the brim with a greenish brownish sludge that surged and lapped against the edges. Magic swirled across the surface, making the liquid ripple and glint.

Costa's sewage treatment facility was tucked into a cove at the bottom of the city, just out of sight from its gleaming walls. This was where her power removed disease and debris from the city's water and recirculated it back up through the tiers in clean pipes.

The swamp monster thrashed in the center of the tank, Costa's power holding it trapped in the liquid. Vola blew out a breath, half relieved and half disgusted. She'd really hoped to be rid of it this time, but at least now it wasn't terrorizing anyone else.

Across the way, Talon slipped into the sludge to wade toward the beast. She'd left her enveloping hood at the edge of the tank, guarded by Gruff, the big black wolf. It meant Vola could see her grimace from here.

"Hah hah," a voice called. "It worked."

Costa stood at the edge of the tank, hands on her hips. The princess of sewage management wore a pair of thick gaiters and goggles. Vola glanced down at her soaked and smeared armor. Gaiters probably wouldn't have worked anyway, even if she'd asked for them this morning. They'd been climbing around in the sewers for weeks hunting down the swamp monster.

At first, it had seemed like a simple job. The creature couldn't possibly have wanted to stay in the sewers. But after days and days of filth and close calls, Vola and the others had finally settled in for the long haul.

Hopefully, it paid well enough to buy them all new clothes. Even after multiple baths, Vola still noticed people hurrying to the other side of the street as they passed.

There was a pop, and Lillie appeared beside them.

"Would you like a ride out of this pipe?" she said. And before they could answer, she'd tucked her hand in Rilla's arm, and the two disappeared only to reappear beside Costa. Sorrel danced around the edge of the tank, small feet sure on the narrow surface. The halfling sang a little ditty at the top of her lungs.

> *"There once was a swamp beast from Water's Edge,*
> *Who had some very sharp teeth in its head.*
> *It evaded the law,*
> *It was ugly and flawed,*
> *Now its evil butt will be put to bed."*

"That was terrible," Talon said, halfway across the tank with the swamp beast.

"Thanks," Sorrel said and did a little spin before bowing.

Vola jumped as Lillie appeared beside her in the pipe again.

Lillie cocked her head and smiled. She tucked her hand in Vola's elbow. "You didn't think I'd forget you, did you?"

The spell pulled them into the air, and for a second, it felt to Vola as if every piece of her had been scattered to the four corners of the world. It only lasted a moment, and then the two of them were standing with the others at the edge of the tank, watching Talon coax the swamp beast back to dry land.

"I guess that teleportation spell is really coming in handy," Vola said, taking some deep breaths. She hated that method of travel already, but she didn't have the heart to tell Lillie.

Sorrel gave Talon a hand up out of the tank, and Vola moved to take the lead rope and tug the swamp monster up, too.

It scrambled up onto the ledge and pulled its lips back to bare its teeth at Vola.

"Careful," Talon said, shaking out her arms. "I think it's more ill-tempered than usual."

"Well, it did just spend three weeks as the god of Glenhaven's sewer system." Sorrel cocked her head to study the creature. It looked like a cross between a crocodile and a donkey with a head cold. "It's probably not ready to live among mere mortals again, yet."

"You'd think it would appreciate the fresh air," Lillie said. "I know I do."

"Yay, no more sewers," Sorrel said, throwing her hands in the air. "I'll be happy if I never have to see another toilet again."

Talon made a face. "I don't think that means what you think it means. You seem to like plumbing well enough."

"From the outside, yes," Sorrel said. "I'd rather leave the insides to the experts." She waved a hand toward Costa, who examined the pipes where they'd reappeared.

"I think that's why the Sewage Management Throne chose me," she said without looking up. "I really like the insides of things. Well, most things. Not people. I'll leave that one to the Health Throne." She straightened and pushed her goggles up until they perched on her head, leaving red rings around her eyes. "We managed not to break anything in this whole mess. Well done. Well done indeed. What do you intend to do with it now?" She squinted at the swamp monster.

Sorrel sighed. "What we always do. Drag it along with us until hopefully one of our adventures finally kills it for real."

Vola kicked her.

"Ouch," Sorrel said. "What was that for? I know you're all thinking it."

"Yes, but none of us were so uncouth as to say it," Lillie pointed out. "It is a living, feeling creature...I think. And it deserves some modicum of respect—"

The swamp monster reached out and tried to take a bite out of the wizard.

Lillie yelped and teleported behind Vola. She leaned out to glare at the creature. "Although, Costa, you did mention wanting to dissect it. Are you still interested in some research?"

"I'm always interested in some research. I'd especially like to know how it survived down there for so long. I'll take it off your hands. You guys deserve a celebration. Dinner. At the nicest restaurant in the city. I'll pay." She wrinkled her nose. "After we've all changed, of course."

She turned with a raised eyebrow to Rilla, who had stood uncharacteristically silent since they'd emerged into the fresh air.

Vola raised her chin and met their employer's eyes hopefully.

"Good work," Rilla said, almost as if it pained her. Then the princess of the Dagger Throne spun to follow Costa back into the city.

Vola's shoulders slumped. Apparently, they'd need to work harder to make up for their mistakes.

TWO

A COUPLE of hours and several baths later, they headed up the stairs to one of the city's highest tiers. Built into a cliff, the city of Glenhaven rose level after level and ended in the palace where the princesses ruled over Southglen from the fifteen Thrones.

Just one tier down from the palace, they found the fanciest restaurant Vola had ever seen. It perched on the very edge of the terrace, looking out over the plains where several canals cut across, forming diamond patterns up to the foot of the city.

She sniffed her sleeve surreptitiously, making sure she didn't catch a whiff of the sewer. She'd left the armor back in their rooms and gone with a clean white dress. She didn't wear skirts often, but Lillie had picked this one out for her, and Vola liked the way the white made her look like an avenging angel.

Sorrel had traded her gray tunic and monk trousers for black, and Lillie wore a flowing blue gown. Talon had elected to wear a pair of trousers and a bodice that cinched at the waist giving the illusion of curves.

For once, they didn't get any odd looks from the restaurant patrons, and Vola's shoulders relaxed. A balmy breeze drifted through the wide windows, which hadn't bothered with the whole glass thing.

"Do you think the food's as good as the view?" Sorrel whispered as they stepped up to the podium just inside the door.

Lillie glanced at her. "You remember the party where we arrested Lord Tildon last month?"

"How could I forget?"

"This will be better than that," Lillie said.

Vola stepped up to the podium. "Excuse me, we're—"

"Mishap's Heroes," the man finished for her. He beamed. "Princess Costa made sure we were expecting you. Please, right this way."

"Well, he didn't barf, so the baths must have done the trick," Sorrel whispered.

Vola hissed at her and followed the man to a table set directly at the balcony railing.

Costa twiddled her fingers from the far side. She'd made a concession for the occasion and had ditched the gaiters for a wrap-around tunic in a subdued green. But there were still red marks under her eyes from the goggles.

No one around them seemed to notice her, completely oblivious to the fact that she was one of their most valuable princesses.

"You may order whatever you'd like," the waiter said quietly as they moved toward the table. "The princess has asked me to put everything on her tab."

He gave them a little bow and scuttled off.

"Wow," Sorrel said. "Fancy."

"I like this place," Costa said, picking up a menu. "It's classy without being overbearing. And you can't beat the view. What do you want to drink?"

"Tea, please," Vola said.

Costa snorted. "To celebrate?"

"Vola doesn't drink," Lillie said.

"And that's okay," Sorrel said, eying the menu.

Costa just blinked. "Fair enough."

"Where's Rilla?" Vola asked as the others fanned out, choosing their seats.

Costa winced. "She, uh…something came up. She decided to stay at the palace to handle it."

Vola mirrored her grimace. "Ah."

That could have been true. The princesses had a lot of clean up to do after the coup. And they had to track down whoever had been trying to steal the power from the Thrones and the bastard who'd managed to take over both Kellan and Finn.

But Vola had a feeling it was more personal than that. The princess distancing herself from a strike team that had let her down.

As Vola reached for the back of the last chair, another waiter appeared at her elbow, holding a polished silver tray.

"Knight Volagra Lightbringer?" he said.

She frowned. "Yes?" She wore her shield still, incongruous with the dress, but as a paladin, she was never without it. But that wouldn't have given the man her name, only her rank.

"This is for you." The waiter held out the tray. A pristine white envelope lay on the gleaming surface.

"Thank you." She took the envelope, and the waiter whisked away before she could ask him who it was from.

She squinted at the back and froze, the edges of the paper crumpling slightly in her tight fingers.

"Would you like me to read it for you?" Lillie asked quietly.

Vola shook her head even though she knew the letters would swim and squiggle. But she recognized the wax seal, and she didn't want anyone else reading something from the paladin council. She'd struggle through it herself if it killed her.

She broke the seal and pulled the paper from the envelope.

After a deep breath, she read,

Knight Paladin Lightbringer,

You will appear before the paladin council at the All-Virtue temple in Glenhaven immediately upon receipt to answer questions regarding your actions and those of your protégé during the palace coup in Glenhaven three weeks prior.

Knight Commander Imralen

"What's wrong?" Sorrel said, voice serious.

Vola shook herself and willed her heart to keep beating. She could deal with this. She'd known it was coming. That was why she'd sent Finn to Henri when she did. He was safe, and there was little the council could do to hurt him now.

"Nothing," Vola said, folding the page again.

"It's not nothing," Talon said. "We could all see your face."

"The paladin council wants to see me. Immediately."

Lillie bit her lip as Talon and Sorrel exchanged a look. "Because of what happened with Finn?" she said.

"Yeah." Vola rolled her shoulders and stood up straighter. "But I planned for this. They're here to punish me by taking Finn away. And they can't take him away if I don't have him, right?"

She tried for a smile, to reassure them, but they didn't buy it. She needed them to buy it. If they didn't think anything was wrong, then *she* could pretend nothing was wrong.

"I did it to protect him. There's nothing else they can do to us now," she said.

"What about something worse?" Lillie said.

Vola's teeth clenched. "Not without a full quorum, and they'll only send a representative here. I was never worth much to them. There's no way they'd get off their butts to bring the full weight of the council all the way out here, just for me."

"We'll come with you," Talon said, pushing her chair back.

Vola held out her hand. "No. This won't take long. Order me something nice, and I'll be back as soon as I've talked with the representative." She just hoped it wasn't the one that had followed her around Water's Edge. She could just imagine his smug smirk.

"I'm sorry, Your Highness." She bowed to Costa, who gave her a little nod.

Vola made her way through the tables and out into the night. She wished she still had her armor on, dirty as it was. It would have made her feel less vulnerable. Like she was convincing her friends just to convince herself.

The All-Virtue temple in Glenhaven was misnamed. The temple was only dedicated to the Greater Virtues. The Lesser Virtues had to make do with their own altars around the city, along with the Greater and Lesser Obstacles.

The temple sat smack in the middle of the city on one of the broad terraces that led to the higher tiers. Bright marble glinted in the last rays of the sun and metalwork shone from the big double doors. The portico soared above Vola's head, and as a half-orc, that was really saying something.

Vola strode up the steps of the temple and caught a couple of acolytes off guard. They jumped and clutched their brooms. Vola recognized the look well enough to know they had only registered her height and the green shade of her skin before bothering to look any closer.

She made sure to turn her shoulder, so the setting sun flashed from the mirror-bright surface of her shield, and the acolytes relaxed a fraction.

One of them nodded. "Paladin," he said. "They're waiting inside."

"Thank you," she said, shrugging off their initial response. It wasn't anything she hadn't seen before.

She stepped inside and was immediately plunged into dim light and cool air.

The temple stretched in a perfect immense circle under the soaring dome of the roof. The last bit of daylight speared down through an opening above them, lighting up the Greater Virtues in their alcoves set around the room. Maxim, god of strength and courage, Ona, goddess of honor, Bierhel, goddess of joy, and so on down the line until the pattern was paused. The Broken's statue was set apart from the others, cut off, and left dark in this particular temple.

Five figures stood in the direct center of the space, taking advantage of the last little bit of light in their gleaming mail and white surcoats.

Vola stiffened. This was not a representative or a committee. This was the entire paladin council, here in the flesh.

And everything about their choice of meeting place and their position under the dome was meant to intimidate her. Her own goddess, Cleavah, had no statue or altar here being one of the Lesser Virtues.

"Brace yourself," Cleavah's voice said, a tiny breath of wind in her ear.

Vola touched the emblem on her chest, seeking comfort. The miniature fish knife that hung from a chain pricked her finger.

The masters of the five paladin academies stared in stony silence.

She knew the one in the middle the best but refused to flinch as he stared at her with light gray eyes in a face as hard and smooth as granite. Knight Commander Imralen. Tall, noble, implacable, and the epitome of the old human men who ran the paladin academies. This one had been her own commander while she'd been training. And she'd thanked her goddess every day for a year when she was finally out from under his control.

The rest of them looked just as hard and unforgiving. They could give the statues behind them a run for their money.

Vola took a deep breath, reminding herself that Finn was out of their reach and she was a full paladin. She'd done everything she could to earn their respect, claiming her shield despite their opposition, and if they still hated her, there was nothing she could do about it.

It didn't make her feel any better.

But she could still beat them at her own game. She didn't just play the part of the faithful paladin. She'd lived and breathed it for years. She'd had to be the best just to survive, and she'd had to prove it over and over again. None of these men could say the same.

She stepped across the flagstones, her sandals making a shushing noise. She missed her armor. She hadn't expected to be facing down the full council in nothing but a dress, but at least she'd chosen white.

She halted ten paces from the council, held her fist to her breast, and bowed. Then she placed her sword and shield on the ground in front of her as tradition demanded and knelt on the chilly flagstones.

The council let the silence stretch an uncomfortable moment.

"Knight Volagra Lightbringer." Knight Commander Imralen's deep voice echoed in the vast space of the temple. "We've called you here to answer for your actions during the Glenhaven palace coup, three weeks past. As well as the actions of your protégé."

"Commander," Vola grated out. It wasn't a question, and she'd be damned if she answered it like one this early in the game. She met his gaze without flinching.

"You have been traveling as a full paladin for nearly two months now," the master on the far left said. "In the company of a group of adventurers you put together in Water's Edge. Correct?"

"Yes, sir," Vola said.

"And when you arrived in Glenhaven, you took in a boy to train. A human boy."

"Yes."

"You thought you were the best choice to teach him?" Imralen said.

Vola's teeth creaked as she clenched them. She inhaled through her nose and called up an image of Henri, short and stout, loyal and unruffled. The direct opposite of these lean, washed out men. Then she blew out her breath and unclenched her fists. "Yes, sir."

"You didn't think it would be best to send him to the academy?"

"I did not." She left it at that, refusing to say that she'd never send a vulnerable child into that nest of hate and vitriol.

"Your first mistake," Imralen said.

"It is allowed," Vola countered. "A knight may choose to train their own paladin candidate if they want. I broke no rules."

Imralen snorted through his nose, and the master directly on his right took up the thread. He seemed like a direct copy of the Knight Commander, the only difference being the cut of his hair.

"And by taking him in and agreeing to train him, you took full responsibility for him."

"I do," Vola said, deliberately using the present tense.

Imralen smiled like he'd caught a knight making a beginner's mistake. "Yes, and while under your care, this boy —"

"His name is Finn," Vola said.

"This Finn murdered an innocent."

Vola refused to flinch. "Finn was under someone else's control. An enemy capable of mind control used him."

"Which you could have prevented if you'd been paying attention."

Vola hung her head. She couldn't argue with that. It was the same thing she'd been telling herself for the past three weeks. It was the same reason Rilla was still upset. As much as she would love to blame the spell caster who'd hurt Finn, they'd had warning, and Vola had done nothing to protect him.

Imralen shook his head slowly, taking her silence for assent. "Volagra Lightbringer, as your protégé's protector and mentor, you were charged with his care. His actions are your actions. Therefore, his honor is your honor, and his crimes are your crimes."

Vola's head snapped up. It was no less than what she'd agreed to, but his choice of words was unsettling.

Imralen held her gaze as he brought out a sealed document and unrolled it in front of her. She couldn't have read it from this distance, even if the words didn't swim away from her.

"You are no longer Lightbringer. You took an oath as a paladin to uphold the law, to hold honor and virtue above all other worldly treasures, and to protect the innocent even unto giving your own life."

Vola held her breath as Imralen shook his head again. "Instead, you allowed an innocent life to be taken. You are a murderer."

"He was under a spell," Vola cried.

"And you were his protector." Imralen's gaze remained implacable. "You were his shield. Or would you like to renounce your duty to him?"

Vola snapped her mouth shut, the air hissing in and out through her nose. Never.

Seeing her answer in her eyes, Imralen raised his chin and delivered his final judgment. "By failing this duty, you have failed yourself and every other knight paladin to come before you. I name you Volagra Lightless. You are declared Oathbreaker, and from this day forth, all shall know you as faithless, without honor, and a danger to yourself and others."

The two masters on either side of Imralen reached to take her shield from where it rested on the flagstones in front of her.

Vola lurched to her feet, heart pounding loud enough it echoed in her ears. "No."

The remaining two masters stepped forward as if to restrain her, and Imralen smirked.

Vola realized this was exactly what they wanted. They needed her to fight; they needed her to turn violent. To prove their decision was the right one. To prove this half-orc should never have carried a shield in the first place. They'd been waiting for this opportunity since Henri had declared her a full paladin. They would use any show of opposition against her.

That was the only thing that stopped her from rushing them. From yanking her shield from their traitorous hands.

And she refused to dishonor Henri or Finn. She would not prove these men right.

That was the only thing that kept her spine straight as they took her shield. Imralen raised his hand, and holy fire spat forth to blacken and curl the bright shine and smooth edges of her shield. The soot and char creeping across the surface would never be polished away, no matter how much she scrubbed.

They tossed it back at her feet, stained and warped, and it gave a dull clank as it hit the flagstones.

Her breath came in short puffs as Imralen stepped close to her. Red licked the edges of her vision as he reached for Cleavah's emblem hanging around her neck.

"You can't take that," she growled, panic threading through her veins.

His lips curled, and he yanked the chain from her neck, severing her connection with her goddess in one short jerk. The presence that hovered at her shoulder like a nosy friend faded until she shivered in the encroaching cold.

"Without a god, you are not a paladin. Go, Volagra Lightless. You do not belong among us anymore."

THREE

THEY COULDN'T PHYSICALLY THROW her out of the temple. Not if she didn't want them to. She was still a fully trained half-orc even if they'd stripped her of her rank and her calling. But they did throw her blackened shield down the steps.

And she stumbled after it like a drunk, snatching it up off the pavement.

She'd worked too hard, and that one sheet of metal meant too much for her to just let it sit in the dirt. Not to mention oathbreakers were required to carry the evidence of their crimes to warn others of duplicity. And Vola was nothing if not a rule follower.

She staggered through the crowded streets, hugging the blackened shield to her chest. The sun had set, but the streets of Glenhaven were lit with bright lanterns and lamps of wizard's fire.

The lights and colors blurred as she wandered aimlessly, thought fragments flitting in and out of consciousness.

She ran into someone who turned to shout at her. But their gaze dropped to the black shield in her arms, and they gasped and skipped back. Vola didn't even register if they were human or not. Male or female.

As she walked, more pedestrians whispered and nodded to the shield, stepping back or retreating out of her way.

Having green skin and tusks had always been bad enough. Orcs were already seen as violent and untrustworthy. But everyone knew what a blackened shield signified. Everyone knew it marked her as a paladin who hadn't kept her oaths.

Oathbreaker. Dishonored. Lightless.

Vola ducked her chin and ran. The streets in front of her miraculously cleared as she sprinted, escaping the looks and the gasps by the simple expedient of outrunning them. Blood beat in her ears, and her fingers ached where they clenched the edges of the shield.

The inn where Rilla had put them up was only one tier down, and she headed straight for their rooms. She slammed the door behind her, dropped the shield with a clatter in the corner, and then braced her hands against the wall, breathing heavily. Air raced in and out of her lungs, uneven and uncontrollable.

The room spun around her, and she swallowed hard to keep from barfing.

Silence pressed on her ears so she could only hear the harsh edges of her breath. The room stood empty behind her.

The others must not have returned from dinner yet. That was good.

She had no idea how to tell them.

She blinked, and the blackened face of her shield caught the soft flicker of lamplight. She squeezed her eyes shut again.

She had no idea what to *do*.

She raised her hand in front of her face, half-expecting it to waver and fade from view as if she wasn't anchored to this world anymore. She didn't feel anchored. Maybe if she just let go of the wall, she'd float away.

She should try it. Float and never come back.

A picture of Henri flashed in front of her, and his voice spoke in her ear. "Try again, Vola."

Vola flinched. But her hands stayed firm against the wall, fingertips pressed to the wood. And eventually, her breathing slowed, the sharp heaves of her chest evening out.

She had to face this. Had to think about it. She'd never run from a fight in her life and this was no different. A fight in her own head, but a fight nonetheless.

She forced her eyes open and stared down at the blackened shield. Henri's shield. Broken for her mistake. Gods, what would he say if he could see it now?

She swallowed.

She'd been so wrong. She thought she was protecting Finn, but the council had used that against her. They'd used it to finally get her where they wanted her. On the wrong end of their judgment.

But it wasn't like she could have done anything differently. Except not make the mistake in the first place. That, at least, they'd been right about.

The council hadn't just taken away her profession. They'd taken away who she was. Volagra Lightbringer was a paladin. A knight. A protector of the weak and defender of right.

Who was Volagra Lightless? Who was she if she wasn't a paladin?

So much of her life she'd spent focused on her shield. Either earning it or using it. She'd been fourteen the last time she remembered having a goal in her head that didn't have something to do with that symbol of everything she loved and honored in the world.

Even the last few months had revolved around using that shield to protect her party. How was she supposed to protect them if she didn't have it anymore?

She managed to turn, to thunk her head back against the wall, and shut her eyes.

Lillie rinsed her hair with rose water every other day, and the scent pervaded everything. Talon's leather and Sorrel's sweaty sandals all smelled like roses. It made Vola's nose itch and her eyes water.

They'd be affected by this, too. Their honor was bound up in hers, and they'd be as blacklisted as she was. Every job they took from now on, every town they visited, or villager they talked to would look at Talon, Lillie, and Sorrel the same way they looked at Vola.

And Rilla was already angry with her. What would the princess of the Dagger Throne do when she learned that the paladin council no longer endorsed the leader of her strike team?

Vola knew.

The only good thing in all of this was that Finn was far away. He didn't know what he'd done; he didn't know what Vola had done to keep him safe. And he didn't have to know. Ever. Henri was wise enough to keep it from him indefinitely. Or at least until the boy was old enough to take it in, understand what had happened to him, and use it as a strength.

But she would never be able to keep this from her party. The evidence lay at her feet, and she wouldn't lie to them anyway.

And the princess of the Dagger Throne would find out sooner or later. It was her job, and she was good at it. As the kingdom's spymaster, she'd have the information on Vola's disgrace faster than anyone else. If the paladin council hadn't sent it to her directly already.

Vola rubbed her face. She knew what she had to do. The one last thing she could do to protect those she'd sworn to protect.

She just didn't want to do it.

She dropped her hands from her face and finally forced herself to look around the room. Sorrel's things were strewn across her bed, the black underwear she'd thought so scandalous draped across the bedframe, a book on Jodin Battlecalled, the hero of her order, open on the pillow.

Talon didn't own very much. But her quiver and bow stood propped in the corner, and the oil she used to soften her leather was open on the bedside table, and the robe Lillie had given her was flung across the end of the mattress.

As usual, Lillie had piles of books all over her side of the room. She'd acquired more since they'd gotten to the city, or they were spawning somehow and creating little booklets to carry on their legacy.

Vola rubbed her chest where a dull ache had grown into a piercing pain. She hadn't known them that long, but they were each as dear to her as the shield had been.

Which was why she had to leave. It was the only way to keep them from being pulled down with her. Her disgrace would not ruin them if she had any say in the matter.

And if she was a little honest with herself, she thought as she stepped across the room to rummage in Lillie's things for a pen and some paper, she couldn't bear the thought of facing them holding a blackened shield.

She couldn't tell them the story. And she couldn't accept the comfort that would come after.

No, this was best.

Her handwriting was spiky and wavering since the letters didn't want to sit still in her head, but she trusted Lillie to be able to decipher it.

She placed one note on the mantle where the others would be sure to find it.

The other she slipped under Rilla's door.

Then Vola left Glenhaven, taking the evidence of her disgrace with her.

FOUR

Sunshine didn't have any right looking that cheerful, Vola thought as the line of warm light passing through the breezy curtains crept down her pillow. Vola had played a game with it every morning for the last couple of months, seeing how long she could lay there before it stabbed her in the eyes and forced her to move.

Her record was nothing. Nothing, because who cared about stupid sunshine.

"Vola!" a high voice sang from downstairs. "Time to wake up! I've made your favorite."

Vola let out a great gusting sigh and threw the covers back to push herself up. She was already fully dressed in a loose linen shirt and a pair of patched trousers. She'd been dressed since she'd woken up before the sun rose, but certain people noticed when you didn't sleep. And sighed all the time. And then certain people started whispering things like "moping all day" and "is she going to live upstairs forever, now?"

She thumped down the narrow stairs making as much noise as she could. The first morning she'd been home, she'd caught those certain people in a very awkward position on the kitchen table, so it paid to act louder than she actually was.

Gauzy curtains hung in the open window, shifting in the pleasant breeze. A curvy figure knelt before the oven, humming a war hymn under her breath as she yanked a tray of muffins from the beating warmth.

"Good morning, sweetie," Vola's mother said, turning to slide the hot tin onto the table. Then she stood on tiptoe to kiss Vola's cheek. "You dressed quickly."

Vola glanced at Lydia's own attire with a raised eyebrow. "And you're not dressed at all, apparently."

Lydia frowned down at herself. "What are you talking about? This is my best armor. If any marauders come to raid the village, I'll be all ready."

"Mom," Vola said, rolling her eyes. "It's a leather bikini. No one in the world would call that armor."

Her mother twisted to examine her butt, which was barely contained by the material. Two strips of fabric hung in the front and the back, giving the barest illusion of a skirt. But the cleavage was a little much.

Vola's father glanced around the edge of his newspaper, tiny glasses perched on the end of his bulbous green nose. "I like it."

"Your opinion doesn't count in this case," Vola said and pulled a chair out from the table. There was still a gouge on this side from Vola's first run-in with a murderous gnome. "Mom, that outfit wouldn't protect you from anything. You can't claim to be wearing armor if I can see more skin than leather."

Lydia planted her hands on her hips. "I'll have you know, this armor got me through the Battle of Verha-Kah."

"Ooh, that was a good one," Gorgo said, folding his paper. He at least wore a robe over his bare chest and a fur-lined loin cloth. "You were conceived on that battlefield, Volly."

Vola made a gagging sound.

Lydia tossed her curly mass of red hair over a burnished bronze shoulder. "Barbarians survive by being tougher than the thing trying to hit them," she said. "I'd be a poor mercenary if I let the first little stab wound stop me."

Vola couldn't argue with the number of scars her mother carried. No one was tougher than Lydia Battlemane. She just wished her mom wouldn't flaunt them at the breakfast table.

"I suppose I could add some chain mail," Lydia said, glancing down at her cleavage cross-eyed. "A little here and there might be a nice accent. What do you think, Gor?"

Gorgo grunted and reached for a muffin.

Lydia slapped his hand. "Those are for Vola."

Gorgo thrust his lower lip out between his tusks. "What? All of them?"

"She's still growing."

Vola rolled her eyes again and grabbed a muffin. "If I grow anymore, it'll be sideways, and then I won't fit into *my* armor anymore." She tossed her father a muffin.

He caught it in one hand and winked at her before he pulled his wife down onto his massive lap. "I've got muffins enough here." He rubbed his bristly face against Lydia's neck.

Lydia squealed.

"Oh gods, I'll eat in my room." Vola pushed back from the table.

Lydia scrambled out of Gorgo's lap and slapped him on the shoulder before darting into the open doorway. "No, no, don't go. We'll stop. Your father's just a bit energetic in the mornings."

"That. That right there. These are things I don't want to know. I'm glad you two are still healthy and in love, but I do *not* need to know any more than that." Still Vola slumped back into her chair. It wasn't like she had anywhere else to go. And Lydia might be a head shorter than her and lithe as a spring sapling, but she could put Vola on the floor nine times out of ten as their daily workout sessions had proved.

After leaving at fourteen and earning her way into the paladin academy, Vola had never expected to move back in with her parents. But the little cottage in the middle of a human-orc farming community was the only place she could think of that didn't have any associations with the paladins or their council.

Vola fought down the feeling that she was running away and hiding from the problem. She wasn't. She was protecting what little she had left by making herself scarce. Of course, it was hard to convince herself of that.

"What's everyone doing today?" Lydia asked with a pointed look at Gorgo.

The orc chieftain cleared his throat and sat up. His robe had little yellow ducks and crossed spears embroidered all over it. He ran a broad hand through his shaggy black hair. More silver glinted in its strands than Vola remembered from when she was growing up.

"I've got clan council meetings all day," he said, taking his spectacles off and folding them nicely on his newspaper. "And I have to find time to corner the elders about the rogue orcs that keep leaving."

He glanced at Lydia, who sat with her back straight.

"I'm baking all morning. I was thinking a cake would go nice with dinner tonight. And this afternoon, I have a contract to clear the goblins out of Marin's cave."

She paused before she and Gorgo looked at Vola.

Vola stayed silent, picking her muffin into little bits and leaving crumbs all over the table.

Lydia cleared her throat. "You could come with me, sweetie. I could use an extra sword. And you can see if the mercenary life is appealing to you."

Vola's mouth twisted.

Gorgo banged his fist on the table, making them jump. "Well, you can't just sit around on the couch all day. So you got your shield taken away. So what? Pick yourself up and get back out there."

Lydia placed a hand over his. "What your father is trying to say is, we love you, Vola. And we will support whatever decision you make. Whatever you want to be, we will be behind you all the way. But you have to choose."

Vola stood and paced to the window where cheery yellow curtains framed a view of the kitchen garden. The turnips looked nearly ready, and the flowers along the edge flourished. Because her mom was good at everything, whether it was homemaking or bashing things on the head.

"I don't want to fight just for the sake of fighting," Vola said. "Taking meaningless contracts for the sake of some coin."

"Some coin is what you need to survive unless you plan on living in the attic till you die," her father said.

Lydia glared at him. "Which is perfectly okay, too."

Gorgo sighed and stood to stand next to Vola. "Or you could enlist. I hear the princesses are building up the army. You wouldn't have to show any credentials if you wanted to try being a foot soldier instead of an officer."

Vola hid a grimace. After commanding her own squad as an elite strike force for the princesses themselves, enlisting as a grunt sounded even worse than taking mercenary work.

"Or the local bar is looking for a good bouncer," Lydia said.

"What happened to Megan?" Gorgo asked.

"She took a sack full of rocks to the face. It's gonna take a while to find all her teeth."

Vola waved a hand, hoping to get them to stop. "I'm sorry. I didn't mean to dump my problems on you. I'm an adult. I have lots of skills. So why is it so hard to find a place for a godless paladin?"

She did her best to ignore the stab of pain that accompanied that thought. For the first time in years she was alone in her own head. The council had taken her emblem, her connection with Cleavah. None of the gods could talk directly to their followers without an emblem, let alone a Lesser Virtue.

Gorgo rolled his eyes. "It's not. We've given you lots of options. You're just too picky."

Vola glared at him.

"If being godless is the only problem, you could always join the Mulgash cult." He clapped her on the shoulder. They were almost the same height, but Gorgo had full orc blood running through his veins and the blow nearly staggered Vola. "I'm sure the orc god could use some more dedicated followers."

Vola gave him a slant-eyed look. "He's one of the Obstacles."

"So?" Gorgo shrugged. "Obstacles aren't evil. They just represent the darker reflections of Virtues. Rage, jealousy, cruelty. That sort of thing."

"And you don't see anything wrong with that?"

Gorgo held his hands up defensively. "Look, I don't follow him. Not religiously. I only go to services on High Holidays. But there are a lot of the clan who do, and they're decent, hard-working orcs."

Vola shook her head. "Mulgash represents rage. Which I've been trying to fight my entire life. I'm not going to forget about that just because someone took a torch to my shield."

Her father's thick brows drew down. "Why are you trying to fight your rage?" he said. "It's a part of your heritage. Are you saying you're trying not to be an orc?"

"I'm saying orcs are more than just their rage. I'm saying we're more than just thugs and fighters and barbarians. No offense, Mom."

Lydia's eyebrows rose. "Offense taken, I think."

Vola sighed. "Mulgash is one of those stereotypes that hurts how other people see orcs. They see us as violent. Untrustworthy. And that's not true. We can be whatever we want to be."

"Like a paladin," Lydia said quietly.

Vola deflated and collapsed at the table again. "Yeah. Like a paladin."

"I don't understand the difference between a paladin and a fighter," Gorgo said. "Why are you so determined to be this one thing when you can swing your sword at something and call yourself whatever the hell you want?"

"Because paladins are different. They choose to be different. And they're seen different. I want to change the way people see orcs. I want to change myself and prove that we can be something better."

"Better than an orc?" Lydia said.

"Yes. No." Vola ran her hands through her hair. "I don't know."

"Yoohoo," a voice called from the front door. Vola's Aunt Urag stuck her head in the cottage.

"Urag," Lydia said, standing and holding out her hands in relieved welcome.

"Hi. I'm not interrupting, am I? Oh, you're just eating. Muffins. Yum." Urag shuffled to the table and snagged a muffin from the tin. Her bristly white hair stood straight out from her head in a frizzy cloud. Vola figured she'd either been trying out her new homemade shampoo or she'd gotten in a fight with a lightning bolt. Knowing her aunt, it could have been either one.

"Did you need something, Urag?" Lydia said with a frown.

"Oh, just came by to say the wargles are back. Ate three patches of my potatoes this morning. I need someone to bash their heads while I blast them out of their cute little tunnels."

"I'll get my ax," Lydia said.

"No, Mom, I'll do it," Vola said, heading for the bench by the door where three pairs of boots waited. "I need to get out of the house, anyway."

"Well, I wasn't going to put it like that, but…" Lydia said.

But Vola had been spending way too much time moping. She needed to fight something she could see and touch and make bleed.

Gorgo sighed and gave her a look that said they weren't done talking. The orc chieftain hated talking about as much as Vola did, but in their thirty-year marriage, Lydia had finally ground it into him.

"I know, Dad," Vola grumbled. "Later, all right." It wasn't like she didn't know her life was going nowhere. But she needed time to pull herself out of the mire.

She pulled on her boots and yanked her sword from where it hung on a peg by the door before slinging it over her head. She hesitated, her gaze sliding to the blackened shield propped in the corner. She winced, then grabbed it and ducked out the door.

She could have just left it. It wasn't like anyone from the paladin council was going to stake out her little village in order to ensure she was following the rules. But carrying it was a little like poking a bruise. She needed to see if it still hurt.

Urag lived with most of the orc clan around the edges of the village. They'd lived in uneasy peace with the humans for as long as Vola had been alive at least, the villagers relying on the orcs to protect them from the frequent raiders off the coast, and the orcs depending on the villagers not turning on them all when there weren't any raiders.

Humans might have been squishy, but they outnumbered the orcs five to one.

Urag's cottage was neat and tidy and sat just off the main village path. The flowers tumbled over a little picket fence, so you hardly noticed the wargle blood painted along the fence in precise sigils meant to ward off disease and calamity.

Sure enough, big holes surrounded by freshly displaced dirt marred the perfection of the lawn. If Vola wasn't careful, she could break a leg in one of them.

Urag shuffled to the door where she'd left a crooked staff, bird feathers ruffling from the top. "Stupid wargles are upsetting the balance of my spring flowers," she muttered. "Time was I'd just blast them myself, but if I send fire into their tunnels, I'll char all my roots and have to start over."

Vola winced, strongly reminded for a moment of Lillie. Her aunt's hands were green and gnarled, but they wielded fire as deftly as the half-elf wizard had done.

"So, send water through," Vola said, drawing her sword and hunkering down beside one of the holes. "It'll flush out the wargles and water your garden at the same time.

Urag laid a finger alongside her nose and winked. "Good idea. Two birds," she said.

"Any reason you wouldn't want blood on the lawn?"

Urag shrugged. "Give em a good whack with your shield. Blunt force trauma is just as effective and won't make as much of a mess. Pieces of wargle are hard enough to clean out of your hair."

Urag knelt and conjured a jet of water into one tunnel opening. Across the lawn, a thirty-pound rat with sharpened incisors flew into the air with a squawk.

Vola darted forward and swung her sword around to smack the creature with the flat hard enough to send it into the opposite fence.

"That's it. Let's see if we can knock any into old Fustus's lawn. I haven't pissed him off in a full day."

Vola spent the morning running after overlarge flying rodents, trying to ignore the glee in her aunt's cackle. It was not fun. It was not full of glory. But it kept her moving. And distracted her from the way the future stretched wide open and empty.

By noon, Vola leaned against the fence, panting, her sweaty shirt stuck to her shoulders, blackened shield propped up at her feet.

"Wait there," Urag said. "That was a full day's work done in three hours. You deserve something for that. I've got some gold around here somewhere." She shuffled into the cottage, her bunny slippers adroitly missing a spray of wargle blood across the stoop.

Vola wiped her forehead as a snicker floated across the dirt path.

"Ugh, what smells?" a voice said.

Vola's chin snapped up. Three girls stood across the lane, willowy figures almost identical, their pale skin perfectly rosy from the sun. The only thing that differentiated them was the shade of their hair. One had a perfect mahogany, another had smooth waves of red, and the last had gold that shone in the sunlight.

The blonde girl met Vola's eyes. "Oh. I didn't realize how far we'd wandered."

Vola's teeth clenched and her lips thinned. She knew from experience it made her tusks stick out more, but she couldn't control the surge of heat that left her face burning in its wake.

She took a deep breath and reminded herself she wasn't twelve anymore. Ella Cormo had no power over her now.

Yeah, right.

"Volagra," Ella said in bright tones. "I didn't know you'd returned. How wonderful to see you."

Vola forced her jaw to unclench. "Ella," she said with a sharp nod. "Elsie, Ellen. I didn't know you still lived here."

"It's our home, silly," the brunette, Elsie, said. "Where else would we live?"

"Weren't you off at some academy?" Ellen, the redhead, said. At least Vola thought it was Ellen. She hadn't bothered keeping track of them in her head for years.

"I graduated," Vola said. "A while ago. Made full knight."

"Riiight," Ella said. "I did hear about that. Your parents were so proud. What was it you were calling yourself?"

Vola took a shuddering breath. "Lightbringer," she said, her voice only wobbling a little.

Ella tilted her head. "Yes, that was it. Only…I heard it was Lightless now." She tilted her head pointedly at the blackened shield at Vola's feet.

She cursed herself for bringing the damn thing with her.

"Oh," Elsie said. "I'm so sorry."

"At least you're home now," Ellen said.

"Yes. And you did get to pretend for a good long while. You even managed to fool those paladins into letting you be one of them for ages."

The girls laughed, identical voices tinkling against Vola's ears as red crept across her vision. The bones in her hands creaked as her fists clenched.

Nothing you say will make a difference to them, Vola told herself. *You can only make it worse. They've seen the shield. They know you were a real paladin. At least for a while. It doesn't matter.*

It. Does. Not. Matter.

"Feel free to join us for our knitting circle on the weekend, Volagra," Ella said as she minced away down the street. "Your hands are still too big for the needles, but you have loads of time to practice now."

Vola closed her eyes so she'd stop seeing red and concentrated on breathing. Deep breaths to ease the pain and the rage clawing their way up from her chest.

Someone cleared their throat behind her.

Vola opened her eyes and turned.

"Couldn't find any gold," Urag said. "Must have hidden it good enough to fool myself. But I have several charms here." She held up a fist. Five bits of wood and feathers dangled from leather strings. "They're worth a fair bit. You can keep them or sell them. Or you can shove them up Ella's ass."

That surprised a laugh out of Vola. "Thanks, Aunt Urag."

She took the charms and rubbed the back of her neck with her other hand. The rage still simmered under her skin, but there was nowhere to direct it. With no one to fight, she could only practice breathing until it went away.

"I need a job," she mumbled. "Need to be doing something." This wasn't a sprint. Hell, it wasn't even a marathon. This was her life now, and she needed to do something other than mope in her parents' attic.

"I hear they need a bouncer at Frog's Bottom," Aunt Urag said. "The pay isn't great, but there are perks."

"Like what?"

"All you can eat wargle ribs. And you get to bonk people on the head when they annoy you."

"That sounds about perfect, right now."

FIVE

VOLA SURVEYED the Frog's Bottom common room, gaze sweeping across the tables crowded with orcs, half-orcs, and the seedier humans from their little village.

Thorack, the largest of the orcs, and the one who gave her father the most trouble, eyed one of the humans and cracked his knuckles.

Vola caught his eye and scowled, folding her arms over her chest, so the leather across her shoulders creaked.

His eyes narrowed as he thought about giving her trouble, too, before he grumbled and settled back on his bench.

Vola sighed. She hated being a stereotype; the brute standing in the corner intimidating everyone else into behaving. But it was a job. And it got her out of the house and doing something. As long as she was moving, as long as she had something to do, she didn't have to spend any time thinking.

And she had a place to direct the rage.

It bothered her how often the red had tried to take her over recently. The rage that was so much a part of her heritage lived much closer to the surface these days, and if she didn't have a safe place to expel it, things got broken. Her mother had nearly kicked her out after the third shattered plate.

So now, Vola came here and knocked heads together whenever said heads got uppity.

The Frog's Bottom was the most peaceful place in the village now.

The door swung open with an enormous creak, and Vola's eyes were drawn to the three lithe figures standing in the doorway.

She sighed and said goodbye to the peace.

Ella, Elsie, and Ellen smirked at the crowd of orcs staring at them before sashaying up to the bar.

Vola wasn't the only one to sigh and shake her head. It wasn't exactly against the rules for the girls to be in here. But the orcs of the village tended to stay at the Frog's Bottom while the humans frequented the Lord's Purse down the lane. Everyone agreed without so many words that it was better that way. Less fights, fewer misunderstandings.

But there were *some* people who thought it was fun to step over that line for a night and walk on the orc side. And most of the orcs in here knew exactly what the girls were doing. And those who weren't quite as bright still knew that they were trouble.

Vola could have told them that years ago.

She could remember the exact twist of Ella's smile as she called Vola a monster and a halfbreed.

Vola couldn't believe there had been a time when she'd desperately wanted to be just like the blonde beauty.

She hoped she'd gotten over most of those hang-ups by now.

She kept her gaze on Ella and her friends as the girl accepted her drink from the surly bartender and sauntered over to a table in the back corner of the dim bar.

Oh, great. She couldn't believe it was an accident that Ella had chosen the spot. The table hosted one orc, Bothank, who dug in his nose with a finger and then examined his find like it might tell him the secrets of the universe.

Vola had spent most of her life trying to prove orcs weren't big dumb brutes, but even she had to admit there was a range of intelligence, just like humans. And Bothank sat at the very bottom.

Ella knew full well most of the orcs in here were wise to her game, so she'd picked the one most likely to think with his pants and not his...well, brain was a generous term when it came to Bothank.

The big orc, Thorack, saw the direction of Ella's attention and thunked his head on the table. But he didn't do anything to get up and stop her. Even though he'd been the one to whisper the rumors in Vola's ear.

Ella flirted with orcs. Ella lied to orcs, promising them love and all sorts of sweet things only big green men with soft hearts would believe.

And then she went crying to her father claiming they'd taken advantage of her and got them run out of town.

A fun game with only one winner.

Vola's lips pulled back from her tusks with a growl, and she pushed herself off the wall and headed for the back table where Ella was just pulling out a seat. Her friends watched avidly from the bar.

Vola tapped Ella's shoulder as her butt hit the chair.

"Ouch," Ella said and rubbed her shoulder before turning to look up at Vola. "You should trim your nails a little before you hurt someone."

"Stand up," Vola said. "You're not sitting here."

"What do you mean?" Ella said, blinking long eyelashes. "Of course I'm sitting here. Are you blind?"

"Are you deaf? I said, get up."

"No. I'm having a nice conversation with...I'm sorry, I missed your name."

"Bothank," Bothank said with a lopsided grin.

"Bothank," Ella said, keeping the grimace out of her smile but not out of her voice. "Hello, Bothank. You're very big for an orc, aren't you?"

Bothank's eyes widened, and his gaze darted to Thorack, who was at least a half a head taller and could bench press an ox.

Vola rolled her eyes. "Stop it, Ella. I know what you're doing. You should get out of here. You don't belong in the Frog's Bottom."

"I have as much a right to be here as anyone," she cried, voice rising. "Just because you're jealous—"

Vola smacked her forehead. "You think I'm jealous?"

"Of course you are. I'm pretty enough to get orc boys when no one even wants to touch you."

Vola groaned. It was like they were teenagers all over again. Except Vola had grown up enough to see how ridiculous this was, and Ella hadn't.

"If you'd just smile once in a while, no one would even notice the tusks. But you scowl all the time, giving yourself that little line between your bushy eyebrows. It's no wonder you don't have any friends."

That hit like a punch to the gut, making the air whoosh from Vola's lungs. Crimson light flickered at the edges of her vision, highlighting Ella's pout, which morphed into a mean smirk when she saw her words had hit home.

Vola's fists clenched, her nails biting into the skin of her palms, and a growl rose up the back of her throat.

It would be okay to hit her, a voice whispered through her mind. *Just this once. Strike her down.*

The whisper stopped her cold, a shiver traveling down her neck, raising the hair along her spine.

It would teach her to mind her tongue, the voice said. *You would be defending your people. You would be doing a good thing. A thing worthy of a paladin.*

Vola sucked in a breath. The voice didn't sound like Cleavah. She'd heard the goddess enough to know her voice as well as she knew the sky was blue. And Cleavah couldn't speak to her now anyway. Without her emblem, Vola was cut off from the goddess like a knife stroke through a cord.

But there was someone out there who condoned rage. Whose power grew with every act of unrestrained violence.

Mulgash. Greater Obstacle. Patron of orcs who didn't care what other races thought of them.

How could he talk to her when Cleavah couldn't?

Vola shook her head. It didn't matter how he'd done it. Maybe she'd given him a way in by giving in to her rage in the past. Whatever the method, she would not be his puppet now.

She closed her eyes, took a couple of deep breaths, and unclenched her fingers. The voice was a lot easier to ignore when she put a hated name on it.

"Ella, I only draw this sword when I intend to use it. Don't make me draw it here."

Ella lifted her nose in the air and sniffed. "Only ugly girls have to make threats to get their way. The rest of us know how to use our charms." Her friends at the bar smirked.

Vola laughed, making Ella jump. "Do you think that actually works? Calling people names." She leaned closer. Ella's eyes widened as their faces came level. "I've been insulted by people far subtler than you. Knights of the realm. Traitors to the throne. Lords and ladies and paladin commanders. You think I'm going to bother swatting a gnat when I've struck down dragons?"

Her pretty little mouth fell open. Bothank had long since abandoned the table, deciding it wasn't worth getting into it with either of them.

"You…you can't say things like that to me. My father…"

Vola snorted. "Not a great tactic. I've already had everything I care about taken away from me. Threats won't work because I have nothing left to lose."

She cocked her shoulder, so Ella's gaze flicked to the black shield on her back. Vola's boss preferred she carried it. A lot of the full orcs wouldn't respect a half breed. But they always looked at the shield and wondered. What had she done? What was bad enough to get a paladin kicked out of her order?

"I can literally throw you out of here any time I want," Vola said, straightening. "I was just giving you the courtesy of landing outside on your feet instead of your behind."

She just avoided wincing, wishing she'd said ass instead, but old habits were hard to break. It still felt like Cleavah was watching over her shoulder, ready to send a lightning strike whenever she swore.

Ella swallowed. The girl picked up her drink and pushed her chair back before heading to the bar and the safety of her friends.

Raised voices from the front of the common room plucked at Vola's attention, but she kept her gaze on Ella.

The girl sat on a barstool and flicked a glance at her. "I'm going to sit here and finish my drink. Which I paid for. And I'm not going to talk to anyone except my friends. Is that all right?" Her voice went sharp and nasally.

There was a crash from the front of the bar, and Thorack's voice bellowed in anger.

Vola's lips thinned. "Excuse me," she said through her teeth and stepped quickly toward the altercation. She was paid to kick out unruly patrons, not protect orcs who didn't know better than to get mixed up with Ella Cormo. Hopefully, the girl knew what was good for her and stayed put for once.

Vola pushed through the leering spectators, using her shoulders to pry open a path. "Thorack. We've talked about this before. You beat someone up, you get kicked ou—"

The biggest, meanest orc in the village lay on the ground beside his table, whimpering.

A halfling dressed in a gray tunic and trousers with her curly hair tied up in a bun sat on top of him. One hand held Thorack's arm pinned behind him; the other raised a beer to her lips.

A lovely half-elf with long blonde hair and a hooded figure with a large, black wolf waited at the edge of the crowd.

Vola swallowed.

"Hi Vola," Sorrel said with a sharp smile. "Fancy meeting you here."

Vola couldn't even find it in herself to be surprised.

SIX

"Do you want some help?" Lillie asked Sorrel, little streaks of lightning dancing through her fingers as she raised her hand. "Or are you having fun up there by yourself?"

"Nah," Sorrel said. "I think I got my point across." She leaned down, twisting Thorack's arm to speak in his ear. "I like a good bar brawl as much as the next girl, but I'm not here for trouble. Halflings aren't toys, all right?"

Thorack whimpered, and Sorrel let go of his arm and slid to the ground while the orcs around Vola grumbled.

"She's just a halfling," someone muttered.

"You want to argue with her? Thorack broke my arm three years ago like it was a toothpick. He didn't even get a hit on her."

Sorrel patted Thorack's shoulder and helped him stand. "Why don't you put some ice on that, buddy. Before it swells up. It's definitely dislocated."

Thorack was the biggest and the meanest orc, yes, but he was not the dumbest by far, sitting on the other end of the scale from Bothank. He shuffled away from Sorrel, who remained standing beside his table, hip cocked nonchalantly.

"Well, that was fun," she said.

"For you, maybe," Talon grumbled, pushing herself from the wall. "The rest of us didn't even get to hit him."

Vola stepped forward against the flow of the orcs, her heart in her throat. "What are you guys doing here?"

"You can have the next bar fight," Sorrel told Talon, brushing imaginary lint from her arms.

"How many do you plan to start?" Lillie asked.

"Guys, what are you doing here?" Vola spoke louder this time.

"As many as it takes," Sorrel said.

"For what?" Talon said.

"To prove a point."

"Guys!" Vola's throat closed on a lump, and she had to swallow.

Sorrel pinned her with a glance. "What? You don't like being ignored? Don't like it when we don't talk to you? When we don't let you have a say in what's happening or answer your questions—"

Vola didn't let her finish. She closed the distance between them and swept Sorrel into her arms. The halfling's legs dangled.

"I'm sorry," Vola said, voice muffled in the monk's shoulder. She hadn't let herself think about them. There was a whole list of things she hadn't let herself think about in the last couple of months, but it was a lot harder with them standing right in front of her.

Sorrel sighed into her ear and patted her back.

Somewhere behind them, Thorack grumbled. "I got thrown on the floor when I tried that."

Vola cleared her throat and set Sorrel down again. The monk straightened her tunic.

"You have to earn the right to pick up a halfling," she told the orc.

She patted Vola's hand and gave her a tentative smile, like she'd already forgotten Vola's mistakes. But Vola wasn't too worried about her. Sorrel wasn't the one who held a grudge.

Talon was.

Vola raised her gaze to the hooded figure. She didn't like seeing Talon's hood up. It generally meant the ranger felt like she had something to hide. Her face or her emotions, sometimes her entire identity.

Talon didn't lower the hood, but she did deliberately point it straight at Vola, so Vola knew she was being glared at. But when she spoke, her normal growl was softer by a fraction.

"I tried to run away once," she said. "It was you who talked me out of it."

Vola shuffled her feet.

"I'm angry you didn't give me the same chance. But I do understand it."

Vola had to blink. She started to turn toward Lillie, opened her mouth, but the movement made Lillie's eyes dart over her shoulder, locking on her shield. She gasped.

Vola bit her lip. She wasn't doing this here. Not with a dozen orcs and their friends looking on.

She hurried them toward the door, shooing them like a herd of sheep.

"Vola! Where are you going?" the bartender yelled. "Your shift doesn't end until dinner."

"I'm the bouncer, aren't I?" she called back. "I'm bouncing the trouble-makers out like I'm supposed to."

She closed the door on his grumbles and took a deep breath. Then she turned to face her party. They stood at the edge of the lane, watching her as several passersby stared at them curiously. The village didn't get very many visitors, so strangers stuck out a bit. Especially strangers who weren't orcs or obviously human.

Vola rubbed the back of her neck.

"All right," Lillie said quietly. "Let us see it."

Vola reached back and drew the blackened shield from her back, avoiding its marred face.

The three of them remained silent, taking it in. Even Sorrel couldn't find anything to say.

She'd expected them to fill the air with platitudes or tell her everything would be all right.

This was better somehow. They took in her pain and made it part of their own.

Finally, Lillie reached out a finger and rubbed at the once shining surface. The black didn't come off on her fingertip.

"How did they even—"

"Holy fire," Vola said. "The effect is permanent."

"Why didn't you tell us?" Talon said.

"I did." Vola shifted the shield on her arm. It felt heavier somehow. "I left a note."

"What note?" Sorrel said.

"The note…" Vola shook her head. She'd left it right where they'd find it. Goddess, had they come all this way without knowing what had happened?

Sorrel's mouth went round. "Oh, this?" She pulled out a sheet of paper, crumpled from her pocket, and held it out to read. "I'm leaving, blah, blah, blah. Stripped rank, blah, blah, blah. I'm stupid, and I don't think anyone will ever love me anymore."

"That's not what it says." Vola lunged to snatch it from her.

Sorrel yanked it out of the way and glared Vola back a step. "This is not a note," she said. "It's an insult."

Vola ran her hand over her braided hair. "I'm sorry, all right. I didn't want to talk about it. I didn't want you to know at all, but there wasn't a way I could keep it from you."

"Well, you sure tried."

"You could have at least told us where you were going," Talon said.

Vola shook her head. "How did you find me anyway?"

Talon jerked her hood at Lillie.

"I triangulated the most likely options based on orc populations, the academy you originally attended, and the town where we all met the first time. I made an educated guess where you might have grown up," Lillie said, head cocked like it was obvious.

"She makes it sound so easy. We had to shake down three different villages before we finally got here," Sorrel grumbled.

Vola had wanted them to stay in Glenhaven. She'd wanted them to keep working for the princess. That was the whole point of this, to keep them from being scarred by her mistake.

But even if they'd ruined all that, she was still glad to see them.

Vola wasn't usually a hugger, but she couldn't seem to stop reaching out to the ones she'd convinced herself to leave behind.

Talon sidled back so Vola could only grip her shoulder. Talon wasn't a hugger either. But Lillie let her draw her into a one-armed embrace and then patted her awkwardly on the back.

"So, you do still have something to lose," Ella said from the door of the bar.

Vola stiffened, and Lillie drew back, blinking in confusion.

Vola glanced over her shoulder at the blonde girl who smirked, eyes calculating.

"What do you want?" Vola growled. She'd kept her calm as well as she could inside, but here she was confronted by the thought that Ella was looking at her friends, sizing them up to see where she could do the most harm. She'd left Elsie and Ellen inside apparently, probably terrorizing more orcs.

Ella placed a delicate hand on her chest as if affronted. "I'm leaving the Frog's Bottom like you asked me to. Don't you remember? It seemed important to you, so I thought I would do you that favor."

Her eyes narrowed on Vola's party, and she sauntered forward, her hips swinging hard enough to knock over a grown orc. "Hi. I'm Ella. Vola's oldest friend."

"Heurgh," Vola said, struggling between a laugh and a cry of outrage.

Lillie shot a look up at her, fair brow crinkling.

Ella sidled up beside Talon, glancing up from under her eyelashes at the hooded figure.

"I love a man of mystery," she said, voice sultry as she walked her fingers up Talon's arm.

Sorrel choked. At Talon's feet, Gruff rumbled and the fur stood up on the back of his neck.

"Do you like women of mystery?" Talon asked, flat and cool. "Because I haven't been a man in a while."

Ella drew back, her mouth pulling in a frown as she eyed the wolf and the ranger. "I don't understand. Are you making fun of me?"

"Is there something we can help you with?" Lillie asked, her posture morphing into something much more formal and stiff than she'd shown in the bar.

"Oh, I just wanted to meet Vola's friends." She glanced at Sorrel, opened her mouth, and then closed it before choosing Lillie as the most likely target. "Pleased to meet you." She offered the wizard her hand.

Sorrel met Vola's eyes surreptitiously behind Ella's back and jerked her chin at the local girl.

Vola rolled her eyes toward the sky and shook her head the slightest bit.

Sorrel's lips tightened as Lillie extended her hand cautiously to Ella.

Ella slipped her fingers in Lillie's with a grin and then froze, gaze caught by the ring on Lillie's finger. Vola had only seen it once or twice before. When had Lillie started wearing it openly?

"That's the Ephyra crest," she said, breathless.

Lillie tried to draw her hand back, a flush creeping across her cheeks.

"You…you must be Lilliara Ephyra, fourth child of Lord Ephyra and the elven maiden, Shereille."

Lillie made a face, and Ella drew her hand back to clutch them to her chest. "I have the entire book of nobility memorized," she said. "The old priest used it to teach us our letters. Vola always had trouble reading, but I was top of the class."

Lillie opened her mouth, but Ella went on right over top of her. "You are so much prettier in person than I realized you would be. I love your hair. How do you get it to shine like that? I'd heard about the trouble in the capitol just a couple of months ago. Were you one of the loyalists who saved the day?"

"Er," Lillie said, face red and starting to sweat.

Ella wielded flattery the same way she had when they were kids. Like a wide stick swung in a broad arc designed to hit just about anything. But she'd picked exactly the wrong tactic with this noble if she wanted to get on Lillie's good side.

Ella gasped and glanced at Sorrel and Talon. "Oh, is this your adventuring party? How wonderful. I've always wanted to see a party of adventurers in action. I'll bet you have loads of stories."

She linked her arm with Lillie's and hesitated a split second before drawing in Talon's arm. "You must meet my friends. They've heard all about you, too. They'll never believe that I met you unless I bring you to them in person."

Lillie cast a helpless glance back at Vola and Sorrel. She'd never been good at saying no. Fortunately, Talon was.

"No thanks," the ranger said, sidestepping so that Ella missed her next step and stumbled.

Lillie took advantage and stepped back as well.

"Sorry, Lola, was it?" Sorrel said with a vicious little smile. "We're not interested."

"What? Why not?" She looked like she genuinely couldn't comprehend why anyone would turn her down.

"We're not here to sightsee," Lillie said.

"We came for our leader," Talon said, jerking her hood at Vola. "She misplaced herself for a few weeks there."

Ella's eyes narrowed as she looked between Vola, Lillie, and Sorrel. Then she let her mouth drop open. "Oh. Oh, you poor things, you have to follow Vola? Well, you don't have to worry about that anymore. She's been disgraced."

Vola's teeth creaked together.

Ella tilted her head. "Hadn't you heard? She came here to hide her shame."

Lillie went still, her face a perfect mask of politeness. "You need to refresh yourself on the definition of shame," she said, low and calm.

Sorrel crossed her arms. "Vola has done nothing but make us proud since we chose to follow her," she said. "You want to look at her and see one mistake? Go ahead. But I look at her, and I see the weapon of a greater god that she helped retrieve." She touched the staff rising over her shoulder.

"I see the entire town she saved from slavery," Talon added.

Lillie bit her lip. "And I see the princesses of Southglen. Whom she saved from traitors and corruption."

"So what was this shame you were talking about?" Sorrel asked, head tilted.

Ella spluttered. "Her—her shield. It's black. An orc just can't be a real knight."

"You're not very clever, are you?" Sorrel said.

"What? How dare you—"

"Vola has three people willing to follow her into fire no matter what color shield she holds. And you keep trying to get us angry. The smart move would be to walk away. Now."

Ella's nostrils flared, and she raised her chin. "You're right. There must be something wrong with you, too." She spun and stormed off down the lane.

Lillie whispered under her breath, and Ella tripped and fell splat into a puddle that wasn't there a second before.

"Nice work," Sorrel said, tapping her lip.

"I hate bullies," Lillie said with a glare.

Talon shook her head. "Maybe there really is something wrong with us."

Vola hurried them through the gate and down the other end of the lane as Ella pushed herself out of the puddle with a cry of rage. "Let's get out of here before she starts screaming."

"Weren't you working?" Lillie said with a glance over her shoulder.

"I'm paid to keep trouble out of the tavern. And I think right now I'm the trouble."

She herded them down the dirt road lined with cheery little houses toward Lydia and Gorgo's cottage.

"So you decided you'd rather deal with that than face the truth with us?" Talon said, cocking her thumb over her shoulder at Ella.

"I didn't pick her over you. She's just an unpleasant side effect," Vola said. "Besides, she's been spitting poison since we were kids."

"You grew up with that?" Lillie said. "You mean she was telling the truth when she said she was your oldest friend."

"We grew up together, but that doesn't mean we were friends. I didn't have any friends until I met you guys."

Lillie froze in the middle of the path, and Vola nearly ran her over. The wizard glanced down at herself and then back toward Ella.

"Oh," she said, eyes widening. "Oh, my gods. No wonder you hated me when we first met."

Vola hissed through her teeth and gestured Lillie on. "I didn't hate you. I had very complicated feelings that we worked through and don't ever have to touch again. All right?"

Lillie bit her lip, her eyes filling.

Vola sighed. "You're nothing like her," she said fiercely to Lillie alone. "Nothing at all, okay? Now please forget about it."

She pressed ahead before Lillie could demand more feelings.

Talon slipped around the corner of the Frog's Bottom, a familiar lead rope in her hand, and Vola groaned.

"Oh no. Do not tell me the swamp monster had to come, too."

The beast glared at Vola balefully, chewing on something that crunched.

"I thought Costa was going to study it?"

"She was," Sorrel said, shifting from foot to foot. "Until it ate her favorite cat."

"There might be one or two laws banning swamp creatures of unknown parentage, now," Lillie said, not meeting Vola's eyes.

Vola raised her gaze to the sky. "Just don't let it eat my mom's petunias."

"We're meeting your parents?" Sorrel said, trotting to catch up.

Vola led the group to the cottage surrounded by a healthy garden full of spring flowers and tubers.

Her hand closed on the door handle before she thought better of it and knocked first.

"Mom, Dad? You home?" She gave them plenty of time before opening the door. But she needn't have worried. Her parents sat fully clothed—or at least as fully clothed as they ever were—at the kitchen table with her Aunt Urag.

"Volagra?" Lydia said, standing. "I thought your shift wasn't over until after dinner…"

She trailed off as Vola ushered Sorrel, Lillie, and Talon through the door into the living room.

"Uh, sorry to spring company on you," she said. "This is—"

"Your party." Lydia's hands flew to her mouth before she grabbed her husband's shoulder. "Her party, Gorgo. She brought her party home to meet us."

"Mom."

"Oh, I have to make something for you to eat." Lydia flitted to the counter, the ends of her long loincloth fluttering with her movement. "Cookies. Or muffins. They're Vola's favorite."

"Mom."

"You like muffins?" Sorrel asked with a raised eyebrow.

"I like Mom's muffins," Vola said with a sniff.

"So do I," Gorgo said with a leer.

"Dad, ew. Not right now, I beg you."

"Which part is the muffin exactly?" Lillie said. "I've always wondered."

"I've never wondered that," Talon said. "Literally never. Until you brought it up."

"It probably depends on which part is poofier," Sorrel decided to add.

"Oh my goddess," Vola groaned. "Stop talking about my mom's muffins."

"You started it," Sorrel said.

"I started it," Gorgo said. "About twenty-five…er…six years ago. How old are you again, Vola?"

Vola smacked her forehead.

"Don't pretend it didn't start long before she was conceived," Lydia said, grabbing a muffin tin so old it had developed its own personality along with its patina. She slid it across the worn counter and cast Gorgo a look from under her eyelashes.

"This was a bad idea. We're leaving," Vola said. "I'd rather brave Ella and all her friends than this."

"No," Lydia cried and darted between them and the door. "We'll be good. We promise. Right, Gorgo?"

"I am an orc chieftain and a retired mercenary. I have never been described as good."

"Close enough," Lydia said. "Urag. You promise?"

"I haven't said anything yet." Urag's eyes sparkled as she rested her gnarled hands on the table. "This is the best entertainment I've had in ages. I'm not doing anything to get myself kicked out."

"There, see," Lydia said, turning back to them. "Weapons on the racks by the door. You're all staying at least for the night. Now, Vola. Be polite and introduce us."

"Hardly a need. They know everything they need to by now," Vola muttered, but her mother glared at her. She sighed. "Guys, these are my parents. Lydia Battlemane and Gorgo, leader of our clan. And my Aunt Urag. She lives down the lane."

"Battlemane?" Sorrel said. "*The* Lydia Battlemane? Geez, we learned about you in the monastery. You guys helped free Hestenford from the goblin hoard."

Lydia beamed, her cheeks going pink.

"And you must be Sorrel Thornbough. Vola has told us so much about you."

"Not that much," Vola grumbled

"You wouldn't shut up about them for two weeks straight." Gorgo leaned back in his chair, balancing on two legs. "Every time you said 'I don't want to talk about it,' you'd insist on talking about it."

"I did not," Vola said affronted.

"And this is Talon," Lydia said, nodding to Talon. "And Lilliara Ephyra. Oh, I'm so pleased to meet all of you finally. A daughter's first party is a big occasion, and we didn't get to see it."

"We're pleased to finally meet you, too," Lillie said, with a polite nod.

"More of you than we expected," Talon muttered, glancing at Lydia's outfit.

Vola cleared her throat. "It's armor," she said. "Or so I've been told."

Lydia bustled around, pulling up mismatched chairs to the kitchen table and dumping a bag of cookies onto a plate while Gorgo lumbered to his feet and tried to look like he was helping.

Sorrel placed her staff on the rack by the door and scampered up onto a chair. Talon eyed the rack until Vola very deliberately stashed her sword and shield.

"Sorry, house rule," she said. "No weapons at the dinner table."

Then the ranger unsheathed her daggers, hung them on the pegs, pulled her bow out from behind her, and stashed it with her quiver. Then she pulled two more knives from her boots and tossed them beneath the rest.

Vola raised her eyebrows. "Anything else?" she asked mildly.

Talon pushed her hood back a fraction, just enough to level a glare at her. "Only if you count Gruff."

Vola eyed the big black wolf and pointed to the fireplace in the living room. "You want to curl up on the rug? I'll bet mom has a leg of something lying around."

The wolf huffed but circled the rug twice and flopped down with his head on his paws.

"You can sit by me," Aunt Urag told Talon. "I like the quiet types." She snapped her fingers, and her familiar, a grizzled badger, appeared to push a chair across the floor toward the table. The badger grumbled some badgerish complaint before curling up at Urag's feet.

Lillie stared. "Can you teach me that? I've always wanted a familiar."

Urag grinned as Talon sat gingerly on the edge of the chair, ready to bolt if the opportunity arose.

Vola glanced around the table at Sorrel, swinging her legs munching on a cookie, Lillie beaming at Vola's mom, Vola's mom beaming at Lillie, and Vola's dad pushing his reading glasses back onto his nose.

"I'll admit. This is not something I ever thought would happen," she said.

"What brings you three here?" Lydia asked. "Not that I'm complaining, but Vola seemed convinced you'd stay in the capitol."

Talon shot her a look. "Only because she didn't consult us about it first," she muttered.

Sorrel swallowed a bite of cookie, ignoring Talon and Vola both. "We came because we have a job. And we need our paladin."

Vola's heart clenched, and cold tingled along her arms. "What? I thought you were just visiting." She'd thought they were just defending her when they'd told Ella they needed their leader back. She hadn't thought they'd actually come to collect her. To rip her out of her carefully constructed indifference.

Lydia clapped her hands. "Oh, wonderful. Vola, you'll need your armor. I'll run and polish it for you."

She raced up the stairs.

"No, Mom…" She turned back to glare at Sorrel. "I left for a reason. It's not like I can just come back."

"Why not?" Sorrel asked, licking her fingers.

Heat beat in Vola's cheeks. "You know why not. Don't make me say it."

"Because they took your shield?" Lillie asked quietly.

Vola looked away. "It means I'm not a paladin anymore. I'm not Volagra Lightbringer. I'm literally not allowed to call myself that anymore."

"Then call yourself something else," Sorrel said. "Brainsplitter. Spellsword. Oo, what about Blademaster?"

"That's not what I mean. I can't *be* your leader. I can't *be* a paladin."

"But you can be a bouncer?" Lillie said, cocking her head. "You're still allowed to work, are you not?"

"Yes, but…"

"But it's not what she wants," Gorgo said. "She's got this hang-up that she's got to be called something specific. Something about knights and doing good. We've never really understood it."

"It's not about the title." Vola glared at her father. "It's about what I'm doing. I'm not going to fight just for the sake of fighting. It has to be *for* something. Something important."

"How has that changed?" Talon asked. "Didn't you always fight for us?"

"Yes, but it's different now," she said through gritted teeth. Red started to beat at the edges of her vision.

"How?" Sorrel said.

"Did they take your skill?" Lillie said.

"No! Yes..."

"Can you swing your sword?"

"Yes, but—"

"Can you hold a shield?"

"Yes—"

"Can you heal?"

"No."

They finally fell silent in the face of her answer.

Vola swallowed the lump away and stared at the grain of the table between her hands, so she didn't have to meet their eyes. "Your power comes from study," she said, gesturing toward Lillie. "And from nature." She included Urag and Talon. "Mine came from Cleavah. The only way I could heal was by using Her power. And they took Her away from me."

She touched her chest where her emblem used to hang. "A Lesser goddess can't work through a mortal without some sort of connection."

"I told you," her father said. "Get another god. Mulgash—"

"Mulgash is a god of rage," she said, rolling her gaze toward Gorgo. "I doubt he'll give me the power to heal. More likely to kill."

She raised her gaze to meet Lillie's and Sorrel's and Talon's in turn. "I can't heal without Cleavah's power."

"Do you know that for sure?" Lillie whispered. "Have you tried?"

She clenched her teeth. "I can't talk to her anymore. Is that enough?"

Lillie flushed and bit her lip.

"So we'll fight this," Sorrel said.

Vola shook her head.

"We'll fight the council," Talon said. "Gladly. We can find you another way to Cleavah. Another emblem. Something."

"Prove you're still worthy of being her paladin to the very source. Even the council can't gainsay a goddess," Lillie said. "Right?"

"It's only done when you stop fighting," Sorrel said.

Vola's lips pressed tight, trying to keep everything inside, and plunged into her last argument. "I was trying to protect you. You shouldn't be traveling without a healer. But also, Rilla won't want me working for her. You'll be guilty by association. If you follow me, we'll never get another legitimate contract. It'll all be mercenary work."

"As if that's a bad thing," her father grunted.

"Guess again," Sorrel said, pulling an envelope from the folds of her tunic. She held up the crisp, expensive-looking paper.

Vola found herself reaching out without having made the decision to do so.

Lillie didn't offer to read the note, probably on purpose. Vola needed to read the words herself anyway.

There wasn't an address, but she recognized Rilla's handwriting easily enough.

You're allowed to be an idiot for exactly how long it takes this to get to you. There, you're not an idiot anymore. You're my employee. Now act like it. Just because you're not a paladin anymore doesn't mean you're fired. I decide when you're fired, and have I ever let someone else make my decisions for me? No. Now get off your ass. We have a lead on the bastard that took control of Finn's mind. Track them down, eliminate the threat, and figure out how it relates to our primary enemy. The one trying to take the power from the Thrones. And when you're done with all that, I need you back in the capitol. You've been allowed to mope. Now it's time to work.

"How many times did she call you an idiot?" Talon said.

"I'm not saying." Vola kept her gaze down, staring at the end of the note. There was no address. No signature. It read like orders. And it made Vola sit up, her spine responding when the rest of her refused.

Vola raised her gaze finally. Lydia stood at the bottom of the stairs, Vola's armor under her arm, shining as bright as her shield was black. She couldn't help glancing at the shield propped by the door.

She'd wanted something to do. Something to keep her moving. This was more than that. This was something to fight *for*. This was revenge. This was vindication.

She'd protected Finn from the paladin council, but she hadn't protected him from this threat. Now was her chance to pay back that pain and that suffering.

They weren't very paladin-y thoughts. But then...she wasn't a paladin anymore.

"We can go after the guy who hurt Finn," she said.

"Yeah," Sorrel said. "Unless you're done fighting?"

Vola bared her tusks. "Never."

SEVEN

IT FELT SO MUCH BETTER to be moving rather than sitting in place and rotting from the inside out. Even the swamp monster couldn't break Vola's good mood, and she made sure to load it up with extra weapons, camping gear, and several tins of mom-made muffins.

The swamp beast gave her a familiar glare, and she actually patted it on the nose, darting out of the way before it could bite her.

They might not even get to use the camping equipment, though. Rilla's lead pointed them down the road from Vola's village, and they weren't going far.

Vola checked the notes again, though Lillie had read them to her several times already.

After a month of sifting through the wreckage Lillie's brothers had left behind, Kellan had found the instructions they'd used to subvert him. Lillie had gone on about some complicated spell that could be done from a distance, but the part that Vola had understood was that the mind mage had taken over Kellan's thoughts from a distance, forcing him to help with the coup.

And then the mind mage had transferred the spell to Finn, leading him to kill an innocent young woman.

Vola carefully folded the notes again so she wouldn't accidentally crush them as her fingers clenched.

Kellan had pinpointed the origins of the instructions. And now they were on their way to avenge him and Finn against this unknown mind mage. It wouldn't be long now.

Vola let the grin spread across her face. There was no one to hide her tusks from here.

Sorrel trotted out front with Lillie following, her nose buried in a book as usual. Talon scanned the surrounding tress, her bow drawn and ready. The ranger had already sent Gruff to scout their flanks. The forest thinned in places along the road, but the wolf still found ways to disappear in the undergrowth.

"How much farther before we should expect to see people?" Sorrel called back to Vola, who brought up the rear.

"Any minute now," Vola said. "Deersford is only an hour away from home."

"That seems convenient," Talon said. "Do you think you have a lot of mind mages lingering around your village? Or just the one that has something to do with you?"

Vola's brow furrowed, and she sped up a little to catch Lillie's attention. "Are you sure Kellan meant Deersford here in eastern Southglen? I'm sure there are other Deersfords out there."

Lillie glanced up from her book. "He was specific. He said he couldn't pinpoint it more than that, but the message that Xavier and Innis received detailing how they were supposed to set up his subversion came from this area."

"It's just a coincidence, Vola," Sorrel said. "It's gotta be, right?"

Vola growled under her breath. "You stop believing in coincidences when you've got gods meddling in your life constantly."

The thought made her wince, and she glanced up at the sky where gray clouds threatened rain. There'd be no more meddling from Cleavah.

She took a deep breath and cracked her neck. It was...well, she couldn't say good. But she could use this as an opportunity to learn who she was without the mantle of the paladin weighing her down. She had been pursuing honor and duty for so long she didn't know who she was without it.

She was interested to see who she really was underneath.

So far, she swung wildly between feeling loose—like an unanchored ship in a swell—and on edge. Nervous and ready to jump on anything that moved wrong.

Not like herself at all.

She shrugged her shoulders to settle her shield and the ax that was strapped to her back.

Sorrel glanced back in time to catch the movement, and she sighed. "I can't believe your mom is Lydia Battlemane. And I got to meet her. *And* she gave you her battle-ax."

"It's just her secondhand one. You think she'd let me touch her work ax?"

"Lydia. Battlemane's. Ax." Sorrel said again. "I don't think you grasp the significance of this."

"You carry Maxim's Warhammer," Vola said. "How is my mom's old ax a novelty?"

"Do you know how much I wanted to be her when I was a kid?"

"I'm surprised you didn't ask her more questions at dinner, then," Lillie said, still perusing the pages of her book. She'd have to put it away soon if she didn't want it to get drenched.

Sorrel flushed. "I might have cornered her in the kitchen later and asked her to give me a blow-by-blow account of the battle of Verah-kah." She buried her face in her hands. "She probably thinks I'm just some silly sycophant, now."

Vola pressed her lips together to suppress a smile. "Actually, after you all went to bed last night, she told me you were very wise. And anyone who could brow beat me into submission was worth listening to."

Sorrel froze in the middle of the road, and Lillie passed her without even looking up. Vola came even with the halfling and nudged her so she stumbled forward with them again.

"The thing is," Vola said. "You can all do that. You just have to look at me the right way, and I cave. Some leader I am. I don't know why any of you bother to follow me."

Talon rolled her eyes, and Lillie smiled a little smile.

"You wouldn't," Lillie said. "But that's why we do."

Vola made a face. "That doesn't even make sense."

Sorrel trotted along beside her, chortling to herself and rubbing her hands together. "It's too bad your parents couldn't come with us," she said finally. "It would have been fun to work with legends. Your dad's pretty famous, too."

Vola shook her head, making sure to keep an eye on the surrounding woods. Gruff would alert them if he saw anything besides trees and the occasional bunny, but it never hurt to be careful.

"Dad had other things to look after," she said. "Some of the orcs from the clan have been wandering off by themselves without leave from the chieftain. A couple I've kicked out of the bar before."

Lillie glanced back at her with a raised eyebrow. "And that's not allowed? Are they prisoners?"

"No, nothing like that." Vola shook her head. "It's just when humans think of you as violent troublemakers, it pays to keep your own people accounted for. Dad likes to keep track of his clan to keep them safe from unfounded accusations and people like Ella Cormo."

Lillie scowled, and Vola kicked herself for reminding them both of her. Vola was over her hang-ups, but she couldn't deny Ella had left scars almost as deep as the one that made Lillie limp.

"What are you reading this time?" Vola said. If anything could distract the wizard, it was talking about books.

Lillie glanced at her before tipping the book in Vola's direction, revealing a page full of indecipherable equations.

"Your aunt gave me her notes on how to summon a familiar."

Vola snorted. "Aunt Urag makes her spells up on the fly. She's never written anything down in her life."

Lillie cracked a smile. "All right. She talked, and I tried to write it all down. Our magic works very differently. Hers is tied to the land, and mine was learned. But the wonderful thing about that is I think I can learn what exactly she's doing."

"And summon a familiar."

Lillie's focus went distant. "I like the idea of an instant friend and companion. Don't you? Someone who loves you unconditionally."

Vola scratched her nose. "Well, yeah. But I guess I'd prefer if it came from a real person. Connection comes from a relationship that's grown naturally."

Lillie blinked then glanced around at the others. "Yes, I guess so. I just didn't have that growing up. Magic seemed like the solution to loneliness at the time."

"Buildings ahead," Talon growled, and Vola straightened.

Lillie put away her book, and Sorrel slung her staff off her back and used it like a walking stick. It looked a lot less like a weapon that way, but Sorrel wouldn't need more than a split second's warning to put it to good use.

The town they approached was bigger than Vola's home but not by a lot. The main street sported a bar, a general store, and a post office. All front and center. The late morning rain shower finally arrived as they strode into town and several figures darted out of the weather. They looked at Vola and the others the way anyone would look at strangers but not as if they weren't welcome. Vola took that to mean they saw enough orcs and halflings from the surrounding area to make them familiar.

They decided to start with the post office. If the message from their enemy came from here, it had probably come through the post office.

The man behind the counter squinted at the battered envelope Lillie handed him.

"If it didn't have a return address, I can't help you," he said, shaking his shaggy head.

"We were hoping you might recognize it or the sender," Lillie said.

"Plenty of messengers come in here to post stuff from all over. This is rural country. Lots of remote homesteads and camps, the occasional orc clan that moves around." He spread the envelope on the counter and leaned over it. "I don't personally remember them all. It probably came in delivered by some kid looking for an extra coin. And probably got sent to the city the same way."

"Right," Vola said as they stepped back out into the damp. Rain pinged from her pauldrons. "So, our quarry is too clever to put a return address on something. Should have expected that. But we can question some of the locals. Look for someone who might have taken the messenger job."

"And if our mind mage has been experimenting nearby, there is probably a trail to find," Lillie said. "People acting strange, like Finn and Kellan."

"Or disappearing completely," Talon said ominously.

Sorrel leaned against the railing outside the post office and surveyed the street. They were getting some curious looks. Or at least the swamp beast was. Most people steered clear as if some primitive sense recognized a threat when it saw one.

A lot of the passersby trickled into the bar across the street.

"You know," Sorrel said, tapping her teeth. "It is almost lunchtime."

Talon gave her a look. "You're angling for a drink, aren't you?"

"No. Well, I mean, I'm always angling for a drink, but this will serve two purposes. Where do you suppose we can gather the most information at once?"

Vola sighed. "The bar. All right, come on."

"It isn't a surprise Vola found a job in a bar," Lillie said as they trotted across the street and tied the swamp monster up outside. "We spend so much time in them she probably felt right at home."

"Nothing interesting happens in the woods," Sorrel said, pushing the door open. The sign above read THE LONG WAY HOME. "This is where all the best quests start."

"I see what you mean," Talon said, gazing around at the half-empty common room and the drab-looking citizens loitering at their tables. Someone had scrubbed the beer stains recently so at least it didn't smell. "This looks like the start of something very exciting. Like the mystery of who stole the cook's second favorite ladle. And if we skip to the end, you'll learn the cook misplaced it himself, under his second-best apron."

"Don't analyze it," Sorrel said with a sniff. "Watch. Something will happen. I promise."

Sorrel made a b-line for the bar and hopped up on a stool. "Your best lager, please," she said.

Vola eyed the premises and decided there was very little in the way of threat lurking here. But a few chairs scraped as patrons surreptitiously scooted away from her.

Vola pursed her lips and jerked her chin at Talon and Lillie. "I think you'll do better without me. See what you can learn."

The ranger and the wizard exchanged a glance and separated, Lillie to sit down with a table of housewives and Talon to prop herself in the shadows close to a boisterous group of lumberjacks.

Vola sidled up next to Sorrel at the bar and leaned on the counter. A hush followed her across the room. She glanced over her shoulder, but the patrons of the bar avoided her gaze. A couple ducked out the door as if to escape.

She looked back at the bartender.

His gaze flicked between her armor and her shield before finally landing on her face. And without asking, he slid a foaming mug in front of her, fingers trembling.

Vola gave him a sidelong look. "I didn't order this."

"No?" he said. "On the house then. Er, if you wouldn't mind taking it outside, though. Maybe around the corner."

"Hey," Sorrel said, brow drawing down.

The bartender held up his hands. "Nothing against orcs. The best drinkers are orcs. It's just...the shield. Black paladins tend to bring the mood down."

The shield. Of course it was the shield. For just a second, she'd almost forgotten it back there. She didn't use it anymore. It felt heavy on her arm and sat better behind her.

"Black paladin," she said. "Is that what you call us?"

"Not just me. It's just...better than oathbreaker, right?"

Red beat at the corners of Vola's vision. *You could prove him right,* a voice threaded through her thoughts. *It might be kind of fun.*

Vola shook her head to clear out the voice and the rage that went with it.

"I'll tell you what," she said. "Answer some questions for me, and I'll get out of your hair."

"Sure. Sure. That seems fair. I don't want any trouble."

Neither did Vola, but it was hard to pass up an advantage when it was handed to her. She leaned her elbows on the bar, bringing her face—and tusks—into the bartender's personal space. "We're looking for anything strange that's been going on around here. Any threatening strangers coming through…besides us."

She traced the grain of the bar and thought back to what it had been like to watch Finn run a girl through with a sword he'd barely known how to use. "Anyone acting strange or not like themselves."

The bartender had already started nodding. "Yeah, sure. You'll want the next town over. Smallville. Town of halflings."

"They named their town Smallville?" Sorrel said.

"Straightforward," the bartender said. "Thought you might have been from there at first. There's been some rumors of a disease. Something making people go funny in the head. Halflings wandering off into the forest; others are losing memories. Some just acting out of character. Our elders have barred travel between our two villages in case it is a sickness. Or something in the water."

"That's…surprisingly helpful," Sorrel said. She cast a glance at Vola. "We can use that."

The bartender nodded. "Yeah? Yeah. Good."

Vola pushed herself up with a grimace. "Thanks. I'll clear out and let you serve the lunch crowd. A deal's a deal."

She shot a look at Sorrel, who stayed on her stool, and snagged the beer the bartender had given her. Vola didn't drink. But the man was already trembling hard enough to spill half his profits on the floor. It seemed mean to intimidate him anymore.

She made her way to the door, and as she passed the last table in the corner, a chair scooted across the floor to block her path.

She glanced up to see a clean-cut figure in a shiny silk doublet with silver buttons down the front, a pair of buckskin breeches, and knee-high boots sitting in the shadows of the corner. The man tilted his head, and his lips quirked in a smile under a neatly trimmed black beard.

"You could go outside like he wanted," he said. "Or you could sit with me, black paladin. No one will notice you here in the corner, especially if you face that shield to the wall. No one except me, of course."

If he wiggled his eyebrows, she was dumping him on the ground and pouring the beer on his head. But he just waited, chair pushed out expectantly. Only when she hesitated too long did he arch one eyebrow, not suggestively, but in question.

She glanced at the bartender. She had promised him she'd leave, but if she tucked her shield against the wall, then she wouldn't scare away his customers.

She made up her mind and sat, clanking a little, but she didn't like traveling without her armor anymore. It did no good sitting outside on the swamp beast.

She propped her shield against the wall, black face tilted away from the common room, and tried to relax in the chair.

"You know, I don't normally like the fully armored types," the man said. "The ones with more metal than brains on them."

Vola's brow drew down, and she slid her beer onto the gouged table top. "Was there supposed to be a 'but' at the end of that sentence?"

"Wouldn't you like to know?" the man said, his mobile lips pursed in a little smile as he sipped his own drink. It was pink and had come in a delicately tilted glass.

Her eyes narrowed. "I guess I would. So I can decide whether to be insulted or not."

"Who would dare insult someone so..." He gestured from her armor to the ax rising over her shoulder. "Well defended."

Vola's lips twisted. "You'd be surprised."

"Well, I'm cleverer than that. I try not to piss off the lady who can break me in half. I'm more of a lover than a fighter anyway."

Vola's eyes searched him for a weapon. He sat still and smirked while she perused him. The neck of a lute rose over the back of his chair, and from the signs of wear and tear, she guessed that was his weapon of choice, not the rapier at his hip.

"Bard?" she asked.

He tilted his head in acknowledgment. He wore his shoulder-length black hair tied back, and a silver hoop glinted from his ear.

"Anyone I would have heard of, Mr..."

He shook his head. "I think this is more fun without names. Don't you?"

Vola's brow furrowed as he raised his drink to her and took a swig. "Is this flirting? Are you flirting with me?"

He choked on his drink and coughed. Vola took it as a good sign that she could surprise him.

"It's not working, is it?" he spluttered, wiping his mouth on his sleeve.

"No," Vola said with a small smile. "Does it usually?"

"Erm, yes?"

"I guess that means you just have to try harder."

He raised his glass again. "It does. Luckily, I find that more appealing than someone who swoons into my arms at the first compliment."

"Let me give you a hint. If there's something out there strong enough to make me swoon, you're better off running."

He laughed out loud, throwing back his head to show off his teeth.

He held out his hand to her. "Cyrano," he said. "Traveling minstrel."

"Volagra Lightless," she said, taking his hand and giving it a good shake. "Er, black paladin. Apparently." She gestured to the shield again, deciding to just own it.

"What's a black paladin doing around here? Deersford is a little off the edge of the map."

"We're looking for something."

"Halflings?" he said, raising an eyebrow.

"You were listening."

He wrinkled his nose. "It's not a very big bar. What are you planning on doing with the halflings?"

She looked at him out of the corner of her eye. "I'm not sure. We haven't gotten there yet."

"I'm not sure if I should wish you luck, then, or not."

"That's up to you. I've been out of luck a lot recently."

"Hmm," he said. His gaze didn't even flicker toward her shield. "You know orcs don't tend to fit in well with halflings. Their buildings are short."

"What are you getting at?" From anyone else, she would have thought it was a threat.

"What are you really looking for?"

All right, that was enough of the...well, whatever this was. She crossed her arms over her chest. "That's really none of your business."

He shrugged and glanced at her out from under his eyelashes. "No. But it was worth a shot."

Cyrano rose and threw back the last of his drink before gathering his things. "I guess I can't really hope that you find what you're looking for, then." He touched his forehead. "Lightless."

"Cyrano," she said with a nod.

As he pushed out the door, Sorrel skipped to Vola's side. Lillie and Talon weren't far behind her.

"Holy cow, were you just chatting up the best-looking guy in here?" she said.

Vola rolled her eyes and stood. "I think he was chatting me up. The question is, why?"

"Why not?" Lillie asked, affronted as Sorrel examined Vola's undrunk beer and started in on it. "You are very attractive. Why wouldn't he want to have a conversation with you?"

"A conversation that could lead to more...conversing later," Talon said.

"A conversation that could lead to more information," Vola said. "He heard us talking at the bar and was far too interested in what we were doing. He was pumping me for information, Lillie. Nothing more."

Lillie bit her lip. "It could be innocuous..."

"Or he could be working for the bad guy," Sorrel said, clunking the empty mug back on the table. "That would be about right for us."

Lillie sighed. "You aren't wrong."

"How about we don't tell our plans to strange men in bars," Talon said. "Come on, Vola. Keep your pants on while we're working."

Lillie and Sorrel chuckled and followed Talon to the door as Vola trailed behind them. "Hey!"

EIGHT

ANOTHER HOUR down the road from Deersford, the rain lifted and the sun came out from behind the clouds. Lillie stopped them all and rummaged in her satchel. She produced four chains hung with a pendant made from woven silver wire.

"Kellan and I made these," she said, tossing one over Sorrel's head. "Before we left."

"What do they do?" Sorrel went cross-eyed trying to examine the pendant.

Lillie stepped up to Vola, who obligingly bent down so the wizard could slip the chain over her head. "They should protect us from the mind mage's invasion," Lillie said, quietly not meeting Vola's eyes. "I didn't think it was a good idea to go into their territory without any precautions."

Like they had last time. Vola touched the pendant, the metal cool against her fingers. It was heavier than Cleavah's emblem and felt clunky and obtrusive. But would something like this have kept Finn safe?

She pursed her lips. What was done was done, and she was paying the price for it. All she could do now was try to do better.

They found the halfling village of Smallville tucked in among the trees. The houses were all built from lumber and plaster with thatched roofs. And they were short enough Vola could see over them by standing on her toes.

"Now this is more like it," Sorrel said with a grin, striding down the lane and looking for once as if she fit.

Halflings went about their day, milling along the road, trading their cabbages and hand carved knick-knacks, and calling to one another about the weather and the price of meat.

"I feel...tall," Lillie said, glancing down at the family who bustled past them, giving them curious, welcoming smiles. She glanced up at Vola. "Is this how you feel all the time?"

Vola winced. "It's not usually this bad. Most humans are near enough my height."

She tripped back a step to avoid running over a gaggle of children chasing after a ball.

"Ho there, friends," a male halfling with a dark gray beard and weathered brown skin hailed them from the front of a large building that looked like a half-sized inn.

"How are you?" Sorrel asked, bouncing up to his front step.

He beamed. "I'm doing all right. It's a nice day, now, so I can't find much to complain about."

"You own this establishment?"

He glanced over his shoulder. "I do. Not much in the way of an inn since we don't get lots of folk wanting to stay the night. But as a drinking hole, you won't find anything better. At least not within a hundred feet."

Sorrel laughed along with him. "Good thing that's my favorite thing to do."

He stuck out his hand. "Reed Hearthstone."

"Sorrel Thornbough."

"Oh my gods," Talon whispered to the rest of them. "Is this where she gets it from?"

"Gets what?" Lillie asked.

"This." Talon gestured to the two halflings. "The constant cheerfulness thing."

"It must be a halfling thing," Vola said. "Orcs definitely don't stop you on the street just to say hi."

"You from around here?" Reed asked Sorrel. "There's some halfling enclaves in the woods I haven't met all of yet."

Sorrel shrugged. "Nah, I grew up in Maxim's monastery up on Gorm's Peak."

"That's not so far. We won't hold it against you, then. You passing through or looking for someone in particular?" he said.

"More like some*thing*," Vola said, not so under her breath.

The man stroked his beard as he eyed her. "We don't mind strangers.

We get lots of humans from Deersford. And some orcs even. But we tend to keep to ourselves. We don't need trouble."

"No trouble," Sorrel hurried to reassure him, glancing back at Vola.

Vola made a face and crossed her arms, but she let Sorrel talk.

"We heard you had been having some trouble yourselves. We thought it might relate to ours. If anything, we're here to help."

The man's glance took them all in, roving over Lillie's hopeful and open face, Talon bristling with weapons, and finally landing on Vola's shield. His eyes narrowed a fraction.

Vola could read body language well enough. She gritted her teeth and stepped back, placing herself subservient to Sorrel and the others.

Reed rolled his shoulders as if making a decision. "You should come on inside," he told Sorrel. "I'd invite you all, but I doubt our ceilings are tall enough. If you wait here, I'll send the boy out with something to quench your thirst."

Sorrel glanced at Vola, and Vola gave her a sharp nod. Sorrel touched her fingers to her temple as if in salute and hurried after the erstwhile innkeeper, ready to play her part as information gatherer.

Talon and Lillie each took a seat on the front porch where they didn't look quite so oversized.

"It's just so…cute," Talon said, the growl in her voice softening. Gruff circled once, then flopped down at her feet to doze. Even the swamp monster gave a half-hearted snort before putting its head down and lipping at the top step of the inn.

A couple of older women in kilted-up skirts and aprons passed, calling a friendly hello. Their smiles shriveled the moment they saw Vola, and they hurried away.

Vola ground her teeth. Her shield felt heavy on her back, throwing her off balance.

Lillie would draw more of the locals to her with her smile, and Talon would eavesdrop, but only if Vola wasn't standing there scaring everyone away.

She stepped to the corner of the inn and leaned against one of the porch supports, trying to make herself look smaller and less obtrusive. She raised her gaze to the sky and pretended that she was fine. It was all fine.

A bright *tink, tink, tink*, rang in her ears like a fingernail on a metal cup.

Vola glanced down. A little halfling girl tapped her shin guard, admiring herself in the mirror-bright shine of Vola's armor.

She did it again and then grinned up at Vola, her gap-toothed smile pulled wide. "You're very shiny," she said.

Vola fought down a grin and carefully knelt, so the little girl wasn't quite so far away. Even crouched, she was still twice as tall as the child, but the girl beamed up at her, brave as a full knight.

"I just polished everything this morning. It's important to take care of your equipment."

"It's shiny," the girl said, running her finger down the metal. "But there's all these scratches."

"That's because it's been through a lot. Never trust a knight in perfect armor."

The girl sucked on a curl. "Why?"

"It means they're not out helping people. The ones that are all scratched up and dirty are the ones who are helping people. The first job my friends and I ever had was in a swamp. It was a lot of work, and we didn't look very pretty afterward. But we rescued a lot of people that day."

"A swamp?"

"Yeah, a really dirty smelly swamp. It's like a forest with water underneath."

"Did you fall in?"

Vola laughed. "A lot more than I'd like to admit."

A hand wrapped around the girl's middle and yanked her up and away from Vola.

Vola blinked at the girl's mother, who held her child like Vola was about to snatch her away. The halfling woman's eyes were wide enough to see the whites around them, and she stumbled back a step when she met Vola's gaze.

"Mama, I wanted to see the shiny."

"Hush now, that's a black paladin. We don't go near them or they'll corrupt us, too."

Bile rose in the back of Vola's throat as the woman staggered away, dragging the little girl.

We could do something, said a voice in the back of her head. *We could prove them wrong. Or…we could show them they're right to fear you.*

Vola lurched to her feet, shaking her head as if she could fling it from herself entirely. "Get out, Mulgash," she muttered under her breath. "I didn't invite you in. Get out of my head."

I don't need an invitation, little mortal. I only need your rage. You wear my emblem in your heart every time you lose your temper.

Vola shivered. She'd thought she knew lots about the gods. She'd served one after all. But she had no idea how a Greater Obstacle slithered into your soul. Rage was something she'd been born with, but she refused to accept it was something that she couldn't change. But without Cleavah, she had no shield against his whispers.

She staggered back to the others. Sorrel reappeared with two drinks in each hand, which she distributed to Lillie, Talon, and Vola.

Vola sniffed and was surprised to find it was a mild cider.

Sorrel winked at her. "I figured you'd rather not pass out on your first job outside the city."

"Good call," Vola said into the mug, then took a swig.

A young woman lingered behind Sorrel, her dark, curling hair pulled back into a braid, her eyes wary on their faces.

"Guys, this is Sandry," Sorrel said. "She thinks her brother might have this mind-changing disease they were describing back in Deersford."

Vola straightened as Lillie and Talon stood up from their sitting positions.

"Go ahead, Sandry," Sorrel said.

The young woman's eyes darted between Talon's hood and Vola's shield.

"These are my family," Sorrel said quietly. "I trust them more than I trust the monks who raised me. If anyone can help, it's them."

Sandry seemed bolstered by this and gave Sorrel a nod before speaking in a quiet but clear voice. "There's been folk doing strange things. People going missing who have never even left home before, some speaking up out of turn when they've always been the quiet one and vice versa. My brother, he's little, not more than twelve, and he walked off one day into the woods. I lost him near the creek, and I haven't been able to find him."

"He doesn't normally wander in the woods?" Vola asked gently.

The girl still jumped. But she raised her chin and met Vola's eyes. "No, ma'am. I know other boys his age like to break the rules and go out on their own, pretending to be grown and all, but Erron, he isn't like that. He's shy. He doesn't have a lot of friends. We're all that's left of our family, and we've always stuck together. He wouldn't just leave while I ran after him yelling. It's not like him at all."

Vola blinked, Finn's normally amiable face twisted into something ferocious as he stabbed a serving girl in the back. She shook her head, trying to get rid of the memory.

Sorrel looked at her, lips thin, before turning to the girl. "We'll find him, Sandry," she said. "We'll find him, and we'll make sure he's himself again."

"You think you can?" Sandry asked.

Sorrel gave her a lopsided grin. "We're getting really good at finding missing people now."

NINE

THEY LEFT IMMEDIATELY to try and pick up Erron's trail near the stream where his sister had lost him. The rest of them let Talon go on ahead, where she could slink through the old growth, trying to pick up traces of halfling footprints in the loam of the forest floor. Gruff ranged along their right, nose to the ground.

Talon examined each stalk and leaf as if it told a story. The ranger talked to animals. Maybe she could talk to plants as well.

But the sun was starting to creep lower, sending the light angling through the trees differently, and Vola glanced at it with her eyes narrowed.

"Is this working?" Sorrel whispered to Vola and Lillie. They kept far enough back so their movements wouldn't obscure any of the traces Talon looked for.

"I think we need to be patient," Lillie said. "This is a delicate process. Or at least it looks like it."

"It's getting late." Sorrel gestured to the darkening sky through the canopy. "Erron's only twelve, and he's already been out here a day and a half. I don't want to leave him out here another night if we don't have to. Do you?"

Lillie bit her lip.

"Talon?" Vola asked tentatively. "Are you finding anything?"

Talon pushed her hood back to glance at them, lips pursed. "I think so. But there have been many others through here, leaving their own trails and markings. And Gruff isn't finding his scent. Could be too old or could be he knew enough to walk in the creek to confuse pursuers."

"He doesn't seem like the experienced woodsman," Sorrel said.

Lillie wrung her hands. "But if his mind is not his own..."

Finn hadn't been a cold-blooded killer until the mind mage had taken over.

"I think Sorrel's right," Vola said. "We should keep pressing on until we find something to go on. You said there were other trails?"

"Nothing suspicious," Talon said with a sigh. "Lots of halflings coming through. Lumberers and hunters. I smell smoke, so I'll bet there are some charcoal burners around here somewhere, too."

Sorrel nodded. "That lines up. The village doesn't do a lot of farming. They mostly make their living from the forest."

"Can you keep following what you have?" Vola asked Talon. "Maybe we can find something clearer further out."

Talon slunk away, following a trail only she could see while the rest tried to keep up without crashing through the undergrowth.

Less than half an hour later, Talon picked up the pace. "Here."

Vola's pulse sped up as she pushed past a low-hanging branch and lumbered after Talon. The ranger slipped around another tree and cried out.

Vola lunged out of the tree line onto the bank of a creek and slid to a stop.

She'd expected to find the halfling boy. But the figure standing on the bank with her hands on her hips was a lithe human woman dressed head to toe in black leather, her dark mahogany hair tumbling down her back in perfect waves.

The woman spun, and even Vola could see the way her boots marred the small footprints in the soft ground, obscuring the last of Erron's trail.

"What are you doing?" Talon said, throwing up her hands.

"I'm looking for the missing boy," the woman said, startled into answering. She lifted her chin and glared. "Why? What are *you* doing?"

"Our job," Sorrel said, coming around the tree.

"You couldn't have found anywhere else to stand?" Talon knelt in the mud, her fingers brushing the edges of the ruined tracks. "If you were looking for the boy, why would you mess up the tracks?"

"What tracks?" the woman said, staring down at her feet. Then she shook her head. "Never mind. You're in my way."

"*Your* way?" Sorrel cried.

Vola shushed her with a glance. "Why are you looking for Erron? Sandry sent us."

The woman tossed her hair over her shoulder. "No one had to send me. I'm an adventurer. Rescuing people is what I do." Her face fell for a moment. "At least, it's what I'm supposed to do."

"Look at this," Talon grumbled. "There's nothing left. And he didn't cross the stream so there's no fresh trail. We're back at square one. I just don't believe it."

The woman's mouth hardened.

"What's your name?" Vola said, forestalling a reaction.

"My name doesn't matter. Only my work."

Vola made a face.

"Of course your name matters," Lillie said, far more gently than Vola would have managed.

The woman hesitated. "Naraya."

"Well, Naraya. Maybe you could step to one side so Talon can see if there's anything to salvage."

Sorrel bent to help Talon as the woman very gingerly stepped out of the mess of boot prints.

Talon tsked through her teeth.

"I don't have time for this," Naraya said. "This path is a dead end. Erron's not here, and it's getting dark. I want to find him before that."

"Then we have similar goals," Lillie said.

"Maybe we can work together," Vola said quickly. They'd encountered other adventurers before, and she had no desire to end up in another race with someone trying to find the same boy. They didn't have to trust her completely to work with her, and who knew? Maybe the woman had hidden skills she could add.

But Naraya shook her head. Her leather outfit creaked with the motion. There was no way it was functional. Anything thin enough to show off that much off her figure was too thin to actually protect the important bits.

"I work alone," Naraya said. "That way, no one can get hurt but me."

"That's stupid," Sorrel said from her knees. "Who helps you when you get hurt, then?"

"I don't need help," Naraya snapped. "Just stay out of my way."

The woman clenched her fists and stalked away into the forest, pushing aside branches that snapped back to whip the back of her head. She yelped as she disappeared.

Vola rubbed her forehead with a sigh.

"Were we ever that incompetent?" Sorrel said.

"More so, probably," Lillie said. "But I like to think we weren't as arrogant about it."

"Is there anything left, Talon?" Vola said. The woman might have derailed them, but at least she was gone now.

"Nothing useful," Talon growled. She glared up at the strip of dark sky over the creek. "And I won't be able to see anything else in the dark. We're screwed."

"I guess we should break out the tent," Vola said. "We can start fresh in the morning."

"Oh, wonderful, more camping," Lillie said, eying the tent strapped to the swamp monster's back.

"We've had a lot more practice," Sorrel said dubiously. "We should be better at it by now."

Talon just snorted.

"What if we could see in the dark?" Lillie said, tapping her lip.

Vola raised an eyebrow and pulled the tent from the swamp beast's back. It thrust its head out to snap at her, its teeth scraping down the plate armor of her arm.

She glared at it. "It would make setting up a little easier."

"I mean, would we be able to keep searching?"

"We still wouldn't have much of a trail to go on," Talon said.

"Because we've been looking down here. What if we could see in the dark and see the forest from above?" Lillie beamed. "Perhaps we would be able to see something we missed before. Not seeing the forest for the trees and all that."

"Do you have a spell that can make you fly?"

"Not me," Lillie said. "A familiar. We need help, yes? Well, I can summon some that can both fly and see in the dark."

Gruff wound his way through the trees and rubbed up against Talon's back. She reached out to scratch his ears.

"Go for it," she said. "Maybe you'll have more luck than we did."

"Why not?" Vola strapped the tent back onto the swamp beast. "It couldn't hurt."

Talon and Sorrel built a small fire while Lillie bustled around the stream bank, arranging spell components.

She patted a little pile of salt into place and took a smoldering stick of charcoal from the fire. Then consulted her notes.

Vola cocked her head. "How long will this take?"

"A few minutes, not much more. I need to be sure to call something fleet and loyal." She grinned at Vola. "I've always wanted to do this." She hummed to herself, and Vola got the impression she'd almost forgotten they were there.

"Someone fierce and clever," Lillie murmured. "Someone cuddly."

Sorrel looked up from the fire. "What does cuddly have to do with it?"

"Hmm?" Lillie said. "What about cuddly?"

"You said cuddly."

"No, I didn't. Why would I say cuddly?" Lillie said.

"I don't know. It's *your* dream animal," Sorrel said.

Talon crouched on the other side of the fire, watching as Lillie sprinkled a bit of ash across her components. "Are you enslaving a wild creature?"

Lillie looked up, brow creased. "It's not enslaving. Not like that at all. It's more like calling and binding the spirit of an animal to this plane of existence." She pulled out a long white feather and cupped it in her hands. "It will have form and personality, but it's closer to being a construct than a real animal."

Talon subsided, sitting back on her heels, waiting.

Lillie placed the feather carefully at the apex of her diagram and held her hands over the components. She murmured, sitting as still as Vola had ever seen her.

Vola sat on her heels beside the fire, waiting for something to happen. Gradually, the feather began to glow, a soft blue that grew and infused the night with the faint ruffle of down.

Vola blinked and glanced around the empty clearing, half-expecting to see wings.

The salt and charcoal shivered and seemed to melt, tendrils drawing into the feather as if it was sucking up the other spell components.

Vola held her breath as the feather swelled and morphed and bulged in different places until a white owl stood blinking in its place, little black markings along its shoulders and wingtips.

"Oh my gosh, it worked," Lillie breathed.

"You weren't sure if it would?" Vola asked.

Lillie ignored her. "He's perfect. Hello, little one."

The owl blinked and let out a bland "hoo."

Lillie held out her hand, knuckles curled as if to let it sniff her. "Hi. I think you and I are going to be great friends."

The owl startled back and flapped. Then launched itself in the air and flew in a circle around their fire.

"Wait! Where are you going? Come back?" Lillie called

A voice chuckled from the trees overhead.

Vola drew in her breath and stood, circling to see who was watching them. Her hand went to her hilt.

Lillie scrambled to her feet and limped after the bird. "Wait, you're supposed to be my friend."

The owl hooted, alarmed, and veered straight into a tree. It dropped to the ground in a poof of white feathers.

"Er, I take it that wasn't supposed to happen," Sorrel said as Lillie stared at the fluttering feathers in consternation. Nothing was left of the bird except a pile of loose down.

The voice in the trees laughed again, directly over Vola's head.

She craned her neck and stepped back enough to see a large black raven perched on a branch overhead.

"Anyone else seeing this?" Vola said, staring at the black bird.

"I am," Talon said.

"I didn't know ravens could laugh," Sorrel said.

"Maybe it learned to mimic like a parrot," Vola said. "I've heard some birds can sound surprisingly lifelike."

Lillie stomped back to the stream bank, carrying a handful of white feathers.

"What are you doing?" Vola said.

"I'm trying again," she snapped. "Clearly, I did something wrong and the owl was not what it was supposed to be."

It took less time this time around, or maybe Vola was just looking for the different parts coming together now.

The owl stood in the center of Lillie's working, staring at them. It twisted its head around. "Hoo."

Before it could fly away again, Lillie very carefully reached for the owl and brought him gently to her chest.

"There," she said. "You just have to be careful not to startle him, that's all."

"Or you could try something with more brains," the voice said.

Lillie jumped, and the owl screeched in alarm, buffeting her with its wings. She let go with a cry, and the owl flapped away.

Straight into the swamp monster's jaws. It's teeth closed with a snap, and feathers spurted out the sides of its mouth.

"Fuck," Lillie said.

Vola drew her mom's ax and leveled it at the raven. "It talks," she said.

"That doesn't sound like mimicry," Talon said.

Sorrel threw up her hands. "Is no one going to mention the fact that Lillie just swore?"

"I honestly can't decide which deserves more attention," Talon said. "The talking bird or the fact that Lillie knows that word."

"You all are funny little things, aren't you?" the bird said, cocking its head as the voice definitely came from its beak. "I think I'll keep you. Oh, is she going to try again?"

"You stay out of this," Lillie told the bird, her hands full of bloody feathers as if she'd reached down the swamp beast's gullet to retrieve them herself. The swamp monster just looked smug, a piece of down stuck to its slimy lip.

Vola looked back and forth between the raven and Lillie as the wizard knelt to begin her summoning again. "What the heck?"

"Can you still not swear?" Sorrel said.

"Habit," Vola said with a shrug. "I haven't actually tried yet."

"What do you mean you'll keep us?" Talon asked the raven.

"You can be my pets."

"That's rude," Sorrel said.

The raven ruffled his feathers. "People keep animals as pets all the time. See?" He jerked his beak at Lillie. "Why would it be any different?"

The wizard's components began glowing again.

"Do you suppose it's under a curse?" Talon said, gazing up at the raven.

He eyed her back, cocking his head. "Of course I'm under a curse. Do you meet a lot of talking ravens?"

"I'm a ranger. I talk to animals all the time."

"Oh, well, you don't count."

"Gee, thanks," Talon said.

"You need to feed it a mouse or something," the raven told Lillie as the components came together to form the third owl in less than half an hour. "Help it bond to you."

"It's supposed to be loyal and dedicated from the first moment," Lillie said. She pulled a strip of dried meat from their packs before dangling it in front of the owl. "Here, you silly thing. Please take it. We need you to help us find a halfling boy. Do you know what a boy is?"

"I know what a boy is," the raven said.

"I think it's a spy," Talon said, mouth pursed in thought.

"I am definitely a spy," the raven said. "But is that all I am? People can be more than one thing, you know."

"Are you a person?" Sorrel said. "I mean, technically speaking?"

The raven ruffled its feathers. "You can think whatever you want of me. I know what I am."

"You just can't tell us outright, is that it?"

"Where would the fun be in that?"

Vola's brow drew down. "You remind me very strongly of a bard I met this morning. He couldn't give a straight answer, either."

"A bard?" the bird said, focusing black eyes on her.

"A halfling boy, you stupid creature," Lillie said, waving the piece of meat. "Can. You. Take. Us. To. Him?"

The owl snatched the meat from Lillie's hand and flapped up into the night. This time it shot straight up, missing any trees and swamp monsters, and disappeared over the forest.

They watched it go in silence.

"Well, you really can't expect much from owls," the raven said. "All they do is sleep and hunt things that squeak and barf up little hairballs of bone and fur. They're like the cats of the sky. Skittish, aloof, and not interested in anything but themselves."

Lillie slumped. "I really wanted it to work…"

The raven flapped down from its perch and landed on the ground next to her. It hopped forward a couple of feet and rubbed its beak against her hand.

Vola's grip tightened on her ax. From this angle, the bird really was enormous. But it didn't seem to be causing them any harm…

Lillie lifted her hand to cautiously stroke the bird's head.

He sidled under her arm. "Honey, don't let that stupid thing hurt you. You were too good for it anyway. I know talent when I see it. You want to find a halfling boy, yes?"

"Yes," Lillie said, head cocked.

"About twelve, grubby like he's been away from home a couple of days."

"Yes," Sorrel said, crouching beside the bird and Lillie.

The raven hopped out from under Lillie's arm and flapped up to a low-hanging branch. The swamp monster snapped at it on its way, but he swerved adroitly around the flashing teeth.

"Easy enough," the bird said. "I know everyone in these woods. I can take you right to him."

TEN

THE RAVEN DOVE between the trees as Lillie followed, limping through the underbrush. Talon trotted along with her as Sorrel and Vola brought up the rear dragging the swamp beast.

"Do you trust this…bird?" Sorrel whispered to Vola.

Vola pursed her lips and shook her head. "Not even a little. He actually told us he was a spy."

"Yes, but a spy for who?"

"Does it matter? He's working for someone else. And if it was a friend, why wouldn't he just say?"

Sorrel dodged around a tree laden with poison ivy and glanced toward the bird. He was nearly invisible in the night, but he kept calling out to keep them on his tail.

"He might not be able to," she said. "If he's under a curse. A lot of those come with a geas that says you can't talk about it."

The raven fluttered up to a branch and jerked his beak at the ground. "Here," he said, his voice just short of a caw. "He slept here last night."

Talon knelt beside the spot indicated and touched the trampled greenery. Then she glanced up at the rest of them. "He's right," she said quietly. "And I'm not sure I would have found it myself. Not with everyone else tromping around in these woods."

Vola bit her lip and glanced at Sorrel, who shrugged and said, "It's hard to argue with someone who's helping you."

The raven just looked on with bright beady eyes.

"Ready?" he asked.

Vola sighed. "Lead on."

The raven took off again, his wing beats sending a wash of cool air over them. "This way."

Vola kept her ax in her hand. Trusting the bird enough to follow him didn't mean she couldn't be ready for an ambush, too. And why did he know so much about Erron's whereabouts? What about the boy had caught his attention? Maybe he had some connection to the mind mage.

He soared high, then dove, careening around a trunk directly in front of them, keeping far enough ahead to lead but doubling back enough that they never really lost him.

Vola scanned the forest on either side while Sorrel watched behind them, moving quickly but quietly through the underbrush, staff ready.

"Here, he took a drink from this stream," the raven said.

Talon paused to confirm, then gave Vola a subtle nod. At least the bird was telling the truth so far. Vola's grip relaxed on her ax handle.

"You said you were under a curse," Lillie called ahead to the bird. "Is there anything we can do to help you?"

"Why do you think I'm doing this?" He circled back to land on her shoulder, careful not to buffet her with his wings. "If you like me, you'll be more likely to help me with my own problems."

He clacked his beak in her ear, and she made a face before stroking his head.

"And having pretty girls give you scratches has absolutely nothing to do with it either, right?" Vola asked with a snort.

The raven leaned into Lillie's caress. "I never said there weren't perks. If you can get the spot right between my wings. It's always itchy, and this neck doesn't bend that way. Yes, right there."

"What's your name?" Lillie asked him. "It seems impolite to call you bird."

"Well, aren't you sweet? You may call me Raven."

He launched himself into the air with a caw that sounded a lot like a laugh. "We're close now. I'd suggest moving quietly. He may get spooked."

"Do you know what's wrong with him?" Sorrel asked.

"His mind is not his own. More than that I can't tell you. I only know that I've watched villager after villager succumb to the same problem, leaving their family and friends and traipsing into these woods."

He dove low under a branch. "Here," he said. "Softly. Follow me." Raven cupped his wings to stop short in the air.

Then with a startled squawk, he disappeared in a flash of purple light, bright in the dark.

Vola threw up her arm to shield her eyes and blinked away spots.

"Where'd he go?" she whispered. She fell into a ready stance and spun, searching the dark tree trunks. Nothing moved between them.

Sorrel ranged out cautiously, pushing leaves back with the end of her staff.

Talon scowled and shook her head. "I don't know. He just up and popped out of existence."

Lillie walked to the spot where Raven had disappeared and held out her hands. "No. No, I recognize this. I was just doing it myself."

"What do you mean?" Vola asked.

"This is what a summoning looks like from the other side. That is, if you're summoning a real creature or person and not a construct."

"Are you saying Raven is someone else's familiar, and they just called him home?" Sorrel said.

"That's what it looks like."

Vola shifted to the balls of her feet. "Do you think he's a prisoner? That didn't look voluntary."

"I don't know. Wizards never summon a real person as a familiar. It's too much like slavery. It's possible he entered into the contract willingly. But..."

"But probably not," Vola finished for her. "Not with the way he was talking about breaking a curse. He needs help."

"Whatever he is, he led us close enough to the boy's trail that I can pick it up from here." Talon crouched between two beech trees, examining the soft dirt beneath. "He's close. He passed this way not long ago."

Vola signaled the others. Talon out front, stepping quietly as a wolf, Sorrel and Lillie in the middle, and Vola guarding their rear.

Vola caught Lillie's worried look in the dark.

"Don't worry," she whispered. "We'll look for Raven after we find Erron."

Only steps away, they found a halfling boy, bedraggled with stains on his clothes and leaves in his curly hair, crouched between the roots of an elm tree. He blinked up at them as Talon came into view, moving as slowly as possible. Sorrel moved up beside her, hands out.

"Erron?" she said into the quiet night. "Erron, we're here to help. All right? Your sister is worried about you."

The boy blinked up at them, blankly. Then he stood, and with wooden movements, he started trudging away.

"They were right. He's been subverted," Sorrel said flatly.

"Just like Finn," Vola said. "And Kellan."

"Well, we know how to deal with that," Lillie said, raising her hands. "Don't we?"

She spoke three sharp words, and a shield sprang up around Erron, cutting him off from the outside world and the influence of whoever was controlling him.

He paused, foot raised and then collapsed.

Lillie let the shield fall as Sorrel rushed forward to catch him.

"Just like Finn," Sorrel said, easing the boy to the ground. She looked up at them, brow furrowed in anger. "There's our proof. The enemy is here. Somewhere. And he's stealing halflings to subvert."

Talon glanced around. It wasn't exactly a clearing. The trees concealed anything that might be sneaking up on them. "And we know he can only subvert one at a time. Now that we've broken his hold on Erron, he'll be starting again on someone new."

Lillie bit her lip. "I didn't think about that. Maybe I should have left him be. That way, we would have known who it was."

Vola shook her head. "No, we have no idea how he would have reacted if we'd tried to take him home in that state. He could have tried to fight. And if this person has total control and knows what their victim is doing, he would have figured out we had Erron and dropped the spell anyway. You made the right call."

"Why would the mind mage want halflings?" Talon said, cocking her head.

Sorrel bristled. "Why wouldn't they want halflings? We're just as good as any other victims."

"What an odd sort of argument," Lillie murmured.

"I meant, what are they doing with them?" Talon said. "Why would they want Erron just wandering around the woods?"

"Maybe he was trying to make his way to wherever the mind mage is," Vola said.

"Oh, then I really should have left him." Lillie covered her cheeks. "We could have followed him to the culprit."

"No," Sorrel said. "We need to get him home. Finn was ill for days after he killed that girl. And he was only affected for a few minutes. Erron's been under for days."

"Good point," Talon said. "Let's go."

"Vola, will you check him?" Sorrel said, rearranging his limbs more comfortably. "To make sure he doesn't need healing—" She froze.

Vola stiffened. Her fingers curled around her weapon.

"I'm sorry," Sorrel said quietly. "I forgot."

"It's all right." Vola took a deep breath and rolled her shoulders, shrugging away the pain. She stepped forward, fighting down the thought that she was failing her party by leaving them without a healer, and lifted Erron from Sorrel's arms. The boy was rail thin and a halfling to boot. Her armor weighed more than he did.

"Talon, I'm assuming you kept track of where we are. You know how to get back to the village?" Vola said.

Talon didn't even answer before leading them back the way they'd come.

The forest remained quiet, late-night animals making their rounds as silently as they did. Talon unerringly led them around any large predators that might have given them trouble, and Vola trusted her to know which direction they were going. She carried Erron in her arms. They could have slung him over the back of the swamp monster, but Vola didn't want to chance it. With their luck, the thing would assume they'd brought it dinner and try to eat the boy.

Vola's legs had started to ache, and she figured they had to be getting close when Talon froze and dropped to a crouch.

She held up a hand, and Vola and Lillie held dead still. Sorrel spun to guard them from behind.

Vola waited. Talon gave her the hand signal to hold, then crept forward and melted into the brush.

Vola held her breath. Nothing stirred in the forest, sending a shiver down her neck.

Talon reappeared and gestured to Vola. She placed Erron, gently on the ground and stepped forward, careful to keep her armor from clanking.

"What is it?" she breathed.

Talon pulled aside some of the screening leaves, and Vola ducked to look.

Ahead of them, two figures spoke beside the creek. The same creek where they'd met Raven.

Vola squinted. The only reason she could recognize them was because one had a ball of light floating over his shoulder, illuminating dark hair tied back in a tail and a lute slung over its back.

Cyrano the bard.

He spoke with the woman they'd encountered earlier that day. It was hard to miss the black leather which shone in Cyrano's light and the sullen set of her expression.

Talon laid a finger to her ear, and Vola listened.

"You're getting in the way of my investigation," the woman snapped.

"I'm doing no such thing, my dear." Cyrano rolled his eyes toward the sky as if asking for patience. "You can go that way. And I can go this way."

"I mean, you're tromping around this forest, scaring everything within a league, including the boy that I'm looking for."

Talon scowled. "Hey," she whispered. "That's my line."

"I have my own path to follow," Cyrano said. "It has nothing to do with you."

"Then get out of my way, or I'll make you get out of the way."

Even from here, Vola could see Cyrano's eyes narrow. "You don't want to make that threat, darling."

Naraya threw back her head. "Why? You think I can't follow through. I'm tougher than I look."

Cyrano took a deep breath through his nose and casually swung his lute into his arms. He began plucking strings as he talked. "That's not my point," he said, and his voice fell into a sort of sing-song-y cadence. "My point is, you seem more than capable. But a wise woman would recognize her match and choose to fight a different way. And you're a wise woman, aren't you?"

She seemed transfixed by the movement of his fingers on the fret of his lute. "I am."

"There. See, that means there's no problem. Right?"

"Right."

"So why don't you run along on your quest and leave me out of it. I have my own places to be, and a wise woman doesn't need to pick a fight where one isn't needed."

"And I'm a wise woman," she said, her voice soft, without inflection.

Vola inhaled sharply.

"Does that seem normal to you?" Talon asked in her ear.

"Not even a little," Sorrel said on her other side.

Vola just kept herself from jumping. When had she and Lillie joined them?

"Well, now we know why he was chatting Vola up," Sorrel said.

"It's him," Lillie whispered. "He's the one subverting people. And he made it look so easy."

"You are not allowed to ask him to teach it to you," Sorrel said under her breath.

Lillie opened her mouth, but before she could respond, Vola had exchanged a look with Talon and Sorrel. "Are we doing this?"

"Well, we can't let him get away now," Sorrel said.

Vola jerked her head at the prone body of Erron behind them. "Great. Stand guard over Erron."

Sorrel started to protest, but Vola signaled her to stand down. "It's just one bard, and we have these." She touched the pendant around her neck. "We'll be fine, and Erron is vulnerable."

Sorrel subsided with a grumble.

"All right, then," Vola said. "Three, two, one."

ELEVEN

VOLA SPRANG FORWARD, the branches parting with a snap.

Cyrano had slung his lute back across his back and was leaning down to grab a coat he'd tossed across a nearby log. He paused, then straightened when he heard her approach.

"Lightless," he said. "I knew you were in the area, but I didn't expect to see you so soon."

Vola leveled her ax at his throat.

He raised his eyebrows along with both hands to show he wasn't holding his weapon. "I like a woman who gets right to the point."

Vola tilted her head. "Really? You thought this was the perfect time to get clever?"

"I'm sorry. I can't really turn it off. It's part of the whole package."

Talon emerged from the trees, bow drawn and trained on the bard. Lillie rushed for Naraya, who stood listlessly beside the creek.

"What did you do to her?" Vola said, jerking her chin at the woman.

"Nothing," he said.

"Right, try again."

"She was trying to keep me from reaching my goal. I have no quarrel with her or with you. I'd rather just be on my way. All right?"

He started to lower his hands, and Vola stepped forward. "You think we're just going to let you leave after what you did to her? And what about Finn? And Kellan?"

"Finn who?" His face fell. "Oh, do I have some competition for you?"

Vola snarled. "That's it."

She took another step, and he leaped back. "Whoa, wrong tactic. Sorry, didn't mean to strike a nerve."

She kept coming, and he darted back, then drew his rapier. "I don't want to hurt you, Lightless. But if you try to get in my way, you'll end up just like her." He pointed his sword at the woman. Lillie was gently slapping her cheeks without result.

Vola's lips pulled back from her teeth. "Was that a threat?"

"Sounded like a threat to me," Talon said.

"Yes, but if we're fair, a lot of things sound like a threat to you," Sorrel's voice called from the thicket where she guarded Erron.

Cyrano's eyes flicked to the sound of Sorrel's voice and back to Vola. He gave her a little bow. "Clearly, you have me surrounded. Very well."

He feinted and thrust with pinpoint accuracy at the weak joint between Vola's shoulder plates.

Vola spun, taking the tip of his rapier against her armor and letting it slide harmlessly to the side. She followed the momentum around, bringing the edge of her ax to his neck.

But suddenly he wasn't there anymore. He'd skipped back to the edge of the creek.

"You're quick," he said. "Much quicker than most knights."

Vola's lip tilted in an unconscious grin. "Not a knight. Not anymore." She drew her sword in addition to her mom's ax. Now that she wasn't using her shield, she could fit a weapon in each hand.

"Then I guess I should look out for more surprises."

He ducked and parried, slashing for her ankles. Vola leaped over his blade and charged forward. He stooped and scooped up water with his free hand, then flung it at her face, making her close her eyes and fumble in her charge.

"Vola, look out," Talon called.

Vola instinctively fell to the ground and rolled as a breath of air flashed over head.

She opened her eyes to see Cyrano standing where she'd been a moment before. There was a zing, and he danced back a step as an arrow sprouted from the ground between his feet.

"Careful now," he told Talon. "You have to buy me dinner first if you want to get any closer than that."

Vola rolled to her feet, clanking a little. Something tickled her ear, and she flinched. A sound almost like someone laughing echoed over her shoulder. She couldn't help glancing to find the source.

And Cyrano attacked.

She saw his movement out of the corner of her eye, and instead of wincing away or ducking, she stepped into his blow, taking the stab across her chest. His blade slithered across her plate, leaving a long scratch and a squeal in her ears that didn't quite drown out the strange laughter.

Cyrano himself wasn't expecting the move, and he stepped right into her and bounced off her chest.

He landed on his rear and scrambled back out of her reach.

Vola paused long enough to breathe and rub at her ear. The voice still giggled and chuckled, drawing her attention away from the immediate threat.

"Are you doing that? It's...clever," she said.

He shrugged humbly. "I've fought knights before. Unless you're a strong brute able to hack away at all that armor, the key is distraction so you can get in close."

"Too bad it didn't work."

"Too bad," he said, but he grinned at the same time.

"I feel like you're not taking this seriously."

"Oh, I'm sorry, would you like me to?"

"That would be nice, yeah. I like people to pay attention when I try to kill them."

Vola skipped forward, brought her ax around as if to slash at him, and when he dodged, she brought her elbow around to bash him in the face.

He staggered back, dropping his sword. He held his streaming nose, then pulled his hand away to squint at the blood.

"Wait. You're serious," he said, eyes wide.

She cocked her head. "Deadly. I'm not forgetting Finn any time soon."

He huffed a laugh and then winced. "And I thought we could be friends." He reached for his dropped sword. "Don't you want to be friends, Lightless?" His voice went melodic and rhythmic.

She took a step forward, but fuzz rose in the back of her mind, like fog sweeping up a riverbank at night. Why were they fighting again?

The mind control. Right. That was it. She should be angry about this.

She shook her head, but the fog clambered deep inside her, creeping down her limbs making them feel heavy and stiff.

An arrow landed at their feet, but not like Talon was shooting at them. More like she'd let her string go by accident, half drawn.

Her party. She had to keep him from subverting her party. Goddess, she was failing.

Vaguely, she was aware of hands on her, guiding her down.

"Really, Lightless. I adore competent people, but I can't afford distractions right now. Even lovely ones. You understand. And I'd hate to have to kill you. We were both lucky, I guess. I can only use that spell once in a fight. And I'm completely useless afterward."

Something tightened across her chest, and she struggled feebly. He could slit her throat right now, and she'd let him.

He clapped her on the arm. "Shh now. It won't last much longer."

She floated for a while, wondering if he had actually killed her. Was this what death was like? Who would come to collect a black paladin? It wouldn't be Cleavah, that was for sure. Mulgash seemed to have taken an interest in her, but she'd been fighting him every step of the way.

Vola blinked. Her eyes felt dry and gummy. Like she'd been sleeping. The creek burbled nearby, low and pleasant and not a bad way to wake up.

Wake up.

She hadn't been sleeping. She'd been spelled.

Early morning sunlight, gray and pink, streamed between the leaves above, lighting up the clearing and glinting from the creek's clear water.

She jerked and found resistance against her chest. A rope tied her to a nearby tree and prevented her from standing.

She whipped her head around and found Lillie beside her, head nodding over their bonds. Across the way, Talon and the annoying leather-clad woman were tied to another tree. And beside them, Sorrel and the halfling boy.

All of them alive. Despite their helpless state.

The swamp monster stood at the edge of the stream slurping.

"You couldn't have eaten him?" she asked.

The creature raised its dripping muzzle, a string of spit hanging from its lip, and it bared its teeth at her.

Lillie stirred at the sound of her voice. "Vola?"

"Here," Vola growled.

"Why does my head feel full of cotton?" Talon said across the way.

"It's like the hangover without any of the fun," Sorrel groaned.

"Have you ever even had a hangover?" Lillie asked.

Sorrel hesitated. "I've heard of them."

"Gruff?" Talon said.

The big black wolf whined. He was tied to the tree like a dog. His tail thumped sheepishly.

"He did his mind control trick on us," Vola said.

Lillie hesitated, lips pursed in thought.

"And then he tied us up."

"But we should have been protected," Talon said, squinting down at her chest. She went cross-eyed trying to see the pendant.

"Why tie us up?" Sorrel said. "If he was the bad guy, why wouldn't he just kill us?"

"Instead, he went out of his way to collect us and our belongings." Talon jerked her chin at the pile of their gear beside the bank. "And made sure we wouldn't wander off in our foggy state."

He tied you up, the voice whispered in her ear. *He bested you and tied you up to mock you. He's baiting you, and you're letting him.*

Vola scowled. She'd let him mock her the whole time. And if she was honest with herself, she'd enjoyed it. She'd enjoyed trading blows and wit. But then he'd tricked her. He was going to get away with all this because he hadn't faced her fairly.

Finn won't be avenged. Or Kellan. Or Erron. What kind of paladin lets the bad guy escape?

Red swept across her vision, painting the clearing in blood. "He's getting away."

"Vola," Lillie started.

"He's getting away, and we're letting him."

"Vola, it's morning. He's long—"

Vola couldn't see anymore. Nothing but red. Nothing but the heat that beat in her blood and her temples, filling her limbs with desperate energy. She needed to chase, to fight, to win.

She strained against the rope, heard Lillie and Sorrel and Talon calling to her, heard the rope snap.

She was free. She stood. Her weapons had been taken from her, but she still had fists. She still had teeth. She'd fight him with every piece of her.

She stepped forward.

Hands on her chest, pressure holding her back. A voice in her ear.

"Vola."

She shook her head. Red. All she could see was red.

"Vola. Stop."

That voice was important. There'd been a time when she hadn't listened to it like she should have, and it had cost her dearly.

"Vola, what's going on? Can you hear me?" The voice took on a deeper quality. It rang with bells and the sound of roaring wind. And it reminded Vola.

Deep breaths. Concentrating on the voice. She closed her eyes. Closed her eyes until she could see more than just red.

Vola blinked. The blood bled from her vision, leaving a cheery clearing drenched in morning sunlight. "What—what just happened?"

Lillie stood in front of her, palms pressed to her breastplate as if the wizard could physically keep her there if she tried. Talon was still tied to her tree, but she was sawing away at the rope that held her with one of the knives she kept in her boot.

"You snapped the rope like it was tissue paper," Sorrel said, eyes wide. She still sat tied to her tree as well, the boy slumped beside her.

"I think you wanted to go after Cyrano," Lillie said. "Without any thought or caution."

"Or a weapon," Talon muttered. The rope came free under her blade, and she stood, shedding the pieces of it. Naraya still sagged against the tree. Whatever Cyrano had done to her lasted longer.

Vola took a clean breath of air as Talon moved to free Sorrel. Whatever had happened had passed. Lillie had snapped her out of it. She stepped to the pile of weapons and snagged her sword and ax.

"Vola?" Lillie asked.

"We're not going after Cyrano," she said. "Not yet anyway. He could have killed us, and he didn't. And that spell. That affected all of us at once. Not one at a time. And it wore off. Not like Finn or Erron." She glanced at Lillie.

Lillie swallowed and nodded confirmation. "That's what I was thinking. He's clearly in this up to his neck, but…"

"But I'd rather not confront him again until we have ourselves in order," Vola said. She glared down at the pendant. "And we have a better plan to protect ourselves."

"They're supposed to work against the mind mage. Not against whatever Cyrano was wielding."

"We need to get Erron home," Sorrel said. "We can regroup there. Make a better plan."

Vola gave a short nod as the others retrieved their weapons. "All right, then."

She stepped away to go catch the swamp monster.

"Vola," Lillie said behind her. "What was it that happened to you?"

"What do you mean?" Vola said, back still turned.

"Just now, when you woke. You…you broke your bindings. Went into a rage. It was like you couldn't even hear us."

"It's an orc thing," she said.

"You've never done it before," Sorrel said.

"Maybe you don't know everything about me," she snapped.

Lillie drew back, biting her lip, but Vola wasn't going to apologize. Lillie would just ask more questions, and Sorrel would need the answers. And Talon would just look at her with the steady gaze of a wary wolf.

And she wasn't going to tell them about the voice in her head. The only thing worse than a black paladin was a black paladin with the backing of a Greater Obstacle.

TWELVE

THEY BROUGHT Erron back to the village, arriving just as everyone was leaving their homes for the day's work. The boy rode in Vola's arms, head propped on her armored shoulder. His eyes were open, but he seemed pretty bleary and tired.

"Erron!" The halfling girl, Sandry, ran out into the dirt road to intercept them.

Before she could run headlong into their party, Vola knelt and let Erron stand. Sandry reached them and caught her brother up in her arms. With their curly heads pressed together it was impossible to tell where the sister ended and the brother began.

Sorrel stood out front as the village halflings gathered around them, murmuring questions and awed praise.

"You brought him back," Sandry said. "You brought my brother back."

"I told you we would," Sorrel said quietly.

Vola took a few steps back from the villagers, anticipating their looks and suspicions, but one or two smiled at her, and the rest crowded around behind so she didn't have an escape route.

"He'll be a little disoriented for the first few days," Sorrel told Sandry. "And he probably won't remember what happened. But he'll be all right. Just let him recover."

"How…how do you know he'll be all right?"

Sorrel touched Erron's shoulder. The boy's eyelids were already

drooping again. "This happened to Vola's protege. And Lillie's brother."
She gestured over her shoulder to the wizard, who bit her lip and nodded.

"You've seen it before then," Sandry said.

Sorrel nodded. "We're looking for the one that did this. So no one else
has to wonder what happened to someone they love."

"Thank you," Sandry whispered. "Thank you." She steered the sleepy
Erron back down the road, and the crowd parted for her, pressing against
the picket fences lining the street.

"Breakfast," Reed Hearthstone said, pushing forward. His gray beard
bristled at the corners of his mouth as he beamed at them. "I'd say you've
earned some breakfast."

Halflings swarmed around them as Reed directed them to bring tables
and chairs from the inn, and they erected an impromptu meal right on the
main street through town so the bigger folks could fit, too. Vola couldn't
even tell where Reed's family ended and the other villagers began. Or
maybe the innkeeper was just related to the whole village.

Sorrel sat at the head of the table with three young halflings stationed
at her elbow just to keep her tankard full. More of them pulled Vola,
Talon, and Lillie down to sit and filled their plates with sausage and fried
potatoes.

And no one rushed to hide their children from Vola.

It was turning out to be a pretty good day, despite the fact Cyrano had
managed to escape.

One thing at a time.

Naraya sat sullenly at the far end of their table, her black-clad legs
stretched out under the surface. She scowled into her cup, probably still
miffed they'd woken her up and explained Cyrano had gotten the better
of her.

The halflings stepped around her when they had to venture down to
that side, eying her with exasperation.

Vola concentrated on her food, but Sorrel couldn't get a bite in as the
other halflings pestered her. She didn't seem to mind it, though.

"You sure you're not from around here? We'd love to claim you as one
of ours," Reed told her.

Sorrel shrugged. "My parents left me at the monastery when I was a
baby. I don't even know who they are."

"And you haven't tried to find them again?" Reed asked.

She took a swig of her drink. "Nah. They couldn't afford another
mouth. And the monks took good care of kids. So they did their best by

me, I suppose. The monks were my family, and when I outgrew its walls, I found my own people." She raised her tankard to Vola and the others.

"More potatoes?" a halfling asked Vola.

"Oh, I've had plenty, thank you," Vola said.

"Nonsense," the woman said.

Vola's eyes narrowed. She was pretty sure this was the same mother who'd snatched her child away just the day before.

The woman flushed. "We get orcs through here sometimes from the next town over. They can always fit another plateful. I imagine it takes a lot of food to fill up someone as big as you, and we have plenty."

Vola just took the second helping without comment. She didn't draw attention to the fact that the woman hadn't trusted her with her children yesterday, and the woman didn't mention it either. She just kept bringing Vola more and more food. It was a kind of apology, and Vola was willing to take it as such.

"It's still a nice thing to know where you've come from," Reed told Sorrel. "To have a place you can call home at least some of the time."

Sorrel cocked her head to scan the village. "I guess even if it wasn't this village, my parents would have been from somewhere very much like this."

Reed clapped her on the back. "You're welcome to us whenever you like."

Sorrel grinned, but her gaze was thoughtful.

Personally, Vola wanted a home where she could sit with her legs under the table and not worry about knocking all the plates into the dirt.

Breakfast was clearly a welcome break for most of the village, but they did have lives to get back to, and after a while, they started drifting away, off to work.

Sandry replaced the halflings who'd been waiting on Sorrel hand and foot, offering her a refill for her juice.

"How's your brother?" Vola asked her.

"Resting. Like you said he would. But when he was awake, he claimed I was smothering him, and that's pretty normal, so I think he's back to being himself."

Sorrel leaned forward, and Sandry straightened, her gaze focused on the monk.

"Did anyone come through the village in the last few days?" Sorrel asked. "Before Erron walked off. Anyone different that your brother might have talked to."

Sandry shook her head. "No, but I don't follow him around the whole time. At least, I didn't. I probably will now."

Sorrel exchanged a look with the rest of them.

"We know the mind mage has worked from a distance in the past," Lillie said. "They really could be anywhere around here."

"Oh goody, more traipsing through the woods," Talon said.

"I thought you liked woods," Vola said.

"These woods are entirely too full of people and bad guys."

Sandry stared at them, biting her lip. "You're leaving again?"

"We have to find the one who tried to kidnap your brother," Sorrel said.

Her face fell. "Oh. Well, I guess that's good." She traced the grain of the table with her fingertip.

"What's wrong?" Sorrel said, her gaze sharpening on the girl.

Sandry shrugged. "Nothing really. I just feel safer with you here, is all."

Sorrel's brow drew down. "The settlement has guards, right? To keep you safe from bandits and raiders and such."

Sandry shook her head. "Nah. We just band together with pitchforks if anyone attacks. And I don't really know how to use a pitchfork. We don't pitch a lot of hay around here."

Sorrel's lips thinned. She threw her fork down with a clatter and snatched up her staff, which leaned against the table beside her.

"Come on," she said.

Sandry's eyes went round. "What?"

Sorrel trotted to a clear spot in the dirt road and pointed in front of her. "Stand right here."

Sandry bit her lip and cautiously slid into the spot Sorrel indicated.

Sorrel used her staff to nudge Sandry's feet into position. "Feet apart, weight on the balls of your feet." She moved around Sandry, touching her shoulder, hip, and knee, guiding her into the first set of forms Vola recognized from Sorrel's daily exercises. "I'll teach you to fall properly in a second, but it might make you feel safer if you know how to punch someone back."

The monk demonstrated, extending her elbow so her fist shot out.

A couple of other young halflings crept closer in the street to watch as Sandry tried to mimic Sorrel's movements.

A snort drew Vola's attention to the end of the table where Naraya sat scowling at the display.

"What?" Vola snapped.

"She's wasting her time," the woman said.

Vola ground her teeth. "Teaching is never wasted," she said, thinking of Finn.

She winced. She'd expected the sudden stab of pain the memory brought. But it should not have hit her like a knight in full armor charging into her side.

The woman sniffed. "I guess. You might have time to sit around, but I have more important things to do."

"Like what?" Talon said, shifting closer. "We saved Erron. If that was your goal, then it's done."

"My work is never done," she said, staring at her plate as she pushed potatoes around with her fork. "You might see the end of a job as a chance for a vacation, but I can only think about all those people out there who still need my help."

Vola opened her mouth, but Talon beat her to it. "What is your problem?"

Vola fought down a snort. She would have chosen a more sideways approach, but Talon didn't suffer fools gladly.

"My problem?" Naraya glared across the table.

"Yes. We saved your ass, and all you can do is whine that we're not doing enough."

"You're adventurers. Just like me. Adventurers are supposed to be out there helping people. They're not supposed to be sitting around eating breakfast."

"Well, I'm glad you can save people on an empty stomach," Vola said, forking another scoop of potatoes. "I can't swing my sword when I'm hungry."

"You have to pace yourself," Talon said. "And you know, be a real person. Not an ideal."

"I am a real person, thank you. My mom…She walked off into the woods. Just like all these other folks. Walked off, never looked back, and she walked off a ridge. Everyone called it an accident, but I knew someone was to blame. And I don't want anyone else to lose someone like I did."

The woman glared at them and stood, making the table shake with her movement. "If you slow down, people think you're soft. Too many people have told me I can't do it. I'm not giving them any more opportunities to belittle me."

She stalked away toward the trees.

"Well, she's super fun," Sorrel said, popping up at Vola's elbow.

"She's going to get herself killed," Talon said quietly. "Can't imagine that would have made her mom happy."

"If she doesn't want to listen, there's little we can do to make her." Vola gestured to Sandry, who was falling forward to roll across the dirt the way Sorrel had shown her. "Did you ever think you would teach?"

Sorrel gave her a wan smile, not nearly as perky as her usual self. "Maybe one day, if I'd lasted long enough at the monastery."

She crossed her arms and sighed.

"What's wrong?" Vola said. "She seems to be doing well."

"Oh, yeah. She's quick and bright. It's just...I was realizing this could have been my life. Or at least something like it if I hadn't left the monastery."

Vola tilted her head. "Are you hankering for farming?"

Sorrel made a face. "No, not like that. But maybe staying in one place wouldn't be such a bad thing. Finding a place like this that could use someone like me. I just always thought that was a really long way off. Now...I don't know. It might be nice."

Vola opened her mouth, not sure if she should be horrified or encouraged that Sorrel had found a calling other than kicking ass.

A flutter of wings interrupted her, and a dark shape descended on the table beside them.

"Hey, are these potatoes for anyone?"

Raven eyed the woman's half-eaten plate sidelong before he snatched up a bite.

"Raven!" Lillie said.

"Hiya, honey. I see you brought Erron back. Well done."

"Where did you go?" Vola said. "You disappeared right before we got to him."

The raven's shoulders drooped. "Unfortunate side effect of the job."

"You're someone's familiar, aren't you?" Lillie asked.

He ruffled his feathers then fought to smooth them, and when he spoke again his voice had gone weary. "It's not as glamorous as it sounds. I'm beholden to my master and have to come when she calls."

"You're a prisoner," Talon said flatly.

He sighed, then shrugged and hopped to Lillie's shoulder to run his beak through her hair. "Yes, but you're going to free me, aren't you?"

"What?" she said with a chuckle. "How could you tell?"

"I know an altruist when I see one." He cocked his head at Vola. "Am I wrong?"

Lillie bit her lip to hide her mirth as Vola glared at him. "No, but that doesn't mean I like being manipulated."

"No manipulation," he said quickly. "Just a fair trade. I'll help you. I can give this lovely one the same benefits as a familiar; let her see through my eyes, yadda yadda. And in return, you can help me get rid of my bond with my real master."

Lillie glanced at Vola. "We could use some help finding Cyrano."

The bird perked up. "Cyrano? The bard? He's here?"

"Yes," Vola growled. "And causing trouble."

"Well, that's what bards do best."

What did Raven know of the bard? Vola would have suspected Cyrano was Raven's master except Raven had referred to his captor as she.

"I'll help you find him." Raven hopped down and wove around a couple of plates and a tankard. "Is it a deal?"

"Deal," Vola said and stuck out her hand before realizing the bird wouldn't be able to shake.

He solved that problem by hopping up to perch on her fingers and bobbed up and down.

"Excellent," Raven said. "I've always wanted a party of my very own."

Raven flew overhead, searching the terrain for signs of Cyrano as they trudged along below. Every so often, Raven would swoop down to give them directions.

"Veer right here."

"Let's try north. There's something moving up there."

"Nope, just some ogres. Keep straight if you want to avoid them."

By midafternoon, they'd passed through thinning trees and found the land beyond the forest was much rockier, with low scrub and deep gullies. They stopped to rest in the shade of one of the last scraggly trees.

Raven perched on Lillie's shoulder and clacked his beak as she fed him tidbits of dried meat from her belt pouch.

"All right," Sorrel said, staring at them as Vola passed Talon the water-skin. "So you're someone's pet."

"Familiar," Raven and Lillie said at the same time.

"Sorry," Sorrel said, holding up her hands. "Familiar. But I still don't get how you can talk. That owl Lillie summoned didn't seem that eloquent."

Raven snorted. "That's because owls suck."

Lillie tapped him on the nose. "No, she's right. Most familiars don't talk. Even the ones that are real animals and not just constructs. So why do you?"

"I didn't start as a familiar. I started as a person. I had several beast forms I could take. But I was trapped in this one when my master summoned a familiar and got me."

"You can shape change?" Lillie said as Raven hopped down from her shoulder. She stood. "Can you teach me?"

"Uh, no. I'm trying to get back to my human self, if you'll recall. Thinking about ravens is the last thing I want to do, thank you very much."

He flapped to the top of the nearest rock. "Come on. You walk so slow."

"What's your name, then?" Sorrel said, bouncing to her feet. "In real life?"

"As opposed to fake life? This is real life, much as I hate it." He flapped to another rock as they readied themselves to move. "And would you believe my name is actually Raven?" He shook his head with a sigh. "I thought it was so ironic at the time…"

He flapped away and circled back, letting them catch up before he winged away again.

A few minutes later, he came spearing down again. "There's a wyvern in a ditch up ahead. You can go straight down in or go around pretty easily."

Vola cocked her head. "We'll go around. Wyverns are only a problem if you get too close. They'd rather run than fight."

They heard the beast before they saw it. Throaty bellows echoed up the walls of the gully, and scales slithered against dirt and rock.

Vola narrowed her eyes. If the wyvern was already in a bad mood, then they really, really didn't need to get any closer. She led the party around the rim, casting glances down below to make sure they remained unseen.

At the end of the dry creek bed, a brownish-green back humped above the edge of the gully before slapping back down again.

A cry rang out between the rock walls.

Vola exchanged a glance with the others. "That didn't sound like a wyvern."

"Raven?" Lillie said.

Raven swooped up high over the opening.

Below, Lillie's eyes went distant. "He's letting me see," she whispered. "Oh, no. It has someone trapped down there."

"Someone who didn't get the memo that wyverns are better left undisturbed?" Talon said with a sigh.

Vola growled under her breath and trotted toward the edge of the gully.

"And of course, we're going to run straight into the thick of it," Sorrel said.

"Isn't that you're favorite? Lillie, got any advice on wyverns?"

"Besides avoid them?" Talon grumbled, but she was pulling her bow from her back.

"They need a lot of space to get into the air. Usually, they climb to the top of something tall they can drop off of. They're not very fond of cold, and they're sensitive near their wings."

The sides of the creek bed were steep enough that it was a one-way trip down. The wyvern twisted and writhed at the end, brown-green scales flashing in the sun. It raised filmy wings but didn't try to take off.

They'd fought dragons before. Well, one. But this looked more like a snake with wings. Its long sinuous body coiled on the floor of the gully.

It had something trapped up against the steep walls.

Vola drew her ax and her sword with a battle cry and slid down the rocky slope to land directly behind the creature. Instead of following like a normal person, Sorrel took a running leap from the top of the dry bed and flew across the distance to the wyvern's back.

The wyvern shrieked and jerked upright just long enough that Vola could see the woman in black leather it had trapped against the end of the creek bed.

"Oh my goddess, you again?" she cried.

Naraya barely had time to sneer before the wyvern whipped around, and she had to duck its tail.

That left Vola with the snapping jaws.

She threw up her arm, and its teeth scraped across her arm guard, catching in her chain mail. Vola winced but took advantage by yanking the creature's head forward and slashing it between the eyes with her blade.

The wyvern hissed and twisted its neck in pain. It pulled free of Vola and reared back.

Before it could lunge again, a wall of sleet slashed down between them. The wyvern shrieked and slithered back, revealing Lillie standing on the ridge above, hands raised and glowing with the spell.

Sorrel spun around on the thing's back and brought her staff down on the wyvern's left wing, right where it connected with its body.

It jerked and threw Sorrel off. The monk landed, rolling to her feet in the dust of the creek bed.

A caw overhead made Vola look up, and Raven dove for the wyvern's head. He went for its eyes as it tried to snap at Sorrel. It twisted its jaws, trying to catch the raven instead.

He flapped away, taunting the wyvern. The creature followed as far as it could, stretching its long neck into the sky and spreading its filmy wings.

A twang cut across the noise, and an arrow went clean through the wyvern's right wing, leaving a gaping hole in the delicate scales.

Sorrel ran for the wall of the creek bed and scrambled up like a squirrel before she leaped over the open space, brandishing her staff. Her trajectory would take her in for a direct hit.

Naraya slid between the wyvern's coils, a dagger in each hand. She cried out as she slashed straight through its tail.

The wyvern screamed and twisted, catching Sorrel in midair and flinging her across the chasm to strike the opposite wall.

The monk slid to the ground and landed in a bloody heap.

"Sorrel!" Vola screamed, heart in her throat.

Another wave of sleet drove the wyvern back down into the creek bed while vines full of thorns sprang out of the dusty ground and wrapped themselves around the creature, courtesy of Lillie and Talon. The creature thrashed to escape, but the vines snaked higher, tying it to the ground.

Vola lunged forward and brought her ax down across the wyvern's neck, severing its head completely.

She stood there panting for a long moment, black blood seeping into the dirt beside her boots before she threw down her weapons and raced for Sorrel's broken body.

"No," she whispered. "No, no, no." She couldn't heal this. She couldn't do anything to help with Cleavah out of reach.

Sorrel felt small and limp as Vola gathered her in her arms. The dust clung everywhere but didn't quite cover the blood welling in the teeth marks up and down her body.

Water gathered in Vola's eyes as she clutched Sorrel helplessly. Her fingers were empty of power, completely useless against Sorrel's torn skin.

The afternoon sunlight reflected in her tears, burning her eyes, and she clenched them shut.

There was a sliding sound, and Talon landed beside them. Lillie huffed, half-climbing, half-falling down the wall after her.

"Vola?" Talon said. "Let us see. There might be something we can do."

Vola concentrated on opening her eyes and unclenching her hands so Sorrel rolled down her forearms.

The halfling's body shuddered. "Something you can do about what?" she said. Then she coughed.

Vola sucked in a breath.

Sorrel shook her head and struggled out of Vola's grip to sit up. "Gah, that hurt."

"You…you're all right," Lillie said, skidding to a halt beside them. "I thought…gods, I thought you were dead."

"Me too," Talon said.

Raven landed on the rocky wall beside them. He tilted his head, staring avidly.

"I don't know," Sorrel said, twisting to look down at herself. "I don't feel dead. Beat up, maybe. But I'm pretty sure death would be more interesting than this."

Sorrel bent to dust herself off as Vola stared. Blood stood out on her tunic, but the giant slashes where the wyvern's teeth had ripped into her seemed to be no more than scratches now.

"Huh," Sorrel said. "That was lucky."

"You did say you were a *black* paladin, right?" Raven said, head cocked.

"This wasn't me," Vola said. Though she did surreptitiously check that she hadn't managed to acquire Sorrel's wounds somehow. She felt beat up, sure, but without stripping out of her plate and chain mail, she couldn't know if the aches were hers or Sorrel's. They had to be hers. Cleavah couldn't heal without a mortal to work through, and Vola was cut off from her.

Sorrel must not have been as bad off as they'd thought. Lucky indeed.

Vola cracked her neck and leveled a glare at Naraya. "You know the best part about being a black paladin is that I can get angry at whoever I want. Even stupid victims."

Talon stood and glowered at the woman as well. "You could have gotten us all killed," she said. "Not to mention yourself."

"You're getting mad at me for attacking a creature that was clearly going to terrorize the village?" she said.

"It wasn't doing anything of the sort," Lillie said with a huff. "Wyverns are very skittish. They'd rather run away from a fight, and they know enough to steer clear of humans. What you did wasn't helping anyone. It was just reckless."

"You think a wyvern is going to scare me?" she shouted. Then her lips thinned, and she looked away. "Nothing scares me anymore."

"Then you're an idiot," Vola said. She took one last look at the monk to be sure she was all right before climbing to her feet. "Or you're suicidal. Which is it?"

"If you'd seen what I've seen, you wouldn't ask me that," the woman said in dark tones.

"Wake up, woman," Talon said. "Everyone's seen things. The world is a dark place. The only problem is when you let it make you dark, too."

Naraya opened her mouth but couldn't seem to find anything to say.

Talon shook her head. "What is it you want? What are you trying to do? Or be?"

"Strong," Naraya whispered like her throat was as dry as the gully. "I need to prove I'm strong, and then no one will be able to mock me again."

"And is that worth other people dying?" Talon said. "Endangering them because of your ignorance and your quest to prove yourself? If you're going to be an adventurer, you need to do better. Or you'll end up being one of the villains we come after. Because we're the ones that keep people like you from hurting everyone around them."

The woman stared at her feet, sufficiently cowed.

"Take the carcass," Talon said, conveniently ignoring the fact that it was three times her size. "Maybe you can get a good price for ridding the countryside of a menace." She turned her back on the woman.

"Well," Raven said. "If we're all done sitting on our asses, maybe we should get moving. I think I've found Cyrano."

THIRTEEN

RAVEN LED them down the dry gully as the fastest and easiest way north. And Vola liked it because it meant they were hidden from prying eyes up where it was too dry and rocky for much to grow. And Raven was sure to swoop down and warn them of anything hiding out in the twists and turns of the gully ahead.

Less than an hour later, Raven cupped his wings and dove, landing on Lillie's shoulder.

"He's ahead, where the gully slopes up and meets the meadow above." The raven cocked his head. "What are you planning to do with him?"

Vola's gaze flicked to the others.

Sorrel examined her fingernails. "I don't know. Last we heard, Vola wanted to murder him on the spot, so…"

"That's about normal for a bard," Raven said.

"I'm not going to kill him," Vola said. "At least not yet. We need him to talk first."

"Why?" Raven said. "What does he know?"

"It's not what he knows. It's what he can do," Lillie said. "He managed to control Naraya with just a couple of words."

"And he managed to hypnotize all of us in one go," Talon said. "That's the sort of power we're looking for. Even if he didn't kill us…"

"You're looking for the mind mage," Raven said. "Of course you are. Don't know why you'd be here doing anything else. But I don't think it's the bard."

"Neither do we anymore. We just want to see what he has to say." Vola kicked a stone and it skittered away, raising little puffs of dust.

"Bards are twisty with words." Raven ruffled his feathers. "But if you wear them down long enough, you eventually get to the truth."

"That's if he doesn't attack us on sight," Vola said. "And if he doesn't just send us all into a fog again."

"Provoke him," Lillie said.

"What?"

"Make him use that spell on us again."

"Yeah, because that worked so well last time," Talon said, rolling her eyes.

Lillie gave her a mild glare. "Trust me. I have an idea."

"I generally like Lillie's ideas," Sorrel said with a shrug.

"Alright," Vola said. "Take him down without killing him. Then we'll make him talk."

"We're moving into my master's territory," Raven said. "I'm not sure I'll be able to help you. And I might have to disappear. I don't want her knowing you're so close to her."

Vola tilted her head. He hadn't made any secret of the fact he was a spy, but she didn't really get a sense of malice from him, either.

"Who is this master? Anyone we know?"

"No," Raven said, but Vola caught his hesitation.

She ran through a list in her head of everyone they knew in the area but came up blank. Unless Sandry or Naraya were keeping their summoning skills a secret.

"You've gotten us this far. That's pretty good," Vola said, meeting his eyes deliberately. "And you've more than earned our help. If we can find a way to free you, we will." But that didn't mean she had to drop her guard.

Raven opened his beak for a sharp caw.

Vola signaled Sorrel and Talon out of the gully to sneak up on Cyrano and flank him before Lillie and Vola came up the middle.

She gave the others enough time to get into place before she led Lillie right up the dry stream bed. The ground rose, and the walls around them fell away leaving them on a plateau with some scraggly trees and light scrub leading back into the forest on their left.

Cyrano crouched in the dry dirt, referencing a book as he drew diagrams at his feet.

Raven swooped overhead in the signal that Sorrel and Talon were in place.

Vola deliberately stepped on a twig that snapped in the still air.

Cyrano whirled, dropping the book in the dirt. Vola could practically hear Lillie's outrage.

"Lightless," Cyrano said, straightening up. His voice held a note of amusement and resignation. Vola was gratified to see his nose and eyes were dark with severe bruising. Good, she'd broken his nose.

"I should have known you'd find me. You just couldn't stay away, could you? It's a good thing I find competence so attractive."

Above them, Raven cawed indignantly and wheeled into the sunlight.

Cyrano squinted up, a slight frown marring his lips.

"Cut it out," Vola said. "You know what's not attractive? Taking away a person's will."

"It was only for a couple of hours," Cyrano said, rolling his eyes. "And I wouldn't have had to if you weren't so blasted good at getting in my way."

"I'm so sorry to thwart your evil plans."

"Evil?" His eyes narrowed. "I'm not the one with a black shield."

Vola stepped back as if slapped.

"Hey," Lillie said, hands on her hips. "Off limits."

Cyrano's lips quirked even as his nostrils flared in irritation. "I take it the rest of your band is around here somewhere. The halfling and the mystery girl."

"Just waiting for you to make the wrong move."

"I only ever make right moves," Cyrano said with a raised eyebrow. "I'm efficient like that."

"Sure," Vola said. "Does that mean you want to answer our questions now or after we tie you up?"

"Since you clearly long to fight me again, we might as well get it out of the way first." He drew his rapier and swished it twice, falling into a ready stance.

Vola glanced back at Lillie.

"Go ahead," the wizard whispered. "Pull out all the stops. I'll be ready."

Vola turned back to Cyrano. "It's your choice," she said with a shrug.

She rushed the bard, sweeping up with her ax and down with her sword. He spun out of the way but she'd just been charging to distract him from the others.

A stream of arrows fell from the sky, making the bard swear and dance out of the way. One clipped him on the shoulder, and he winced.

Sorrel chose that moment to pop up behind him and sweep his legs out from under him.

He rolled and sprang to his feet, gasping.

"I'm disappointed," he said. "You know what I can do when pressed. You really want this to end that soon?"

"I think it's really weird how much you enjoy this sort of thing." Vola slashed.

He met her slash with his weapon, twisting it so her blade slid right off the end of his rapier.

"As if you don't like it, too."

She grinned and brought her elbow around to bash him.

This time he ducked, shook his head, and started to croon. Just like last time. "Friends, Lightless. I don't know why we're fighting."

Vola staggered back a step, recognizing the note in his voice, but even as he started to speak, Lillie raised her hands and spoke her own spell.

Cyrano choked.

He cleared his throat to speak, but the spell he'd tried to weave was broken and shattered beyond recall.

He gaped, then coughed and brought his weapon up too slow to keep Sorrel from kicking it out of his hand.

He stumbled back, into Gruff, who snarled and took hold of the back of his doublet and flung him to the ground.

Vola stepped forward and placed a booted foot on his chest. "Thank you, Gruff," she said. "I'll take it from here."

Cyrano glanced up Vola's leg, gaze finally landing on her face. "This is promising."

"She has you at sword-point, literally under her boot, and you're still flirting?" Lillie said as Talon coalesced from the surrounding scrub.

"It's my defense mechanism," Cyrano said with a pout. "You don't like it?"

"I'm all right with it," Sorrel said, raising her hand. "I'm immune."

"That's because he's not using it on you," Vola huffed.

"I could." He turned his gaze on Sorrel. "You know height difference doesn't matter when you're horizontal."

"Aw, that's so sweet." Sorrel made a kissy face at him. "You're kind of cute when you're not a threat."

He recoiled. "Oh, gods. Is that what I sound like?"

Vola pulled some rope from the swamp beast's pack and tossed it to Talon. "You know how to tie someone up?"

"Oh, better and better," Cyrano said as Talon went to work securing his limbs.

She glared at him, and he winced as she yanked the cord around his wrists.

"Maybe not so tight?" he said.

"This was your choice," Vola said. "I gave you the chance to answer questions willingly."

Talon finished, sitting the bard up and cinching him into that position.

Raven fluttered down to land on the tree just behind Cyrano, staring at the bard with his bright eyes.

"Now," Vola said. "This is more like it. Are you ready to talk about what you're doing here?"

"Magic," Cyrano said.

"What kind?"

He grinned, showing off straight white teeth.

"Lillie?" Vola said.

The wizard stepped over to the diagram Cyrano had been drawing and squinted down. She tilted her head and finally spoke. "It's a communication spell. You were trying to call someone—" She stopped, and her mouth fell open. "Oh." She glanced back at Cyrano whose cheeks had gone pink.

"What is it?" Vola said. "Who was he trying to call?"

Lillie opened her mouth, but it was Cyrano who answered first.

"My beloved," he said through gritted teeth.

The power went out of Vola's annoyance.

Raven made a coughing noise, and Cyrano yanked his head around to see who was behind him, but his bonds didn't allow him to go that far.

"What happened to them?" Talon asked, voice rough.

"He disappeared. Somewhere in this area," Cyrano said. "But I'm going to find him, no matter how many enthusiastic adventurers get in my way."

"Vola," Lillie said quietly. "If he disappeared here, like the halflings…"

Vola licked her lips and cleared her throat. "Cyrano. He…he might not be the same anymore."

"There's someone in this area who can use mind control," Lillie said. "They can subvert a person's will and take away whoever they were as a person."

Cyrano's head jerked back, and he stared at them. "I know that." His brow drew down in suspicion. "But how do you?"

"We're hunting them," Vola said.

"To be fair, we thought it was you," Sorrel told Cyrano. "You did make Naraya all dopey and complacent."

"And you put all of us in a fog and managed to escape," Lillie said.

"I can only make that last a couple of hours." Cyrano rolled his eyes. "And I can't make you do anything you don't want to do. Only suggest things and see if they take."

Lillie flipped through her spell book to a clean page and started writing.

"You're saying we wanted you to get away?" Sorrel said.

Cyrano shrugged. "I'm saying you didn't really want to kill me. And I didn't really want to kill you." His gaze hardened on Vola. "But I will if you keep me from finding my love."

"I don't want to keep you from doing anything," Vola said, throwing up her hands. "But that would have been a lot easier if you'd just told us the truth in the first place. Why do you have to be so squirrely about everything?"

"Why should I trust you?" Cyrano said, struggling a little against his bonds. "I don't know who it is who is subverting people. And…well, I kind of thought it was you as well."

"What?" Talon said. "Why?"

"You've got a wizard." Cyrano's eyes slid to Vola's shield. "And a black paladin."

The blood drained from Vola's face.

"She has to have done something to earn the black on her shield. It could easily have been using a god's power to subvert people's wills."

Sorrel, Lillie, and Talon stared at him, faces set like granite.

He glanced between them, deflating a little.

"I *earned* the black by making a mistake," Vola said, forcing the words through her tight chest. "A boy I was training, a boy I cared about, was subverted in the middle of the palace coup a couple of months ago. He ended up killing an innocent while under the enemy's influence."

"Vola took responsibility so Finn wouldn't have to bear the consequences," Lillie said. "And the paladin council kicked her out for it."

"Their loss," Talon said. "'Cause if the bastards had been looking closely enough, they'd have seen she was protecting someone."

"Just like she's always done." Sorrel leaned on her staff, glaring at Cyrano.

Cyrano hesitated just a moment before inclining his head to Vola. "My mistake, paladin."

She shook her head. "No, you were right. I'm still a black paladin. I still have a black shield. I made a mistake. It just wasn't the one the council accused me of. Mostly, they thought I was wrong because I'm an orc."

Cyrano winced. "I've known plenty of orcs I would love to have behind me in battle. And plenty of humans I wouldn't."

Vola cocked her head. "So you believe us?"

"Do you believe me?"

Vola took a deep breath then gave him a curt nod. "I do."

"Good, because I'm getting a crick in my neck. Do you have to be so blasted tall?"

As Vola leaned down to slash his bindings, Raven took off with a caw and disappeared into the trees.

Cyrano stood, rubbing his arms and legs as if to get the feeling back in them. Then he straightened and held out a hand.

"Will you work with me?" he said. "If we find this mind mage, we find my beloved. And we can avenge your Finn and your shield."

To be completely honest with herself, Vola wouldn't have minded if Cyrano's flirting had actually been serious. He was good looking when he wasn't being annoying. But he was clearly devoted elsewhere and there was a lot to respect in that.

"Deal," Vola said and shook his hand.

"Good, keeping you off my tail was exhausting." He touched his bruised nose. "And painful."

FOURTEEN

VOLA WAS ready to track down the mind mage, but she had to admit they did need some supplies, and they didn't have much in the way of direction yet. Even with Cyrano on their side.

So, they trudged back toward Smallville, hoping to talk to some of the others that had experienced blackouts and relatives wandering off in the middle of the night.

Less than a league away from the village, Talon lifted her chin and sniffed the air. Gruff's ears went back.

Vola's gaze trained on them. "What is it?" she whispered. But then she smelled it, too. The unmistakable scent of fire and blood on the wind. They'd seen enough fighting to know the smell of battle when they encountered it.

"It's coming from the village," Talon said.

"Go." Vola signaled them forward, not bothering with stealth.

Flickering light drew them through the trees like a beacon. At the edge of the forest, Vola gasped. The stable beside Reed's inn blazed. So far, it was the only building on fire, but that wasn't the worst of it.

Orcs tromped down the dirt road dressed in an eclectic collection of armor. Chain mail and dented breastplates stamped with smears of paint. Something that looked like a staff crossed over a red eye.

They herded terrified halflings down the street toward a line of orcs waiting with clubs. Any time a halfling broke for the forest, an orc scooped them up and kept them running toward the line.

Vola stared, her mouth hanging open. Her personal nightmare coming to life before her eyes.

Beside the inn, Sandry stood with three others, a staff made from a rake handle in her hands as she fought desperately against the orcs.

"Charge!" Vola yelled. She drew her sword and her mother's ax and raced for the defenseless halflings being herded by the orcs.

Sorrel, only a step behind her, leaped for Sandry and the others defending their home.

Vola hit the nearest orc running and knocked him off his feet into the dirt. Lillie caught the halfling he'd been herding before the housewife could escape into the woods and directed her to the well.

"Help me put it out," she yelled, and the two set about drawing up buckets of water.

Vola took the orc's head in her hands and slammed it into the ground until his eyes rolled back.

Yes, the voice said in the back of her thoughts.

Vola gasped and stumbled back. She stared at her hands. She'd always fought to stay in control of her anger, but this was infuriating. How could she fight without letting Mulgash in anymore? How could she keep him out when all she wanted to do was smash the orcs who were hurting people?

Cyrano darted past her, rapier out and ready. He gave her a concerned glance before running the next orc through.

"Lightless?" he called.

She shook her head to clear it. "Fine," she said, but her voice croaked. She cleared the smoke and fear from it and tried again. "Fine! Can't you do something to get them to stop? Charm them or whatever?"

He scowled and wove his hand through the air. The orc in front of him shrugged his shoulders and kept coming.

"Nothing I have left is powerful enough. I used the big stuff on you guys already. It'll have to be blades from here on out."

Vola let Cyrano and Talon take the orcs in the street and lurched back to join Sorrel. If she was defending someone, she could keep the rage at bay. She could convince herself her anger was her own on behalf of the halflings and not some product of Mulgash's favor.

She knocked another orc off her feet and swung her ax. The halflings had rallied at the first sight of their saviors, and Sandry gave a blood-curdling yell as she raced for another orc.

Three steps into her charge, she stumbled. The halfling raised a hand to her head. And then dropped her weapon to stand listlessly in the middle of the road, the battle raging around her.

"Sandry," Vola called, cold racing down her limbs.

"Oh, shit, shit, shit," Sorrel chanted behind her.

Not again, Vola thought, Finn's face supplanting Sandry's in her mind's eye.

"Lillie," she screamed. "Lillie, we need a shield now."

Sorrel raced forward to grab Sandry's arm.

Sandry turned, fists raised, and Vola lunged to snatch Sorrel back. Sandry flew at them, her movements far more confident than they'd been that morning.

Raven swooped out of the smoke and cawed, beating his wings and clawing at Sandry until she stopped advancing. He flapped and retreated to the roof of the inn.

"Look out," he cawed.

All around them, halflings went still and blank-eyed.

"No," Vola whispered, retreating a step with Sorrel in hand. "It's only supposed to be one at a time."

The usually cheerful Reed picked up a sickle from the ground at his feet and turned to face them, wicked blade glinting in the light of the flames.

"Reed," Sorrel called. "Sandry. Don't do this. Don't succumb to it. Fight it off."

"Kellan said there was no way to fight it," Vola said. She lurched back to avoid Reed's swing. Sandry advanced. "Lillie?"

"I can't shield this many," the wizard called. She limped around the well as the woman who'd been helping her chased her. "Oh my gods, it's all of them."

"Lightless, what do we do?" Cyrano called from the middle of the road. He put his shoulder to Talon's as they faced a line of advancing halflings, the orcs lurking behind them in the smoke. The enemy had expected this. They'd come here for the halflings specifically.

Vola's gaze darted from one group to the other, her mind racing.

"Retreat," she said. "Retreat to the forest. Go."

"But—" Sorrel gestured helplessly to Sandry and Reed, her grief taking in the entire village.

Vola kept her grip on the back of the monk's tunic and kept walking backward. "Later," she said in Sorrel's ear. "I don't want to hurt them, do you? But we'll have to if they keep fighting us."

"We can't leave them like this!"

"We aren't. We can't free them now, but we *can* follow them back to the mind mage. We can save them and take the bastard out."

Sorrel subsided but with an angry grumble.

The ruse worked. As they faded into the edge of the trees, the halflings lowered their weapons, their shoulders slumped, and the orcs herded the lot of them down the road.

It killed Vola to watch them walk away, their victims going along thoughtlessly.

As the orcs disappeared down the road, taking the halflings with them, Vola crept back out of the trees to stand beside Reed's inn.

Movement caught her gaze, and she glared at the orc she'd beaten into the ground earlier. He groaned and tried to push himself to his elbows.

With a fierce grin, Vola knelt on his chest. "At least we can get some of our questions answered."

"But they're getting away." Sorrel flung her hand out. "We'll lose them if we wait."

Cyrano sheathed his rapier. "If you trust me, I'll take your best tracker, and we'll keep an eye on them. Make sure we can find them when we need to—Oh."

Talon signaled Gruff, and the wolf raced out of the village, nose to the ground.

"Try to keep up," she told Cyrano before following the wolf.

Cyrano raised his eyebrows. "Careful. Don't make me fall in love with you. You'll only break my heart."

Vola shook her head as the bard took off after Talon. The ranger could take care of herself. And Vola had a lot of questions she needed answers for.

She turned back to the orc coughing under her knee. Her eyes narrowed, and she knocked the round helm from his head.

Beady black eyes, lank hair that was too long, and nostrils wide enough to park a cart inside. She knew this orc.

"Arag," she said.

Arag turned his head and spat.

"You know this...person?" Lillie said, stepping up beside Vola and Sorrel.

"Vaguely. He drank at the Frog's Bottom," Vola said. "Until he decided to disappear."

She studied his eyes, but his gaze wasn't blank like the halflings had been.

"You didn't just walk off," she said. "Your mind's your own. Where have you been Arag? Dad's been worried sick about you. You and the others." Her gaze flicked toward the road. She hadn't gotten a close look at them, but she'd bet the rest of the attacking orcs had been the rogues her father had been trying to track down.

Arag rolled his eyes. "Gorgo needs to mind his own business. Can't even take a piss without the chieftain asking if you drank enough water today."

"I think that means he cares about you, you dunce," Sorrel said, popping her head over Vola's shoulder.

"Or he's got a stick up his butt bigger than yours." He jerked his head at Sorrel's staff.

Vola gave Arag a shake. "Hey, that's my dad you're talking about. He's just trying to keep you safe. Humans like to blame everything on orcs who wander off."

"Exactly why we need to change things. Show them what we're capable of."

Vola's eyes narrowed. "Yeah. I know. But somehow, I don't think you and I are talking about the same thing."

"Of course we are. Inga knows what she's doing. And she's strong. Why else would you be working with her instead of your old man?"

Vola jerked back, nearly letting Arag go. She resettled her grip.

"Inga," she said. "Who's Inga?"

"The mind mage." Arag worked his fingers free and twirled them around his ear. "She makes people follow her. Including the holier-than-everyone Vola."

"Why do you think Vola is working for this person?" Lillie said. "She sounds dreadful."

"You have her familiar."

Sorrel drew in a breath. The back of Vola's neck prickled as she followed that realization to its end.

She turned her head and stared up at the roof where Raven sat, his wings hunched.

Well, fuck. She didn't quite dare say it out loud yet, though she dearly wanted to.

"Lillie, put Arag to sleep," Vola said quietly.

"It won't matter," Arag said as Lillie knelt beside them. "Inga knows you're coming. She knows everything. You won't be able to get to her—"

Lillie laid her hand on his head, and the orc's eyes rolled back.

Vola stood, careful not to wake him. She rubbed the back of her neck.

"I have to get a message to my parents. We found the other end of their problem."

"What about...?" Sorrel's eyes flicked to the roofline.

To Raven's credit, he hadn't fled.

Vola gazed at him. "So," she said.

He shivered, then shrugged and hopped off the roof to glide down and land on the railing of the inn. "So," he said, voice weary.

"You work for the mind mage."

"She is my master," Raven said, raising his beak. "I do not work for her. There is a difference."

"It's a pretty small one," Vola said. " Were you sent to lead us astray?"

Raven cocked his head. "Have I led you astray?"

Vola hesitated. "No. But you haven't given us much to go on."

"I told you I can't. I thought this was a good idea, but I can't *do* anything. I can't tell you anything you need to know." He ruffled his feathers and shook them out.

"Why did you find us in the forest in the first place?"

"I was looking for you. I thought you would be able to help me."

"You pretend to help us, and we help you. Is that it?"

"It's more than that," Raven said with a glare. "Inga. She's obsessed with you. A paladin who's also an orc. She won't stop talking about you. I thought you'd be the perfect one to counter her and help me break my curse."

"But you didn't know I was a black paladin," Vola said flatly.

His gaze met hers without hesitance. "No. I didn't. But that didn't change anything really. Not once I saw you work."

"You still lied to us," Lillie said.

"To protect you." He shook his head hard enough to unbalance himself. He raised his wings. "But now I think Inga's been one step ahead of me this whole time. She knows you're coming. And if I try to help you, I'll only end up hurting you."

He spread his wings.

"Wait," Lillie said.

"No. She'll make me betray you. As much as I hate it, she's my master. She'll force me to hurt you."

"No, I have an idea."

Raven launched himself into the air.

Vola trusted Lillie's ideas. And she didn't exactly want Raven flying back to Inga with everything he knew. She lunged and caught him around the middle, pinning his wings to his sides. He struggled in her arms and yanked a wing free, buffeting her ear, but she held on.

"Raven, stop," Lillie said, reaching for him with both hands. "What if *I* summon you?"

Raven froze.

"Would that break your connection with your master?" Lillie asked.

Raven opened his beak for a second before he responded. "I think so. I don't think it would prevent her from summoning me again. But it would mean…"

"You'd be mine," Lillie answered for him. "I would be your master instead. I didn't want to do it before because you would be bound to me the same way you're bound to Inga. You would have to trust me."

Raven wiggled a little, and this time, Vola set him back down on the railing. He stared at Lillie for a long moment. Then each of them in turn.

He bent his neck and pried a large feather free from his wing then held it out to Lillie. She took it between two fingertips.

"Anything," he said. "Anything to get away from Inga."

FIFTEEN

VOLA KEPT watch for Cyrano and Talon down the road while Lillie set up her spell just off the steps to the inn. The stable smoldered in the background, casting the cute gabled houses in an orange glow, too far away from the woods or the inn to jeopardize them.

Raven flew to the roof of the inn to get a better view and watched the wizard's movements with interest as she drew her diagrams and placed the salt and the charcoal carefully.

"It's a little different to summon a specific creature," she said, nudging the charcoal into line. "Especially if you want it to come out the other side alive."

Vola made a face, and Sorrel shot a glance up toward the raven.

"But it should be much easier with Raven's feather. The spell will have no problem recognizing him."

Raven gave a harsh caw. "This had better not roast me. I don't taste like chicken."

"How would you know?" Sorrel said as Lillie winced and finished by laying Raven's long black feather in the direct center of her spell.

"Only something super dumb would taste as good as a chicken. It's their only purpose in this world," Raven called back. "I am clearly too clever to taste good."

"Your logic might be flawed," Sorrel said, squinting and holding her hand over her eyes so she could see him. He was really just a black blur against the night. The only light came from the fire, edging his feathers in orange.

"Would everyone please be quiet?" Lillie said. "I need to concentrate."

Sorrel mimed locking her mouth shut. Vola just leaned back against the inn's railing and crossed her arms, waiting with her jaw clenched.

Lillie started chanting. Above them, Raven shifted from foot to foot.

The diagram began to glow just as it had in the forest.

"What is Lillie summoning this time," Talon said from just beside Vola.

Vola jumped, making her armor clank. "Geez! How did you sneak up on me? I was watching for you."

"You watch with your eyes, not with your ears," Talon said.

"What's going on?" Cyrano said, coming down the road like a normal person. "I thought we were going after the halflings?"

"Shh," Sorrel said.

Raven cawed, and Cyrano jerked his head up, but just then, the bird disappeared in a snap of blue light.

"Wait." Cyrano stopped dead in the middle of the street. "Was that—"

The blue light surrounded the feather between Lillie's hands, and she pulled her palms apart.

Raven didn't grow from the spell components like the owl had. Instead, he snapped into existence in a flash of blue light accompanied by the smell of singed feathers.

Raven shook his head, then craned his neck around as if to check that he was put together right. He fluffed his feathers.

"Inter-planar travel always makes me feel squished and unstable," he said. "Like my head's going to fall off."

Cyrano gasped, a sharp jagged sound that made Vola reach for him without thinking.

"Raven," he said. His voice broke on the name.

"Hmmph," Raven said.

Cyrano gulped and dropped his lute in the dirt. "Oh my gods, Raven!" The bard lunged forward, arms outstretched as if to scoop the bird off the ground and hold him tight.

But Raven squawked and flapped out of his reach to land on Lillie's shoulder. The bird stretched out his neck and hissed.

"Don't you dare," Raven said.

Cyrano stopped short, blinking. His mouth opened and closed. "My love, what...what's wrong?"

"You," Raven barked. "I can't believe you."

Cyrano shut his mouth with a click and planted his fists on his hips. "What? What about me?"

"You standing there like nothing's wrong."

"Believe me. There's plenty wrong. I've been worried sick about you. I came all the way out here looking for you, thinking you were dead or worse. I'm here to rescue you."

"And how much of that time have you spent flirting with every adventurer you came across, huh?" Raven flung a wing out to indicate Vola.

She just raised her eyebrows, watching with interest.

A bright, painful-looking flush stained Cyrano's cheeks.

Vola wouldn't even have thought the bard could blush.

"Don't try to deny it."

"I'm not. But I flirt with everything. It's part of my charm." The bard looked up under his eyelashes. "It was one of the things you said you loved about me.'

"That was when I wasn't missing," Raven said with another hiss. "It was cute when I was the one you came home to. Now I'm wondering if you were out here trying to replace me."

"Never." Cyrano stepped forward, trying to meet Raven's eyes, but Raven spun around on Lillie's shoulder. "Love, please. Talk to me. I love you. I miss you. I looked all over for you. These guys were just a means to that end. Lightless never took me seriously. Right?"

Vola snorted. "A passing amusement. Hey, by the way, we found your boyfriend."

"You mean, I found you," Raven said.

"Why don't you change back, and I can welcome you the way I really want to," Cyrano said, cocking an eyebrow.

"Because I'm stuck, you libidinous outlaw."

Cyrano jerked back a step. "Stuck?"

Raven mantled and then tried to smooth his feathers. "Yes, stuck."

"That's never happened before," Cyrano said. "You're much too good a shape-changer to get stuck."

"I suspect divine meddling."

Vola raised her chin. "What do you mean?"

"I was scouting in this form when Inga summoned a familiar and got me. She's got the backing of one of the Obstacles, and I think he helped her snag a less than willing subject."

A pit settled in Vola's stomach. "Let me guess, Mulgash?"

Raven cocked his head. "How'd you know?"

Vola avoided their eyes. "Just a gut feeling." It was too much to be a coincidence that Mulgash took an interest in her just as she crossed into one of his other followers' territory.

"But you're free of her now," Lillie said. "She's not your master anymore. Can't you change back?"

"Wish it were that easy, sweetheart. But something's keeping me this way. Some curse she laid on me when I was first dragged into her summons. That is..." His gaze slid to Vola, and he cocked his head. "Unless someone can heal me."

Vola straightened. "No."

"Hey, we had a deal."

"I'm not saying I don't want to help you. I'm saying that I can't."

"Come on. Paladins are good at that sort of thing. Healing, breaking curses, that sort of thing."

"Black paladin," she said shortly. "Remember? Not paladin. I'm a black paladin without a god."

"But you said it wasn't really your fault that they took your shield," Cyrano said, folding his arms and looking thoughtful. "That you were protecting someone. Surely that's got to count for something with your god."

"It would if I could talk to her," Vola snapped. "But I can't. Lesser gods can't talk to their followers without an emblem, and the paladin council took mine. All right?"

"You healed Sorrel in the gully," Raven said quietly.

Vola swallowed. "I didn't. I wanted to, but I didn't. She didn't need it."

They all looked at Sorrel. There were still a couple of red marks that looked like old teeth punctures. Or like they hadn't exactly broken the skin in the first place.

Sorrel chewed her lip as if in thought. "It...it didn't really feel like one of Vola's healings."

"What did it feel like, then?" Lillie asked curiously.

Sorrel cast a sharp glance at her. "Like I hit a wall and had the silly knocked out of me."

Raven slumped.

"If I can't heal you, what other options are there?" Vola said.

"I'll have to sneak back into Inga's stronghold. Break the curse from there. She has to have some sort of focus or anchor for the spell."

"We," Vola said.

Raven hunched his shoulders. "You'd still help me? Even though I didn't tell you everything."

Vola's lips thinned, but she nodded. "I still trust you."

"You do?"

"You trusted us enough to go through the summoning. And we had a deal. You helped us find Erron. And Cyrano. We can help you against Inga. Besides…" She cracked her knuckles. "We're headed that way anyway."

"We do have some unfinished business with her," Lillie said.

"We left Gruff trailing the orcs and the halflings," Talon said. "They will lead us right to her stronghold."

Sorrel spun her staff. "About time."

Cyrano retrieved his lute from the road.

"Where do you think you're going?" Raven said.

"I'm coming with you, obviously."

"Like hell you are."

Cyrano pointed at him. "I'm not letting you out of my sight again. And you're not big enough to argue with me."

"Yeah, I wonder how pretty you'd look with talon marks down your face," Raven muttered. "See how well you flirt then."

SIXTEEN

RAVEN'S GRUMPINESS was only matched by Cyrano's sheepishness. The bard spent the next two hours trailing Raven, listing apologies. When he got to the end of the list, he floundered for a second and then started over again in alphabetical order.

Raven rode on Lillie's shoulder, doing his best impression of someone who did not care.

"Are you sure it was a good idea to leave Arag behind?" Lillie asked Vola as they moved from the thinning trees to the rolling hills beyond.

"Dad will find him. Especially with the burning barn to serve as a beacon. And we don't really need him if we've got Raven."

"He's going to get wet if Gorgo waits too much longer," Talon said. "I smell rain."

Vola squinted upward but the night was pitch black. "So will we. Where is this Inga's stronghold, then?" she asked Raven.

"About half a day's journey from where you found Cyrano. He would have tripped over it if his ego wasn't big enough to block his sight."

"Hmm," Cyrano said, raising his chin to gaze into the distance. "It's funny. The feathers hide that stick up your butt really well."

"What can we expect when we get there?" Vola said, ignoring them.

"Magic probably," Raven said with a shrug.

"Well, that's super helpful," Sorrel said.

Raven sighed. "I was mostly trying to escape her. I wasn't paying that much attention to the traps she set around the fortress to keep people out."

"So, traps," Vola said. "At least there's that."

"Lots, around the entrance. Some magical, some mechanical. I think it will mostly be things to discourage people from getting too close. Charms and misdirection to hide the stronghold itself. Then once you get up on top of it, it'll be fire and pits and things that hurt enough to make you turn back."

"Is there any other way in?" Talon said. "Besides the front door?"

Raven opened his mouth as if to say no and then paused. "Well, actually. I think she has an escape tunnel. A way to bail out if everything blows up."

"It's likely protected," Vola said.

"Yes, but maybe not as much," Lillie said. "And if we can get past a few traps, then we might have a clearer way in."

Talon hissed and held up a hand, signaling them to freeze. Vola glanced around, hand going to her ax handle. "What is it?" she whispered.

"We're catching up to Gruff and the orcs."

Talon motioned them forward but low. They crouched along the hills, going around wide gullies. It might have been pitch black, but there was no reason to alert the enemy if they didn't have to.

Gruff appeared beside them, a silent shadow in the night, and Talon held out a hand to greet him. At the next hill, Vola signaled Cyrano to wait with the swamp beast as the rest of them crawled to the crest, hiding in the long grass.

Raven launched himself into the air and circled.

Vola reached to part the blades of grass in front of her.

Figures traipsed on the wide road below them, all walking with the wooden expressions and jerky movements they recognized from the few times they'd seen someone subverted by Inga's will. The orcs watched the sides of the road diligently, herding the halflings along at a steady pace.

Vola blew out her breath. "I thought she could only control one person at a time," she whispered. "She had to abandon her hold on Kellan so she could take over Finn."

Raven swooped to land beside them. "You mean, you don't get better at things with practice?"

Vola's shoulders drooped.

"It started one by one," Raven said, eying the prisoners below. "But that was months ago. She can do twenty, forty, fifty. She has an entire village under her thumb at the stronghold."

"Why?" Sorrel asked. "What does she do with them?"

"In the end? I'm not sure. She sends them off to someone else. Someone bigger and meaner than her, I think."

"The enemy Rilla wants us to find," Sorrel said. "This guy has his fingers in all the plots, apparently."

"It sounds just like Lord Arthorel and the way he kidnapped people to send to the enemy," Lillie said. "Except these people can't protest or fight back."

"Not yet," Vola said. "But we can fix that as soon as we get to Inga's stronghold. We'll figure out how to free them."

They watched silently as the figures jerked and made their way down the road.

"It starts with one," Raven said. "One person hearing a voice in their head, and it spreads to the others."

Vola gulped. "What kind of voice?"

Raven turned to eye her. "Mulgash, I believe. Whispering things that seem perfectly sensible."

Vola's jaw ached as her teeth clenched.

"Shit," Talon said under her breath and started shimmying back down the hill.

"What?" Vola turned to follow. "What's wrong?"

"We're not the only ones on the trail." Talon jerked her head to the other side of the road. "Gruff says Naraya is over there."

Vola blew out her breath and looked at the sky for guidance before remembering she was on her own.

"Shit is right," Sorrel said, pushing herself back down the hill. "If she screws this up here, we won't get the chance to rescue them later."

Vola tried to stay quiet, but she was nowhere near as stealthy as Sorrel and Talon. "Can Gruff stop her?"

"Not without alerting the orcs. People tend to yell when he grabs them."

"Who is Naraya?" Raven said, hopping after them.

"Shit," Cyrano said, overhearing them. "She's determined to screw up everyone's plans, isn't she?"

"Stay here with the swamp monster," Vola said. "This needs to be quiet.

Cyrano eyed the swamp beast. The swamp beast eyed him back.

Vola sprinted after the others down the hill where they'd been hiding. Talon had circled back, crossing the road far enough behind to stay out of sight of the orcs. Vola kept one hand on her breastplate and the other over her shoulder on her shield to keep from clanking.

There. A few feet from the edge of the road, Naraya waited, the little bit of moonlight glinting from her shiny leather angles.

She stood as the orcs passed her.

And Talon struck her from the side.

They went down in a tangle of limbs. Talon slapped her hand over Naraya's mouth to muffle her scream as Vola and Sorrel dragged the two of them away from the edge of the road. Lillie puffed up beside them, and they all crouched in the grass, holding their breath.

The orcs hesitated on the road. One glanced their way.

Lillie raised her hands, ready in case they were spotted.

And then the orcs moved on, herding their charges a little faster.

Vola let out her breath and hung her head. Talon waited until they couldn't see the orcs or the halflings anymore before she finally released Naraya.

"What the hell do you think you're doing?" Naraya whispered.

Talon scowled. "Keeping you from getting yourself killed."

"You're welcome," Sorrel told her.

"I could have handled it," the woman said. "It was only a couple of orcs."

"And two dozen halflings all under the control of a maniac," Vola said. "They wouldn't have thanked you for the rescue. They would have turned on you and torn you to pieces, even if you'd managed to kill the orcs. Which I doubt."

Lillie whispered, and a little ball of light appeared in her hand, just enough to illuminate Naraya's angry flush. Raven settled on Lillie's shoulder.

"Why can't you just leave me alone?" Naraya wailed. "I get the job done by myself."

"Yeah, but you don't," Talon says. "Your habit of jumping into things too big for you is making all of our lives harder. Why do you keep doing this?"

"No one looks down on me, okay? No one looks at me and sees a weak woman."

"Yeah, well, you're not a strong woman either."

Naraya deflated. "I'm trying."

"How?" Sorrel asked. "Strength isn't about how much leather you wear or how stubborn you are, you know?"

"She should know. She follows the god of strength and loyalty," Talon said.

"You think I like leather?" Naraya snapped. "It's hot. And don't get me started about how far up my butt it is right now."

"Then why do you wear it?"

"Because you have to look the part if you want people to respect you. You have to dress like you're tough. You have to talk like you know what you're doing even if you don't. You can't ask for help. And you have to hit anyone who dares question you."

"So, you have to be an annoying brute?" Cyrano said, coming up on them with the swamp beast in tow. He was missing a chunk out of his silk doublet, and the swamp monster looked smug.

"Sounds like you're not trying to be strong," Talon said. "You're trying to be a man."

"Hey now," Cyrano said. "I'm not like that, am I?"

"Only when you think it will get you laid," Raven said with a snort.

Cyrano spluttered.

"Yes," Naraya said. "You have to be masculine if you want to be strong." She hesitated and gestured to Talon. "But you're not. You keep doing a better job than me, but you're not a man, and I don't understand what I'm doing wrong. I needed to understand."

"So, you threw yourself at the enemy in order to understand what exactly?" Talon said. Her brow was drawn but a lot of the anger had filtered from her voice.

"You asked me yesterday if my quest was worth getting people killed. It's...it's not. That's the point. I just want to keep people from losing their mothers, too. From getting hurt. But my dad and brothers, they said I wasn't strong enough to do anything about it." She bit her lip hard enough to turn it white. "They said I wasn't strong enough to protect anyone else. I wanted to prove them wrong. But I've just been proving them right. Over and over and just moving further and further away from myself." She sank to the ground and hugged her knees. A couple of tears trickled down her cheeks.

Vola glanced at Talon.

Talon watched with pursed lips, and then hunkered down beside her.

"Are you a man?"

"What?" Naraya swiped at her tears. "Are you mocking me?"

"No, that was a legitimate question coming from her," Lillie said.

"Then, no. I'm not a man. I'm a woman."

"Then why do you keep trying to be one?" Talon asked. "You don't have a man's strength. You have a woman's strength. Female strength is many different things, but the one thing it's not...is masculine."

Talon produced a handkerchief. Vola would have sworn up and down Talon owned no such thing.

Naraya took the little cloth square and ran her thumb over it. "How do I get your strength?"

Talon blinked, pink tinging her cheeks. "I don't recommend my method," she said slowly. "It involved a lot of self-doubt. But find people who accept who you are and who you want to be. Not who everyone else thinks you should be. Strength comes from knowing who you are and being able to hold tight to that in the face of everything else."

Naraya blotted her nose. "I don't even know who I am anymore. I'm not the girl who watched her mother walk away. But I'm not someone my dad and brothers can be proud of either."

"Then your first step is finding out who you are now."

"How do I do that?"

"I'd start with a change of clothes. No one feels like themselves with that much leather up their butt."

SEVENTEEN

THE SUN CRESTED THE HORIZON, lining big black thunderclouds with gold as they came upon the edge of a giant pit mine. The cliff dove sharply away from them, leaving no safe way to the mine floor.

"Here," Raven said, alighting on Lillie's shoulder.

Vola stared at layers of bare earth and rock, but as far as she could tell, there wasn't anything else in the derelict space.

"You're sure?" Sorrel said. "There's nothing here."

Lillie frowned, then touched the circlet she wore that allowed her to see magic. Her mouth dropped open as she stared.

"Oh," Vola said flatly. The place must have been crawling with illusions and tricks.

"It's not just magic that hides it," Raven said. "It's also the natural lay of the rock and earth. She's used optical illusion to hide her stronghold. Come on. This way."

He winged away around the edge of the pit.

Vola started to follow, but Lillie took her arm.

"What?"

"There's a trap there," Lillie said, pointing ahead of them. "I think. Whatever it is I don't want you stepping in the big, bubbly-looking magic."

"Ew bubbly," Sorrel said.

"Maybe you should lead for once," Vola told Lillie.

Lillie's lips thinned, and she nodded. She stepped out ahead of them and wove her way around the top of the pit, following Raven carefully with a winding, circuitous route that took her around invisible pitfalls the rest of them couldn't see. Vola and the others followed her one by one, stepping only where she stepped.

Raven led them to the top of a sloping ramp plunging away into the pit mine. Here ancient bits of scaffolding crumbled against the walls, and broken tools scattered the floor far below.

As they came even with the ramp, the air at the far edge of the mine shimmered and fuzzed like the heat haze on a summer day.

Slowly, a massive fortress came into view. Black towering walls soared into the air. There was nothing so pretentious as a tower along the whole edifice, just squat battlements with square crenelations guarding whatever was inside. An enormous gate stood in the center, keeping the world out.

Sorrel let out a whoop. "It's a real live, evil stronghold," she said. "I've always wanted to lay siege to one."

Talon hissed. "Maybe keep your voice down? We don't need to announce ourselves more than necessary."

"What are you talking about, anyway?" Vola asked Sorrel. "We've stormed plenty of bad guys where they've holed up."

Sorrel rolled her eyes. "A rundown noble's manor, an empty research facility, and your own captured palace don't count. This is more fun."

"Has this always been here?" Vola said.

"I don't know. I don't think so," Raven said. "I think the orcs built it for her."

Gruff circled the space above the ramp and then sat with a huff.

"Well, there's no way we're going in the front door," Talon said. "Where's this escape tunnel?"

"Around the side. But this is the only way down to the mine floor. We'll have to go down this way anyway."

"Lillie, you go first. Make sure we don't set anything off," Vola said. "Can we avoid everything?"

Lillie squinted down the path. "I think so. I see a clear way if we're careful."

"So, we'll be careful."

Lillie trod carefully down the steep slope. Vola followed her, one hand on the wizard's shoulder. Sorrel and Talon came next, and Cyrano brought up the rear with the swamp monster. He kept casting suspicious looks at the creature though all it had done so far was nibble on his clothes a little.

They reached the bottom of the ramp, unscathed, and Vola blew out her breath in relief. "Well, done," she said. "Thanks, Lill—"

Ahead of them, the front gate creaked open. The drawbridge dropped down all inviting and safe.

"Welcome, Vola," a female voice said from the opening.

Vola suppressed a shiver.

"Soo, that's really creepy," Sorrel said, glancing at Vola.

"I told you, she knew you were coming," Raven whispered.

"You also said she was obsessed with Vola," Lillie said. "What exactly does that mean?"

Vola's teeth clenched as Raven cast a surreptitious look at her. "I figured she must be an old friend. Or enemy."

Vola shook her head. "Not that I know of."

"Then how does she know you?" Sorrel said.

Vola assumed it had something to do with Mulgash. If Inga was working with the Obstacle of Rage, he might have pointed her out.

"Well, we're still not going through the front door. No matter how inviting," Talon said.

"All right, then," Vola said. "This doesn't change what we need to do."

"I mean, it changes how I feel about this whole situation," Sorrel said. "What is her deal? Is she watching us all the time? Does she have *plans*?"

Vola glared at her. "It doesn't change the fact that we still have to get in there and take her down."

"Oh, right, that," Sorrel said with a shrug. "Yeah, I'm still on board with that."

"How?" Talon said. "If she knows what we're planning?"

"She can't hear us," Raven said. "At least not out here. She can only see. It might be a different story once we get inside. I'm not sure what she's capable of."

"Where is the escape tunnel?" Talon said.

Raven bobbed his head. "Down the wall a ways. But someone will have to go over to sneak in."

Vola scowled. "What? Why?"

"It only opens from the inside. That's one of the features protecting it."

"Why didn't you tell us this before?" Vola said.

"I didn't think I'd have to," Raven said, hopping from one foot to the other. "Of course it only opens from the inside. Obviously, it wouldn't be as safe if you could break into it from the outside."

Vola growled under her breath.

"So, someone has to sneak over that wall and open it for the others," Talon said flatly.

"I vote Raven," Sorrel said.

"I'd do it," Raven said with a squawk. "I promise I would. But I don't have thumbs."

"It's all right," Sorrel said, slinging her staff onto her back and rubbing her hands together. "And it's better we didn't know. No time to panic this way. Just get me to that wall, and I'll get over it."

"I'm better at sneaking," Talon said.

"And I'm better at climbing. I've scaled prison walls, remember?" Sorrel gave her a look. "And I'm small enough that I'll have the advantage inside as well. As long as Raven's not hiding any other surprises."

"None," Raven said hastily. "I've got a pretty good map of the place in my head so I can get you to her rooms without any missteps. And since I'm this lovely lady's familiar, we can keep in touch while we're separated." He ran his beak through Lillie's hair.

"Don't think flattery will get you off the hook if you've left anything else out."

"Nothing, I promise."

"But clearly Inga is watching us," Talon said, a frown creasing her forehead. "How do we get in without alerting her? Sneaking through her escape tunnel does no good if she sees us do it."

"No worries," Cyrano said, swinging his lute into his arms. "Get us to the gate, and I'll cover your way to the escape tunnel. Inga will be so riveted on me, she won't notice you're gone till much later."

"Fine," Vola growled. "If this is the only way."

"Unless you want to climb up the pipes in the bathroom," Raven said. "It is."

"We've totally done that before," Sorrel said, following as Raven launched himself into the air.

"That sounds like a story," Cyrano said. "Ouch!"

Vola glanced back as Lillie began showing them the way across the safe ground to the gate. "Did the swamp monster get you?"

Cyrano rubbed his elbow, glaring at the creature who just chewed menacingly. "Yes. What diseases am I likely to get?"

"We're pretty sure it doesn't turn you into a swamp beast, if that makes you feel any better."

"It doesn't."

Ahead of them, a gout of flame shot up from the ground. Sorrel stood just a foot away, staring at it with her head cocked.

"What are you doing?" Lillie yelled at her. "I clearly walked around that spot."

"I know, but I was bored. I wanted to see what would happen. It's not like Inga doesn't know we're coming."

Vola snagged the back of Sorrel's tunic and dragged her back a step onto the safe path Lillie had demonstrated for them. "No more experiments. Let's just get to the wall."

"If you insist," Sorrel said with a sigh.

They made it the rest of the way to the wall without incident. Vola expected guards outside the gate, but it stood clear, open, and inviting. Surely Inga wouldn't expect them to take that obvious bait, though.

Cyrano stepped forward, strumming his lute, and suddenly he seemed like the most riveting thing Vola had ever seen. His eyes gleamed clear and enticing and his shoulders strained against his silk doublet. He tossed his thick hair out of his eyes and Vola fought not to drool.

Cyrano hummed under his breath. "Get out of here, Lightless. I'll join you as soon as I can."

Vola shook her head and Cyrano went back to his normal self. Well put together but nothing extra special.

She gestured the others away from the gate.

"That was disconcerting." Sorrel shuddered.

"You can say that again," Lillie muttered.

"Is that what attraction feels like? Glad I don't have that in my life."

Vola shushed them and led the way around the stronghold, hugging the wall until they found the shortest section. Sorrel grumbled about not getting a challenge, but Vola just rolled her eyes as she cupped her hands. The monk rubbed her palms together and used Vola as a springboard to swarm up the wall.

Vola watched, heart in her throat, but Sorrel found handholds in the completely smooth wall and was perched on the top before Vola could call out a strangled, "be careful!"

She gave them a jaunty way and dropped over the other side.

Raven swooped over them one last time.

"Keep her safe," Vola hissed at him. "Don't let her do anything stupid. And if anything happens, I'm blaming you."

"Yes, well. I would, too." Raven ducked his head before sweeping up the wall. "The tunnel comes out another sixty feet down the wall, around the corner. Meet us there."

Raven soared up the wall and dove over the other side.

Vola didn't immediately hear an outcry from any guards. There were no sounds of fighting, and she had to assume they'd made it without being seen.

"I can see them," Lillie said. "Raven's letting me use his eyes. They're making their way into the kitchens."

Vola let out her breath. "Let's get into position, then."

They crept along the wall, this time Vola taking the lead. She walked with her weapons drawn, her shield still hooked to her back. She was getting used to not drawing it in battle. There wasn't a rule that said she couldn't use it; she just didn't like waving a blackened shield around.

Lillie walked behind, gaze distant as she kept track of Raven and Sorrel.

They reached the corner without incident. Vola almost stepped around it without thinking, but a prick in her gut stopped her mid-step. Instead, she paused and peeked around the corner.

A small grate looking suspiciously like a sewer opened in the stone wall just as Raven had said. Two orcs stood guard on either side. One leaned against the wall, arms crossed. The other picked his nose and examined the contents. Like Arag, she recognized these as more rogues from her village.

Vola turned back and signaled Talon. "Two," she mouthed.

Talon nodded and stepped forward.

Vola put an arm out and shook her head.

"What?" Talon whispered.

"We don't need to leave a trail of bodies for Inga to follow."

Talon humphed and crossed her arms.

"Lillie, how close are Raven and Sorrel?" Vola asked.

"Raven says not far."

"Tell him not to come out until we get rid of the guards."

They needed another distraction. Vola had the vague idea of stepping out and trying to convince them she was their replacement, but they'd recognize her as Gorgo's daughter and know she was a fake.

Her gaze landed on Gruff, waiting patiently beside them, his tongue lolling.

"Talon, can Gruff draw them away?"

Talon and Gruff exchanged a glance, and Gruff stood to shake himself. Then he slipped around the corner.

The big black wolf trotted right up to the orcs without even bothering to hide. The one on the right jumped.

Gruff woofed and lowered his body like a dog who wanted to play. He woofed again and then leaped back.

"Here," one of the orcs grumbled. "What are you doing here?"

Gruff trotted out across the mine floor a little ways before he looked back over his shoulder. His tail wagged.

"Not now, dog," the other orc said. "You're cute, but Inga will kill us if we leave."

"There's no way that's a dog. It's huge."

Gruff whined and wagged his tail. Talon made a gesture down by her thigh, and Gruff streaked away across the mine floor.

Vola glanced at her curiously. "What?"

"Just wait," Talon whispered.

Within moments, Gruff was back again. This time something glinted between his teeth. He stopped far enough away Vola couldn't tell what he'd brought.

"What's he got?" the nearest orc asked.

"Don't know. Something shiny."

"Here, boy," the orc said. "Bring it here."

Gruff cavorted just out of their reach while the orcs tried to coax him closer. Vola covered her mouth to keep from laughing.

"Come on, what have you got?" one of them said.

Gruff gave a muffled woof and jumped away across the mine floor.

"I'll get him," the nearest orc said.

"And cut me out of whatever you find?" the other asked. "No way."

The two took off, chasing the big black wolf out of sight.

"Way to go, Gruff," Vola said.

"Are we just standing here?" Cyrano said, coming up behind them.

"Not anymore." Talon stepped up to the grate. Sure enough, it opened from the inside.

Vola stood outside the wall, staring down the black opening, chewing her lip.

"Lillie?" she said.

"Not long." The wizard remained calm and focused inward, following the path of their missing companions.

"Let's hope it's soon," Cyrano said. "I don't think my diversion at the gate will hold for much longer."

Vola tried to relax her shoulders, keeping one eye on the black behind the grate and the other out in the mine, waiting for the orcs to come back.

Vola blew out her breath. She was worried about Sorrel, yes, but she had to admit that if anyone here was going to be subverted, it was Vola herself. She was the one hearing a voice. She was the one who had to fight for control of her own thoughts whenever she got angry. Lillie's charm didn't seem to work against Mulgash. Maybe because Vola was an orc.

Her mother might be human but used anger all the time. She always claimed it made her stronger. She'd just go berserk, and a battlefield would turn into a slaughtering house. Her father had always told her that orc rage was the same thing, only buried in the blood. It was a tool, something that could be pulled out when all the other options were exhausted.

It was no wonder her parents had gotten together.

"They're here," Lillie said, just as there was a click from inside the opening.

Sorrel hopped out. "Did you miss us?"

Raven swooped through the opening and headed for Cyrano's shoulder before veering at the last second and landing on Lillie. Cyrano's face fell.

"Any trouble?" Vola asked, even though she knew Lillie would have told her if there had been.

"Nah. A couple of guards. But we got around them easily. Funny how people don't think to check under the furniture when they're patrolling."

Gruff streaked back across the mine floor and into the tunnel.

"Those guards will be right on his tail," Talon said.

"Everyone inside, now." Vola herded them all into the opening and closed the door behind them.

"Follow me." Raven dropped from Lillie's shoulder and skimmed the ground of the tunnel. The others followed.

The swamp beast seemed right at home in the cramped space. Probably reminded it of its domain in the sewers, Vola thought. But she didn't dare bring it all the way into the keep. It would give them away for sure, and it wasn't like they could hide it. She found a grate far enough into the tunnel to be hidden from both sides and tied the rope to one of the bars to keep the beast in the tunnel. Then she hurried to catch up.

The others were just emerging from the back of a storage room somewhere near the kitchens. Vola could tell by the smell of frying fat.

"How big is Inga's operation?" she whispered as she surveyed the sacks of grain and barrels of preserved foodstuffs stacked in the closet.

"She has about twenty staff who work here under their own free will. Cooks and guards and maids. Not sure where she picked them up," Raven said. "Before my time. Plus the ones she's subverted."

And the rogue orcs she'd hired. They definitely hadn't been subverted.

Vola listened at the door, then cracked it open when she didn't hear any movement.

"Raven, which way?"

"Left," Raven said. "Then up the stairs to the upper level of the great hall. There shouldn't be any guards up there now, and it's the straightest shot to Inga's rooms."

"Left it is. Take them up."

Raven hopped off Lillie's shoulder and waddled through the door. He jerked his head, and the others followed him out and down the hall.

Vola brought up the rear, checking to be sure no one was coming from the other direction.

They padded down the hall. Raven paused at a corner that opened onto a large room. Metallic clangs rang through the opening.

Raven waited, then said, "Now. Quietly." And he swooped across the open space to a staircase on the other wall.

Lillie held her breath and scurried after him. Her uneven gait scuffed the flagstones, but Vola doubted anyone could hear it over the clanging.

Talon and Sorrel moved as silently as Gruff. And Cyrano just raised his head and strode purposely as if he had every right to be there and somewhere important he was headed.

Vola followed, ducking across the open space as the others made it to the safety of the staircase.

"Hey, what are you doing in here, guard?" a voice called, making Vola freeze. "You know you and your lot aren't allowed in here before meal times. I've caught too many of you snitching food in between."

Vola hid a grimace and turned to face the human woman who brandished a ladle at the other end of the kitchen, where a couple of ovens belched savory steam. Several waifish scullery maids stared at Vola from the shadows at the edges of the kitchen.

The cook advanced, her curly red hair escaping from its bun in flyaways around her red face. Vola didn't dare glance at the others for fear of giving them away.

"Er," Vola said. "I'm here to collect Inga's lunch." She straightened herself up as official as she could manage. It was a good thing Inga employed orcs. She'd never have blended in in any other establishment.

The cook's eyes narrowed. "It's not time for her lunch. She always eats after she addresses the new ones."

Vola gulped and struggled to find something to say. "I don't question my boss," she said. "It's worth more than my job. I just do what I'm told. You should, too." Vola tried a smile, stretching her lips wide across her teeth.

The woman's eyes fixed on her tusks, and they went round.

"Y-yes," she said. "Of course. Inga is allowed to do whatever she wants. I won't keep you. Here." The cook rushed back over to the stove, ladled something thick and creamy into a bowl, and then threw it onto a tray. She thrust the tray back at Vola.

"There. And don't let me catch you back in here before it's the guards' meal rotation."

"Yes, ma'am," Vola muttered and raced for the staircase carrying the tray.

The others rushed ahead of her until they were out of earshot of the kitchens.

"Geez, I thought we were done," Raven said.

"It's a good thing Inga employs a lot of orcs," Talon said.

"Hey, were you planning on eating that?" Sorrel said as they reached the top of the staircase.

Vola rolled her eyes and slid the tray onto a side table. The hall stretched out ahead of them, clear of any guards or servants.

"Guys," Lillie said, peeking out from behind a pillar. "Look."

She pointed down over a balcony into a cavernous room that had to be the center of the stronghold.

Vola crept up to join her, keeping most of her bulk behind the pillar.

Below them stretched the great hall, pillars rising like great trees to support the second floor where they stood.

Rank upon rank of figures stood on the bare stone floor. More than fifty. More than a hundred. Most dressed as simple villagers.

"That's way more than she could do yesterday," Raven whispered.

"Sorrel," Vola said, voice tense. "On the far side."

The rank of figures opposite them was a lot shorter than the others. The halflings. Even from here, Vola could make out Sandry's curly hair and Reed's gray beard. They looked healthy, just blank-eyed and wooden.

"They're not the only ones, Vola," Lillie said quietly.

Vola glanced to where she pointed, and a chill raced down her spine.

In the line closest to them stood a row of familiar orcs. Behind them, several humans waited, including a willowy figure with long blonde hair and a vacant expression.

"Ella," Vola breathed. "Oh, gods. She got my village."

EIGHTEEN

Vola searched the group below, and yes, behind Ella were Ellen and Elsie of course. And she recognized several of the orcs from her clan, including Thorack and the gullible Bothank. His vacant expression hadn't changed much as far as she could tell.

She didn't see her parents. Or Aunt Urag.

"Your family isn't there," Lillie said from beside her. "That's a good thing, right?"

Vola's shoulders slumped, but the relief was short-lived. "Maybe. Or she could have already captured them. They could be somewhere else in here. They could be wandering the forest all blank and empty."

Lillie touched her arm as Vola's voice rose.

Vola stared down at the villagers she'd known her whole life. She'd left them behind at fourteen, thinking she could get away from that life and the prejudices that came with it, but here she was again.

An orcish woman stood on a dais at the front of the crowd in a dark blue gown, fitted through the torso and slitted to the thigh. She wore her long dark hair down her back and carried a gnarled staff in one hand.

"Inga," Raven hissed.

"Oh," Vola said, voice flat.

"What?" Lillie whispered.

"I do know her. I think. She lived outside our village, but I saw her sometimes. Her parents didn't let her come to school with the rest of us."

But instead of sympathy, the familiar heat rose and red beat at the edges of Vola's vision. This woman had been her neighbor. She'd grown up with Ella and the others, at least at a distance.

And she'd kidnapped them all, subverted their wills, and hurt so many people.

Vola's pulse pounded in her ears. *You could show her what a mistake she's made. You could go down there and rescue them.*

"We could rescue them," she growled, hardly aware when her lips started moving. "We could take her out, and everything will be okay again. The villagers would be free."

"Well, yes, that is what we're planning, aren't we?" Lillie said.

Vola stepped out from behind the pillar and put her hand on the railing.

"You mean now?" Lillie squeaked. "Vola, no, think about this." The wizard snatched Vola's arm and hauled her back a step. "Vola, there's over a hundred of them. She has her own army of mind-controlled servants."

"And we have to stop her," Vola said, her voice sounding strange in her ears. A red haze washed over everything she could see, painting the great hall below them with blood.

"Vola." Lillie's voice faded in her ears. But another rose to replace it. Something soft and ringing at the same time, full of the rush of wind. "Vola, listen to me. You are not yourself."

Vola took a deep breath and closed her eyes tight so black drowned out the red. She forced herself to breathe, in, out. And focus on the feel of Lillie's hand on her arm.

Finally, she blinked. "Sorry," she slurred. "Lost...my train of thought there for a minute."

Sorrel and Talon stared at her wide-eyed from the next pillar over. Somehow, Lillie had hauled her back behind their own pillar. Vola suspected magic. Or maybe it was a subconscious reaction on Vola's part.

Cyrano cocked his head to glance at her. "I've heard of orc rage before, but I've never seen it sidetracked like that."

Vola rubbed her face. "I don't want to talk about it."

"This isn't the place to do so," Raven said, mantling. "Listen."

"Take them to the courtyard," Inga said to her guards, her voice sonorous and carrying. "The wagons are waiting."

The guards turned to the villagers as Inga spun, her skirt flaring. She held out her staff, and a glowing doorway appeared in the air behind the dais. Flickers of black laced the edges of the portal. Inga stepped through, disappearing in a swirl of sparks.

"Shit," Vola said. "She's gone." There was a little zing along the back of her neck, like a stray bit of lightning, and Vola glanced around them. But they remained alone on the balcony.

"She'll be in the courtyard," Raven said. "She usually oversees the loading of the wagons before retreating to her rooms."

"How do we free the villagers?" Talon asked.

"If we take her out, will the mind control be released?" Sorrel said.

"I can only assume yes," Raven said. "She is the key focus point for her spells. The power comes from her god, but she is the center. If she goes, the spells go."

"Then we have to stop her in order to free the others," Vola said. Below them, the guards began herding the villagers toward the back of the hall, and the party's noises were lost in the general hum of activity.

Raven took off and circled them once. Then winged his way down the hall toward another staircase. "This wa—"

Raven disappeared in midair with a flash of purple light.

Lillie gasped and doubled over.

"Where'd he go?" Cyrano said, stepping forward. "Raven!"

"He's gone," Lillie said, clutching her head. "Inga has summoned him again."

"So, he's her familiar again?" Talon asked.

"Well, call him back," Cyrano said, striding back to them. "You can do your own summoning, can't you?"

Lillie shook her head. "It would take too long. And Raven didn't give me another feather. Besides, how long can we keep summoning him back and forth?"

"Then we have to get to her and break his curse. We have to save him."

"Guys," Sorrel said from the railing, her brow drawn tight as she stared down at the villagers disappearing into another hallway. "If we don't save them soon, they'll be on their way to Inga's boss and who knows where."

"But Raven," Cyrano said, his voice as lost as Vola had ever heard it.

"We have to get to Inga to save him. And we have to get to Inga to save the villagers. All roads lead to her right now." Vola held his gaze. "We aren't abandoning him. I promise."

Cyrano's lips thinned, and he glanced between them and the staircase where Raven disappeared. After a long moment, he gave her a tight nod. "Let's go, then."

She gave them the signal to move out, and they stepped down the hall-way. They just had to find a staircase that led down. Inga had mentioned wagons and a courtyard. They hadn't come through a courtyard, but it was a pretty good guess that it would be below them.

The balcony led around three sides of the great hall, and they followed it all the way around, looking for another staircase down. They were nearly to the other side when the air shivered against their skin, and Lillie stopped dead in her tracks.

She looked up and around, eyes narrowed.

"What is it?" Vola said, searching herself. But she didn't see anything.

"I've been waiting for you, Vola," a voice said out of the air.

Vola drew her ax as the others gasped and spun, looking for the owner of the voice.

"Inga?" Vola said. She glanced at Lillie, who was muttering a spell under her breath.

"I'm glad you finally showed up. It's a lot harder to talk to you outside this stronghold."

"It's just a spell," Lillie said. "She's not actually here."

"No, but it means she knows where we are," Talon said.

"Where you are, what you're doing," Inga said. "How many hairs are on your chin."

Both Vola and Talon's hands went to their jaws, and Inga's laugh tinkled in the air.

"What do you want, Inga?" Vola said.

"Hardly anything. I'm just going to sit here and watch."

"Watch what?"

"You."

"What do you have against me?"

"I want to know if you're real."

Vola glanced down at herself. "Pretty sure I'm real. Why? Do you have a lot of imaginary friends?"

Inga laughed again. "I mean, I want to know if you really believe everything that you say and do. You're so...good. But here's the thing. Nobody is that selfless. Altruism is always an act. Something that will get you something."

"Maybe in your world," Vola said. "Why me? Why focus on me?" Raven had said she was obsessed. But Vola couldn't think of a single reason why she would care about Vola. Neither of them had been near each other in years.

"Do you remember me?"

"I do." She didn't mention that her only memory of Inga was of a blurry little girl several years younger. Vola hadn't paid much attention.

There'd been plenty of other orc children and she'd been so busy with her own misery, she hadn't had time left over to spare.

"They always talked about you after you left. Your parents. Even some of the other villagers. You had become a paladin. You had the backing of a Virtue. They talked about you like you were some sort of paragon. But I knew it couldn't be true. Everyone knows Orcs are evil." Sarcastic irony almost managed to cover the resignation in her voice.

"So here's the thing. You can save your villagers, if you'd like. If you're strong enough. But you will have to get through me and everyone I employ to get to them. Or…"

Below them, the big doors at the end of the great hall opened, and through them, they glimpsed the empty pit mine they'd traversed just an hour before.

"Or you can leave now, without anyone getting in your way. Without anyone you love getting killed."

"And what happens to the villagers?" Vola asked.

"They will remain mine," Inga said. "But rest assured, they will be well treated. Just because they don't have their minds does not mean we wish to hurt them."

"You're already hurting them," Sorrel said. "They don't know who they are. They can't fight back."

"You assume everyone's goal should be fighting."

"No deal, lady," Talon said. "This was just the way we were going to do things anyway."

"Vola?" Inga said. "Is that true?"

Vola glanced at their faces.

Cyrano glared back at her. "I'm not leaving without Raven."

Lillie raised her chin, letting a little lightning dance through her fingers. Sorrel's knuckles went white on her staff, and Talon drew her daggers.

"Send us your worst," Vola said.

There was the sound of boots tromping up the stairs at the end of the halls. The stairs they'd been trying to get to in the first place.

"Very well," Inga said.

A dozen fully armed and armored orcs poured from the top of the stairs, and Vola drew her weapons.

She opened her mouth, but before she could speak, Inga said, "Charge."

Vola cut down the last orc and rubbed the sweat from her eyes. They'd barely made it down the stairs, meeting swarm after swarm of Inga's followers on the way. Their goal could be just around the corner or miles away, but it made no difference if they couldn't even get down these stairs.

The wood paneling on the walls was singed and smoldering in places. Evidence of Lillie's contributions. And several of the corpses at their feet had throats ripped out. Courtesy of Gruff.

Gods, how many of her father's people had she killed today?

She stared at one of the green faces trying to remember if she'd ever kicked him out of the Frog's Bottom.

"They chose Inga," Lillie said beside her, sensing her thoughts. "They didn't have to fight you, but they did."

"Much good it did them," Talon said.

"Much good it does us." Sorrel leaned against the wall. "Are we any closer?"

Vola took a moment in the lull to catch her breath and survey her team. Talon didn't even have the decency to look ruffled. She stroked Gruff's head while surveying the damage. Sorrel leaned on her staff three steps down from Vola, but she didn't dare go any further because every time they tried to advance, Inga sent more guards at them.

Lillie's hair was in wild disarray, and her face was red with exertion, but she attempted to stand straight when Vola looked at her.

Cyrano grimaced at his bloody rapier and bent to clean the blade on an exposed bit of shirt peeking out from under a dead orc's breast plate.

"How long are we going to do this?" Talon said.

"Until we give up or we're dead," Sorrel said. Then she grinned. "I know which one I vote for."

"You can leave any time," Inga said. "No one would blame you. It is insane what you've gone up against. What I still have to throw at you. Cut your losses, and everyone will understand."

"Stay out of this," Lillie snapped. "We already know your opinion."

Vola shook her head. "I don't know if this is a good idea anymore. If someone gets hurt, there's nothing I can do."

"You know our opinion, too," Lillie said, glaring at her. "We're staying right here."

"So you're not giving up?" Inga said.

"Never," Cyrano said, raising his chin.

Vola grinned and stepped down to join Sorrel.

"Keep it coming, Inga," she said. "You're going to run out of people at some point."

"Will I?" Inga said as another orc came around the corner, yelling a battle cry and wielding a greatsword. "I have orcs from all over the country. Orcs who are tired of being blamed for every little problem. Orcs who want to be more than what the world says they can be."

Vola stepped down sideways and took his legs out from under him.

"They're just like you, you know," Inga said. "Just like me."

Vola's heart ached, but she continued down the steps. "Then why are you treating them like cannon fodder? You're no better than the rest of the world."

"I don't want to be better. I wanted to be the same. But the world only ever saw the orc half. Never the human. I wanted to show them what the orc half could do."

A fireball zipped by Vola's ear and took out the orc rushing up the stairs. Vola kept advancing.

"You left," Inga said. "You left and the paladin academy handed you a shield."

Vola scoffed.

"You paved the way. But none of the universities would accept a half-orc. Magic is for noble races, they said. Not half-breeds. Not violent savages."

"I see how you overcame that prejudice," Vola said, stepping down to take the next orc's head off his shoulders. "Kidnapping people—" She heaved in a breath. "Sending waves of innocent orcs into certain death."

Inga chuckled. "I've learned better since then. You can't expect the world to respect you unless they are afraid of you. I've learned to embrace the orc half and let it serve me. Rage and violence have a place in this world. Of course, you could prove me wrong. You could just lay down and die for me."

"This is your decision, Inga," Vola said. "Not mine."

"It could be yours, too. What will you do to protect people? In order to be who you were supposed to be?"

"What did you do to become who you were supposed to be?" Lillie said. "This is not university-sanctioned magic."

"Of course not, they refused to teach me, remember?" Inga said. "I went to someone else who had no such reservations. Mulgash was perfectly willing to make a deal with me."

"Deals with the Obstacles hardly ever work out the way you want them to," Vola said. "The darker emotions of the world don't help anyone."

"So says an avatar of the light. Oh, wait..."

Vola growled, the weight of her shield digging into her shoulder.

"I knew you must have cheated. You must have gotten lucky. And then, one day, your shield was black. And I knew I was right."

"Cheated like you cheated?" Vola panted. "You couldn't do it without an Obstacle, so you think I couldn't either?"

"What did you do to blacken your shield, Vola?" Inga said. "Protected the wrong person?"

"No."

"No." Inga sounded thoughtful. "No, I don't think so either."

"What's your deal with Mulgash?" Talon said, aiming her bow at the next orc to rush up the stairs. "You sell him your soul, and he gives you everything you want?"

"My soul was hardly worth so much," Inga said. "He gave me the power and knowledge I was looking for, and all I have to do is be his representative here. I gather followers for him, and he grows stronger with every new mind that is now bound to him."

"Does Mulgash know you're sending those followers to someone else?" Sorrel sailed down the steps, feet first to smash the next orc. "Cause that seems like something he should be aware of."

"Silly, Mulgash doesn't care where they are or what they're doing. As long as he has a bond to their mind, he gets stronger."

"That's all it takes," Cyrano said. "A bond."

"A bond. A touch. A whisper in the ear. I don't know, Vola, how would you describe it?"

Sorrel slipped down a step. "What? What's that supposed to mean?"

The last orc went down under a spout of fire, and ice raced along Vola's nerves as Lillie turned to stare at her.

"What did you do to blacken your shield, Vola?" Inga whispered, but everyone heard. "How long have you been hearing his voice?"

"You...you've been hearing voices?" Lillie said. She stood with her hand on the wall.

"Orc rage comes from Mulgash," Inga said. "And he's been after hers for a while now. He likes you, Vola."

"This is a trick," Talon said with a growl. "Inga is trying to get to us, and lying is the only way she knows how."

Except it wasn't a lie. Not exactly.

Vola's limbs refused to respond. Her feet stuck to the floor as if Inga had frozen them there, and her hands had gone numb on the handles of her weapons.

"Every time you got angry, every time a little bit of red threatened to overtake you, you let him in."

Vola opened her mouth, then shut it. Then tried again. "No."

"You lost your shield by breaking your oaths to Cleavah. Because you already belonged to Mulgash."

"No, I didn't hear his voice till after."

"You do hear him then," Talon said. "It's not a trick."

"For how long?" Sorrel said.

Vola rubbed her face on her gauntlet. "Since I got home. Look, it's my problem. Not yours."

"Sounds like it might be our problem now," Talon said.

"It's fine. I'm handling it."

"Are you?" Lillie said quietly. "Like you were handling it on the balcony. And after Cyrano escaped."

Vola couldn't think of anything to say.

"Cleavah always shielded you, didn't she?" Inga whispered in Vola's ear. "What's it like living without that protection?"

"You don't know what's in my head," Vola roared into the air.

"I think I've proven that I do."

Vola's breath shook.

"She knows you, Vola," Sorrel said.

"If Mulgash has been in your head this whole time, he could know you better than we do." Lillie bit her lip, and Vola's heart caved.

"He's not a part of me." Her voice wobbled.

"You don't want him to be," Talon said. "But that doesn't mean he isn't."

"What do we do?" Lillie said. "Should we go back?" She was not talking to Vola.

"The villagers still need saving," Sorrel said.

"Then we go on," Talon said. "Inga already knows we're coming anyway. Apparently, Mulgash will tell her whatever we do even if we try something different."

They weren't asking her. Like at the bar when they weren't talking to her, except this was way worse.

Vola closed her eyes. She couldn't watch them pulling away from her. Even after she'd lost her shield, they'd followed her home. They'd followed her through treason and dishonor.

But this was how she finally lost them. Here on the steps of Inga's stronghold.

A touch on her hand made her jump. Vola opened her eyes to meet Sorrel's wary gaze.

"It's not that we don't trust you," she said.

"It's that we don't trust Mulgash," Talon finished.

But in that moment it was the same thing. Even if they denied it. They couldn't bring Vola without bringing Mulgash.

Sorrel spun and headed down the stairs.

The way was clear now. No one stopped them as they continued down and found the courtyard opening at the bottom of the staircase.

None of them looked at Vola. Except Cyrano, who just stared at her, eyes worried and lips thin.

None of them trusted her. As if that had been Inga's intent all along.

NINETEEN

THE COURTYARD STOOD at the back of the keep, the walls surrounding it on all sides. A large opening in the back led out to the pit mine and a winding ramp that climbed up the steep walls.

Several orc guards loaded the listless villagers into five wagons like cattle being hauled to market. The halflings climbed into the wagons nearest them, and Vola caught sight of Ella's bright head down the row.

Inga stood to one side, stark and beautiful in her blue gown. Raven sat on her shoulders, feathers ruffled, head down, and eyes dull.

She turned toward them with a wide smile as they poured out of the stairwell into the courtyard.

Vola was close enough to Cyrano to hear his pained gasp as he caught sight of Raven.

Inga gestured broadly to the guards who closed up the backs of the wagons.

Sorrel stepped out in front. "Lillie, keep those wagons from going anywhere," she said. "Talon, cover me."

Vola's heart clenched as her team sprang into action, leaving her behind. She gaped for a split second, everything within her numb, as Sorrel raced for the wagon carrying the halflings, and Talon shot at the guards, forcing them back under cover.

Vola shook herself when Cyrano let out a cry and charged for Inga. Alone.

Her grip tightened on her weapons and she followed. Her team could handle a couple of orcs. She went for the half-orc spellcaster, hoping to catch her off guard.

She should have known better. Inga smiled, showing off her tusks, and held out one hand to blast Vola with dark purple fire.

Vola dove out of the way, the flames licking her boots, and she rolled to her feet. Cyrano darted in with his blade drawn, but suddenly Inga wasn't there anymore. The bard stumbled, balance thrown as Inga appeared behind him and raised her hands.

Raven shrieked and clamped his beak on Inga's ear.

She jerked, and her dark fire shot into the sky. Inga growled and reached for the bird, but Raven back-winged off her shoulder and slashed at her hands with his talons.

She tilted her head to smirk up at him. "You can run, but you know it won't work. You're trapped."

He hissed at her.

Instead of appearing angry or ruffled, Inga just planted her free hand on her hip. "You say that now, but you always come when I call."

Cyrano cried out and lunged for her.

Inga spat a sharp word in his direction, and he tripped and fell to his knees, his blade ringing against the flagstones. Cyrano rubbed frantically at his eyes and ears.

"Cyrano!" Vola called, but the bard didn't respond, and when he stared around himself, his eyes searched unseeing.

With her nearest ally blinded, Vola charged, ax drawn back for a blow. But Inga stepped back, and purple fire sprang up between them, stinging Vola's cheeks. She skidded to a stop and flung up her arm to protect her eyes.

"Really, Vola. You can't surprise me. I know the inside of your mind."

Vola tried to back up a step, but the fire raced around behind her, closing the circle, cutting her off from the others.

Beside the wagons, Sorrel swept the last guard's feet out from under him and smashed his head in.

Lillie stepped up to examine the underside, looking for ways to sabotage the vehicle.

Sorrel hauled on the latch and yanked the back of the wagon open. Then she held out a hand to Sandry, who sat closest.

"Come on, now," she said gently. "We're taking you home."

"I know everything you're going to do, Vola," Inga crooned in her ear.

The heat beat against Vola's face, and she fell to one knee. She wiped the sweat trickling down her temple, trying to see Sorrel. "You really don't," she said, but there was little force behind it now.

"I do. Because I'm you. I'm you without Cleavah. I'm you without your friends."

Vola shook her head. "Stop talking at me and fight."

"I don't have to."

Lillie was busy setting fire to the wagons' axles, making them unusable, while Talon went down the line and threw open the tailgates, letting villagers free.

Sandry stared at Sorrel's outstretched hand for a moment before she reached out to take it.

Sorrel froze and shivered. Her eyes grew wide, and her face went slack.

Vola sucked in a breath. "Sorrel?"

Sorrel turned and stepped toward Lillie, who bent to start another fire under the halfling wagon.

The monk spun her staff straight at Lillie.

Lillie gasped and ducked just in time to take the blow on her shoulder instead of her head. She cried out.

Then Lillie's eyes went wide. "Oh, no. Sorrel? Sorrel, answer me."

Lillie lurched upright, just avoiding another blow, and grabbed hold of Sorrel's shoulders as if to shake her.

The wizard froze.

"No, no, no, how are you doing this?" Vola groaned. They'd shielded themselves. The pendants. They should have kept Inga out of their heads.

"It was tricky figuring out how to get past all those shields," Inga said. "But Mulgash gave me the answer."

Lillie turned in slow motion to Talon. The ranger backed up a step.

"Talon! Look out!" Vola called. But Lillie was already moving, trying to place a hand on Talon.

Vola rocked back on her heels, held her arm over her nose and mouth, and leaped over the dark purple flames separating her from the others.

Talon skipped back and spun. Instead of letting Lillie get close, she stuck out the end of her bow and tripped her.

The wizard went down with an "umph."

Talon straightened just as Lillie's hand shot out and grasped her ankle.

Talon froze.

Vola skidded to a halt in front of her. "Talon?"

The ranger blinked.

"Talon, snap out of it. You can fight this."

"Who are you without them?" Inga asked in her ear. "Who are you without Cleavah?"

Vola's fingers clenched on her weapons. She had no way to heal this. No way to fight it. Not unless she wanted to cut down those who were dearest to her.

She cried out wordlessly and didn't even try to duck as Talon reached out to touch her shoulder.

A voice slithered through her head. *You don't have to let them go. You can join them. They'll leave you otherwise.*

It would be so easy to entertain the thought. Just for a moment. Let the idea take root and wonder what it would be like to just let go. She could stop making decisions. If she was with them, she'd still be able to keep them safe, right?

But they wouldn't be themselves anymore. She wouldn't be herself. And who knew what Inga would make her do.

You don't really know her. It might not be so bad.

Bad enough. And wasn't giving up her own choice the worst sin of all? Sure, it was hard to choose sometimes, but she'd rather be choosing as herself than as Inga's pet.

"No," she whispered.

You are by far the stubbornest of all my creations.

"I am not yours."

A sharp pain lanced down Vola's cheek, and she jerked back to awareness, Talon's reaching fingers inches from her face. Raven swooped between them, claws ready to scratch again.

Raven's wings beat so close to her face, she flinched. He drove her back again.

She shook her head. "Stop. Stop!"

"Focus, Lightless," Cyrano's voice said behind her. "This is not a time to be drifting off."

"Fuck off," she said.

Lightning zapped the ground in front of them, and they leaped back. They looked to Inga.

Inga raised her hands and pointed to Cyrano.

"Get out," Raven cried. "Get Vola out of here."

He flew at Inga, talons outstretched.

Cyrano threw an arm around Vola's chest and dragged her backward, toward the opening to the pit mine.

Talon stood staring at her with blank blue eyes as Lillie and Sorrel stepped up to flank her.

Vola struggled in his arms. "No, I'm not leaving them!"

"You don't have a choice unless you want to *be* one of them."

"What are you going to do, paladin?" Inga called as she ducked another of Raven's attacks. "Flee or fight the ones you swore to protect?"

"Flee," Cyrano whispered, hauling her back another step. He had to throw all of his weight back to get her to move. "Flee in order to fight later."

He yanked on her again, and with a cry, she let him.

Raven battered at Inga's head and shoulders while Cyrano hauled Vola to the opening in the wall.

As they disappeared through the wide archway, Raven broke off and flew after them. Inga straightened up behind him, her laughter ringing in Vola's ears.

The pit mine's walls rose on one side, and Vola pulled herself from Cyrano's arms in order to sprint blindly across the floor. Maybe she'd hit one of Inga's traps and never come out again.

An arm snaked around Vola's chest and threw her sideways into a bush.

Vola came up swinging as Cyrano leaped after her with a cry.

"Easy, Volly," a voice growled. "It's me. It's me."

Vola shook leaves and dirt from her eyes and focused on the figure crouched beside her.

Her father, Gorgo, knelt in the brush beside the rough road leading from Inga's stronghold. Her mother guarded his back.

"Friends?" Cyrano asked, checking with Vola before lowering his weapon.

"Family," Gorgo said with a glare at the bard. "Why? Who're you?"

Raven fluttered into their cover, startling Gorgo and Lydia. Lydia brandished her favorite ax.

"Peace, peace," Raven cried. "I promise I would taste really awful."

"We're not hunters," Gorgo said.

"We got Vola's message about the orcs that have wandered off," Lydia said.

"And eventually Urag got Arag to tell us where this stronghold was hidden. We're here to stop Inga."

Cyrano reached for Lydia's hand. "Then we are here with common purpose, beautiful."

"Seriously, it's not a personality trait anymore. It's a flaw," Raven muttered, settling onto a branch.

"You'll want to refrain from flirting," Vola told Cyrano flatly. "Considering that's my mother. And that's my dad." Vola pointed to Gorgo.

Cyrano gulped.

Gorgo shot a look up and down Cyrano and then sent Lydia an amused glance. "I'm not worried."

"Vola, honey, what's going on?" Lydia said. "Where are Lillie and Talon and Sorrel?"

Gorgo glanced over the bushes at the smoke billowing toward the sky. "What the hell happened in there?"

Vola crumpled, dropping her head into her hands. "I lost them. Oh, goddess, I lost them all."

TWENTY

LYDIA AND GORGO exchanged a look and then seamlessly switched places so Lydia could fold Vola in her arms while Gorgo guarded their back and flanks. An ancient badger snuffled into view. Beside him, the dirt mounded, and Aunt Urag climbed out of the soil, carrying her gnarled staff.

"We're safe here for now, but we shouldn't linger." Her gaze lighted on Vola. "Oh. I take it things have gone to shit already."

Vola shook her head, her throat too tight to speak.

"Honey, I'm so sorry," Lydia whispered.

Vola resisted the urge to throw her mother off. Words wouldn't do anything to help them now. And the words didn't help the black mass of sticky guilt and pain writhing in her chest.

"It's not like they're dead," Cyrano said sharply. "Just subverted. They can be retrieved and rescued. If you'd just get off your ass."

A growl built in the back of Vola's throat, but before she could answer, Inga's voice threaded through the air around them, soft and sweet enough to make Vola's teeth hurt.

"Yes, but Vola won't fight her friends. She's a paladin. Her entire job is to protect them, and she failed. She won't risk hurting them further."

Lydia stiffened as Gorgo snapped around, searching for the owner of the voice. "What is that?" he hissed. "Is someone there?"

"It's Inga," Vola said, low and rough. "She's been following me for who knows how long. Talking to me. She knows me better than she should. And she's right."

Vola raised her gaze to Cyrano. "I won't risk hurting them."

"Then what were you doing back there?" He threw his hand back, indicating the courtyard where the wagons still smoldered from Lillie's handiwork. The few orc guards remaining were herding the prisoners back into the stronghold, down another set of stairs. Inga had disappeared.

"If you weren't going to fight them, what were you doing?" Cyrano said. "Joining them?"

She glared at him. "No...maybe. I could have...I could have fought Inga."

"By yourself. Right, so you were going to die and leave your people without someone to rescue them." He snorted. "I'd heard orcs were dumb, but you're the first one to prove it."

Gorgo's growl started low and rose, heading toward a roar at break-neck speeds. Lydia reached out and laid a hand on his arm, freezing the noise in his throat.

Vola's lip lifted and her fists clenched so hard they creaked. "You're walking a thin line, bard."

He folded his arms over his chest and jerked his chin up. Raven eyed them back and forth.

"If you're not stupid, then prove it, Lightless," Cyrano said.

She shook her head in frustration. She was the one with the tactics, yes, but usually, she had an entire party to work with. Scenarios circled her head, and they kept running up against the diamond-hard wall that said 'you're alone. You don't have them anymore. You failed.'

The evening sun plunged behind roiling gray clouds just as the sky opened and rain came sheeting down. It battered Vola's head until she bowed under its weight.

"How?" Vola said. "How do you fight someone who knows every move you're going to make before you do. She's literally listening right now."

"Don't follow your own rules," Cyrano said. "She knows your character? Then break character."

Vola froze.

If Inga knew her better than she knew herself, then the only way to beat Inga was to be someone new.

She touched the blackened edge of her shield over her shoulder. She'd been trying to hold onto herself, trying to hold onto the good paladin, since they'd taken her shield.

But...that wasn't who she was anymore. She wasn't a good paladin anymore. She was a good paladin who'd been blackened. She was different. The old Vola would never fight her party.

The new Vola didn't have the luxury of that choice.

Her spine straightened as rain pinged against her pauldrons. "How?" she said again, but this time the tone was one of thought, not despair. "I don't have Lillie to break Inga's spell. Or Cleavah to heal them." Her throat closed, but she pushed through the pain. "How does Inga's magic work? Why were the others taken but not me?"

"Relationship," Raven said from the bush. "It's relationships that allow Inga's magic a foothold. Your monk had a relationship with the halfling girl. She cared about her enough to allow the infection to spread despite protections. And from her to the others as well. The care you have for them invites the rot in. Mulgash corrupts the best in us."

"Then why didn't I succumb?"

Raven shrugged. "You're used to fighting him? Then I distracted you."

Vola touched her cheek where he'd slashed her in the courtyard. "But that won't work after its already taken hold. Would it?"

"I doubt it."

Vola frowned and glanced at her father. "You use orc rage all the time. But you don't succumb to Mulgash. You don't seem controlled to me."

He snorted. "Just because you hear a voice doesn't mean you have to listen to it. And even when you do agree with it, that doesn't make it your master."

"You make it sound so easy."

Gorgo tilted his head. "The rage was a gift to orcs from Mulgash. But once a gift is yours, it's yours. You use it the way you want. Or don't. And you don't owe anything to the giver. Do you still use that hideous scarf your aunt knitted you when you were twelve?"

"No," Vola admitted. "I used it to stuff my first set of armor so it would fit."

Urag sniffed. "I'll remember that the next time your birthday comes around. See if you get any homemade gifts again."

"My point is," Gorgo said with a glare at his sister. "Mulgash has no say in how you use his gift."

A breath of wind touched Vola's cheek, easing the sting of Raven's scratch. "Not all anger belongs to Mulgash," a voice breathed in her ear. Not Inga's. This was a voice full of the rush of wind even within a gentle breeze. A familiar voice she'd never thought to hear again. It had been following her since Glenhaven, hiding in the whisper of other people's words.

Even as her breath caught, her memories raced. She couldn't help thinking of the devotee in Cleavah's temple—before she'd known it was Cleavah herself. The woman had drawn a fish knife on a trouble maker. She'd fought, over and over again, even when fighting didn't look the way it did for other people.

Vola had spent so much time trying to ignore the rage that was a part of her blood that she'd forgotten there was such a thing as righteous anger.

Her lips pulled back from her teeth in a feral grin as rain slipped down her face, tasting fresh and clean. Someone was going to have to fight her friends, if only to get to Inga and end her reign over this area. And who better to fight them than one who knew them so well. Knew their strengths and weaknesses. Knew and cared about them so much.

Surely if something like Inga's control could spread like an infection through that bond of caring, then something good could spread through it as well.

TWENTY-ONE

VOLA CROUCHED at the edge of the brush and peered back toward the courtyard. The storm clouds blocked out the last rays of the sun, and Vola had to squint to see anything.

"If you're going back in, that's the only way," Urag said over her shoulder. "Everywhere else is locked down."

"Inga will know you're coming," Raven said. He flitted from the nearby branch to Vola's shoulder.

"Inga already knows I'm coming," she said. "I'm not trying to keep it a secret."

"You're going in alone?" Cyrano said.

"I have to. Inga can just take anyone who goes in there with me. We thought we were protected. Apparently not."

"She can do that to us out here, too," Cyrano said. "Would you rather have a team that could turn on you in there? Or an unknown number of enemies coming at you from behind?"

She twisted on her heels to raise an eyebrow at him. "Are you saying you want to come with me?"

"Nothing's changed from my perspective," he said. "And you're still the best ally I've got."

"Are you dumb enough to follow a dumb orc?"

His lip twitched. "No. But I'm smart enough to follow a smart one."

Vola stood. There was no sense in hiding behind the bushes. Inga knew where she was. Inga knew she was coming. She didn't have to tie herself up in knots over it. Physically or mentally.

The rain rapidly turned the dust on her armor to mud. She brushed at it and only succeeded in smearing it around, grinding it into the scratches in the metal.

She gave up and reached behind her to unsheathe her mother's ax. She turned to hand it over to Lydia.

Her mother met her eyes.

"I thought you might like this back," Vola said. "I'm sticking with my own from now on."

Lydia took the ax and slung it behind her while Vola drew her longsword. Then she pulled her blackened shield off her back and stared at it before she settled it on her arm. She'd earned that shield. And everything she did with it was a reflection of who she was. Not the mistakes she'd made.

She cocked her head at Gorgo and Lydia. "What do you think?" she said. "I don't suppose I can convince you to go home. If Inga uses relationships to subvert people, you're the ones with the most risk."

"You mean we're the ones with the most experience resisting," Gorgo said, standing and stretching so his leather belt creaked and the muscles across his torso popped.

Vola rolled her eyes.

"We've got a lot of people to rescue in there. We can do it better together," Gorgo said.

"Oh," Lydia said, eyes shining. "This will be just like that family camping trip we took when you were seven. Remember, Vola? The one where you took out your first horde of goblins."

"I remember Dad second-guessing every move I made." Vola leveled a glare at Gorgo. "Is that going to happen this time, too?"

"I have more experience—"

"I am a graduate of the Paladin Academy."

"You're barely more than a grunt—"

Lydia thrust her elbow into Gorgo's ribcage. "Just follow your daughter without complaining, please." She lowered her voice to hiss in his ear. "She needs this."

"Thanks, Mom," Vola said with a sigh.

"I'm coming, too," Urag said. "Though I can't help noticing that no one bothered to ask me."

Vola put a hand to her chest and faked surprise. "You're still here, Aunt Urag? I assumed you would have stormed the castle by now."

"It's too late to try to sweet talk me now."

"I can't help you," Raven said, dropping his head between his shoulders. "I'm still under Inga's power. If I try, she'll just anticipate your moves or summon me again." He shuddered. "And I don't want to think what that will be like now. She can't be happy with me."

Vola reached up to stroke his head. "We're not trying to sneak up on her. Remember?"

"Good, 'cause I'd have to tell her. She'd force me to."

"Then maybe we should fix that first."

They didn't try to hide. Or sneak. Or flank. They just strode right back into the courtyard, Vola at the head of her new—er, eclectic—party.

She had an ax-swinging berserker, an orc chieftain who liked to fight with his fists, a sweet-talking bard, a crotchety nature mage, and a bird.

Well, she was used to it by now. If the events in Water's Edge had taught her anything, it was that anyone could work together as long as they had a good leader.

Whether or not she was still that leader remained to be seen.

"Very discreet, Vola," Inga whispered in her ear as they strode past the wagons smoldering in the rain. It was full dark now, and the sputtering embers flickered against the doors of the keep, which were shut and barred.

"We're not trying to be discreet," Vola said and pointed her father at the door. "You wanna get that?" she asked him.

"Only if you don't think you can get it yourself." He gave her a tusky smile.

"I'm delegating," she said. "Making you feel useful. Aunt Urag could set it on fire, I suppose."

Urag held out her hand and watched the rainwater pool in her palm. "Might take a bit. And it'll smoke like a sailor on watch."

Gorgo rolled his eyes. "I didn't say I didn't want to."

Her dad stepped up to the door, cracked his knuckles, took a deep breath, and punched the door in.

The solid barrier, half a foot thick, thudded to the floor inside.

Gorgo shook out his hand. "It's not the wood you have to worry about. It's the hinges."

"You're not fooling anyone." Inga's voice floated through the rain. "I know what you're doing."

"Yeah?" Vola said. "Here's the thing, I don't think you know me as well as you think you do. If you did, you would have known not to touch them. But you did. Now you can sit back and watch and know that you did this."

That shut Inga up. The ghostly voice in her ear disappeared as they surveyed the dark corridor beyond the door. Stairs led up from the landing, and another set led down.

"The prisoners will be below," Raven said. "Until she can get new wagons."

Their purpose wasn't to be discreet, Vola thought. But it was to be unexpected. So what would Inga expect her to do.

The paladin in her wanted to free the prisoners. To make sure they were on their way to freedom first. Which meant she couldn't do that.

"All right. Up it is," Vola said. "Raven, you're up first. The curse she has you under, it has to have an anchor, right? where is it? Is it on her? Is this a case where if we kill her, it'll free you?"

"I don't think so. It's too big. I would have noticed if she'd been carrying it around with her."

"Too big? What is it that's binding you then?"

"She stole my ability to shift. I shape change by letting the spirits of other shapes inhabit me. But she captured those shapes, including my true self. Without them free, I'm trapped."

"You mean she's got a freaking zoo locked up here somewhere? Where are they?"

"I don't know. You think if I knew, I would still be here?"

"Fine, it won't be that easy then."

She paused for a second, chewing her lip. She had to think like Lillie. Solving problems. She cocked her head.

"Cyrano."

"Lightless?" he said.

"You were creating communication spells out in the wild. Trying to contact Raven. Did they work?"

"No," he snorted. "They were supposed to target his physical form, which he wasn't wearing, so..." His eyes went wide as he caught her drift.

He didn't bother connecting the dots out loud. He just pulled his lute from his back and strummed a chord.

"What just happened?" Gorgo asked as Cyrano started up the stairs.

Vola shook the rain from her face and wrung out her braid on Inga's carpet. "Cyrano can target Raven's true form now that he knows that's what he's looking for. And if Raven's true form is trapped with his spirit forms..."

"Then we can find them," Urag said.

Inga didn't bother sending waves of her orc minions to try to stop them this time. Either because she'd run out of them or because they'd decided they had a better life expectancy somewhere else or for some other nefarious reason. Vola didn't bother trying to speculate.

They reached the top of the stairs, which led back out onto the balcony above the great hall.

"This way," Cyrano said and ducked into another stairwell, still strumming. Walls closed in on them from either side, creating a narrow space spiraling up the inside of a tower.

The staircase ended in a flat ceiling and a trap door above them.

"Stand aside," Gorgo said, ready to ram the door again.

"Please," Cyrano said, lifting a hand. "Not everything requires brute force." He placed his hand on the trap door and whispered a word. The lock glowed and clicked.

"That's handy," Vola said.

Cyrano gave her a wink. "I might have been a burglar in another life."

Gorgo snorted. "Not everything requires brute force," he muttered. "But brute force is more fun."

Vola craned her head to listen at the door, but nothing moved on the other side. And considering the ceiling was the floor of the room above, they should be able to hear every step like the inside of a drum.

Vola lifted the trap door and peered around the room. Raven clenched his claws on her shoulder in order to stay in place.

Vola expected to see Raven's true form propped in a corner of the tower room like a creepy full-sized doll. Or maybe some sort of obviously magical device that kept his animal forms trapped.

What she did not expect to see was a lion standing less than a foot away from her, whiskers twitching.

The lion's growl rumbled in its throat, and it took a swipe at her.

Vola ducked and slammed the trapdoor shut behind her.

"What the hell was that?" Gorgo asked.

"Lion," Vola said.

"That would be my magic," Raven said. "My spirit forms taking a physical shape."

"How many of those do you have?" Urag said.

Raven cocked his head. "Erm. Twenty? I'm not sure. I've lost track."

"Great. I thought it would be as simple as finding your true form and just sort of..." Urag pressed her palms together. "Squishing them together."

"Inga's magic is keeping me from reabsorbing them," Raven said.

"I don't think your spirit forms are going to let us get close enough to assess the situation," Vola said, frowning at the trapdoor. The floor above creaked. As if a lion paced across the planks.

"So what do we do?" Gorgo said. "This was supposed to be a fairly simple magical rescue."

"We fight," Raven said. There was something in his voice. Some resignation she hadn't noticed before now. "Tire out the spirit forms and then we can get close enough."

Vola grinned at Gorgo. "When clever doesn't work, then try hitting it head-on."

Lydia rubbed her hands together as Gorgo whooped. "Lion taming," she said. "Bring it on."

Vola counted to three then threw open the trapdoor. She ducked the lion's first swipe and vaulted up into the room above.

Raven launched himself from her shoulder as she came out into the round room. Rain slashed against three windows, but they were covered by a shimmering magic that locked Raven's spirit forms inside.

The lion stood directly over the trapdoor as Lydia and Gorgo peered out from under its paws. Vola swept a blow toward the lion and backed up, luring it away from the opening so the others could come through.

The lion sprang at her, and Vola planted her feet, catching the blow on her shield. She heaved and sent the great cat flying across the room. Goddess, it felt good to use it again.

The lion twisted in midair and morphed into a giant eagle.

Lydia leaped from the trapdoor, catching the bird in flight with her ax. It screeched and fell to the floor.

Raven faltered in the air and recovered.

The eagle's body thinned and twisted, scales sprouting in place of feathers until a snake slithered across the rough floorboards. It reared back, then lunged forward and wrapped itself up Gorgo's leg. Gorgo fisted one hand and smashed the creature on the nose.

Raven's wing dipped, and he hit the wall.

Vola hesitated, eyes on Raven as he flapped upright and circled above them.

The others swarmed the snake as it shook its head and morphed into a huge brown bear. Aunt Urag raised her staff and shot a spray of fire at the massive creature.

This time when Raven plummeted from the air, Vola was ready. She lunged to catch him. He lay limp in her arms.

"This is hurting you," she said, voice tight.

Raven shook his head as if to clear it and struggled upright. He used his talons to climb to her shoulder, where he clung to the edge of her armor.

"There's no other way," he whispered. "I can't control them, Vola. Either you kill them—and me as well—or they will kill you."

"No." Vola shook her head as she stepped out of the way of the fight, pressing her back against the wall as Cyrano clashed with a giant crocodile. It snapped at him, and he barely managed to dart out of the way without losing a foot. Lydia brought her ax down, cutting off the end of its tail.

Raven drooped.

"Raven!" Vola cried.

"Vola, this is the only way I'll be free. If you can't break Inga's magic, then the only way I'll escape her is in death." His head lolled. "Just do it. But please. Don't tell Cyrano until after it's done. He'll try to talk me out of it."

"*I'm* trying to talk you out of it."

She almost called the others off, but the deadly barrage of creatures hadn't stopped. The crocodile had shifted into a wyvern now, nearly filling the space, spitting fire at Lydia and Gorgo. They couldn't retreat. Raven was the only one weakened by what they'd done. The spirit forms fought for their lives as viciously as any creature.

"You knew this coming up here, didn't you?" She pulled him from her shoulder and held him in her hands. He lay there, chest heaving.

"I knew back in the village when you said you couldn't heal me. Death was the only freedom I could look forward to. But I wanted to help you as much as I could before that."

Vola bowed her head over him. They had nothing else to try. But the choice couldn't be kill him or leave him enslaved.

"We'll kill Inga," she whispered. "That will free you."

"And what happens if you can't? Would you leave me like this forever?"

She shook her head, her vision going blurry.

"Urag! Tie it down," she called. "Trap it."

Her aunt gave her a concerned glance before nodding and raising her hands. She pulled up from the floor, and vines sprang out of the wood planks, lashing around the creature.

It morphed from one shape to another, thrashing to free itself, but

Urag's vines stretched and shrunk to accommodate it until finally, it lay still, exhausted.

Vola stepped to the bound shape. It lay in the form of a great eagle, tethered to the ground, its eye fixed on Vola.

In the sudden stillness, Cyrano caught sight of the limp form in her arms.

"Raven?"

"Do it, Vola," Raven whispered. "Please, free me. I'm tired. And I hurt. I don't want to hurt anymore."

Vola laid a hand against the eagle's throat.

Something pulsed under her palm. An oily touch that retreated the moment she tried to focus on it.

She frowned and closed her eyes, reaching out with a sense she hadn't realized she still carried with her. A shadow of Cleavah standing over her shoulder, whispering in her ear.

Behind her eyelids, Vola could see dark purple sludge surrounding a bright prick of light that lay in her arms, smothering it like a wet blanket tossed over a flame. It stretched toward the shape on the floor, and she could see the vague outline of the eagle even through her eyelids. Purple, the same shade as Inga's dark fire, wrapped the creature and connected it to Raven, keeping them separate but trapped together.

She could see the curse. She could see it and not do anything about it. How stupid was that? How stupid was it that Cleavah herself was cut off from Vola? A goddess in her own right. A minor one, yes, but what did that have to do with anything when faced with the divine light Vola had always seen in Cleavah.

She'd seen how powerful her goddess was. Seen how righteous and compassionate and mighty. Nothing could stop her if she didn't want it to. If something was in her way, she went right through it. Or she found a way around.

And she'd chosen Vola for those exact same qualities.

If Cleavah couldn't reach her through an emblem...then Vola would just find a way to reach back to her.

She lowered Raven to her lap and placed her palm over his chest, his keel bone fitting under her broad palm. Now they were all three connected. Raven, his spirit form, and herself.

This time, instead of reaching out, she reached back over her shoulder. Toward her goddess. Or at least toward the place where she'd always found her.

The barrier stretched between them, a paper-thin veneer, making Cleavah's light fuzzy and dim.

But it was still there. Beyond the veil that separated them.

Vola stretched out her hand in her mind, dirty and bloody but covered in shining mail. The veil bent and stretched.

And her fingers punched through, shattering the barrier into a million gray pieces. It fell, crumbling around her.

On the other side stood Cleavah with her golden skin and dark hair curling down her back. Her hand already held outstretched toward Vola.

As if she'd been waiting.

"Ah," the goddess said with a soft, fierce smile. "There you are."

Their hands clasped, and power poured into Vola, filling the space inside her as if it had never left. A vast ocean of divine power just waiting for her to use it.

It didn't go through an emblem. It simply speared deep into her chest.

She breathed deep.

"Lady bless," she whispered.

Light shone from under her hand, making Cyrano and the others cry out and stumble back, shading their eyes.

When Vola blinked and finally pulled her hand back, a man lay on the floor in front of her. Completely naked, tall and lanky, full of sharp angles and knobbly knees with chin length brown hair in wavy strands across his face.

Cyrano's small gasp filled the room, and Vola fell back as the bard fell to his knees with uncharacteristic awkwardness.

"Raven." His voice broke on the name.

Raven's chest moved, and he blinked up at them, eyebrows coming down in a frown. He lifted a hand and held it in front of his face, wiggling his fingers.

"I can't help but notice this is the opposite of what I asked for, Vola," he croaked. His voice still sounded very much like the raven's, but she imagined it'd clear up with some use.

"You're welcome," she said. She stared at her own hands, her breath coming faster than normal. What...the hell had just happened? She flexed her fingers, feeling the tingle along their edges. And inside her chest, Cleavah's power still rested.

Cyrano threw his arms around Raven's bare shoulders and hauled the other man into his lap.

Raven pushed the hair from his eyes and glared at the bard. "I'm still not talking to you."

"Sure you aren't, love," Cyrano crooned. "And that's fine. I'll do all the talking, and you'll be back to loving me eventually."

"Get off of me, you flirt." Raven shoved half-heartedly against Cyrano's chest.

"Oh, I'm the flirt?" Cyrano said with an unrepentant grin. "I'm not the one who went to extraordinary lengths just so Lightless here would get me naked."

Raven's cry sounded like an undignified squawk.

"Sorry, Raven," Vola said as Gorgo gave her a hand off the floor. "Not really my type. Your butt is too skinny."

Raven huffed a defeated laugh and leaned his forehead against the bard's shoulder.

TWENTY-TWO

"YOU TWO SHOULD GET OUT NOW," Vola said while Cyrano helped Raven to his feet. "While you can. I've got plenty to work with here." She gestured to her family.

Lydia beamed. Gorgo flexed. Urag snorted.

Raven rolled his eyes while Cyrano laughed outright. "We're not going anywhere, Lightless. We're helping you get your party back. And we have a stake in the fight against Inga." The bard flung out his arms. "We have each other and an enemy to fight. What more could we want?"

"I'd settle for some clothes," Raven muttered, trying to find a strategic place to put his hands.

"Aw, why would you want to ruin the effect?" Cyrano said.

"We all know you're enjoying the view," Raven snapped. "But there are...dangly bits. I don't like dangling."

"We'll find you a curtain or something." Vola said with a raised eyebrow. "How are you feeling otherwise?"

"Fine. Good even. I won't be shape-changing any time soon, but I don't feel half-dead anymore."

"Curious that," Urag said. "How'd you know how to break the curse, Vola?"

"She's a paladin," Lydia said, beaming at her daughter. "That's what they do."

At least part of that was right. But Vola wasn't exactly sure it was true for a black paladin. And if it wasn't, then what the hell was she now?

"Come on," she said and jumped back down through the trap door to the spiral staircase.

"We're going after Inga, right?" Cyrano said, hurrying to keep up.

Raven followed him, a little more warily.

"Eventually," Vola said. "But Inga's not going to make this easy. She'll be hiding behind Sorrel, Talon, and Lillie. Using them as a shield."

"So, you either have to give up on getting to her or fight them," Raven said.

"Yeah," Vola said flatly.

"So what are you going to do?"

"Well, I'm not leaving them here."

"So you're going to fight them."

Vola stopped at the bottom of the stairs and checked around the corner to ensure none of the orc guards had decided to come back and play at brave soldiers.

"Think about this, Lightless, before you do anything you can't take back," Cyrano said. "Think about what you're prepared to do."

Vola glanced back over her shoulder. Cyrano and Raven waited at the bottom of the stairs, her family spread out up the steps behind them. They all stared at her solemnly.

Vola met Raven's eyes. "I'm not leaving them," she said again.

He nodded, knowing exactly what she meant.

Cyrano blew out his breath. "All right then," he said quietly. "Raven, which way?"

"Right. To the top of the keep."

"Oh, Raven," Inga's voice said into the air. "You didn't like being my pet?"

Raven stiffened, and without a shirt, Vola could see his flush spread all the way down his chest. "Fuck off," he said.

"Language," Inga said. "I knew you'd never love me, but we could have at least been friends."

"We have very different ideas of friendship," Cyrano said. "Come down and I'll educate you."

"With your blade? How original."

"Just ignore her," Vola said and stepped out into the empty hallway. "Remember what Dad said. Just because you hear a voice doesn't mean you have to listen to it."

"Aw, you do pay attention to your old man," Gorgo said as they followed her.

"That's all right," Inga said. "This way I can focus better on Vola."

"Still not listening," Vola said and paused when she realized they were missing one person. "Raven? You coming?"

Raven waved a hand from where he stood, staring up at the curtains lining the tall windows. "Keep doing whatever you're doing. I'll catch up."

Vola raised an eyebrow but didn't argue.

She found another set of stairs that led up and trotted up them. The whole stronghold was eerily silent aside from the rain pounding the windows.

Had they really killed that many of Inga's guards?

On the next floor, a long hall stretched ahead of them, lined with doors.

"The guest wing?" Vola said.

"How many visitors do you suppose she gets?" Lydia said.

"How many visitors do you suppose she lets leave?" Gorgo grumbled.

Vola started to step forward, but Urag stopped her with a hand on her chest.

"Traps," Urag said. "Dozens of them." She leaned down and blew. Symbols lit up and sparkled the entire way down the hall, covering the floor space completely.

Vola scowled at the carpet. "You couldn't have made this easy, Inga?"

"Oh, you're talking to me now?" Inga said.

"Yeah, you're right. Never mind."

Lydia and Gorgo put their heads together with Cyrano. "I can dance my way through," Cyrano said. "Looks like a standard two-step will keep me out of the worst of it. Ms. Battlemane looks pretty light on her feet. I'll bet she can follow my steps."

Gorgo narrowed his eyes at the bard. "I say we just smash the nearest one, jump back, and see what happens."

Lydia rolled her eyes. "Men," she said with a sigh. "Spells set this close together are usually tied to each other with a single thread. If we just find the thread, we can unravel them one by one."

Vola exchanged a look with Urag. The old orc rolled her eyes toward the ceiling. Then she swept her staff out, sending a wave of water sweeping across the carpeted floor. Traps sprang right and left, some sending up gouts of flame—which turned to steam under the wave of water—some lighting up with ineffective binding magic. One at the end brought down a chunk of ceiling which splashed harmlessly into the water.

As soon as the wash of liquid had swept through every crevice and cranny of the hall and even splashed up the walls, Urag extended her staff again, and the water surged back toward them.

Her staff sucked it up with a slurp, leaving only the damp carpet and dripping wallpaper.

Lydia, Gorgo, and Cyrano blinked.

"Or…we could just do that," Cyrano said.

There was a jingling behind them, and they all spun, weapons out.

Raven looked at them, his hands full of the deep blue curtains hanging at their end of the hall. "What?" he said. There was a long pause. "Would someone help me get these down?"

"What was wrong with the ones downstairs?" Cyrano said as he and Lydia moved to help.

"I decided I didn't like the color."

"You didn't like the color?" Cyrano said.

"I'm not a fan of red. It reminds me of blood."

"And that was what you thought was important right now?"

"Hey, I have spent the last few weeks dressed in nothing but black feathers. I will pick a color if I want to. And if you have a problem with that, you can just shove it."

Cyrano blinked, then he seized Raven's face between his hands and kissed him fiercely.

Meanwhile, Lydia measured the curtains along her arm and folded and tucked and knotted until she could throw the result over Raven's head.

Vola led the way down the damp hall, Urag stepping behind her, a smug grin lighting up her face. No traps remained for them to spring, and they reached the next stairwell unscathed. As they started up, Cyrano, Raven, and Lydia joined them, Raven dressed in a draping robe of deep blue with a gold tasseled belt.

"Stylish," Vola said.

"Thank you," Raven said, lips tilting in a smirk.

They reached the top of the stairs and froze.

"Oh," Vola said weakly. "So this is where they all went."

Ahead of them stretched a wide hall probably used for balls or receptions or other large gatherings. Vola didn't know.

The only thing she cared about was the twenty or thirty orcs spread through the hall, armed in an eclectic variety of armor and armed with everything from pikes to two-handed battleaxes. They'd splashed red paint across their chests—even those without armor—in a semblance of Inga's crest. A staff crossed over a red eye.

She'd killed a lot of orcs today and she was getting kind of tired of them standing in her way.

"Dad," Vola said over her shoulder. "Think you can talk them down?"

Gorgo frowned at the mass of orcs. "Doubt it. Most of these aren't mine. Inga must have been gathering them from all over."

"Vola," Lydia said quietly and pointed.

Far across the hall stood three figures, one short, one with long gold hair, and one with a hood pulled low to cover their face.

Vola's breath blew out like someone had punched her in the gut.

"This," Inga said. "This is the fun part. Show me your paladin nature. Flee. Or kill them to get to me."

"Black paladin, remember," Vola said and drew her blade. "All you're going to find out is what happens when you take everything away from me."

She advanced. "Cyrano, you're on point. Dad, guard the spell casters. Mom, you're with me."

"Oh, I'm so happy," Lydia said, skipping up beside her. Gorgo groaned.

Vola glanced at Lydia. "You want to get angry? Now's the time to do it."

"What are you talking about, Vola?" Inga said sweetly. "You never condone anger."

"Guess again," Vola whispered.

A shiver went through Lydia Battlemane, and her stance changed just a fraction. She opened bright eyes, and her lips pulled back in a feral grin.

She opened her mouth, and a fierce roar grew in her throat. "Uuuuur-ryaah! My baby girl wants to fight! You thought her dad taught her that? Moron! I eat moron's for breakfast! Haaaaaggghhh!"

Sweet, calm Lydia flew at the nearest orc with the same enthusiasm with which she baked cookies.

"Stay out of range of Lillie's spells," Vola called back to her motley party. "Talon and Gruff will try to flank you. Watch for that. And what-ever you do, don't let Sorrel get close."

Vola charged the front ranks of orcs, sliding in beside her mother's battle frenzy, weaving around the flying battle-ax. She caught a blow on her black shield and threw the orc off his feet before taking his head from his shoulders.

"Yeah, those are my girls," Gorgo yelled from the back.

Cyrano darted forward, humming under his breath as he cut his way through the swarm of orcs.

Vola kept one eye on the battle around her and the other eye at the front of the hall where Lillie was raising her arms. Talon was already slip-ping off to the side to disappear while Sorrel ran straight down the middle.

Right. Time to end this. Her heart couldn't ache any more than it did right now.

"Mom, with me." Vola stepped back from the next orc. He grinned at her and pressed forward just as a gust of wind seized him by his feet and swung him upside down over the battle.

Vola waved at Aunt Urag and darted around the armored orcs, eyes surveying the terrain. There, a clear area toward the back with a good line of sight but no immediate enemies, protected by the ranks of orcs.

Vola grabbed her mother's shoulder and hauled her in close. "Mom. Get to Lillie. Charge her fast. Faster than she can dodge. Don't hold anything back. Go. Go now."

Lydia's wild eyes widened, but she didn't take time to question Vola. She raced up the middle of the hall. She dodged around an orc, cut down the next one in line, and used his body as a springboard. She sailed the last few feet, ax aimed for Lillie. If she landed, she'd split the wizard in two.

Lillie blipped out of existence, and Lydia landed on a bare patch of ground, her ax splitting the wood floor.

Vola sprinted for the open space she'd noted before.

Lille appeared, just where Vola had predicted.

The wizard saw Vola coming and raised her hands. Flames shot out, singing Vola's eyebrows. She ducked, but the end of her braid caught fire.

Vola rolled, putting out the flame, but she was forcibly reminded of the time when Lillie had incinerated a copy of Vola. It had been easy.

It couldn't be easy now. If she let Lillie burn her up, this would never work. Because she had the sneaking suspicion she was the only one who could do it.

Vola scrambled to her feet in the breath of time Lillie had to take to form the next spell.

"Yes," Inga said.

Vola tossed her blade and her shield aside and launched herself at Lillie.

She took the wizard to the ground and there was a crack. Vola desperately hoped it wasn't anything important. Like Lillie's head. Around them, Urag's vines held the orcs back, and she had a moment of clear air.

Lillie glared up at her. This wasn't the blank stare of Finn or Kellan or Sandry. This was pure hatred. How deep had Inga crawled into her friend's mind? How many claws had Mulgash sunk into the wizard?

Cleavah's power rose in her chest. Divine. Light and good. But how did she use it? This wasn't a curse like Raven's. No oily black coated Lillie's form just under her surface. If there was anything, it was buried deep inside Lillie's head, and Vola didn't have the first clue how to get to it.

She swallowed down panic. Lillie struggled against her, and Vola pinned her arms to keep her from casting any spells. The wizard spat in her face, but Vola held, teeth clenched against the pain in her chest.

Relationship, Raven had said. If Inga could spread rot through a relationship, then Vola could spread healing.

She closed her eyes and reached for the power. At the same time, she pictured the very first memory she had of Lillie, standing in front of her table in Water's Edge, straw in her hair and a buried panic in her eyes. She remembered Lillie with fire in her hands; she remembered her sitting at a desk telling Vola she forgave her for the mistakes she'd made. She remembered Lillie's face, determined and despairing as she cast the spell that banished her brothers to the void between worlds.

"This is who you are to me," she said in her mind, the power rushing through her into Lillie. "You are fire. You are worry. You are determination and strength. You are forgiveness. Please, come back to me."

Her throat closed, and she bowed her head. If this didn't work, she had nothing left.

Lillie's body remained rigid for a long moment.

Then, "Vola?" Her voice was strained, muddled. But full of everything that was Lillie.

"Oh, thank the goddess," Vola breathed. She rested her head on Lillie's shoulder for a bare second before she lurched to her feet.

Lillie propped herself up on one hand, the other going to her head. Vola wanted to kneel there and make sure she was all right, but the rest of the orcs around them were slowly hacking their way free of their bonds.

"Dad," Vola called. "Here."

Gorgo used his bare fists to bash his way through the line of orcs. Urag followed, holding her gnarled staff. She knelt beside Lillie.

"Thanks, Aunt Urag," Vola said. "Keep them safe, Dad."

"Vola?" Lillie tried to push to her feet.

Vola ignored her and snatched up her shield and sword before pressing back into the sea of orcs.

"What?" Inga said over top of it all and for the first time there was a note in her voice that wasn't mocking or confident. "How did you…"

Vola double-checked everyone else. The ranks of orcs had thinned considerably. Vola suspected her mom, who was closing in on Sorrel. She was still in battle rage, but she remained wary of the monk's speed and agility. Good.

"Cyrano."

"I can't find Talon," Cyrano said, appearing at her elbow.

Vola glanced around, looking for a furry black shape close to the ground and found it sneaking up on Gorgo from behind.

"Forget Talon."

"Okay, that's not what I thought you'd say." Cyrano cocked his head.

"I mean, go for Gruff." Vola pointed.

He gave her a dubious look, but Vola was already moving. She took out another three orcs on her way to the wolf who slunk along the wall, stalking the big orc chieftan who guarded Lillie and Urag.

She made sure to telegraph her movements, make it clear who her focus was on. And then she charged, yelling a battle cry.

The wolf yelped.

But before Vola could hit him, a shape flew between her and Gruff.

Vola grinned as Talon lunged at her, knives drawn.

"Leave him alone," the ranger growled.

"There we go," Vola muttered.

"Don't touch her!" Inga yelled, and Vola wasn't sure if she was talking to her or Talon.

Talon lunged again, and instead of dodging, Vola grabbed her wrists.

Gruff snarled and charged her, but Cyrano was there to wrestle the wolf down.

Vola gripped Talon's wrists and let the power surge forward. She breathed slow and steadily as images sprang into her mind. "This," she murmured. "This is who you are."

Talon calling out Vola's mistakes in the basement of Lord Arthorel's manor. Talon pulling her aside to tell her she was a girl, not a boy. Talon sitting in front of the fire while Vola shaved her chin.

"Stop that. Stop whatever you're doing." Inga's voice rang against her ears, but she was easy to ignore now.

Talon blinked, eyes clearing away a fog Vola hadn't even registered before that moment.

"Oh," Talon said, breath leaving her all at once.

Cyrano let go of Gruff, who shook his shaggy head and staggered.

Talon pulled away from Vola and knelt to put her arms around the wolf and bury her head in his neck. Vola let her.

Vola swallowed down all the things that tried to climb up her throat and turned away. They still weren't done.

None of the orcs had survived. They'd whittled away at the horde until no one remained standing.

No one, except Sorrel.

"You're not following the rules," Inga whispered.

"I made new rules."

"Fine. Then I'll just concentrate on this one. A formidable warrior. How will you get to her?"

Gorgo, Urag, and Lydia surrounded Sorrel. The monk sprang from punch to kick to blow as fluidly as water. And she wielded Maxim's Warhammer with deadly accuracy.

She landed a blow on Gorgo, and lightning arced across his skin. The orc chieftain stumbled back with a grunt.

"Don't let it touch you," Vola called.

"Yeah, thanks," Gorgo grumbled.

Sorrel planted the staff and used it to launch herself at Lydia. Lydia caught the monk and spun, turning the blow into a throw.

Sorrel sailed into the wall. She landed on the floor and rolled to her feet. Without even a moment's rest, she planted a kick in Raven's ribs when he got too close.

Vola circled, looking for an opening. Sorrel's eyes weren't angry. They weren't desperate. They were thin and calculating.

Vola lunged, but Sorrel dodged back and sprang at Urag.

The orc spell-caster raised her staff to summon her magic but Sorrel's blow struck Urag's wrist and the staff went flying. Urag cursed and cradled her arm against her chest.

Sorrel spun, her limbs a blur. All they could do was try to keep her contained. Her speed versus their strength. But even the halfling could be overwhelmed if they timed it right.

Vola signaled her family behind Sorrel's back. Urag nodded as Vola and Lydia surged forward, driving Sorrel ahead of them.

Urag cowered until the last moment before she reached out with her good hand and snagged the monk's wrist. As soon as she slowed, Gorgo pounced and wrapped his arms around her.

Sorrel's head snapped back, and Gorgo took the blow on his jaw with a grunt.

Vola approached.

Sorrel snarled at her.

Vola took the halfling's small hand in her own. "This is not you."

She closed her eyes and let the memories surge along with the power.

Sorrel plopping down next to her at her table in Water's Edge, asking what the adventure was. Sorrel telling the monks she wouldn't be returning with them. Sorrel dancing through fighting forms surrounded by the thrones of Southglen.

Sorrel sitting on top of Thorack in the bar, saying, "Fancy seeing you here." Having come all the way from Glenhaven to collect Vola.

The power flared bright and white, and Sorrel blinked, then sagged in Gorgo's arms. Gorgo carefully laid her on the ground.

Vola knelt beside the monk.

"Mmuuugh," Sorrel said, trying out her mouth. "I was wrong. This. This is what a hangover feels like, isn't it?"

Vola laughed and hung her head, too weak with relief to do anything else.

Lillie slumped to the floor beside them. Talon crouched.

"Inga got us, didn't she?" Sorrel mumbled, still groggy. She tried to push herself up and only succeeded in rolling over and mashing her face to the floor.

"Yeah," Vola said. She still couldn't lift her head properly.

"Well, crap." Sorrel tried again, and this time managed to sit up.

Lillie pressed her hands to her cheeks. "I can't believe I threw fire at you. I mean, without protecting you. I haven't done that since —"

Vola threw out her arms and pulled them all in as tight as they would go. Sorrel made a noise like "huerrk," and Talon wriggled a little. But Lillie patted her on the back while Vola just took a moment to breathe.

TWENTY-THREE

Vola just sat there, waiting until her face wasn't quite so wet. Talon was the first one to move.

She cleared her throat and said, "Your armor's not very comfortable, you know."

Vola sniffed and withdrew her arms. "Sorry. I uh…For a few minutes there, I thought Inga was going to win."

"Never," Sorrel said with a growl that normally belonged to Vola or Talon. She started struggling to her feet.

"Sit," Lydia said. "Stay there. You are still recovering."

Sorrel sank back and tipped her head back to stare at the assorted faces around them. "Vola, am I hallucinating, or are your parents here?"

"Well, you're not hallucinating," Gorgo said as Lydia twiddled her fingers in hello. "Though it's probably polite to remember when you try to kick someone in the balls."

Sorrel's eyes widened.

"Let's be fair, dear," Lydia said. "She didn't try. She did an excellent job. Even I had a hard time keeping up."

Sorrel made a noise in the back of her throat and spoke out of the corner of her mouth. "Ohmygods, I fought Lydia Battlemane. And she complimented me."

Lillie was staring at Raven, dressed in his draping curtain, like she was having a hard time placing him. He just stared back, a small grin playing with his lips. "Would it help if I sat on your shoulder?"

"Raven!" Lillie cried. "How…"

Raven's eyes flicked to Vola. "With a little help."

"Great, now that we're all introduced again," Talon said with a snort. "Can we not stand in the middle of an enemy fortress like sitting ducks?"

"All I'm saying is maybe you should rest for a minute or two," Lydia said, holding out a hand to keep Sorrel seated.

The halfling used it to haul herself to her feet instead. "There is a bad guy in here somewhere who just tried to take my brain away from me. I am not going to sit down again until I have smashed her face in a few times." She used her staff to prop herself up, and little bits of lightning zipped up and down the intricately carved mahogany. She looked like a slight breeze might knock her over, but considering the beating she'd just dealt out to Vola's parents, no one was willing to mention it out loud.

Talon stood and threw back her hood. She hadn't had a chance to shave in a day or two, so her chin bristled a little, but the set of her lips and the lines around her narrow eyes dared anyone to comment. She at least had no trouble standing.

Lillie didn't try standing yet. But she met Vola's eyes, and as calm and cool as a princess of Glenhaven, she said, "I'm going to burn this place to the ground."

Her smile made Vola shiver.

Gorgo cleared his throat. "As much as I agree, there are still prisoners held here somewhere."

"Then I suggest you remove them before I start," Lillie said.

"Okay, scary Lillie aside," Vola said, climbing to her feet. "That's not a bad idea." She braced her hands on her knees for a second.

Lydia put a hand on her shoulder. "Are you all right?" she said quietly.

Vola tried to flash her a grin, but it was a little weak. "Mostly," she said. She still hadn't quite wrapped her head around Cleavah's power flowing through her. There were rules, laws of the universe, and gods just couldn't reach their followers without a touchstone in the physical plane. It was immutable. But if that was true and Cleavah could still reach her, what did that mean?

She shook her head. Time enough to figure it out later. Inga could be escaping while they lingered here. And there were innocent people to be rescued as well. Vola straightened.

"Dad, I need you and Aunt Urag to get to the prisoners. There are enough of us now to go after Inga, and I'd feel better if I wasn't worried about all of her captives."

Gorgo's thick brow drew down. "You're sending me to babysit civilians? No way."

"Are you following my orders or not?"

"Not if I want to fight the bad guy at the top of the tower."

Vola put her hands on her hips. "I believe we had this conversation outside. And it ended with, 'yes, ma'am.'"

Gorgo rolled his eyes toward the ceiling. "Fine."

Vola's eyes slid to Urag.

Her aunt shrugged. "No arguments here. I like rescuing civilians. They're so squeamish when someone with tusks says, 'come with me if you don't want to die.'"

"I should go with them," Raven said, reaching for his tasseled belt. "They'll get there faster with help."

Cyrano frowned. "No. We're not splitting up. I told you, I'm not letting you out of my sight."

Raven placed his hand on Cyrano's arm, halting his protests. "I'm not leaving the stronghold without you. I promise. And if I go help them, I can still fly back to you faster than anyone on foot."

"I thought you didn't want to shape change any time soon."

"I didn't." Raven touched him on the cheek. "But this is more important."

Cyrano's scowl didn't let up, but he also didn't stop Raven when he gracefully dropped his makeshift curtain robe and shifted seamlessly into the great eagle shape they'd fought in the tower.

The eagle nosed the curtain pooling on the floor. "You can hang onto this for me," he said. Then he nudged the bard's hand like planting a kiss on it.

"Maybe I'll just lose it. Strategically," Cyrano grumbled.

Raven glared at him before launching himself up into the air and winging toward the stairwell. Gorgo and Urag followed him with varying expressions of disgruntled and smug.

Vola gave Lillie a hand up while Sorrel staggered to the end of the hall, where stairs led to one more floor above them. Lydia watched with a slight frown.

"You sure you're all right?" she said.

"Peachy. Just push me back upright if I fall over. Inga had better watch out."

"I'm sure she's shaking in her boots," Cyrano muttered.

"Give her a second. She'll be fine," Vola said. "I've seen her bounce off harder things than walls."

"You hear that, Inga?" Sorrel yelled toward the ceiling. "We're coming for you!"

For once, Inga seemed to have nothing to say to this. Vola would have been relieved by the quiet if it didn't creep her out so much. Inga had to be lurking up there, preparing for them. She hadn't had anything to say since Vola had disrupted her plans.

The staircase at the end of the hall was wide and carpeted and led to the last level of the keep where a set of wide double doors waited. Sorrel and the others had gained considerably more vigor by the time they reached the top. Maybe Vola's method of reviving them had given them strength. Or maybe they were just really excited to kill Inga.

As Vola's foot hit the top step, the doors swung open.

Inga stood at the end of a wide hall, bright against windows darkened by night and the storm clouds outside. She held her staff propped at her side, a curved piece of light wood with a loop at the top. The skull of a small mammal hung in the open circle.

"Vola," Inga said as if to a particularly troublesome child. "I suppose this is where it ends."

Vola advanced down the middle of the room, letting Sorrel, Talon, and Lydia take one side, and Lillie, Cyrano, and Gruff take the other.

Inga's gaze followed them. "I still can't figure out how you did it. A black paladin shouldn't be able to heal."

"I did it the same way you did," Vola said, drawing her sword. "I wormed my way in."

"I've been in their heads, now, you know. I know how they work. All their tricks. All their strengths and weaknesses."

"You knew that before. When I was fighting them," Vola said. "And I still knew them better than you. You're stalling." She leveled her sword at Inga. "Because you're scared."

Inga's lips spread in a tight smile, showing her tusks. "I'm cornered. There's a difference." She raised her free hand in a careless gesture. "Mind if I bring a friend in? Since you have so many. And you took my familiar."

Before Vola could answer or move, she extended the end of her staff, and Vola realized the floor wasn't carpeted like the previous two levels had been.

"Look out," Lillie called.

A diagram lit up, dim purple light spreading across the floorboards from Inga's staff all the way to their feet. It looked a little like Lillie's summoning spell but way bigger.

Vola skipped back a step.

"Hey, spell fingers," Cyrano called to Lillie. "Want to stop whatever creepy thing is going on?"

"Be my guest," Lillie snapped back. "I don't know a counterspell big enough for this."

Purple smoke shot through with bits of black glitter rose from the circle, making Vola's heart drop in her chest. A hulking shadow rose in the center.

The figure gained weight and substance, gathering the smoke into itself as if it could turn shadows solid. It towered over them, head hunched under the peaked roof. Red and bulbous, with black gleaming at the ends of its fingers and feet and wingtips.

Oh goddess, *wings*.

"Lillie, what is that?" Vola called, backing up another step.

"Uuuuhh," was Lillie's response.

"It's a Nightfiend," Sorrel said, leveling her staff at the creature. It would squash her under its big toe if it stepped forward, but she glared at it anyway.

"A what?" Vola said.

Sorrel gaped at them. "Wait. I know more than Lillie?"

"What is a Nightfiend?"

"Just a second. Let me savor this moment."

The creature grinned, showing off huge black teeth, and took a swipe with its club, making Vola and Lydia dive one way and Lillie and Cyrano the other.

Geez. Nothing that big should be able to move that fast.

"Just tell us what it is!" Cyrano cried.

"Okay, okay." Before it could withdraw, Sorrel jumped to the club and raced up the stick to land a solid blow on the creature's knuckles. It roared, and she hopped off again as it jerked back. "A Nightfiend is a physical representation of an Obstacle. In this case, I'm gonna guess Mulgash."

"So, he's here?" Vola's heart pounded as she stared up at the shadowy form. She'd never ever wanted to actually see Mulgash. Hearing him was bad enough. She gripped her sword and darted in to slash at the Nightfiend's legs, hoping to hamstring it. It dodged, and she only managed to nick it.

"I mean, sort of. It's a little more complicated than—"

"Sorrel!"

"Yeah, for all intents and purposes, that's Mulgash."

The creature leaned down to stick its head in Vola's face and grin.

"Boo," it said.

The familiar voice made Vola's chest constrict, like Mulgash himself sat on her chest.

Vola gritted her teeth and slashed. The Nightfiend howled and jerked upright, blood dripping from its nose.

"Well, like my mom always says, 'end the caster, end the spell.'"

"You remembered," Lydia said. "I'm so proud."

Vola's eyes fixed on Inga's staff. It wasn't just Virtues that needed an emblem to work through their followers. All gods were bound by the same rule, including Obstacles. So she just had to separate Inga from her emblem, and Mulgash would be powerless here.

But Cleavah hadn't been playing by the rules recently. Could Mulgash circumvent them as well?

Vola gritted her teeth and lunged for the enemy. There was no way to find out unless they tried it. And it wasn't like she had any better ideas.

Talon stood to one side, aiming at the Nightfiend's head. Cyrano darted back and forth, his lute pulled forward so he could pluck a tune while he dodged. Vola hoped it was actually doing something, and he wasn't just composing their victory song.

Lillie cast fireball after fireball that seemed to bounce off the thing's thick skin, doing little damage. Finally, she growled in frustration and pulled both hands down from the sky as if drawing fire from the heavens themselves, and flames erupted, engulfing the room.

Lydia yelped in surprise, but while the flames seared the Nightfiend, making it roar, they didn't dare touch Lillie's allies.

The massive creature roared and swept the ground with its club. Sorrel leaped over it easily, but Lillie, Talon, and Vola went down in a heap against the wall. The Nightfiend raised the club again.

"Vola," it crooned with Mulgash's voice.

Vola shook her head. "No." She ignored the way her stomach clenched and hauled Lillie out of the way as Talon raised her bow. The ranger took a wild shot, striking the Nightfiend's hand.

It hissed and drew back. The overwhelming presence lessened, and Vola could breathe again.

Lydia darted in and laid another thick slice across the Nightfiend's leg.

A screaming cry streaked through the air above them, and Vola glanced up to see a great eagle attach itself to one of Mulgash's ears. The Nightfiend swatted at the bird, catching him between its fingers and throwing him toward the wall. Raven recovered in midair and tried to dart past the giant manifestation. But the Nightfiend swung its club, knocking him back.

This was not working. Between the flames and bits of purple mist, Vola could see Inga standing by the window, watching the fight with her hands raised. Sweat stood out on her brow, but Vola couldn't get close. Not with Mulgash's Nightfiend in the way. And how did you fight a god?

"With another god?" a voice spoke in her heart, making it sing.

"Cleavah," she whispered.

"Finally," the goddess said. "I'm not going to be able to spoon-feed you forever, you know."

Vola stepped back and did something she'd never done before. She concentrated on the seething bits of frustration and injustice waiting just below her surface, the hurts she'd carried with her from the first moment Ella had called her 'hulking,' the unfairness of her demotion, the smirks, the jibes, the prejudice.

All of it made her see red.

But as the wash of blood crept across her vision, Vola welcomed it in, instead of pushing it away. She welcomed the slights, the insults, the injustice. And focused it all into the thought of "What am I going to do about it?"

She growled under her breath as her sword began to glow.

Yes, there was bad in the world. Yes, there was wrong and injustice.

But she was a paladin. And she could fight against it. She was also an orc, and hardship made her stronger.

Rage belonged to Mulgash. But righteous anger belonged to Cleavah.

The red sharpened her vision, focused her attention, so the battle seemed to slow. The flames flickered at half time and the Nightfiend's next blow slowed to a crawl.

Vola lowered her shield in front of herself and charged.

Beyond the Nightfiend, she smashed into Inga.

The other half-orc went down with a surprised 'oof,' her staff rolling away with a clatter.

Sorrel had followed, unnoticed, and she leaped on the staff, snapping it in two.

The Nightfiend behind them vanished with a roar.

Vola leveled her sword at Inga's throat.

Inga's lips pulled back in a snarl, and she raised her hands in a helpless gesture.

"Do it," she said, cool as the rain streaking the windows.

"No," Vola said. "I am not an executioner."

"Then what are you?"

"I am Cleavah's chosen," she said.

The others stepped up around her.

"As I was Mulgash's," Inga said. "See how well that worked out. The gods don't care about us, Vola. I was only powerful as long as I was useful."

"Maybe you picked the wrong god."

Sorrel knelt beside Inga's head. "I promised to bash your face in when I got the chance," the halfling said. Then her eyes flicked to Vola's. "But I have a better idea. Tell us who you were sending the prisoners to in order to keep me from bashing your head in."

"I thought you weren't executioners?"

Sorrel snorted. "She's not," she said, cocking a thumb at Vola. "I have no problem with it. Pretty sure the others won't either."

Inga's gaze flicked to the rest of the room and the flames climbing up the walls. Talon stood just within sight, bow drawn and ready. Raven had found a perch at the top of the window and he stared down at her with angry golden eyes.

"Point taken," she said. "I was sending them to a man named Anders. At the edge of the kingdom. Before you ask, I don't know the rest of his name, and I don't know what he was going to do with them."

"That was fast," Lillie said.

"I owe no loyalty to him. He needed warm bodies, Mulgash needed usurped minds, I needed power. It all lined up."

"Why the halflings?" Sorrel said, face drawn.

Inga grinned. "They were convenient. And a link to you. If I took the halflings, I could get to Sorrel and through Sorrel, to all the rest of you."

Sorrel drew back, and Talon put a hand on her shoulder.

"What does Anders want with all these people?" Lillie asked. "This isn't the first time he's solicited kidnapped souls."

"No idea."

"You were sending them to him without any idea of what he would do with them?" Lydia said. "Have you no conscience? No heart?"

"No," Inga said and brought up her hands too fast to catch.

Vola pulled her sword back to strike, and Inga used the moment to blast them off their feet. A wave of air knocked them all back.

Vola's breath burst from her lungs as she struck the ground and slid. She scrambled to her feet, but Lydia beat her.

Her mother sprang up, ax in hand, and leaped for Inga, who had already stood.

Inga hissed, and her eyes went wide and black. Dark purple fire shot from her eyes, her mouth, and her hands, striking Lydia from the air and slamming her against the far wall.

Vola roared and raced forward. Inga turned the dark fire on her, but Vola flung up her shield, and the flame glanced off the blackened surface.

She ran straight into the other half-orc, ramming her off her feet.

Inga stumbled. And lurched into the wide windows behind her.

Nothing but shattered glass stood between her and the black night, and she fell through the storm with a lingering scream.

TWENTY-FOUR

VOLA STEPPED CAREFULLY to the edge of the broken window and leaned out to peer down into the blackness. Nothing. She blew out her breath, the end of her braid lifting in the wind of the storm.

"Vola," Lillie's quiet voice called her back, and she turned.

Lillie knelt beside the wall, Lydia cradled in her arms. Cyrano was there already, checking her, hands gentle. He looked up at Vola, lips thin and shook his head.

Vola swallowed and stumbled back to them. Sorrel and Talon crowded close but left enough room for Vola.

Vola's knees hit the floor with a clank, and she fought the panic crawling up her throat. Lydia was broken and bloodied, scorched from Inga's dark fire. Her eyes fluttered as if she fought for consciousness.

Raven morphed back into his own form and stood behind Cyrano.

"I told you you should wear more armor," Vola said, her voice breaking.

The corner of Lydia's mouth lifted in a weak show of humor. But that was the only response.

"What about all that berserker nonsense, not letting the first hit take you down and all that? Mom?"

Vola fought for calm. This was nothing. Before her demotion, this would have been easy to fix.

But it had been a long time since she'd tried truly healing anyone.

Cleavah had helped her break the curse on Raven and the mind control on the others. But there were rules and without them Vola had no idea what Cleavah would and wouldn't do.

She set aside her sword and shield and placed her hands on Lydia's hands.

"Vola," Lillie said quietly. "Do you think you can? You reached us somehow. Even without Cleavah."

And she'd used much of that power already.

But if she knew one thing about her goddess, it was that she wasn't very good at following the rules.

"Lady bless," Vola whispered, reaching for the power within her. And reaching out for the goddess around her.

Lillie gasped, and Vola felt hands cover hers. Light shot out from under Vola's palms, and she had to squeeze her eyes shut. She felt the others shift around her as if flinging their hands up over their eyes.

Warmth flowed into her from that unseen touch and poured back into Lydia through her.

Even before the touch withdrew, Vola knew it would be enough. Her mother breathed deep and painless under her hands.

Vola forced herself to open her eyes before it ended. To look up through that blinding light to find Cleavah kneeling on the other side of Lydia.

The goddess met her eyes. And smiled.

"Take up your shield, knight," she said, her voice the soft rush of wind in Vola's ears.

Vola didn't think Cleavah meant figuratively. She reached for her shield and settled it on her arm.

Cleavah reached out a hand and touched the blackened surface. The shield heated under her fingers, burning Vola's arm. But she didn't even think of drawing back.

It was moments before Cleavah withdrew and Vola glanced down at the shield. Henri's shield, which she'd destroyed by her actions.

Black still covered its surface, but Cleavah had burned through the stain left by holy fire, leaving a clear shining mark in the center. Two hand-prints spread to look like a pair of wings.

Vola looked back up into her goddess's eyes.

"I am never out of reach," Cleavah said. "As long as you are reaching for me. I am not something that can be taken away from you, Vola."

"Yes, lady," Vola whispered. "I'm sorry it took me so long to figure out."

Her lips quirked in that gentle smile. "You can forget over and over again. I will never tire of reminding you."

Vola swallowed. She didn't want to forget. She wanted this to always be how she remembered who and what she was. Kneeling on the floor with her goddess smiling at her.

Between one blink and the next, she was gone, and Vola knelt with only her mother and her party and the friends they'd made along the way.

Lillie gaped opposite Vola. They'd all seen Cleavah before. But not without layers of obfuscation and confusion. Sorrel rubbed her eyes, and Talon shook her head as if to clear spots from her vision.

Lydia glanced at the rest of them and realized they were having a moment, and no one was going to help her. So she sat up herself.

She raised her arms and checked them for damage. Nothing seemed broken, the skin clean and pristine. Lydia nodded in approval. "I think you even got rid of some wrinkles. Not sure how I feel about that since I earned them."

"Was that...?" Cyrano said. "Did you just...? Who...?"

"Cyrano the bard at a loss for words, everyone," Raven said. "Congratulations, Vola. I've never seen that happen before."

"I thought...I thought she couldn't contact you," Lillie said. "Isn't there a block? Or a rule? Without an emblem, a god can't work through their followers."

Vola glanced at Sorrel, the only other one who had any training in divine matters.

Sorrel pulled a long chain out from under her tunic. At the end hung a pendant made from knotted silver. "That's what we were always taught. Of course, Maxim's never used mine. Cleavah's the only one I know of who actually shows up despite the fact she's a minor goddess." Her voice trailed off as she chewed her lip.

The four of them exchanged a glance.

"She's never been good at following the rules," Talon said.

"And you did say once that there was nothing minor about her," Lillie said.

Vola fingered the wings on her shield. It wasn't just minor deities, though. It was all of them who couldn't reach into the mortal plane without an emblem.

She took a deep breath. She had no idea what Cleavah really was exactly. But she knew she was going to choose to follow her. Over and over and over again.

Vola started to stand when there was a rumble beneath her feet. She stopped and darted a look around her.

"What was that?" Cyrano said.

Something groaned ominously above them, and Vola eyed the ceiling. Most of the floor smoldered, and a lot of the room was still on fire.

"Lillie?"

"I don't think that's me...Wait." The wizard touched the circlet on her head, the one that allowed her to see magic. Her eyes widened as they traced invisible lines around the room, ending at the broken window where Inga had disappeared. "Uh oh..."

"What uh oh?" Cyrano said. "It's never good when a wizard says 'uh oh.'"

"This whole place is collapsing," Lillie said.

"What?" Sorrel said.

"Inga must have had spells tied in with her death. To destroy this place if she was ever defeated or maybe to keep it upright while she was alive."

"You don't know which?" Talon said.

A piece of the roof came down in the middle of the room, making them jump.

"Would you like me to take the time to find out? Or would you like to escape first?" Lillie snapped.

"Escaping sounds good." Raven yanked his makeshift curtain robe back up his body as he ran for the door, Cyrano following him.

"Dad's still in the basement," Vola said, helping Lydia to her feet. Then she held out a hand to Lillie, who always had a tough time standing after kneeling on the floor. "We need to get down there and make sure he and Urag got all the prisoners out."

They raced for the stairs, following Raven, who knew the fastest way down. At the balcony around the great hall, Vola paused. There'd been a lot of staff in the kitchen when they'd come up. Maybe they'd fled after all the fighting, but maybe they hadn't. There was more rumbling under her feet, and a crack snaked up the wall, separating the stones of the keep.

"Kitchen it is," she muttered. The others were already halfway down the next flight toward the dungeons, but she could catch up.

Vola sprinted for the stairs they'd climbed from the kitchen to the great hall. She burst into the kitchen, forgetting how the staff had reacted to her the last time.

But she needn't have worried. They weren't paying any attention to her. All eyes were on the creature standing at the other end of the kitchen, which chomped and slurped its way through a cake as tall as it was.

"Oh, great," Vola said.

Still, no one noticed. There were whimpers from the kitchen staff, who remained huddled in the far corner as far from the swamp monster as they could physically get.

The swamp beast reached out its long neck and snagged a half-cooked chicken from the sideboard. It swallowed it in one gulp, the bulge visible as the poultry slowly slid down its throat.

There was a loud crack and a rumble somewhere above them, and Vola wondered if a tower had come loose to crash to the floor of the mine.

"Hey, people, this castle is coming down. You'd better get out," she called.

Still nothing. Just wide-eyed fascination as the swamp monster took a large bite out of a pot hanging over the stove.

Vola heaved a sigh. "Fine," she said. She stomped over and hauled the swamp beast's head around by the jagged lead rope it had obviously chewed through. Again. "We're going to have to find one reinforced with wire," she muttered. Then glanced at the pot with the bite taken out of it and thought again. "Though, you'd probably just eat that, too."

She turned back to the kitchen staff, dragging the swamp beast away from its perusal of a souffle. "All right, I've rescued you. You're all free. Now I suggest you leave before the castle comes down on top of you."

There was a small aborted movement toward the door but nothing substantial or helpful.

Vola gritted her teeth, took a deep breath, and roared. Orc lungs were good at this. And her mother had sung her all sorts of battle cries as a baby.

That finally got a response. The staff stampeded for the door just as a beam broke free from the ceiling and crashed down. Vola flung up an arm and stumbled back. The swamp beast just chewed in sullen silence.

Something crashed down the chimney, scattering bits of the fire around the room.

"Time to go," Vola said and dragged on the swamp beast's halter. She managed to wrestle it to the end of the hall, where a promising-looking set of stairs led down.

Down had to mean dungeons, right?

Vola bashed her head on a low ceiling about halfway down. But as she stopped to rub her forehead, she could hear her father's voice, raised but still calm, and she made her way toward it. That led her to a large cavern underneath the stronghold.

Large pens trapped herds of villagers below ground, dead guards strewn around them.

Gorgo stood at the gate of one of the pens, ushering frightened villagers out and up the stairs at the opposite end of the room where Urag stood beside an open door. Her staff blazed in her hand, providing a beacon for the panicked people.

At least the villagers didn't seem blank now. They had full control of their minds, even if all they were feeling right now was fear. Cyrano and Raven coaxed the more reluctant prisoners from their cells. Talon and Sorrel ran from Urag to Gorgo, keeping the villagers moving even when the rumbling overhead grew alarming. And Lillie was popping in and out of existence, teleporting small children to safety.

Vola tugged on the swamp monster's lead, but it balked. Vola didn't care anymore. She tossed the lead over its neck and left it on the long ramp that led down to the cavern floor. She trotted down to meet her father.

"We need to hurry," she said. "I don't know how much longer we have before the stronghold collapses entirely. We don't want to be trapped down here."

"We're going as fast as we can," Gorgo said calmly. His eyes traveled over each villager as they passed under his nose, clearly cataloging them as he cataloged his own clan. "It's much better now that the villagers are free of Inga's control. It was impossible before that."

Another familiar figure appeared at the door above them and waved.

"This way," Naraya called.

Vola almost didn't recognize her in a pair of loose-fitting pants and a bulky jacket.

"Naraya!" Talon said, exasperation lacing her voice.

"I have the refugees organized outside," she said. "Hurry now."

Vola raised her eyebrows while Talon gaped. Well, that was new.

A couple of boulders rumbled loose from the ceiling and crashed beside them, knocking them out of their hesitance. Vola winced, but it certainly sped things up. The last of the villagers fled their cages and raced for the ramp up to Urag and Naraya.

"That's it, then," Gorgo said. "Let's go." He gestured the others to follow and herded the villagers like a bunch of sheep.

Vola moved to follow but felt a tug in her gut. Something that told her she was missing something. Go back, it whispered. It was a feeling she normally associated with Cleavah. A feeling she trusted.

She doubled back, trotting around the fallen boulders, following the feeling.

"Vola?" Cyrano said as he passed.

"Hold up. I think we're missing someone."

Sure enough, at the back of the last pen huddled an older orc woman. She squinted up with eyes gone nearly white with age.

"Sorry, grandmother," Vola said. "We'll have you out of here in a second. Cyrano."

Cyrano hurried up to help her. They lifted the old woman to her feet, and with Cyrano's hand under her elbow, she started shuffling toward the opening in the pen.

There was a sniffle behind her, and Vola turned to squint into the darkness. Urag's light barely reached this far. A figure stirred beneath a pile of moldy straw, and it took Vola a second to recognize the dirty face.

"Ella?"

The girl sniffled and rubbed her nose with her sleeve.

"What are you doing just sitting there? Why didn't you run with the others?"

"It's dark," she said. "And there were all these orcs around, and no one told me what to do."

Vola rolled her eyes and lunged for the girl. "Well, I'm telling you what to do. Get out. Come on. Let's go. If you want to be rescued, you have to at least try."

"Can't I be rescued by someone else?" Ella said, trying to pull her arm from Vola's grasp. "Like him?" She fluttered her eyelashes at Cyrano.

Cyrano gave Vola a look with one eyebrow raised as if to say, "is she serious?" Vola just rolled her eyes.

There was a crash and a roar from upstairs, and they instinctively ducked.

"Did Inga have explosives?" Cyrano yelled.

"Sure sounds like it. Conversation over." Vola ducked and, without asking, threw Ella over her shoulder with a grunt. The girl shrieked.

Cyrano gave the orc woman a little bow. "Excuse me, grandmother. Let me help." He hoisted her into his arms, and the two of them rushed for the ramp out.

"Vola! Vola! Put me down. This is assault. This is—"

"It could be worse. I could be making you ride that." Vola jerked her chin at the swamp beast, which was snuffling around the base of the cavern. "Come on, you stupid thing, time to escape." Vola tried to grab its halter again, and it snapped at her. "Fine, have it your way."

"Ew, what is that thing? Don't let it near me."

Trying to deal with the swamp creature put Vola a few steps behind Cyrano by the time they reached the top of the ramp on their way to the courtyard.

She hissed and stepped back a step, flinging her hand up to protect her face from the heat. Everything up here was on fire now. The curtains, the upholstery, even the rugs.

Ella screamed.

Vola winced. "You have to stop doing that. It's right in my ear."

"It's hot. Oh, gods, we're going to die."

"We're not going to die," Cyrano called from ahead of them. "The courtyard is just down this hall—"

Spikes shot out of the walls on either side of them, burying their wicked tips into the floor. Vola jumped back.

The shafts created a barrier, blocking the hallways between her and the bard. The last of Inga's traps.

"Vola!" Cyrano called.

Vola reached to shove one out of the way, but the metal shaft burned her fingers.

She shook her hand with a hiss. "We're all right. But we're going to have to find another way out."

"But—"

"Go, Cyrano. Get out with the others."

Through the flames, she could see his hesitation.

"Go," she said.

"See you on the other side. Good luck, Lightless."

Vola spun, surveying the burning stronghold with narrowed eyes. If they could get back up the stairs and around the great hall, then they could go through the kitchens and get back to the tunnel where they'd come in originally.

Vola ran.

But at the top of the steps to the kitchen, she stopped short and wobbled at the edge of a pit. It looked like the stairs had caved in. Probably all the way down to the cavern below.

"Shit," Vola said.

A lightning bolt struck the ground beside her, and Ella made a little peep of surprise.

Vola glared at the burning ceiling. "Some situations call for swearing, my lady," she yelled.

A voice came out of the air beside her, sending a wave of calm and cool over her. "But if I just let it go, you'll become complacent."

"I promise I won't. You want to get us out of here?"

"Head for the front door." Cold settled across Vola like a soothing blanket, and she could take a breath a little easier now.

Vola spun around again, but they were on the balcony of the great hall, and all the stairs down were either blocked or collapsed.

Vola wiped her brow.

"Who was that?" Ella asked quietly.

"My goddess," Vola said shortly. She squinted at the balcony.

"Your goddess talks to you? Just like a real person?"

"I guess she likes me." She made her decision. "Hang on. This could save our asses. Or it could go very, very badly."

Before Ella could protest, Vola ran for the balcony railing and vaulted over it.

Ella screamed.

They crashed to the ground, and for a second, Vola was terrified she'd miscalculated, that the floor was made of wood and would just collapse under their weight. Instead, they slammed into the stone, and Vola grunted with pain. But they were still in one piece. Even if Vola's knees were yelling obscenities at her.

"Vola," Lillie's voice came to her in her head. It was getting a little crowded in there these days. "Where are you?"

"Front door," Vola said with a cough.

"It's blocked," Lillie said, voice sharp with worry.

"Of course it is." Vola could see it through the haze of smoke, big double doors broken near the top so she could see the light of dawn just beginning to turn the sky pink.

"Wait where you are a second."

There was a sizzle and a pop, and Lillie appeared beside them, bringing with her the overwhelming scent of fresh air.

It calmed Vola even as the fire raged around them.

"I can only take one with me," Lillie said as Vola set Ella on her feet.

"Take Ella," Vola said without hesitation.

"You would say that," Lillie snapped.

"Of course I would. I'm a paladin. Take Ella."

"I don't know how many more trips I have left in me," Lillie said, glancing at the ceiling which groaned ominously. "This might be the last one."

"Then take Ella. And go. What do you expect me to say, Lillie?"

Lillie's face crumpled. "Exactly that," she said quietly. "But I'm coming back for you."

Vola eyed the ceiling. "Better not," she said as Lillie touched Ella's arm, and the two winked out of the stronghold.

With them went the breath of fresh air.

Vola eyed the door. It was thick. It was blocked. And it was on fire. But maybe the flames would weaken it.

"Can I get through?" she asked the air.

"Go," Cleavah said.

A massive crack echoed above her, and the ceiling bulged low.

"Go now. Do not wait."

Vola took a deep breath, raised her shield, and charged. Flames licked up her legs and arms before the cooling feeling took over again. Wood splintered and burst around her as the great hall collapsed at her heels.

Vola roared and suddenly shot out the other side into clear, clean air.

She hit the ground rolling, and there were hands there, dozens to pull her away from the wreckage of the front door.

"Or I suppose you could just bash your way through the problem," Lillie's exasperated voice said in her ear.

Vola huffed a laugh and opened her eyes. Sorrel, Talon, and Lillie knelt beside her while Cyrano and Raven and Vola's family hovered behind them. Ella stood off to the side, face stricken.

"What is it?" Vola growled. "Why is everyone looking at me like that?"

Talon tilted her head. "You were…er…glowing."

"What? Like I was on fire?"

"Well, yes," Sorrel said. Then held up her hands. "But not like in a bad way."

Inga's stronghold exploded with a roar.

They all flinched. Except for Vola, who'd had divine hints that it was going at any minute.

Gorgo whistled, surveying the flaming mass, inferno licking the sky, and smoke billowing up in a massive cloud. "I guess Lillie really meant it when she said she'd torch the place."

Lillie tilted her head to examine the mess. "I believe I'm only responsible for about half of that," she said. "The rest is Inga's."

"I think that's plenty," Talon said.

"We did already know not to make you angry, right?" Sorrel asked with a grin.

"Did everyone get out?" Vola asked, climbing to her feet.

"Everyone except the swamp beast," Sorrel said. "And all the orcs we killed."

"But we have about three villages worth of people here," Talon said. "Between the orcs, the halflings, and the humans. Plus, the staff who decided working here was no longer an option."

"Yeah." Sorrel gazed at the halflings gathered beyond them with a little frown between her eyebrows.

Naraya moved between little clumps of people, pulling packages of bandages and food and full waterskins out of her bulky coat and passing them out.

She caught them looking and flushed a deep scarlet. "What?" she said. "I still want to help."

"We never said you couldn't help," Talon told her. "It was just the way you were going about it."

Naraya handed over a waterskin to the ancient orc grandmother Cyrano had carried to safety. "Maybe I'm not a warrior. But I can fight bad guys like Inga in other ways."

"I think that makes you as much a warrior as anyone," Talon said quietly.

Naraya gave her a small smile and ducked her head. "I'm glad you think so."

Vola's eyes flicked between the two, and she held her breath.

"Maybe…maybe I could see you again," Naraya said.

Talon's hand fluttered like she wanted to tug her hood over her face, but instead, she rubbed the back of her neck. "I, uh, think I'd like that."

Sorrel planted her hands on her hips. "Well, I think we should get all these people home first."

Lillie squeaked and glared at Sorrel as Vola rolled her eyes.

"Way to ruin the mood," Vola said.

Sorrel's lips pulled in a frown. "What mood?"

Gorgo snorted. "Don't worry. We'll escort them all home and make sure everyone ends up where they're supposed to be."

"Wait?" Lydia said, shading her eyes to look back at the stronghold. "What's that?"

A figure coalesced out of the flames and smoke, stepping through the rubble.

"Oh, you've got to be kidding me…" Sorrel said.

"Do you suppose it's indestructible?" Lillie asked, head cocked. "Or immortal?"

The swamp beast picked its way out of the blast zone and sauntered over to the group. It immediately tried to eat Lydia.

She ducked out of the way. "Hey. I almost died once already today. I'm not going to be taken down by wannabe crocodile."

"What?" Gorgo said with a start. "What do you mean you almost died?"

Vola winced. "Long story. No time. Let's get these people home, shall we?"

TWENTY-FIVE

VOLA, Sorrel, Talon, and Lillie made sure the halflings made it back to their village safely while Lydia and Gorgo led the humans and captured orcs back to where they belonged.

The halflings wanted them to stay, to eat and drink and celebrate their safe return. And Vola was perfectly willing to put off returning to her own home. But Sorrel's lips thinned, and she looked away from Reed, who stood on the inn's steps, hands outstretched in welcome.

"Sorry," she said. Her voice would have sounded bright and cheerful to anyone who didn't know her that well. "But we've got an appointment to keep."

Vola opened her mouth to ask what appointment but took one look at Sorrel's face as she walked away and shut up. She'd ask later, after they were out of earshot.

But she didn't get the chance. As the four of them left the village, a voice called from behind them, and Sandry puffed up the lane.

"Sorrel. Sorrel, wait." She skidded to a stop, hardly winded. "Please don't leave. We need you here. To protect us."

Sorrel winced before she turned to face Sandry. "I'm not staying," Sorrel said gently. "Because you really don't need me. We got rid of Inga. You'll be safe here without her. And if you keep practicing, it won't be long before you'll be the one who can defend your people."

Sandry's face brightened at Sorrel's words. "You think so?"

"Of course." Sorrel grinned. "Just remember to keep your elbow up during a block. And your shoulder down when you roll."

The rest of them waited patiently while Sorrel gave the other halfling a fierce hug and sent her scampering back to her people.

Sandry herself went with a smile and a wave. But as soon as the other halfling was out of sight, Sorrel turned back to the road, a frown tugging at her lips.

"Do you really think she can defend her village?" Talon said quietly.

Sorrel looked up, surprised. "Of course. Eventually. I told her that, didn't I?"

"You just seem glum," Lillie said.

"Did you really want to stay?" Vola asked. Before the stronghold, there had been a day or two when Sorrel had been seriously thinking about it. Realizing that living a quiet life in some village didn't sound half as bad as it used to.

Sorrel's brows drew down and her mouth hardened. "No."

Vola tilted her head, inviting more.

Sorrel sighed. "Our job is necessary. It's also dangerous. We all knew that going in. But it's not just a risk to us. We carry risk to every single person we meet. Everyone we get close to. We drag danger around with us. I don't want to settle down in one place until I'm sure that I've taken care of enough of that danger in the world. And that I'm not bringing any of that back to whoever I'm settling with."

"Inga had her eye on that village before we ever got there," Vola said quietly. "Whatever she said. You know that, right?"

"Yes, but we brought more trouble to their doorstep. She took them and the ones from Vola's village so that she could use them against us."

Vola remained silent while Talon and Lillie exchanged a look. They couldn't argue with that.

"I don't think I'll retire until I'm sure there's no one like that still after me."

"So you're just not going to retire?" Lillie said and ducked her head to hide her grin. "Face it, Sorrel. You enjoy making enemies almost as much as you enjoy defeating them."

Sorrel opened her mouth to argue and thought better of it. "Well, then I guess I'll just have to retire with you guys. If anyone threatens you, I know you'll be able to take care of it." Her eyes caught on Vola's shield. "And you'll probably have help."

Vola hadn't taken it off her arm yet. It somehow seemed lighter than the whole time she'd been carrying it around since she'd left the capital.

"Well, that's one more thing to look forward to," Lillie said with a smile.

"What?" Vola asked.

"The mystery of who Cleavah is."

"Cleavah is Cleavah," Vola said.

"And more," Talon said.

Lillie rubbed her hands together. "She did something today that all the priests agree that gods aren't supposed to be able to do. It's a mystery."

"And you like mysteries." Vola's lips twisted indulgently. She didn't add anything, but she couldn't help the niggling thought that she wanted to know, too. She'd follow Cleavah anywhere—the goddess had proven herself over and over—but even as she answered questions in Vola's mind, more cropped up to take their place.

The day brightened as they passed through the ancient forest, the last of the storm clouds receding until nothing but a bright blue sky remained. It was beautiful, but Vola was feeling every single hour of the last three days. Every ache, every worry, and she was looking forward to collapsing into her own bed, even if it was in her parents' attic. Knowing Lydia, she'd probably already made up the couch and hauled out the old adventuring bedrolls to accommodate them all.

It was well past noon by the time the thatched roofs of the village came into sight over the next hill. Vola squinted. Was it laundry day? The road seemed more cluttered and colorful than usual and a dull roar made its way to them. Not the idyllic silence of a country village in the middle of summer.

She stopped short where the wilderness ended and the village started and blew out her breath.

Banners crossed the lane, little purple, green, and blue triangles strung between the houses at the edge of the village. Mismatched tables and chairs lined the road that led straight through town, each laden with an assortment of food offerings. Pies, roasted vegetables, cookies Vola recognized as Lydia's usual.

"Aw, they're throwing a party," Sorrel said, leaning on her staff.

The entire population milled under a giant banner splashed with purple and gold letters that sparkled saying, "Welcome Home! Vola!" Orcs and humans alike. Vola had never seen them all in one place without bickering before. The clan usually stayed on their side of town and the humans on the other.

"What's happening?" Vola said, eyes wide. "I'm not...I'm not sure what's going on." Had Inga survived the fall? Was she doing some more mind control, trying to throw Vola off in new and unpredictable ways?

"It's called a party, silly," Lillie said and poked her in the back. "You're supposed to smile. Don't look so grim."

"Like you want to smash something," Talon said. Then she cocked her thumb over her shoulder. "I think I'll join you guys later. Gruff and I will just hang out out here —"

Sorrel snagged the back of Talon's cloak as she tried to slink away. "No, you don't." She pushed Talon forward as Lillie did the same with Vola. The swamp monster ambled behind them, still smelling faintly of smoke and eying the food on the tables as they approached.

The crowd saw them and gave a cheer before Vola could decide how she and Talon could escape.

A lithe figure slipped between a couple of big orcs and ran up to seize Vola's hand.

"There you are," Ella said. "Seriously, it's just like you to miss the start of your own party."

She hauled Vola through the crowd. On one side, Thorack and a couple of other orcs lifted their mugs to Vola as she passed. On the other, a human man with a tuba and another with an accordion made an impromptu band. Ella pushed and prodded her way all the way to the stoop of Lydia and Gorgo's house, where the biggest table was set. Lydia and Gorgo themselves lounged on one side, watching everything with puzzled smiles.

Ellen and Elsie perched on the other side.

Ella shooed them away. "Go on. This is Vola's spot. And there's room for all her friends, too."

"Ella," they complained. "You gave away the best spot."

"You aren't heroes," Ella said, hands on hips. "And you don't have a goddess who talks in your ear."

She pushed Vola onto a chair and directed Sorrel, Lillie, and Talon to sit as well.

"You settle in here," Ella said. "I'll be back with some food and drinks." She disappeared through the crowd.

Vola blinked. "What is happening?" she said again.

"Relax, Lightless," a lilting voice said from the other end of the table. "You've never had a town throw you a party in thanks before?"

"This is different. I grew up with these people." Vola glanced down at Cyrano where he sat with his feet up. Raven sat beside him, digging into an entire chicken with gusto.

"It's weird." Talon fingered the tablecloth suspiciously.

"I think it's adorable," Lillie said, gazing around them with bright eyes.

"Careful, Lillie," Sorrel said with a grin. "Your noble is showing."

Lillie flushed.

Gorgo pulled Lydia to her feet. "Come on, darling. We've got music and food. The only thing left is dancing." He spun Lydia across the road.

"Hey, hey," Sorrel said and vaulted the table. "I can get behind that."

"Are you feeling better, Raven?" Lillie asked. Possibly to get him to lift his head from his food for a second and take a breath.

Raven nodded and kept eating.

Cyrano watched with an indulgent smile on his lips.

"Where are you two headed next?" Vola asked.

"Probably west," Cyrano said. "I think we'd like to stick to a quiet circuit, for now, playing at inns for our keep."

Raven finally pushed his plate back with a sigh. "I really missed cake," he said.

Cyrano nudged him, and Raven glared at the bard.

"I'm getting to it," Raven said. He stood and turned to Lille, Vola, and Talon. Sorrel was in the middle of the road, gyrating to tuba music.

"I feel bad that I'm leaving you without a familiar," he told Lillie.

Lillie's mouth formed an o. "Oh, no. You shouldn't. I knew you weren't truly mine to keep. You were a lovely companion, but you don't owe me any loyalty."

"Ah, but I do," Raven said. His grin reminded Vola of the cocky raven who'd cackled at them in the woods. "You rescued me. All of you. But especially you, Vola." He raised an eyebrow at her. "That deserves a lot more than mere thanks. I owe you. Everything; not just loyalty."

"We would have helped you, regardless of the deal we made," Vola told him quietly.

"True," he said. "But I still want to give you something."

He held out his hand and pulled a shape out of his palm. Blue smoke twisted into a shape that resembled a raven. It solidified until it looked just like the real thing.

The raven cocked its head at them.

Lillie offered it a bit of meat leftover from Raven's plate, and the raven hopped to her arm to accept it. She beamed.

"It's the spirit of my raven form. The one you freed me from," Raven said. "It will work and act like a real raven, but you can summon him whenever you like. He's yours now. As much as any bird belongs to a person."

The raven snatched a piece of cake out from under Talon's nose and flapped to a nearby roof with a squawk.

Raven winced. "He'll have my personality, though. Sorry."

"Raven," Lillie said. "I can't accept him. Don't you need him for your magic?"

Raven shrugged uncomfortably. "I have many other shapes I can still use. This one...this one isn't one I want to keep."

Lillie bit her lip as the spirit raven hopped back down to her shoulder and ran his beak through her hair. He left a trail of crumbs.

"Don't look so worried," Raven said with a laugh. "It's only a little piece of me you'll be carrying around. A piece freely given. And he's a lot more clever than some owl."

Raven winked as Cyrano stood and slung an arm around his shoulders.

"We're off," Cyrano said. "You know what you've done for us. We'll come if you ever need us." He jerked his chin at Vola. "Good luck, Lightless."

They wended their way through the crowd, pausing to give a funny look to a woman who leaned against the side of Vola's parents' house. She wore a dark green leather jerkin and sleek pants lined with throwing knives. Her hair rose in frothy curls around her head as she surveyed the party with light brown eyes.

The woman gave Cyrano and Raven a look back as she straightened up out of the shadows.

She sauntered to their table and sat in the place Cyrano had vacated.

"Your Highness," Vola said.

"Just Rilla today, please," the princess of the Dagger Throne said, her lips quirked in a smile. "I'm blending in."

Talon snorted.

"What?" Rilla said.

"You hardly blend in," Lillie said diplomatically. "You're born to stand out."

"It works well enough in the city."

"What she means is, this is a small village," Vola said. "Everyone knows each other."

"Hey, Rilla," Sorrel said, bounding up. "Saw you a million miles away. How'd you get here?"

"I have portals I can use when the occasion calls for it."

"Here you are, Vola." Ella interrupted them, sliding a plate and a mug onto the table in front of Vola. "And there's lots if your friends want to some, too." Her gaze slid to Rilla, and her eyes widened. "Oh my gosh.

You're Princess Allellarilla. Guardian of the Dagger Throne. Ruler of Southglen." Her mouth dropped open.

Rilla's annoyed gaze slid to Vola, who was trying to swallow a laugh.

"Told you," Vola said.

"I am one of fifteen," Rilla said. "Definitely not the only ruler."

"But still. You sit on a Throne. You helped defend Glenhaven when the nobles tried to take it over."

"You've heard a lot about me," Rilla said.

"I have the whole book of Southglen nobility memorized. I can show you around if you'd like. We have a very nice village, compared to others."

"No, thank you," Rilla said. "I'm here to speak to Vola and the rest of my team."

Ella's wide eyes darted to Vola. "You speak directly to goddesses, and you work for a princess?"

Rilla leaned forward, fixing her gold gaze on Ella. "Clearly, you're at the wrong table. Shoo."

Ella squeaked and scampered away.

"That wasn't very nice," Lillie said. "I'm pretty sure she arranged this whole party."

Rilla glanced around. "I take it you're celebrating a victory then."

"Inga is gone," Vola said. "And her mind control magic with her."

"You killed her?"

Vola rubbed the back of her neck. "She...fell out a window."

"After blasting Vola's mom," Talon muttered. "Pretty sure none of us felt sorry for her after that."

Rilla's lip twitched.

"She gave us the name of the man she was working for. She was sending the prisoners to someone named Anders. On the west edge of the kingdom."

"That's all she had?"

"It's more than we've had before," Sorrel said. "This is the same man who was buying people from Lord Arthorel. Who was funding Myron Vidal's necromantic research. And who tried to steal the power of the Thrones a couple of months ago."

Rilla examined her fingernails. "A worthy enemy indeed. He does keep sticking his nose where it doesn't belong." She looked up at them. "You want to go after him?"

Sorrel shot her fist in the air. "Yes, ma'am!"

But Rilla kept looking at Vola. "Are you done moping, Lightbringer?"

"It's Lightless now," Vola said. "That's the name the paladin council gave me. It's the name I'll keep. Thanks."

Rilla's brows came down. "So not done moping, then."

"I didn't say that." She gave Rilla a look and made sure her shield was placed to catch the light. Rilla's eyes latched on the spreading wings, shining through the black. "What kind of paladin would I be if I was afraid to walk through the dark?"

SCENES FROM CREATION AND CALAMITY

VOLA

ONE

VOLA SWUNG HER AX, a hand-me-down from her mother, chopping the last goblin's head clean off his shoulders. It rolled down the hill away from the cave mouth and stopped at the feet of a massive orc dressed in a fur-lined loincloth and a leather harness. He leaned on his greatsword and propped his foot on the goblin's head.

"There, see, now you've got the feel of it," he said with a wide grin. "Just remember to keep your weight on your toes."

"And remember to clean your blade afterward." A short lithe woman with bushy roan-colored hair placed her boot on a dead goblin's back and yanked her own ax out of its spinal cord.

"You know when normal people go on family camping trips they don't make detours to wipe out the local pests," Vola said, stooping to clean her weapon. Her mother might have been the deadliest woman east of Fire-watch, but she was also a real stickler for cleanliness.

"I thought we were having fun," Lydia Battlemane said, stopping to pout at Vola.

Vola sighed and rolled her eyes, then made sure there was no goblin blood on the backs of her hands. It was hard enough showing up in town with gray-green skin and tusks that stuck out no matter how nicely you tried to smile. Add in some decorative blood splatters and the local humans would be lunging to grab their pitchforks and torches.

"The mayor asked us to clear the cave out on the way back," her father said. As the chieftain of their clan, Gorgo had the most dealings with the humans. He was much better at smiling nicely when they cowered.

Vola didn't say anything as she slung her ax across her back and trudged home. Their cottage wasn't far now, and as much as she loved her parents, there was only so much of them she could take. An entire weekend outdoors with constant reminders to keep her eyes open and her blade sharp had her on edge.

It wasn't that she didn't like beheading goblins. Oh sure, there were plenty who were peaceful and left the village alone, but these had been kidnapping baby sheep and stealing young maidens for their rituals. The mayor had already tried reasoning with them, but they'd just kept stealing and kidnapping. And sometimes it was nice to let off steam with some well-sanctioned blood shed.

But that was all the village saw them as. Exterminators. The orc clan that had settled on the outskirts of the village was tolerated as long as they kept the bandits away in the winter and stayed on their side of the street.

Yes, fine. Vola was good at bloodshed. Almost as good as her parents.

She just wanted to be good at other things as well.

Too bad no one saw the daughter of an orc chieftain and a human barbarian as anything other than a sword for hire.

"What's wrong?" Gorgo asked, catching up to her as she broke through the forest at the very edge of the village and stomped up the stairs to their cottage. Her mother's daylilies bobbed beside the door.

"Nothing," Vola said. "It's just...don't you ever get tired of swinging your sword for no reason?"

Gorgo blinked and opened the door. "There were a lot of dead goblins in that cave when we were done. That's plenty of reason."

"That's not what I mean," Vola mumbled.

"Boots off," Lydia said behind them. "Weapons by the door. If I have to scrub mud or blood out of my rugs, I'll be very put out."

Vola obediently hung up her weapons, chewing her lip between her tusks. "I just mean don't you ever want to do something more?"

Gorgo beamed and slung his arm around her shoulders. "Of course."

Some of the tension melted from her shoulders. "Really?"

"That just means it's time to find you a job. I'll talk to some of our old adventuring buddies and we'll get you set up as a mercenary. Plenty of gold to be had clearing out goblin caves and wargle nests."

Vola winced and pulled out from under his arm. "Not really what I was going for, Dad."

Lydia smacked Gorgo's arm. "Don't go pushing her into a career. She's only sixteen."

Vola retreated up the stairs to her attic room while her parents whispered not so subtly behind her.

"Well, how else do you explain this mood? Orcs need to get out and bash things now and then to feel normal."

"It's not the bashing. She just spent all weekend bashing, and it didn't help. She's a teenager. Let her figure herself out."

Gorgo sighed gustily, and Vola echoed him as she pushed through her door and shut it behind her, cutting off their voices. She didn't even glance at the bed or the comfy chair her father had built from rough branches and wargle fur. She went straight to the window and flung it open, then climbed up to sit on the sill with her feet dangling out.

From here she could see the town hall where the humans gathered to talk about whatever it was humans talked about. Vola wasn't sure. Lydia wasn't a great example of human normalcy being married to an orc chief. And the humans all screamed and ran whenever Vola tried to smile at them. Hardly a way to make friends and fit in.

Across the way on the orc side of town, she could just make out her Aunt Urag chasing a couple of children out of her yard with a broom. They squealed as she swatted them, and the end of her broom scorched the earth as it passed. Aunt Urag was pissed apparently. They must have trampled her nightshade.

Vola tilted her face up toward the sun. Really, her parents were both wrong. But she had no idea how to explain herself to them. She needed to do something. But mercenary work wasn't it. Fighting was fine—in fact, fighting was the one thing she was really good at—but it had to mean something.

But every time she got there in her head, she asked herself, "mean what?"

And she still couldn't come up with an answer.

The next morning, Vola passed a group of orcs raising a pole in the center of their encampment. Blood red streamers flowed from the top, drifting in the breeze.

She raised a hand to shield her face and ducked through old man Terrence's back yard before any of them could notice her. She'd forgotten it was the orcish New Year, a time to celebrate orc rage and all the other hardships that made them strong.

As the chieftain, her father attended all the High Holy Days, but he'd never insisted Vola and Lydia be *religious* about it all, and Vola wasn't about to start now.

Through a hedge of raspberry bushes and over the next fence Vola found herself on the human side of town, just across the street from the temple. The last bell chimed as she slipped into the back and joined the other students jostling for places on the benches.

The other human students.

A couple in the back gave her wide-eyed looks or sniffed like they smelled something rotten, but mostly she avoided the notice of the rest.

Until she tripped over the leg of a bench, sending it crashing to its side and dumping a row of students on the flagstones. They cried out and suddenly everyone was looking at her.

Vola took a deep breath, fighting the urge to flee or draw her blade. Her long adolescent limbs only seemed to want to cooperate when she was fighting.

"Sorry," she mumbled. Then she stooped to right the bench and picked up the other students one by one to set them back in their places, fast enough none of them could muster a protest.

She plopped herself on the bench against the back wall, hunching her shoulders so her bulk wasn't so noticeable.

A slim girl in the front tossed her long blond hair over her shoulder and leaned in toward her friends. "When do you think the monster will give up and run off into the woods where it belongs?"

The girls all giggled while Vola bristled. At least the other students mostly ignored Vola. When she wasn't knocking them over. But Ella and her nearly identical friends Ellen and Elsie were always looking for someone to torment. A green someone.

The door at the end of the long musty temple opened and a man in a long drab robe with his gray hair growing out of a tonsure stepped to the lectern at the front of the room.

The old priest's glare scoured the class and found Vola against the wall.

"Oh, you're back." His nasally voice was as sour as ever.

Vola raised her chin. He said the same thing every day, but it still hadn't driven her away.

"You know I'm not wasting my time on someone without the aptitude to appreciate my tutelage," he said. "You'll get no special help."

Vola ground her teeth, tusks rubbing her top lip raw. "I'm aware."

"She probably doesn't even know what 'tutelage' means," Ella whispered.

The old priest cleared his throat. "Ignore the distraction, please," he told the others. "And open your books to your last lesson."

Vola ground her teeth and spread the pages of her primer, ready to force herself through the lesson yet again.

The words swam before her eyes, twisting on the page until she couldn't discern the difference between them. Why did humans all write their p's and q's exactly the same anyway? And she didn't even want to think about b's and d's.

Vola had to concentrate on each letter one at a time to get them to stand still, but she would get them to stand still. Even without help.

Because the priest might be right about it being harder for Vola than for everyone else. But he wasn't right about it being a wasted effort.

And she was far more stubborn than some spindly human.

By the end of the day, her head hurt, but she'd made it through the whole page. Maybe she wouldn't bother showing up the next day. She was already teaching herself; why did she put herself through the torture of all the sidelong looks and snide comments, anyway?

Because she wanted them to see. She wanted them to see her trying harder than all the rest of them. Because maybe one day, that would make a difference.

The older boys all jostled to leave the temple first while Vola stood and collected her book and papers.

As she moved to the door, Ella pushed past with a huff.

"Really, Vola. I know you're huge, but you could at least try not to take up the entire doorway."

The girls laughed.

Red crept from the edges of Vola's vision and threatened to overwhelm the whole temple.

She closed her eyes and took a deep breath, forcing down the rage that belonged to the orc half of her. *Words*, she told herself. *Use words. That's what humans value.*

She was just forming an appropriate comeback when gasps and frantic shuffling filled the echoing space of the temple. Her eyes snapped open, and she found her classmates retreating to make room at the door.

A man in gold-washed steel armor strode down the center of the temple, the light from the high windows reflecting from his breastplate so Vola had to squint to get a good look at him. A sword hung from his hip. Jewels glinted from the cross-guard but the hilt was well used.

The warrior raised his helm and winked at the girls oggling from the sides. Ella swooned into a friend's arms.

With a start Vola realized the man had sharply pointed ears.

She'd heard of elves, but she'd never seen one before.

Vola waited for the priest to make some snide comment about non-humans in the temple but the old man fell over himself to greet the newcomer at the front of the temple.

"Welcome, paladin," he said, holding out his hands. "Welcome. What can I do for you? Are you here on a quest? Do you need accommodations? Refreshments?"

The elf flashed a grin. "A place to pray is all," he said. "Henri? Will you take care of the horses?"

Vola hadn't even noticed the other man who'd come into the temple in the paladin's shadow. His cropped gray hair and eclectic choice of leather and plate armor made him easily overlooked.

The second man, Henri, grinned and lifted his fingers to his forehead in a lazy salute. He turned to exit the temple, and over his shoulder, Vola caught sight of a gleaming white charger stamping its hoof in the stable yard.

The priest turned and saw the rest of them gawking near the door and hurried to shoo them away.

Vola went just as reluctantly as the others.

"Who is he?" she whispered without realizing she was going to say it out loud.

"A paladin," the priest answered, putting his hand on her shoulder and pushing when she took too long to leave.

"What's a paladin?"

"A white knight, a holy warrior chosen to protect the people who can't protect themselves," the priest said. "They spend their lives fighting evil." He glared at her. "Which means you should get out of here."

Vola's cheeks went tight and hot as he shut the door in her face. That word had plagued her all her life. It shouldn't bother her so much now. Especially coming from the priest who'd abused it so much it had lost its meaning.

But he'd just welcomed another non-human into the temple. He'd treated an elf with a reverence he only showed for old wine and soft cheese. She'd never heard him speak of anyone with such respect.

And Vola couldn't help but wonder which meant more. The fact that the man wasn't an orc? Or was it that he was a paladin?

Vola bit savagely into her sandwich letting loose bits of bread and barbecued wargle fall on her plate.

She had an idea floating around in the back of her head that she couldn't quite articulate yet. Something that poked and prodded at the discontent that had been boiling under her skin but didn't quite fix it. Not yet.

They spend their lives fighting evil. Which means you should get out of here.

Hmph. The priest wouldn't know evil if it bit him in the ass.

Not that that was new. It was just…she couldn't get the image of shiny armor and that white charger out of her head. But that little scrap of daydream was all wrapped up with his sibilant voice in her ear.

She growled as she took another bite.

Her mother came into the room and stopped short when she saw Vola at the table. "You're supposed to be in school."

"Yeah, I am," Vola said to her sandwich. But she was teaching herself anyway. What difference did it make if she did it here instead of there?

Lydia eyed her sidelong across the rough table. "Everything all right?"

"Don't want to talk about it," Vola muttered.

Lydia's lips thinned, and her eyes went crinkly around the corners like they did when she was worried. "You know it's not healthy to keep all that anger inside, right? Letting it out and facing it will make you stronger in the end."

Vola snorted. "That's what the orcs believe."

"You are half orc," Lydia said. "And I've lived with your father for long enough that I think they have the right of it."

"You're probably the only human who's ever thought orcs were right for worshiping the Obstacles."

Lydia opened her mouth to respond, but the cottage door swung open, smashing into the weapon rack on the wall. Gorgo stood on the threshold.

Lydia's outraged cry died when she saw her husband's face. "What—?"

"Bandits," Gorgo said, reaching past the door to grab his greatsword. "Attacking the village."

Vola's chair banged behind her as her mother raced for the door.

"They're out of season." Lydia grabbed up her ax and followed Gorgo out into the street.

"You want to try telling them that?"

"I will," Lydia said with a huff. "With my weapon."

"Coming, honey?" Gorgo said over his shoulder.

Vola was already pulling her own ax from the wall. "Woohoo, another fun-filled family outing."

"That's the spirit." Gorgo laughed and raced down the dusty street, a few paces behind his wife.

Vola hurried after them and froze on the corner, all the sarcasm rushing from her in a flood, leaving her limbs heavy.

Human villagers fled to the safety of their homes while the orcs streamed toward trouble. But from the screams carrying across the thatched roofs and the smell of smoke in the air, this wasn't just a brief raid from a couple desperate thieves. This was a concerted assault planned and executed to deal the most amount of damage in the least amount of time.

Vola's grip tightened on her ax haft, and she stepped forward to follow Lydia and Gorgo who were already disappearing toward the trouble.

A lithe figure ran smack into her back, knocking her off balance. She stumbled and turned, catching the blonde girl around the elbows.

"Ella, what are you doing?" she snapped. "You're running the wrong way. Get inside."

Ella whimpered and tried to pull out of her grasp. "They're coming from the other side of the village. They've set fire to the temple with the priest still inside. Nowhere is safe."

Vola's breath came quicker. The attack on the orc side of town had been a feint, a ruse to draw the orcs away from the human village.

Vola thrust Ella toward their cottage. "Get inside," she said. "You'll be safer in there."

"Ew, but that's your house."

Vola slammed the door in her face, trying not to feel too happy about it.

Then she cracked her neck and raced for the human half of town.

At the corner where the bakery backed up to the pub, she found the mayor crouched between the walls of the two buildings, several other townsfolk with him.

Vola slid to a halt beside them and peered out into the street. Sure enough, several buildings were on fire, sending thick black smoke billowing into the afternoon sky, including the temple across the street.

"Where are they coming from?" Vola asked the mayor before he could open his mouth.

He had more presence of mind than Ella and gulped before he pointed a steady finger. "They've been smashing through the shops, taking what they can carry. They're in the bakery now."

"How many?"

"At least six here," the mayor said. He mopped his red forehead with his sleeve and grimaced at the streak of sweat and soot he left on the white cloth. "I don't know how many total."

Vola tapped the corner of the building. Six goblins weren't that much. They fought berserker style, and as long as you didn't let them get too close, they couldn't mob you. But six bandits were bad. And these had already proved they were smart.

She was starting to regret not grabbing her parents before rushing over here. They were on the wrong side of town completely.

Vola's thoughts raced. The fires flickered from a copper bottomed pot in the nearest window, reminding her of sun on gold plate.

"The paladin," she whispered. They needed the paladin. She stuck her head out again and scanned the streets, looking for shining armor and a white horse.

Nothing. But she did hear a quiet nicker from behind the inn beside them. Vola signaled the mayor to stay put and crept to the corner, heart in her throat.

Please let him be here. She wasn't even sure who she prayed to. Anyone who might listen she guessed.

The horse in the alley behind the inn wasn't white. It was brown and the man at its side was dressed in an eclectic mix of leather and plate armor.

Henri. The man who'd been with the paladin in the temple. He carefully and quietly lifted three children up to sit on his horse. Their pale faces had gone blank with shock.

Vola's breath left her lungs in a whoosh. "Hey," she said quietly so as not to startle him. "That paladin you came with. We need him."

Henri glanced at him. The glint of humor in his eye was gone, replaced by calm determination.

"He's on the other side of town. Where the fighting started."

Vola huffed and ran a hand through her hair. "That was a feint. The bandits drew away the orcs, and now they're attacking here."

"I know. I'm trying to get as many people out as I can. Then I'll get him back over here."

Vola's lips thinned. "That may be too late."

"The bandits set fire to the temple with the priest still inside," a woman beside the mayor said. "He'll be dead before anyone can help. The gods have abandoned us."

Vola chewed her lip between her tusks. Maybe the woman was right.

The gods hadn't left anyone around to help these people. She stared down at her hands.

Then her fingers clenched.

"Sir," she said to paladin's companion. "Er, knight?" How did she address him?

The man smiled. "Just Henri. I train knights. I don't claim to be one."

But his armor was well cared for and showed signs of battle. Clearly he knew how to use the blade that hung at his hip and the round shield he carried on his back.

"Will you get these people to safety?" Her gesture took in the children he'd already loaded onto the horse and the group with the mayor.

"Of course," Henri said swiftly. "What will you be doing?"

Vola called over her shoulder as she stepped out onto the main street, "Guarding your back so you can get away."

The door of the bakery smashed open, and Vola didn't have time to check their progress. She rushed forward before the bandits had a chance to make it out into the street.

The first one she caught bottle-necked in the doorway, his arms full of bread. His laughter cut off with a gurgle as she slashed her ax across his throat.

The three bandits behind him froze in the shop's front room, staring down at the body. The first to react was a woman, her hair tied up in braids and a slash of green paint across her face.

She screamed and rushed Vola.

Vola planted her feet, leveled her ax, and ducked the woman's charge.

The bandit went tumbling over her back into the street. The next one went for a blow to her head, and she met his sword with a block, the blade biting deep into her ax haft. She grunted and heaved and even a half grown orc's strength was better than a spindly bandit's. He staggered back into his fellow and they both went down in a heap.

There was an intake of air, and Vola turned to catch the woman with the face paint lurching at her, club raised. Vola pulled her elbow up awkwardly, caught in the narrow doorway, and managed to take the blow on her forearm.

She cried out and stumbled back, dropping her weapon. She tripped over the two fallen bandits and smashed them flat against the rough floor boards with her weight.

Vola winced and scrabbled for her ax. It lay just out of reach. He mom was going to kill her for that mistake.

One of the fallen bandits pushed her legs aside and surged to his feet, the woman right behind him.

The woman raised her club.

Vola kicked the man's groin and he fell back with a cry. Right into the woman's blow. He went limp, his dead weight falling into her, and together they crashed through the front window.

The last bandit wriggled under Vola's legs, and she stretched to grab her ax. The bandit had barely freed himself from her weight when he looked up to catch Vola's blow descending.

"Oh, shi—"

Her ax silenced him.

Vola climbed to her feet, using the counter to help, and she leaned there, breathing hard.

Then she lurched to the door to check the two bandits in the street. The man lay still, unconscious or dead, Vola couldn't tell. But the woman struggled under his weight, growling under her breath.

Vola didn't wait for her to free herself. She planted a solid kick in the woman's temple and watched her go limp.

Then she braced her hands on her knees and stared around the empty street.

She'd been lucky—so, so lucky—that she'd caught these by surprise. But the mayor had said there were at least six. So where were the other two?

The shops along the streets stood quiet except for the flames licking at their roofs. Broken glass strewn across the street reflected the fires, but there was no movement in any of the empty windows.

A raised voice came from the open door of the temple. Vola glanced at the roof, holding her breath. The flames licked up the sides, but the structure was much bigger and had been built much sturdier than the rest of the village. Vola hoped it would hold.

She stalked forward. Her wounded arm ached and sweat ran into her eyes and burned. At the door of the temple, she stopped and swiped her dirty sleeve across her face before she peered around the edge.

No one lurked in the main temple where they held lessons and services, but smoke wafted through the rafters.

Vola held her arm over her nose and ducked inside, avoiding the benches. Behind the main sanctuary, a door opened onto the priest's private rooms. Vola put her back to the wall and listened.

"—last time. Where's your treasure, old man?" a woman asked.

"I have no treasure," the priest answered, his voice gone hoarse from coughing or screaming. "I'm here to serve the gods."

"All temples have treasure. Altar ornaments, gold offerings."

"We're a small village—Ahh!"

Vola's teeth clenched at the sound of his scream. The priest might have made her life miserable, and a very, very small part of her felt vindicated by his pain, but the rest of her squirmed with it.

She took a deep breath and stepped around the doorframe.

Three bandits, not two—the mayor needed to go back to school for a bit—stood with their backs to the door. The priest lay across the floor, blood trickling from his neck. The lead bandit, a woman with more green paint, pressed her spiked mace against the wound.

The priest's eyes went wide as Vola slipped through the door, ax in hand.

"M-monster," he cried.

The woman rolled her eyes. "You don't think we're falling for that one, do you—"

Vola swung and the lead bandit fell under her ax. Surprise was the best ally, her dad always said. Take out the leader first, her mother would tell her. There's a good chance the rest might scatter if their head's been cut off.

The other two bandits jumped and stared at Vola, and she paused to see if they were the type to run or fight.

The nearest looked at her face then looked down at the bandit leader. Then he lunged at her.

Fight it was, then. Vola raised her ax and blocked his first blow. Then she ducked around the priest's desk and shoved. The solid piece of wood struck the man in the gut, and he doubled over gasping.

The second bandit threw himself across her back, and Vola staggered. His arm closed around her throat, cutting off her air.

She choked and coughed, her vision going dim. *Think, think, think.* Her parents would never forgive her for dying to two measly bandit.

With a heave, she slammed her attacker into the wall, once, twice, three times until she finally heard a crack and his grip loosened.

She shook the bandit's limp form off her back, and he slumped to the ground, blood running from his cracked skull.

Her last enemy growled and started around the desk.

Red tinged the edges of her vision, and Vola knelt to grasp the bottom of the priest's desk. She flipped the heavy piece of furniture into the bandit.

He collapsed between it and the wall.

Vola coughed, trying to draw a decent breath in the smoke filled room. She stumbled to the priest.

"Let's go," she said, stooping to grab him under the arms.

He pushed feebly at her hands. "Leave me," he said, closing his eyes. "I go to be with my gods now."

She squinted in the flickering light. Nothing seemed to be wrong with him except for some bruises and the stab on his collarbone.

"You'll be fine," Vola said. A creak from the ceiling above made her wince. "As long as we get out before the roof collapses."

He cracked an eye to glare at her. "If my gods wanted me to live, they would save me."

"They sent me to save you, you dingbat," she cried.

He spat. "An agent of the Obstacles? Never."

Vola ground her teeth. He would rather die than be rescued by an orc.

Well, she wouldn't give him the satisfaction.

She hauled his dead weight over her shoulder and climbed to her feet. His moans and litany of whining buzzed in her ears as she limped through the temple proper and out the door.

She gasped in the clear air outside and stumbled the last few feet to the temple yard gate. Then she dumped the priest unceremoniously in the street.

"Vola!" Her mother's voice cut through the priest's complaining, and cool hands smoothed the soot from her face. "Are you all right?"

Vola coughed once more and raised her burning eyes to gaze at the villagers gathered in the street. Henri stood at the temple fence, squinting up at the roof.

"What happened?" she croaked. "They were supposed to get out."

"We've swept the town and driven the rest of the bandits out," Lydia said. "The paladin and your father are setting up patrols to make sure they're well and truly gone. But the mayor said you'd gone into the temple and hadn't come out."

"Dishonoring my death," the priest moaned.

Lydia glared down at him.

"Don't mind him," Henri said, turning so the flickering flames lit up the scar that pulled from the corner of his eye all the way down his cheek. "You did good and deserve all the thanks he's not giving you."

"I didn't do it for the thanks," Vola said before she'd realized it was true.

Henri tilted his head. "Then why?"

Vola surveyed the villagers standing in the street. The mayor seemed unscathed and aside from his moaning, the priest was alive and well, too.

A surge of pride made her chest swell, and she was surprised to find that the priest's words didn't actually matter. Who cared if he would rather die than be saved by a "monster?"

"I did it because it was the right thing to do." She'd saved them because they couldn't save themselves, but she could.

For the first time in a long time, the itch behind her breastbone that urged her on and scratched at her until she didn't know whether to run or fight died down.

She knew how to fight. But now she knew why she wanted to fight. She could spend her life fighting evil, because it was the right thing to do. But also so that one day people like the priest would look at her and see more than a monster.

TWO

Vola used her wooden practice shield to lock up her opponent's weapon, then spun so the winter sunlight shining across the training yard blinded him.

But the paladin trainee didn't need to see her to crowd into her, lips spread wide in a sneer.

"Go home, monster," he hissed.

Her eyes narrowed, but she kept her head. The old priest had more venom in his little toe than this boy did in his entire being. She grunted and used her shield to dump him on his butt in the dirt.

The trainee swiped sweaty blond hair out of his eyes in order to glare up at her.

"Get out of the ring, Geston," one of the knight trainers called from behind the fence. "You let her beat you, now get over it. Do better next time."

The trainee, Geston, climbed to his feet and spit. Vola didn't bother stepping back. She'd had four years to get used to the other trainees and all the ways they could make her life miserable.

They weren't the ones that mattered. They gathered at the edges of the fence, churning the slush into mud in order to grumble any time she won a practice bout.

The knight trainers didn't matter either, in the end, even if they were the ones to mark down her progress.

No one mattered except the Paladin Council and the gods. They were the ones who would decide her fate. Everyone else was just window dressing.

Vola moved to the edge of the ring, the sun beating on her head even though the air was cool with winter's chill. The mud of the practice ring would freeze into solid ruts tonight after dark. She made a mental note to watch her feet during training tomorrow. The week of vigils would be a hell of a time to break an ankle.

A few men gathered behind the boys at the railing. They turned their backs as Vola climbed over and returned her practice gear to the racks. Some were trainers, some were full knights here to choose a candidate to mentor. None would look her in the face without a smirk or a snub. Even though after four years of training she'd grown into her limbs, and now she was the strongest trainee at the Whiteshield Academy.

She swiped her towel from the fence and wiped her face and neck before making her way through the throng to the building that held the Knight Commander's offices.

The yard was packed this time of day. Most of the trainers reserved the mornings for classwork and the afternoons for practice and drills. So Vola had to duck around several groups of students. The ones in her year turned their shoulders and closed ranks. As if she didn't already know she wasn't welcome with them.

Some of the younger ones waved a greeting before being shushed by their peers. She'd made a few friends among them, giving some extra fighting lessons. But they'd learn soon enough not to address her in public. Not if they wanted the respect of the Paladin Council.

A low rumble started beside the door to the council offices, as the rest of her year-mates gathered near the board on the wall. Vola stopped at the edge of the crowd and lifted her chin. She was tall enough to see the little scraps of paper that hung there, leftovers from previous announcements. But there wasn't a list. Not yet at least.

Her heart hammered in her chest. She hadn't missed the vigil assignments, but that didn't keep her mouth from going dry.

After four years of trainee status, the vigil was the only thing separating her from becoming a true paladin candidate. All the classes on tactics and monster types and fighting styles, all the training in the ring, and all the snubs and insults from the trainers and her year-mates would be worth it after this week.

As long as one of the gods found her worthy enough.

She shook her head. That was what the vigil was for. A trainee stood vigil in the chapel all night to acquaint themselves with the gods they might serve. And in the morning, if one of those gods had chosen them—and a knight master agreed to mentor them—then they were considered an actual candidate who could earn their shield.

That last bit, that was the important thing. Because the last few years of training happened outside of the academy. Under the direction of a knight master.

If her vigil went well, if a god chose her and a knight master picked her, then she could leave this place forever. Finally.

And Knight Commander Imralen wouldn't be able to do anything about it.

A squirrely looking man with prominent teeth and a pair of dirty spectacles sliding down his nose pushed through the door.

The Knight Commander's toady. In four years Vola had never learned his name because even the Knight Commander had never used it. The man had inserted himself so firmly into Imralen's shadow, that was all he was ever remembered for.

The man frowned at the crowd of trainees and pushed his spectacles up his nose before he turned and nailed a list to the board beside the door.

The trainees surged forward.

Vola held her ground, her breath coming faster.

She let the surge of the crowd part around her before deliberately stepping out and clearing a way for herself. Her bulk alone made the others step back so she could peer at the list. The letters twitched and tried to scramble off the page, but she concentrated, running her eyes down the names, looking for her own.

Volagra. Volagra.

It wasn't there.

She started again from the top. Letters always squiggled and refused to hold still. Maybe her name had just gotten lost for a second. She didn't have to panic. Yet.

Geston and a couple of his friends stepped up beside her, found their names immediately, and turned to sneer at her.

"Looks like the Knight Commander agrees with us," he said. "You'll have to go home, monster."

They guffawed and left Vola standing in front of the board, staring at a list that didn't have her name on it.

Her fists clenched, nails digging into her palms hard enough to draw blood as the rest of the trainees trickled away, whispering about their vigils.

Her name wasn't on the list. She hadn't been assigned a vigil. Without a vigil she couldn't be chosen by a god. Without a god she wouldn't get a mentor. And without a mentor she would never earn her shield.

Four years wasted. Four years of taunts and back-breaking work.

Vola straightened her spine. No.

She'd had to fight her way in here in the first place. She'd had to fight every day to stay. This was no different. If Knight Commander Imralen thought she was going to run home just because her name wasn't on some stupid list, he clearly hadn't been paying attention.

She strode for the door to the offices.

The squirrely man held up a hand to stop her. "Trainees aren't allowed in today."

"Screw that." She picked him up and set him down out of her way.

Her boots made a satisfying thump as she stomped up the steps to Knight Commander Imralen's office.

Vola didn't bother knocking.

The door struck the wall as she slammed through, making the tall gray-haired man at the desk beyond jump. His flint hard eyes narrowed, and his jaw clenched.

"Volagra," Knight Commander Imralen said.

She made a concerted effort to unclench her teeth and speak. "I wasn't assigned a vigil." As if he didn't know.

He raised an unimpressed eyebrow and went back to his paperwork. "You're not ready."

"Not ready?" Vola said. She threw out an arm to indicate the rest of the academy. "Every trainee in my year got an assignment except me. How am I any less ready than them?"

"Every now and then we have a student who doesn't keep up with the rest of their peers. You just happened to be the one for this year."

She poked her finger at his paperwork, forcing him to look up at her. "I'm the best damn trainee you have, and you know it."

The lines around his mouth deepened as he stared at her offending finger. "And yet, I've decided you're not ready to be a candidate."

"Give me a reason," she said. "Just one."

He steepled his hands in front of him. "You want a reason? Fine. I cannot allow your evil to taint this academy, Volagra."

She drew back, brows lowering. "What evil?" she said quietly. Though she could guess. It was the same reason mothers pulled their children away from her on the street. The same reason men with torches and pitch-forks drove orc families away from their neighborhoods.

"Orcs worship the Obstacles," Imralen said, casually straightening his papers. "Paladins only ever represent the Virtues."

She shut her teeth tight on the flood of arguments that she wanted to use. The Obstacles weren't evil. They just represented the darker side of human existence. Things like rage and shame and jealousy. And orcs revered them because overcoming hardship was the fastest way to become strong. Nothing about any of that made orcs evil.

But Imralen knew all that.

"I haven't worshiped an Obstacle even once in my life," Vola said through gritted teeth. And attending the occasional High Holy day with her parents hardly counted. Everyone did that.

"Nevertheless, I can't allow you to set foot in that chapel and risk the possibility of an Obstacle choosing you."

"Obstacles don't choose paladins."

"And if that's true, then you can wait until I'm certain you are virtuous enough that you won't taint our chapel or our academy."

He waved her out and then bent back over his papers, dismissing her before she was even gone.

Vola stood there, swallowing over and over again, the red beating at the edge of her vision a direct contradiction to the calm she struggled to exude.

Imralen didn't mean a word of what he said. He didn't actually believe an Obstacle would choose her. He just didn't want an orc graduating from his academy. And he could say she wasn't ready over and over and over again until she gave up and went home.

Or she snapped and proved his words right.

She cracked her neck and fought down a pleasant daydream of leaping across the table and wrapping her hands around his neck. It might be pleasant but the paperwork would be the real murder.

Though the snapping thing was still a possibility. She couldn't stay here another month let alone another year or ten, trying to prove herself to men who'd already made up their minds about her.

But she also wasn't going home. Now that she knew what she wanted to be—what she was *supposed* to be—she would not retreat. She would not settle for something less than knighthood.

Imralen might have been stubborn. But Vola was half orcish. Her mother had often said her head was thicker than a stone wall and twice as hard to tumble.

She wouldn't let him beat her.

Imralen glanced up at her. "Did I not make myself clear, trainee? What are you still doing here?"

She didn't give him the respect of an answer. She just turned on her heel and left the offices.

Imralen didn't dictate her future. She refused to leave her life in the hands of a man who saw her as nothing more than a beast to be humiliated and broken. There was only one authority she needed to become a paladin.

Time to see if the gods agreed with the Knight Commander or with Vola.

The vigils for the current batch of trainees were supposed to start the next evening. So Vola didn't have long to make this work.

As soon as the sun went down and the training yard cleared, Vola crept out of the dormitories and made her way to the chapel on the other side of the yard. It should be deserted this time of night.

She wore a simple linen shirt and a pair of loose pants, and the chill winter air cut right through them, but nothing touched the fire burning under her skin. She was getting out of here. She was finally taking her future into her own hands, and as long as everything went right, she'd be riding away from this place in the morning.

As long as the gods didn't agree with Imralen.

She wouldn't think about that possibility.

A lone trainee wandered across the dark yard and stopped to take a swig of something contraband he'd secreted in his coat. Vola pressed herself into the shadows of the wall, waiting for him to move on.

Finally he staggered to the threshold of the dormitory, and Vola was free to move toward the chapel again. She darted to the big carved doors and reached for the handle.

Locked.

Dammit. Who kept a chapel locked at all times? What if someone wanted to pray in the middle of the night?

Or sneak in to hold an unsanctioned vigil?

Vola chewed her lip and stared up at the imposing facade. She'd always figured that if she was going to talk to a god it would be better outdoors where she could see the sky and feel the wind. But tradition was set in stone around here, so she wasn't about to mess with the vigil ritual. And vigils were held in the chapel.

Well, if Imralen couldn't stop her, a measly little locked door was nothing. She slipped around the edges of the building checking for windows.

The ones along the sides were all tall and stained glass. Not only would she feel bad about breaking them, the noise would bring every paladin and paladin trainee in the academy.

Imralen would have no trouble throwing her out, then. The only reason he hadn't yet was because she'd been very, very careful not to break any rules. You know, besides the unspoken one about being an evil orc.

She turned the corner to the back of the chapel. There. A normal looking window was set high over the back door the priests used. She might even fit through it.

She just had to figure out how to get up there.

If she remembered correctly, there were some moldy crates hanging out by the stables this morning.

She tiptoed to the outbuilding, avoiding the hostlers who played cards around the wood stove, and grabbed a couple crates. She could fit four of them under her arms as she huffed back to the chapel. There were some advantages to being tall.

Vola stacked the crates, eying the window to line them up.

They wobbled precariously as she settled her weight on them. She grabbed the sill to steady herself and tried the window.

It was locked, too. Dammit. Maybe the gods really didn't want her to be a paladin.

She squinted, trying to see the latch inside.

The crate under her feet creaked. That was all the warning she had before the moldering wood gave way, and she crashed through to the ground.

She stumbled out of the debris and landed on her butt in the dirt. A grunt escaped between her lips, but she managed to stifle the rest of her cry.

That had hurt more than any paladin trainee would be willing to admit. She rolled to her side to survey the wreckage. Bits of rotten wood littered the ground, but at least none of the splinters were in her butt. That would have been hard to explain in the morning.

Nothing stirred the still air, so her dramatic fall hadn't woken the entire academy. A small blessing but one she'd grab with both hands.

She grimaced and climbed to her feet, cracked her back, and then glared up at the window.

"It certainly is up there," a voice said.

Vola jumped and whipped around.

A man lounged against the corner of the chapel, arms crossed over his chest. He wore an eclectic mix of plate and leather armor, well used and well taken care of. The moonlight illuminated his steel gray hair and glinted from the scar that pulled at the corner of his eye and traveled down his neck.

He grinned at her, wide and friendly.

She blew out her breath, relaxing just a little. Of all the people to have caught her, Henri was by far her best prospect.

The old trainer wasn't at the academy all that often—usually he was off with a paladin candidate, helping them earn their shield, like the elf he'd worked with in Vola's village. But he showed up every now and then and always went out of his way to treat Vola like any other trainee.

She specifically remembered him bent over a book of tactics, explaining the troop movements to a frustrated young woman who couldn't make the words sit still long enough to read them.

She'd gotten a lot of grief for that one. All the trainees spoke about him in hushed tones and they all hoped to be his next candidate. Clearly he was too good to be helping an orc. Even if he wasn't a full knight.

"I, uh, don't know what you mean," Vola said, eyes flicking to the window.

Henri's grin grew broader. "Then I guess you'd better try harder. Or smarter."

He pushed himself off the wall with a wink and then disappeared around the corner of the chapel.

Leaving a ladder propped where he'd been standing.

That definitely hadn't been there before.

Vola gulped and peered around the corner, trying to catch a glimpse of Henri. But he was gone already. The yard stood clear and empty.

No one to see her. And a convenient ladder where there hadn't been one before.

Was this a trick? A trap to get her to thrown out?

If it was Imralen or any of the paladin council, she'd believe it in a heartbeat. But Henri was different.

Every candidate he'd ever trained had gone on to become paragons of justice and mercy. Holy warriors dedicated to the good of the world.

Vola blew out her breath. She could either believe he had good intentions and seize her chance to get out of here. Or she could second guess everything until the sun rose and she was truly stuck.

Her choice.

She grabbed the ladder and dragged it into place.

The window would still be locked. But maybe once she got up there, she'd be able to jiggle it open. The shutters in the dormitories were cheap enough that if you leaned on them the right way they popped open. A trick many tardy trainees had used in their time here.

The window swung open at her touch.

A shiver went down Vola's spine. She'd checked it. She *had*, she knew she had.

She shook her head. Maybe it had just been stuck before.

The frame squeezed her sides as she shimmied through and dropped to the floor inside. None of the acolytes actually slept here since the chapel was really only used for vigils and High Holy days, so the back rooms were just for storage and stood empty tonight.

A lone candle burned in the main sanctuary, sending flickering shadows up to the faces of the gods painted on the back wall. A massive mural stretched from one side of the chapel to the other, depicting every Greater Virtue as benevolent giants with hundreds of Lesser Virtues gathered at their feet.

The only ones missing from this pantheon were the Obstacles.

Vola gazed up at the shadowed faces of the Greater Virtues. Maxim and Ona looked especially unforgiving in the wavering light. And they were the two who chose the most paladins. The Greater Virtue of Strength and Loyalty and the Greater Virtue of Honor.

Vola gulped. She was here. She'd made it inside. Now she just needed to sit her vigil.

The older candidates had described it as a night of contemplation and prayer. Of supplication to the gods you were about to serve.

Vola had never been much for praying. Orcs in general didn't really like to ask for help. It defeated the purpose of suffering and hardship if you asked for help getting out of it. And Vola's parents had always been so competent. They'd taught her to be competent, too.

But knights were supposed to be humble as well as strong. Their power didn't come from inside themselves. It came from the god who'd chosen them. And Vola desperately needed a god to choose her.

It wouldn't be too hard to pray for that. She'd been wishing and hoping for it for four years. And praying was only a step away from hoping.

She knelt.

A clinking from the front step of the chapel startled Vola from her reverie. She blinked, her neck stiff and her knees numb from kneeling on the stone floor. Light came pouring through the tall windows lining the chapel.

How had she missed the sun rising?

Something jingled, like a ring of keys dropped on the threshold outside.

"Just open the door." Imralen's voice cut through the thick doors, like an ax through a board.

"I'm sorry, Knight Commander. We never usually lock it."

"Yes, well, I didn't want any vermin infesting the place the night before we begin the vigils."

Vola staggered to her feet, heart in her throat. This was it. If she was going to become a paladin this was the moment the gods had to choose her. There was no more waiting. If Imralen dragged her out of here, they would have lost their chance.

She craned her neck to look up at the Greater Virtues. How did this work? None of the paladin candidates had ever said. They told the younger trainees that the moment was secret and sacred between them and their god. She'd always assumed it would become obvious once she'd gotten here.

A key clicked in the latch behind her. The bell toll that said her time was running out.

She closed her eyes. "Please," she said. Everything she'd had to say she'd said during the night. She'd poured out her arguments into the still wintry air. She'd laid out the logic of choosing her. She'd even revealed the deepest desires in her heart. The will that drove her to be better and stronger than the ones who doubted her. Who doubted all orcs.

"Please," she said again as the hinges creaked.

Nothing. The gods stood silent above her, their painted faces flat and expressionless in the bright morning light. As disapproving and uncaring as everyone who'd ever looked at Vola and said "no."

She was on her own the same way she'd been for the last four years.

"Volagra." Imralen's voice cracked across the empty space.

She flinched, her teeth grinding hard enough to creak. It was the hardest thing she'd ever done to turn and face the ending of her dream. There was no way Imralen would let her stay now.

The Knight Commander stood just inside the chapel, his mouth thin and white and his eyes hard as he stared at her. An acolyte shifted his feet beside him, hands playing nervously with the ring of keys. Several members of the paladin council including Imralen's toady crowded behind him.

"Commander," Vola said, voice grating. Her breath puffed in the cold air. She didn't say anything more. If he was going to kick her out, she was going to make him work for it.

"How dare you violate the sanctity of our chapel —"

"I haven't violated anything. I was praying. Standing vigil. That's what it's for, right?"

"I did not give you permission."

"No, you didn't. I've earned the right to try so I had to take it when you wouldn't give it to me."

Imralen strode to the center of the sanctuary which left the door clear enough for the rest of the council to shuffle in. Behind them, several of the knight masters crowded and trainees peered over their shoulders to see what was going on.

Vola straightened her shoulders.

"You do not belong there," Imralen said through his teeth.

"I've spent four years proving I belong just as much as anybody else. All I wanted was the chance to try."

His expression smoothed, and his eyes traveled up to the mural behind her. "Fine. You've tried. Was your vigil successful?"

He dropped his gaze to hers as she went hot and then cold all over. The blood pounded in her ears. She could argue forever that she deserved the right to stand here, but it wouldn't change the fact that the day had dawned and she stood here alone.

Vola opened her mouth just as a breeze touched her cheek. It took her a moment to realize why that sent a shiver down her spine.

The breath of air hadn't come from the door.

It had come from the mural at her back.

Imralen's eyes went wide as a light grew behind Vola, sending her jagged shadow stretching across the floor. The air changed as if someone stood behind her shoulder.

A hand clasped her shoulder, making Vola draw in a sharp breath. She wanted to turn, to see who stood there, but she was afraid to break the moment. She was afraid if she turned the hand would drop and she'd face empty air again.

"Not alone," a voice said out of the gentle breeze. Right into her ear as if it was meant only for her. "Not empty air."

The voice rose, a shush of wind and the shing of a blade being drawn. "Hello, Imralen."

Imralen jerked. "You," he said. "You choose her?"

"I do."

He barked a laugh. "That's fitting."

Who exactly was standing with her? Vola fought the urge to shrug, not willing to disconnect herself from the presence behind her. A god was a god. It didn't matter who had chosen her as long as she was chosen.

"Laugh again and you'll discover why I'm called the lady of sharp implements," the voice said.

Imralen made a cursory effort to wipe the smile from his face. It didn't quite work. He still smirked as he said. "Yes, my lady."

"Carry on, Vola," the voice said in her ear, and Vola got the impression she was the only one who could hear it again. "You have much work to do. But I know you are up to the task."

"Yes, my lady," Vola whispered, keeping her voice much more respectful than Imralen's had been.

The presence behind her shoulder faded, and the light dimmed until her shadow spread evenly from the morning sun.

The hand lingered a moment longer, and Vola tried to memorize the feel of it, the weight of it on her skin.

Gods had always been so abstract to Vola. Virtues and Obstacles alike. None had ever felt so real or complicated, like a sister calling to her from just over her shoulder.

She looked up at Imralen, a fierce grin making her cheeks ache. "You have to make me a candidate, now," she said.

His smirk remained in place, souring her pleasure. "Of course," he said. "As soon as you have a mentor. You might have a god, but you need an earthly knight to train you until you earn your shield."

He threw out his hand, indicating the knights gathered in the doorway.

"Will any of them agree to train an orc with a laughingstock of a goddess?"

Vola's gaze swept the array of figures. It was just one step. A small one, too. She'd already convinced one of the pantheon to take her on. Surely there had to be one mortal in the entire world who believed an orc could be a paladin.

As she looked over them, the knight masters shuffled their feet. None of them met her eyes. Some of them found their fingernails fascinating, others glared at her feet. None of them spoke up.

One face in the crowd actually looked at her.

Henri lounged against the wall beside the door, eyes on her. His grin twitched as if to say "let's make some mischief."

"I'll take her," he said loud enough to carry across the chapel.

Imralen started and spun around. His eyes narrowed on Henri. "You aren't a knight."

"You've never made that distinction before. No, I'm not a knight. I'm better than a knight. I train knights. I train the best damn knights who come out of this academy." He tilted his head. "And you know it or you wouldn't let me ride away with them every year."

"I have plenty more promising trainees I was saving for you to look at—"

"I like Volagra," Henri said. "I'll take her."

"You can't—"

"I said, I'll take her." Henri's chin raised as his voice went firm and final.

Imralen's lips stretched thin over his teeth. His nostrils flared, and Vola waited for him to dash her last chance. He could order Henri to stand down, to take someone else. The old trainer would ride away with another candidate, and Vola would be alone again.

Imralen swallowed. "Fine, Trainer Henri."

Vola bit her lip on any noise she could have made. Knight Commander Imralen was caving? Gods, she'd never seen such a thing.

"I can see my words won't dissuade you," Imralen said through his teeth. "But know this. Her evil will break through eventually. One day it will crack that facade of good she's fooled you with and it will be your downfall."

"You're right," Henri said, hands in his pockets. "Your words mean very little to me."

Imralen's lips twisted. He cast one more poisonous glance at Vola and swept out of the chapel. The rest of the paladin council scrambled to follow.

Henri stepped across the flagstones to Vola as the others all trickled out into the yard.

He cocked his head up at her. She was taller than him by a good four inches.

She looked down at this man who would train her and travel with her for the years it took to earn her shield. He didn't look like much in his mismatched armor with his face seamed by weather and scarring. But he'd trained the best knights in Southglen. And he'd faced down the paladin council for her.

"So do you want to rest today? Or do you want to get out of here immediately?" He cast her a sidelong look like he already knew the answer.

"I want to get out," she said. It wasn't like she had anyone to say goodbye to. And she looked forward to the next phase of her life, following this man with the easy grin.

"I don't blame you," he said, turning for the door.

Vola stepped to follow him and an unfamiliar weight clunked against her chest.

She glanced down. A pendant hung from a silver chain, dangling over her heart. A long hooked fish knife. The symbol for Cleavah, Lesser Virtue and goddess of Vengeful Housewives.

Vola spun to search the mural. All the Lesser Virtues crowded at the feet of the Greater Virtues. It was nearly impossible to make them out individually. But near the bottom right, Vola thought she saw a hand clenched around the handle of a fish knife.

Imralen had called her goddess a laughingstock. But at least she had one now. Her hand curled around the pendant. It was her emblem. Her connection to the goddess. It would allow her to contact Cleavah and Cleavah to work through her.

Never alone, she'd said. Not anymore.

Vola turned to follow Henri.

He waited on the threshold of the chapel, a sheathed sword across his palms. "It's tradition. When a knight master takes on a candidate he gives them a sword. To signify they are ready to use their strength to serve. I'm not a knight, but you're definitely a candidate."

Vola took the blade from him, her fingers sliding across the worn leather sheath. It didn't look like much. But it was more about what it meant. She'd always used hand me down axes from her mother, but this settled into her hand like a long lost memory.

"Thank you," she said, meaning so much more than just those two words.

"You'll need a name," Henri said, tilting his face up toward the sun.

She cocked her head. "What?"

"A paladin name. You choose one when you leave the academy to earn your shield."

Vola turned her face up to the sun as well. It warmed her despite the winter air. Leaving the academy with Henri at her side and Cleavah at her back felt like stepping out of a dark cave into the morning light. Out of loneliness into the company of two people who believed in her.

But she didn't just want to be the one stepping into the light. She wanted to be the torch. No, even that was too small. She wanted to be the blazing sun.

"Lightbringer," she said. "I want to be Lightbringer."

MISHAP'S HEROES

5

Sparks and Scales

It just had to be dragons this time...

KM MERRITT

MISHAP'S HEROES

5

Sparks and Scales

KM MERRITT

BLUE FYRE PRESS

For Arielle, Miranda, Lacey, and Seth. Thanks for spinning fate with me.

ONE

Vola counted quietly under her breath, listening for the sounds of movement from the others. There was the soft tread of a sandal on loam from Sorrel. A gasp and the heavy exhale of someone not used to the wilderness from Lillie. And nothing, not a sound or a breath or a whisper from Talon.

"Twenty-eight, twenty-nine, thirty."

Vola whistled the signal and surged upright in the underbrush. She charged forward with an orcish battle cry, and crashed her sword against her blackened shield, making as much noise as possible. Her charge flushed the family of warg out of hiding.

The big dog-like creatures startled and bolted out of the screening cover of the shrubs, across the empty dusty gully. Panicked grunts rang from the rocks. They tried to plunge back into the scrub on the other side, but a gray-clad halfling leaped from the underbrush, swinging a staff overhead, which crackled with lightning.

"Not today, beasties!" Sorrel cried.

The alpha warg skidded to a stop with a snarl, its rough gray fur standing on end. It spun to bolt through the opening the halfling had left to the north. Before it could escape with the other warg, a line of fire sprang between them and freedom.

Behind the flames, Vola could make out a plump woman, her eyes narrowed in concentration and hands outstretched. Lillie's outline wavered with heat, and her long blonde hair fluttered.

The lead warg spun, its lips pulled back, well and truly cornered. The female and the little wargs circled the alpha's legs, whining.

One opening remained to the south. But a new figure had appeared in the gap, cloak thrown back over her shoulders, her face obscured by a hood.

The ranger held her hands out in a calming gesture, making soothing noises through her teeth.

The warg's ears lay flat, then swiveled forward as if it couldn't decide between listening and charging.

Vola's fingers clenched on her hilt as a puff of warm air from Lillie's spell brushed her face. "Talon? Are we attacking or not?"

The hooded figure crouched, presenting a less intimidating presence. The warg eyed her warily.

"Give me a second."

Vola cast a glance at Sorrel and Lillie, but they both held their positions, keeping the warg from escaping.

A large black wolf brushed Vola's leg, and she laid her hand on his head, her fingers sinking into his thick fur.

"I know," she told Gruff. "It's not the plan. But I trust her."

Talon spoke quiet words the rest of them couldn't quite make out, and gradually the warg's lip lowered. The alpha lay down and listened with its head cocked.

Vola lowered her sword but kept her grip firm and ready.

Eventually, the alpha warg stood and shook himself. Talon raised her head.

"Drop the fire, Lillie," she said, voice a low growl.

The blonde wizard closed her fists and lowered her hands without hesitation, and the wall of flames fell, leaving nothing but a line of blackened shrubbery.

Talon barked a word and the alpha warg led its family away to the north.

Lillie squeaked and stumbled out of their way, but the warg didn't pay her any attention, their mottled gray pelts helping them blend in and disappear until nothing remained of their passing.

Talon stood and brushed her hands off on her pants as Gruff raced to her and twined around her legs. "They'll stay out of the way of the villagers now," she said. "They don't like conflict any more than other animals, they're just way better at defending themselves when threatened. It makes for a bad reputation."

She pushed back her hood, revealing sandy-colored hair long enough to curl around her ears and the nape of her neck. She'd shaved that morning, and her jaw actually looked smooth for once. Maybe the cream Aunt Urag had given her was actually working.

Her eyes met Vola's and Vola read the question in them.

"It wasn't what I was expecting this morning when the village asked us to go warg hunting. But it worked," she said.

Talon's gaze shifted to the north, where the creatures had disappeared. "They didn't deserve to be hunted for one mistake. Revenge is a human thing. They wouldn't have understood it."

Lillie stepped across the line of scorched vegetation to the ranger. "Do you actually speak their language?" she said. "Or is it more of a spell that allows you to communicate with them?"

"More like a spell," Talon said as Sorrel trotted up to join them, slinging her staff back across her back. The little lightning bolts crackled and subsided. "I'm sorry you didn't get to hit anything," Talon told her.

The halfling monk shrugged. "It's fine. We got the job done. And if Rilla ever gets back with Anders's whereabouts, we'll have plenty of fighting to look forward to."

They turned to head back toward Vola's village to give them the good news that the warg threat had been taken care of.

"What do you think this Anders guy is doing with all the magic he's stealing?" Sorrel hopped over a patch of scrub, making her red-brown curls bounce.

Vola glanced at Lillie, their magic expert. "Any ideas?"

Lillie chewed her lip, watching her feet carefully. Her limp made this type of rocky forest that much harder to navigate. "I don't know," she said quietly. "But it can't be anything good."

"It's too bad none of the people working for him so far have known more than his name and the vague direction they were sending his super nefarious magical shenanigan supplies," Sorrel said. "Inga could have been so much more helpful in that case."

"If Vola hadn't pushed her out the window," Talon said. With her hood down, her smirk was clear.

"She'd just thrown my mother across the room." Vola's frown pulled at her thick eyebrows. "Any one of you could have been next. I was protecting you."

Lillie bit her lip on a laugh and gave Vola a dancing-eyed smile. "Our hero."

"I'm not saying she didn't need to go out the window," Sorrel said. "I'm just saying she could have been much more helpful before she died. She could have told us what this Anders character wants, how he intends to get it, where he normally holes up."

"What kind of defenses he has," Talon said.

"Exactly." Sorrel threw her arms over her head. "Hopefully Rilla is having more luck tracking him down."

Vola sniffed as they neared the village. Someone was barbecuing wargle ribs. Vola had a sneaking suspicion she knew who.

"I imagine the princess of the Dagger Throne will have far more resources than just us," Lillie said.

"And then we can stop killing time," Talon said.

Sorrel took a relieved breath. "Finally." Her eyes widened, and she held a hand out to Vola. "Not that it's not wonderful killing time with your family, Vola. Your mom has so many great stories about her and your dad from when they were mercenaries." She sighed. "I still can't believe I get to spar with Lydia Battlemane every morning."

"And your father is quite funny," Lillie added politely.

Vola's brow drew down. "Everything out of his mouth is a bad sex joke."

Lillie stopped dead in the middle of the dusty lane, her mouth dropping open. "Those were sex jokes?"

"I'm just saying," Sorrel said. "It's nice being here and all, but…"

Vola, Talon, and Sorrel drew up at the edge of the village and stared at the banner hanging across the road between two roof peaks. It glinted with fresh paint and glitter and read "THANK YOU MISHAP'S HEROES!"

"But Ella is really getting annoying," Sorrel finished, her shoulders sagging.

"We should not have told her our name," Talon growled under her breath.

Sorrel planted her hands on her hips. "Just because everyone calls us that doesn't mean it's actually our name. I never voted on it."

"If it was up to you, we'd be called 'super awesome bashing ladies,'" Lillie said.

"Do you think we can sneak back to my parents' house without any of them noticing?" Vola said.

"You wear plate armor," Talon said with a sniff. "You can't sneak anywhere."

"Too late anyway," Sorrel said in a stage whisper.

A slim figure with perfect hair, perfect skin, and perfect fingernails trotted out to greet them, carrying a cake.

"Vola, I'm so glad you've returned safely. Thank you so much for driving off the wargs. You've kept our village safe and we commend you for your sacrifice."

"I didn't even do anything this time, Ella," Vola said.

The girl just shook her head. "You're so modest. It's such an example for the rest of us." She thrust the cake into Vola's hands before she threw an arm around the paladin's shoulders and steered her through the center of town, where half the villagers had gathered to cheer as they passed.

Vola cringed. Sorrel and the others trailed after them, resigned. She could hear them whispering behind her.

"It's been like this the whole week."

"Well, we did save them all from Inga."

"Maybe Vola should have just left Ella there instead of carrying her out."

"Yeah, but a whole week of feasting?" Sorrel said. "Even I'm getting tired of booze and food."

There was a shocked gasp from Lillie and stunned silence from Talon. Even Vola shot a raised eyebrow over her shoulder at Sorrel.

"I didn't say I'd turn it down if offered," Sorrel said. "It's just, the novelty's worn off. Know what I mean?"

Ella slipped her arm through Vola's elbow and beamed up at her. Vola tried to smile through her tusks, but her heart wasn't in it.

This constant celebration certainly beat the ostracism of Vola's childhood. But enough was enough.

Why couldn't there be a place in between? A neutral spot where Vola could walk into a town, do her job, get paid, and move on. Like a normal person. Without the curled lips of her past or the hero worship of her present.

Near the center of the village, where the crowd was the thickest, Vola's parents' house stood. In the shadows, a figure leaned against the wall, surveying the party with amusement.

"Oh, thank Cleavah," Vola said under her breath. She pulled herself from Ella's clinging grasp with a half-baked excuse and hurried through the crowd. Sorrel, Talon, and Lillie were right on her heels having seen and recognized the dark green-clad figure as well.

The woman wore a leather jerkin and tight pants designed to blend in, and curly black hair rose in a frothy cloud around her head. No crown for this princess. She preferred to remain anonymous. And if anyone questioned her, a knife in the ribs worked just as well as royal privilege.

"It's about time, Rilla," Sorrel said.

"Did you learn anything new?" Lillie said. "Are we going to go after Anders now?"

Rilla's lip quirked, her eyes settling on the cake Vola still held. Then her gaze flicked to the party behind them. Ella had hopped to a bench to give a rousing speech about their brave heroes and how they'd defeated the warg pack and saved the village.

"Why? Ready to get out of here?" Rilla said, meeting Vola's eyes.

Vola heaved a relieved sigh. "Oh, my gods, yes. Give us a direction and we'll race you there."

Rilla gave them a theatrical pout. "But where else are you going to get this kind of treatment? Cake every day. Endless feasting and all the tail you could possibly want. Bet you have to beat the boys off with a stick."

Sorrel stuck her finger in Vola's cake and swiped up a huge glob of frosting. "It gets old after a while. Trust me." She stuck her finger in her mouth and grimaced.

Rilla raised an eyebrow at Sorrel, which she didn't notice.

"The cake gets old," Vola said. "She's talking about the feasting, not the boys."

Sorrel's brow furrowed in confusion. "What boys?"

Rilla hid a smile. "Never mind. It's time to pack up. If you can tear yourselves away, I've lined up a job on a caravan headed to dragon country."

"Dragon country?" Talon's voice went sharp and clipped.

"We're going after Anders."

Vola breathed a sigh of relief.

"You're coming, too?" Lillie said.

"Firewatch is out of Southglen's jurisdiction. You'll need my clout to get anywhere." Rilla shrugged. "Besides, I want to get this guy as much as you do. I can always portal back to the capital if I need to."

Talk about royal resources. Lillie could only teleport short distances, and she had to be sure of what was on the other side.

Sorrel clapped her hands. "Road trip!"

"A road trip toward danger," Talon reminded her. "Dragons are worse than anything we've faced so far."

"Yeah, but maybe Vola's mom will bake us cookies. They're so much better than Ella's cakes."

TWO

LYDIA DID MAKE COOKIES. There was also a lot less weeping and clinging than Vola expected there to be when they left the little cottage.

Lydia stood on the front doorstep with her hands on her hips, head cocked so her bushy mane of red hair fell over her bare shoulders.

"Well, to be honest, honey," she said. "We love you, and it was wonderful to fight beside you. But you and your friends don't need to be in our attic anymore." She cast a glance at Vola's father, who was examining a crack in his picket fence with a frown. Lydia licked her lips.

Talon grinned wide enough they could see her teeth even under her hood. "She means we're getting in the way of their fun times."

Vola cast her eyes toward the sky. "Yes, thank you, Talon. I got that."

"What do you mean getting in the way?" Sorrel said. "We're fun."

Talon snorted. "Never mind."

"You're taking your…creature, right?" Gorgo called.

Vola cast a grimace at the swamp monster. "Yes, Dad."

"Good. I think it's been eating the fence."

Rilla stood in the lane, rubbing the smile from her face as she waited for them.

Vola hurried her team and their employer out of her village and as far away from her parents as she could manage.

Visits home always seemed like a good idea. But between local baddies and parents who knew you too well, they always ended up awkward.

Vola's shoulders relaxed the further they traveled from her village.

The caravan Rilla had convinced to hire them was bigger than Vola had been expecting but still small enough to be ignored by most of the world. The owner seemed to know what he was doing, encouraging, coaxing, and cajoling the motley group to get on the road on time. Even with ten different merchants plus their wagons, livestock, and merchandise, keeping them all safe would be easier than a lot of the things Vola and the others had done to earn some coin in the past.

At least until they got to dragon lands.

They rolled along, leaving the familiar forests and plains of Southglen behind. They could have just huffed it across the countryside like normal, but they traveled with the princess of the Dagger Throne now, and she was nothing if not subtle. Not to mention paranoid.

So they walked alongside the caravan during the day and stood watch at night, pretending to be simple mercenaries, disguising their true purpose. Considering someone had already tried kidnapping the princesses of Southglen once that year, Vola wasn't complaining about the extra precautions.

So far it seemed to be working.

Vola strode around the perimeter of the campsite, hand on her hilt, eyes trained on the surrounding hills, even as she kept her ears open for anything unusual coming from within the campsite.

Nothing. Just the low crackle of the fire kept lit in the very center of the circle of wagons. She couldn't even hear Talon on the other side, walking the perimeter as well. The ranger moved like a shadow when she wanted to.

Vola stopped, letting the bulk of a nearby wagon consume the shape of her shadow, and stared into the darkness, letting her ears tell her where to watch.

Still nothing.

She was too used to conflict now. Expecting it around every corner and under every rock. A hazard of the job, but to be fair, it made her sharper than the average guard.

She moved on, stepping around the little hummocks of dry grass and poky shrubs. Nothing taller than a bush out here now. Apparently, the lands ahead of them were even dryer than anything they'd seen yet.

Vola couldn't really find it in herself to complain. This sure beat trekking through a swamp and nearly drowning inside a sinking tent.

Vola shuddered.

She paused at the fifth wagon in the circle, waiting for Talon. This was where they checked in with each other after every other pass.

Vola squinted and a lithe shadow detached itself from the wagon. "Talon?"

"Who else did you expect?"

Talon stopped and stood facing the rest of the world, back to the fire and the caravan. She wore her hood less and less these days. Usually, she only hid her face when overwhelmed by large crowds or inundated by pestering strangers who looked at her and saw a man rather than a woman. It still happened occasionally even though she kept her face clean-shaven and wore a leather cuirass that cinched at the waist.

And Lillie had been doing something with Talon's hair—Vola had no idea what—pinning the ragged ends out of her face for a softer look. Soon it would be grown out enough to braid.

"Anything on your end?" Vola asked.

Talon remained motionless, staring off into the distance.

Vola straightened. "What is it?"

She didn't answer.

"Talon?" Vola whispered.

Talon jerked. "Hmm? What?"

"What do you see?"

Talon shook her head and took a step back. "Nothing. Sorry. What did you ask?"

Vola's brows drew down. "Are you all right?"

"Fine."

Vola crossed her arms and settled against the corner of the wagon. "Sure you are," she said. "Try again."

A couple of months ago, that would have shut Talon up for good. Tonight, she only hesitated for a bare second before opening her mouth.

"We're headed to dragon lands," she said.

Vola tilted her head. "Yeah. That's where Rilla says Anders is heading."

"It's also where dragons nest. Presumably."

Vola's breath blew out in the cool night air as she finally caught on. "Your original pack was killed by a dragon, weren't they?" she said quietly.

"Yes."

Talon had been raised by a wolf pack before she'd rejoined the human world. There were still some times when she looked at Vola and Vola could see the wolf in her eyes. Times when she was sure one wrong word or look would send Talon bolting.

But tonight, Talon turned to meet Vola's eyes, the firelight flickering across her face, and she seemed to really mean it when she said, "I'm fine, Vola. I promise."

"All right," Vola said. "I believe you."

"They're dead," Talon said. "They're gone. And nothing I do can change that. I've moved on. Like Gruff." She gestured to the long shape of the wolf lying beside the fire. He turned his head as if he could tell they were talking about him and his tongue lolled.

"I found a new pack," Talon said and flashed a rare smile at Vola. "But this trip is making me remember them."

Vola frowned.

"Not bad things," Talon said before she could respond. "I just…I want to be sure I remember them well."

"And how do you do that?"

"Honor the things they taught me," Talon said, turning back to the night. "Protect my new pack. Don't make the same mistakes twice."

"I thought maybe you were hoping for revenge."

Talon shook her head sharply. "What good would that do anyone? Besides, the dragon that did it is dead. It won't be hurting anyone ever again. I'm just worried about the ones we're headed toward."

Vola opened her mouth, but in the dark silence of the night, a twig snapped.

Talon's chin came up, and she sniffed the air. Behind them, Gruff rose to his feet, a growl starting in his throat.

Vola gave Talon a signal, pointing her to the right while Vola slipped left. Gruff passed between them, nothing more than a waft of breeze and a shadow against the darkness.

Vola unsheathed her sword as quietly as she could and settled her shield on her arm. She waited, tense and ready. She'd left the full plate armor in their tent, but sneaking wasn't her strong suit, so she stayed put until Talon gave her more to work with.

There. Four sharp whistles that could have been from a night bird but weren't. Then a long, swooping whistle — Talon letting her know what was going on. Gruff had found four enemies to their south.

Vola whistled back. She would close in on them from the left; Talon from the right.

She crouched low and scanned the horizon, waiting for movement. Finally she saw a shadow cross the stars between her and Talon.

She rose and charged the figure. A silent battering ram.

Orcs saw better in the dark, true, but the figure didn't become clear until she was nearly on top of him. He wore a motley selection of armor and carried a wicked-looking knife. Perfect for slitting sleeping throats. And no one friendly would be moving around in the dark without torches or a wizard's light.

Vola hit him before he even realized which direction she was coming from, and he went down without a cry.

There was a familiar sizzle behind her left ear, and she managed to turn a wince into a duck and roll as a flash of fire flew over her shoulder and struck the bare dirt where she'd been standing.

She came up, sword ready, but just as she found the spell caster a few feet away, an arrow sprouted from the woman's eye, and she went down.

"Two more," Talon growled, sliding up next to her.

"There." Vola pointed to two pale faces, fading back into the low scrub. "Tell Gruff to flush them out."

There was a growl, a short bark, and then a snarl. The remaining bandits yelped and leaped from the scant cover of the bushes.

Right into Vola and Talon. Talon tripped one and made sure he didn't get up again. Vola spun and slashed, taking her last opponent down with an anti-climactic sigh.

She stared at the bodies with a bemused frown.

"That was hardly worth the fight," Talon said.

"Tell Gruff to check the perimeter. Make sure there aren't any more of them lurking on the other side. These could be scouts for a larger party." Vola knelt to check the bodies as Gruff slipped away to sniff out any more intruders.

"Anything to identify them?" Talon asked.

"Broke bandits from the look of it," Vola said, emptying their wallets out onto her palm and finding only a few coins.

"Desperate bandits," Talon said. "If they decided four against a caravan was good odds."

"Middle of the night, just before watch change. Probably thought we'd be asleep on our feet."

Talon grinned, teeth flashing in the dark. "Too bad for them, Rilla doesn't hire fools."

Vola stood and dusted off her hands, almost feeling sorry for the enemy. They didn't have anything worth much on them, and their armor and weapons were shabby.

"When did we become the thing to be feared?" She rubbed her face. "Last I remember we were like these poor sods, knocking around Brisbene, trying to earn enough coin to get a bed for the night."

"You want to go back?" Talon said.

"Hel—er, heck no."

A wolf howled from the other side of the caravan, and Talon's head jerked up. "Gruff says it's clear."

Vola cocked her thumb at the campsite and led the way back to the wagons. "Let's make sure everything's still quiet."

A figure hovered in the opening between two wagons, silhouetted against the fire. Gregor, the caravan lead. He'd been the one to hire them, though Vola strongly suspected Rilla had insisted and then made him think it was his idea.

He craned his neck to look past them, squinting into the dark. "I heard something."

His son, Yevan, sidled up next to him, eyes trained on Vola.

She made sure to smile at him. The gangly youth was only twelve, but he reminded her strongly of Finn.

"Sorry to wake you," Vola said. "Just a couple of bandits. Nothing serious. We caught them before they even made their move."

Gregor's shoulders sagged, and he turned to let them back into the circle of firelight. He ran a hand through his shaggy blond hair, eyes darting between them and the darkness behind them.

"Thank the gods," he said. "You five are worth twice your fee, you know that, right?"

Vola gave him a look of mock horror. "Gregor, you're not supposed to tell us that. We might charge you double next time."

"He'd pay it," Yevan said, skipping to keep up with Vola.

"Gladly," Gregor said. "Your goddess must look after you personally." His eyes flicked to her shield with the spreading wings burnished into its blackened surface.

Most people didn't know what to think when they saw her shield. The surface blackened by holy fire was a mark of shame the world over. A symbol of a black paladin. A holy warrior stripped of their rank and position. But the shining symbol cutting through the black had wiped away part of the mark and made everyone she encountered look twice, wondering what it meant exactly. Vola was still trying to figure it out herself.

Gregor had decided after the first night when they'd fought off a family of manticores that she must have landed on the right side of whatever debate the gods had had over her shield.

"Who did you say you served again?" he said, eyes on the shining wings.

Talon glanced at Vola sharply as she hesitated for the briefest of moments. Back in Inga's stronghold, her goddess had proved herself to be something more than a Lesser Virtue. Something more than a Greater Virtue too, maybe. But she hadn't deigned to explain to Vola just who—or what—she actually was.

"Cleavah," she said for simplicity's sake. That was the only name she knew her lady by, so that was the one she would continue to use.

"Goddess of Vengeful Housewives?" Gregor cocked his head so his big nose cast a shadow across his face.

"Yes," Vola said simply and quietly. She couldn't explain the differences even to herself, so getting into it would just give Gregor more questions.

Gregor shrugged. "I hope the lady of sharp implements continues to grace us with her favor," he said and gave her a little bow before herding Yevan back to their wagon.

Vola turned for their tent and Talon followed. A light still burned behind the canvas, casting the shadow of a woman with bushy hair hunched over a camp table.

Rilla stood pouring over her map under a swinging lantern. Sorrel and Lillie were already tumbling out of their bedrolls, rubbing their eyes and reaching for shoes.

"Figured it was about time for a shift change," Sorrel said with a yawn.

"Any trouble?" Lillie asked.

"Couple of bandits," Vola said. "From the south. We're pretty sure we got them all, but keep your eyes open. There's still a chance they were part of a larger group."

Lillie nodded as she tied her boots. "I can do a sweep to check for any signs of life sneaking up on us."

"Have you been up this whole time?" Talon asked Rilla.

The princess glanced up from the map, a frown line between her eyebrows. "Is it that late?"

Vola raised her eyebrows. "Yeah. What are you worrying about?"

"Not so much worrying as trying to imagine all the traps ahead of time," Rilla said, scowling at the lines on the paper. "It saves time later when you're trying to avoid them."

Vola joined the princess at the table. The pictures of mountains, the lines depicting rivers, and the boundaries between areas were all clear enough. But the names scrawled under each landmark swam in Vola's vision, and she blinked. Lillie claimed it was just part of her orc heritage, the main reason they passed down their history orally, but it didn't make it any easier to accept.

Rilla didn't seem to notice. She stabbed a dark finger at the line between an area covered with little pictures of scrub and the area surrounding the mountains.

"This is the border between Southglen and the dragon lands. Beyond that, my authority dwindles to that of a mere dignitary instead of a princess." She flashed a rueful grin at Vola. "That makes me snappy."

"Understandable," Sorrel said, standing on her tiptoes to see the map. Her brows drew down. "This table is not halfling friendly."

"If it was halfling friendly, the rest of us would be sitting on the floor," Talon said.

"What's wrong with that?"

"The dragon lands are not technically part of Southglen," Rilla said. "They're held jointly with the neighboring kingdoms as a sort of neutral zone. A place we all help to maintain where the dragons can roost or nest or whatever it is dragons do."

"Perch?" Sorrel said.

"Sure," Rilla said. "But what it means is that a bunch of humans and other sentient beings, dwarves, halflings, elves, even a few orcs, have made their home there where their former governments aren't technically allowed to touch them."

She stabbed the picture of a city tucked up against the mountains.

"An interesting situation," Lillie said over Talon's shoulder.

"A craptastic nuisance is what it is," Rilla said. "But Firewatch is well established now. They think of themselves as their own little kingdom out here. They've got their own council, their own culture and traditions cobbled together from scraps. And to be fair, they know how to navigate the dragon lands better than the rest of us. I feel like I'm walking into a bloody menagerie. But they live there. And manage to do it peacefully."

"It might not be that bad," Lillie said, chewing her lip while staring at the map. "The *draconis minimus*, the smaller dragons, are fairly ubiquitous. They're intelligent, they don't eat that much more than, say, another large predator like a bear. But they're small, docile, and easy to get along with as long as you respect them. It's the big ones, *draconis maximus*, that you have to worry about."

"Believe me, I'm worrying," Talon muttered.

"But they spend most of their time sleeping," Lillie continued. "They only wake every century or so to eat and…catch up on current events."

"You hesitated," Sorrel said. "Why did you hesitate?"

"Bad things tend to happen when the dragons wake." Lillie's gaze flicked to Talon. "A lot of Firewatch's resources go into making sure that doesn't happen early."

Talon didn't react.

Rilla glanced at Lillie, eyebrows raised. "That was very thorough."

"That's why we keep her around," Sorrel said. "That and the fireballs."

Lillie flushed. "My mother is supposed to be studying dragons." She glanced at the city on the map. "The last my father heard she was in Firewatch."

"If you remember any other tidbits, let me know," Rilla said.

Lillie nodded before slipping out of the tent to go stand watch, Sorrel trotting at her heels.

Rilla crossed her arms and tapped her lip. "My operatives tell me Anders is on his way to the city. If he's using the dragon lands to stage his...whatever it is he's planning, then he's most likely in Firewatch. Or will have a base within easy traveling distance." She straightened suddenly to tap her foot. "Do we still have to worry about the mind control Inga used? Will we have to worry about subverted city officials doing Anders's will?"

Vola raised her chin. "It's still a risk, but we know how to counter it now. Inga used relationships to pass Mulgash's influence from one victim to another. But you can use a relationship to spread the cure as well."

"Would we still need Cleavah to do it?" Talon asked quietly. "You used her power to heal us, didn't you?"

"Yes, but I don't think it's necessary in the long run. It just sped up the process." Vola frowned, remembering those frantic heartbeats staring into Lillie's hate-filled eyes, wondering if that was the last thing she'd ever see. "Considerably."

Rilla turned to plant her butt on the rickety table and pinned Vola with her gold gaze. "I thought you were cut off from her."

"I was," Vola said, spreading her hands. "The paladin council took my emblem."

Rilla froze. "Gods can't work through their followers without a physical connection," she said carefully.

"I think that's still true," Vola said. "For the rest of them. But I don't think it is for mine."

She could feel Cleavah—or the goddess she'd always known as Cleavah—as a burning weighted presence standing at her shoulder. But ever since Inga's stronghold collapsed, she'd had the feeling that all she had to do was turn her head and she'd brush against the goddess herself.

Had she always been that close, just...hidden? Or ignored?

"You can't ask her?" Rilla said.

Vola was dying to turn her head. To ask the question burning within her. Who are you? What's your name? Who am I serving?

But...

"If she's chosen to appear as a lesser goddess, she must have a good reason. I've learned to be careful with my questions. Because my goddess isn't afraid to answer them."

THREE

THEY TRAVELED with the caravan for two weeks, each day blurring into the next. The scenery shifted so gradually that it was three days before Vola realized they trudged through rolling dunes of fine-grain sand broken by rocky gullies instead of low dry scrub and grass. The sand got in their boots. It worked its way into the leather straps of Vola's armor. Lillie had to hold her books upside down and shake them to get sand out of the binding.

The only blessing was that it was dry. Like Talon had pointed out, it was far better than a swamp. Vola even glanced back now and then at the swamp monster trudging along behind the wagons, wondering if it had been such a good idea to bring the creature into a desert. Looking like a cross between a donkey and a crocodile, it was clearly made for the wet.

But the swamp monster glared at the scenery with the same bad temper it always showed. Vola couldn't see any difference in its temperament, and it still ate anything it could sink its teeth into, including the small rodents that ventured too close to the picket line when they camped at night.

On their fifteenth day with the caravan, Vola paused beside the road and shaded her eyes. The wagons rumbled along the stones set deep enough into the ground with magic that the constant wind and bite of the sands would never move them. Dunes rose on either side so the road wound between them, a thin path of certainty in the desert that led to a smear of darkness on the horizon.

"The Firewall," Gregor said, stopping beside her to shade his own face. "The mountains themselves are too rugged to drive a caravan through. We have to make for the passes. But even those can be dangerous with dragons roosting in the heights."

"I thought they were sentient and docile," Vola said, resuming her march.

"Oh, aye. The ones who live in Firewatch aren't a problem. But the wild ones can be a nuisance if you get a clan of young ones all making trouble together. And the city officials always want you to hire a guide, to be sure you don't wake any of the big ones. They're the ones that level cities and start the apocalypse if they wake up early and grumpy."

The dark smudge on the horizon came into focus as they approached, revealing jagged peaks of flame-scoured rock towering over the desert below. The Firewall mountains.

The city of Firewatch sat nestled in the steep valley between two peaks, gold domes catching the light and deep crevices providing homes for the darker industries for a city of outcasts. Bridges connected the different layers, some built from rope and wood, sagging across the empty spaces between, some built from red stone, arching high and wide enough for the city's traffic.

Far above the buildings, a couple of towers perched on the jagged peaks, providing unbroken views across the entire desert.

"Those are the towers Firewatch is named for," Lillie said, staring into the distance. "Even peaceful dragons can be volatile. The residents have learned to live with them and guard against them at the same time."

Yevan, Gregor's lanky son, walked the ridge of a nearby dune, his arms out for balance. He'd been on this trade route often enough to know the importance of staying in sight. Vola spared a glance at him every few minutes just to make sure all her wards were accounted for.

Yevan stopped and raised his hand to shield his eyes, peering across the dunes away from the caravan.

"Dad," he called to Gregor. "There's something there."

"Be more specific," Gregor called back. "'Something's' not helpful. The last something was a dead raccoon. I'm not falling for that again." He muttered the last part under his breath.

Vola bit her lip on a chuckle.

"Dad!" The change in Yevan's tone raised the hair on the back of her neck, and she whipped her head around.

Black shadows crept along the ridge of sand at Yevan's feet, but the sky remained clear of any clouds or birds.

"Lillie…" Vola started. "What is that?"

"I don't know," Lillie said. "But it doesn't look natural."

Vola opened her mouth to call to Yevan, to tell him to get back to the caravan, but the boy skipped back a couple of steps from the creeping black, already on the same page.

The sand shifted under his boots, and he twisted. Yevan's scream pierced the hot air as he tumbled out of sight down the other side of the dune.

"Yevan!" Gregor shot forward, but Vola was already moving.

She grabbed Gregor's arm and hauled him back toward the wagons. "Stay here."

The merchants behind them were already starting to gasp and race for their wagons.

"But Yevan—"

"I'll get him," Vola said. "But it will be a lot harder if I have to rescue both of you."

Gregor gulped, but in a show of wisdom, he stayed put.

Vola signaled for Talon. "Get them all under the wagons," she told the ranger. "Shelter in place until I give the all-clear."

Talon nodded and began herding their charges toward safety.

Vola started for the dune. "Lillie, what am I heading into?" she called over her shoulder.

Lillie raised her hand and then pulled down from the sky, a streak of sparks following her fingers. The sparks flashed and formed the figure of a large raven. He swooped away from Lillie's hand and up into the air. She lifted her face toward him and closed her eyes.

"Rand says it's just black."

Not helpful. Vola clambered up the dune, her boots slipping in the sand. Behind her, Rilla and Sorrel caught up.

Sorrel scampered up the slope on hands and knees, reaching the top before Vola. She gasped and kicked her feet out to slide down the other side and out of sight.

Rilla drew even with Vola as she swore at the halfling's disappearance.

"That's what you get for wearing full plate," Rilla said.

"It always seems like a good idea in the morning. I don't have to stop and put it on before a fight."

Vola huffed to the ridgeline and straightened up to stare out across the desert.

Sorrel was helping Yevan back up the dune, slipping and sliding as they scrambled. But the boy seemed unharmed. Just shaken.

Vola's breath caught.

The desert stretched out, but instead of the golds and reds and warm browns that painted the landscape behind them, this was black. A dead sort of black that seemed to suck up the very sunlight and leave no warmth.

It didn't go on forever. There was a break just a few hundred yards away where the gold dunes started again. But here, this bit of the desert looked...dead.

"What in Ona's name is that?" Rilla said. And if a princess didn't know what was going on, Vola didn't feel so bad about letting her jaw drop.

"Yevan," Vola said. "Are you hurt?"

The boy shook his head as Sorrel stopped trying to drag him up the hill. Tendrils of black branched out from the dead circle, but they didn't move anymore, and Sorrel and Yevan were careful to stay away from the dark sand.

"Not hurt," he said. "Just scared. It was moving. Like it wanted to eat me. Then it just stopped."

Vola stepped forward, sliding down the sand dune.

"Vola," Lillie said, finally puffing to the top of the ridge. "Be careful."

"What else would I be?" Vola said. But she had to get closer.

Lillie's raven familiar swooped above her, keeping an eye out, and she trusted him to call if he saw anything creeping up on them.

She stepped over the sloping footprints where Yevan and Sorrel had passed and carefully approached the edge of the blackness.

She knelt and leaned forward.

Rilla joined her to stare at the blackened area.

"What is it?" Lillie called. But Vola had no answer.

Lillie huffed and slid down the hill. Yevan remained on the dune above them, but Sorrel came closer, watching their backs.

Vola gave Lillie a hand up at the bottom of the dunes.

"Is this common in dragon lands?" Rilla asked. "They breathe fire, after all."

Lillie held her hands out, hovering just on this side of the affected area. "It's not a burn," she said. "This isn't from fire. It's...it's almost like it's empty."

"Empty of what?" Sorrel said, planting her hands on her hips. "Color?"

"Life."

"How?" Rilla said, a frown creasing the skin between her eyebrows. "How is that possible?"

"I don't know." Lillie took an apple from the satchel at her side. She frowned at it, then tossed it into the direct center of the area.

It bounced and rolled to a stop. The shiny green surface gleamed against the black, unblemished by it.

Lillie held up her hands again. "Whatever happened here, it's done now. I think."

"That's not as reassuring as you think it is," Sorrel said. "I'd still like to know what happened."

Lillie frowned at her, then finally stuck her hand out, breaking the plane between the normal desert and the blackened zone.

Vola cried out, but Lillie just turned her hand over and over, watching it for any effect. Vola stood and yanked her back a step.

"You can't just jump into it to see what happens," she scolded.

"Well at some point hypothesis needs to move past observation." Lillie gave her a sidelong look, and Vola let go with a huff.

Lillie stepped forward as Vola held her breath. The black sand parted around her feet just like the normal stuff did, rolling away in a fine cascade of darkness. Vola expected it to glitter in the sun, but it was so black the light didn't even seem to touch it.

Lillie frowned and knelt to take a handful and let it run between her fingers. She squinted at her palm, then reached out to take a blackened twig from some low-lying scrub between her fingers. She pinched, and the twig cracked, but it didn't crumble.

"Definitely not a burn," she said. She took a rock from the area and drew her knife.

Rilla took a deep breath and then stepped across into the black. Still nothing happened. The princess strode to the exact center of what they could see and planted her hands on her hips to glare up at the sky.

Not to be outdone, Sorrel jumped feet first across the line, looked down to check herself, then jumped back.

Vola reached out a toe and nudged some of the blackened sand with her boot.

"Ouch." Lillie hissed in pain and shook her hand.

Vola jerked and stepped across into the blackened area. "What? What happened?"

"Oh, I was stupid. I was trying to score this rock. I thought maybe the black is just on the surface. But I slipped." The wizard dropped the rock and turned her hand to show Vola the slice across her palm.

"Not stupid, and lucky for you, you travel with a healer." Vola took

Lillie's hand in hers and covered the gash. "Lady bless," she said, reaching for Cleavah.

And she came up empty.

Vola's breath froze in her chest. She reached again, but nothing met her except a sort of hollow emptiness.

"Vola?" Lillie asked, a crease forming between her brows as Vola just stood there, gaping at their hands.

"It's gone," she whispered, her voice catching.

"What's gone?" Lillie's fingers clenched on hers.

"Cleavah. Cleavah's power. It's gone. I can't feel it. This can't be happening again. She told me she would never be out of reach. She told me."

"Vola," Lillie said, her other hand reaching to grasp Vola's arm. "Don't panic. If she told you that, then she meant it."

Sorrel gazed around at the blackened area, then focused on Lillie.

"Cast a spell," she said.

"What?" Lillie's eyes still focused on Vola, who was trying to swallow down the panic climbing up her throat.

"Try casting a spell."

Lillie pulled away from Vola long enough to twitch her fingers and whisper under her breath. But nothing happened. Blood dripped down her hand in silence.

Lillie's eyes widened. "I can't cast," she said. Her breath hitched. "Oh my gods, Sorrel is right." She grabbed Vola's hand and hauled her off the black, back onto the normal sand. Vola stumbled over her feet.

"Now try it," Sorrel said.

Finally catching on to what the other two had already guessed at, Vola reached again for Cleavah's power. A well of burning energy rose at her call.

"Lady bless," she said, placing her hand over the gash in Lillie's palm.

White light flashed between them, and when Lillie drew her hand back, her skin gleamed unmarked in the sun. A mirrored cut stung Vola's palm.

"That's better," Lillie murmured. She snapped her fingers and a little ball of fire appeared on her palm, crackling happily.

Vola blew out her breath, relief pounding through her so hard it gave her a headache.

"It's the spot," Sorrel said, frowning at the black sand beneath her sandals. "It's not just dead…"

"It's devoid of magic," Lillie said, stepping away from Vola.

"But how did it affect us?" Vola said. "I'm pretty sure I'm not magic."

"Spells have to come from somewhere. Some of us study a long time to learn how to use them, but the power comes from somewhere." She gestured around her, her hands fluttering through the air. "Wizards learn how to harness the world's magic for their spells. Inside that circle, there is no magic to harness."

"What about me?" Vola said.

Lillie chewed her lip. "Paladins get their power from the gods, yes? Well, the gods are connected to the world in a very fundamental way. They were the ones who created it. They're the ones who guide it. Without that connection..."

"They're powerless," Vola finished. "And that means so was I."

Vola's shoulders sagged. Sorrel and Lillie exchanged anxious ideas and Rilla interjected sharp questions, but Vola pushed all the sound away and focused inward toward that presence that always hovered just over her shoulder.

"Lady?" she whispered.

"I am here, Vola," the voice said. But it came without the normal rush of acceptance and love. This felt...worried with an edge of the same panic Vola had just felt. "I do not know what this is. And that...is not good."

That was the understatement of the century. Whoever or whatever Cleavah really was, if she didn't know what was going on here, it could only mean trouble of a spectacular sort.

"Someone or something stole the magic out of this section of desert," Rilla said, bringing Vola back to the present. "Enough that spell casters and healers can't even reach their own magic or their gods."

"I didn't even know that was possible," Lillie said quietly, wringing her hands.

"Well, we didn't know stealing magic out of dead people or out of the Thrones was possible either," Sorrel said, face unusually sober. "And Anders was managing that. With help."

Another figure came up over the ridge to stand beside Yevan.

"Talon," Vola called and gave her the signal that it was safe to come down.

Talon slid down the slope, sending a cascade of sand before her.

"Sorry," Vola said. "We weren't sure what was going on so we didn't give the all-clear yet...What's wrong?"

Talon's burned, peeling nose and cheeks had gone white, and she stared at the dead spot.

"Are you all right?" Sorrel asked.

"I've seen this," Talon said, voice cracking on the last word.

"Where?" Rilla moved closer.

"When...my pack died. There were spots like this. The dragon left them."

Lillie shook her head. "It's not a burn—"

"I know it's not a burn," Talon snapped. "Believe me, I know the difference. This is empty. The land no longer speaks to me, as if it's dead."

Lillie pressed her lips together and stared at her boots.

"The dragon used these spots to kill my pack," Talon said. "They were all over the forest where we lived and the pack was gone."

They all looked up, searching the skies for the shape of spreading wings. There was nothing but Rand turning and turning above them.

But off in the distance, little draconic shapes wheeled over the city.

"One of the great ones has woken up," Talon said.

"Wouldn't we have seen one of the big ones if it had been here?" Sorrel said. She raised her hands when Talon rounded on her. "I'm just making sure. It's pretty hard to hide anything in this wasteland. Let alone a big honking scaly thing."

"There are many spells that can be cast at a distance," Lillie said quietly. "And...well, there are dragons nearby. We know they sleep in the Firewall mountains."

"Could a dragon really do this?" Rilla asked. She glanced at Lillie.

Lillie put a hand on her hip. "Why does everyone always look at me when they ask things like that?"

"Probably because you usually have the answer," Sorrel said.

Lillie rolled her eyes. "My mother is the one who studies *draconis maximus*. Not me. I suggest you seek her out."

Rilla straightened her shoulders and strode back toward the dune, where Yevan waited, his eyes wide and worried.

"Let's get moving. We need to get to the city."

"Wait, are you really going to find Lillie's mother?" Sorrel asked as she passed.

Lillie gulped.

"No, I'm going to warn Firewatch that a dragon has woken." Rilla turned on her heel to meet Vola's eyes.

Vola raised her chin. "What do you need from us, princess?" she said, quiet and steady.

"Get the caravan to the city. Finish the job. Then get yourselves fitted for an extended expedition into the mountains. A great dragon waking before its time is a threat to Southglen as well as Firewatch. These things start apocalypses when they're angry. So follow this lead until you get to the end and smash the threat into as many pieces as you can manage."

"Yes, ma'am," Vola said as Sorrel gave her jaunty salute.

"Smashing things is our favorite," the halfling said.

"I'll meet you at our inn as soon as I have anything substantial. Maybe this isn't the first of these spots. Maybe the city already knows about this threat."

"Maybe they have leads we can follow as well," Lillie added.

"Go," Rilla said.

Sorrel scrambled up the dune toward Yevan.

Rilla paused far enough away from the dead spot and yanked her hand through the air, tearing open a portal edged with green and black light. Rilla cast one look back over her shoulder before disappearing into the portal with a whoosh. It snapped closed behind her.

Vola turned to herd the rest of her party up the slope, but Talon stood at the edge of the blackened area, staring at the dark sand.

Vola's gut twisted. This was exactly what the ranger had been worried about. And they'd walked right into it. Now, her new pack was in the exact same danger as her old one.

Vola reached to touch her shoulder, but Talon turned to trudge after Sorrel and Yevan, too absorbed in her thoughts to notice.

Vola dropped her hand.

Lillie limped forward to stand at Vola's shoulder, and they watched Talon walk away together.

"Is she going to be all right?" Lillie asked.

Vola didn't answer. Talon insisted she wasn't still affected by her grief and turmoil. But this had to change things. This had to bring back more bad memories. It had to feel like history repeating itself.

"You know that this follows Anders's pattern," Lillie said quietly. "Right?"

Vola's lips tightened. "Are you saying you don't believe her?"

"Of course, I believe her," Lillie said. "But...what if they're connected?"

"Are you saying Anders could be controlling the dragons?"

"I'm not sure what I'm saying yet. I just don't want to be the only one thinking of the possibility."

Vola blew out her breath and pushed her sweaty hair back from her forehead. "Then we're going after the man who was responsible for the death of Talon's pack. I don't think that changes anything. Do you?"

"It makes me angrier."

"Ah." Vola turned to head back toward the dune. "Remind me to point you in the right direction and stay out of your way, then."

Lillie flashed her a smile before they started climbing. Creaks from the wagons and the sounds of whips and curses came floating to them over the ridgeline. Sorrel had obviously gotten Yevan back to the caravan and gotten them underway again. A joke and a smile from Sorrel could move mountains. Which was why Vola counted on her as her second.

"I forgot how disconcerting it is to see Rilla worried," Lillie said, puffing to the top of the dune.

"I'm not sure we've ever seen her really thrown before," Vola said. "Even when she was cut off from her Throne, it made her more angry than anything."

"Forgive me if I'd like to keep her from getting angry again. She tends to stab things," Lillie said.

"I mean, so do we. If we're honest."

FOUR

THEY DIDN'T ENCOUNTER any more trouble on the way into Firewatch. Nor did they see any more dead spots along the road.

The paved path led all the way through the rocky foothills, up into the narrow, jagged valley of Firewatch. There was no gate and no wall. Without a national government to answer to, there was no reason to keep people out. This was a city made for refugees, a city built to escape into. And with the surrounding peaks inhabited by dragons, no one had ever been brave enough to try invading. The little ones breathed fire and flew, dive-bombing their enemies, but the big ones could level armies in a single stoop.

The caravan made its way along crowded narrow streets to park outside a bazaar tucked up under a rocky overhang. There was more shade here with the buildings blocking a lot of the sun but the air hung heavy between the walls, cut off from the breezes across the open desert.

Vola and the others said goodbye to the merchants there. Gregor pressed a hefty bonus into Vola's palm before they left, telling them they had a job with him any time they wanted. Vola still wasn't sure if he'd guessed that Rilla was a princess, and she wasn't about to point it out.

Rand, Lillie's familiar, had left them near the entrance to the city, flapping off to find Rilla. An hour after they arrived, he returned with a message.

"Change of plans. I'm ass-deep in negotiations up here. They didn't even want to let me into the city, bastards. Get up to the council rooms prepared to argue."

At the bottom of the page was an address.

Vola and the others glanced up at the city looming above them. It was a mishmash of pieces salvaged and looted from wagons, land barges, and carriages. Stone from distant lands, pilfered and transported across the desert. Elegant golden domes sat next to rickety towers where dragons had tried to add to the eclectic mix and ended up with something more cluttered than Vola's parents' attic.

"How are we going to find it in all of that?" Sorrel said.

"Was there a map somewhere that we missed?" Talon said.

Vola glanced around, looking for signposts, but all she saw were hundreds of people going about their lives. Carrying produce, hurrying to and from the bazaar booths, gossiping in corners.

Every now and then, a large, horse-sized dragon flew overhead, but no one seemed to pay any more attention to them than you would to say a horse.

Throughout the bazaar flitted little dragons about the size of Rand. The familiar eyed them suspiciously. The swamp beast tried to snatch one out of the air to snack on. The little green dragon trilled and stuck out its tongue before darting away through the crowd.

Vola frowned at it. "I didn't realize there were tiny ones, too."

"I don't remember reading about them along with their larger cousins," Lillie said, holding her hand up to entice one closer. It hummed as it hovered, then dodged away. "Maybe they were bred more as pets."

Vola watched carefully as a nearby group of women lured one of the little dragons in with a piece of meat. When they let it go again, it hovered before them as they followed, going slow enough so that they could keep up.

"Or as local guides," Talon said.

"Rand," Vola said. "Could you catch one and bring it here?"

The raven ruffled his feathers, then launched himself into the air. Gruff watched, and Vola could almost imagine an envious gleam in his eye. The familiar had been a gift to Lillie just a few weeks ago, but he'd already made himself invaluable, as much a member of the party as Gruff was or the swamp beast.

The swamp beast eyed Rand, but its look was much more speculative and hungrier.

Okay, not like the swamp beast.

The familiar circled above, then dove on one of the little dragons. They collided with a squawk. His momentum carried them to the ground at their feet.

Vola swooped in and grabbed the little dragon as Rand extricated himself. And she held up a strip of dried meat from her pack.

"Can you take us to the council rooms?" she said, then read off the address.

The little bronze-colored creature cocked its head and eyed them with a slitted golden pupil. Then it snatched the meat and its wings whirred. Vola let go, and the creature sprang into the air and zipped away over the crowd.

"What if it leads us off a cliff?" Sorrel said, but Vola was already moving. She pushed through the bazaar shoppers, keeping the swamp beast on a tight leash behind her. They'd learned well enough that it did *not* pay to lose track of the swamp monster in an unfamiliar city. That's how it ended up living in sewers, terrorizing the populace from beneath their feet.

The little dragon led them up through the patchwork city, through narrow alleys made from recycled wood, and up big thoroughfares of solid stone. They crossed the valley on a small but serviceable bridge and ended up on the other mountainside.

Their guide stopped outside one of the big white-washed towers with a gold dome. It trilled, then zipped away, its wings whirring too fast to see.

Sorrel squinted at the sign out front and then up at the disappearing dragon. "What do you know; it worked."

Vola tied the swamp beast to a railing she assumed was a hitching post and glared it into submission. "Don't eat anyone," she said as the others filed through the ornate door.

The swamp beast narrowed its eyes and snorted, spitting a wad of yellow mucus onto Vola's breastplate. It sizzled.

She just sighed and scrubbed it off with a spare polishing cloth she kept in her back pocket. It paid to be prepared when traveling with a walking snot factory.

Inside the tower, the others had paused to wait for her. Or to admire their surroundings, one of the two. Vola wouldn't be insulted if it was the latter.

The round reception hall could have fit their entire caravan, and it was paved in a mosaic of colored stone and glass gathered from all over the world. She recognized a bit of blue stone from the quarries near her home and something green she was sure she'd seen on the tor in the swamp near Water's Edge.

Two staircases rose before them, hugging the walls so they curved around and met in the middle of the opposite wall, where a door hung slightly ajar.

A voice floated from that second story opening.

"What do you mean, am I sure? Of course, I'm damn sure. I came all this way up here to argue about it with you. Do you think I'm enjoying myself…Well, screw that. I don't have to cater to your bloody insecurities."

Vola exchanged a glance with Lillie as Rilla stormed through the door above them and stomped down the steps.

Lillie cleared her throat delicately. "Trouble?"

"This level of stupidity is astounding. We have a real problem heading this way, and all the council can do is worry that a princess of Southglen is trying to steal their authority."

Sorrel tilted her head. "Are you trying to steal it?"

"Trust me, it's not worth stealing," Rilla growled. "They can do whatever the hell they want on top of this cute little city they've built. I don't care. What I care about is that there's a dragon out there with the power to suck magic out of the earth itself. But I'm so wrapped up in the local bureaucracy they haven't even acknowledged the threat creeping up on them."

She paced to the foot of the left staircase, then spun on her heel and paced to the foot of the right, her boots clicking against the colored stones.

"I thought it was their job to keep the dragons from waking up," Vola said with a glance at Lillie. "Isn't that what they're so worried about?"

"Yeah," Rilla said. "But they've been doing it for so long that they think they know everything there is to know about sleeping dragons. There's no proof, they said. Nothing to show that a dragon has woken. And by insinuating that one has, I insulted them and their sacred duty."

Vola winced. She could imagine Rilla insulting a lot of people in the course of her job. The princess could be subtle when she wished, but clearly, she did not wish right now.

"Proof?" Talon's voice grated even more than it usually did. "They want proof."

Rilla stopped pacing and faced the ranger. "I'm sorry," she said quietly. "A dead wolf pack however many years ago and miles away won't convince them."

Talon stiffened. "Unfortunately, a dead pack is all I have to offer. What the hell else can I say or do to make them believe me?"

"I believe you," a voice said. A dwarf stepped through the door above them and closed it softly behind him. Squat and round, he would only come up to Vola's belly button in his bare feet. His shoulder-length dark hair was caught in a tail at the nape of his neck and he jingled in a fortune of custom chainmail and leather as he descended the stairs.

"I heard your arguments," he said as he came even with them. "And I believe you."

Rilla's eyes narrowed on the dwarf. "I don't remember you in there."

"I'm not a councilor. I was watching from the gallery. Fedor Gerrickson," he said, thrusting his hand out to Rilla. "Captain of the city militia and professional dragon hunter."

Rilla shook it, keeping her hesitance at an acceptable level.

The dwarf turned to Talon and jerked his chin up to meet her eyes. "You've got a personal stake in this."

"I've seen it before," Talon said. "A dragon killed my family."

"And did you kill it right back?" Fedor asked, eyes boring into her.

The corner of Talon's mouth twitched. "I did. With help."

Fedor waved a hand. "Then you're practically a professional, too."

"I wouldn't have guessed there'd be much call for dragon hunters," Lillie said, clasping her hands in front of her. "Considering the *draconis maximus* are supposed to remain sleeping."

"Yeah, but they don't always, do they?" Fedor said sharply. He gestured to Talon. "Accidents happen and the big beasts have to be put down for the sake of the world. And I have no problem occupying myself in between. After taking one of the big ones down, things like the little horse-sized ones and bears and minotaurs are easy."

"True," Vola said. But she kept her eye on Talon. She didn't look like she'd met a kindred spirit. Mostly, she looked worried.

Fedor took a step closer to Talon. "I know what it's like," he said. "To have everything you love wiped out by something that barely sees you as an ant. That's why I'm here. One day, I'll convince the council that we need to burn out the problem at its source. We need to strike the beasts where they lay and kill them before they rise."

Talon took in a sharp breath while Lillie blinked.

"All of them?" the wizard said.

"'Course. It's the only way to be safe," Fedor said.

Talon's mouth drew tight. "Attacking them for no reason would just wake them up earlier and put more people at risk."

"Not if we do it right. It's called nipping the problem in the bud."

"It's called murder," Sorrel said, cocking her head.

"Do you murder a bear or a boar that's gone savage?" Fedor said. "Or do you slaughter it? *You* understand." He met Talon's eyes.

Talon grimaced. Then she opened her mouth but hesitated.

"Killing them before they threaten everything is the only way to keep everyone safe," Fedor said. "They're much more dangerous once they're awake."

"Which is why we have to deal with this one before it does any more damage," Rilla said, making Talon jump.

The ranger backed up a step, her brow coming down. "She's right. There's one awake right now. We can't deal with a sleeping threat until we deal with the threat that's already here."

Fedor shrugged. "Fine with me. I enjoy killing them either way. Revenge is sweetest when it's shared. Am I right?"

He bumped his shoulder into Talon's elbow making her stagger.

Talon, who didn't like physical contact at the best of times, lifted her lip. Gruff rose from his spot by the door and slunk between them, neatly putting himself in Fedor's way.

Fedor frowned down at the wolf.

"What do you suggest?" Vola said, drawing his attention away from the ranger and her companion. "Since you're the professional."

"Find proof," he said. "Something that will convince the council that you know what you're talking about."

"An expert opinion might sway them." Lillie tapped her lip, eyes distant. "This is where the experts on dragons gather, anyway. They must respect them and their results."

Fedor made a face. "I was thinking find the dragon and show the council the danger. Personally. But yeah sure. Experts. That works, too. There's a monk at the All-Pantheon temple who might be able to help. A Master Bao. He was asking me about where the dragons roost. Maybe he's got something up his sleeve."

"Master Bao?" Sorrel cried. "My Master Bao?"

"I didn't know you had a Master Bao," Talon said.

Fedor squinted at the halfling. "He was dressed a lot like you. Claimed he was from one of Maxim's monasteries."

"That's him, then," Sorrel said.

Vola tilted her head. "Why would one of your masters be all the way out here, looking for dragons?"

"Obviously, that will be the first thing I ask when we talk to him."

"Obviously," Vola said.

"What are you going to be doing?" Talon asked Fedor.

"I have my eye on several dragon lairs around Firewatch," he said. "And associates posted up and down the mountain range. I'm going to check to see if any of them are suddenly empty."

A solid plan. "Good luck," Vola said.

Fedor gave them a jaunty salute and headed for the door, his mail jingling with every step.

"An interesting character," Lillie said, as he disappeared out the door.

Rilla crossed her arms. "He might have been disparaging of it, but I liked your idea of experts. Did you have anyone in mind?"

Lillie flushed. "Sort of. I mean, my mother. She's supposed to be around here somewhere, studying dragons."

"Perfect place to start then."

"Are you sure that's a good idea?" Vola asked.

"Why not?" Lillie asked, shoulders going back. "She's...she's family. And she knows what she's talking about, presumably. And...well, it might be nice to meet her."

Vola's brow drew down, reading a lot more into the pauses than what Lillie was saying. The woman had left the Ephyra family after Lillie was born, having completed her side of the marriage contract. Vola didn't see the worth in a woman who saw a family and children as a contract, but also, she'd gotten to grow up with her own mother. She could see how it would be different for someone who hadn't.

"Do it, then," Rilla said. "You're better able to ask questions than I am, right now." She pinned Lillie with her glance. "And I trust you not to let anything personal get in the way."

Lillie raised her chin. "Of course, Your Highness."

"I'm gonna swear at the wall some more. It'll be good practice for when they let me back in the council chambers."

"You're going back in?" Vola asked.

"I have to get them to admit there's even a problem. Meanwhile, you're going to have to be my eyes and ears and hands."

"Will they let us do our job?" Talon asked. "If they don't like you, why would they like us?"

"I don't think anyone here knows you work for Southglen. Unless the caravan spreads it around."

"I'm not sure Gregor ever guessed you were a princess," Lillie said.

"Probably hasn't met any," Vola said.

"Especially not ones that swear so much," Talon muttered.

FIVE

When Rilla had hired them back in Brisbene, she'd promised them room and board, as well as their salary, and she hadn't disappointed them yet. The hotel in Firewatch wasn't as fancy as the one in Glenhaven, but it was clean and there was actually room service.

Although Rilla's parting words as she left the next morning were, "Have fun, but stay away from the eggs."

"I think I should have listened to her," Sorrel groaned as she and Vola made their way through the winding paths of the city toward the All-Pantheon temple. It stood beside a House of the Broken, a healing center dedicated to the Greater Virtue of Righteousness.

"I don't know why you didn't. The rest of us did," Vola said.

"It was clearly a challenge." Sorrel rubbed her stomach. "You can't just let a challenge like that go."

"It was clearly a warning." Vola squinted up at the facade which comprised three different architecture styles, each story representing a different culture and technique. It was probably supposed to mean something like unity and togetherness, but mostly it came out looking like a badly done puzzle. "So, you seemed pretty excited about this Master Bao."

"He was my fighting master."

"And he treated you okay?" Vola asked, knowing the answer might not be yes. The rest of the monks hadn't been particularly good to Sorrel.

Sorrel grinned, her gaze going distant with memory. "He refused to train me at first. Said I was too small."

"That doesn't sound very nice."

Sorrel grinned. "Well, I was four. But I climbed to the roof where I could see them in the yard and mimicked everything he did until he finally agreed. I was his favorite after that."

They stepped up through the wide archway of mismatched plaster. There wasn't even a door. Just an open portal into the dark interior.

They'd decided that morning to split up. Sorrel had obviously wanted to track down Master Bao while Lillie had to find her mother's address at the city's registry before she had a hope of talking to her.

Talon and Vola had exchanged a wordless look and they split as well, Vola to watch Sorrel's back and Talon to watch Lillie's.

Vola might have had an ulterior motive for following Sorrel to the temple. She could talk to Cleavah anywhere, true, but some conversations just felt better in a place of worship.

The space inside was cool and dim. Only a few worshipers stood beneath the arranged statues to pray. The Greater Virtues all stood lined up under the steep roof while little altars to the Lesser Virtues and Obstacles lay at their feet.

"I'm going to find an acolyte," Sorrel said. The staff across her back sizzled and lightning crackled over its surface, lighting up the statue of Maxim for a moment. "Maybe one of them will know…huh."

"Huh, what?"

"Well, I was going to say maybe one of them will know where Master Bao is, but he's right there."

An ancient human with skin as dark and dry as the desert outside ambled around the statue of Ona, Greater Virtue of Honor. He wore a gray wrap-around tunic just like Sorrel's, and his stark white beard had been pulled together into a long braid.

"Master Bao," Sorrel said, her voice carrying up the walls. She raced to the old man.

As she drew even with him, he stuck one foot between her legs and twisted her over his hip to send her flying across the floor.

Vola cried out and rushed forward, drawing her sword, but Sorrel hit the ground rolling and bounced upright with a grin.

"Just checking your reflexes." Master Bao's voice scraped like leather across the stone, but his lively eyes glinted.

"They're as good as you made them," Sorrel said, stepping back to them. This time Master Bao didn't throw her.

He tsked. "That is not the compliment you mean it to be. They should be better by now. You should have made them better yourself."

Sorrel rolled her eyes. "Master Bao, I thought you'd be back at the monastery, making sure Hazel didn't make any mistakes in her first year as abbess."

"Hazel is doing fine. You were wise to pick her." His eyes flicked to the staff across Sorrel's back, and Vola had a feeling he knew it was the real thing while Hazel had gone home with a replica. "She can do without me. Indefinitely."

Sorrel's brow drew down. "What does that mean? What are you doing in Firewatch?"

His mouth twisted in a self-deprecating grin. "I'm retiring, Sorrel."

Sorrel's eyes went wide, and she sucked in a breath. "No."

Vola's gaze flicked between the two of them. Retiring didn't sound that bad, but from Sorrel's expression, she must be missing something.

"Congratulations?" Vola said.

Sorrel shook her head. "You can't," she cried. "Master Bao, you're not done."

"I am, little one. I have taught many. I have lived years beyond my normal life, thanks to Maxim. I have seen much of this world. And now I'm ready to meditate with my god."

"That actually sounds rather peaceful," Vola told Sorrel.

"You don't get it. When a monk retires, they don't just not work or fight anymore. What it means is they go off into the wilderness to 'meditate.' Forever. No food, no water."

"Until we return to the earth we were born from," Master Bao said.

Sorrel jerked her chin up. "Until they die of starvation and exposure, you mean."

"It is my choice, Sorrel." A bit of steel came into Master Bao's voice.

"Well, it's a stupid one. Some dragon hunter up the hill said you were looking for dragons. I thought you were going to fight one or something."

"I am done fighting. Maxim was once considered the brother of dragons along with the other Virtues. I wanted to spend my final days meditating in a place closer to him."

Vola winced. Personally, she didn't think it would matter all that much where Master Bao chose to do his dying. Maxim hadn't proved he cared.

But it was still Master Bao's choice.

"I'm not letting you do this," Sorrel said.

Vola put her hand on the halfling's shoulder. "Sorrel."

Sorrel shrugged it off. "No. He still has so much left to do in the world."

"Like what?" Master Bao said, more gently than Vola would have.

Sorrel's mouth worked, but she couldn't seem to come up with anything.

Master Bao stepped around them, heading for the door.

"Like helping us with this dragon," Sorrel said, going after him. "A big one is out there, causing trouble."

"And you are the best ones to take care of it." He paused and met her eyes. "I made sure of it."

Master Bao walked out the door empty-handed. He didn't take any supplies or a weapon. He didn't need to.

A range of expressions flickered across Sorrel's face, making her eyebrows twitch and lower and her mouth pinch.

She took a deep shuddering breath and cast a glance up at Vola. "This isn't over. I'm not done arguing. Wait here." And she followed Master Bao out of the temple.

Vola took a step and then shook her head. She wasn't going to be any use in the conversation. She could see both sides, but she didn't have a reason to argue for Sorrel. The halfling argued well enough on her own. And Master Bao was fully capable of making his own decisions. And defending them.

And the thing Sorrel might be too upset to think of yet was that it took a while for someone to die of starvation and exposure. Especially someone who'd spent a lifetime making their body into a weapon the way Master Bao had. They still had time to change his mind.

Vola moved closer to the statues, gazing up at the still marble faces of the gods. As usual in an all-pantheon temple, the Greater Virtues had their statues arrayed around the far wall, towering over the little alcoves where the Lesser Virtues had their altars. There were fifteen. Fifteen Greater Virtues who carried the righteous traits of the world. Gods like Ona, who carried a scale and represented honor. Bierhel, who posed with her arms up in dance, representing joy and honesty. And Maxim, who stood fist to his heart, representing strength and loyalty. His stony face didn't seem to care that Master Bao was heading off to "commune" with a distant god who never answered.

At the end of the line stood the Broken, a scarred woman missing an arm and most of her left leg. Flames climbed behind her like fiery wings.

Vola stood in front of the Greater Virtues, surveying the alcoves at their feet. Somewhere down there, among hundreds of others, there would be an altar to Cleavah. Lesser Virtue of Vengeful Housewives. Mother of sharp implements. A mystery who was more than what she seemed.

The air moved as if someone stepped up to stand behind Vola's shoulder, and she breathed in deep. The scent of warm bread, fresh-cut grass, and the salt breeze from the sea washed over her even here in the desert.

"My lady," Vola said without turning around.

"My knight," Cleavah said in a voice that sounded like bells in the wind.

Vola's fingers twitched, and she just kept herself from touching the shield on her back in response, pride swelling through her. Standing here in the temple with the statues of the Greater Virtues in front of her, it was so tempting to try to match the voice with a face. She knew what Cleavah looked like. As the goddess of vengeful housewives, her altar lay beneath the Greater Virtues' feet. But she belonged up there, standing shoulder to shoulder with Maxim, Bierhel, Ona, and the Broken. Didn't she?

"Do you know all of them?" Vola asked instead of the question she really wanted to ask. She raised her other hand to gesture to the statues. "The Greater Virtues?"

Cleavah hesitated before answering. "Very well," she finally said. "Bierhel might be my favorite. She always knows a good joke. Maxim… well, he's a good man, but a bit dour."

Vola took a deep breath and turned. Cleavah stood in the dim temple, her golden skin glowing slightly, her long curling hair moving as if in an unseen breeze. Just as she'd always looked. She didn't look like she had the power to reach through all the rules and regulations to touch Vola.

"My lady, what happened in the desert? In that dead spot? You told me you could never be taken away from me as long as I reached out for you."

Cleavah's mouth drew tight and her eyes pinched. "I was not taken from you, Vola. But there is something in the desert that is able to steal power out of the world. And a god's power is directly tied to the world. Without that connection…" She spread her hands. "We are left in the dark. When you stepped into the dead space, nothing connected me to you anymore. Nothing connected me to that part of the world."

Vola gulped. "That's possible?"

"It shouldn't be," Cleavah said, her voice growing firm. "It never has been before. But this…this could be something new. It *is* new. And the world has been toppled by new things before."

"What about something that's very, very old but doing a new thing?"

Cleavah tipped her head in question.

"Could it be one of the dragons? They start apocalypses apparently."

Cleavah's lips thinned. "Perhaps. The dragons were there when the gods made the world. They are like siblings. And all siblings squabble."

"So they could be powerful enough."

"All together, yes. But something would have to wake them first."

"One might already be awake."

"I did not know that." Cleavah tapped her lips. "Siblings don't always talk to each other." Her eyes strayed to the statues of the Greater Virtues.

Vola opened her mouth to ask. She was going to do it. Three little words. Who are you?

The shush of sandals grabbed her attention. Sorrel strode across the quiet temple. Her staff sizzled as she passed Maxim's statue again. A bruise was forming under one eye and her clothes shed sand. "Well, he threw me across the street and disappeared, so I guess the argument's over. Hiya, Cleavah."

"Hello, Sorrel." Cleavah waited a beat longer, giving Vola time to ask.

She didn't.

She just watched as Cleavah turned and stepped into the shadows of the temple, heading for the door. Vola's eyes tracked her movement, but by the time she reached the sunlight outside, she was gone.

"Don't worry about Master Bao," Vola said as they exited the temple. There was no sign of Cleavah or the ancient monk outside on the street. "We have a little time. We can still track him down."

Sorrel trudged down the steps, her head down as if thinking.

A raven cawed, and Vola lifted her chin to find Rand perched on the railing opposite them. He flapped up over the crowd in the street and landed on Vola's shoulder.

She lifted her hand, and the raven dropped a note into her palm.

"Did Lillie and Talon find her mom?" Sorrel asked, not looking up.

"She works at the field museum, apparently," Vola said, squinting at the small page. Lillie always made sure to write her letters big and blocky so Vola could read them without them crawling all over the page. "They're headed there now."

Sorrel rolled her shoulders and cracked her neck. "Enough moping, then. Let's go meet them. Hopefully, Lillie's mom will have a better idea where to look for the dragon."

They followed Rand as he swooped over the heads of the crowd and led them nearly to the top of one of the peaks.

The museum itself was built overlooking the city from a rocky crag.

Wide windows glinted in the sunlight and reflected the other side of the city climbing up the mountain opposite them.

Lillie and Talon stood on the steps leading up the last few hundred feet. Lillie's mouth hung open.

"It looks like a ship, doesn't it? Like the cabin of a ship. How did they get it up here?"

Vola squinted at the museum, which did resemble the back end of a ship sticking out over the empty space at the edge of the rock. The building beyond was quite a bit larger but obviously made up of pieces of other vessels and structures.

"Magic," she said.

Lillie spluttered and limped up the steps to the front door. "Of course, it was magic. I meant more specifically. We're miles from any bodies of water. The amount of power and energy it would take to transport this across the desert…"

Lillie continued babbling to herself as they pushed through the doors and stepped into the cool quiet of the museum.

Vola's eyes widened as they adjusted to the dim light inside. Strung across the wide hall was the lithe, shiny skeleton of a dragon. One of the *draconis minimus*, otherwise it would never have fit inside. But it was still larger than any of the other dragons Vola had seen flitting around the city so far. Along the walls stretched murals of dragons in their natural habitats.

The museum seemed dedicated to draconic natural history, but a few other species made appearances here and there. A manticore's stinger sat on a pedestal before a painting depicting the angry beast. And on their left, a tooth from an earth giant rested against the wall, nearly as tall as Vola.

"Huh," Sorrel said, hands on hips as she gazed around. "Maybe we can sell them the swamp beast. It would feel right at home here, I think."

"I agree," Talon said. "I can see it fitting right there." She held up her hands to frame a bare patch of wall across from them. "Stuffed, preferably."

"They'd have to kill it first," Vola muttered. "Which is more than we've managed."

Sorrel cocked her head as several well-dressed patrons passed, ogling the displays. "Who do you suppose is in charge?" she said. "None of these look like they work here."

"Are you looking for someone in particular?" a voice said, accompanied by a slithery, serpentine noise. Like scales on stone.

Vola turned to catch the speaker and found herself face to face with one of the small dragons. This one was red and gold with its wings folded tightly to its back so it didn't knock anything over. It sat on its haunches, waiting.

Vola's eyes narrowed. She hadn't seen that many dragons this close yet, but this one seemed sort of familiar. Its coloring would gleam as bright as flames under a clear sky.

"Hurren," Lillie said, quicker than Vola to place the dragon.

"Mishap's Heroes," the dragon said, the crest above her eyes raised in what looked like surprise. "Well, hi."

"Oh, now I remember," Sorrel said. "You were bouncing for Fang in Brisbene last we saw you."

"And you kicked my tail," Hurren said with a light laugh that didn't seem at all resentful. The dragon purred deep in her throat. "That was fun."

"What are you doing here?" Lillie said.

"Working," she said. "I retired from pit fighting a couple of months ago. There's only so many adventurers you can bop on the head before you get tired of it and go home."

"So, you got a job at the museum?" Lillie said, perking up. "I had no idea you were so interested in history."

The dragon shrugged, her gold scales glittering. "I mostly carry things. And answer the really stupid questions tourists have about dragons. Like 'are you sure you don't want to eat me?' and 'where's the toilet?'"

"Speaking of toilets…" Sorrel grimaced and rubbed her stomach.

"Out of order for the day, unfortunately," Hurren said.

Sorrel sagged. "Figures."

"Rilla told us not to eat the eggs," Talon muttered.

"You don't mind working beside…er, a blatant display of draconic mortality?" Lillie's eyes flicked to the skeleton hanging in the center of the room.

Hurren followed her gaze. "What? Brocker? No, he was a dick. He deserved to be strung up for display. About the only thing nice about him was his bones." The dragon batted her eyes at Lillie. "Unlike you."

Lillie flushed.

"Still casting that net pretty wide, huh?" Vola said.

"Hey, dragons like pretty things," Hurren purred. Her gaze flicked from Lillie to Vola. "And I have a broad definition of pretty."

"Yeah, yeah, keep it in your pants," Sorrel said, rolling her eyes. "We know we're beautiful. But we're not interested in being collected. We have our own questions."

Hurren sighed and settled back on her haunches. "Let me know if you ever change your minds. What would you like to know?"

"We're looking for an elf named Shereille. She works here." Her words were a statement, but her voice rose at the end, betraying her nerves.

"Oh, Shereille." Hurren rolled her eyes. "Yeah, sure. Everyone here at the museum knows Shereille. She's one of our lead researchers."

Lillie's eyes fluttered, and she looked simultaneously terrified and exalted. "Oh. Oh, is she here?" Her gaze flicked around the hall. But all Vola could see were the tourists gathered around the manticore stinger, reading the plaque.

Hurren shook her head, and Lillie's shoulders slumped.

"She's out with her team. Isn't due back for a couple of weeks." Hurren cocked her red and gold head. "I can give you a map, if you'd like. She wouldn't be that hard to find since she studies Listrell—the dragon closest to the city."

Vola glanced at Lillie for an answer.

Lillie pressed her lips together and nodded. "Yes, please. We need to talk to her. Unless...Hurren, if one of the *draconis maximus* had woken, would you be aware?"

Hurren snorted. "Gods, yes."

"You have a connection?" Talon asked. "Because you're all dragons?"

"Nothing as complicated as that. Everyone would know. The world would know. The big guys are noisy, and if one woke up early, it would be angry. Believe me. Everyone would know."

Talon took a deep breath through her nose.

Vola gave her a look. "It's not proof either way. We still need to find an expert."

Lillie squared her shoulders. "Yes. I think we'll need that map, Hurren."

SIX

HURREN WASN'T WRONG. Shereille's campsite might have been well up into the mountains that flanked Firewatch, but there was a broad path leading through the rocky crags and jagged bluffs. The morning sun beat down on Vola's head, making her regret the choice to wear the full armor of her calling.

"Well, it is a desert," Sorrel said, pausing at a bend in the path to shield her eyes and survey the view. She wasn't even panting in her loose linen tunic and trousers. Although she was shifting from foot to foot and holding her stomach.

Talon had pulled her hood low over her face to protect her fair skin. The end of her nose was already peeling from their long trek across the sands the last few days.

At least they'd left the swamp monster stabled back in the city, with Gruff standing guard to make sure it didn't eat anything important.

Lillie's red face glistened, and she stopped to swipe at her forehead with a damp handkerchief. "This is...really quite...oh, I can't even come up with words for how hot it is. Are you all right?"

Vola stopped and rested her hands on her knees to concentrate on breathing. "I think I could double as an oven, right now. There's enough sweat under this breastplate to drown a horse."

Raven swooped over them, cawing.

Lillie shaded her face. "It's just around the bend, he says. There's a camp and people and shade."

"Woohoo." Sorrel scampered up the trail after him. "I hope they have a bathroom."

Talon picked up her pace, too.

Vola started to follow but noticed Lillie hesitate. She turned, ready to offer a hand. The wizard didn't draw attention to her limp very often, but it had to be bothering her going up these hills and avoiding the rocks and gravel.

But Lillie stared up the path, teeth chewing her bottom lip.

"You can make it," Vola told her quietly.

"That's not what I'm afraid of," Lillie said. She met Vola's eyes. "I…I haven't actually met my mother, Vola. She left when I was barely a week old. Is it really childish to say I hope she likes me?"

Vola snorted. "Not at all. You want to make her proud."

Lillie rolled her eyes. "That doesn't make me sound like any more of an adult."

"No. You're right. It makes you sound like a child. But you are her child. No matter how grown-up you are, you will always be her child."

Lillie's lips pulled into a slow, sweet smile. "Yes. Yes, of course. Thank you, Vola. You always manage to put things into perspective. She is my mother and always will be and that counts for a lot." Lillie gathered herself and climbed the path past Vola.

Vola frowned. Wanting to impress a parent made absolute sense. But she hoped Lillie didn't think that impressing her would magically make Shereille into a better mother than she had been.

Vola brought up the rear in case Lillie slipped in the gravel that lined the path. The jagged spires of rock gave way to a little hidden valley between the peaks. Here the sloping mountains flattened out a bit, leaving a broad smooth area large enough for several tents that looked semi-permanent and about a dozen sturdy tables. Crates and baskets of supplies sat in neat stacks between the tents.

There were at least twenty humans and elves dressed in dusty shirts and trousers striding purposely around the campsite. A few leaned over the tables, notes spread before them. A couple manned the cookpot over a central fire-pit, while others checked the supplies, taking notes.

They looked a little surprised to see them appear from the path, but no one seemed ready to kick them out, either.

Sorrel clasped her hands over her heart. "Look. Latrines."

"You're leaving now?" Talon asked as Sorrel started for the line of little tents big enough to hold one person standing up. "What if Lillie needs your moral support?"

Vola was pretty sure Talon was just messing with Sorrel, but the halfling glanced between the latrines and Lillie.

"Oh, all right. I suppose it's not an emergency. Yet." She stopped the first person to pass within shouting distance. "Where can we find Shereille?"

The woman tucked her hair behind her ear and jerked her head toward the large tent at the back of the campsite. It backed up against the nearest peak, and a steady glow shone from the open flap.

Definitely not hard to find. Probably because Lillie's mother wasn't really hiding. She was just living a life free of any kind of familial obligation.

Sorrel trotted forward without hesitation. Lillie stumbled after her.

The tent at the far end of the camp had been erected atop a wood platform, as if the researchers expected to be in one place for a while. Through the flap, Vola glimpsed several full bookshelves, a neatly made cot, and a desk dominating the center.

A tall, slim figure with blonde hair tied up in a no-nonsense bun leaned over the desk.

"Aster, I'm going to need another wizard light in a few hours. Would you be so good as to have one ready when this one gives up?" a lyrical voice said.

Vola glanced at Lillie, but she seemed frozen, her foot just hovering over the step up to the platform.

Well, introductions weren't going to happen any time soon. At least not without help.

Vola cleared her throat and stepped up, her boots clanking against the boards. "Shereille Moonhallowed?"

The woman straightened and turned. "Oh, you're not Aster. I'm so sorry. What can I do for you?" She tilted her head, revealing sharply pointed ears, and smoothed her hands down her front as if she wore a court gown and not a pair of dusty overalls and a stained apron.

"Er," Vola said and glanced at Lillie, waiting for the wizard to take over. Nothing. "I'm Volagra Lightless. Paladin. We're here investigating some disturbances with the dragons. We came to find you because...well, you're the expert. But also, um, Lillie? You want to help me out here?"

Lillie shook her head, like breaking free of a reverie, and took the step up into the tent. "Yes," she said softly. "Um, hello. It's lovely to meet you finally. I'm—my name is Lilliara Ephyra."

The woman blinked. "Ephyra. As in Lord Ephyra. Of Glenhaven?"

"Yes."

Sorrel rolled her eyes and bounced forward. "Yes, Ephyra. Miss Shereille, meet your daughter. Daughter..." She gestured to Lillie. "Meet your mom."

Well, Sorrel hadn't made it any *more* awkward.

Shereille's eyes flickered over Lillie's form, her face, her hair, and eyes. Vola couldn't help comparing as well. Lillie had gotten her stature and a lot of her features from her father. But her hair and eyes, those came directly from the woman standing before them.

"Oh," Shereille said on an escaped breath. "Lilliara." Finally, she beamed. "Welcome. I'm glad to have finally met you."

But she didn't immediately step forward and sweep Lillie into a hug. Vola couldn't tell if Lillie was glad or not.

"You've grown," Shereille said. "You were so tiny when I left."

"That is what babies do," Lillie said with a twitchy little smile.

"I suppose so." Shereille tilted her head. "Elves take much longer to mature. That must be the human part of you. I guess I remember that from your brothers. They were a bit older. I got to know them so I might even recognize them now."

Lille bit her lip hard enough to turn it white, and Vola could tell she wanted to ask why she didn't stay to get to know her daughter, too. But she didn't.

"What do you do with yourself now?" Shereille said as if searching for something to talk about.

"I'm a wizard," Lillie said. "I went to the university in Glenhaven."

Shereille brightened. "Oh. A researcher?"

"Er, no. I took a more practical route." Lillie glanced at Vola and the others. "I help solve problems."

Vola nodded. "Not a bad way to put it."

"Oh, well that's useful, too, I suppose," Shereille said. "I remember your father being very studious. He surely instilled a curiosity and love of learning early. I would never have signed the contract otherwise."

"Are contracts like that common among elves?" Sorrel said, leaning on her staff. Her eyes kept flickering to the latrines.

"Common enough," Shereille said. "Marriage among our own kind is similar to the other races, but we live so much longer than humans, it's hardly practical to find a life mate so young. Especially not one of another species." She paused with a small smile. "Still, Ephyra was nice enough. And we had lots in common so we had plenty to talk about while under contract. It passed the time pleasantly."

"That's...good?" Sorrel said.

"Oh, yes. It's rather dull when your partner can only provide excitement in bed."

Lillie let out a little squeak. "That's all right. That's not something we have to talk about."

Vola bit down a smile. "No, I get it." She turned to Shereille. "It is much nicer when you can rely on someone's wit as well as their...prowess."

"Yes," Shereille said brightly. "Ephyra wasn't as robust as some, but what he lacked in stamina he made up for in enthusiasm."

"Stop talking," Lillie hissed at Vola.

Vola leaned toward Sorrel. "You're right. This is much more fun when it's someone else's parents."

"Glad I don't have any," Sorrel said with a grin.

"Me too," Talon added.

"What about your research?" Lillie asked in a rush. "I'm so interested in what you're doing out here. Please, tell me about it."

Shereille turned her brilliant smile on her daughter and Lillie staggered a little. It must have been disconcerting to be on the other side of that brilliance for once. "Oh, I'm so glad you're interested. We're out here studying the great dragon, Listrell, while she sleeps. She is one of the most powerful of the greater dragons."

"You're not worried about waking her up?" Talon said.

Shereille laughed. "There is very little that could wake a greater dragon. They're tied to the land, and the land sustains them in slumber. They are its guardians even while it shelters them." Her eyes narrowed. "But why are you here? You mentioned something about a disturbance with one of them."

Because meeting her daughter wasn't enough. Vola fought not to huff. "We think one has woken," she said instead. "There are dead spots out in the desert. Places where magic was sucked out of the ground. And the last time anyone saw anything like it, a dragon was involved."

Shereille's frown creased her forehead. "Impossible."

"Excuse you, but we've seen it," Sorrel said.

"I'm not sure what you've seen, but it's impossible for it to have been a dragon."

Talon crossed her arms. "The last one killed an entire village and the local wildlife near my home. There were half a dozen spots just like it and a rampaging dragon on the loose. Don't tell me they're not related."

Lillie wrung her hands, her eyes darting between Shereille and Talon.

"I'm sorry," Shereille said, tilting her head. "But *draconis maximus* are tied to the land. The way the *draconis minimus* are tied to water. They govern it. They would never do anything to harm it. And believe me, if one of the greater dragons had woken up and gone rogue, we would know."

Vola read outrage in the stiffness of Talon's shoulders but also a creeping doubt.

"I have it on good authority that it's possible," Vola said, inching closer to Talon.

"What authority?" Shereille said.

"A goddess. One of the Virtues."

Shereille smiled indulgently. "Well, a goddess isn't really the expert on these things, is she? I am."

Vola's eyebrows went up.

Lillie stepped forward. "Perhaps you would like to examine the dead spot with us. It would be helpful to have a trained eye to see anything we might have missed. And we were looking for an expert for a reason." She gave Vola a look.

"That would be helpful," Vola said, her voice barely above a growl.

"I'm afraid I can't spare anyone from my team." Shereille turned back to her table, shuffling her notes. "Unless you'd like to take a closer look at Listrell. She occupies my time nowadays."

"You're not even curious?" Vola said, glancing at Lillie. Lillie was curious about everything.

"Not really," Shereille answered flatly. "I don't believe it's connected to my work. But let me know if you want a glimpse of Listrell. She's quite fascinating even in this dormant state."

Lillie glanced at Vola. "We could take a look, couldn't we? We might see something that's related to the dead spots."

Vola didn't miss the note of pleading that crept into Lillie's voice. She sighed. Of course Lillie wanted to steal every moment with her mother that she could. She couldn't blame her. And she couldn't be the heartless git that stood in her way.

"Sure," Vola said quietly. "It wouldn't hurt. And maybe Talon will spot something familiar."

Talon hesitated and then nodded.

Lillie turned back to her mother. "We'd love to take a look."

"Wonderful," Shereille said, turning back to her desk. "I'll have Aster show you up to the lookout point. I'm sure you'll love it, and she can answer any questions you have while you're up there."

Vola was close enough to hear the little sip of air as Lillie's chest caved. But the wizard just smiled a strained smile and turned away from her mother who had already gone back to work, dismissing her as easily as she'd done as an infant.

SEVEN

THEY TRUDGED up the hill after Aster, a plump young woman with short curling brown hair and a perpetually cheerful expression. She scrambled up the narrow trail ahead of them, clearly familiar with the terrain. Dry shrubs grew between cracks in the rock. There was a lot more shade here and little depressions and crevices where water could gather so the plant life wasn't instantly vaporized by the desert sun.

"It's not far up here," Aster said, without having the decency to sound winded. "We have a perfect overlook where we can observe Listrell as she sleeps. There's still so much we don't know about the great dragons since they haven't been awake in centuries."

"You almost sound sad about that," Talon said.

"Well, obviously no one wants them to wake up. It would be a disaster. But…can you imagine if one did? Think of everything we could learn."

Lillie hung behind, her attention on the ground in front of her. Vola had expected her to ask a billion questions and take notes. But she didn't even look up.

Rand swooped down to light on her shoulder. He fluffed his feathers and bobbed his head the way he did when he had a gift for the wizard. She held out her hand and he dropped a blue stone into her palm.

"Thank you, Rand," Lillie said, polite even in her distraction.

Vola climbed up next to her. "I'm sorry meeting your mom was awkward."

Lillie's eyes flicked to her and then back to the rocky trail. "I don't know what I was expecting. I'm awkward about everything. I can't help overthinking every word and gesture and so it all comes out stiff. I just wish I could have had all the right things to say. Just once, when it counted."

Vola frowned at Lillie's back as she climbed past.

As she hurried to follow, she stepped headfirst into a draft of air smelling like fire-warmed rock and year-old carrion.

"Whoof, what is that?" Sorrel asked as Vola caught up to the group.

"Listrell," Aster said. "There's a shaft up ahead that vents fresh air into her sleeping chamber."

"And hundred-year-old morning breath out."

"You're one to talk," Talon muttered, climbing the path directly behind Sorrel. "Rilla said not to eat the eggs."

Aster bounced a little as she walked. "We can actually look straight down the shaft and see Listrell's flank move with her breathing. Mistress Moonhallowed often posts someone there to make the daily observations."

"How long have you worked with my m—with Shereille?" Lillie said.

"Almost two years now."

"Is she...a good boss?"

"Oh yes. I mean, she's demanding, sure, but you have to be in this field. She's extremely choosy about who she devotes time to, so it's an honor just to get to work with her."

"I'm sure," Lillie murmured miserably.

If it had been Vola, she would have been glaring a hole in the girl's back, blaming her for stealing Shereille's time. But Lillie's focus seemed to be diving further and further inward, looking for the fault in herself, probably. What had she done wrong? What did she do to drive her mother away?

Vola placed her hand on Lillie's shoulder and leaned to whisper in her ear. "Stop that."

Lillie glanced at her, eyes wide. "Stop wh—"

"I give up!" Sorrel threw her hands in the air, making Lillie jump. She hopped over one of the rocks at the edge of the path and disappeared.

"Where are you going?" Vola asked.

"Where do you think?"

"Why didn't you go back at the camp?"

"I second-guessed myself, okay? You've never done that before? But the non-emergency has now become an emergency. Just keep going. I'll catch up if it really is as close as Shereille said."

Talon stifled a snort behind her hand.

Aster had paused in the middle of the trail. "Is everything all right?"

"Fine," Vola said and tried to start up the path again.

But Talon had frozen, smile falling from her face.

"What is it?" Vola said.

Aster waited above them, blinking at their hesitance.

Talon turned her head, her nose in the air like she smelled something worse than the dragon.

"Talon?" Vola said quietly.

Talon's gaze dropped to the ground and she knelt to place her fingers against the dirt. "It's happening again," she said. "The magic, it's leaving. It's being pulled out of the land."

"Another dead spot is forming?" Lillie said. "Here?"

Vola didn't doubt Talon knew what she was talking about. The ranger's magic came from the land so she could probably feel it even before Lillie. Not to mention she had a personal connection to the problem.

Vola drew her sword and settled her shield on her arm. "Where is it going?" she said. "Where is it being drawn to?"

Talon stood and pointed up the trail. Aster stepped to the side, gazing at them with wide eyes.

Vola led the way, charging up the narrow path and dodging around the sharp boulders that jutted into their way.

"Sorrel, we need you," Lillie called as she and Talon followed.

"Kinda in the middle of something here!"

The trail twisted one last time, hiding the overlook, and Vola barreled around the corner to see the path even out and stretch all the way to a cliff with a sharp drop off on two sides and a steep slope up the other.

A short figure in long brown robes knelt in the center of the overlook. She glanced up as they came around the corner and Vola registered big eyes, wide ears, and round cheeks reddened by the sun. A gnome, dressed in a robe that hung from her waist in long, tattered strips. She held a gnarled staff with a clump of black feathers tied to the top.

Vola skidded to a stop.

She couldn't feel the magic sucking out of the world like Talon, but the colors of the rock beneath her feet writhed and twisted, like snakes or worms wriggling across the stone and sand. It made Vola's stomach roil, and she lurched back a step.

The stone around the gnome's feet grew black, absorbing the light until nothing remained but the darkness. And the black spread out, sending tendrils across the overlook as if stealing all the color from the world.

Vola instinctively crowded the others back with the feeling in the pit of her stomach that it would be very bad to be standing where the gnome was working.

"What...what is happening?" Aster said from behind Vola. She'd managed to keep up.

"It's her," Talon said. "It's not a dragon, it's her."

Vola leveled her sword at the gnome. "Stop that. Stop doing...whatever it is you're doing?" The words felt stupid, but what else could she do?

The gnome grinned at her, showing off a set of wide, perfect teeth. "Well, hello to you, too."

"I said stop it."

The gnome rolled her eyes. "Uh, no. Then the spell will be all ruined, duh."

"You're hurting the land," Talon said, squeezing in beside Vola. There wasn't a lot of room where the trail opened onto the overlook. "You're taking the magic right out of it."

"Well, yeah. That's the point." The gnome sighed like they were being really slow. "I can't use its power if it's locked away in the land."

"It's not yours to use," Talon cried at the same time Lillie said, "Use it for what?"

"Well, it's not yours either," the gnome said, planting her free fist on her hip while keeping her staff planted firmly against the rock. "Why shouldn't I claim some to power my spells? No one's going to miss it." She flung out her hand. "We're in the middle of a desert, in case you missed it."

"Stop it right now," Vola said. "You're stealing power from the world."

"And that's...bad," the gnome said. Her gaze flicked to Vola's shield. "Why would a black paladin care? Aren't you like the expert on bad?"

Vola growled.

Then the gnome's eyes widened. "Oh. Oh, I recognize you now. An orc, an elf, and a..." She waved a hand at Talon. "Whatever you are. You're Mishap's Heroes. You've been wandering all over Southglen doing good. Where's the halfling?"

"Indisposed," Talon growled.

The gnome cocked her head. "Huh."

"What?" Vola yelled.

The gnome shrugged. "Nothing. Nothing at all."

"Obviously you were going to say something," Lillie said, a frown creasing her forehead.

"It's just...you're shorter than I was expecting."

"Speak for yourself," Talon growled.

"Yeah, but I'm a gnome. What's your excuse?" The gnome raised an eyebrow at Talon. "I guess the fact that you're here means you're going to try to stop me."

The blackness spread through the rock under their feet. They were running out of places to stand.

The gnome grinned. "Kind of hard, when you can't get close."

There was a whisper behind Vola's shoulder, and she didn't flinch as a fireball flew past her head to explode at the gnome's feet.

The gnome waved her hand in front of her face and coughed, a little singed but no worse than the sunburn peeling the end of Talon's nose. "Oh, good try. You must be Lilliara Ephyra."

"You have the advantage of me," Lillie grated through her teeth.

The gnome bowed from the waist. "Nargilla Pipwattle, the Unbeaten."

"Nice title," Talon said. "You come up with that yourself?"

"Yes. I'm rather proud of it."

"Enough," Vola said. "Talon, put an arrow through her ear. Maybe that will get her to stop."

"Gladly," Talon said and swung her bow up.

Pipwattle twisted, dodging the arrow meant for her head. "Too slow," she cried. "Aaaand done!" She lifted her staff from the ground, leaving only a large spread of black where the rich reds and browns of the rock had been.

Vola uttered a war cry and charged the cocky figure, shield down, sword ready for a swing.

The gnome raised her staff as if to block the blow.

Before they struck, there was a violent rumble beneath their feet, and Vola stumbled past Pipwattle into the steep cliff beyond.

Vola spun to see if this was some trick. But Pipwattle stared at the blackened ground, a crease along her forehead. "Huh," she said.

"Oh, my gods," Aster said, eyes wide enough to reflect the overlook and the sky beyond.

"What was that?" Lillie hissed.

There was another deep rumble and a noise that started like a shiver at the base of Vola's spine and rose until it became a roar that echoed off the sharp cliffs around them.

"Oh, my gods, the dragon," Aster said. "It's Listrell."

Nargilla Pipwattle stepped to the edge of the overlook and glanced down.

"Phew. I guess they don't have the equivalent of beauty sleep for a dragon, do they?"

Vola gaped at her, but the vibration under her boots was more immediately concerning. The rumble became constant and a waft of smoke curled from the vent beside the overlook, snaking and weaving into the sky.

"The land," Aster whimpered. "Dragons are tied to the land. And you just took all the magic out of this spot."

"Pff, she should learn to share then, shouldn't she?" Pipwattle said.

The peak beside them shivered, like a sleeping bear rising from its hibernation, and between one second and the next, it erupted in a shower of earth and rock that blotted out the desert sun.

A shape so big Vola could barely register its size climbed from the jagged broken mountain, spewing a mouthful of fire into the sky. It unfurled wings of brilliant turquoise as bits of dirt and gravel pattered around them.

The dragon, Listrell, turned her head and opened her jaws to let out a roar that made Vola's sword ring in her hand. She dropped it to clap her hands over her ears.

The dragon's long neck snaked forward and her eyes fixed on the overlook. Slitted gold pupils pinned Vola to the rock against her back.

"Well, that was unexpected," Pipwattle said, gazing up at the giant silhouette against the sun. "But I'll take it."

"What the hell are you guys doing up he—Whoa, that's a dragon." Sorrel skidded to a stop at the top of the path, her mouth wide and her hands frozen on the ties of her pants.

"Nice of the halfling to join us finally," the gnome said. "Just in time to say good bye and good luck."

She spun to give Vola a jaunty salute and then stepped backward off the cliff edge.

Vola lunged forward, landing on her knees at the edge. Pipwattle floated downward as if held by a gentle breeze, her gnarled staff in her hand, and the strips of her robe fluttering around her. She alighted at the base of the cliff among jagged rocks and kept her balance like the distant cousin of a mountain goat. She flashed a grin up at Vola and then vanished among the rocks.

"Shit," Vola said. A little lightning bolt struck the ground beside her hand.

"Not to distract you or anything," Sorrel said. "But we have a much bigger problem heading this way."

Vola glanced up to see Listrell raise her wings, muscles bunched beneath her. She launched herself into the air, wingbeats like thunder that set their bones to shaking.

Listrell turned at the top of her arc and dove. Straight for the overlook.

Vola scrambled backward, snatching at her fallen sword, and she had a split second to wonder what good the blade would do against a dragon.

Then Listrell's bulk blocked out the light, casting a shadow over the blackened surface of the overlook.

Vola stared up at her, turquoise scales shining all along her back, wings slanted overhead, and Vola's gibbering brain said, "well, at least it's shade."

Then she kicked herself into action and raised her shield.

Listrell opened her huge jaw, and Vola found herself staring down the dark, empty stretch of teeth to the flames gathering at the back of her throat.

Fire shot out, but just before it reached Vola, there was a crack of air and Lillie manifested in front of her. The flames parted around them, flickering like they hit an invisible wall.

"Thanks," Vola gasped. "But isn't that usually my job?"

"You'll have plenty of opportunities. I don't know how many times I can do this."

The fire didn't let up.

Sorrel, tiny compared to the beast in front of them, leaped on the dragon's snout. She was no bigger than the dragon's eye, but she slammed Maxim's staff into the dragon's snout, letting a ripple of lightning crackle across the scales.

The fire stopped abruptly as the dragon's breath hitched. Vola didn't squander the opportunity. As Sorrel leaped free of the snout and snapping teeth, Vola lunged around Lillie and swung her blade at the nostrils just within range. She connected with a clang, and her blade slid off the scales. But she swung again and again—it had to at least be making a dent because the dragon grunted and shook her head.

Arrows sprouted from the beast's hide, and Vola glanced back to find Talon sniping from behind a rock on the trail.

Sorrel scampered past and leaped again, using the arrows as handholds to climb up the dragon's slick hide. Her feet were sure as she raced down the length of the snout, and the dragon went cross-eyed trying to keep track of her. Sorrel snapped out and bashed her staff into the beast's forehead, right between her eyes.

Listrell roared, and Vola lunged forward to plunge her sword hilt deep in the dragon's gums.

A precisely timed arc of lightning shot from Lillie's hands into the open maw, and Listrell gurgled in pain.

She jerked back, yanking Vola's sword out of her hand. Vola stumbled a couple of steps as the dragon reared back and Sorrel landed beside her, rolling into the cliff.

With another ear splitting shriek, Listrell pushed off from the overlook, beating her wings and sending a wave of air to press them back. She gained height and spun above them, roaring the entire time.

Then she wheeled and headed toward the city, spouting gouts of flame at the ground as she passed.

"Oh no," Lillie said. "She's going for Firewatch."

"And she took my sword with her," Vola grumbled.

"Well, you did stick it in her mouth," Lillie said. "Sorrel, are you all right?"

"Peachy," Sorrel said. She lay upside down, her feet up the side of the cliff, her arms flat against the ground as she stared up at the sky. Her staff lay in the dirt beside her. "Luckily monks are made out of rubber. You know, fighting dragons sounds so romantic in the stories, but it's a lot of bad breath and just whacking away at something until it falls over."

"Except she hasn't fallen over yet. She's headed for the city," Vola said.

Talon peered behind another rock, finding Aster, who cowered there with her arms over her head. "Get to the camp," she said. "Tell the researchers to evacuate. Get under cover. The camp is too open if the dragon decides to come back and take her revenge on anyone nearby."

"Revenge?" Aster said, sitting up. "Why would she want revenge? We didn't have anything to do with waking her up."

Talon frowned at the sky. "This is exactly what happened to my pack."

Vola straightened and winced when her back popped.

"Is it?" Lillie said quietly.

Talon spun around. "Yes. It's not exactly what I thought it was. It mustn't have just been a dragon that time, either. But I think the dead spots woke it up, and it was angry. It attacked everything in sight. That's the important part. I don't care who's to blame, but if we don't do something about Listrell, many will die."

Aster gasped and followed her gaze. "What about the city?"

"We'll get to the city. You get the researchers to safety."

EIGHT

THEY RACED back down the narrow track, following Talon, who didn't bother to pause at the researcher's camp. Lillie hesitated when Aster split off and rushed for Shereille's tent, but she kept going down the trail before Vola could even open her mouth.

Vola wanted to stop and take stock for just a second, to wrap her head around the fact that they'd just fought a *dragon* and they were heading toward *another* fight with a dragon. But she decided they couldn't spare the time when Listrell made a swooping pass over them, making the air hum, and then she winged away toward the city, flames spouting from her jaw.

Clearly, the threat was ahead of them. And it wasn't like they could find Pipwattle to exact justice.

Besides, Talon had seen this before. And Vola trusted Talon. If the ranger said to hustle, she'd hustle.

It had taken them two hours to walk from the city to the researcher's camp, but they made it back in half an hour.

Nothing kept them from running straight into the city. It wasn't like the dragon had laid siege to it. She was still airborne, doing her best to burn the whole thing to the ground.

Vola hadn't thought Firewatch could get any hotter, but with flames licking up the eclectic collections of wood structures, she was half convinced she was going to melt inside her tin can armor. Civilians ran by, knocking into them in a panic, some running into buildings that still stood. Others tried to escape the burning city with what few belonging they could save. Ash began to gather on the street softening their footfalls.

Vola's nose burned from the acrid smoke as she whipped around, mind racing. What the hell could they do against a dragon? How could they defend an entire city?

She squinted, spotting a familiar figure on one of the stone bridges spanning the gap between the two halves of the city. She gestured to the rest to follow and sprinted up the sloping road to the bridge.

"Now do you believe me?" Rilla waved her hands over her head as she confronted a man in a flowing blue robe with a cream-colored tunic underneath.

"Dragon," the man gibbered towards the sky. "It's a dragon. What is it doing awake?"

Rilla took him by the shoulders and shook. "Your city is literally called Firewatch! You live in the middle of dragon lands. How can you not be prepared for a dragon attack?"

"We haven't had one in hundreds of years!" the man yelled back. "Our strength lies in the ability to reason with and live peacefully with the creatures. The little ones live here as well. They don't want to burn it down."

"Well, you've got a big one trying to do just that! What are you doing about it?"

The man gestured as a civilian ran past with a bucket, water sloshing across the stones at their feet. "Look, the brigades are already forming. They'll pull water from the cisterns inside the mountain."

"Great, so you can save the buildings. Hopefully, there will still be people to live in them! What are you doing about the dragon?"

The man hesitated, his mouth wide.

Rilla growled deep in her throat and turned to Vola and the others as they drew even with her. "This is fucking ridiculous. They built the city to withstand dragons centuries ago, but now when they actually need it, they've forgotten everything they learned." Rilla gestured to the nearest building, which smoldered uncontrolled. "They let people build with wood on top of the stone. And now they act surprised when it's all burning."

"The dragons have left us alone for years," the official said behind her. "Why would one attack now?" His eye caught on Rilla, and he leveled his finger in her face. "You came here talking of a dragon attack. What did you do to wake the creature?"

"It wasn't us," Vola said. "The dead spots out in the desert that she warned you about. We found the one who's doing it. She woke the dragon up by draining the land."

The official clutched his dark hair with both hands. "We must drive it away from the city. Long enough to regroup and put the fires out. Only then can we solve the problem of who woke the thing."

"You four." Rilla pointed to Vola and the others. "You're on dragon duty. Get that thing to leave us alone. Join whatever defense these people have cobbled together."

"Captain Fedor Gerrickson will be on the Heights," the official said, pointing to the jagged peaks. "He's in charge of the city militia."

"The dragon hunter?" Talon said.

"Well, we don't let him go around waking up dragons, so what else is he good for?"

There was a squeal and a shape the size of a horse with nasty teeth and worse breath slithered by, the light of the fire reflecting from its scales. Gruff ran after it with an angry bark.

"Oh no," Lillie said.

"It must have escaped the inn in the confusion," Sorrel said.

Rilla rolled her eyes. "I'll catch your swamp monster. You get to the Heights."

Vola gave Rilla a snappy salute and led the way through the conflagration. She didn't have a map and didn't think it would be helpful with most of the city burning, anyway. But she figured all they had to do was keep moving up, and they'd eventually reach the Heights.

Sparks swirled through the air along the lower levels, stinging Vola's skin as they settled, but the higher they got, the more smoke stung her eyes and caught in her chest.

Vola squinted and led them up the last tower. From there, a wooden bridge spanned the gap to the bare peak, where figures swarmed in the smoke.

She gestured the others across, bringing up the rear, but the wood smoldered under her boots and crumbled behind her heels.

"Go, go, go," she called. "This is a one-way trip."

Lillie took one look over her shoulder and then grabbed Talon and popped out of existence, the two of them reappearing on the peak. Sorrel stopped suddenly and threw herself onto the wood slats.

Vola sprinted past her. "What are you d—"

The rope railing snapped with a violent twang. Vola threw herself toward the end of the bridge but landed halfway over the edge with a painful gasp. She kicked and scrambled her way to solid ground.

"Sorrel!" Lillie called.

Vola leaped to her feet and peered over the edge, expecting the worst, but Sorrel had wrapped her arm through the railing and ridden the bridge down. Their side was still attached so that the loose bridge dangled over the empty space above the city. Sorrel just grinned and climbed up it like a ladder.

"That was fun," she said. "What's next?"

Vola heaved a sigh and coughed on smoke. "Would you not do that?" she choked out.

Sorrel patted her on the back, but there was an ominous flapping noise coming from all around them and Vola didn't dare sit there recovering for any longer.

She straightened and glanced around. A few guardsmen in soot-stained uniforms shot from the peak and a couple more manned an ancient ballista.

"Fedor?" Vola called, squinting through the smoke. "Are you up here?"

The dwarf's head popped up from the other side of the ballista, topped with a smudged helmet. A grin wreathed his face as soon as he saw them.

"Proof!" he cried. "That's some damn fine proof!"

"We're here to help," Vola said.

"Great." He bent his head to aim the ballista. "We'll take anything you can give us. Grab a bow and start shooting. Unless you have anything else that can bring down a dragon."

A gust of wind drove the smoke away from the peak in swathes of swirling darkness, revealing Listrell. The great dragon dove for their tiny defense.

The guardsmen yelled. Fedor fired the ballista, shooting off a great crossbow bolt that struck Listrell's side and bounced off.

"Shit." Fedor lunged out of the way as the dragon landed on the ballista.

The ancient wood crunched beneath her talons. She swung her head around, teeth snapping, and a guardsman leaped from the peak with a scream, not waiting to be dragon food.

Vola reached for her sword and remembered it was still stuck somewhere in the dragon's maw. If she hadn't swallowed it already. All she had left was a pair of matching hand axes.

Before she could draw, Sorrel had charged the dragon, staff crackling with lightning, and got in two solid blows which cracked like thunder.

Listrell grunted. Her muscles bunched, and she sprang into the air again.

Talon was already taking aim beside Vola, and Lillie had her hands raised calling forth lightning or fire. Sorrel couldn't follow the dragon into the air, but she did carry a god's weapon with many uses. The staff morphed in her hand until she held a bow nearly as tall as she was. Vola had never seen her use one, but she'd grown up in a martially-minded monastery and the staff answered to her almost as if she was Maxim herself. So Vola didn't doubt she could use it.

Which left Vola standing there useless unless Listrell chose to land again.

The guardsmen all scrambled to their feet and Fedor called orders for them to form a rank and send a volley of arrows at their enemy. Vola had to give them points for bravery.

She rubbed the smoke and soot from her eyes and followed Listrell's movements. The dragon circled just out of range of the guardsmen's short-bows. The only thing hitting her were Lillie's spells and whatever Talon and Sorrel could fling at her with their longbows.

They had to get closer. Bring the fight to the dragon rather than waiting for her to come to them.

Vola's eyes narrowed. She had a crazy idea, but since the normal ideas weren't going to be enough right now…

She grasped Lillie's shoulder. "Can you get me onto her back?"

Lillie gaped at her, soot streaking her round face. "Get you—? You mean teleport you there? Are you insane?"

"Not since the last time I checked. Look, we have to drive her off, not bring her in closer. Get me up there, and I think I can do it."

There was a roar, and they ducked as Listrell swept past, raking the peak with her claws and taking several guardsmen with her.

"Now, Lillie. Before she kills anyone else."

Lillie's lips thinned like she was going to argue. Then she blew out her breath. "Shit."

"I always know it's a fun idea when Lillie swears," Sorrel said with a grin.

Vola slung her shield across her back—at least it hadn't gone down the dragon's gullet—and drew her axes.

Lillie took her arm and muttered a few words.

Vola's ears popped, and the world went white for a second.

Then slick turquoise scales heaved under her feet and air rushed past her like a storm across the deck of a ship, only way worse. She staggered and grabbed Lillie before either of them could fall from the dragon's back.

"Go," she yelled in Lillie's ear. "Back to the others. You'll be safer there than here."

"Be careful," Lillie said, then flashed out from under Vola's hand.

Vola crouched low, trying to keep her balance as Listrell banked. The dragon's back tilted and Vola lunged to grab hold of one of the spikes marching along her spine.

As the beast leveled out, Vola stood and tripped forward, using the change in momentum to fight the rush of air.

Vola squinted into the wind and caught sight of the peak ahead of them, growing closer by the second. The dragon was going in for another pass.

Vola quit trying to get to Listrell's head and swung her right ax at the spot where her wing met her body.

The dragon screamed and veered to the left, and Vola grabbed a scaly spine. It was a long way down if she lost her grip or her footing.

She swung again, trying not to think about what would happen if she made the dragon fall from the sky rather than flee the fight.

Listrell roared and shuddered, trying to shake her free, but Vola clung to the spike for dear life.

There was a pop, and Lillie appeared beside her with Sorrel.

"I told you to stay on the peak with the others," Vola yelled.

"My fault," Sorrel said. "I was jealous you got to bash her up close."

Lillie just rolled her eyes before teleporting away again.

"All right," Sorrel said. "Let's see if we can annoy her into leaving."

Beside them, an arrow streaked through Listrell's wing, leaving a gap big enough to ride a horse through.

"That'll help," Vola said. She made for the beast's head again, this time with Sorrel in tow.

Vola leaped the last few steps and planted an ax blade between Listrell's eyes. Sorrel followed it up with a blow to the eyebrow ridge. The Warhammer had changed back into a staff for her.

Listrell roared, and Vola kept up the onslaught.

"It's not worth staying," she yelled, wondering if the creature could hear her. "We're just going to keep bothering you."

Sorrel aimed a kick at her eye. "We're very annoying like that."

Listrell jerked, and Vola lost her footing. She flung her arms around the dragon's neck, just fast enough to avoid a long plummet.

Sorrel tumbled down the dragon's back, and Vola gasped. But the halfling caught hold of one of the spine ridges, halting her fall. She adjusted herself, then raised her fist and brought it down with a crack right on Listrell's spine.

The dragon screamed and wheeled again, only this time instead of circling the city, she straightened her course and made for the mountains.

"It's working," Vola called to Sorrel.

"Great, now how do we get off? I can't imagine she's gonna like having stowaways when she gets wherever she's going."

Vola scanned the ground as the city sped beneath them. Then she spotted one of the fire watch towers ahead of them.

It was perfect, but they weren't going to get close enough. Sorrel might be able to make it, but there was no way Vola could jump that far.

Vola squinted, searching for another option. High on the cliff above them, a figure appeared and drew a longbow.

"Talon," Vola whispered.

An arrow whistled through the air, close enough to the dragon's eye to make her grunt and swerve. Now they headed directly for the fire watch tower.

"Thanks, Talon," Vola said under her breath, then she called to Sorrel. "Get ready to jump."

"I mean, I'm always up for jumping but are you sure—"

"Now!"

Vola flung herself from the dragon's back, trusting Sorrel to follow her.

She overshot and had to grab the tower railing as she went by. Her momentum swung her around, and she crashed into the side of the tower, smashing through a plywood wall.

At least that gave her plenty of hand and footholds. She hung there, gasping for a moment, half in and half out of the hole she'd made in the tower.

"Hey, it worked." Sorrel stood above her, leaning nonchalantly on what was left of the tower's railing. The rest lay below them in pieces.

Stupid monk had probably landed on her feet.

"You always sound so surprised when you say that," Vola said. "Don't you believe any of my plans will work?"

Sorrel scratched the back of her neck. "Well, I mean there's believing and then there's *believing*. I will follow you anywhere, but I usually pray for luck before I do."

A distant roar made her glance up to see Listrell hesitate in the air. She hung there for a moment, and her head swung around, glinting eyes finding Vola and Sorrel on their tower.

One last arrow streaked close enough to make Listrell flinch, and the dragon banked away, aiming for the nearby cliff.

"No!" Vola called.

Talon flung up her arm to ward off the dragon, but the creature's claws raked the stone, catching in her cloak. Listrell pushed off from the rock, and Talon dangled from her grip.

The dragon winged away into the mountains, carrying the ranger with her.

Vola cried out and nearly lost her grip on the tower. She fought down her instinct to leap after the enemy who'd snatched her friend. What could she do? She was stuck at the top of a broken tower, and all she could do was watch them disappear.

Gray clouds roiled overhead and a rumble of thunder rolled far closer than any normal storm. In seconds, torrential rain blanketed the city, pouring over the fires still smoldering below.

Above them, on the highest peak, Vola could just make out Lillie with her hands raised, directing the storm to the most damaged parts of the city.

Vola let her head fall back, and the rain washed over her face. Numbness spread from the water's touch, matching the cold inside her.

NINE

IT TOOK CONSIDERABLY MORE effort to climb down from the tower than it had to jump from the dragon's back. And Vola was having a hard time making her hands and feet work through the haze of red that threatened to swamp her vision.

The monk, of course, had no trouble. She scampered around the tower like an insect, finding hand and footholds that were obvious enough that even Vola could see them. And she kept up a steady stream of words, keeping Vola anchored here and now instead of flying away with Talon and the dragon.

"A little to the left. Keep going, you're doing great. Only thirty more feet."

"Sorrel…"

"We'll get down. Don't worry."

"That's not…"

Sorrel met her eyes where she clung less than halfway up the tower. "We'll get her back. Don't worry about that either."

The halfling glanced between Vola's trembling arms and the ground. "Maybe I should go find some mattresses…"

That made Vola laugh, and she found the strength to slip and slide the rest of the way until she planted her feet firmly back on the ground again.

"Hey, with Lillie's rain you can hardly tell what's water and what's sweat," Sorrel said, head cocked as she stared up at Vola's face. "I guess you don't like heights."

"Let's never speak of this again," Vola said. "Come on. We have to find Rilla and Lillie."

They found the princess about halfway up the city with the same official, directing bucket brigades to the parts that still burned. Big wafts of black smoke billowed into the air, obscuring the sunset and making twilight fall a lot earlier than usual.

Lillie limped up from the opposite direction with Fedor. Vola didn't feel particularly steady, but instinct made her catch Lillie as the wizard sagged.

"Good job," Rilla said, pausing long enough to give their soot-streaked forms a once over. "We've saved at least half the city. I think. But damn, there's a lot to do here." She ran a hand over her forehead, leaving a streak of sweat and grime. "We need to get after the one that woke the dragon—"

"We need to go after Listrell," Vola growled. The numbness had spread through her chest and made it hard to breathe, let alone speak the words she needed to say.

Rilla's brows drew down, and she opened her mouth to argue.

"She took Talon," Sorrel said.

Lillie gasped, her body going stiff against Vola's, and Rilla froze.

"The dragon?" she said.

Vola drew in a painful breath. "Talon covered our escape from the dragon's back, but Listrell snatched her just as she left."

"Gods, I'm sorry," Rilla said, jaw slack. In better circumstances Vola would have been proud. They rarely managed to shock the princess.

Fedor pounded his fist into his palm. "Then we go after the creature. Pin it down in its lair and make sure it never harms another soul."

"You're not going anywhere," the city official said. His blue robes were considerably shorter and ended in a ragged, burnt line, but to his credit, he was still on his feet. "We hired you to protect the city. How can you do that if you're gallivanting around the mountains?"

"Gallivanting?" Fedor said. "Listen here, you. I'm a dragon hunter—"

"Which should make you uniquely suited to protect us from dragons."

"Which I can't do if you don't let me go after any."

"Freelance on your own time, Gerrickson. You'd need a permit to hunt one of the greater beasts anyway and the council isn't granting you one. They, however, are another case entirely." The official cocked his thumb at Vola and Sorrel and Lillie.

Fedor glared at them, his eyes glinting from underneath his sweat-streaked hair.

Vola shook off his look. She didn't care about Fedor one way or another. He could be an asset or a hindrance. Right now, she just wanted her teammate back.

She made sure Lillie was steady on her feet before she straightened up. "We're going after Listrell. Now. I'm not leaving Talon—"

Rilla held up her hands. "I'm not trying to stop you, but you just fell off a dragon—"

"Jumped. And we're fine."

"Vola," Sorrel said quietly. "She's right. We're exhausted and half-crisped."

"So is Talon," Vola snapped.

"And we won't be able to do anything to help her if we die on the way there." Sorrel's words were steady and pragmatic and impossible to ignore.

A yip made her start and a long black shape wove through the crowds of refugees and the crates and boxes stacked along the edges of the walkway.

Gruff twined around Vola's legs. The big wolf liked to be touched about as much as Talon did, but now he cuddled against her, seeking comfort. She knelt and buried her hands in his fur. He turned his head to lean his skull against her chest.

Vola gazed up at her battered team. Ash settled on Lillie's pale cheeks, the rain making more of a mess instead of washing it away. Sorrel's tunic hung limp and stained from her thin shoulders.

Rilla didn't look nearly so battered, but she stared back at Vola all the same. She could order them to wait. She could order them to do whatever she wanted. But she didn't. She waited.

"All right," Vola said quietly. "All right. We'll go after her in the morning. We're not prepared for a desert expedition, anyway." And logic said that ridiculous speed wouldn't help them, anyway. If the dragon wanted to eat Talon, there was no chance they'd get there in time to save her. Listrell could move faster than any of them and was probably already settling into her lair. Whatever she planned to do with Talon was already done or started.

All they could do was catch up in order to find out what it was.

"We'll find her in the morning," Vola said, mostly to herself and Gruff. "I promise."

They slept in their hotel, which smelled like damp, burned wood, an unpleasant combination that kept Vola awake for most of the night. Gruff slept curled up against her back. Rilla had tracked down the swamp monster and tethered it back in its stall so the thing couldn't wander off again. Vola strongly suspected the fires were the only thing that had kept it in the city in the first place.

In the morning, they collected their monster and dragged it along with them, visiting the shops and crafters that were still open after yesterday's attack.

Everything in Vola urged her to go racing out of the city, but she was as responsible for Lillie and Sorrel and now Gruff as she was for Talon. While their brief trek to Shereille's research camp had not required much in the way of equipment, a rescue mission did.

The selection was pretty poor. Two out of every three shops were closed along the main pathway down through the city.

Vola paused outside one with a shopfront narrower than a desert snake. It didn't have any writing on the sign, just a pickaxe nailed over top of a coil of rope.

"Camping supplies?" Vola mused out loud.

"I suppose pickaxes and rope are too niche of a market to support an entire shop," Lillie said.

Vola tied the swamp monster up on the railing and pushed inside.

A couple of oil lanterns lit the dim interior. More tools and wares were nailed to the walls.

"To be fair, it is a much easier way to display your goods than say glass cases," Lillie muttered.

"If you buy something, do you have to pull it off the wall yourself?" Sorrel said.

"Ooh," Lillie said, touching the brim of a wide straw hat which hung from a peg.

"Not really your normal style," Sorrel said.

"Who cares if it keeps the sun off my face?"

The shopkeeper stepped through a door in the back wall. "What did you need?" she asked. She was as broad as a horse and almost as tall, and she scowled at Vola.

"We're headed into the mountains for a prolonged mission," Vola said, trying a smile.

The shopkeeper frowned at her tusks.

"Can you tell us what gear we might need?"

The shopkeeper squinted one eye. "I wasn't talking to you," she said. "I'll speak with the humans, thank you."

Vola kept her eyebrow from twitching, but it was a near thing.

Sorrel snorted. "That'll be hard. None of us is completely human." She looked Lillie up and down. "I suppose you're closest."

The shopkeeper spit, apparently not caring that it was her floor she'd have to clean later. "Fine. I'll talk to anyone who's not that one."

"Excuse me?" Lillie said, voice gone calm and quiet. "Vola is our leader. She's the one who speaks for us. It doesn't matter that she's a half-orc, and it shouldn't matter to you."

"Don't care if she's green," the shopkeeper said. "I care that her shield is black." She gestured to the shield slung on Vola's back. "I don't deal with black paladins. Can't trust them."

Red flickered at the edges of Vola's vision. But instead of thrusting it down, she welcomed the surge of anger, letting it rise and holding it at a simmer just below the surface.

"Now what did you need, ma'am?" The shopkeeper focused on Lillie.

Lillie crossed her arms, her mouth set in a thin line.

"Let's not set anything on fire now that we've saved it," Vola muttered to her.

"What about you?" the shopkeeper asked Sorrel.

Sorrel exchanged a look with Lillie. "I'll be outside. You can talk to our leader or you can lose our business." Sorrel trotted outside.

Lillie smiled her coldest, politest smile and followed her.

Vola turned her gaze back to the shopkeeper and huffed a mirthless little laugh. One of her teammates was missing, and this woman was a fool if she thought she could delay Vola for another second.

"Can't help but notice you drove off the only two witnesses." She put her hand down on the counter and leaned. "You know the best part about being a black paladin? No one cares when you break the rules."

The woman's face went white and she glanced at her wares. Vola could see her calculating how much her pride was worth.

A half an hour later, Vola left with armfuls of gear to load onto the swamp beast.

Lillie leaned against an intact portion of the railing, well outside biting distance from the swamp monster. Sorrel squatted next to her, watching as Rand dove over the swamp beast's head, taunting the creature.

"You're going to get your tail feathers snatched," Vola told him.

"He's much too fast for that," Lillie said with a proud smirk.

"So how much did you have to threaten her?" Sorrel asked, examining her nails.

"I didn't threaten," Vola said. "I just leaned. And pointed out the flaws in her logic. That's always more fun, anyway." Vola tossed Lillie the straw hat she'd been eying. "Try that on."

Lillie beamed at her and placed it on her head while Vola dumped the rest of her load onto the swamp beast's back. It had been a while since they'd had enough gear to use the swamp beast for its original purpose, and she grinned at it while it hissed.

Sorrel stood to help and glanced up at the peaks surrounding the city. The one just north was a completely different shape than it had been the day before. The top had exploded out under the force of Listrell's exit, and now the whole peak looked like some giant had taken a bite out of the top with a set of uneven teeth.

"Talon is the priority," Sorrel said quietly. "But Master Bao was supposed to be up there somewhere, too."

Lillie took the hat off and bit her lip before stowing it behind the swamp monster's harness. "I'm sure he's fine," she said.

Vola tried not to wince. He'd been suicidal. None of his self-preservation instincts would have been working properly.

"We'll keep an eye out for him," Vola said anyway. Though she couldn't promise more than that. If Master Bao had been anywhere on that mountain when Listrell had burst through, there wouldn't be a lot left for them to find.

"Do we even know where to start looking for them?" Sorrel asked, turning back to check the swamp beast's straps. "I doubt Listrell has gone back to the same lair where we can find her easily. Dragons are supposed to be smart, right?"

"They are incredibly intelligent," a lyrical voice said. "And no, she would not have returned to her sleeping lair. But I know where to find her now."

They all turned. A tall, blonde elf dressed in sensible trousers and a linen shirt sat on a pile of luggage at the next corner.

"Moth—I mean, Shereille?" Lillie squeaked.

Shereille beamed. "Hello again."

"What are you...what are you doing here?" Vola asked, casting a look at Lillie.

Shereille blinked. "I was looking for you. You're quite famous around town now, you know."

Lillie made a noise in the back of her throat, but before she or Vola could respond, Sorrel said, "You know where the dragon might be?"

"Of course. I am the foremost expert on Listrell."

"You weren't that interested in helping us yesterday," Vola said.

"You were spouting nonsense about how Listrell had caused your dead spots. It couldn't possibly be true and had nothing to do with my research since Listrell was sound asleep." She gestured vaguely to the sky, which was still a little hazy from all the smoke. "Of course, that's all changed now. Fascinating times we live in, don't we?"

"Right. Fascinating." Vola's eyes narrowed.

"Why—" Lillie stopped to clear her throat. "Why were you looking for us?"

Shereille stood, brushing down her trousers. "You are going after the dragon, are you not?"

"Yes," Vola said. "She took one of our teammates."

"I would like you to escort me to her hideout, as well."

"Um..." Sorrel said.

"You are adventurers," she said, her green-blue eyes flicking between them. "You accept money to...solve problems, I believe is how you put it. Well, I wish to study the dragon up close. Now that she's awoken, we will be able to gather so much more information than before. It's a truly unique, once-in-a-lifetime opportunity. And I'm not going to miss it."

"You're hiring us to take you into a dragon's lair?" Sorrel tilted her head. "Don't damsels usually want people to rescue them from dragons?"

Shereille raised her chin and looked down her nose. "I assure you I am perfectly capable of taking care of myself, if that's your concern. You will be paid for your time, and this is a wonderful opportunity for many things." Her gaze landed on Lillie.

Lillie flushed a deep red and cast a beseeching look at Vola and Sorrel.

Vola's eyes narrowed a fraction. Well, maybe Shereille was actually trying to make an effort now. Maybe this was her way of spending more time with a daughter she hardly knew. Motherhood probably didn't come naturally to everyone; some people had to work on it. And she couldn't fault Shereille if she was doing her best and trying to get better.

She cast a glance at Sorrel to assess her reaction. The halfling gave a little nod.

"You're aware that we might be killing the very thing you're trying to study, right? Listrell took Talon, and if we have to kill her, we will."

Shereille surveyed them, a calculating look on her face. "Slaying a *draconis maximus* would provide me with enough research to publish for the rest of my life. If you think you're capable. Just do me a favor and don't mess up the cadaver when you do so. I'd like to do a dissection and lopped off limbs are very frustrating."

"That's...very reasonable," Vola said, trying to find the catch. Oh right, the catch was they'd be trying to kill a dragon. Which they were already heading off to do, so what difference did it make?

"All right then," Vola said.

Lillie squeaked again and covered her mouth with her hand.

Vola raised her eyebrows but went back to Shereille. "We'll draw up the contract. We can't take a wagon up into the mountains, so most of your things will have to stay behind. And we're on a rescue mission so we're moving quickly."

Shereille gave them a serene smile and reached to pluck one case from the pile of luggage. "Don't worry. I am capable of traveling light when it's important. The rest of my equipment I'll have shipped back to my residence."

She came to stand beside Lillie. "Well," she said. "Won't this be pleasant?"

Lillie beamed at Vola, bouncing up and down on the balls of her feet.

Vola just shook her head. *Pleasant is one way to put it,* she thought. *But I probably would have chosen awkward.*

TEN

Vola would give Shereille this. She was right about knowing how to travel light. They tossed her case onto the swamp beast's back with the rest of their equipment, and it didn't seem to bother the creature any more than usual.

Though the swamp beast did its best to bother Shereille.

As they passed out of the city and turned into the desert sun, the swamp monster reached out its long neck and took a snap at the researcher.

Lillie cried out and smacked the beast on the nose. "Millford, don't you dare."

She crowded the beast back and spun to check on her mother. "Are you all right? Did it get you?"

Shereille rubbed her back end surreptitiously. "That creature bit me."

Sorrel leaned over and squinted at the elf's butt. "You're not missing the back of your trousers so you're doing better than most people it eats."

Shereille's eyes widened. "It eats people."

"No," Lillie said sharply, glaring at Sorrel. "It does not eat people."

"Not regularly," Sorrel mumbled.

Lillie transferred her glare to the monk. "We don't let it."

"Because that makes it better," Vola said, but she wasn't sure Lillie heard her.

Shereille eyed the swamp monster, who ambled along through the sand, leaving wide webbed footprints. Slobber dribbled from its chin and hissed when it struck the sand. It stared balefully over the crest of a dune and then squealed and lunged forward. When it straightened up, an armadillo's tail hung from its mouth. It swallowed with obvious relish.

Shereille's eye twitched. "And you keep this thing as a…pet?"

"Not on purpose," Sorrel said cheerily. She whistled as she scrambled up the next dune, then stopped to stare up at the rocky foothills, her hand shading her eyes.

"It's more of a beast of burden," Lillie said.

Shereille did not look convinced.

"It grows on you," Lillie tried to say, and then choked on the words. "Actually, it doesn't. We feel sort of responsible for it. And if we are taking care of it, then at least the rest of the world isn't subjected to it."

Shereille's lips thinned, but then she shrugged and continued walking. "I suppose that is honorable in a way."

The elf didn't notice, but Lillie beamed behind her back.

"I have colleagues who would be fascinated by such a creature," Shereille said. "I, however…" she cast a glance back at the swamp monster, who was drooling again. "I think I would prefer dissection."

"If you can think of a way to kill it, you can have it," Sorrel said.

Shereille did not react, and Vola wondered if she just hadn't heard or if she was pretending not to.

Vola joined Sorrel at the top of the dune and shaded her eyes. "Where is Listrell holed up now?" she asked Shereille.

Shereille pointed along the ridgeline of the mountains. "She will have found herself a new lair, since the old one is no more than a crater. We should follow the mountains."

"And then I imagine we follow the scorch marks," Vola said. She could already see a streak of blackened rock spreading into the next valley.

Valleys in the Firewall range were a bit different than anything Vola had seen before. They weren't the verdant green she was used to in South-glen. Instead, they were uneven trenches zig-zagging through jagged rocky cliffs.

As they climbed into the foothills, Vola kept a sharp eye on the trail, peering around the sudden corners to check for lurking threats, while Sorrel followed with her staff in her hand and her eyes on what sky they could see between the cliffs.

Rand swooped between the rock formations and dropped to Lillie's shoulder. She smiled at him, and he reached out his beak to drop a shiny bit of quartz in her palm.

"Oh, thank you," Lillie told him. "What a lovely gift."

Rand ruffled his feathers in pleasure and croaked, then ran his beak through her bright hair and took off again. Vola trusted him to alert them of anything that might be sneaking up on them from the hidden trail up ahead.

"Your familiar?" Shereille said, eying Lillie.

"Yes." Lillie tracked his flight with her gaze.

"Hmm," Shereille said. "Ravens aren't very majestic creatures, are they? Not like owls. Or dragons."

Lillie's jaw hardened. "He was a gift from a friend. And he's much cleverer than the owls I've met."

"More loyal, too," Sorrel said. "And I've never seen him run into a tree. Not even once."

Lillie turned her frown on her mother, eyes expectant, as if waiting for a response. Any kind of response.

Vola suspected Lillie of reacting indignantly on purpose. She'd seen the wizard hold her tongue against the worst of insults, so maybe Lillie was trying to get a reaction out of her mother.

It didn't work, though. Shereille blinked as if puzzled, then just shrugged. "All right," she said and trudged after Vola.

Lillie's shoulders sagged the barest bit. Vola only noticed because she was watching for it.

Lillie limped unevenly after Shereille. "Do you have a familiar?"

"I am a researcher, my dear. Not a practical wizard. I don't have the same insecurities that require constant companionship."

Vola and Sorrel winced.

"Do you think Lillie would flame her own mom?" Sorrel whispered.

Vola cleared her throat. "Shereille, maybe you should be up here with me."

Shereille tilted her head. "I don't know a lot about combat, but I imagine the front position is the most dangerous."

"Yes, but it's also the closest to me so I can protect you." Because Vola wouldn't be at all surprised if Lillie snapped and ended up killing her. "Besides, you're the one who knows where Listrell most likely went to ground. I'm hoping you can spot her before she spots us."

"I suppose that is true." Shereille gamely trotted to catch up with Vola. Like Aster, she didn't even have the decency to look winded. Researching dragons must involve a lot of climbing and hiking.

The ground under Vola's boots vibrated, making the soles of her feet tingle. "What the—"

"Is the dragon coming back?" Sorrel said, searching the skies.

"Rand says no," Lillie said. "He doesn't see anything unusual from above."

"Well, then, where is it coming from?" Vola glanced down.

Just in time for a round mouth to erupt from the rock at her feet.

"Geez!" She stumbled back, dragging Shereille out of the way.

The mouth gaped, showing off rows of needle-thin teeth as a long tubular body stretched from the rock face.

"What the hell is that?" Vola said. She looked at Lillie.

But it was Shereille who answered. "Rock wyrm. Cousin to the more common sand wyrm."

The thing reared back and up, looming over them where they stood on the narrow trail. It looked a lot like the garden worms Vola's Aunt Urag pulled out of her vegetable patch, except this one was big enough to eat an orc. Purple veins pulsed under its pale hide, and its long thin body ended in a circular mouth designed to latch onto something and suck.

A low moan made its way from the rock wyrm's throat, and Vola had a second's warning before it lashed forward.

Vola dove and rolled, coming up with one of her hand axes drawn. Sorrel shot past her, staff a blur in her hands.

Vola took the opportunity Sorrel gave her to shove Shereille down behind a rock outcropping.

"Stay there," she said.

"I could help—"

"No. Our job is to get you to the dragon safely. To get us all to the dragon. The best thing you can do is stay out of the way."

There was another shiver in the rock below, and Vola danced to the side as a rock wyrm's head gnashed its teeth at her feet. She brought her ax down, but the wyrm ducked back into the rock and the blade rang against stone.

"Heads up," she called. "There's more than one."

The swamp monster chewed silently on what was left of the armadillo while Lillie ducked out from behind a rock and shot a stream of fire at the wyrm still waving above them. It's thick, translucent hide reflected the flames so they bounced right off.

The ground under Vola's feet erupted, and she stumbled back a step, but not fast enough. The second rock wyrm's mouth collided with her torso, and its teeth scraped across her armor with a chilling squeal.

She went down under its undulating body with a yell.

"Vola!" Lillie's voice rang against the rocky cliffs, and a blast of fire made Vola's skin shiver. It charred the rock around them, but the rock wyrm just moaned, and its head shot forward again, oblivious to the heat as it tried to attach itself to Vola's breastplate.

"Ha, hah, yah!" A column of air struck the wyrm in the side and lifted it clear off Vola. Sorrel followed it, fist outstretched.

Lillie flashed out of existence and reappeared on an outcropping above them.

Vola flipped to her feet and charged the first wyrm since Sorrel was busy with the second now. She dodged as it lunged and slashed the long body. Instead of biting into the creature's hide, the ax crunched and slid aside. Almost like she'd struck...

"Rock," Lillie called. "They've taken in the essence of their home and used it as armor."

Sorrel spun in a flurry of fists and feet and then fell back, panting. "Essence of what now?"

"How do we fight stone?" Vola called. She still had her ax but held it at her side since it wouldn't do any good.

"Stand back," Lillie said. Then she raised her hands.

Vola knew that gesture well enough. She grabbed the back of Sorrel's tunic and dove for Shereille's shelter.

With a crack that sounded like the air itself split, lightning streaked from the sky and struck the first rock wyrm just as it reared back to strike. It froze there, bits of lightning crackling over its hide. A second branch arced between it and the second wyrm, limning its outline with blue-white light.

The moans of the rock wyrms rose to screams and after a long moment, they toppled to the ground like giant fleshy trees.

"Bleh," Sorrel said, clambering out from their hiding place. "Rock wyrms win the prize for the most disgusting thing we've fought so far."

"You think these beat the giant flesh golem thing in Myron's lab?" Vola said.

"Or what about the time we crawled through the sewer to fight the traitors in Glenhaven?" Lillie pointed out.

"Those were just human traitors." Sorrel climbed to the top of one of the dead wyrms and turned with her hands on her hips. "How are they disgusting?"

"Well, we were covered in, er—" she glanced at her mother, "—poop at the time."

Sorrel gave a shrug. "Then I think we would be the disgusting thing in that scenario."

Lillie flashed back down to the ground and limped to the rock that hid Shereille. "Mother? I mean, Shereille. Are you all right?"

Shereille climbed to her feet and stared dispassionately at the dead wyrms. "How did you know to use lightning?"

Lillie bit her lip. "I do a lot of research before we enter an area. On its inhabitants—both sentient and non—in order to better understand what we might be up against."

"She was reading almost the entire way here," Talon said.

"But then she's always reading, so it's hard to tell when we should pay attention sometimes," Sorrel said.

"Hmm," Shereille said. "Impressive."

Lillie blushed a brilliant scarlet. Shereille didn't look at all shaken from the attack. She just kept climbing up the path. Lillie scampered after her, her lips twitching in a careful smile.

ELEVEN

"WE'RE LOOKING for a long corridor through the mountains," Shereille said as Lillie sent Rand to circle overhead. "I imagine it will be quite obvious from the air and it should lead us to Shereille's new lair."

"Doesn't that seem a little easy?" Sorrel said. "Like a great big arrow saying 'look at my hideout.'"

"Many texts mention some sort of guardian." Shereille tilted her head. "I imagine the challenges will become clear as we get closer to Listrell."

"Great," Vola muttered.

Lillie's eyes went blank as she watched what Rand was seeing. "I don't see a corridor, yet. But there's another scorch mark to the north," she said. "It looks like they extend straight that way."

"Any sign of Talon?" Vola asked quietly.

Lillie shook her head gravely.

Vola wasn't even sure what they were looking for. What signs would Talon have been able to leave? If she was able to leave any…

She shook her head. They just had to find the dragon. If they found the dragon, they'd find Talon. They had to. There were no other options.

"Any more signs of rock wyrms?" Sorrel asked.

Lillie blinked, her attention returning to them. "No, but we wouldn't be able to see them from above, either. They travel directly through the rock and only emerge where they feel vibrations from their prey." She tilted her head as Vola and Sorrel started climbing again. "I wonder if you could set up some sort of machine to thump the ground and draw them away from high traffic areas."

"That's exactly what we do when we camp near known sand and rock wyrm territories," Shereille said. "Well done."

"Oh," Lillie said on a little puff of surprised air.

"It's a mechanism that looks mostly like a hammer. And it thumps the ground to draw the wyrms."

"In a regular cadence? Or are the wyrms smart enough to recognize the difference between a footstep and something tapping?"

"They do recognize the difference." Shereille's eyes lit up as she spoke. "It was actually an intriguing problem for a while. How to imitate the random noises and vibrations caused by a camp."

Lillie tapped her lip. "I'll bet you could do something with gears. Set up an interlocking system with different numbers of teeth in different sizes to create a randomized output."

"Exactly." Shereille threw her hands in the air, and she and Lillie beamed at each other.

Vola cleared her throat. "I'm glad you're having fun, but are we still going the right way?"

Lillie jerked and glanced up at Rand, who circled lazily above. "Rand says yes." She frowned and squinted. "Wait…" She turned slowly in a circle. "I think I see the corridor Shereille was talking about. That way." She pointed toward a cliff in the distance.

It was too steep to climb easily, so Vola had been angling them parallel to it.

Lillie closed her eyes as Rand dove out of sight behind the rock face. "It's like a valley cut through the cliff. It doesn't look natural." She opened her eyes again and caught Vola's glance. "It follows the scorch marks."

"Any sign of the guardians Shereille mentioned?"

Lillie's brow creased. "No. It's…empty."

Vola huffed up one side of a fall of rocks and slid down the other, leading them closer to the cliff. The path had given up some ways back, and now they had to scramble over the stone and scree.

Vola came up against the cliff face and squinted toward the top. There was no way she was getting up without help. The ridgeline flattened out about three times her height.

"Could you teleport us in?" she said.

"Not blindly." Lillie slid down the rocks behind her and winced. She stood, rubbing her rear end. "And it would take so many trips I'd be useless for anything else if we encountered trouble in there."

Vola surveyed the cliff, then met Sorrel's eyes as she hopped down next to her. "Can you get up there?"

Sorrel didn't answer, just made a noise like "pfft" and started digging in the swamp beast's bags. The swamp monster bared its teeth, and Vola lunged forward to keep it from snapping at the monk.

Sorrel turned with a coil of light rope and a stack of metal stakes.

"Pylons," Sorrel said. "Remember the set we almost sank in the swamp? I wondered if we'd ever need them."

"You mean pitons," Lillie said as Sorrel draped the rope over her shoulder. "Did that nasty shopkeeper sell you these?"

"At a discount, even," Vola said with a vicious grin.

"I'll take the rope up and secure it along the way," Sorrel said. "That way you guys can follow."

"We'll have to rig something special for the swamp beast," Lillie added.

Sorrel snorted. "Good luck with that." She took a running jump at the rock face and stuck to the wall six feet up.

"Will she be able to get up that?" Shereille asked, eyes wide as Sorrel scrambled higher.

"Easily," Lillie said. "I've seen her climb sheer walls. She broke us out of prison once."

Vola cleared her throat violently and shook her head before Lillie could tell that particular story.

Sorrel reached the top of the cliff and stood at the ridge line, hands on her hips. She whistled as she gazed over the far edge. "Would you look at that?"

"We can't yet," Vola said. "Stop gawking and do your thing."

Sorrel tied the end off and tossed the rest down the cliff. Then she climbed down a lot slower, stopping every few feet to hammer a piton into the wall and secure the rope to it.

"All right, let's move," Vola said, stepping to the wall.

Shereille glanced dubiously at the rope trail leading up the cliff, but she gamely took hold and started climbing. Sorrel reached the bottom and hesitated a moment before climbing back up to show Shereille the best hand and footholds.

Lillie froze at the base of the cliff.

"I'll give you a boost," Vola said quietly, guessing at Lillie's discomfort.

"It's really not that hard," Lillie said. "I'd just rather no one watched."

"Well, Shereille is pretty distracted. Come on."

Lillie reached for the rope and placed her foot as high as her leg would go. Quickly enough to stall Lillie's protests, Vola put her shoulder under the wizard and heaved.

With a startled "oof," Lillie rose halfway up the cliff and clung to the rope.

"There," Vola said. "Half the work is done."

"Yes, thank you," Lillie snapped. "But maybe with a little less gusto next time."

"At least I can toss you," Vola grumbled, then turned to the swamp monster, who leveled a glare at her. As if daring her to do the same with it.

Gruff had disappeared, maybe to make his own way up and avoid the humiliation of being tossed. But of course, they couldn't count on the swamp beast to solve the problem for them.

"Wait," Sorrel called from above. "I have an idea." She scampered down and hung on the cliff face at about Vola's height, safely off to one side so she didn't get in the way of the climbers. Then she waggled her butt in the air.

Vola gaped. "What are you —"

"Come and get me, you smelly thing," Sorrel called.

"There is no way that will work."

Sorrel bent over to peer through her legs and stuck her tongue out at the beast.

The swamp monster squealed and launched itself at her.

So fast Vola barely registered the movement, Sorrel scaled the cliff again.

And the swamp monster followed, swift and sure as a mountain goat. At the top, it lunged for Sorrel.

The monk ducked out of the way, and the swamp beast sailed past her and out of sight. There was an indignant bellow from the other side.

"Problem solved." Sorrel brushed her hands off and straddled the ridgeline, swinging her feet.

Vola just shook her head and climbed up after them.

At the top, she had to echo Sorrel's whistle. A long corridor had been carved through the mountains with steep walls and a smooth floor leading north and a little east for as far as Vola could see. Once they were in, it would be a lot harder to get out. Sorrel would be able to manage it, no problem, but the rest of them would be stuck.

Gruff walked carefully down the ridgeline to sit next to Vola, having found his own way to the top.

"This seems like the perfect place for an ambush," she said. "A custom-made funnel, channeling us right to whatever's waiting."

"Listrell, hopefully," Shereille said, lowering herself to the ground alongside Sorrel. "This is the thoroughfare leading us to her lair. That is where you wanted to go, isn't it?" Shereille raised an eyebrow.

Vola surveyed the corridor as Lillie slipped the last couple of feet to the ground and landed with an "oof" next to Sorrel and Shereille.

There was nothing in the corridor now. At least not within sight. And any "guardians" trying to get in to ambush them would have the same difficulties scaling the walls.

Unless, of course, they could fly.

Vola lowered herself uneasily to the ground after the others.

"I'll send Rand ahead," Lillie said. "Do you suppose Gruff can scout without being spotted?"

Vola glanced up at the wolf, who sat dejectedly on the ridgeline. "Gruff," she said, trying to imitate Talon. Then she gave him the hand signal the ranger had always used.

The wolf whined once, then shot away along the top of the wall. His course took him parallel to their path.

They followed the corridor to the north, Rand flying high to check ahead.

Five minutes later, they came across a scorch mark, a streak of black soot that stretched from one side of the corridor to the other.

Shereille knelt and ran a finger through the black. She rubbed her fingertips together. "Is this what you were talking about? Dead spots?"

Vola shook her head. "No. This is just burned. Not dead. The land is still alive."

"The spots that we've found have no magic," Lillie said. "Talon could feel it drained out of the land itself. I couldn't cast spells, and Vola couldn't reach her goddess."

"That is...troubling," Shereille said.

Vola wanted to say it was a damn sight more than troubling, but this was the first time Shereille had acknowledged an interest in something outside her area of research, and it didn't seem prudent to mock her.

They marched on, leaving the scorch mark behind. The sun blazed directly overhead, glaring along the trench they followed so there was no shade.

Sorrel didn't seem to mind at all. Vola felt hot but was pretty sure that was a product of wearing a metal chest plate that could double as an oven if needed.

Shereille pulled a floppy hat from her back pocket that unfolded until the enormous brim shaded her head and shoulders.

Lillie glanced at her, then bounced from foot to foot before she pulled the straw hat Vola had bought her out from the swamp beast's packs.

Shereille raised an impressed eyebrow, and she and Lillie spent the next hour comparing notes on big hats. Vola was glad Lillie had finally found some common ground with her mother, but they really couldn't have picked a more boring subject.

Ahead, shapes came into view, and Vola slowed. Rand swooped over them in the signal for all-clear, but it sure looked like large figures lined the corridor in front of them.

Vola gave the signal to wait, and the others fell silent as she crept forward. On the ridge above, Gruff mirrored her progress.

Vola reached the first figure and huffed a laugh.

"Statues," she called to the others. "They're statues."

"Yes, but of what?" Sorrel said as they trotted forward.

Vola tilted her head to examine the carved stone. They stood almost two heads taller than Vola herself and had been chiseled from the same red-brown rock that surrounded them. The figure was humanoid in that it had two arms and two legs, but a draconic head stared down at them and a scaly tail jutted out behind the figure.

"They're beautiful," Lillie said, creeping closer to the one opposite. She reached out, but her hand stopped before she actually touched the armor carved across the statue's chest. "So lifelike."

"These must be the guardians the texts talked about," Shereille said, voice hushed and reverent. "We must be getting close to Listrell's lair."

"What do you mean?" Lillie asked.

"These statues. I could write so many papers on these alone. Perhaps they were placed by the ancient peoples who worshiped dragons."

"Wasn't Listrell sleeping somewhere else?" Sorrel asked. "In that mountain she destroyed yesterday. Why would these be here and not there?"

"Dragons don't sleep in the same lairs where they spend their time awake."

"Really?" Sorrel said, squinting up at one of the statues. "Why? I mean, besides the fact that she destroyed hers when she woke up."

"Would you want to spend another minute in the bed where you'd just spent a hundred years?" Lillie said.

Sorrel shrugged. "Fair point."

"We spent most of our time near her sleeping lair, so I've never actually seen them before." Shereille stepped right up next to one. "I should have sent an expedition out here to study these before she woke. I always figured we had time. And I hoped she wouldn't wake up quite so angry so I'd have a chance to talk to her."

"But you're sure you still want to study her now that she's trying to burn everything to the ground?" Vola said.

"Oh, of course. Even just five minutes of observation would make a huge difference in our understanding."

Lillie shifted her feet. "I'm not sure you'll have a chance to talk to her. We need to make sure she doesn't go on any more rampages."

Shereille gave her a little smile. "All knowledge is good knowledge. I am very much looking forward to seeing how she fights. I will attempt to take copious notes before you do what needs to be done. I wish I could take the time to sketch these statues as well, but I suppose you want to move on."

"No need to worry," Lillie said, holding up her notebook. "Already done."

Shereille's lips parted on a smile. "You work fast."

"I suppose I've had a lot of practice."

"Good, that means we can go," Vola said.

"Yeah, these things look like they're ready to come alive and jump us," Sorrel said.

A growl rumbled from the surround rock. "You ruined the surprise," the low, rough voice came from the statue in front of Vola.

"Heaagh!" Vola jumped back as the draconic statue moved, stretching its limbs.

It cracked its neck and then fixed Vola with a beady glare. All the statues around them creaked to life, blinking in the sun and shaking out their arms as if they'd been asleep awhile.

Sorrel stared around them with her hands on her hips. Shereille looked absolutely delighted.

"They aren't statues," Lillie whispered. "They're alive."

"We're all watching," Vola snapped. "You don't have to narrate everything."

"How do you do that?" Sorrel tilted her head back to ask the nearest guardian. "Stay so still?"

His lips pulled back from his teeth in a grin. "We enter a fugue state." He seemed to be the only one interested in conversing. The others checked their weapons and armor. All along the corridor as far as Vola could see, hundreds of draconic statues came alive, ready for a fight.

"It slows our breathing and our heart rate so we may remain stationary for centuries if necessary."

"Can you teach me that?" Lillie asked.

"I cannot," the guardian replied. Color returned to his scales as they spoke, streaking the reddish-brown under his armor with subtle flashes of green and blue. "Dragon blood is required. And I believe we will be busy with other things." He rolled his shoulders and settled his massive warhammer in his hands. "We cannot allow you to disturb Listrell."

"Disturb?" Sorrel said. "She's set fire to an entire city and we're disturbing her?"

"We will not let you pass."

The other guardians moved to stand at his shoulders. Each one had a subtle pattern of colors moving along their skin. And each one carried their weapon like they'd had centuries to perfect their skill.

"I don't suppose reasoned argument is going to change your mind," Vola said.

The lead guardian's lip twitched, revealing a long row of very sharp teeth. "No. But it was nice of you to try long enough for my warriors to breathe life back into their limbs."

"You're welcome," Vola said sourly, unsheathing her axes.

"This is not personal," the guardian said. "Only duty."

"Keep telling yourself that, buddy," Sorrel said. She spun her staff so it whirred through the air. "If it makes you feel better."

The guardian lunged for Vola.

She twisted out of the way, trapping the guardian's forward arm under hers. Then she brought her knee up into his gut.

The breath that whooshed from his lungs was dry and hot as the desert wind.

The ridge of scales above his eye that looked like an eyebrow rose. "All right, this will not be as easy as I thought," he wheezed.

"Damn right it won't," Vola said. Then she yanked him around so Cleavah's lightning struck him squarely in the back.

Vola pushed away in time to avoid getting singed.

"I always knew that would come in handy someday," Sorrel said and threw herself at the clump of stunned guardians. She scrambled up one, using its own armor as her footholds, bashed it over the head with her staff, and then launched herself at another.

Lillie stepped aside, muttering over her hands before she shot lightning into the nearest guardian. The arc of energy zipped from one figure to the next, to the next, curving to avoid Vola and Sorrel.

A howl echoed from the walls of the corridor, and Gruff dropped on a guardian. His teeth screeched across scales as he tore at the figure's throat. But the guardian did not fall.

None of them fell. Even the one in front of Vola had regained his wind and pressed forward.

Vola huffed and called out, "Gruff, guard Shereille. Guard!"

The wolf lunged away from the guardian, teeth bared, and then raced to herd the elven researcher against the wall. He circled in front of her, keeping the other guardians at bay while Shereille watched with shining eyes.

As an experiment, Vola slashed the nearest guardian's arm. Her ax blade drew little blood from the scaly skin and the creature didn't seem fazed at all.

The guardians were as living as Vola and the others, but they were nearly as hard as the statues they resembled. Sorrel was having a little more luck with blunt force and Lillie had her lightning, but through the sweat stinging her eyes, Vola could see the inevitable.

The corridor was narrow enough that the guardians couldn't get around their sides to flank them, but the figures stretched ahead of them, nearly endless. Hundreds still waited for their turn to attack the intruders.

Blood beat in Vola's ears. There were too many and they took too long to cut down. She and the others would fight well, yes. Maybe even for hours. But inevitably they'd fall exhausted amid the hordes of guardians. Unless they could pull an ace out of their sleeve.

Cleavah had said the dragons were like siblings. They were there when the Greater Virtues created the world. Did that include the servants of dragons?

Only one way to find out, and they didn't have a lot of options if they wanted to press forward to find Talon. Vola wasn't a Greater Virtue. But she knew someone who was. Maybe.

The lead guardian brought his warhammer down, and Vola caught it on her crossed axes. Her muscles strained to keep the wicked point from falling any further.

"Lady," she croaked.

"I am here." A breath of wind touched her cheek.

"Will they obey you?"

After only the briefest hesitation, the blades of Vola's axes burst into flames.

"Let's find out," Cleavah said.

The guardian flinched away from the flames, and his warhammer slipped against Vola's weapons. She heaved and threw him off. He stumbled back a step and fell to one knee.

He raised his head as if it pained him.

"What—? How are you—?" His slitted green eyes widened. "You are a Greater Virtue."

Vola snorted. "No. But I have one on my side."

The flames flickered in the eyes of the guardians, and one by one they fell to their knees around their leader.

"What will you do now?" he asked.

Vola took a deep breath, her shoulders relaxing a bit. But she didn't dare loosen her grip on her axes.

"It seems to me like this would be the perfect time to get rid of them," Shereille said. "Make sure they don't get back up again or hinder us from our purpose."

Vola winced. She didn't like the idea of leaving an enemy at her back, but she also wasn't in the habit of slaying a thinking creature who knelt before her in submission.

But Talon still waited for rescue.

"Let us through," Vola said.

"I cannot." The guardian dropped his eyes.

"Not even at the command of a greater god?" That was stretching it a little. But Cleavah had just confirmed her place in the pantheon, even if Vola still didn't know her real name.

"No," the guardian said with a growl. "I am bound so that none may pass me while I still live."

"We don't want to kill you," Sorrel said.

"We don't?" Shereille tilted her head.

"No," Lillie said. "They don't fight us while Vola controls them."

"She's right," Vola said. "We don't want to kill you."

"But will you kill Listrell?" the guardian asked.

Vola's lips thinned. "I can't guarantee anything past this point."

The guardian bowed his head. "That is…better than I thought. If I cannot fight you and I cannot let you pass, then I have only one option."

He stood smoothly and signaled the other guardians. In a wave of movement, they all rose from their knees, and together they retreated down the corridor. The lead guardian's eyes remained on Vola until they disappeared from sight.

TWELVE

"ALL RIGHT, I admire your elegant solution to a hopeless fight," Lillie whispered after the guardians had disappeared. "But what are we going to do when we get to the lair? We're just delaying the inevitable. They know we're coming, and they won't let us kill their dragon."

Vola ground her teeth, thinking the same things. "We might have better terrain for an assault when we get there."

"Better terrain?" Sorrel said. "In a dragon's lair, inside a mountain, which she probably picked specifically to be defensible."

"I don't know. I'm just following our normal procedure."

"You mean, making it up as we go?"

Vola made a face. "It sounds so much worse when you say it out loud."

Lillie patted her arm. "Perhaps it will all work out. We're good at improvising. It's why Rilla calls us Mishap's Heroes. Even if Sorrel refuses to acknowledge the name."

Sorrel plugged her ears and skipped ahead. "Not listening," she sang.

Vola shook her head.

"Will you be able to do what you did before?" Lillie said, gesturing to Vola's axes. "With Listrell instead?"

Vola glanced at her weapons. The flames sputtered and flickered out, but Vola could still see the sheen of orange and yellow along the blades.

"No," Cleavah said in her ear, but from the way Lillie and Sorrel straightened, they heard her, too.

Shereille had pulled out her notebook and was scribbling furiously, bright head bent over the page. For that moment, she looked just like Lillie.

"My authority extends to draconic servants," Cleavah said. "But I doubt one of the great dragons will bow to my authority. Even if we called them sisters and brothers once."

"Well, I guess that answers that question," Sorrel said to the air. "You really are a greater god."

"We knew that." Lillie addressed the spot over Vola's shoulder. "The remaining question is which one."

The air remained silent and expectant, and Vola got the distinct impression Cleavah was waiting for her to add something.

"Cleavah is good enough for me," she said.

Sorrel rolled her eyes and turned to start down the corridor. "One day you'll have to as—" She fell in the sand with a grunt.

"What was that?" Vola said.

Sorrel kicked her feet. "I tripped over something."

"You? Tripped?" Lillie said, kneeling to brush the sand away, revealing the cold ashes of a long-dead fire. A couple logs created lumps in the sand.

"It happens sometimes," Sorrel said. "And that's not what caught me. It was this." She snagged the strap of a satchel and pulled it from the sand.

"Wait." Vola lunged forward and caught the bag, so it stopped swinging. She swiped sand from the flap.

A complicated knot was burned into the outside, matching the ones that crawled the length of Sorrel's staff. The symbol for Maxim's followers.

"This was Master Bao's," Vola said. "He was carrying it when we saw him in the all-pantheon temple."

Sorrel yanked the satchel from Vola and tore open the flap to rummage inside.

"Did you literally trip over a clue?" Vola said. "I can't decide if that's good luck or bad."

"Maybe your goddess isn't the only one getting involved here," Lillie said. "I'd believe it was a coincidence if it was me. But Sorrel hardly ever trips over anything. Perhaps Maxim wanted her to find it."

Vola made a face. It would be a first if Maxim decided to pay attention to anything down here.

Sorrel pulled a battered journal from the satchel and flipped through the pages.

"What's in it?" Vola asked. "How does it end? Anything helpful about what might have happened to him?"

"Unfortunately, no. No convenient cause of death."

"When I die, I'll be sure to leave you a written record of the event," Lillie said.

"I really can't tell if you're being facetious or not," Vola said.

Lillie grinned at her.

"There is this, though," Sorrel said, her mouth drawing down at the corners. It was the most unamused face Sorrel had ever managed. She held up the last page of the journal.

Vola squinted to make the words stop swimming and read aloud.

"I've made my choice, Sorrel. Stop following me."

Lillie rubbed her lips, hiding a smile.

"Well, at least now we know it wasn't a coincidence," Vola said.

Sorrel stuffed the journal back in the satchel and stalked toward the swamp beast. "No, he meant for me to find it. This was his last camping spot. He had to have seen Listrell erupt from here, but he's still going through with his plan to up and die in the mountains somewhere."

She snatched the swamp monster's lead rope and avoided its bite to tie the satchel to the rest of their supplies.

"Then we still have time to find him," Vola said. "After we find Talon."

Shereille slipped her pen back in her pocket and snapped her notebook shut. "Of course, Listrell flew this way last night. She could have snatched your master the same way she snatched your teammate."

Vola glared at Shereille as Sorrel went green. "That was so helpful, thanks."

"There's no blood," Lillie pointed out. "Or claw marks. If Master Bao encountered Listrell, he has the same chance of survival as Talon, I imagine."

"Unless the guardians got him." Sorrel brushed the sand from her pants.

Vola shook her head. "They didn't come alive until we started talking about what we would do when we reached Listrell. I think we must have activated their defenses somehow. If he was just camping here, they might not have bothered him."

"Which means Listrell is our best chance of finding both of them right now," Lillie said.

Sorrel nodded and turned to continue down the corridor. This time she carried her staff in her hand, ready.

The sun had started falling toward the horizon, dipping behind the ragged peaks by the time the corridor ended abruptly in a rock wall. A stone doorway large enough to admit a dragon opened into the cliff, the deep black maw stretching into the mountain itself.

"Needs a welcome mat," Sorrel said, tapping her teeth.

"I'm not sure Listrell is really open to visitors," Lillie said.

"How are we doing this?" Sorrel said. "The guardians will be ready for us." She pointed to the sand in front of the door, which was pitted and marked with hundreds of footprints.

"Maybe she has a back door," Vola said and glanced at Shereille. "Any ideas?"

"Her last lair was riddled with openings," Shereille said, examining the facade. "Air holes like the one we made our observations through. *Draconis maximus* might be tied to the land but they still need fresh air."

"Holes big enough to sneak into?"

Shereille pursed her lips. "Usually. An air hole for a dragon is a sizable tunnel for anyone else."

"So we find one of those instead of knocking on the front door. I think this has a better chance of working if Listrell is at least surprised by *how* we come in. Our goal is to save Talon. Not kill a dragon. If we can sneak in to do it, all the better."

"You won't fight her?" Shereille said.

Vola cast her a disgruntled glance. "Not if we don't have to. Not if it endangers our teammate. If we can find and free Talon without risking anyone's life or limbs, then we will."

"I do like my limbs," Sorrel said.

Between Sorrel, who could climb, and Rand's swooping passes, they found a nearby tunnel much more subdued than the big entrance by the corridor. A healthy breeze of hot, dry air threaded steadily into the entrance.

"Hey, it's not stinky," Sorrel said, poking her head into the entrance.

"Well, it hasn't had a dragon sleeping in it for the last century." Vola dragged her back from the entrance. "We're supposed to be sneaking, remember?"

"I'm naturally sneaky," Sorrel said. "People don't see me because I'm so short."

"They can still hear you." Vola rolled her eyes. "Sorrel goes in first. Lillie and I after them. Shereille, you'll stay here with the swamp monster."

"What?" Shereille said with a dubious glance at the swamp creature. "I'm not staying here. I'm supposed to be studying Listrell."

"You can come see her up close as soon as we've...er...subdued the situation."

Shereille opened her mouth again.

"We're not arguing about this," Vola said, putting on her paladin face. "You hired us to get you to your subject safely. So let us do our job." Plus, Vola didn't want to worry about protecting her while they were trying to find Talon.

Shereille scowled, but she snapped her mouth shut and didn't argue again.

Vola signaled Sorrel forward while Shereille sullenly grabbed the swamp beast's halter.

Lillie bit her lip. "Just don't get too close to its head," she told her mother. "It really doesn't care what it eats."

Vola dragged her into the tunnel after Talon and Sorrel.

"You didn't have to be so harsh with her," Lillie whispered fiercely. "She just wants to see her life's work fulfilled."

"And I'd prefer she stay alive while she's doing it, wouldn't you?"

Lillie shut up.

The tunnel was narrow and close, but Vola could stand most of the way upright, which was better than a lot of places they'd stormed. She tried to walk carefully without a lot of clanking and made sure she didn't scrape against the rough walls. Gruff stayed pressed against her side.

Air still streamed past them, as if something on the far side sucked it through a straw. They hadn't lit any torches, and Lillie kept her spells dark and silent, so Vola trailed one hand on the wall and trusted Sorrel to lead them through the dark.

Gradually, Vola realized a faint glow grew ahead of them, mostly blocked by Lillie's head. The tunnel continued to lighten until Vola could make out Sorrel silhouetted against the lighter cavern opening.

The halfling turned and held her finger to her lips but didn't signal them to wait, so Vola and Lillie crept up behind her.

An enormous cavern opened beyond the mouth of the tunnel carved into the very center of the mountain. Massive amounts of stone had been chiseled away, leaving great columns stretching to support the arch of the ceiling so far above it was lost in darkness.

The rock face sloped away from their feet down to the cavern floor where rank upon rank of draconic guardians had gathered. They knelt in a wide circle, weapons ready and facing out, as still as the statues they'd originally mistaken them for. Behind them they could finally see what made the cavern glow.

Listrell paced back and forth from one end of the cavern to the other, her turquoise scales pulsing with her anger. She was the light source for the entire cave.

As impressive as the sight was, it wasn't what Vola had been looking for.

"Where's Talon?" Lillie whispered.

Vola didn't see any sign of the ranger. And it wasn't like there were a lot of hiding spots, at least ones that weren't directly under the dragon.

"Maybe she escaped," Sorrel said, eying the other openings around the cavern

It was a nice hope, but Vola couldn't seem to fit it around the knot of pain and worry in her gut.

"Look," Lillie said, her voice flat. She pointed, and Vola and Sorrel followed her focus to the dark cloth caught in Listrell's claws.

It was just black fabric. It shouldn't have made Vola's insides twist with pain. But she'd seen that cloak every day for months now, and her gut recognized it even before her mind had caught up.

Her sharp inhale echoed in the tunnel behind them. "Talon."

The ranger herself was gone. All that remained was that tattered bit of clothing slashed almost beyond recognition.

"She can't be—" Sorrel choked, cutting off the rest of what she was about to say.

Lillie held her hands over her mouth.

Vola's fingers clenched on the edge of the ledge, and she forced herself to breathe as little flickers of red licked at the edges of her vision.

"We can't..." Lillie cleared her throat. "We can't assume. Look. The guardians haven't noticed us yet. We can still leave. We'll follow Listrell's flight path back to the city. She might have dropped her somewhere in the mountains—"

A squeal of rage rang from the walls behind them, making Vola jump.

Lillie and Sorrel flattened themselves against the wall, and Vola ducked as a shape came charging down the tunnel.

"Oh, fu—" Vola lunged for the swamp beast's halter as it sped past, but she missed, and the creature shot off the edge. Straight into the sea of guardians below.

Listrell didn't even wait for the guardians to defend her.

She lurched forward, head snaking out on her long neck. The dragon's jaw snapped shut on the swamp beast, who disappeared with a cut-off snort.

Vola froze at the edge of the tunnel and stared.

"Uh, so that just happened," Sorrel said.

Boots pounded up behind them, and Vola turned to catch Shereille skidding to a stop, her eyes wide. "I'm so sorry. I couldn't catch it."

"Guys," Sorrel said.

Hot air blasted past them, and Vola glanced up to find Listrell looming over them, her nostrils glowing as she took a deep breath. Her eyes focused on them in the tunnel mouth.

This…this thing had killed Talon. Eaten her as easily as it had eaten the swamp creature. Vola welcomed the red that smeared her vision, welcomed the rage that swelled through her, and lent strength to her limbs. She opened her mouth and roared at the dragon.

"Well, this is happening," Sorrel said. "Lillie, cover us from the right. Vola, I assume you want to go down the middle with me."

"Yes," she growled.

"Great, don't get crisped."

"I'll just…stay here and take notes, then?" Shereille said behind them.

Lillie popped out of existence and reappeared on a shelf halfway up the wall to the right.

Vola crouched, holding her shield over her head. Sorrel leaped onto its flat surface, and Vola heaved, flipping her into the air.

The moment Sorrel was airborne, Vola ducked and dove out of the way as a stream of fire struck the wall behind them and sparks flew. Shereille didn't even flinch. She just pulled out her notebook and started taking down her observations.

Sorrel landed on Listrell's snout as Vola hit the slope and turned her dive into a roll. She found her feet at the bottom and raced between the guardians, who shifted and stood. Gruff hit the ground seconds behind her and dove into the fray with his teeth bared.

Sorrel spun atop the dragon's muzzle and brought her staff down between Listrell's eyes. "Ha!"

Listrell shook her head violently, but Sorrel clung to the ridge over her eyes, flapping around like a shirt on a washing line.

Gruff snarled and snapped, then suddenly he froze, sniffing the air. He threw his head back and howled long and high. Without any other warning, he shot off toward one of the other air holes in the opposite side of the cavern.

"Gruff!" Vola called. Talon would never forgive her if the wolf got himself lost or killed.

But before she could follow, Listrell swung her head and snapped at Vola. Vola threw up her shield and deflected the dragon's snout, glistening teeth closing inches from her face.

A boom echoed above them, and a wash of heat heralded Lillie's first fireball of the day.

Listrell raised her head, and Vola darted into the space she'd left and swung her hand ax at the dragon's claw, right where the talon met the skin.

Listrell shrieked and pushed herself up to stand on two legs, wings spread. Vola's eyes widened as she realized how big the cavern really was if she could do that without clipping her wings on either side.

A voice full of roaring wind spoke in her ear. "Behind you."

Vola spun in time to catch the lead guardian's warhammer against her shield. But in the moment she was distracted, the dragon fell back onto all fours and whipped around.

Vola yelped and brought her shield up. But instead of snapping at her again, the dragon's tail whistled through the air and caught her from behind.

Vola flew through the air and struck the wall with a clang. She crumpled to the floor, one long ache. The cavern spun around her, and she blinked, trying to focus through the pain. Vague shapes started converging, and she tried to remember why that was a bad thing.

"Vola!" she heard as if from a great distance.

Claws descended and pinned her to the ground. She still held her ax, but she couldn't even lift it, not with the dragon's strength holding her down.

She blinked at the guardians who leveled their weapons at her as she tried to call back the red rage that lent her strength. But she just felt empty, her chest caving inward under the crushing weight of her armor and the dragon's claw.

"Why do you invade my home?" a voice boomed above her, and Vola focused her watering eyes on the dragon.

"You...killed my...friend," she wheezed.

"It's possible. I kill anything that threatens me and mine."

Vola bared her teeth, but that was all she managed. She tried to struggle, but her wrists just flopped uselessly against the ground. Even at full strength she'd have been pinned, and hitting the wall had knocked her silly before that.

The dragon arched her neck and sucked in a huge breath, the air whistling past Vola. Little flames flickered at the corners of Listrell's mouth.

Vola refused to close her eyes, even though she knew what was coming.

A figure, blurred through Vola's pain, leaped onto the dragon's claw. Vola gasped as their weight landed. The figure planted two long daggers in the foot that pinned Vola.

Listrell shrieked and yanked her claws back, shaking the figure loose.

Vola raised her head and blinked the fog from her eyes.

The figure stood between Vola and the dragon and all the guardians surrounding them. A figure wearing a dark cuirass with sandy-colored hair growing out of a short cut. Gruff growled beside her.

Vola heaved in a painful breath. "Talon," she wheezed.

THIRTEEN

TALON STOOD THERE, features outlined in blood and soot and her clothes torn. But her eyes were bright and fierce. She looked like she'd fallen off a cliff. Or got in a fight with a dragon.

Listrell drew back her lips, baring teeth as silver as Talon's blades.

Vola rolled, ignoring the grating pain in her chest, and pushed up onto her elbows. She needed to rise, to defend and protect. This was about to go so badly. Talon had said she didn't want revenge on all dragons, but this one had attacked her new pack. What was going through her head?

Black crept across Vola's vision and she collapsed on the ground again.

Listrell lunged.

Talon spun aside, dodging the teeth, and slashed her twin blades across the dragon's face.

Most of Vola's blows had just slid off the impervious scales, but Talon must have hit something sensitive. Listrell yanked back with a hiss and raised her front claws to hold her face.

A collective gasp went through the guardians, and they pulled their weapons back as if to charge.

Talon spoke, her voice as harsh as usual, but her words were guttural and unfamiliar. They rang against the cavern walls, echoing back to them a hundred times. It wasn't a language Vola recognized, but Listrell certainly did.

The dragon snorted and jerked her head up. The guardians fell back a step, shaking their heads in confusion. The lead guardian they'd talked to in the corridor tilted his head back and stared up at Listrell as if asking for orders.

A skidding sound distracted Vola, and suddenly Sorrel's sandals appeared in her view. "Talon!"

Lillie's boots joined them a few inches from Vola's nose. "We thought you were dead." Her voice quavered, as if she still didn't quite believe the truth.

Vola tried once more to lever herself to her feet, using the wall for balance. Lillie rushed to help her, sliding her shoulder under Vola's arm. They wobbled for a precarious moment before Vola gained her feet.

Talon remained between them and the dragon.

Listrell waited, eying them with a swirling green eye.

"Talon," Vola grated. Her voice didn't sound right, either from the damage in her chest or the way her heart squeezed, Vola wasn't sure.

Sorrel stepped up beside the ranger, leveling her staff at the guardians and the dragon beyond. "Shall we finish this?" she said with a feral grin.

"No," Talon said.

"What?" Lillie said as Sorrel's mouth dropped open.

"No."

"I heard that part," Lillie said. "Perhaps I should clarify the question. Why not?"

"She killed you," Sorrel said. "Er, well, I mean, I guess she didn't actually kill you. But we sure thought she did. And she carried you away. And she ate the swamp beast and set fire to the city."

Talon remained poised, knives in her hands, eyes trained on Listrell. But she didn't make a move to attack.

"We're not going to kill her because she didn't kill me," Talon said. Her voice grated like normal, but she spoke with grudging respect. "And because she's not killing us now." She gestured to the dragon, who waited beyond her wall of guardians, watching them warily.

"What did you say to her?" Vola asked.

"I said I knew she was Pipwattle's victim."

"That is surprisingly reasonable," Listrell rumbled. "I don't meet a lot of reasonable adventurers. And definitely not any that speak my language." She lowered her head to gaze at them steadily. "Truce?"

"Truce," Talon said.

"Great," Vola wheezed. "I never really set out to slay dragons, anyway."

Sorrel shrugged and let her staff fall from its guard position. "Yeah, it's no fun to kill things that aren't trying to kill me back."

Since the guardians had all lowered their weapons and the dragon sat back on her haunches, staring at them with her head tilted, Vola finally felt safe enough to drop one of her axes and take care of the rib stabbing her lungs.

She laid her hand over her chest and whispered, "Lady bless."

Power flowed out of her center and then in through her hand, resetting bone and knitting it. The pain eased.

"You have the power of one of the greater gods," Listrell said.

"It's more like she lets me borrow it." Vola finally took a deep breath and straightened away from Lillie's support. She faced Talon.

"I thought you'd been killed," she said. "We came out here to rescue you and when we couldn't find you, we thought you'd been eaten."

"Ha," Sorrel said. "Then you saved us instead."

Talon's lips twisted in a little smirk. Blood had dried in a streak down the side of her face. "I appreciate the thought, at least."

Vola wanted to throw her arms around the ranger to make sure she was real and unhurt. But Talon wasn't a hugger. She held herself apart, even from them, and probably wouldn't appreciate almost seven feet of paladin blubbering on her shoulder.

"No offense, but why aren't you dead?" Sorrel said.

"She dropped me," Talon said. "As she flew over some of the closer peaks, she let me go. It took me this long to catch up with you."

Which explained why Talon looked like she'd rolled off a cliff.

"Are you all right?" Vola asked quietly.

Talon rolled her shoulder and winced. "A little banged up. Nothing a couple of full nights of rest won't help."

Vola glared at Listrell.

"She could have circled back and eaten me, Vola," Talon said to her personally. "She didn't."

"That doesn't make her good," Sorrel said, glaring at the dragon. "That's like the lowest standard of living, not eating people. And she set fire to the city."

"An emotional reaction, I assure you," Listrell said. She covered her mouth with a claw and let out a loud gassy burp. Then cleared her throat. "Excuse me. You've never woken up on the wrong side of the cave?"

"Of course, except when I wake up angry, I don't level whole cities." Sorrel planted her hands on her hips.

"I don't usually," Listrell said, avoiding their eyes sheepishly. "But I don't respond well to pain. It's a personal flaw that I'm working on." She burped again and looked surprised. "I'm sorry, something I ate isn't agreeing with me."

"What do you mean, pain?" Lillie asked.

"The land I am tied to, I am its caretaker. But also, it is my source of power. And someone drained all the magic out of a piece of it. It woke me up early, and it feels like a hole burned right through my hide." She scratched the side of her belly.

They exchanged a look.

"The dead spots," Lillie said.

"They hurt her," Talon said. "It's like someone stabbing you awake."

"You understand," Listrell said, leveling her gaze on Talon. "I like this one. I was thinking about eating you. That's why I grabbed you. But the moment I flew away from the city, you stopped fighting me."

"Because there wasn't a reason anymore. We were just trying to protect the people there."

"The way I was just trying to protect my people and the land we are connected to." She jerked her snout at the guardians.

"We have a common enemy then," Talon said.

"The one who's draining magic out of the land," Vola said.

"The gnome," Listrell added.

"How did you know that part?" Sorrel asked.

Listrell shrugged her massive shoulders. "I have resources."

Then she made a gagging noise, covered her mouth, and hunkered down to heave something big and wet onto the floor of the cavern.

The swamp monster rolled to its feet and shook the goo from its scaly hide.

The party ducked with various cries of disgust and outrage.

"I'm so sorry," Listrell said. "Usually I'm a very neat eater. But bleh, my mouth tastes like three-day-old fish."

FOURTEEN

"I'M NOT surprised it didn't agree with you," Vola said as Sorrel took advantage of the opportunity and snagged the swamp monster's halter. "It's never agreed with anyone that we can tell."

"But you still let me eat it." The guardians around Listrell shifted out of their combative stances and moved away toward the edges of the cavern, leaving only the lead guardian they'd talked to in the corridor.

"Should we hang a sign around its neck that says 'may cause stomach upset?'" Sorrel asked.

"If we're on the same side, then we can't go around talking about who ate whose swamp monster and who attacked who on a cliff outside Firewatch," Talon said, crossing her arms.

"I already apologized for that. Oh, you mean before I flamed the city." Listrell shuffled her feet. "Fair point. Wait, then are you the ones..." She dug around in her mouth with a claw and winced as she pulled Vola's sword from between her teeth. "That's been bugging me something awful. Finally managed to work it loose." She handed it down to Vola. "Is this yours?"

"Er, yes. Thank you." It was a relief to take the hilt in her hand again, even if it was covered in slime and a little bit of dragon flesh.

Pebbles cascaded down the slope behind them, heralding the arrival of Shereille as she slid down to join them on the cavern floor.

"How many of you are there?" Listrell asked.

"That's it," Vola muttered.

"I'm not really with them," Shereille said, making Lillie sag yet again. "I hired them to bring me here. Greetings, Great Listrell. It is so wonderful to finally meet you in person."

Shereille made a big show of bobbing her head to the dragon.

Listrell glanced between her and Talon. "Customs change so much when you sleep for hundreds of years. Are the cults that worship dragons still around, then?"

"I don't think so," Talon said. "I think this is just Shereille being Shereille."

"Oh, good. High Holy Days were always so awkward. How many times do you have to say, 'no unwilling sacrifices?' A nice roasted ox does the trick without all that tying up and screaming part."

Shereille froze, hands raised in some exaggerated gesture before she dropped them to her sides. "I'm not a worshipper. I'm Dr. Moonhallowed. I'm the lead researcher on the *draconis maximus* team based out of Fire-watch. I've been studying you for nearly ten years now."

"Studying?" Listrell said.

"While you slept," Shereille said.

Listrell's whirling green eyes narrowed. "That's...unsettling."

"I was just hoping to ask you some questions." Shereille pulled her notebook and pen from her pocket.

"And you thought now was a good time? When we have someone draining magic out of the land and waking dragons before their time? If you think I was bad, you should see old Bothard when he's startled."

Shereille blinked. "That just means this is the best time. I must get all my answers before the world ends."

"I'd rather keep the world from ending," Listrell said and turned her shoulder, effectively cutting Shereille off with her bulk. "Now," she addressed Talon and Vola. "I know where you should start."

"With Nargilla Pipwattle," Vola said. "She's the one doing the draining. Do you know how to find her?" Perhaps dragons could sense the draining before it got out of control, the way Talon almost had.

"Yes, Pipwattle," Listrell said. "What an awful name. I've captured someone who works for her."

"Really?" Lillie said.

"I've actually rounded up several people wandering around my moun-tain in the last day. There are certainly a lot more of you little almost-humans than there were the last time I was awake."

"Master Bao!" Sorrel exclaimed. "You found Master Bao."

"Oh, I have no idea. I can't actually tell you apart most of the time.

You're too small. And every time I stick my head in their cave to get some answers, they do nothing but scream. That's where you come in."

"You want us to interrogate your prisoners?" Vola said.

"They're only prisoners because I didn't want them escaping to Firewatch and bringing an army back here. They'll be free to go as soon as we move to another lair, and Renvick and the others have been taking good care of them in the meantime. He at least can tell them apart."

She nodded to her lead guardian, the one with green and blue streaks through his red-brown scales.

"I will show you to them," Renvick said with a small bow.

Sorrel scrambled to keep up with him as the big draconic figure strode off toward the other side of the cave. Talon followed, but Lillie hesitated.

"You coming?" Vola asked.

Lillie bit her lip and glanced at her mother who had wasted no time filling the sudden silence with questions. Listrell grumbled under her breath.

"I think I'd better keep an eye on Shereille," Lillie said. "You can fill me in when you're done."

Vola just raised an eyebrow and followed Renvick and the others.

Across the cavern, the lead guardian disappeared into one of the wider air holes dug into the rock of the mountain. Not too big by Listrell's standards, but wide enough to sleep their entire party if need be.

The back end opened onto a cave about the size of the all-pantheon temple in Firewatch where several figures lounged on crates and canvas sacks. One small figure puttered around a pot over a fire against the far wall.

Sorrel scanned the small crowd, and her shoulders drooped. "I don't see Master Bao."

The prisoners eyed them curiously over cups of fine porcelain.

"More captives, Renvick?" one asked. He was a tall, slim elf dressed in hunting leathers with his hair tied up in intricate knots.

"Not today," Renvick said in his deep rumble. "But they're here to help. Then we can get you home faster."

The hunter shrugged. "No hurry. I haven't eaten so well in a long time."

The others made agreeable noises.

Vola addressed the hunter. "You're doing okay, here? Do you need rescuing?"

The hunter snorted. "Renvick's guardians are keeping us in fine fashion. They're better hunters than me. And the last one they brought in was a merchant who'd lost the rest of his caravan in the mountains. He was so grateful not to die on some mountain peak that he donated his goods. It won't hurt any of us to hang out here for a few days. Just so long as the dragon stays on that side of the wall."

"She will not fit in here anyway," Renvick said.

"Probably the only reason they're all so calm," Talon muttered.

Vola cleared her throat. "Um, do you know if any of you worked for a gnome named Nargilla Pipwattle?" She wasn't even sure it was a good question. Would someone who'd worked with Pipwattle volunteer that information?

The hunter spun on his crate and pointed. "You want Doddleben. She left him out on the mountainside for no good reason. But lucky for him, he ended up here."

"Thanks," Vola said. She moved the way he'd indicated with Talon and Renvick close on her heels.

Behind her, Sorrel asked, "Hey, while you were out there, did you happen to see an old monk?"

Vola left her to her questioning. Towards the back wall, an older gnome bustled around a makeshift living area wearing an apron over his tattered robe. He hummed while he transferred a steaming pot from a camp stove to a big rock made up like a table. Complete with a checkered table cloth and some mismatched plates.

Vola cleared her throat, and the gnome looked up startled.

"Oh, hello Renvick," he said, looking at the guardian. "Visitors?"

"I heard you were with Nargilla Pipwattle," Vola said.

Doddleben sniffed. "Worked for. Briefly." The old gnome straightened his tablecloth with gentle hands.

"We're looking for her. Any information you have would be helpful." From the hunter and Doddleben's reaction, it didn't seem like the old gnome was particularly loyal.

"Of course, of course. Join me?"

Vola blinked as Doddleben flounced to the other side of the makeshift table and sat down with a flourish. He stared up at her, waiting.

She felt eyes on the back of her head and glanced over her shoulder. All the prisoners watched her now with varying expressions of wariness.

Vola clanked over to the rock and sat, pushing her sword so it didn't catch against the ground.

Talon hunkered down beside her, her arm around Gruff.

"Would you like some tea?" Doddleben asked.

"I would love some tea," Vola said.

Talon grunted.

The gnome poured tea into tiny floral cups and slid them over. Vola took the porcelain carefully in her hands.

All around them, the prisoners breathed sighs of relief as Doddleben beamed. Like she'd passed some sort of test.

"Even when one is a prisoner one can never be caught without a tea service," he said. He eyed them both. "What do you think?"

Vola surveyed the floral pattern and was strongly reminded of Becky's Tea and Tap Room in Water's Edge, where she'd met the others.

"It's lovely," she said. "It reminds me of happy memories."

The gnome blushed. "Thank you. Nargilla was always making fun of my teacups. She preferred something a little more rugged, I guess. It irks me to no end to think of her throwing them out after I was gone."

"What happened?" Vola took a sip. The tea tasted like wilted grass but she didn't dare spit it out.

"She left me out there," he said, waving a hand vaguely at the wall. "Hoping I would draw the dragon's attention. I think she expected me to die. Luckily, I've found some new friends who appreciate the finer things in life."

He raised his cup to the other prisoners, and they all raised theirs back to him in a silent salute.

"Nargilla just left you?" Talon growled.

Doddleben shrugged. "It happens with people like me."

"No." Talon's hand sliced through the air. "You were her pack. Even if she was paying you. She was responsible for you. She should never have just left you behind."

The old gnome's eyes grew misty, and he reached across to pat her hand. "Thank you."

"We want to stop her," Vola said. She placed her cup back on the tablecloth and leaned forward. "We need to know how she's draining magic out of the land so we can keep her from doing it again."

Doddleben shook his head. "I'm sorry. You'd want one of her magic team for that. I was just looking for new places for her to hole up. She prefers old dragon lairs. They're spacious and they already have a link to the land that she's looking for." He brightened. "That means she could be nearby. She'll be trying to find another abandoned lair in the nearby peaks."

Vola nodded. "At least that gives us a place to start. What's she even trying to do? Why does she need all the power?"

"Oh, she has plenty of power. It's money she's after now. She's sending it along to her boss. Anders," the gnome said sipping his tea. "He's paying her for it. He'll be here to collect it soon."

Vola shot a look at Talon.

"Well, we knew it had to be connected," Talon said under her breath. "He's been stealing magic this whole time. Of course he'd be involved with Nargilla."

"And now we know why Rilla's sources said he was coming here."

"I have no idea what this Anders fellow wants to do with it," Doddleben said. "Except try to rival the gods."

Vola's chin jerked up. "What was that?"

"Oh, just a joke." He laughed to himself. "It's the next logical step, isn't it? If you control the magic of the land just like the gods. But a man can't rival the entire pantheon. Even one god couldn't control all of them. They threw out the Broken just for being powerful enough to think about it."

Vola wasn't laughing.

"Thank you," Talon said, glancing at Vola and evidently noting her wooden expression. "I hope Listrell lets you stay as long as you like. You seem at home here."

The gnome gave them a cheery smile. "I am. Which is good. I can't imagine leaving would be good for my health. Nargilla will not hesitate to finish the job if she found out I talked to anyone."

FIFTEEN

IN THE MAIN CAVERN, Lillie had started making camp, unpacking the bedrolls and cooking supplies from the swamp beast's packs. It seemed like most of their gear had survived the experience of being ingested at least. Though they were missing one or two pots that had been tied directly to the saddle. Vola wondered if they'd make an appearance again in a week or so.

The dragon herself shuffled around the immense cavern followed by Shereille, who chattered non-stop. As far as Vola could see, Listrell wasn't actually answering any of Shereille's questions. In fact, it looked more like Listrell was trying to run away, but Shereille had her trapped in her own lair.

Finally, the dragon flopped down, making the floor shake, and pulled her tail over her eyes.

Renvick stepped up beside Vola with the dry hiss of scales against his armor. "Listrell told your friends to make themselves comfortable."

Sorrel trotted up to the campfire Lille had lit with a quiet word and plopped down with a sigh.

"Any luck finding Master Bao?" Lillie asked.

"None," Sorrel said. "Waste of time."

"Well, not entirely," Vola said. "We did figure out where to look for Nargilla. But it will have to wait for morning, I think."

Renvick cast Sorrel a sidelong look. "Would you like to prepare for sleeping, as well? I am told I make an excellent bed."

Sorrel craned her neck to look up at him. "Do you mean you make the bed or you are the bed?"

"For you? Either."

Vola choked and tried to turn it into a cough. Lillie's eyes went wide, and she bit her lip hard enough to turn it white.

Sorrel's brow creased. "I think you're confused. Usually, people flirt with her." She cocked her thumb at Lillie.

"I am not familiar with flirting," Renvick said. "I only wish to make another warrior comfortable."

Sorrel frowned. "Then talk to Vola. She has what you want. Probably. I don't know. I'm not really well versed in..." She waved a hand. "All that."

Vola decided she should save the halfling, even if watching her deal with Renvick's attention was as amusing as hell.

"Come on, Renvick," Vola said. "You can show me a place where I can see the sky. I have someone I want to talk to."

Renvick gave a slow blink. He had two sets of eyelids. The first, an almost transparent flap of skin that slid over his eyes just before the scaled set did. "Very well."

He led her around the edge of the cavern. There were more alcoves like the one that held the prisoners, and Vola was struck by the idea that the cavern could hold nearly an entire city and they wouldn't even be crowded.

"Did I say something wrong?" Renvick rumbled once they were out of earshot.

"Maybe not wrong, but...unexpected? She's right. We're used to people going for Lillie. I'm not sure Sorrel knows what to do if your interest is serious."

"I have fought wizards before. Magic—and those who wield it—are uninteresting to me. And while you are an excellent warrior, you fight with blade and shield. Also very traditional. But I have never met so much skill and vigor in someone so small. It is fascinating."

"Then I suggest you focus on that. Sorrel's not much for romance, but if you present her with a good challenge and something she can fight, you'll go a lot farther."

Renvick made a noise somewhere between a laugh and a groan. "Thank you for the advice."

They passed a massive opening where fresh air gushed, tasting of dry desert night.

"That is where Listrell comes and goes," Renvick said. "But up here..."

He led her up a set of crude steps carved into the wall to an archway that led immediately to a long, wide balcony open to the night sky. "This is where the guardians come to watch when she flies."

Vola stepped into the cool breeze and lifted her face to the sky, which had gone black and deep, sprinkled with pinpoints of faraway light. The mountain stood between them and the city, so no human-made light marred the night.

Renvick didn't say more. He just stepped back out of her way. She could feel him standing beside the archway, either guarding her or guarding Listrell. But she didn't mind. She'd stopped caring if there were witnesses to what she was about to do.

"My lady," she said softly, and immediately another presence joined her on the balcony. Warmth pressed against her skin, like the arm of a comrade.

"My knight," Cleavah said, and her voice reminded Vola of the rush of wind as she'd stood on Listrell's back. A shaft of moonlight appeared beside Vola, and the beam coalesced until a figure stood there clothed in white, face too bright to stare at for long. The glow faded to reveal a woman with gold skin and dark curling hair that fell to her waist.

"You heard what the gnome said," Vola said. "About Nargilla."

"I did. I am...concerned."

From the feel of alarm that crackled through the air between them, Vola guessed that was an understatement.

"You think Anders really wants to rival the gods?"

"Perhaps that is his goal, but Doddleben is right. One man cannot take on the entire pantheon."

"Even with the magic of the world in his possession?"

"The gods still have their power. Which we might have to use if Anders gets much farther in his plan."

Vola had thought that was a pretty big worry. But if Cleavah was concerned about something else, that meant there was something even worse Vola didn't know yet.

"What's concerning you, then?" she asked.

Cleavah's lips tightened. "I am more concerned about Nargilla's ability to cut the gods off from their followers. You and I have one of the strongest bonds the pantheon has ever seen."

Vola blinked.

"And Nargilla severed it with one dead spot. If she can do that to us, it means she can sever the gods from the land itself. We would lose our ability to influence the world."

"And the rest of your power."

Cleavah shook her head. "It's not about keeping our power. We are the stabilizing influence of the world. We created it. Stripping the gods of their power would mean stripping power out of the world. It would end it, Vola."

Vola sucked in a breath. "End the world."

Cleavah attempted a smile. "We are not there yet. But..."

"But we could get there fast if Nargilla goes unchecked."

"Yes. It should be a concern for the entire pantheon."

"Even greater gods?" Vola asked carefully.

The goddess Vola had known as Cleavah hesitated. "Yes. Even us greater gods." Cleavah turned her head. "You know what I am."

Vola bowed her head. "I do."

"And yet you've never asked for my name."

Vola raised her chin and tried to meet Cleavah's gaze. The moon's brightness had faded, but the goddess's eyes still held an intensity that made Vola shake. "No."

"Why not?"

"I spent a long time worried about what people called you. What people thought of you. But in the end, it doesn't matter what any of them say. I know who you are to me. Your name won't change that."

Cleavah held her gaze for a moment longer before rolling her eyes. "Finally. Do you know how long I've been trying to teach you that particular lesson?"

"I guess I have a thick head," Vola said with a grin.

"Not as thick as some mortals. You were right to be worried about Nargilla. I will have to warn the rest of the gods."

"Will they listen?" Vola said. "They don't really listen to us, but if you're the one who's worried..."

"They do have a history of not heeding me, but I'm worried because I'm the prudent one. If I worry about everything, then nothing can surprise me. Personally, I think it's a better stance than some of my fellows who wallow in their presumed power and safety." She huffed a laugh. "I'd love to see Helleron actually heave himself off that sofa for once."

Her chuckle faded as the moonlight dimmed, and her presence retreated to that constant hovering just over Vola's shoulder.

"Your goal has not changed," Cleavah whispered in her ear. "Find Nargilla. And protect your people while you do it."

A nudge pushed Vola toward the right, along the railing. Vola followed, trusting Cleavah even in her confusion, and she found a small ledge wrapped around the side of the mountain. Two shadows sat hunched at the end, where another air hole opened to the sky.

Vola rubbed her hands over her face and leaned against the railing as close to Talon and Gruff as she could get.

Talon's hood was gone, torn to bits under Listrell's claws, and the ranger sat now with her face to the sky, her left hand buried in Gruff's fur. The wolf pressed the top of his skull into her side, leaning like he did when he was reassuring her. Without the cloak, her pink tunic was a lot starker against her dark cuirass.

"Hey," Vola said quietly. It was amazing how wonderful it was to see someone doing something as boring as sitting when the day before you'd thought they were dead.

Talon leaned her head back against the rock wall of the mountain, her overlong hair flopping away from her eyes.

"The others are bedding down in the cavern," Vola said.

"I'll come in a minute," Talon said. Her voice was still growly, the way it was when she wasn't paying attention and had something on her mind.

Vola waited. Cleavah wanted her to take care of her people, and taking care of Talon often meant giving her space to speak in her own time.

Finally, Talon spoke. "I wanted to thank you."

Vola tipped her head.

"For coming to save me. Even if I didn't end up needing it. I thought... when she dropped me I figured you'd think I was dead and...I didn't know what you'd do. I followed you through the mountains, trying to catch up."

"You made really good time."

"Well, I know what it's like to think someone's dead, but never know for sure. I didn't want you to live that way for too long."

"It was two of the hardest days of my life." Vola scratched at the rough stone of the railing. "And thank you. For coming to save us. You rescued me from a dragon."

Talon folded the edge of her ragged tunic over and over again, making the seams fray.

They were all alive, and they had a lead. So why was Talon still so agitated?

"What's wrong?" Vola said.

Talon surged to her feet and edged along the pathway back to the balcony. Gruff followed her, moving fluidly.

She vaulted the railing and paced from one end to the other. "I don't know."

Vola watched, silent, waiting for Talon to explain more.

Finally, she stopped beside the railing and gripped it with both hands. "I'm...I'm angry," she said.

Vola leaned back on her elbows. "Yeah, you look angry."

"And sad and frightened and-and guilty."

"Guilty about what?"

"The dragon that killed my pack. It was a victim, just like Listrell. It was forced awake, and it retaliated. And then we killed it. For nothing."

"Not for nothing," Vola said softly. "It was on a mindless rampage. You had to do something. The same way we had to do something about Listrell. You saved lives."

Talon sagged. "I still feel guilty about it. But it wasn't just the dragon. Nargilla is the one causing these dead spots. She was the one who woke it up. She has to have known what it did, but still, she came here and did the same thing. Who knows how many times she's done it since then?"

She pushed away from the balcony, her fists opening and closing like she wished Nargilla was standing right there, her neck ready to be wrung.

Vola wasn't sure she'd ever seen Talon truly angry. Even when Vola had screwed up so royally in Lord Arthorel's cellar, Talon had been more disappointed than angry.

"You're allowed to be angry, you know?" Vola said. "She killed your pack."

"Yes, but what do I do about it? It's been years. I put it behind me. I recovered and moved on. It wasn't affecting me anymore." She gestured to Gruff, who lay at her feet, tongue lolling to take advantage of the cool air. "Like a wolf. Wolves don't dwell."

Vola wanted to put her hand on the ranger's shoulder, but she knew it wouldn't be appreciated. "But you're not a wolf. Not really. You're human. And you're allowed to have feelings and to remember."

Talon collapsed against the railing and clasped her hands. "But I don't want to remember if it makes me angry. I don't like being angry." She glanced up at Vola, who had plenty of experience with anger, both wanted and unwanted. "What do you do with it? How do you keep it from swamping everything else?"

"It's...hard. I try to make sure I'm using it for something. It's easy enough to stomp around and break things. But I want to make sure my anger changes the things that are wrong. When Inga kidnapped you all and turned you against me, I used my rage to get you back. I used it to beat Inga and make sure she never did it again."

"So I should use it," Talon said, staring at her hands. "That's the only way to get rid of it?"

"You could ignore it, I guess. But orcs believe that's not healthy." Of course, that didn't mean that Vola hadn't spent years trying to do just that.

Talon was silent for a long moment. "I'm not out for revenge. I don't want to be like Fedor Gerrickson, on a quest to kill every dragon just because one made a huge mistake."

Vola snorted. "I think you can seek justice without being like Fedor. Justice is different from revenge."

Talon took a deep, sweeping breath. "Wolves protect, they defend, and when they fail, they forget. I think I'd rather be a wolf." She rubbed her hands over her face. "But you're right, I'm not. I won't forget. I'll learn. And I'll use my anger to protect better the next time."

She put her hand on Vola's forearm and Vola just kept herself from jumping. "I won't let Nargilla Pipwattle take my new pack from me."

SIXTEEN

VOLA SLEPT like the dead that night, despite the fact that a dragon rumbled just a few feet away. The night before at the inn had been awful, and then there'd been all that traipsing around the mountains, fighting said dragon, and bouncing off a wall. After all that, Vola was one long ache.

For the first time since she could remember, she slept in. She woke to the sizzle of bacon and the metallic shing of a fork scraping the bottom of a pan.

"Breakfast, Vola?" Lillie said, tilting the pan toward her, revealing a wealth of grease and protein.

Vola didn't need to be asked twice. She threw her blankets back and reached for her pants. It was always nice when they found a spot safe enough that she could sleep without her armor on, and Listrell had assured them that the guardians would keep anyone from bothering them. Or at least give them enough warning that she would have time to armor up.

"I don't remember packing bacon," Sorrel said, skipping to the fire while Vola pulled on her boots.

"It was the guardians," Lillie said. "Apparently taking care of Listrell also means taking care of her guests. And Listrell said they don't need sleep."

"Wish I didn't need sleep," Talon said, rubbing her face as she settled down on her heels beside the fire.

Vola snagged up some bacon before it disappeared entirely and then stood back to survey the cavern.

Talon reached as if to pull up her head only to find it gone.

"We can get you another one if you miss it," Vola said.

Talon hesitated, then shook her head. "No. I'm sorry it's gone because it was a gift from someone who's gone now. But I don't need it anymore. And she would have been the first to understand that."

Listrell tromped up, shaking the ground with her footsteps while Shereille trotted along, trying to keep up.

"But I just wanted to know—"

"It is rude to ask," Listrell boomed. "Any decent person should know that."

"Yes, but I'm not a person. I'm a researcher."

Vola's mouth pulled, caught between a grin and a grimace. Shereille was certainly inhumanly persistent.

Lillie's glance flitted between her mother and the dragon. "Mo— Shereille, would you like some breakfast?"

Shereille eyed the pan full of grease and bacon. "Oh, no, my dear. My body just doesn't need that much fat in the morning."

Lillie flushed bright red and dropped her gaze.

Talon took a vicious bite of her bacon. Without her hood, she couldn't hide the glare she sent Shereille.

"We need to plan our attack," Vola said, deliberately drawing attention away from Shereille. "Listrell, do you think you could lead us to the old lairs in this area to look for Nargilla?"

"No."

Vola's mouth fell open.

"What?" Sorrel said. "I thought you were on our side now."

"I am. My priority is to keep any more dragons from waking early."

"Can't you do that by tracking down Nargilla and keeping her from draining any more spots?" Vola asked.

"Finding one gnome is too small for me to see clearly. But it is the perfect sized problem for you."

Sorrel narrowed her eyes up at the dragon. "Are you sure you're not just using that as an excuse to not even try?"

Lillie choked.

"Listrell's right," Talon said. "We don't want to repeat the dragon attack."

Listrell inclined her head to the ranger. "Your wisdom shines once again."

It was hard to argue with that, but Vola had really been hoping to have a dragon on their side. "Finding Nargilla would be a lot more helpful with you."

"I will go with you," came another rumble, not nearly as deep as Listrell's. Renvick stepped up to their fire and bowed his head. The firelight glinted across the green and blue streaks in his scales.

"I thought the guardians protected you," Lillie said, looking at Listrell.

"They do," Listrell said. "But they are many, and Renvick can make up his own mind. He will be able to lead you to any empty dragon lairs nearby," Listrell said. "Then at least you will be able to search out your enemy without wandering in circles."

"Thank you," Vola said, making sure she included both Listrell and Renvick in that.

"I'll go with Listrell," Shereille said, notebook clutched in her hands. "My research is barely begun and—"

"No, you will not," Listrell said.

Shereille gaped. "What?"

"I am not babysitting you anymore. I go into danger, and I will not protect you the way these four chose to. Your incessant questions will likely wake any dragons we come near anyway and defeat the entire purpose of my mission."

"But...but you're my life's work. You can't leave until I've learned enough to publish at least one paper."

"I'd like to know how you plan to stop me." The dragon snorted, a flicker of flame shooting between her lips, long enough to lick at Shereille's boots.

Shereille stumbled back a step and tripped over a bedroll. She landed on her butt amid the blanket.

She cast a glare at Vola. "This wouldn't be happening if you'd just killed her when you had the chance. I could be dissecting her right now."

Listrell ducked her head, smoke flowing between her teeth. "You planned to cut me apart?"

A low growl rose from the guardians arrayed around the edges of the cavern.

"Er, no," Shereille said, scrambling to her feet. "At least not originally. I just wanted to talk to you, so I tried to get closer. But then the swamp monster got loose and there was going to be a fight, anyway. I figured if there was a body left over, then I could examine it."

Vola rolled her eyes to the ceiling. This woman could not read a room to save her life.

"You should probably shut up now, Shereille," she said.

"Why is that so surprising?" Shereille glanced between the seething dragon and the guardians. "She wouldn't have been using her body anymore. Why not dedicate it to science?"

"I prefer not to share my space with people who only see me as a thing to be studied," Listrell rumbled.

"Give it up, Shereille," Vola said. "Your test subject has decided not to be a test subject, oddly enough."

"I'm an observer," Shereille told Listrell. "I see and learn and then I write about it. You can't just decide not to participate."

"Watch me," Listrell said. "You may take her with you, or I will take her out to the desert and drop her," the dragon told Vola. "Your choice."

Lillie's head shot up, and she cast a beseeching glance at Vola. Vola pretended not to notice.

The wizard scrambled to her feet and took Vola's arm so she could speak in her ear. "We can't let Listrell drop her," Lillie said. "Please, Vola."

"Her carelessness nearly got us killed, Lillie. I don't know if we can trust her if all she cares about are her results."

Lillie bit her lip. "It's actually a compliment, don't you see? She knows we can take care of ourselves."

Vola made a face. Lillie was being unusually dumb when it came to her mother, but she wasn't about to say that out loud. Vola's parents might have been super supportive, but that just made it more obvious how awful Shereille was and how Lillie deserved better.

Vola blew out her breath. There was a grain of truth in Lillie's argument. They could handle themselves, for the most part. They'd even gotten out of a fight with a dragon, albeit unconventionally.

But Vola was responsible for Lillie and Talon and Sorrel, and if Shereille was going to put them in harm's way, then Shereille was a threat.

Lillie stared up at her, big blue-green eyes wide. Vola sighed.

She also wanted to protect Lillie's feelings and convincing her that her mother deserved to get dropped from a dragon wasn't exactly on her list of things to do today. Maybe Shereille would take this one last chance and actually impress Vola and give Lillie the validation she was looking for.

Or maybe Vola was going to regret this. A lot.

"Fine. She can come with us. But only until we can figure out how to get her back to the city unharmed."

Lillie squeezed her arm and beamed. "Thank you, Vola," she said quietly, as if she knew the only way Vola would have agreed was for her sake.

Shereille moped and moaned the entire morning as they left Listrell's lair and followed Renvick through the hidden paths of the mountains. She was a lot less likable when she was complaining all the time. And Vola hadn't liked her much to begin with.

Lillie tried to distract her, asking about her research, but Shereille always managed to circle back to how they'd destroyed her one chance to study a *draconis maximus*.

Sorrel scrambled to the top of a jagged rock and then hopped from one rock to the next as they threaded their way through the rough terrain. "She's annoying the crap out of me," she told Vola. "But I'm a little disappointed, too. It would have been nice to just point and have a dragon swoop in to burn our enemies."

"She's preventing our enemies from doing more damage," Talon said. "That's our goal in the long run, isn't it?"

"Yeah, but it still seems like she's running away from the danger, not toward it. Hey, Renvick," Sorrel called to the guardian making his way through the boulders. They weren't even on a path, but he moved as light-footed as a goat, despite his size. "You're pretty handy with your weapon."

He paused a few paces ahead of them and glanced back, the ridge above one eye raised. "I am very skilled with my weapon. Yes."

Vola choked on the euphemism. Talon covered her eyes and shook her head.

Sorrel just ran right on by without even noticing. "Great. Would you rather stand at the castle door to guard it against intruders? Or track down the threat and root it out at the source?"

"I am here with you, searching for the enemy. So what do you think?"

"Ah, good point. Good point." She turned to call over her shoulder. "He's a charger, guys."

"I am glad you noticed."

Vola snorted, and Sorrel paused on top of another rock.

"Oh," she said, her mouth screwing up with distaste. "There was another whole conversation happening there that I didn't even notice, wasn't there?"

Before Vola could think of an explanation, Renvick blinked his first set of eyelids and gave her a toothy grin. "I was speaking of battle. It has been many centuries since I've gotten to travel with worthy warriors."

Sorrel examined him out of the corner of her eye, but he just gave her a mild look and stepped up the path to a spot marked by a massive standing stone, carved with ribbed wings and claws.

The draconic warrior hunkered down beside it and put his shoulder to the rock. He heaved the stone and it shifted almost like it was on wheels, revealing a dark tunnel, similar to the one they'd crept through to invade Listrell's lair. Only this one was vertical and ran straight down into the mountain.

"Ooh, what's down there?" Sorrel said, sticking her head in the entrance.

"Another lair," Renvick said. "Possibly our enemy. Hopefully no rock wyrms."

Vola glanced back at their party. Lillie and Shereille still spoke, Lillie looking more red than usual and Shereille looking bored. Behind them trailed the swamp monster, which made grumbling noises and ground its teeth.

"I don't think lowering us down one by one is a great idea. Sorrel, do you want to do some scouting? Just don't alert anything to our presence."

"Sneaky, sneaky. Got it." She gave Vola a mock salute and disappeared down the tunnel, clinging to the walls like a spider with Maxim's Warhammer across her back.

Vola stepped back to see if she could rescue Lillie.

"I thought you were going to take me back to the city," Shereille said as soon as Vola came within earshot. "If I can't continue my studies in the field, I at least need to get back so I can lead my team. Maybe we can find another dragon who's still sleeping."

"I said you would come with us until we could find time to take you back to the city. Besides, I thought this trip was supposed to be an opportunity for other things, too," Vola said, nodding significantly to Lillie.

Shereille's pinched expression didn't change. "I'm not saying it wasn't. But now that's done, I really must get back to what's important."

"I'm beginning to see why you left Glenhaven in the first place," Lillie snapped.

"Oh, good," Shereille said. "I was worried you would never understand."

Lillie opened her mouth, but the only thing she could come up with was a wordless cry. Sorrel returned in that moment, interrupting them.

"Nothing's down there," she said, climbing from the hole and dusting her hands off on her pants. "But it looks like some kind of big operation might have been there a few nights ago. Probably Nargilla if that old gnome is to be believed."

"He seemed pretty pissed at her," Talon said. "I doubt he was lying to protect her."

She knelt and touched the ground.

Lillie's mouth went round. "Oh, can you feel if there are dead spots nearby?"

Talon grunted.

"Wait," Vola said. "Wouldn't Listrell be able to feel one if it was so close? We've only been walking a few hours."

Renvick shook his head. "We passed out of her territory. This is unclaimed since there's no one living in the lair right now."

"So, Nargilla can wreak whatever sort of havoc she wants," Vola said with a growl.

Talon's breath hissed through her teeth, and they all focused on her.

"Where?" Vola said.

"That way." Talon pointed. "I don't know how long ago. It doesn't feel like the last one felt, but it's there now."

She stood, then clambered up the slope. The rest of them hurried to follow. Even Shereille had shut up for once.

Talon was the first to make it to the ridge, with Renvick not far behind. Vola could tell something was wrong as soon as Talon froze, silhouetted against the sky. The moment Renvick joined her, he stiffened, the colors in his hide shifting into more vibrant hues.

"Another dead spot?" Lillie called.

"Yes," Renvick said at the same time Talon said, "Worse."

She turned back to them. "You'd better get up here quick."

Vola vaulted boulders to get to the ridge. At the top, she sucked in a breath.

It *was* another dead spot. A spreading, flat black, just like the one in the desert and the one outside Listrell's first lair.

But this one had a shape inside it. A body sprawled across the darkened stone, pale and limp in the harsh sunlight.

"Geez," Vola said and started skidding down the slope.

She lurched to a stop and fell to her knees beside the man, who lay face down against the rock. Her gaze raked him up and down, cataloging his hurts. But the thing was, he didn't seem to have any. His back moved with his breath but barely. She reached for his shoulder and tried to draw up enough healing power to tell what was wrong with him.

But it was like reaching blindly for a railing and finding it missing.

Damn, she had no connection to Cleavah in the dead spot, and therefore no way to heal.

The others skidded down the slope, sending gravel flying past Vola as she turned the man over gently.

She gasped. She hadn't paid any attention to his clothes while he lay there, but now she could see his face, she recognized him.

"Master Bao!" Sorrel said her breath escaping on a gasp.

The old monk didn't stir.

"Vola?" Sorrel said.

"Help me get him out of this spot," Vola said. She didn't need any help. She could just hoist the thin figure into her arms, but Sorrel needed something to focus on.

The halfling scrambled to lift his feet as Vola supported the old monk's shoulders. They dragged him out of the blackened area and laid him down in a clear spot.

"What's wrong with him?" Sorrel asked. "Is he hurt? Sunstroke? Did Nargilla do something to him?"

"I don't know yet," Vola said. "He doesn't seem wounded. And he hasn't been out long enough to have suffered from dehydration and starvation like he was planning."

Vola reached for Cleavah's power again, searching out the damage in Master Bao's wiry frame, but all she could see was an overwhelming grayness. The place where a person's bright spark of life usually resided was shriveled and colorless.

"It's like...his life is being drained."

Lillie sucked in a breath. "He must have been in the spot when Nargilla drained the magic out of it."

"But we don't have any magic," Sorrel said. She touched the staff over her shoulder. "I mean besides what little Maxim gives us."

"All creatures have magic," Lillie said. "It's attached to our life force. Those of us with more of it get a special connection to the land or it's gifted by a god." She gestured to Talon and then Vola. "The rest of us learn to use what's already in the world." She touched her chest. "Or we fight with more mundane means." She gestured to Sorrel. "But everyone has at least a little."

"So...she drained his life force?" Sorrel said, face going slack with horror as she surveyed Master Bao.

"Not all of it," Vola said. "Just the magical part."

"That still looks pretty bad," Talon said.

"Quiet, I'm going to see what I can do." Vola closed her eyes while the others held their breath.

Vola reached again for her healing power and poured it into the old monk, trying to sop up the gray like a dishtowel. When that didn't work, she tried infusing him with the power, repainting him from the inside to get rid of the frightening blankness.

He seemed to soak up the power like dry ground soaking up the rain, more and more and more, but none of it seemed to make a difference. Vola was left panting and shaky and suddenly she realized she was at the end of what she could provide.

She pulled back and her shoulders drooped.

Talon supported her before she fell over. "Are you all right?"

"No," Vola said, voice hoarse. "I can't fix it. I can't fix whatever is wrong with him. He's alive, but only barely. And whatever it is about being drained can't be fixed by healing."

"You are nothing if not predictable, Mishap's Heroes," a cheerful voice said.

Vola tried to stand too quickly and ended up on one knee as black rushed to crowd her vision.

At the opposite edge of the dead spot stood a cheeky gnome in a tattered robe.

"Nargilla," Vola growled.

SEVENTEEN

"I WILL ADMIT, I'm impressed you didn't get eaten by a dragon," Nargilla said, tilting her head to survey them. "Or burnt to ash in the burning city. But here you are after only a slight delay. Maybe this will be fun after all."

"You knew we would be here," Vola said.

"Like I said, predictable." Nargilla shrugged. "I knew you would be coming after me. Your honor would demand it. So I made myself easy to find."

"What did you do to him?" Sorrel asked, still supporting Master Bao.

"Pff, hardly anything. He tried to stop me from taking the magic out of this spot. And that's what happens when you get caught in the spell. It harvests you, too."

"Is he going to die?" Lillie said.

Nargilla looked affronted. "It takes your magic, not your life."

"Would you want to live without magic?"

Nargilla tapped her chin. "Huh. Hadn't thought of that."

Vola drew her sword.

Nargilla shook her head. "See. Predictable."

"I know how to deal with being predictable," Vola growled stepping closer.

Nargilla snorted. "What? Because you dealt with Inga? That stupid orc. She was a special case. She was obsessed with you."

Vola jerked. "You knew Inga?"

"Is there some sort of evil villains club?" Sorrel said. She was swinging her staff behind Vola ready for a fight.

"There's no such thing. We worked for the same boss, dummy."

"Anders," Lillie said.

"What does he want?" Vola said. "And what are you getting out of it?"

"Money, power, sex," Nargilla said with a shrug. "What else is there? He pays me, I get to keep the excess power from what I siphon off for him, and he's got the best butt I've ever seen. And believe me, at my height, I've seen a lot."

Renvick crept closer to the gnome from the other side and met Vola's eyes. Vola gave him a minuscule nod. And as Nargilla drew her next breath, Vola lunged.

Before Vola could touch her, Nargilla collapsed, as if she'd melted directly into the very stone. Vola stumbled, her momentum carrying her forward over the spot where Nargilla had disappeared.

Renvick glanced around, his weapon in his hand. "Where did she go?"

"Yoohoo," Nargilla waved from the top of a rock pile.

Vola ground her teeth.

"Talon, Lillie—"

"Already on it," Talon said, bringing her bow up. Lillie was whispering over her hands.

Vola turned to the most troublesome member of their little group. "Shereille, stay with Master Bao. And keep the swamp monster out of the way this time."

"I don't have to take orders. I was the one who hired you."

Vola ignored her and turned back to the fight.

Talon and Gruff had moved to flank Nargilla on her distant rock. Together, they drove the gnome back down to flat ground where Sorrel, Vola, and Renvick could engage.

Vola charged, swinging her sword around to cut the gnome's feet out from under her. Nargilla spun away, the tattered ends of her robe flying. Vola planted her leading foot and pivoted, bringing her shield around in a bash that should have taken Nargilla's head off.

But the gnome ducked and bounced back. "Ew, I don't want to touch that," she said, gesturing to Vola's black shield. "The evil might rub off on me."

"You're literally stealing the world's magic for money and sex," Lillie cried. "How is that not already evil?"

"Details," Nargilla said.

Renvick took advantage of her momentary distraction and swiped his warhammer through the air. Nargilla stepped back, tripped on her tattered robe, and fell, narrowly missing getting her head bashed in.

"Ooh, that one was close. I guess you guys aren't as bad as I thought."

Sorrel yelled a battle cry and leaped for the prone gnome.

She flew through the air, but halfway through her jump, the stone at her feet erupted, and Sorrel struck the unforgiving hide of a rock wyrm. It loomed over the halfling, who shook her head and tried to push up from the ground where she'd fallen.

Rock wyrms sprang from the stone all around in showers of dirt and gravel, making Vola and the others stumble back.

Nargilla climbed to her feet and brushed herself off. "There, see. I have friends, too."

"Lovely to meet you all," Lillie said, sourly.

The rock wyrms pulsed, their purplish veins throbbing under translucent skin. One leaned and lunged at Lillie.

Vola darted between them, sliding the last few feet on her knees, and caught the attack on her shield. She heaved upwards and threw the wyrm backward so that Lillie could throw lightning at it.

Sorrel flew by, her staff alight with crackles and sparks. She landed on the back…front?—it was impossible to tell—of one of the wyrms and clung there, beating the thing over the head.

A squeal rang out behind them, and Vola spun to see a rock wyrm lunging for the swamp monster. Shereille dropped its lead rope and cowered, covering her head.

The rock wyrm's mouth gaped wide enough to swallow the swamp beast whole. But somewhere between descending on it and eating it, the swamp beast twisted, and suddenly the rock wyrm was writhing on the ground as the swamp beast shook it from its neck.

Well, at least their rear was guarded. Vola remained beside Lillie, guarding the wizard as she rained lightning down. Renvick followed Sorrel, trying to guard the halfling's back, but getting left behind half the time.

In the center of the chaos, Nargilla stood, grinning at her rock wyrms.

Silent as a wolf on the hunt, Talon sprinted for her.

Nargilla pulled a hand up as if dragging something from the ground and spiky thorns sprang out of the rock, wrapping around Talon's boots and tangling in her cloak.

Talon's step hitched, but she spat out an angry word and the thorns let go as if they'd been burned, retreating underground.

Nargilla's eyes widened a split second before Talon tackled her.

"Ow. Hey, you're not actually supposed to get near me."

"No one told me that part," Talon said and drew back her fist.

Nargilla gasped and melted into the rock just as Talon's blow connected.

Talon cried out and cradled her hand against her chest, alone on the ground between all the rock wyrms.

"Talon," Vola called. She glanced back at Lillie.

"Go," Lillie said, face set.

Sorrel was atop yet another rock wyrm, her staff limned with lightning as she bashed the creature over the head. It moaned and threw itself on the ground, trapping Sorrel with its weight. She cried out.

Renvick rushed to her aid, hacking at the thick hide of the creature until it parted with a spurt of blood.

Vola skidded to a stop, halfway between Sorrel and Lillie with Talon on the ground at her feet. She couldn't reach everyone at once.

Lillie threw her arms up and pulled one last bolt from the sky, sending it arcing through the last rock wyrm. The wyrm moaned, but with its dying gasp, it lashed out, catching Lillie and throwing her into the rock pile where Nargilla had stood.

"Lillie!" Vola wavered. They all needed her help, but Nargilla was still lurking in the ground, waiting for her chance to strike.

Vola spun, surveying the battlefield, but the rock wyrms lay quiet, leaking dark purple blood into the dirt and rock, and no deranged gnomes leaped out of hiding.

"I think she's gone," Talon said with a grimace. She tried to uncurl her fist but hissed in pain and cradled the hand to her chest.

"Sorrel?" Vola asked Renvick.

The guardian heaved aside the rock wyrm's carcass and pulled Sorrel out from underneath its thick hide. He met Vola's gaze and nodded. "She will live."

Vola helped Talon climb to her feet, and together they stumbled to Lillie where she lay crumpled against the rock.

Vola fell to her knees as Talon propped herself up against the rock.

"Lillie?"

The wizard was breathing, and she had her eyes open, blinking at the sky. "I used...I used to think I would like flying," she said.

"What?" Vola laid her rough palm on Lillie's face, trying to get her to focus. One pupil was sluggish to respond. And the wizard wasn't making sense.

"It's not as much fun as it looks," she said, her words slurred. "Flying through the air."

Vola huffed a laugh. "It was only the landing that gave you a problem, little bird."

Lille tried to laugh, and her face went green. Vola rolled her onto her side in time for the wizard to barf up all her breakfast.

"How bad is it?" Talon asked.

Concussions had been common among the paladin candidates at the academy. Put a bunch of half-grown warriors in a ring with blunt weapons and grudges to work out and heads were bound to crack.

"She hit her head really good," Vola said. "She's gonna be loopy and dizzy for a while."

Lillie groaned. "No loops. No more flying, please."

"No more flying," Vola promised. She reached for the well of healing power in her soul but found it still empty. Just pulling a little thread out to examine Lillie's injuries made Vola break out in a cold sweat, and her hands started to shake. She cut off the thread of power before she could heave up her own breakfast.

Renvick stepped up to them, Sorrel in his arms. He'd crossed his forearms, gripping his elbows, and Sorrel sat in the seat they made, feet dangling.

"You all right?" Talon asked.

"The rock wyrm broke her leg," Renvick said as Sorrel winced.

Talon glanced at Vola. "What can you do?"

It was Vola's turn to wince. "Nothing. I'm out. I spent everything trying to heal Master Bao." She held up her hands so the others could see how they shook. Lillie went cross-eyed trying to focus on them.

"We can't stay here," Talon said. "We have to get back to the city. These two need healing, and Nargilla could still come back and decide to finish us off."

Lillie and Sorrel weren't the only ones who needed healing. Talon tried to hide it, but she still cradled her hand against her chest. And Master Bao remained motionless beyond the dead spot while Shereille dithered beside him, trying to yank the swamp monster away from the carcass of the rock wyrm it had killed. It was trying to eat it.

"Right. Renvick, can you handle Sorrel?"

The guardian's mouth twitched, flashing the end of a fang. "I am very capable of handling the halfling, yes."

Sorrel gave him a suspicious look. "There's a double meaning in there, I just know it."

Renvick, wisely, did not respond.

Talon sidled up next to Vola. "Why did Nargilla leave?" she said quietly. "If she was waiting here for us?"

Vola shook her head. "Maybe we were too much for her and she decided to cut her losses and retreat."

They exchanged a look, neither of them believing that explanation.

Vola gathered Lillie in her arms, trying not to jostle her too much. Vola would prefer to carry her the whole way to the city if only to keep an eye on her, but the draining and the fight had left her knees shaky as well. She'd never make it all the way back without some help. Lillie's head fell back, and she stared blearily at the sky.

Talon stalked up to Shereille and took the swamp beast's halter. She held it still while Vola placed Lillie on its back.

"No, anything but the monster," Lillie slurred.

"Shh," Vola said. "This is half the reason we have the dam—darn thing."

EIGHTEEN

THEY MADE it back to the city as night fell. Talon sent Gruff to the hotel to find Rilla while Rand circled above them, guiding them through the darkened streets that still smelled like smoke and wet, charred wood.

Vola had specifically asked the familiar to find a House of the Broken. The Broken might have been the Greater Virtue of Righteousness, but she had hospitals all over the world along with courts and homes for the homeless.

As they passed the first bridge in the city, Shereille stretched her arms out with a yawn. "Well, I appreciate your escort, but it's time I returned—"

Vola slung her arm around the elf's neck. "It's time you stayed with your daughter to be sure she's all right? Yes, I agree," she said, glancing back at Lillie. The wizard swayed on the back of the swamp beast. Talon wouldn't let her fall asleep, poking her when it looked like she was about to nod off. But she definitely wasn't completely aware of her surroundings, either.

Shereille opened her mouth as if to protest and stopped when she saw Vola's big, tusky grin. "Yes, of course," she said meekly.

The House of the Broken was clearly lit with lanterns and some wizard's fire lamps. This wasn't anything like the elegant marble facade of the hospital in Brisbene, but it was still bustling despite the charred roof and late hour.

Vola loved competent people. Less than half an hour later, they were all ensconced in a large treatment room that had been whitewashed to cover the eclectic patchwork walls. Nurses and healers in calming blue uniforms floated in and out, putting together cots and bringing extra blankets, while others gently straightened out Sorrel's leg and laid Lillie's head down on a fresh pillow.

Beyond the open door, a couple of traveling judges dressed in red passed, whispering worriedly. And warriors hired to maintain the peace tiptoed by, doing their best not to clank.

No paladins, though. Paladins were chosen by their gods directly. And everyone knew the Broken had never chosen a mortal to act for her. The other gods had ranks and ranks of paladins called to serve their divine master on earth. But the Broken had always stood apart. In deed as well as appearance.

"There. You're all knitted up," one of the healers told Sorrel. "Be sure to keep the leg immobile through the night, though. The break is still weak and could be re-fractured." The healer brushed bushy black hair over her shoulders as she rose gracefully from the edge of the halfling's cot.

She moved down the row. Someone was already tending to Lillie who stared blearily at the ceiling from the next cot over, but the healer stopped at Talon and gestured for the ranger's curled hand.

More healers murmured from the far corner where Master Bao lay, all by himself, limp and unresponsive. His herd of caretakers shook their heads, as baffled as Vola had been up in the mountains.

Renvick stood in the corner, as still as a statue once again. His scales gradually faded from vivid streaks of blue and green to the red-brown color of rock.

"Do you need to sleep?" Sorrel asked him.

"This is my sleep," he rumbled, words coming slow and slurred. "Do not worry about me, fierce one. I will wake when I am needed."

Both sets of eyelids drifted shut even as his scaly lips pulled back in a draconic grin.

Sorrel stared at him, lips pursed and eyebrows drawn down.

"There is no lasting damage," the healer beside Lillie said. "And I have taken away the pain of the headache. I want you to try sitting up now."

Lillie cautiously pushed herself upright. She didn't immediately turn green and barf, so that was an improvement.

Lillie's healer moved on to check on Vola.

"I'm fine," Vola said. She'd taken off most of her armor, and now she was just stiff.

"Physically, yes," the healer said. "But I believe you are depleted in here." The healer touched her collarbone. "Allow me to bolster you, and you will replenish yourself faster."

Vola blinked. She hadn't even known that was possible, but then she was more of a field medic than a full doctor.

The healer lay a hand on her shoulder and closed her eyes. Vola felt something like a poke deep inside where her well of power normally resided.

The healer hissed and drew back, shaking her hand.

"What?" Vola asked.

"You...stung me." The healer tilted her head. "Your magic feels like the sun on a hot day. I don't think I can help you."

"I get my power from my goddess," Vola said with an apologetic smile. "So maybe it doesn't work that way. It's already coming back; I just have to be patient."

The healer's eyes narrowed. "I've worked with paladins before," she muttered as she moved away.

But Vola was more concerned about watching her party, making sure they were really okay, now. Talon was flexing her hand, and Lillie was cautiously craning her neck around, checking her range of motion.

Sorrel heaved a huge sigh.

"What's wrong?" Vola asked.

Sorrel's lips twisted, and she glanced at the motionless guardian out of the corner of her eye.

"Do you think he can hear us?"

"He did say he'd wake if he was needed."

Lillie's attention focused on him. "I think it's more of a passive awareness, though. Why?"

Sorrel plunked her head back on her pillow. "What am I supposed to do with him?"

"Whatever you want?" Talon said with a sly grin. "He seemed to make that very clear."

Sorrel glared at her. "That's just what I mean. He's persistent, and I don't know how to deal with that."

"If you aren't interested, you just have to tell him," Vola said. "There's nothing wrong with that."

Sorrel stared at the ceiling, her thumbs twisting over and over. "It's not that I'm not interested..."

Vola sat up as Talon spun around.

"Oh?" Lillie said, carefully.

"I'm just worried that I'm not interested in the same way other people seem to be. I like him. He's fun to talk to and fight with, but I'm still not into all that love and sex stuff. That's just not who I am."

Vola exchanged an amused glance with Lillie and Talon. That wasn't news to them.

"You know, you can like and spend time with someone without the expectation of sex," Vola said. "It's a hard concept for some people, but there are other kinds of relationships. You like us, don't you?"

"Of course."

"But you're not ready to jump into bed with Lillie or Talon or me."

Sorrel screwed up her nose. "No, thank you."

"And that doesn't make how you feel about us any less important."

"Romance is only one type of relationship," Lillie said quietly. "It's up to you to decide if it's a necessary one for you. And if it's not...then it's not." Lillie shrugged.

"Yes, but how do I know if he'd be okay with that?" Sorrel asked.

Vola snorted. "You ask him. You won't know anything if you don't talk to him and tell him exactly what you're feeling."

"Communication is key," Shereille said, startling them. She'd been lurking beside the door, looking uncomfortable. "I recommend a contract. It is the only way to be sure hearts won't be broken."

"I'm not so sure of that," Lillie said sourly.

Shereille pressed her lips together. "Yes, it seems even that is not fool-proof." She heaved a sigh and edged toward the door. "Well, since I'm not needed anymore, I will bid you farewell."

Lillie swung her legs over the side of her cot. "That's it?" she said, voice higher than normal.

Rand hopped from the little nightstand to her shoulder.

"Is what it?" Shereille lifted her chin. "I'm not a healer, Lilliara."

"No, I imagine such practical magic is beneath you," Lillie spat.

"Er," one of the healers said.

"I mean, don't you care at all?" Lillie said.

Shereille's brows drew down. "Care about what?"

"Anything!" Lillie threw her hands in the air.

"What a silly question. Of course, I care about things. I care a great deal about my research, which you might have noticed if you were paying attention."

"I mean about things that matter. People. Lives. Family. I was hurt. And...and you're just trying to get back to your books."

Vola raised an eyebrow. She'd never thought she'd hear Lillie admit that there was something more important than books.

"Let's be honest, Lilliara," Shereille said. "I barely know you."

The blood drained from Lillie's face. Vola would have leaped between them to spare Lillie this pain, but Lillie hadn't been willing to hear about it from Vola. Maybe Shereille herself was the only one who'd be able to convince her.

"What about people you do know, then?" Lillie said. "My brothers. The boys you helped raise when they were little. Did you know two of them are banished now? They tried to start a coup."

"That wasn't very smart of them."

"I had to do the banishing."

Shereille looked at Lillie like she still didn't get it. "Good for you. That's a hard spell."

Completely missing the turmoil and the anguish Lillie still felt over that decision.

"You really don't care, do you?" Lillie's shoulders sagged, and she sank back against the wall at the head of her cot.

"I never promised to care," Shereille said, and that was the gentlest tone Vola had ever heard from her. "It wasn't in the contract."

"That's what I mean. It's not that you don't care as a mother. You don't care as a person." She raised her gaze to meet Shereille's eyes, lips set in a hard line. "You care more about your research than you do about the people around you."

Shereille blinked. "Yes. I thought you understood that when I hired you."

"We thought you hired us to spend more time with Lillie," Vola said pointedly.

"I hired you to do a job," Shereille said. "The expectations were in writing and everything. You were supposed to help me study a dragon and you couldn't get it right. Even when I forced the issue, you still couldn't provide me with a subject."

"Forced the issue?" Vola said as Talon said, "Subject?"

"You stood at the end of that tunnel dithering for so long, and then you were just going to turn around and leave without letting me talk to Listrell. I figured a fight to the death would give me what I needed for my research."

Vola's stomach clenched. "You let the swamp beast go on purpose, to instigate the fight. You drove it into the cavern so we'd have no choice but to kill Listrell."

"You were talking about leaving!" Shereille cried. "That is not what I hired you to do."

"So you alerted her to our presence, made her angry, and risked all of our lives." Vola stood, looming over Shereille.

The elf shrugged. "You're adventurers. You risk your lives every day. What's the difference?"

"The difference is that we decide what's worth it and what's not. Your research is not worth our deaths."

"Maybe not to you," Shereille said with a pout.

They stared at her. Lillie stared at the ground, a heavy crease between her eyebrows.

"You risked her life, too," Vola said quietly, pointing to Lillie. "Was that worth it?"

Shereille remained silent, and Vola wondered if she even saw her daughter or just a means to an end.

"I can understand that you used me," Lillie said, her hands clenched together. "After all, I am only the result of a contract. But you manipulated me into endangering them. They could have been killed, and it would have been my fault." Her eyes snapped up to her mother's face. "Mine and yours."

"Lillie," Vola started, but Lillie held up a hand, her eyes implacable as she stared at Shereille.

"I'd like you to leave, please," she said. "I won't bother you again."

Shereille didn't even hesitate. She walked out the door without looking back or pausing. As if she was finally free of an annoying obligation.

Vola reached across to take Lillie's hand.

Lillie remained staring at the empty doorway, but her fingers gripped Vola's hard enough to hurt. Vola didn't wince or pull away.

Sorrel hopped off her cot and hobbled over to put her arms around Lillie from behind.

"Immobile," the healer yelled. "You're supposed to keep the leg immobile! That means not moving!"

Sorrel jumped and guiltily tried to clamber back into her cot. But there was a stirring from the bed in the corner, and the healers in the room froze.

"What's the yelling about?" Master Bao said, voice as dry as a desert wind.

NINETEEN

SORREL IGNORED the cries of the healers and hopped across the room. Vola caught her halfway and scooped her up so the healers would stop yelling.

"Master Bao," Sorrel said. "Thank Maxim, you're awake."

The old monk blinked at her for a long moment, and Vola found herself holding her breath. "Sorrel?" he finally said.

The color seemed to be leeching from his skin now, and his hair, which was already white and wiry, was going limp as well. But his eyes were alert and trained on Sorrel's face.

"I guess I'm glad you didn't stop following me," he said.

"You must have met Nargilla, then," Sorrel said as Vola placed her on the edge of his bed. The healers glared at her, but Sorrel didn't even notice.

Master Bao put a hand to his head and wheezed. "The gnome from hell? Yes, we're acquainted now. She interrupted my meditation to create that dead spot. I figured one last fight before I died wouldn't hurt anything. Except I didn't die, did I?"

"She drained the magic out of you as well as the land," Vola said.

"I'm sorry to say it's still happening," the closest healer said. "It seems to be a continual leeching process. But I don't know how to fix it."

He shook his head. "Forget that. We have a bigger problem."

"The dragons?" Talon said. She'd joined them with her bandaged hand.

Lillie sat on the edge of her cot looking like she was trying to get up. One of the healers rushed to her side and pushed her back down.

"I said you could sit up. Not that you could go jumping around."

"No," Master Bao said. "The...the city. Nargilla is going to drain the city. One big dead spot with all the power sucked out of it."

Vola gasped, and Sorrel went completely rigid.

"The spots she's already drained, she's using them as anchors. That's how her magic works. It builds on itself. If she drains even one more..."

"The whole city will be gone," Sorrel said. "Worse than burnt."

"We have to evacuate," a voice said from the doorway. They turned to see Rilla with Gruff beside her. Soot still streaked her green leather jacket, and she smelled like the burning city. Clearly, she hadn't slowed down in the days they'd been gone.

Fedor Gerrickson lurked just behind her, looking even more bedraggled. His beard was snarled and his shoulders drooped under the weight of his dirty chainmail.

Rilla stepped into the room and did a double-take when she saw Renvick beside the door. She cocked a thumb at him. "Did you guys stop to rob a tomb along the way?"

"Does it count as robbing if the artifacts walk away with you?" Renvick's voice rumbled through the room.

Fedor jumped and pulled his double-headed ax from his back.

Rilla tilted her head as the color started to pour into Renvick once more, greens and blues suffusing the guardian's scales.

"Does it count as an artifact if it talks back to you?" Rilla asked.

Renvick grinned, showing off a row of sharp, gleaming teeth. "It does not." He cracked his neck. "You are evacuating the city?"

"You heard?" Vola said.

"I hear everything in my fugue state.

Sorrel gulped. "Everything?"

"How else do you think I would know when to wake?"

"I don't know. Instinct?"

"Instinct is just action without thought. Thought alongside action is decision. You and I will talk, fierce one. But not immediately, I think."

He stretched his limbs, and Vola thought she heard a creak. Then he turned to Rilla. "I would like to offer the sanctuary of my mistress's old lair. If the people of Firewatch are in danger, we will shelter them."

Rilla raised an eyebrow. "Okay, I've missed a couple of steps here." She glanced at Vola.

Vola gestured to Renvick. "Rilla, this is Renvick. Guardian of the dragon Listrell and her representative at this moment. Renvick this is Rilla. Our boss."

Renvick gave Rilla a respectful little bow.

"Listrell," Rilla said, eyes narrowed. "And we're all friends now?"

"More or less," Sorrel said. "It helps that she didn't eat Talon."

Rilla glanced at Talon, who'd been half-hidden behind Vola. Talon gave her a little wave.

Rilla shook her head and raised a hand to rub her forehead. "Okay... okay, we're going to have to move fast so I can't ask all the questions I really, really want to. I trust you. That's why I hired you."

Fedor snorted loud enough to draw the gaze of everyone in the room. "You really believe this creature? This agent of dragons?"

Rilla's eyes narrowed. "I believe my people."

"They've been duped. Dragons are monsters."

"No," Talon said, standing so Fedor was forced to look at her. "We were wrong."

"How can you say that? Dragons kill and destroy."

"So do humans. So do dwarves and elves and orcs and every sentient creature. That doesn't mean we should make war on each other."

Fedor gaped at her. "You were the victim of a dragon. But you stand here and defend them to me."

"I was wrong. And an innocent creature died for it. I don't want to be wrong again. Listrell is not our enemy. Nargilla is. We have to go after her."

"This enemy can't be bigger than the dragon that is looming over all of us!" Fedor threw his hands over his heads.

"Is your revenge really more important than the lives of everyone in this city?" Talon said.

Fedor's face went hard as granite. "My revenge is everything," he said. "My heart still bleeds for the people I've lost. Your heart must be shriveled in your chest if you can forget what you've lost and feel regret for the death of even one of those creatures."

Talon reared back as if he'd struck her.

Vola stepped forward. "That's enough. How dare you judge what's inside someone else's head and heart?"

Fedor spat on the floor, making the healers cry out in disgust. "There's nothing wrong with *me*, paladin. But I'd seriously question the commitment of anyone in my party who backed out of their duty so easily."

"Good thing you're not in charge of my party, then," Vola said, dark and dangerous.

Fedor shook his head. "Don't expect any help from me. I have one priority. And it's to hunt this dragon down and kill it so that at least my honor will be satisfied."

He spun on his heel and slammed out the door. Renvick jerked as if to stop him before thinking better of it.

Talon stood frozen in the middle of the room, eyes wide and blank.

Sorrel caught Renvick's gaze across the room. "You want to go protect Listrell from that maniac?"

"I do. But I will first lead your people to a safe lair." He nodded to Rilla again.

She jerked her chin up. "I appreciate it. But I hope you don't mind if I vet this Listrell and her lair first."

"That sounds wise to me," Renvick said.

"While I do that..." She pointed to Vola and Talon. "I want you tracking down Nargilla. Your instincts are right, whatever that nutter says. Track her down and get rid of her. If there's no spellcaster, then there's no spell."

Talon remained quiet. So Vola answered. "We'll start, but we don't even know where—"

"I need a map of the city and the surrounding area." Lillie brushed aside the healer, who was trying to get her to lie back down, and snapped her fingers. "Now, please."

"You can find her?" Vola asked.

"The dead spots outside the city. She's using them as anchor points, which means I can predict where she'll need to cast her final spell."

"I can tell you how she forms her spells," Master Bao said from his bed. "So you will have a better chance to stay out of it. Unlike me." He cracked a weak grin.

"Then I leave you in good hands," Renvick said. He met Sorrel's eyes and gave her a solemn nod before leaving with Rilla.

One of the healers rushed into the room with a map for Lillie.

Vola stepped up to Talon and put her hand on her shoulder. The ranger didn't like to be touched, but Vola got the impression Talon needed something anchor her just then.

"Maybe he's right," Talon said.

"He's not," Vola said without even bothering to ask about what.

"Am I just running from a fight, though? Maybe it's human to want revenge and I'm more animal than I thought I was."

"Maybe you can be both," Vola said as Lillie did something arcane with rulers and a stick of charcoal across the map. "Take the best parts of both worlds. Animals run to protect themselves. But at some point, you have to stop running, Talon. At some point the best way to protect yourself is to turn and fight. Defense has to turn to offense. Or you'll be running forever."

Talon's shoulders straightened under Vola's grip. "It's not cowardly to want to protect what's important to you. To want to keep it as far away from the fighting as possible."

"No," Vola said. "Definitely not. But you don't have to do it alone. Your pack is with you."

Talon huffed a grim laugh. "Yes. That's what I'm afraid of."

TWENTY

LILLIE'S MAP had all sorts of lines slashing across it by the time she was done, but she assured Vola that the one they wanted was a dark angry x-mark near the top, a few miles north of the city.

"What do we do when we get there?" Sorrel said. "If Nargilla's there, too?"

"We disrupt her spell," Lillie said.

"Just like we've done the last two times, huh?" Sorrel said.

Lillie looked hurt. "We know so much more now than we did then. Master Bao can give us the details we need." She gestured to the old monk who lay on the cot, his head turned toward them. "If her magic works with anchors, on a large level as well as on a smaller level, then there have to be anchor points for the spell, anchoring on Nargilla herself when she draws power."

"Let me guess, we just have to find those and break her connection to them," Vola said. Sometimes magic could be so predictable.

"Exactly," Lillie said.

Master Bao cleared his throat. "They look like crystals."

"How do we keep from dying while we find them?" Sorrel said. "She's thrown us around before and your head has to hurt as much as my leg."

"We couldn't get to her before because she was in the middle of the spell. And if we're caught in there, we'll end up just like Master Bao. But she couldn't move either..."

"If she's trapped there until she's done, then we can use that," Vola said, catching on.

"I also remember her being pretty good at dodging, whether she was trapped or not," Sorrel said.

"So we concentrate our fire. Sorell, that staff does lightning too, right?"

"Yeah." Sorrel touched Maxim's Warhammer and static crackled across its surface. "And I have a couple of bolts I've been saving especially for her."

"What about the rock wyrms?" Talon said.

Lillie raised her chin. "Leave those to me. I think I can take them out of the equation entirely."

"Then, you, Talon, and Sorrel concentrate on Nargilla," Vola said. "I'll have to go for the anchors. But be ready. Once we disrupt the spell, she can move again and I can't imagine she'll be happy."

"We have your back," Talon said. "Don't worry."

"Mountains look so much flatter on paper," Sorrel said the next morning as they made their way from the city.

This terrain was much harder than the meager trails they'd been following through the rest of the Firewall so far. Here there was no trail. There was no pass. It was just one ragged peak after another and finding ways to scramble up them.

Higher and higher they climbed. Vola tried to go slowly for the others. Talon's hand was fine, but Sorrel still limped and Vola didn't want her rebreaking anything. Lillie never complained, but every now and then she held her hand to her forehead as if the world still spun a little.

Vola tried to go slow, but she could still look over her shoulder and see glimpses of Firewatch through the peaks. It buzzed with the frantic movements of thousands of people trying to evacuate. They didn't have time to go slow.

"Lillie, how far?" Vola asked.

Lillie squinted at the map in her hands and then gazed around them. "We should be getting close. I don't know whether we should hope she got there first or not."

"Why would we hope that?" Sorrel said, puffing as she climbed up onto the next ridge.

"Because then we'd know for sure we got the right place," Talon said.

Lillie gave her a lopsided smile. "The map is not wonderfully detailed. I'm mostly just aiming us in the right direction."

"Great," Vola muttered under her breath. "Talon? Can you find her the way you did last time, now that we know where to look?"

Talon shook her head. "I don't feel anything. She must not have started yet."

It took them a few hours canvassing the area Lillie had marked on her map, but finally, they found a flat-topped cliff in the distance. A lone figure stood silhouetted against the early afternoon sky, and magic tingled against Vola's skin.

"There." That was all she had to say. They were as ready as they could make themselves even if Vola still felt shaky.

They converged on the peak.

At the top, it seemed like a god had taken a greatsword and sliced off the top, leaving a broad flat area with little peaks off to the side, serving as short edges to the bowl.

Nargilla stood in the center, staff planted in the rock. Black gathered at the tip in little tendrils, as if she'd just started.

The gnome sighed as the party climbed to her plateau.

"You know, you guys were fun at first. But your tenacity is beginning to irk me. Do you know what it's like when an annoyance just won't die?"

"Actually, we're familiar with the feeling," Vola said. They'd left the swamp monster with Rilla, who'd promised to put it to work evacuating the city. But if it managed to slip its leash and escape in the chaos...well, none of them would shed a tear over it.

"So, we're doing this again?" Nargilla said, leaning heavily on her staff.

"Unless you stop your spell," Vola said, drawing her sword.

Nargilla snorted. "Well, that's not going to happen. I've already explained this. If I stop the spell, then it doesn't get done. Does it?"

"That's the plan."

And Lillie hit her with a fireball.

When the smoke cleared, Nargilla coughed and brushed soot from her robe. "Good one, but—"

Lightning came from the other side as Sorrel let loose with Maxim's staff and Talon let loose an arrow.

Nargilla could only dodge one at a time and came out the other side, looking a bit singed. "Hey. Stop that. Do you know how hard it is to set this up? I'll have to start all over if you knock me out of sync."

Lillie sent another gout of fire at her, and when she tried to twist out of the way, Talon struck her with an arrow.

Nargilla cried out, Talon's arrow sprouting from her shoulder. "Fine." She panted. "I can work with this."

She reached down as if grasping a piece of earth and yanked upward. Just like she had when summoning the rock wyrms.

They all stared at the ground.

Nothing happened.

"Were you looking for your friends?" Lillie pointed over Nargilla's shoulder at a peak they'd passed on their way there.

A thumper like the ones the researchers used was positioned on top, just visible through the swarming bodies of half a dozen rock wyrms. Every rock wyrm in the area would be drawn to the thumper instead of them.

Nargilla's mouth thinned and her brows drew down. Sweat stood out on her brow as she clutched the end of the arrow with her free hand.

"You can end this now, Nargilla," Vola said. "By choice. Or it can be by force. Which will it be?"

Nargilla snapped the feathered end off the arrow, making the rest of them wince. "Guess," Nargilla said, eyes going to narrow slits.

She raised her blood-covered hand and dark clouds rushed to swirl over their heads.

Vola didn't wait to see what other spells she could call while working to drain the land. Nargilla was distracted, and that was all that mattered.

"Now," she shouted and rolled away to the edges of the plateau.

Behind her, her teammates pummeled Nargilla. They couldn't get close enough to hit, but they could send a variety of unpleasant things her way.

Vola sheathed her sword to give herself a free hand and leaped to the raised rock surrounding the plateau. The spell anchors would look like crystals, Master Bar had said. Vola scoured the ground, looking for anything out of the ordinary glinting among the rocks.

Thunder rumbled above and suddenly the heavens opened up. Except it wasn't rain that threatened to soak them.

Hail pounded the top of the mountains. Huge pieces of ice as big as her fist whistled past Vola's ear. She flung her shield up to cover her head and ran crouched over, hoping the others would be able to hold up under the onslaught.

She slipped and slid over the treacherous ice. Finding a crystal in this would be ten times harder. Vola kicked pieces of ice out of her way and noticed the others backing up a step out of the corner of her eye. The black was spreading from Nargilla's staff.

There, a glint of blue among the blanketing white.

Ice continued to pour out of the sky, hammering her shield and making it ring as she cleared the crystal of ice.

Perfect. She pulled her hand ax from her belt. Then slammed the blade into the crystal. It shattered, the sound of tinkling glass getting lost in the pounding of hail.

One down. Five more to go.

From the center of the circle, Nargilla screamed. She whipped around to fix Vola with a glare.

Vola stopped for long enough to meet her look. *See*, she said to silently. *We're going to make you stop.*

Nargilla lowered her chin. The ice storm ceased, a few last hailstones falling to the ground with a clatter. Then she lifted her staff, pulling it free from the spell.

Vola took a startled step back. She hadn't actually expected Nargilla to stop. They were supposed to force her.

The gnome disappeared into the earth, traveling through the rock itself, presumably. Vola skidded across the hail stones, trying to guess where she would come up.

"Where'd she go?" Sorrel asked. The three of them backed up, meeting Vola halfway as they scoured the mountaintop.

"Shit, we can't pummel her if we can't see," Talon said.

Lillie faltered, putting a hand to her head. "Does anyone else feel...woozy?"

"Is it your head?" Vola said. "Maybe we shouldn't have climbed so fast."

"I feel it, too," Sorrel said. She stared at her feet.

Vola reached for them both, pulling at her healing energy while she did.

Except she couldn't reach it.

It felt like a half-empty well, the surface of the water too far away to touch.

"What?" She gasped, and on a hunch, she knelt to clear away the hailstorms.

The ground was black, the last of the red-brown of the rock swirling away.

"Oh, gods," Vola said. "How did she—how did we—?"

"I had a second circle." Nargilla's voice came from the raised edge of the plateau, and they whipped around. She sounded weary, and she sagged against her staff as she glared at them.

From her knees, Vola swept armfuls of hailstones aside and found another line of crystals outside the first.

She looked back up at the gnome.

"I knew you'd turn up, so the first one was always supposed to be a decoy. Thanks for making it work."

"Oh, no," Vola whispered. "No, no, no." She tried to spring to her feet, to lunge at Nargilla, but a wave of weakness washed over her.

Around her, Lillie, Sorrel, and Talon fell to their knees and slumped over.

Vola growled, welcoming the wash of red across her vision. Rage would give her strength. She levered herself to her feet, using her knees to brace herself.

The breath left her lungs and suddenly she found herself too weak to draw another. Black crowded her vision, and she fell.

Laying on her side, the last thing she saw was the tattered ends of Nargilla's robe as the gnome stepped across the blackened rock to stand between her and her party.

She had no idea how long it took her to wake, but her dry mouth tasted like she'd licked the swamp monster when she finally cracked her eyelids open.

Short figures bustled around a large sprawling skeleton hung from a ribbed ceiling. The scene seemed familiar, but when would she have seen a floating skeleton like that?

Vola blinked, trying to clear the fog from her mind, trying to make sense of what she saw.

Light streamed from high windows, dawn from what she could tell. It had been early afternoon when they'd found Nargilla.

The windows stuck out over open space, like the back end of a ship but from the inside. And the skeleton was…?

A dragon, a piece of her mind answered its own question.

The field museum. She was in the field museum in the middle of Firewatch. How the hell had she gotten there?

Vola tried to sit up but a wave of weakness and disorientation kept her pinned to the ground as if she'd been tied there. Instead, she stuck out her elbow and heaved so she could roll.

Talon lay beside her. And beyond, she glimpsed Lillie's gold hair and Sorrel's brown arm.

At least they'd stayed together, whatever else had happened.

But what *had* happened?

The black. The crystals. Nargilla had trapped them in a second spell. She'd drained them along with the land. Just like Master Bao.

Vola's heart pounded, and she reached, trying to find Cleavah. But there was nothing there. No connection. She was empty inside, no healing and no calming presence.

Oh, gods. She groaned.

One of the small figures bustling around the skeleton heard and came toward them. Vola recognized the tattered hem of Nargilla's robe from her spot on the floor.

"Ooh, one of you is still in the land of the living. So exciting. I always work better with an audience." Her misplaced cheer was back, and she leaned over so her face hung in Vola's sight, grinning ear to ear.

"Fffuck. You."

No lightning bolt. That was scarier than anything.

Nargilla clicked her tongue. Behind her, the skeleton dropped from the ceiling, bones shattering against the tile floor. Vola winced.

Talon stirred and tried to push herself up on her elbows. She didn't succeed any more than Vola had. "What...?"

"I'm clearing space," Nargilla said. "We're gonna need more room."

As she spoke, the gnomes behind her, dressed in shapeless gray shifts, made short work of sweeping the bones into a messy pile across the room. There was a low rumbling and another group of gnomes appeared in the doorway, rolling several tanks fitted with copper wiring into the center of the room.

Vola's eyes narrowed.

"You recognize them," Nargilla said, eyes on Vola. "Myron Vidal's work, you know. The man was an idiot if he thought he could get away from Anders, but he did have his moments of genius. These tanks can store the power I siphon from the land as easily as they stored the power he siphoned from the dead."

One of the tanks clanged as the gnomes stood it up in the center of the room.

"Careful with that," Nargilla said.

Lillie groaned and Sorrel thrashed about, trying to right herself.

"Well, I'd better get back to it, if I want to get those tanks filled. Anders will be here to oversee the draining of the city and to take the tanks back with him. I only get my bonus if I can prove it works." Nargilla straightened up again.

Vola tried to get her elbows under her to push herself up, but ended up panting, too spent to do anything besides stare at the floor. "Why haven't you killed us?"

"I thought about it. But I thought maybe Anders would prefer to do it. I'll also admit, I'm curious what the draining will do to you eventually. It'll be so much fun to watch. Thanks for clearing out the city, by the way. Much shorter commute now."

"They'll never let you live," Vola grated out.

"Who?" Nargilla paused. "The city counselors? They're not brave enough to come back. The dragons? They don't care enough to do more than defend themselves."

"The gods," Vola said, thinking of Cleavah and the burning anger she'd spoken with outside Listrell's lair. "They know what you can do. They won't let you threaten them or their people."

Nargilla's eyebrows went up. "Ha. Yes, that was a problem. Yesterday. Today, however, I've discovered a workaround. A happy little coincidence."

She flicked her fingers behind Vola, then trotted away, humming.

Vola fought the heaviness of her body and rolled to her other side. She sucked in a gasp and her vision went fuzzy.

One of the exhibits stood behind her, empty of everything except some fake rocks and lichen. And a figure bound to a stake.

Golden skin had gone dull in the dawn light and dark curling hair fell limp to her waist. Cleavah stood tied to the stake, her eyes closed and face wreathed with pain as gold light flowed out of her, spilled onto the floor, and flowed to one of the empty tanks.

TWENTY-ONE

VOLA FOUND A SURGE OF STRENGTH—OR at least, a surge of not weakness—and pushed herself to her hands and knees while her friends gaped at the captured goddess.

Vola shuffled to the display and fell over the railing into the diorama of the surrounding mountains made of foam and dry lichen. A fake rock disintegrated under her weight with a puff of dust.

"Lady," she whispered. A clear pane of spell glass separated her from her goddess. She pressed her fists against the smooth surface. She wanted to pound on it, but all she could manage was a dull thump.

Vola reached for her connection with Cleavah. It had always been there. Even when the paladin council had stripped her of her rank and stolen her emblem, Cleavah had still been there, just wrapped in fog, separated by the thinnest veil that Vola had spent too long shying away from.

Buried deeper than she'd ever looked before, Vola found her connection to Cleavah. At the very bottom of her well, power pulsed through a thin thread. It was pulled taut and stretched to the goddess. Was this how Cleavah normally fed her power? Except now, power sucked through that string, into Vola, and then immediately out and away, toward the closest of Nargilla's tanks.

A side effect of Nargilla's spell. Vola was connected to her goddess, therefore draining Vola meant draining Cleavah. The goddess had been right. Nargilla did have the power to rival the gods themselves. It was just way, way worse than they'd thought.

As if the end of the world wasn't bad enough.

Cleavah's eyelids cracked open, and she stared blearily at Vola. Even a greater goddess had been brought low by the maniacal gnome.

Vola thumped the glass again. It was just a simple ward spell to keep something valuable in and potential thieves out. Lillie could have broken it in a heartbeat. Vola could have smashed through it with no problem. Yesterday.

"Lillie?" Vola whispered. She knew the answer, but they might as well make sure.

"I'm out," the wizard said. She couldn't even muster the energy to sound grim. She just stared at the ceiling. "She's taken the magic out of our very selves. Even here where the world's not drained, I'm cut off." She raised her hand and a single sad little spark spluttered against her fingertips before dying out.

Vola definitely couldn't use Cleavah's power to heal. She was already the reason the goddess was hanging there, being bled like a butchered animal. How did Nargilla even get her physical form? Had Cleavah manifested while Vola and the others were knocked out? Or had her spell sucked Cleavah here like a summoning spell?

"I can't feel the land," Talon said. "I can't call on it anymore."

"Can't feel the land?" Sorrel said. "I can barely feel my legs." She rolled to her elbows and tried pulling her knees under her.

"Where's Gruff?" Vola asked. Maybe they had a friend on the outside, a lone wolf waiting to slink in and save them.

"I can't feel him either," Talon said. "He could be out there looking for me, but if he can't hear me..." She shook her head. "How can Nargilla cut me off from him? He's family."

"It's just like Master Bao," Lillie said. "She's tapped into our life force and is draining it away."

"Still?" Vola said. "She isn't done yet?"

"No, or we wouldn't be able to talk or move."

Vola swallowed. "So how long do we have?"

"I'm not sure I have all the tools I would need to calculate —"

"Then guess."

"A few hours."

Vola couldn't help the gasp that escaped her lungs.

"This appears to be much faster and progressing at a rate exponential to that of Master Bao's experience," Lillie said, discussing numbers like what she wanted for tea that afternoon. "Nargilla has stepped up her timetable, apparently."

The gnomes in the rest of the hall had finished setting up the rolling tanks and fiddled with the copper wiring between them. They'd seen the same kind of tank in Myron's laboratory so many months ago. He'd used them to collect magical energy from the dead and ship the result to Anders. This was no different, except it posed a threat to a much broader area.

Not to mention their own magic was swirling around in those tanks somewhere.

If they could just smash one...

Vola tried lifting her arm experimentally. Her fingers twitched.

The others didn't look like they were in any better shape. They'd all stopped trying for a minute, taking a breather to just lay there.

Vola squeezed her eyes shut. What could they possibly do against Nargilla now? She'd been toying with them all along, if this was an example of the kind of work she could do normally.

The city was empty. There was no one left to help them, and really, there was no one left for them to save.

"We shouldn't have gone after Nargilla," Vola said, slumping to the rough floor of the exhibit.

"What?" Sorrel said.

She could hear Talon shift, but Vola kept her head down. It was easier than trying to wrestle it up.

"Why?" Talon said.

"We should have run with the others. We should have helped evacuate the city and stayed out of Nargilla's path. Then we'd be out there planning a siege that might work, rather than in here with no hope."

Vola could barely keep her lungs working, and she wasn't exactly sure why she was still trying so hard. She had nothing left to fight with. All she wanted was to lie down among these fake rocks and admit she'd been beaten.

It was a new feeling for her.

There was a long moment before Talon's voice finally came from outside the exhibit. "You've never lost everything before, have you?"

Vola opened her mouth and had to stop. She'd lost lots of things in her life. Given up a lot of things, too. But had she ever lost everything? Even when the paladin council had taken her emblem and burned her shield, she'd still had her team. She'd tried to give them up, but they'd followed her, anyway. She'd had her team; she'd had her family. She had so much that she'd never even thought of before.

"No," she said. "This would be a first for me."

"It's definitely not my first time," Talon said quietly. "I know what it's like to hit the very bottom of yourself and still be alive. When you still have to go on despite everything that's happened because the world didn't have the decency to kill you."

Talon pushed herself to her feet, looking haler and healthier than she had any right to. "Maybe we should have run."

Vola stared.

"But you were right, when you said there's a point where you can't run anymore. Because you've hit a cliff or a pit or a wall. Or because you've run so far and so long that you're stronger now than the thing chasing you."

Talon stumbled to the railing of the exhibit and held out a hand to Vola. How did she have the strength to stand upright?

"There's a point when you have to turn and fight because you're human, and the only other option is to get slaughtered like an animal."

Vola felt like a slaughtered animal already. She had nothing left to give, nothing left to try. But neither did Talon, and she still stood there, waiting for Vola to take her hand. Waiting for Vola to find the last bit of hope or strength or sheer stubbornness that would propel her until she had the momentum to move on her own again.

Vola glanced back at the trapped goddess, around at the green tanks, and over at her team trying to pick themselves up.

Then she reached up and clasped Talon's hand.

Talon hauled her to her feet. Or at least halfway, and Vola ended up draped over the railing of the exhibit.

"Very motivational," Sorrel said from the floor. "But what the hell are we going to do against Nargilla if none of us can even move?"

"We'll figure it out," Vola said, huffing against the railing. "Rilla called us Mishap's Heroes for a reason. We take misfortune and spit out gold."

"If that were true, we'd be a lot wealthier," Sorrel said. "And what if the misfortune kills us before we have a chance to get to the second part?" But she sighed and heaved herself to her feet, using the railing beside Vola as leverage. She and Vola reached down to give Lillie a hand up.

"It helps if you just concentrate on breathing," Talon said, once she was upright. "Keep the air going in and out and let muscle memory do the real work."

"You make it sound so easy," Sorrel grumbled.

"We haven't lost everything," Vola said. "Like Talon said, we're still alive. And we have a lot more than just magic. Nargilla didn't take Lillie's mind. And she didn't take the rest of our skills."

"So, ideas?" Lillie asked.

Talon's chin jerked up. "Can you distract her?"

They all stopped and looked at Talon. She was the only one who managed to stand there without support so far.

"Distract?" Sorrel said. "We can still talk, so yeah, we can be distracting as hell."

"Why?" Vola said, eyes narrow.

"I'm going for help."

Vola straightened and nearly blacked out. "What?"

"How can you go for help?" Lillie said. "She took your magic."

"I don't need magic to talk people into something they should already be doing. That's language, not spells."

"Talon, being a pack works both ways. You don't want us to put ourselves in danger. But we don't want you haring off by yourself either," Vola said.

"That time has passed," Talon said. "We're out of options." She met each of their eyes in turn. "Trust me."

"We do," Vola said without hesitating.

"Then distract her. Slow her down. Anything to kill time. And don't die."

"Only if you promise the same," Vola said.

Talon's lip twitched with a smile. "Promise."

"Then go. We're counting on you to get us out of this."

TWENTY-TWO

NARGILLA'S GNOMES eyed them as they wobbled on their feet and Vola hung her head trying to appear non-threatening. The gnomes left them alone. Like they didn't consider the party a threat in their current state.

They probably had the right of it.

Vola glanced around, taking quick stock of their equipment. All their weapons were missing, but Vola still wore her plate armor. Which seemed a bit silly right about now.

She yanked at the leather straps as she surveyed the room. Everything the gnomes did seemed to center around those tanks. She fumbled with the clasps of her pauldrons, and Lillie reached to help her. Vola pulled the armor from her shoulders and limbs. There, that felt a lot better. A piece of her was screaming that she needed that protection. It did no good on the ground. The rest of her was sighing in relief.

"All right. Distractions it is. Sorrel, I want those tanks to blow up or leak or something."

"I'll make it happen," Sorrel said. Instead of trying to walk, she flopped to the floor again and just rolled. Like a loose sausage rolling off an inn table.

"I'm hungry," Lillie said, absently.

Sorrel paused to let one of the gnomes pass, laying there like a dead thing. The gnome sniffed and stepped over her. As soon as she was unobserved again, Sorrel rolled between the legs of the tanks and disappeared from view.

A gnome stopped to peer underneath, and Vola's breath hissed through her teeth. She exchanged a look with Lillie.

The wizard wobbled a couple of steps to the center of the room and touched her head. "Oh, I feel so faint," she said and toppled over.

Vola lurched to her and fell to her knees. "Oh no, she's fainted. She's too delicate for this. Someone help, please!"

Lillie snorted, her arm over her face.

At least her cry had drawn the attention of the gnomes and while she couldn't hear it, she knew that somewhere behind her, Talon was slinking into the shadows.

There was a small clank from under the tanks, and someone swore.

Smoke poured out from under the glass containers and the mess of copper wiring and tubes.

The gnomes yelled and spun back to the tanks, racing to find the problem.

Vola didn't immediately feel an influx of power, so it probably wasn't their magic leaking into the air. That might take more work. But they'd obviously caused a problem, and that was the best she could hope for right now.

The smoke rolled over them as Sorrel crawled back to them.

"This will only work for so long," she whispered. "And we're too visible."

"Scatter," Vola whispered back. "Under cover of the smoke. If Nargilla's looking for us, she won't be looking for Talon. Stay out of sight. Sabotage what you can. And whatever you do, don't get—"

"Killed?" Sorrel said.

"I was going to say caught, but yeah, that, too."

Sorrel flopped onto her back and rolled away like a frenetic sausage. Lillie army-crawled her way toward a back hallway, and Vola heaved herself to her hands and knees and shuffled in the opposite direction. She found a table and ducked under it as the gnomes yelled frantically from the center of the room.

She peeked out long enough to check the high windows. Sure enough, someone yanked the edge of a pink sleeve free from the casement, and the window slapped shut, unnoticed by anyone below.

Good. Talon was away. Now they just had to keep her disappearance a secret from Nargilla for as long as possible.

Vola spotted a door that presumably led deeper into the museum and crawled towards it before the smoke could clear from the room. It wouldn't do Talon any good if she was caught here in the first chamber.

The hallway stretched long and skinny back into the mountain the museum perched on. Bare and utilitarian, this one was obviously not meant for the public. But Nargilla's people had been here already to lay down lines of copper tubing. They'd never experimented with smashing Myron's tanks to see if that released the stolen magic, but now Vola wished that they had. Not that she was strong enough to smash anything right now. But it would have been a nice goal to work toward.

As it was, she stopped several times to concentrate on breathing and yank copper tubing apart. She left a little trail of destruction along behind her.

It was not the most rewarding of battles, crawling along the hall breaking things. It didn't feel heroic at all.

But that was Talon's point. This was what they could do at the moment. This was how they could go on after Nargilla had taken everything away from them.

Maybe she could find the anchor points to Nargilla's spell. No, those would be somewhere beyond the city. Probably near those dead spots. Maybe they were the dead spots themselves. She would have to ask Lillie. Either way, she wouldn't find them here.

But she could follow this tubing to wherever it led. And screw up whatever she found there.

Voices from down the hall made Vola jump, and she scanned the corridor for an escape. Doors lined the hallway, most with windows at the top, but they were too high to see through when she was on her hands and knees.

It was a unique experience for Vola to be too short.

She picked a door at random and ducked inside, trying to close it quietly behind her.

She came face to face with a familiar elf, red-gold hair falling out of her bun, her blue-green eyes wide with surprise.

Vola slapped her hand over Shereille's mouth before she could scream or do anything to give them away.

They froze, locked together as the voices outside came closer.

"This had better not be like Myron or Inga," someone said. A low male voice Vola had never heard before.

"Those jokers?" Nargilla's voice scoffed. "I'm ten times better."

"Mishap's Heroes has managed to thwart me at every turn. Don't underestimate them."

"I've declawed those four. They won't be a problem anymore. Maybe we can take care of them for good together. And can I just say how fabulous your butt is looking today?"

"Please don't."

The tread of a sturdy pair of boots moved down the hall, accompanied by the patter of Nargilla trotting to keep up.

Vola slumped against the door and released the breath she'd been holding. "Anders is here," she whispered, heart pounding against her ribcage. "Gods, we've been chasing him for so long, and now he's right on the other side of the door, and I can't do anything about it."

Her gaze fell on Shereille, and she scowled. "What are you doing here?" She was glad to find that curiosity and outrage fueled her muscles better than anything else right now.

"What do you think I'm doing?" Shereille pushed her hair out of her eyes with both hands. "Trying to stop that little shit, of course."

Vola raised her eyebrows at Lillie's mother's language. "I'm sorry, but you? You're trying to stop the bad guy?"

"You don't have to say it like that."

"Yes, I do. Not only have you had no interest in stopping Nargilla, you've actively gotten in our way when it's served your own purpose." Vola's mouth pulled down. "Unless...did Lillie's words actually get to you? Is that why you didn't evacuate with everyone else? You felt bad?"

"Felt bad about what?" Shereille said, shattering that idea. "This master plan of Nargilla's is completely interfering with my research. First, they tried to get me to evacuate with the others. As if I would leave my work unfinished. Then that gnome came in and started draining the magic out of everything. If anything is going to affect my results, it's that."

Of course. She wasn't doing this because it was the right thing to do. She was doing it because she was just as self-centered and determined as ever.

Really, it was a shame. Shereille and Lillie were so much alike in so many little ways. It was just the big ones that had sent them careening away from each other. Shereille was just Lillie, without any of the feelings attached.

"Why are you crawling around on the floor?" Shereille finally said, looking askance at Vola. "And don't you think you'd be more useful with armor and a weapon?"

"We were captured," Vola said shortly. "And Nargilla drained all the magic out of us. I'm crawling because it's easier than walking."

Shereille sat there gaping, without anything useful to say.

"What about you?" Vola said. "Have you made any progress? How can we beat her?"

"There might be a way to reverse what's happened. At least, to release all the magic back into the world that Nargilla has stolen. But it will require magic."

"You can't just smash the tanks?"

Shereille looked horrified. "Who knows what that would do? You could completely destroy us and yourself in the process. Or worse, Nargilla would absorb that power into herself."

Vola's stomach dropped. "No, no, no, she can't do that. She has the power of a goddess trapped in there. Cleavah herself is being drained. Through me."

"Oh my gods," Shereille said, eyes wide.

"Exactly."

Shereille bit her lip, and her eyes went unfocused and distant. Vola knew what that look meant when it was Lillie.

"What are you thinking?" she asked. "Do you have an idea?"

Shereille blew out her breath through her nose. "Only that if Nargilla has the power of a god, you will need a god's power to counter her. I wonder if any of the priests stayed in the city or if they were all sensible and evacuated."

Vola froze, hand raised to her head. "Not a priest," she said. "A weapon. We need to find wherever Nargilla stashed our weapons."

She scrambled to her knees and leaned up to check the hallway through the window.

"What good will that do if you can't even carry one?" Shereille said.

"Sorrel's staff," Vola said. "The staff she carries and fights with. It's part of Maxim's Warhammer. I've seen it shear through just about everything before. She can usually call it to her, but it must be locked away behind a door or a spell right now. If we can find it…"

Shereille pushed Vola aside—it didn't take much strength—and opened the door.

Vola hauled herself to her feet using the door frame, and surprisingly, Shereille slipped her slim shoulder under Vola's arm.

"Where would she have stashed our weapons?" Vola asked her. "We were unconscious when she brought us in."

"There's a back door by the delivery bay. Besides the visitors' entrance, that's the most likely. It seems to be where most of the equipment is being brought in."

They shuffled down the hall. Vola kept checking over her shoulder to make sure they weren't spotted. No one used the hallway right now, but they could hear shouting coming from the main room where she and the others had woken up.

Nargilla must have learned of their absence by now.

"I think they'll be coming after us shortly," Vola told Shereille. "Let's pick up the pace."

"Easy for you to say," Shereille said. "You're not the one hauling around a half-dead half-orc."

Vola glared at Shereille as she puffed, but for once she was pretty sure that had been a joke on Shereille's part. Huh. Maybe the woman did have a sense of humor.

The long hall ended in a doorway and light spilled through the cracks around the door.

"There are storerooms here," Shereille said. "If she brought you in this way, which seems likely, then she probably stashed your weapons here somewhere."

They checked the first room. Nothing but brooms and mops. The second held crates of antiquities.

"Oh, the Longbarrow collection came in," Shereille said. "I was looking forward to that exhibit."

"Focus," Vola said.

The third door they checked was locked.

"Bingo," Vola said. "Can you get it open?"

Shereille's mouth dropped open. "What do you think I am? Some common adventurer?"

"Mostly I was just hoping for helpful."

Shereille made a high-pitched squeak. "I am plenty helpful in my own field, thank you."

"Your daughter is much better at this." Vola twiddled her fingers. "A little bit of fire. A little bit of wind and ta-da. Magic is useful."

"Just because I refuse to debase myself for something so common—"

"You mean common like survival? You're right, you're too good for that."

Shereille let out a little scream and laid her hands against the door. Flames flashed out and licked at the dry wood.

By the time Shereille stepped back, the door was black and charred.

"See, that wasn't so hard," Vola said.

Shereille stared at her. "How did you know how to make me do that?"

"I've been traveling with another stubborn elf for a while now. Her block is self-confidence. I just have to goad her enough that she forgets to be worried. Your block is pride. Prick that and you'll bleed a river."

Shereille's mouth worked.

There was a yell from the end of the hall, and several figures appeared.

"We're out of time," Shereille said.

Vola let all of her dead weight fall against the door and it crunched open. They tumbled inside, and Shereille pushed it closed behind them.

She examined the rough surface. "I can hold it for maybe thirty seconds."

"It'll have to be enough," Vola said. She climbed heavily to her feet again as Shereille set her back to the door.

There, flung carelessly across a table in the middle of the storeroom, was their equipment. Vola pushed aside Lillie's spell book and Talon's daggers to grab Sorrel's staff. In her hands, the staff changed into a longsword.

"I appreciate the sentiment," Vola said. "But I can't do anything with you right now."

Her hands lingered on her own sword and shield, but there was no way she'd be able to carry them, let alone hide them from Nargilla and her people.

There was a thump against the charred door, and Shereille was knocked back a few inches. "Thirty seconds," she said, resettling herself against the barrier.

Vola glanced at their weapons again. She had to choose and choose fast. But with her arms feeling like noodles, there was no way she was going to get away with any of these.

"We can only take what we can hide," Vola said. Then she held out Maxim's Warhammer, disguised as a sword, and addressed it directly. "Work with me, please, and I'll get you back to your rightful owner. I need something small. Something I can hide."

The sword shuddered for a second, as if choosing, and then its surface rippled until she held a butter knife.

"That'll work," she said and stuffed it in her shirt.

The next thump on the door flung it open, and Shereille stumbled back into the table of weapons. She fell to the ground with a clang as Vola's sword and Talon's daggers cascaded around her.

Vola just slumped against the other end of it and refused to flinch as a couple of Nargilla's gnomes poured through the door into the little storeroom.

They were caught. No use fighting it. Her entire purpose had been to stall the inevitable. Well, that and get the Warhammer back. Hopefully they'd taken up enough time that Talon was well on her way to finding help.

The gnomes had no trouble manhandling Vola. They patted her down roughly, to see if she'd hidden any of the weapons from the room, but they didn't find the butter knife tucked between her breasts.

They hauled Shereille to her feet and gave her exasperated looks when she flinched and screamed with every sharp movement and word. Even Vola couldn't help rolling her eyes. They might have been caught, but there was such a thing as dignity.

The gnomes herded them back down the hallway Vola had so painfully traversed just a few minutes ago. Vola had to use the wall to stay upright, but Shereille walked with a stiff little hitch in her step despite the fact that she'd been perfectly fine before. Vola tried to catch her eye, but she stared straight ahead, her lips thin and her eyes pinched and worried.

Back in the massive foyer, one of the gnomes nudged Vola, and she lost what little balance she'd regained. She sprawled across the tile floor.

Shereille avoided the same fate by skipping forward to kneel beside her.

Lillie lay nearby. Not moving.

"Where are the others?" Nargilla snapped from somewhere over Vola's head.

"We haven't found them yet," one of the gnomes replied.

Nargilla's nostrils flared, and she glanced at a man who stood examining the tanks with a clipboard. His short brown hair was combed precisely away from his face, and he wore a pair of fitted trousers and a leather vest.

"I'll find them myself," Nargilla muttered. "Make sure these don't escape. Again," she told her gnomes.

The man didn't bother glancing up when Nargilla trotted off. He just turned another page on his clipboard and ran his finger down a list.

Vola narrowed her eyes. Was this Anders? The sinister presence they'd been chasing for years? The man who'd orchestrated the coup on the Thrones and hired Myron and Inga and Nargilla to steal all the magic out of the different pieces of the world?

Her fingers itched for her blade. He might be unassuming and unarmed, but she wouldn't fall into the trap of underestimating him.

His eyes met hers, almost as if he could tell what she was thinking.

But he didn't react. He just stepped around the tanks to examine the other side.

Vola's fingers flexed against the tile, but she was still weak as tepid water. And Lillie still wasn't moving.

"Lillie?" Vola croaked. She rolled onto her side.

"I'm all right," Lillie said without opening her eyes. "When one of them grabbed me, I tried to blast him. Fun fact: trying to draw magic you can't reach has unpleasant side effects."

"Good to know. I won't reach for Cleavah again if I can help it." She glanced over to the exhibit where the goddess stood trapped. Her head had slumped forward, so it was hard to tell, but Vola thought she looked paler than before. The stream of golden power flowing from her to the tanks had steadied, and no longer pulsed.

"On the bright side, I did fall down and manage to trip him at the top of the stairs." Lillie's expression hardened. "He won't be getting back up again."

"One down," Shereille said. "That's useful."

Lillie's eyes shot open, and she turned her head to stare at them. "Shereille? What are you doing here?"

"Long story short, Shereille is learning how to be an adventurer," Vola said.

Shereille made a face and opened her mouth.

Cries and the sound of fists on flesh interrupted them, and Nargilla returned with two gnomes dragging Sorrel behind her. The monk was nowhere near as fast as she usually was, but she did manage to get in several hits before the gnomes tossed her on the ground beside them.

Sorrel struggled to her feet while Nargilla stalked toward them.

"Where's the last one?" she said.

Vola glanced around and used her finger to count. "One, two, three, four." She shrugged at Nargilla. "Last one who?"

Nargilla growled. "The other one. Used to wear a hood. The one with the wolf. That one…" She pointed to Shereille. "Is new. I don't know where you picked her up, but where is the other fighter?"

"No idea," Vola said. The butter knife poked her in a rib but she didn't dare try to slip it to Sorrel now. Even if she did hand it over, there was little chance they'd be able to fight back. All that would accomplish was letting Nargilla know how special the Warhammer was. And who knew if Sorrel would be able to use the Warhammer's power without her innate magic?

Vola glanced at the others. "What about you guys?"

Sorrel shrugged expressively while Lillie shook her head on the floor.

"Sorry," Vola said. "Can't help you—"

Nargilla's fist struck her across the face, and Vola sprawled against the floor.

"Try again," the gnome said, cocking her head.

Vola rubbed her jaw.

Nargilla knelt and grinned at her, but the mirth didn't reach her eyes. "I can do anything I want to you in this state," she said, voice low. "You have no magic to protect you. No goddess. And your strength is draining out of you like water. Now, where is the last one?"

"I already gave you my answer once before. Fuck you."

Nargilla cocked her head. "I thought you didn't swear."

"My goddess doesn't like it. But you took her away, so..."

Nargilla smirked like she conceded the point.

"I told you not to underestimate them," Anders said, voice bland. He folded the papers smooth on his clipboard and hung it on the nearest tank. "This all seems to be in order. Do you need any help with them?" His brown eyes narrowed on the party laying on the tile floor.

"No," Nargilla said. Then she muttered, "Having a great ass doesn't make you better than me."

She struck Vola again.

Vola, who prided herself on her reflexes, couldn't even dodge.

"Stop that," Lillie said. She tried to push herself up on her elbows.

"Would you like a turn next?" Nargilla asked.

Vola glared Lillie down. She couldn't fight back, but Vola could still take a punch better than the rest of them. And she just had to hold out until Talon fetched help.

Nargilla struck her again.

Good gods, she was going to be beaten to death by a gnome with a god complex.

"You just have to tell me where she is," Nargilla said calmly, squinting at her knuckles. "If not, I'll see if any of them want to tell me." She gestured to Sorrel and Lillie.

Vola spit on her. It seemed like the only response. Her jaw burned when she pursed her lips.

Nargilla raised her fist again. "Where?"

A rumble rattled the tanks and made the floor vibrate under Vola's back, and the screeching sound of tortured metal stopped Nargilla.

They all turned their faces toward the ceiling.

A crack of light appeared between the top of the walls and the roof. It grew wider as the screeching sound grew louder.

And suddenly the entire roof lifted off, flung open like the top of a treasure chest, and standing over the opening like the scaliest treasure hunter in the world was Listrell.

She peered inside the museum, one arm holding up the roof and one braced against the far wall as her wings spread far enough to blot out the sun behind her.

Talon rode just behind her horns.

"Looking for me?" she said.

TWENTY-THREE

A FIERCE WILD light burned in Vola's chest as five of the smaller *draconis minimus* climbed up over the walls and hung there above them all. Vola recognized the red and gold scales of Hurren.

The front doors burst in, and Rilla and Renvick led a troop of guardians into the foyer, each one bristling with their choice of weapons. Behind them crowded the old gnome, Doddleben and his squad of former prisoners, now freed from Listrell's lair. They brandished broken teacups in the direction of Nargilla and her gnomes.

Beside the tanks swirling with magic, Anders shook his head. "Sorry, Pipwattle. You're on your own for this one."

He put his left hand on the tank that held Cleavah's power. The golden glow had filled it nearly halfway by now. Anders raised his right hand and a blue crystal glinted in his palm.

"Vola." Lillie struggled to her hands and knees. "He's getting away."

"No!" Vola lurched to her feet and lunged for Anders, but he was most of the way across the foyer.

The blue stone flashed and crackling light washed over Anders and the tank. They disappeared just as Vola hit the ground a foot away, her hands closing on empty air.

She whipped around to check Cleavah. But the goddess still hung from her bonds. Her power drained into one of the other tanks now, along with the power pouring in from the city.

"What?" Nargilla screamed. "You're just going to leave me with all this? Fine," she muttered, lunging for the rest of the tanks. "Anders can live with that little bit of power. I'll take the rest."

"Stop her," Rilla shouted, gesturing to the guardians to spread out around the room as Nargilla yanked a copper tube from the tank where Cleavah's power was being siphoned to. She attached it to something else Vola couldn't see.

"Uh oh." Vola rolled onto her elbows.

"Vola—" Sorrel called.

"I know."

Myron had done the same thing once. And had become nearly invincible in the process. It had taken a god's weapon to stop him. And Nargilla had access to a goddess's power herself. That changed things.

Vola plunged her hand into her shirt for the butter knife.

"Sorrel," she called. "Here."

"What the—" But the monk's reflexes were better than Vola's right now, and she caught the knife. The moment her hand touched the handle, the Warhammer pulsed and flexed and became the quarterstaff Sorrel always favored. The Warhammer's magic didn't seem to mind Sorrel's state.

"Oh, yes," Sorrel said and surged to her feet.

Nargilla bent and attached the copper tube to a different tank.

A boom rocked the room and pressed Vola flat on her back again.

"What a rush," Nargilla said from the middle of a cloud of smoke. Slowly it cleared, revealing the gnome, who was flexing her fingers.

Listrell lowered her head enough that Talon could slide down to the floor with them. "Hit her now," the dragon said.

Sorrel stumbled forward, then her gait evened out as if she drew strength from the Warhammer. Finally, she sprinted flat out and raised her staff.

"Hah!" She brought it down on Nargilla's head.

There was a flash, and Sorrel flew back. Listrell caught the halfling before she could slam into a wall.

Nargilla chuckled. "Oh, good try. But you're just a smidge too late." She held up her thumb and forefinger half an inch apart.

Nargilla raised her hands and a howling wind whipped around the foyer. Vola clutched the smooth tiles to keep from being blown away.

Rilla reached Vola's side with Renvick a split second behind her. The guardian gave Vola a hand to her feet and handed her a hand ax.

"Thanks," she said.

The guardian bent to lift Sorrel to his shoulder, and she clung there with one hand, her other holding her staff. "Watch my back," he said.

The wind tore at their clothes as Shereille hauled herself to her feet and produced Talon's daggers from the folds of her shirt. She tossed them to Talon. The ranger leaned out from Listrell's head to snatch them before the wind could fling them aside.

Vola stared. "When did you get those?"

"When the gnomes were busy trying to grab you. It's funny how if you scream and whimper, no one suspects you of conniving."

Vola laughed. "Connive away. Will you be Lillie's feet?"

Shereille nodded and stepped to help Lillie stand against the maelstrom.

Rilla hauled on Vola's arm. "I can't guarantee I'll keep you upright," she said. "But I can keep the worst from knocking you over."

"Sounds good to me," Vola said, ducking her head to keep Rilla between herself and the worst of the wind.

"All right. Spread out," Rilla said. "Maybe if we hit her all at once."

"Gods, you're taking forever," Nargilla said, rolling her eyes so hard her whole head moved. "Are we doing this or not?"

Listrell snapped at the gnome. Anyone else would have disappeared into the giant teeth-lined maw. But Nargilla's whole form flashed, and Listrell yanked her snout away with a snort.

"Ouch," the dragon said.

"She's basically a god right now," Vola said.

Rilla raised her daggers and stalked forward. "Not for long."

Vola followed, for the sake of staying upright. Rilla blocked at least some of the wind.

Those that could wield their weapons without falling over attacked. The five smaller dragons swarmed across the tile floor, trying to get close while Doddleben and his band of tea-toting prisoners darted in from the other side.

Nargilla swung her staff around, and Cleavah's gold light spilled out in a wave, knocking them all over before they reached her or the tanks.

"Again," Rilla called. "All at once."

Vola just tried to keep her fingers clenched around the haft of the ax. It wouldn't do her any good on the floor. Not that it was doing her a lot of good with the blade tipped toward the floor, but at least she felt better holding it.

Nargilla swept the ground again. Her staff scraped the tile and sparks sprayed out.

Rilla stumbled back into Vola, and they went down in a tangle of limbs. Vola managed to keep from stabbing the princess but only just.

"This isn't working." Vola's gaze focused on the golden light flowing from Cleavah to the gnome. Every move Nargilla made kept her between the goddess and her rescuers.

"We have to disconnect them," Vola said, pushing at Rilla with weak hands. "She's drawing away Cleavah's power. But if we can separate them—"

"Maybe it'll pull the power away. Got it." Rilla rolled off Vola's legs and helped haul her to her feet. She gave orders for the right ranks to close in and the left to give way, driving Nargilla away from Cleavah.

But the gnome narrowed her eyes and struck the ground with her staff. A rumble beneath Vola's feet told her what was coming a split second before the head of a rock wyrm broke through the tile.

"Shit," Rilla said, as rock wyrms erupted all over the floor.

Listrell snapped the head off of one, but three more rose to take its place.

It was no use. Nargilla would never let them get close to the source of her power. They just needed to do it from here.

"Sorrel," Vola called across the battle.

Sorrel still clung to Renvick's back, but she twisted around to make eye contact.

"We have to break the shield on Cleavah."

Sorrel looked down at the staff in her hand and squinted across the battle at the trapped goddess. "This is the first time in my life I think I've ever said this, but…I can't make that jump."

Vola opened her mouth, but Sorrel shifted her grip on Renvick and called across to Talon. "Talon, catch!"

She threw the staff like a javelin, and it whistled as it parted the air.

Nargilla's eyes widened when she saw it. It wasn't affected by her winds at all.

Vola's heart dropped as Nargilla reached out, close enough to intercept it.

But Listrell snatched the staff out of the air and twisted her head to offer it to Talon.

Vola let out her breath, but before Talon could take the staff, a cry echoed above them.

"Death to dragons!" A short squat shape leaped from the top of the museum wall, plummeting toward Listrell's head.

Fedor Gerrickson struck her snout and caught her eye ridges. Listrell grunted in surprise and dropped the staff which clattered and rolled between her feet.

Vola started for the staff, cursing under her breath, but she'd never get there before Nargilla. That had been the whole point of throwing it.

Listrell shook her head with a roar, making Fedor's feet whip through the air. And finally, with a snap, the dragon hunter flew across the room to strike Nargilla.

Clearly, she hadn't expected an armed and armored dwarf to fly at her or thought to guard against it, and she went down under his weight.

Talon slid down Listrell's flank, reaching for the staff.

With a cry of rage, Nargilla slammed her fists into Fedor's chest, and he flew across the foyer. Vola glimpsed his wide eyes and gaping mouth just before he struck the wall and slid down to lay still.

In Talon's hands, the staff shifted into a longbow complete with its own quiver.

Nargilla growled under her breath and leveled her free hand at Talon who lifted the bow and set an arrow to the string.

Listrell lunged, pulling more of her bulk over the museum wall, and threw her head between Nargilla and Talon.

Nargilla's god power struck the dragon square in the jaw and the dragon roared as Talon released her arrow.

Her shot sped toward Cleavah, ripping through the power Nargilla threw to stop it.

It whistled and struck the shield around Cleavah with a crack that shook the entire foyer. The shield shattered and dissolved in bright flames.

Talon tossed the longbow to Vola, and Vola dropped her ax to catch it.

"Listrell!" Vola called.

The dragon swung her snout around, and Vola flung herself aboard. Listrell cocked her head and sent Vola flying at the goddess, who stood tied to the exhibit.

The longbow warmed in her hand, responding to her touch, and it morphed into a longsword. It's keen edge hummed and sliced through the power Nargilla threw at her as she landed. A surprised rock wyrm fell in two pieces, and she stumbled across its corpse into the fake lichen of the exhibit.

Nargilla screamed as Vola righted herself.

Cleavah's eyes fluttered, and she tilted her head enough to stare blearily at Vola.

Vola brought the sword edge down to slice through the goddess's bonds. They sizzled as flames licked across the ropes and burned away the remaining strands.

Cleavah slumped, and Vola reached to catch her without thinking. Her arms went around the goddess, but her knees buckled and they fell.

For a moment.

And then that moment froze. The sounds of battle faded, Nargilla's scream muted, and Vola stared up into Cleavah's serene face. The goddess's eyes fluttered closed, and she breathed deep.

The gold power flowing out of her across the floor to Nargilla stopped. Then it started flowing the other direction, pouring back into Cleavah, filling her skin with golden light. Light so bright, it burned Vola's eyes.

She scrunched them shut and suddenly sound returned. Nargilla's scream still echoed around the walls, and she could hear the moans of the rock wyrms and the clash of weapons.

Cleavah's arms closed around Vola and gently lifted her to her feet. Strength filled her limbs until she felt like she would split in two and pour herself out into the world. Her own feet held her again and her fingers closed around the hilt of her sword, lifting it without any trembling.

Vola could still feel the searing heat of Cleavah's light against her face, and she held a hand over her eyes as Cleavah finally let go of her.

Vola could feel the goddess through their bond once more but more clearly now than ever before.

Cleavah had always felt like that friend standing just over her shoulder, waiting to be called on. But this...this was the burning of rage. This was the feel of righteous anger held barely in check. Vola could feel Cleavah as a white-hot torch shot through with her cool concern for the mortals in the room. If she released her true power, if she allowed herself to act on her rage, she would incinerate everyone and everything. Friend and foe alike.

A touch left a mark of heat on the back of Vola's hand. And then the burning presence moved away. Cooler air stung Vola's sensitive cheeks, and she gasped still hiding her eyes.

This was ridiculous. She was a paladin. Her goddess had returned to her strength, and Vola was too afraid to open her eyes to see it?

Finally, she pulled her hand away. One glimpse. One little peek was all she needed.

A figure stood at the edge of the exhibit, but that was all the detail Vola could discern. The blinding radiance of the goddess's true form burned across her vision, blotting out everything else in a figure of white light.

The burning goddess stepped down from the exhibit. Listrell's guardians and Doddleben's squad cowered back, ducking their heads and hiding their eyes from the searing light.

Vola couldn't look away.

Neither could Nargilla. She stood frozen in the center of the room, her eyes fixed on the dazzling figure. Tears streamed down her cheeks and the skin around her eyes went tight and red, but still, she didn't break away.

The goddess's expression remained implacable as she brought her hands together, and Nargilla's tanks exploded in a shower of light and glass. Someone screamed. Several someones. But it wasn't Nargilla or Vola.

Glass rained down, tinkling against tile, claws, and scales. But the power remained in the air, floating over Nargilla's head, flashes and sheets of color that looked like streamers in a carnival sky.

The goddess tipped her head back to gaze at the power hanging in midair. She held up one searing glowing arm and seemed to gather it to her. Her other arm hung limp at her side, blending in with the brilliance of the rest of her.

The power roiled and eddied and flowed toward the goddess and then she flung her hand out.

The power exploded. Like the tanks, but this time it was like a cloud of light fractured into a million tiny motes of dust that sped out back into the world.

Three streams of it gathered and speared toward Talon, Lillie, and Sorrel. The three of them clutched their chests and fell to their knees as their strength and magic returned.

The goddess shifted, and her burning aspect turned until she looked directly at Vola. Coal-black eyes rested in that light, the only break in the expanse of burning divinity.

Nargilla squeaked and finally broke her frozen terror. She darted away only to be grabbed by a glowing golden spear that could have been a hand.

She struggled in the goddess's grip but couldn't rip away.

The goddess's eyes never left Vola's face and as they stared at each other, the burning aspect dimmed and subsided, drawing in as if her skin absorbed the light and fire of her true self until she was something fit for mortals once again. Her figure didn't shrink or hunch. It just drew the light together into a more compact space.

She subsided until she had the same golden skin which Vola could now tell held all the light of the world underneath. The same dark curling hair, but now it was cropped short, curling around an ear. She was missing an

arm and one leg was gone from the knee down. Half of her face was that
serene beauty Vola had met in a defaced temple in Brisbene. The other
half was covered in a mess of scars. Burns that had left the shining skin
puckered and marred.

The same black eyes stared back at Vola, and the figure of light had
been burned into Vola's gaze so that it hung like a halo around the self-
contained outline of the Broken.

"Lady," Vola croaked. Her eyes burned from the memory of light, and
she rubbed the moisture from her stinging face.

"Volagra," the Broken said, her voice the same sound of rushing wind
that it always had been.

Nargilla tried to struggle again, and the Broken raised wings of flame
to steady herself against the unbalance.

The Broken glared at the gnome in her hand, and Nargilla shrank
away from the wrath of a goddess.

"Righteousness demands I don't kill you," she said. "But you should
know, it's going to be very, very hard for me."

Glass tinkled as those present picked themselves up off the floor where
they'd been thrown after the tanks exploded.

Rilla was the first to her feet, brushing the bits of broken glass from
her clothes and hair. A cut across her forehead was bleeding down the side
of her face.

The princess raised a bloody finger. "Er, hi. Yes. That's our prisoner."
She pointed to Nargilla.

Vola climbed carefully out of the exhibit and made her way to her
team. Talon stood, shaking her head as if trying to clear it. Renvick set
Sorrel on her feet, and the monk winced as she cracked her back. Vola
started to reach to help Lillie up, but Shereille was there already with her
hand under her daughter's elbow.

The Broken's eyebrow raised as she looked at Rilla. "Yes. And your
point?"

Rilla's head jerked. "My point is, I want to take her in for trial and
judgment. She nearly leveled this city. She's stolen power out of the
land—"

"And from the gods themselves," the Broken said. Her eyebrow
remained raised without even a twitch.

"Yes," Rilla said. She wasn't easily cowed, though Vola could see her
thumb shaking. "But you can't just walk off with her."

"You think your authority supersedes mine?"

A stupid question if ever there was one. Rilla was not stupid, and her mouth snapped shut on any sort of answer she could give. But she still fumed a little as the Broken took Nargilla more firmly in hand.

The Broken paused for a second. "Would it make you feel better if I told you there is no reprieve where she is going? I have friends in high places. The Greater Virtue of Justice for instance. She'll be more than happy to see this one serve for eternity."

Nargilla gulped.

"I suppose that makes it slightly better," Rilla said. She glanced at Vola and added. "My lady."

The Broken also glanced at Vola and the twitch in the unburned corner of her mouth was so reminiscent of Cleavah's grin that the last of Vola's uncertainty fell away. Vola gave her a little shrug.

The Broken gave her an almost imperceptible nod. "I like you. And Vola says you'll do, so we'll be speaking again."

Rilla flashed Vola a wide-eyed look as the Broken spread wings of flame. Instead of leaping into the sky, the goddess wrapped the fire around herself and Nargilla before they disappeared in a swirl of sparks.

TWENTY-FOUR

LISTRELL SWOOPED low over the blackened earth, and Vola hung out over her shoulder to get a good look.

"Looks the same to me," the dragon rumbled.

"Talon?" Vola called across the dragon's scales to the ranger, who clung to the dragon's other shoulder.

"The magic has returned, but the land...it's still dead," she said over the rushing of the wind.

"All right, put us down at the city gate, Listrell."

The massive dragon took another lazy turn and had them back to Fire-watch in less than five minutes. Vola and the others covered their eyes to guard against the sand and grit kicked up by the dragon's landing.

"Thanks for providing transport," Lillie said as she crept carefully down the dragon's side to the ground. Vola jumped down and stepped to offer her a hand.

Sorrel leaped without looking and landed on her feet. "Very handy having a dragon in your back pocket."

"It was no trouble," Listrell said. "I was curious as well. I could feel the spot still, but the others are outside my territory."

"Firewatch isn't in your territory either, is it?" Sorrel said.

The dragon tilted her head. "Firewatch doesn't belong to any one drag-on," she said. "But to all."

"So if the magic is back but the land is still dead, what does that mean?" Vola said.

"It means that whatever Nargilla did caused permanent damage," Lillie said.

Listrell's massive shoulders rolled. "And we don't know what that will do in the long run. At least the culprit is gone for good."

Vola winced. Nargilla might have been gone, but Anders had escaped and she didn't want to think about everything that could mean.

Still, Listrell was right. They'd succeeded yesterday. Won the battle if not the war.

"Thank you for coming to help," she said, walking around to the front of the dragon so Listrell didn't have to crane her neck to hear.

"You saved our butts," Sorrel said.

"Talon just said she was going for help. She didn't say she was going to come back with you." Lillie beamed up at Listrell.

"I didn't want to promise something I didn't know if I could deliver," Talon said, coming around the dragon's massive forearm.

"I'm sorry it took me as long as it did. I...did not want to believe that such small things could affect me or the other dragons. But Talon convinced me small bodies can contain big enemies." Listrell shook her head like a dog. "But this is the time for all of us to focus on one threat. Are you headed for the meeting? I can give you a lift."

Vola shook her head. "We wanted to check in on Sorrel's master first. We'll meet you there."

"Suit yourself," Listrell said. "And cover your eyes."

The dragon launched herself into the air, sending up another cloud of dust and dirt. When they could finally look up to track her flight, she had already alighted on the cliff above the field museum.

Lillie chewed her lip as they turned to start their trek up into the city. "I don't like that those dead spots are still dead."

"I definitely thought it would all go back to normal when Cleavah...I mean...the Broken did her thing," Sorrel said.

"Have you spoken to her yet?" Lillie asked quietly.

"Not since she left with Nargilla," Vola said. And she wasn't sure what she would say when she finally did. There was so much roiling around underneath Vola's skin that she wasn't sure what would rise to the top when she finally stood face to face with her goddess again.

She could feel her there, deep inside, still connected. If she needed to heal someone or if she really needed to talk, she could just call and the goddess would be there as always. But the Broken hadn't reached out to her yet, and Vola wondered if the goddess needed her space as much as

Vola did now that the truth was known. She had to have been hiding herself, making Vola think she was a lesser goddess for a reason.

Outside the House of the Broken, where they'd brought Master Bao, a scaled creature with a filmy green crest and a menacing expression stood tethered to the railing by a thick chain.

"Oh, dear," Lillie said.

"I'll admit I kind of hoped it would disappear during the evacuation," Sorrel said.

Talon grabbed a note that had been tucked under the swamp beast's halter, deftly dodging its teeth. "It says it tried to eat one of the patients, so they left it behind. Too bad it's still here. They also said please, please don't bring it back."

"I'll second that, since I was the patient it tried to eat," a voice as dry and cracked as the desert said behind them.

They turned to see a slim, straight figure in a monk's tunic leaning against the doorframe.

"Master Bao," Sorrel said.

She trotted up to him, and he smiled in greeting. Then she took his hand in hers and flipped him over her shoulder.

The rest of them cried out as the martial arts master hit the ground rolling and sprang back to his feet.

"What are you doing?" Lillie cried.

"Making sure he feels better," Sorrel said.

Vola forced her shoulders to relax as Master Bao grinned.

"Much better," he said. "I never thought of myself as magical before, but it's amazing how not having any takes it out of you."

"It's a matter of balances, sir," Lillie said with a brilliant smile. "All life carries some magic and without it, a body has a much harder time just existing."

"I don't know, I felt like I was getting used to it, by the end," Sorrel said.

The rest of them stared at her, and she raised her hands.

"I'm not saying I wanted to stay like that. I just had an easier time convincing my body to fight after I had a chance to get used to it."

"I'll take your word for it," Master Bao said. "All I know is I felt like a long-dead weasel beaten against the rocks until it's nothing but a bag of skin holding some bones and some mush."

Vola made a face.

"That's exactly how I'd describe it, too," Talon said.

"But I'm back to normal now," he said, raising his chin.

Sorrel crossed her arms. "Great, so you can go back to trying to kill yourself."

Vola rolled her eyes. She didn't disagree, but there was such a thing as tact. She'd have to introduce it to Sorrel sometime.

The old monk examined his nails. "Actually, I'm heading back to the monastery."

Sorrel eyed him sidelong. "You are?"

"There was a point there while I was watching a psychotic gnome drain the life out of me when I realized I wasn't done fighting. If I was, I wouldn't have minded someone else taking the choice away from me. But it turns out, I do mind. And I don't want someone like that taking the choice away from the rest of the world either."

"We think that's what Anders is trying to do," Vola said.

He met her eyes, his glinting with something much stronger than steel. "Yes. I'm returning to the monastery to rally Hazel and the others against this threat. This is much bigger than even Maxim."

"It's a threat to the world," Sorrel said. "Maxim is only part of it."

Now that he was recovered, Master Bao was the last person in the world who needed an escort to the edge of the city, so they collected the swamp monster reluctantly, and continued up to the field museum.

The roof still hadn't been replaced after Listrell hinged it open like a huge treasure chest, and considering that she was still coming and going over the edge, it didn't seem likely that she would replace it any time soon.

The dragon herself was overseeing the transformation of the foyer under the bright desert sun. One of the museum's employees shuffled by with a broom, sweeping up the last of the broken glass from Nargilla's tanks while others righted the fake lichen and the mossy rocks in the exhibit where the Broken had been tied. Still more followed Listrell's directions, hauling square tables together in the center of the room.

Rilla stood arguing with the councilman of Firewatch and the curator of the museum while Renvick looked on with his arms folded over his chest.

A glowing portal of dark green stood open behind the princess, and as they watched, the Princess of the War Throne and the Princess of the Defense Throne stepped through. And behind them came the Princess of the Magic Throne. Four rulers of Southglen in one room together. Rilla must be worried.

No one had seen them yet where they stood beside the door, and Vola took a deep breath before starting forward. She nearly ran over a young woman with short, curling brown hair.

"Aster?" Vola said, recognizing Shereille's assistant.

"Oh. Hello," she said with a bright if harried smile. "Sorry, I didn't see you. We're in a hurry."

Vola caught sight of Shereille directing the rest of her crew to collect the crates just inside the door. Vola's lips thinned. "I can imagine."

She stalked over to the elf woman. "Heading out again?"

"Oh, you know how it is," Shereille said. Her bright hair was perfectly contained in its bun again, and she didn't seem any worse for wear from her adventure the day before. "There are still undergrads to harangue and research assistants who absolutely need to finish by a certain time or they won't receive their certification."

"What can you possibly be studying?" Lillie asked. "Listrell said they're going to be waking all the dragons to warn them of the threat and enlist their help."

The lines around Shereille's mouth deepened for a moment. "All the more reason to hurry then, isn't it? If we want to talk to any of the *draconis maximus* before they leave dragon lands, we must go now."

Especially since Listrell still wouldn't talk to her.

"You don't care that Anders is going to try what he did here again?" Talon said.

Shereille blinked. "Why would I? Nargilla is no longer a threat to my research. Tell your goddess thanks for that, by the way. Aside from that, my life is going back to normal."

Vola glanced at Lillie, but the wizard just watched her mother calmly.

"Good luck, then," Lillie said.

"Thank you." Shereille bent to pick up a crate and then thought better of it. "I'm sorry," she said abruptly, meeting Lillie's eyes. "I'm sorry I'm not the person you wanted me to be. I actually feel rather guilty about that."

"Don't worry," Lillie said with a thin smile. "I'm sure you'll get over it soon enough."

"You know, I'm sure I shall," Shereille said, completely missing the veiled insult in Lillie's words.

"Goodbye," Lillie said, voice steady and firm. And Vola noticed she didn't say anything like "see you later" or "be sure to visit for the holidays."

Shereille lifted the crate in her capable hands and didn't even look back as she followed her team out the door of the museum.

"Are you all right?" Vola asked Lillie, who stared after her.

"I am not going to fall apart if that's what you're asking," Lillie said quietly. "But that's as good as it's going to get right now."

"I'm sorry," Talon said. "We all are."

Lillie shook her head and squeezed her eyes shut. "You shouldn't be. She is who she is. I cannot force her to be someone else just because I had silly dreams as a child. She cares about her research and only her research. A fact I should have picked up on long ago. Even before I met her."

"We're still sorry," Sorrel said.

"I know. But not every story has a happy ending." Lillie's mouth firmed, and she lifted her head. "My father more than made up for her. And I prefer the family that I have now." She glanced at them from under her lashes. "The one that I chose."

Rilla spotted them, finally, and waved impatiently for them to join the others at the makeshift council.

Vola and the others took their places along one side of the pushed-together tables beside Fedor Gerrickson, who still served as the captain of the city militia even on the injured list. He sat with his arm in a sling and his bandaged leg propped on a stool. The stout dwarf was missing his ax and his chainmail, but he glared at Listrell as if he wished he still had both.

Vola cleared her throat. "I hope your recovery is going well," she said as politely as she could manage. A growl still managed to rumble through the good intentions. This man had interrupted at exactly the wrong time and could have ended the world with his misplaced fanaticism.

Fedor glanced at her, breaking his stare at Listrell. "A few broken bones." He winced. "And some ribs. Dwarf bones are sturdier, but that makes them harder to heal, too."

"What will you do now that the dragons are all on our side?" Lillie asked. "Surely you're not here to ambush Listrell." She chuckled, but her eyes flickered between the dragon and the dragon hunter.

Fedor grunted. "I guess I'll have to find something else to hunt."

Talon settled herself on the chair directly beside him. "What about your revenge?"

He met her eyes, and his mouth screwed up in a grimace. "My revenge completely misses the point if it hurts other people," he said. "I can't claim to be protecting others if I'm just trying to get them killed. Besides, I have another personal target now." He raised the arm that was still in a sling. "Nargilla threw me against a wall while she was under orders from this Anders fellow. I'm ready for a little payback." He cracked his knuckles.

"So…more revenge," Sorrel said as Renvick stepped up beside her and pulled out a chair.

"Is this seat taken?" he asked.

Sorrel glanced at him. "No. Be my guest."

He settled himself so his tail draped comfortably to the side.

Lillie leaned over to whisper in Sorrel's ear. "Have you had your conversation yet?"

Sorrel batted her away with a mild glare. "No, and this isn't really the time for it." She cast a look at Renvick full of chagrin and a little bit of longing. "I think we're both okay with leaving it at that for now. Maybe when this is all over, we can figure out what our relationship will look like."

Vola raised her eyebrows but did her best to hide her expression. Sorrel might have wanted to stay non-committal, but it sounded like there was a relationship there already, whether they'd figured it all out or not, yet.

The leaders of Firewatch arrayed themselves along one side of the tables, and Listrell had her own side opposite them. Rilla sat with the three other princesses directly across from Vola and the others.

Rilla stood. "We know now the threat Anders presents." She braced her hands on the tabletop in front of her. "He is trying to drain the magic from the world."

There was a sudden hush in the museum's foyer. The councilman of Firewatch shifted in his chair. "I hate to say it like this, but Firewatch is one city outside of any country's jurisdiction. An attack on us hardly indicates an attack on the world. How do you come to this conclusion?"

Rilla's eyes narrowed, but she jerked her chin at Vola's group without speaking.

Vola stood and ticked points off on her fingers. "He was using a necromancer to suck magic out of dead people. He tried to steal the magic from the Thrones of Southglen. And we know now he's been using Nargilla to suck the magic out of different lands for years."

"And when we first met, he was buying living people from desperate nobles," Lillie said. "We thought it was for slavery, but now I'm sure he was going to steal their magic out of them, the same way Nargilla did to us just a couple of days ago."

Rilla nodded. "And these are only the incidents we know about. We've thwarted him so far, but we know he has these capabilities. He has Myron's tanks and Nargilla's spell. He can set up shop whenever he likes."

"If this is true," Listrell said, her voice making the tile under their feet rumble. "It means war. We cannot allow him to take what does not belong to him. But more than that, we cannot allow him to destroy so much of the world to do it."

"Yes," Rilla said. "This means war. War with Southglen, war with the world."

"And war with the gods themselves," a voice like rushing wind said.

Vola felt her before she turned her head to see the Broken standing just behind her right shoulder.

The goddess's presence was muted somehow, as if she was holding some of herself back so as not to scare the mortals. She wore her Broken aspect, the scarred, unbalanced body with the hint of fiery wings raised behind her.

Vola's breath caught in her throat, and she forced herself to swallow. "My lady," she said quietly.

The Broken's eyes flicked to Vola, and the scarred corner of her mouth lifted.

Rilla gave the Broken a respectful nod. "We welcome all the help we can get, of course."

The Broken winced. "I don't know how much help it will be. Anders escaped with a piece of my power."

A gasp went through those assembled.

"With it, he can cut the rest of the gods off from the land and thereby end the world."

The councilman clutched his chest and swayed in his chair.

Rilla didn't flinch. The only reaction Vola could see was the twitch at the corner of her mouth that looked like a split-second grimace.

"Well," Rilla said. "Won't this be fun?"

The Broken actually smiled.

Vola felt torn. There was a big piece of her that felt like she stood beside a stranger. A benevolent leader who had taken a strange interest in her. She didn't know this woman, this entity that had chosen to stand beside her.

Except she did. There was an even greater piece of her that recognized Cleavah in the figure beside her. The aspect was different, but the feeling of comaraderie, benevolence, and humor was the same. The bond that pulsed in Vola's center was the same that had been there for five years as she'd trained and worked under Henri and Cleavah's leadership.

Everything she knew about the Broken came from legends and myths surrounding the mysterious Virtue. She was the Greater Virtue of Righteousness, but since righteousness could rule over all the Virtues and

Obstacles, they'd tried to throw her out. They'd tried to burn her. They'd only let her return to the pantheon on sufferance with the understanding that she would remain an outcast, a recluse who wasn't allowed to seize power for herself.

But everything Vola knew about Cleavah was something she'd learned firsthand along the way. And if the two were one and the same...then Vola knew more about the Broken than any mortal alive. Maybe even more than the gods who'd harmed her.

"Then the gods are declaring war on Anders," Rilla said, her diplomatic princess face stretched thin across her features.

Vola wouldn't have noticed it if she hadn't been standing right beside her, but the Broken flinched.

"*I* am declaring war on Anders," she said firmly.

The Broken had once been powerful enough to rule the rest of the gods. Even apart from the pantheon, she would be a formidable ally.

Rilla gave her a formal nod. "I'll assign a liaison to serve as a go-between for you—"

"I like Vola just fine," the Broken said.

"I know that," Rilla snapped, then she cleared her throat and straightened her jacket. "She's obviously your chosen, my lady. Though she might have called you by a different name. I just meant I would make it official. That is if you don't mind making that information public."

The princesses stared at the Broken. Listrell and the Firewatch officials looked a little more confused. They might not be as well versed in Pantheon politics or realize that the Broken had never taken a mortal representative within written history. She'd never chosen a paladin or a prophet or even a heroic farm boy to carry out her will. Probably because the other gods would assume she was maneuvering to assert her dominance.

The Broken put her good hand on her hip and cocked her head. "Have you ever tried to shove a cat back into a sack once it's escaped?"

Rilla's mouth quirked as she saw the goddess's point.

The Broken pointed her thumb at her own chest. "Cat," she said. Then her face and form shifted to that of unblemished Cleavah for just one second. "Bag. Vola is my chosen. For good or ill, I'll not forsake her now."

The words meant more than just what she was saying to Rilla. Vola's hands tightened on the edge of the table, and she swallowed down the sudden knot in her throat.

"Unless Vola has a different opinion," the Broken said quietly.

This was her out. She hadn't signed up for this. She'd just wanted to be a normal paladin. Not the first and only paladin to serve an exiled Greater Virtue. She was rocking the boat enough just by being herself.

But she didn't have to imagine herself without Cleavah or the Broken or whatever she chose to call herself to know how miserable she would be. She'd lived that life already.

"My opinion has not changed, my lady," Vola said, voice steady and strong in the quiet foyer. "Although…" She glanced up and met the Broken's black bottomless eyes. "We are going to have a talk about this, you and I."

Her chest tightened as the words left her mouth. But she'd earned a little familiarity after all of this.

The Broken's throaty chuckle filled the empty spaces of the room, and it was Cleavah's laugh and everything was okay.

"I can't wait till someone explains this to the paladin council," Talon muttered. Vola caught the amused glance she shared with Sorrel and Lillie.

"I came to tell you where we will find Anders," the Broken said, ignoring them for the moment.

Rilla straightened. "Nargilla talked?"

A toothy grin spread across the Broken's face. "She didn't have to. I do have some friends in the pantheon. And once I'd convinced them of the threat, the Greater Virtue of Perception found him easily enough."

"And since you didn't just snap your fingers and disintegrate him just as easily, I'll assume he's going to be a tough nut to crack," Rilla said, raising an eyebrow.

"War was an understatement," the Broken said. "Muster your strength. This is going to be fun."

SCENES FROM CREATION AND CALAMITY

TALON

ONE

THE CHILD SHIVERED beneath a spreading pine tree. Water dripped from the branches to splash the dry needles at his feet. The rain was the only reason he was alive. Otherwise he'd be dead with the rest.

He shoved the thought away. Too much. Too soon. He rocked himself gently, arms around his knees, the way his mother had rocked him when too many people crowded him or too many voices babbled.

There weren't too many people now.

He buried his head against his knees. There were no more tears left. He'd spent them already.

He couldn't remember what happened, even though it was just a few hours ago. All he remembered was fighting with his mother over some-thing silly. Something about the pretty ribbons she didn't want him to wear.

He'd stamped his feet and screamed. Screaming had never worked before, but he didn't have words for the feeling that tightened in his chest whenever she she told him boys didn't play with dolls or ribbons.

Then someone else was screaming and there was cursing and noise and heat. His mother's face had gone white, and he'd fallen silent in the face of her terror. She pushed him under one of their wagons.

"Hide there," she'd said. "I'll come for you when it's safe."

It was the last thing she'd said to him.

Then the bad men had come, and he'd hidden his face in the dirt for a long time. Until the fire had raged, and he'd thought he would burn under the wagon.

When the rain finally smothered the flames and the world fell still, he knew his mother wasn't coming back.

He'd made it as far as the tree before the shaking started, and he couldn't stand anymore.

The smell of smoke tickled his nose, and he shivered again as a trickle of rain slipped under his collar.

He missed being warm and dry. His father had always kept them warm and dry and fed. The lump in his throat nearly choked him, but he swallowed down more tears.

He had to find someplace to sleep. Something to eat.

He could concentrate on that, those simple tasks. He stood, using the tree trunk to steady his small frame while dried pine needles crunched and slid under his feet.

He trudged, forgetting to look up and around more often than not. But as the sky above the trees grew dim, he caught sight of a rock shelf and remembered camping away from the caravan with his father. They'd used a site like this.

He slid and skid down the hill under the overhang, skinning his hands and knees before he tumbled into the cool, dry cave underneath. Someone or something had dug into the soft dirt at the base and hollowed out an area big enough to feel cozy and safe.

The child curled into himself and slept, too tired to worry about a fire or food.

A wet snuffle woke him a few hours later, and he sat up. Shadows slunk between him and the opening of the cave, long and low. His heart beat in his throat, and he drew his knees to his chest but he didn't cry out or scream. What if the bad men had come back? What if they'd found him?

The largest shadow crept closer, sniffling, and the child realized it was a big black wolf with gray around its muzzle.

The wolf sniffed at his hair and torn clothes and snorted. Then it cocked its head.

What are you doing here, human cub?

It wasn't a voice. More like the hand gestures the caravaners used when communicating from one end of the caravan to the other. But the child realized he could read the words in the tilt of the wolf's head and ears.

He shook his head and tried to shrink deeper into the back of the cave. "I'm lost," he managed to say, voice hoarse from the smoke.

Where is your pack? the big wolf said.

The child shook his head. He still couldn't think about it. Couldn't concentrate on the images of blood and smoke that swirled just out of his reach.

The big black wolf stared at him a moment longer with gold eyes before it huffed. Then it stepped forward and nudged the child with its nose.

Lay down, cub, the gesture seemed to say.

And the child lay down, too spent to be afraid. The wolf curled up around him and others padded forward to join them. One red-brown. One gray. Another brindled. A whole pack surrounded him, laying in a heap, sharing their warmth and the comfort of their presence.

And the child slept deeply.

For weeks, months, and years the wolves shared their cave with him. And when he was strong enough to venture into the filtered sunlight of the forest, they taught him to hunt as they did, with cunning and perseverance.

He grew stronger, until he could keep up with them.

They never took him back to the dead caravan.

But they took care of him the same way his parents had. They kept him warm and dry and fed. They brought him things. Clothes from a broken crate they'd found. A jacket stolen from a wash line. A bow and a quiver from a hunter who'd fallen from a cliff.

They talked to him and he talked back and eventually he learned to talk to them over distances. They didn't use his name, and he was content to forget it. It had never really fit, anyway, and it belonged to that other life. That mother and father who were gone now.

The wolves accepted him no matter what he was called. And they didn't name themselves the way humans did. They named each other for how they were related. Sister, Mother, Brother. The big black wolf was Father to them all.

They called him Cub. And Hunter. And Friend. And that was enough for him.

The hunter knelt in the snow beside the corpse of a wolf. This one had been known as Nuisance to the rest of the pack. He'd been someone's brother or cub, too, but his flighty personality had made even the most loving of family snap at him and label him a troublemaker.

He wouldn't be playing any more tricks or pranks.

The hunter touched the arrow shaft protruding from the wolf's side. Nuisance must have been shot closer to the human village at the end of the valley and still had enough energy to escape before he died. Otherwise the human hunters would have retrieved their arrow. They would have skinned the wolf and hung the rest of him up outside their wall to warn away the rest of the pack.

A big black wolf with sleek shining fur panted beside the hunter.

It's the humans, isn't it? Brother said.

"Yes," the hunter said. He grabbed his bow out of the snow and slung it over his back.

Why do they hunt us? We only seek to feed ourselves the way they do.

"The sheep in the barns and behind gates. They think they belong to the village. They get angry when we eat them."

Father padded up beside the hunter on his other side.

We have little choice, he said. *When the humans take all the deer and the sheep, too.*

"The pack can't move?" the hunter said.

Normally, yes. But we are surrounded with mountains and cliffs on two sides, the human village at the one end of the valley, and another pack at the other. We can't leave without risking a fight with one or the other or braving the perils of the high passes.

"Then we will have to learn to share the valley," the hunter said.

We are trying, Father said. *We are not the problem.*

Father turned and pushed his way through the snow, his big paws leaving divots in the drifts. The other big black wolf known as Brother followed.

The hunter paused for a moment and then mounded the fresh snow across Nuisance. He might have been annoying but he was still pack.

Father waited at the edge of the trees where they could just see the smoke rising from the human village.

We need someone to speak for us, Father said as the hunter joined them again. *Someone whose teeth do not scare them.*

The hunter snorted.

You will convince them, Father said.

"What?" The hunter froze, snow trickling into his second-hand boots.

As much as you have been loved by the pack and raised by us, you are still human. They are more likely to listen to you.

Father rose from his haunches and trotted through the trees, back toward where they'd left the rest of the pack. *Let us know when you are done.*

"That's it, then?" The hunter planted his fists on his hips. "Just, 'see you later?'"

Brother shook the snow from his ruff. *Father has never beaten around the bush.*

"He could have at least said good luck," the hunter grumbled.

You don't need luck. You have the human language. They will listen to you. Brother stepped forward and licked the hunter's chapped knuckles. *What's wrong?*

"Well..." The hunter rubbed his neck. "I haven't spoken to a lot of humans in the last few years, believe it or not."

Brother tilted his head. *Running around the woods with a bunch of wolves will do that to you.*

The hunter snorted as Brother leaped from one snow bank to the next.

Come on, Brother said. *Or don't you want to get this over with?*

The hunter sighed and followed.

The human settlement sat tucked against the mountain on the west side of the valley with the snowy meadows and forest stretched out in front of it.

The hunter's nose wrinkled as they got closer to the gates. He'd hated the smell of woodsmoke ever since...ever since he'd lived with the wolves. Especially when it was damp, and the village was rife with it.

"Stay close," the hunter told Brother. "I don't want them getting the wrong idea about you."

What? That I'm a wolf? I think that's the right idea.

The gate stood open, but a couple human hunters guarded the rough wooden palisade, their weapons in their hands.

The hunter raised a hand in cautious greeting.

The humans glanced between him and the big black wolf, but finally they waved him through.

"Looking for someone specific, boy?" the nearest one asked as he passed. The man didn't seem unfriendly. The squirm in the hunter's gut had to be his own nerves.

"I'm just—just looking for someone in charge to talk to," he said. There. Had that come out too much like a wolf? He never had to worry how growly his voice was with the pack. Half the time he didn't even need to speak out loud with them so it tended to be rusty with disuse.

The man didn't seem to mind. He wiped his red nose and pointed to a fenced in area directly in the middle of the village. Little houses with thatched roofs surrounded the clear space.

"The elders meet on the green around noontime. You won't have long to wait. If you'd like, there's a pot of something hot to drink set up by the smithy. You're welcome to pour yourself some."

The hunter dug deep for manners his mother had taught him long, long ago. "Thank you," he said.

"You're welcome, boy."

The hunter flinched, and the man eyed him. But the hunter escaped into the village without another exchange.

Brother stuck close to the hunter's side. A couple of women in thick winter skirts and shawls wrapped around their shoulders goggled at the big black wolf and skipped aside to let them pass.

The smithy rang with the sounds of hammer and anvil so the communal pot wasn't hard to find. A middle aged woman stirred it, her chapped hands steady on the ladle.

The hunter held out a battered cup he'd found in a burnt out shack beside the river last summer. He didn't mind sticking his face in ponds and streams like the wolves did, but sometimes it was nice to be able to carry a cup of water somewhere.

The woman smiled, revealing crooked teeth, and she ladled something dark and hot into his cup.

"There you are, young man."

The hunter's chest tightened, and he coughed. Why did his cheeks burn and his hands shake? He steadied them on the cup and bobbed his head in thanks before he escaped.

What's wrong? Brother said, pressing against his side as they walked.

"I don't know," the hunter whispered. "I just…don't feel right."

Are you sick? The wolf said. *I can find a spot for you to drag your butt if you need to.*

The hunter grimaced. "Ew, no. Not like that. It's just…It's when they talk to me. There's something not right. Like I don't fit what they're seeing."

Well, I've always thought you were more wolf than human on the inside. Maybe they're only seeing the human.

"Maybe," the hunter said. "At least that's close."

He'd felt this before in that long ago time before the wolves. He'd been different then, too. But different how? If he could just put a name to it maybe that would make it better.

Maybe Brother was right. The walls of the settlement leaned in a little, feeling like the edges of of a cage. Maybe he'd lived too much of his life running in the open to feel comfortable inside walls.

He shook his head and made his way to the open space the gate guard had indicated. The village green was hemmed in by a rough log fence. A circle of stumps provided basic seating, and the hunter plopped down on one, cradling his tin cup in his hands, preserving the heat.

No one had gathered on the green yet except for one ancient woman who hunched over her knitting. Her gnarled hands moved with surprising grace and skill, fingers flashing in and out despite the half gloves covering her palms.

She gave the hunter a grin wide enough to split the seams of her face.

"Haven't seen you before," she said. "What's your name?"

Her smile invited him to grin as well even though the squirm in his gut intensified.

"Um, I don't...I don't really have one," he said.

She tilted her head, attention on him, but her knitting didn't even slow. "Everyone calls themselves something."

"The wolves call me the Hunter," he said, glancing at his companion, who'd curled up at his feet, keeping them warm. "And I call him Brother." Except the word came out sounding like a growl and a bark.

Her needles paused for a second before resuming. "They talk to you," she said, eyebrows raised in surprise.

"I...guess so," he said. Deep down he'd known that was unusual, but he'd been so little when they'd found him that it hadn't really registered. His lips pressed thin. Great. Another thing to make him different.

"You don't need to look like you've stuck a lemon up your butt."

That surprised a laugh out of him. "What?"

"So sour. Nature magic is a gift from the gods."

"I don't know that it's really magic."

"Why not? I know some spell casters up in the hills who talk to their animals. And rangers can work with the land and its creatures."

The hunter barely knew what magic was, let alone how to cast spells. That certainly didn't fit. But talking to the wolves felt so natural, and he'd always been able to find water and game.

"Maybe," the hunter said reluctantly.

The woman didn't seem put off by his reticence. "I'm Nan," she said. "Least that's what everyone's called me so long it's stuck. So what do the wolves want?"

The hunter's mouth dropped open.

"Oh, don't look like that. It weren't hard to figure. A stranger comes in with a great big beast like yours tame as kitten, claiming to talk to the pack. Clearly you're with them. And it's been a hard winter on all of us, so I'm sure they want something."

"That's...true. The wolves are just trying to survive. I've steered them away from the sheep as much as I can, but still the human hunters here kill us. I mean them." He gestured back toward the gate and the armed guards.

"The hunters think it's their duty to protect us," Nan said. "From wolves and bandits alike. If the wolves stray too close, they're going to feel threatened."

The hunter shook his head. "We're not threatening anyone. At least we're trying not to. But with the hunters taking all the game in the valley, the wolves have to range further and further to hunt for themselves."

"Can't they find new hunting grounds?"

The hunter raised his chin. "This is their home, too. Besides, they can't make it over the passes in the mountains, the village blocks this end of the valley, and there's another pack that's claimed the territory at the other end. We risk violence and death on all sides."

"I see."

Several villagers drifted onto the green and took places on the stumps around them. The hunter sat back, biting his tongue. He'd have the chance to argue his case, and Nan had been kind so far. She wasn't the one to take his frustration out on.

A man in fur-lined gloves and a wraparound coat took his place in the center of the circle. "All right, let's do this quickly. Even we don't have enough hot air to stay warm out here for long."

The gathered villagers chuckled. The hunter's fingers tensed on his cup, rehearsing his words in his head.

"Nan, you want to get us started?"

The hunter whipped around to focus on Nan, who creaked to her feet.

She stood and cracked her back. "I'll keep talking as long as you all keep listening to me. We have a request from the wolf pack of the valley." She gestured to the hunter.

The hunter swallowed as all their eyes focused on him.

A man across the circle snorted, making his frost covered beard ripple. "What could a bunch of wolves have to say?"

"'Stop killing us' was the gist of it, I believe," Nan said, raising an eyebrow. "Right?"

The hunter nodded. "That's about it."

The man with the beard scowled. "Maybe they should learn to stay further away."

"Maybe we should learn to work with them," Nan said.

The hunter started.

"This is Lod, our lead huntsman." Nan gestured to the bearded man. "Lod, what was the complaint you were going to bring to the elders today?"

Lod crossed his arms, breath huffing between his lips like a cloud. "The huntsmen are spread too thin. Between the bandits we have to fend off and the wolves, we hardly have time to keep the village fed. And that's our first priority normally."

Nan tapped her teeth. "Hunter, can you see a way to work together on this?"

The hunter opened his mouth and hesitated. It would never work, would it? The humans would never trust the pack. But Nan stood there handing him the answer and all he had to do was grab it and run.

"We could make a deal," he said. That was a thing humans did. It's what his parents had done all the time. "The wolves will patrol the valley and keep the bandits away, if the village promises to stop killing them and…and pays them."

Lod looked like he was about to scoff again, but instead he paused a moment to think. "What would they want for helping us?"

"Game," the hunter said immediately. He glanced down at Brother. "If you provide a buck a week or a couple of sheep every now and then, the wolves will have enough time to hunt the bandits. And if you're not hunting bandits or wolves you'll have enough time to hunt game."

"The wolves can't eat the bandits?" someone muttered, but Nan glared them into silence.

"Lod?" Nan said. "Is this acceptable?"

The huntsman ran his hands over his face and beard. "We'd have to trust wild animals."

"Not so wild," Nan said, glancing at Brother. "You've worked with rangers before."

"Gods help us, but it makes sense," Lod said, dropping his hands. "Very well. It's a deal."

The hunter's chest swelled, and he held his breath a moment to make sure it was all real. Had he really just helped? He'd argued and they'd listened.

Nan shuffled across the green to him. "Don't look so surprised. Words matter, kid." She handed him a pair of fingerless gloves made from a bright purple yarn. The ones she'd been knitting as they talked. "Those are for you. But feel free to come back and trade other things, too. Wolves are good company, sure, but maybe you want some friends with less teeth sometimes."

The hunter shifted the pack on his back and followed the stream, which was swollen with snow melt.

Brother trotted beside him, leaving big paw prints in the muddy bank. The black wolf stopped twice to look over his shoulder, back at the woods they'd left behind.

"What is it?" the hunter said.

Brother shivered, his hackles settling. *I don't know. I just don't feel right leaving the pack today.*

The hunter tilted his head. "Why? We've left them dozens of times this winter. It's always been fine."

It just feels different today. Can we hurry?

"Sure," the hunter said. "Nan said she'd meet us on the green and we don't have any other business."

He picked up his pace and headed for the bridge near the human village. Normally he'd just hop across the stream, but with the banks flooded for spring, he didn't quite dare.

The guards at the gates greeted him with smiles. "Good hunting, boy?" one of them asked.

The hunter tried to smile back. "Good enough," he said and hurried past them, Brother on his heels.

Nan waited on the green, tubs of wash water at her feet. It was warm enough she'd rolled up her sleeves to scrub the winter grime from her blankets and sheets.

"Ho, Hunter," she said. "What have you brought us today?"

The hunter slung his pack to the ground, avoiding the biggest puddles of mud and flipped open the top. A variety of weapons lay inside. Some were good quality but most were cobbled together out of sharpened metal plates tied to rough clubs.

"Hmm," Nan said. "You'd think with winter being over the bandits would be a bit less desperate and a little more organized."

"I think it's taking them longer to recover than it took you. These were scrawnier than usual and didn't put up much of a fight. I counted fifteen."

Nan raised her eyebrows and sank back on her heels. "Your pack took on fifteen? I'm impressed." She eyed him up and down.

The hunter flushed and shrugged. "They listen when I tell them how and when to attack…"

"And?" Nan said, guessing there was more.

"I can hear the land. Like you were talking about. And it responds."

Nan smirked. "Told you you're a ranger. I take it you've been practicing?"

The hunter's lip twitched, and he held a hand over the soft ground. A vine surged up through the mud, swaying in the slight breeze before it wrapped gently around Nan's wrist.

"Well, look at that." Her eyes shone as she stared. "You're learning to listen to it."

She shook her hand and the hunter let the vine collapse with a word.

"I love it when I'm right," she said.

The hunter snorted. "I'll bet."

Nan kicked the side of the pack. "These are worth a buck and a sheep. I'll have Lod haul them out to the normal place for your pack to retrieve. And tell them thank you."

"You're welcome," the hunter said.

"I've laid some things aside I thought you could use. That coat you're wearing is nothing but patches now, and I think I found one in your size. And there's a nice new knife if you think you want it."

The hunter perked up. "I loved the last one you gave me."

"Sure thing. Helen, would you grab the goods from the smithy?" Nan asked one of the other village women.

Helen straightened and dried her hands on her apron. "Of course." She returned a moment later with a dagger the length of her arm and a new coat. "Here you are, young man."

The hunter flinched and just managed to take the things without fumbling. He mumbled his thanks and backed up a step.

Helen didn't seem to notice, returning to her work without comment. But Nan speared him with a glance.

"You've been welcome here for months," she said quietly. "Why are you still so skittish around us? Do you distrust all humans or just us?"

The hunter shook his head. "No. It's not…not trust."

"Then what is it?"

"I'm not sure I can explain."

Nan turned over an empty washbasin right there in the mud and plopped down on it like she had all the time in the world. "Try," she said.

The hunter scratched at the patchy beard on his chin. It had gotten thicker every winter for a couple years and his old knife wasn't sharp enough to shave it down now.

"I don't even know that I have the words for it." But that wasn't exactly true. He'd spent most of the winter trying to place his feelings every time he came into the village. The wolves didn't help. They felt things and moved on. They didn't get stuck in the sinking pool of discontent. Like spring mud that just wouldn't let go.

"I feel like everyone here looks at me and sees something I'm not. They see something different than I do when I think about myself."

"Do you think of yourself as a wolf?"

The hunter shook his head. "It's not that. It's...deeper than that somehow. And more specific."

She raised an eyebrow. Waiting.

The hunter blew out a breath. His tongue stuck to the roof of his mouth. The last time he'd voiced anything close to this, he'd been too small to know better. And it had made his mother sad.

"I don't like it when people call me 'boy.' Or 'young man.' It's just...not quite right."

Nan didn't say anything. Which was better than running away screaming. Or getting that white face, pinch-lipped look that made his insides squirm.

"The wolves, they always called me Cub or Hunter. Never Brother or Sister. I think because they know that neither fit."

The hunter smoothed a seam on the new jacket, not meeting her eyes.

"That's hard," she said without having to think about it. "It makes you different. People count on what they can see to tell them about the person underneath."

The hunter flinched. "Great," he said.

Nan held up a hand. "I didn't say it made you wrong. Just different. And the outside doesn't match the inside for a lot of people. It's just not usually so drastic. People look at me and see a doddering old woman whose mind is probably going."

"And they'd be wrong," the hunter said with a grin.

"Dead wrong. And it's their fault they made the assumption. But that's not going to stop them from making the same mistake with everyone they meet. We're creatures of habit."

"So, there's nothing I can do."

"There's nothing you *have* to do." Nan wrapped her knuckles on his knee. "Not your job to change their thinking. That's up to them."

"So, I just have to ignore it."

Nan shrugged. "Or grow strong enough that it doesn't bother you anymore."

"Because that sounds so easy."

"Didn't say it would be, Hunter. It's also not fair, which you haven't pointed out yet, but I'm sure you were getting to."

The hunter rubbed the back of his neck. "I'm not sure I like the human world."

"You can't tell me wolves don't have gender. I know your friend there is male." She gestured to Brother.

"They do," the hunter said. "They just don't use it or abuse it the way humans do. It's not...important in the same way. And they might have the right of it. This whole thing makes me want to run back to the woods and hide. At least there I don't always feel looked at. Examined and judged to be different or wrong."

Nan regarded him for a moment before she stood and shuffled to the clothesline strung across the village green. Her deft fingers shuffled through the linens hung there until she came to a long drape of black fabric. She took it down and tossed it to him.

"No retreating," she said. "You're out of the woods now. Sure you can go back in and not come out if you really want. But you don't have to. And I don't think it's good for you. You've grown so much in the last few months, interacting with your own kind. But you can still hide. If that's what it takes to make you feel safe. If that's what it takes to keep growing, keep getting stronger, you can hide yourself. At least until you know what face you want to force the world to accept."

The hunter spread the damp folds of cloth to find a cloak with a deep hood. He'd be able to pull it low over his face, keeping it in shadow no matter what the weather.

His fingers stroked the tight weave. None of the other villagers felt the need to hide. Half of them didn't even wear hats anymore now that the air had warmed up.

It was a step. Maybe in the right direction. Maybe not. But it was a step either way. A decision he'd have to make.

A declaration that he was different. If only to himself.

He didn't remember his mother's face anymore. But he could remember her tight lips. The way her eyes had gone confused and unhappy.

"Maybe," the hunter said, but he couldn't keep the reluctance out of his voice.

She didn't make him explain it this time. "I'll keep it for you," she said. "You can decide later if you like."

"Thank you, Nan," he said quietly, handing the cloak back to her.

"Don't thank me. It just means I'm forcing you to visit me again."

He grinned as he stood. "Clever. I'd better go. I promised Brother we wouldn't stay so long."

She turned back to her washing. "Remember what I said. You'd better be back to visit before too long."

Brother surged to his feet and shook himself before following the hunter back out into the wilds. The hunter kept his head down to avoid goodbyes from the villagers. Most of them were used to him by now, but some still tried to waylay him and get him to talk. And they were never as soothing as Nan.

Maybe she was right. Maybe he did need a way to hide from the world without retreating entirely. Would wearing a hood make it easier to talk to people? Maybe it would feel like carrying the forest around with him.

He shook his head as they crossed the bridge and plunged back into the trees. He already had a hard time fitting in with the villagers. If he wore a hood all the time, he'd just have to explain that instead of himself.

An hour later, he still wasn't closer to deciding, but they should have been getting closer to the pack. He lifted his nose to the wind. The wolves had been moving dens up near the north end of the valley.

He couldn't smell them yet.

The hunter stopped to listen. "Do you hear them?"

Brother's ears twitched to and fro and his nostrils flared. *I do not.*

There was something else though. A low whooshing sound far off but getting closer. It sent a shiver down the back of his neck and he realized if he'd had hackles they would have been raised.

He didn't recognize the noise and these were *his* woods. He should have recognized everything in here.

The hunter pulled his bow from his back and turned just as a massive shape blotted the sun, casting a shadow over a good section of the forest.

"What the —"

A roar rang through the trees, and the hunter clapped his hands over his ears as the sound ricocheted off the nearest peaks. Brother whimpered and pawed at his head.

The shape swooped low and the trees rocked, showering the forest floor with leaves and pine needles.

The hunter threw himself to the side, behind a trunk, as a column of fire poured out of the sky.

Brother dove beside him, cowering. The hunter threw his arms around the wolf to shield him from the heat, but the fire crackled up the trunks, racing through the spring-damp undergrowth as if it was dry kindling.

The massive shape beat scaly wings, fanning the flames. It raised its snout to roar again, then swept away across the valley.

Heat made the hunter's skin tighten and ache, but he sprang to his feet and darted to an outcrop of rock where the flames hadn't reached to squint at the retreating monster.

"Was that...was that a dragon?"

Who cares what it was? Brother said, circling his legs. *It tried to kill us.*

"Shit. The entire valley is on fire."

*The entire valley...*Brother whined looking out over the flaming trees. Cinders fell through the air like snow.

"The pack," the hunter whispered.

They turned as one and dashed through the flames. The dragon fire had burned fast enough that it was already retreating from a lot of the spring-damp forest, leaving a trail of blackened trunks and foliage in its wake.

Brother and the hunter sprinted through the burnt trees to the new den.

But the pack wasn't there. They exchanged a worried look and traced the path the pack would had taken.

Over a ridge the hunter stumbled to a halt, mouth falling open. Spread on the downhill slope, a black swathe covered what had been verdant land just that morning. The hunter recognized the peaceful glen, but now it was blackened, darkness climbing the trees until they spread thin empty branches across the sky.

Brother whimpered and slunk closer.

A wolf's corpse lay smoking just at the edge of the black.

The hunter knelt. He could barely recognize Father by his grizzled muzzle. The old wolf looked like he'd been caught in a blast by the dragon.

It was hard to tell with so much of the world burning, but this spot... this black spot was different. The trees weren't charred, they were just dead as if all the life and color had been sucked out of them.

The hunter held a hand over the blackened ground and tried to call forth a vine. Nothing happened.

The dragon? Brother said, ears laid flat against his skull.

"I don't know what else it could be. But this place isn't burned. It's just...dead."

Whatever it did, it killed Father.

"Yes," the hunter laid a hand on the old wolf's head, fighting against the choking feeling in his throat. It was so similar. The smell of damp burning wood. The grief and loss.

"The pack. They have to be around somewhere. They wouldn't have tried to escape the valley without Father." They'd be scattered without his leadership.

Brother searched. All up and down the valley he sniffed, following the wolves' trail. The hunter followed close, looking for evidence of their passing. Tufts of fur, prints, the scent of fear.

Nothing.

Nothing except three more dead spots and swathes of fire blackened forest crossing what little traces of the wolves they could find.

At last, exhausted and shaking, they stopped at the edge of the southern forest. Brother raised his head to howl, calling for their family one last time.

The forest smoldered under the moonlight, but the air was still and silent. No one answered his call.

TWO

Two days after they'd visited with Nan, Brother and the hunter stumbled back up the valley to the human village. Black smoke billowed into the sky though it seemed like most of the fires had been put out. The rough wood palisade tumbled on the side facing the woods, charred until it had crumbled under its own weight, and many of the thatched roofs still smoldered.

Figures dragged bodies to the village green, laying them out in neat rows. The process was strangely quiet, the remaining villagers hollow-eyed and close-mouthed as if they'd already done their weeping.

Lod greeted the hunter at the edge of the green, taking in his soot-stained clothes and shaking hands.

"You too?" the huntsman said quietly.

The hunter just stared, eyes burning. They hadn't stopped burning. "I can't find the pack. I don't know...I don't think they made it."

Lod ran a hand through his hair, leaving bits standing on end, stained dark with soot. "If they faced what we faced, there might not be anything left."

Too many houses smoldered nearby. Too many bodies lay on the green.

A familiar figure was tucked beside the fence. Someone had crossed her arms over her chest.

The hunter's throat went thick and tight as he knelt beside Nan. He wanted nothing more than to throw his head back and howl his grief like Brother. But no sound made it past the tightness in his chest. No howl, not even a whimper.

"She wasn't running," Lod said behind him. "She was making sure everyone got out okay."

"But not everyone did."

"No. It's funny. She was the same age as my grandma. But I always thought she would outlive me."

Lod pulled a long piece of black fabric from the fence where it had hung. "She left this for you. Said you'd come back for it if you wanted it."

The hunter took the cloak between his hands. Even with her laying there still and silent he couldn't imagine a future without Nan chiding him, pushing him, asking him to visit her.

He slung the cloak around his shoulders and fastened it. He'd wear it as a tribute to her kindness and wisdom. It hurt to look at, to remember, but he relished that pain right now. It felt better than the numbness.

Brother sat beside the gate to the green, head bowed, panting. The hunter wasn't sure what the wolf was feeling, but if it was the same emptiness, then he would let him be. The hollowness rang inside the hunter's head, begging to be filled with something, anything.

"What now?" he said mostly to himself. How many times could you lose a family and start over? How many times could you stand back up after that?

"I sent Markus to track the dragon," Lod said, voice growing firmer. "He came back this morning with the news. The beast is holed up in the north mountains. I don't want to risk the entire village, but we can't stay here if that thing is going to come raiding every time it's hungry. We're going after it."

Lod leaned on the fence and focused on the hunter. "We could use a man with experience in the woods and tracking down monsters. You want to come?"

Blood pounded in the hunter's ears. It surged under his skin, making him feel itchy and antsy. The missing howls of the pack rang around the emptiness in his head and heart. He could fill that emptiness with something. He could fill it with anger, with rage. And he could direct those at something that deserved it. The dragon would never take another family. It would never burn down another village, or strike down an old woman before her wisdom had changed the world.

He took a breath and his chest swelled. The acrid smoke lit up familiar memories of pain and fear. But this time...this time there was something he could do about it.

"Yes," the hunter said. "Yes, count us in."

They left the next morning when the sky was still gray and the air clear and chilly. The hunter wrapped Nan's cloak tight around his shoulders, but he didn't pull the hood up. Not yet. It seemed like an admission, and he wasn't ready to admit anything to himself or to the other huntsmen yet. And it seemed silly to try to hide any part of himself when they were trekking up the side of a mountain to confront a dragon.

No one in their little valley had ever hunted such big game before. Even basilisks and rock wyrms were scarce here. Lod claimed he'd slaughtered a tunnel drake once, but it had been long ago.

Brother stuck close to the hunter's legs as they trudged through the forest and made their way into the foothills.

Why are we going toward the big scary thing that wants to eat us? he said. *We should be running away. This is stupid.*

"What else are we supposed to do?" the hunter asked. "We can't let it kill anyone else. You saw what it did to the forest. Not just the burning but those dead spots, too."

We can move, Brother said. *We can sneak through the other pack's territory at the end of the valley. We can leave. We don't have to fight.*

The hunter scowled as he picked his way up the goat trail the huntsmen were following. "Don't you want to fight? Aren't you angry? This thing killed all of them. It killed Father, and it killed our brothers and sisters and the cubs."

And now we don't have a pack, Brother said. *A wolf without a pack should run away. He has no one to guard his back.*

"I'm not running," the hunter snapped. "I want to do something. I *have* to do something."

Brother whined, but he didn't turn around and go back. He padded along with his head down.

Clearly the wolf didn't feel the same burning ache in his chest. He didn't feel the tingle in his legs that called him on, further and further up the mountain to where the threat lay. How could he not feel the anger simmering under his skin?

Lod climbed just behind them, bringing up the rear of the party. He gave the hunter a look, and the hunter realized he'd spoken out loud to the big wolf. He flushed.

"Different opinions?" Lod said.

The hunter blew out his breath. "Wolves don't confront bigger predators unless they have the whole pack to back them up."

"Smart." Lod squinted up the trail. "Maybe smarter than we are right now."

The hunter shook his head. "But we have to do this. The valley won't be safe again until that beast is dead."

"True. It's necessary. But that doesn't make it smart. If we all wanted to live, we'd leave the valley. But then plenty of us would die out there trying to make new homes for ourselves, so…" Lod shrugged.

The hunter frowned at his boots. The trail wound up the side of a peak, disappearing around a bend ahead of them.

"Nan, said you could speak to them," Lod said, jerking his chin at Brother who trotted tirelessly upward, body low and ready, eyes alert. "Can you talk to all animals?"

"Only the ones who listen," the hunter said. "Most don't want to have anything to do with humans or wolves."

"So you're screwed on both sides."

The hunter huffed a laugh. "Yeah." Ahead of them the first of the huntsmen disappeared around the bend in the trail, placing their feet carefully since it got narrow here.

"Do you think you can talk to the dragon?"

The hunter was surprised enough to stop dead in his tracks and stare back at Lod. Lod just returned his look placidly.

The hunter's brows drew down, and he spun to continue climbing. "I'm not talking to the beast that slew my family."

"Fair enough," Lod said behind him. "I'm just looking for ways to be smarter about this."

The hunter hugged his elbows, concentrating on his footing. At the bend he straightened and flattened himself against the cliff face and shuffled around the corner.

"Nan called you Hunter," Lod said, following. Brother picked his own way across the treacherous path. "Is that your name?"

This was more conversation than the hunter had had with one human being in his entire adult life. Except for Nan, but she'd always had a way of talking without expecting anything in return.

"I have no name," the hunter said.

"Everyone needs a name, boy."

"Well, it's definitely not 'boy,'" the hunter snapped.

Lod was quiet a moment. "I'm sorry. You're right. It's patronizing. It's just, you remind me of my son."

The hunter took a steady breath and unclenched his jaw. "I didn't know you had a son."

"He died three days ago when the dragon struck."

The hunter stepped onto a wider part of the path and paused long enough to meet Lod's eyes.

"I'm sorry," he said.

Lod nodded, lips pulled in a sad smile. He gestured the hunter on.

"You can always pick one, you know," he said behind the hunter's shoulders. "A name. Not having one already can be a blessing that way. You can pick something that fits you."

The hunter was so fixed on Lod's words he didn't notice the man in front of him had stopped until he almost ran into him. He stumbled back a step, and Brother flowed up beside him to steady him.

"What's wrong?" Lod called ahead.

"Trail disappears," the man in the lead called back. "The damn goats might be able to go on, but we're not getting any further this way."

Lod frowned up at the mountainside.

The hunter peered around the men as well. High up on the peak ahead a trickle of smoke led them like a beacon. The dragon itself wouldn't be hard to find as long as it kept smoking. But the men were right. The trail ahead flattened against the slope, disappearing like a ripple on a pond. Any further that way and the men would risk breaking legs and ankles, or worse, falling to their deaths among the rocks below.

There was no point in losing good men before they even got up to the main threat.

Lod sighed loud enough to echo from the rocks around them. "We'll have to go back. Find another way up and around. Damn."

"Wait." The hunter held out a hand to forestall him.

"What is it?" Lod said.

"Let me try." He could feel the land under his feet. In the forest it had always felt like a faint singing, something he hadn't even noticed until Nan had pointed it out and made him practice listening to it. Here the rock seemed to mumble, like a restless sleeper.

Lod gestured him ahead, and the hunter climbed carefully around the other men to the head of the party. The trail dropped away leaving nothing but rocky scree and a steep slope, but the hunter closed his eyes and listened.

To the left the murmurs of the mountain faded into the open air, promising a swift death after a long fall. To the right the slope spoke in sharp whispers. It wouldn't be impossible, just very tricky.

The hunter placed his feet carefully, following the more gentle mumblings, trying to avoid the short sharp warnings of the treacherous rocks. Brother stepped carefully to follow him, planting his paws on the path the hunter laid out.

"Follow him," Lod said. "But carefully. Don't stray off the path he marks or you may start a rock slide."

The hunter climbed, inching along on tiptoes or dropping to all fours to lead the party of would be dragon slayers up the steep mountain. The trickle of smoke above grew steadily closer as the hunter's heart pounded faster and faster.

Were they climbing to their deaths? Brother was right, with no pack to watch their backs this was suicide. The men…they were better than no pack, but they didn't have the same rapport; they didn't have years of experience hunting together to mold them into a cohesive family.

Would it be so bad if they all died on this mountain? What else was left for them down in the valley? The hunter had already lost two families and the only human friend he'd ever made.

His fingers curled against the rocks under his hands. There were only two options for the end of this day. Either the slayer of the pack lay dead at his feet. Or he and brother would never have to worry about being lonely again.

The peak grew steeper and more treacherous the higher they got. A couple of snowflakes drifted past. It might be spring down below but up here, the last traces of winter bit at exposed skin. Just above the hunter's head, a ledge jutted into the open air, a trickle of smoke outlining it against the afternoon sky.

The hunter's shoulders tensed. The dragon.

He took a step without bothering to listen to the land, and his boot skidded against the loose rock.

He fell forward, catching himself on his hands as he slid down the slope a few feet.

The man behind him hissed and grabbed for his belt.

Brother yelped and lunged forward to drag the hunter up the slope.

The hunter dug his fingertips and toes into the mountain to keep from sliding any further.

"Quiet," Lod whispered from below. "Don't alert the dragon!"

A rumble shook the ground, making pebbles cascade down the slope around them. Smoke poured down over the edge of the ledge, choking them.

"Too late," a man called.

"Shit," the hunter muttered. There was nothing for it now.

He scrambled up the slope, finding desperate handholds among the rock. Just as he reached for the ledge, a massive shape barreled over head. The man behind him jumped back with a yell, lost his footing, and plum meted to the rocky crevice below.

The hunter gulped as the dragon pumped its huge wings and veered over them. He reached for the ledge again and hauled himself over. Brother scrambled after him. The hunter ducked as the dragon swooped overhead. Then he leaned over the ledge and offered his arm to the next man to help him climb up.

As soon as the huntsman was safely up, the hunter leaped to his feet and drew his knives.

The dragon roared, a great green-scaled storm of fury and teeth plunging at them over and over from the sky.

The hunter flailed wildly every time the beast swooped close, but he couldn't even begin to reach. Behind him, the rest of the men were still climbing up onto the ledge.

Finally Lod pulled himself over, just as the beast dove again.

The hunter saw the dragon's claws outstretched for the older man and he screamed and leaped for the vicious talons.

His blade barely scored the thick hide, but the dragon hissed and the claws clenched on empty air before it pumped its wings and curved away.

"We have to ground it," the hunter said. "Bring it down. We'll never get it while it's flying."

"Its wings," Lod called. "Aim for its wings."

The hunter sheathed his knives and pulled his bow from his back as the others spread out across the ledge, raising their bows to sight along arrows.

The dragon circled overhead and many of their arrows didn't make the distance, arcing harmlessly below the swooping monster.

The hunter raised his bow and sighted along his arrow, tracking the dragon's movement. Its wings cupped the air and the hunter counted, one, two, three, before releasing his arrow.

It streaked toward the dragon's wing and just as it heaved to flap again, tore a hole through the delicate membrane.

The dragon screamed.

"Aim before the upswing," the hunter called. He loosed arrow after arrow as Brother circled his feet.

Lod stepped up next to him with a longbow nearly as tall as he was.

With specific instructions more shots found their mark and the dragon faltered in its path.

"Duck," the hunter yelled as the beast lumbered into a turn and opened its jaws wide. He dove to the side as the stream of flame passed directly over the ledge. There was little cover here on the naked mountain top, and one of the other men stumbled over the edge, beating at the flames licking his arms and legs.

"Down, down," Lod mumbled, climbing to his feet beside the hunter.

"Yeah, but once its down, how do we keep it from knocking us all into the abyss?" the hunter said, gesturing to the edge of the ledge. There was nowhere to retreat to. Back down the mountain was nearly as treacherous as trying to continue up the last of the peak.

"We should have brought rope," Lod said.

The dragon came back for another pass but it dipped and shuddered in its flight and instead of another gout of flame it landed heavily on the ledge, plowing into the stone as if it had trouble controlling itself.

"Now," Lod called and the village huntsmen converged.

The hunter shook his head. "Wait."

The dragon's tail lashed around, throwing one of the men into the side of the mountain, and the hunter winced.

They might have grounded it but they'd never have a chance against the beast if they didn't contain it somehow.

Ropes, Lod had said.

Well, the hunter had the next best thing.

He reached toward the ground and then yanked up, pulling life from the earth itself. Vines sprang from the rock, showering them with pebbles as they snaked around the dragon's body.

The dragon thrashed as vines snapped closed, pinning its wings to its body and its tail to the ground. It tried to shake itself like a wolf after a swim, but the hunter held the vines firm.

"Now, Lod," the hunter called.

Lod gave him a grateful nod and sprang for the dragon's back with his ax drawn. The others all found places to climb up the creature's limbs. Even Brother leaped to close his jaws on the dragon's snout.

The beast roared but could not break free.

The hunter watched, eyes going wide as the village huntsmen hacked the great animal to pieces.

This was what it deserved. It had killed the pack. It had killed Nan. In fire and fear it had destroyed half the valley, and it deserved to be put down.

But that didn't stop the hunter's stomach from clenching and acid crawling up his throat.

Blood flowed across the rock but the dragon still screamed and struggled.

He should want this. Why did it make him want to throw up?

He shook his head and tossed his bow to one side. Then he sprinted for the dragon's head. His muscles bunched, and he leaped to the beast's head, past Brother who clung desperately to its snout.

The hunter planted both knives deep in the dragon's eye.

The beast shuddered and lay still.

Tension dissolved from the hunter's shoulders and hands, and he tumbled from the dragon's head, rolling at the last minute to keep from breaking anything against the stone ledge. And then he lay there panting, fingers pressed into the cold rock beneath him as if that would keep the world from spinning.

The vines pulled away from the dragon's corpse and slithered back into the ground.

Brother jumped down beside him and came to lean his head into the hunter's side.

The hunter slung his arm around the wolf.

The rage that had sustained him the whole way up the mountain poured out of him, leaving nothing but an echoing cold.

The hunter knelt there with his face buried in Brother's fur as the village huntsmen cheered and kicked the dead dragon. They cavorted around the ledge, drunk on their victory and survival.

He concentrated on breathing trying to keep his breakfast down. Brother remained silent, breath warm against his cheek as the wolf panted.

Footsteps crunched on the loose gravel the vines had dislodged, and Lod crouched beside him.

The older man didn't say anything for a long moment.

"You all right?" he finally said. "Anything hurt."

The hunter shook his head, not trusting his voice right away.

"I don't—" He had to stop and swallow. "I don't know why I feel so sick. I've killed before. Plenty of times. I've killed to eat and I've killed to protect. But nothing has ever felt like this."

He turned his head just enough to see the bristle of Lod's beard out of the corner of his eye. "I wanted to slaughter that thing. It was all I could think about as we climbed. But as soon as the slaughter started, I just wanted it to stop."

Lod pulled off his hat and swiped his sleeve across his brow. The men still laughed and called out beyond them, but Lod seemed quiet. "This wasn't like killing to eat or survive. It protected others, sure. The valley is safe now. But it was also revenge for a lot of them." He gestured to the others.

The hunter grimaced and buried his head in Brother's fur again.

"It's not a bad thing to be averse to revenge. It's not a bad thing to keep your head in a fight when passion and grief should cloud it." Lod tilted his head back to the sky and closed his eyes as a couple of snowflakes settled in his beard.

The men began migrating toward the edge of the ledge, some carrying grisly trophies from their kill. Mostly scales and a few claws. They lowered themselves over the edge, taking care on the slippery slope.

"You coming back to the village?" Lod said. "This snow is going to get worse before it gets better. Best to be down by then."

"I don't...I don't know."

Lod nodded. "You did well today, boy," he said. "You'd make a good dragon hunter. And if you've no stomach for that after all this, you can always settle in the village. I need more huntsmen if we're going to survive another winter."

"I'll think about it," the hunter said. "I'll make my way down soon. I just...need a minute." He just needed time to think without the press of unfamiliar human voices. He needed the pack's warmth around him. But he wouldn't get that part.

"See you down there, then. Keep your footing."

Lod hesitated and then clapped him on the shoulder before following his men on their journey to the valley below.

The hunter waited until even the echoes of their passage faded before he finally turned to sit with his back against the dead dragon. Brother curled into his side.

What do we do now? he asked. He turned his nose up to the hunter.

"I don't know yet," the hunter said and rubbed his face. He still felt like he could be sick if he really wanted to, but at least now it wasn't hanging out in the back of his throat, threatening every breath.

Dragon hunter. The very word made the bile creep up his throat again. He hated the dragon that lay silent and dead behind him. That hate had sustained him the whole way up the mountain. But he couldn't even begin to imagine killing another one. The blood and ooze covering his hands made them tingle, and he couldn't wait to get to a stream or pond to rinse it off.

Killing the dragon hadn't brought his pack back to life. It didn't make Nan's death mean anything. It didn't even make him feel better. The opposite in fact.

So what was he supposed to do now? Hunting more dragons was clearly out. At least in terms of revenge. He had no stomach for a kill that meant nothing. Unless it was a way to protect others from a rampaging monster, he couldn't do it again.

Miraculously, he and Brother sat here alive. But they still had no pack. No family. No one to watch their backs, no one to grieve with or celebrate with or grow with. They still had each other, but that seemed somehow hollow when they both needed the stability of a pack working together.

Strange. The thought of family still brought up images of Father and the rest of the wolves, along with dim recollections of his actual parents. But it also stirred memories of Nan with her swift fingers and tart tongue.

Maybe he was ready for a more human family.

He could take Lod up on his offer. He could make his home in the village. It wouldn't be that bad would it? Nothing like the woods, of course.

But it didn't bring him comfort. Facing the villagers still made him want to hide. It made him extra aware of the cloak hanging from his shoulders. If he started wearing it now, after getting to know so many of them, they'd want to know why, and he could barely explain it to himself let alone to a group of nosy humans.

And while Lod was kind, the hunter wasn't ready to be a replacement son. The word was wrong, and he wasn't ready to find the right one.

It would all take too much fixing. And he didn't have the energy, not without Nan's wisdom.

He raised a hand to stroke Brother's head. At least it felt like his hand again instead of some numb piece he couldn't exactly control.

"We'll go back to the village for a little," the hunter said.

Brother's ears came forward.

"Just for a bit, to make sure they're okay. But I don't want to stay."

What do you want to do? Brother asked. *Go back to the woods?*

"I don't think we can go back there either. Not alone. It might be time to leave the valley."

Brother stood and shook himself, and the hunter prepared for an argument.

And then what? Brother said.

The hunter blinked. "That doesn't bother you?"

Not as long as we remain together. You are my pack, small as it may be. I will stay with you, guard you until we find a bigger pack, a bigger home and a place to belong.

The hunter bit his lip and buried his hand in the wolf's ruff as a sort of hug. "Yes," he said, voice thick. "That's what we'll do. And when we find one, we'll do better. We'll protect them. The way we couldn't with the pack."

Brother stood and shook the gathering snow from his fur. Then he hopped over the ledge and started his controlled skid down the mountainside.

The hunter stood and looked back at the dead dragon. He would not apologize to it. But he wanted to remember it. So the memory of it flaming the forest stood side by side with this dead thing which he had killed.

Then he pulled his hood over his head, allowing the deep pocket of fabric to hide his face. Until he was ready. Until he knew enough of who he was to show the world.

MISHAP'S HEROES

6

Wastelands and War

It's time to
finish this
fight...

KM MERRITT

MISHAP'S HEROES

6
Wastelands and War

KM MERRITT

BLUE FYRE PRESS

For all the gamer girls. Keep kicking ass.

ONE

"WHAT ARE you supposed to pack for war?" Sorrel said, holding up a loose white shirt Vola had never seen her wear before. The monk always wore the same gray wrap-around tunic and loose pants tied close around her calves.

"I suppose the same kinds of things you've always packed before," Lillie said. Her lilting voice, which would have done well when paired with a lute, was distracted as she stacked books in her saddle bag. Vola was waiting for her to drop something on her foot because she wasn't paying attention.

"Knives, swords, daggers, bows, quivers, armor, two pairs of pants, boots, and new gauntlets from the vendor down the street." Talon ticked off the list on her fingers.

"That's oddly specific," Lillie said, pausing with her head cocked. "Especially for Sorrel who doesn't wear armor and fights with a glorified stick."

Talon looked up, blue eyes confused. "What's Sorrel got to do with anything? I was going through my bags."

Lillie rolled her eyes. "Sorrel was asking what to pack for war."

"I think Lillie's right," Vola said, folding her own shirts. "Just pack normal."

"Sexy underwear it is, then," Sorrel said and tossed a couple of scraps of black fabric at her bags without folding them first. "Might come in useful."

Talon snorted under her breath. "If you like to wear it for yourself, that's fine. But I think you might have to actually have sex to call it useful."

"Bleh," Sorrel said, making a face. "Whatever for?"

"Maybe because you love someone," Talon said.

"And want to feel close to them." Lillie's gaze was distant and unfocused again.

Vola scooted a stack of books closer to her reaching hand so she could grab them without having to look down.

Vola was already packed. She'd spent the night rearranging it all over and over again, mulling over what they were about to do. Heading to war wasn't something she took lightly. Too bad she couldn't repack her thoughts out of the way where she wouldn't trip over them every five minutes.

"Not sure I need to be that close to anyone," Sorrel said, shoving another shirt into her pack and sitting on it to make it close.

"Not even Renvick?" Lillie said with a sly smile.

Sorrel opened her mouth and hesitated. She and the draconic guardian had been circling the issue for a week, but they weren't any closer to defining what exactly they were to each. And with the impending conflict, they likely wouldn't even see each other for a while.

Sorrel shook her head. "I doubt we're going to be that type of couple. If we're going to be a couple at all..."

Lillie's face fell and her fair skin flushed bright red, clashing painfully with her strawberry blond hair. "I'm sorry."

Lillie's familiar, Rand, flew through the open window of their hotel room, the sun glinting from his black feathers and turning them nearly blue. He clacked his beak and dropped a shiny bit of broken jewelry into her hand before lighting on her shoulder. She smiled and stroked his head.

"It's alright, Lillie," Vola said. "We all know you're a romantic."

"Says the woman with a couple of cheap romance novels in her bag," Talon said.

Vola didn't flush the way she used to. She just shrugged. "It's research."

"For what?" Sorrel's brow furrowed. She pulled her bag off the bed. It was nearly as tall as she was.

"I'm trying to figure out how to weaponize your underwear." Vola spun for the door while Sorrel spluttered in outrage.

Talon swung her saddle bag over her shoulder and stood, the big black wolf, Gruff, flicking his ears at her feet. It was strange to see her without her cloak, so the light from the window hit her sandy-colored hair, now long enough to curl around her ears.

"Come on, Lillie," Talon said. "If the books don't fit, you'll have to leave some behind."

Lillie's mouth fell open. "No!"

"How did you even have time to acquire more? I swear your books procreate by themselves," Vola asked as Lillie tried to tighten the straps over the last couple of tomes. She winced when she heard a seam pop. "We've spent all of the last week running after dragons and putting out fires."

Sorrel sighed with a smile. "Good times. Hey, remember that day and a half when we thought Talon was dead?"

"You thought that was fun?" Vola said.

"Well, not the thinking she was dead part, but the finding out she wasn't part was great."

"I'm not leaving any of my notes behind," Lillie said, ignoring the ominous popping and trying to hoist her bag over her shoulder. "We need everything we have to go up against Anders. He has Nargilla's plans. Between those and the piece of the Broken's power he stole, I want every advantage we can get."

The others went quiet and sober for once, and Vola took the pack from Lillie without saying anything.

They left the hotel room that had been their home since they'd arrived in Firewatch and headed down the narrow, creaky stairs.

"At least now we have a god on our side," Talon said. "That should give us an advantage, right?"

They entered the common room which was patched together with a variety of woods and pieces of wagons and it was empty this time of day.

"Has Cleavah—I mean the Broken said anything to you, yet?" Sorrel asked Vola. "She likes you. A lot. And Maxim has never been the talk in your ear sort of god, so he's not saying much."

From everything Vola had heard since she'd met Sorrel, Maxim wasn't the sort of god to give his followers any sort of feedback. There'd been a time when Vola had envied Sorrel for her connection to the Greater Virtue of Strength and Courage. It had taken her a while to realize just how worthless a connection it was when the Virtue refused to use it.

"She hasn't said anything to me since we met with everyone at the museum the other day," Vola said quietly. "She might have declared war on Anders, but I'm not sure how much help that's going to be in the end."

"Why?" Lillie said, tilting her head.

Vola ran a hand over her dark braid and tried to come up with a coherent argument for what she was thinking. It wasn't just about the knot in her chest and the way she felt a little woozy every time she thought about her goddess. Vola had served the minor goddess known as Cleavah for years now. She'd grown in so many ways, some very unexpected for a paladin, all with the goddess's help.

But now Vola knew that Cleavah wasn't just Cleavah, Goddess of Vengeful Housewives. She was actually the Broken. The Greater Virtue of Righteousness. One of the greater gods and quite possibly the greatest god in the pantheon. If the others would ever agree to such a hierarchy.

"The Broken isn't exactly popular with the rest of the gods," Vola said. "She has some friends, some of the Greater Virtues on her side, I think. But there's a reason they call her the Broken."

"She was cast out, wasn't she?" Talon said. "Kicked from on high when the other gods realized that righteousness could rule all the rest of the Virtues and Obstacles."

"Yes," Vola said quietly. "She fell in flames and was missing from the pantheon for millennia while she recovered. She's still marked by it." The figure who'd broken free from her bonds and blazed her image across Vola's vision while she'd shattered Nargilla's magic tanks had been that of a woman with one arm and one leg, burn scars masking the left side of her face.

"So you don't think she's going to ride into the pantheon on a cloud and tell the rest of the gods what to do," Sorrel said.

"Actually, that sounds like the beginning of another Divine War," Lillie said. She tapped her lip. "Perhaps I should take notes the next time we see her."

"They didn't even trust her to hold Nargilla after she captured her," Vola said. The gnome was being held by the other gods.

"Yeah, but we don't have time for another Divine War," Talon said. "If the gods take it into their heads to beat their problems out of one another, Anders will have stolen all the magic of the world and we'll be better off dead."

"Maybe that's why the Broken chose a paladin for the first time ever," Sorrel said. "To convince the gods that this threat is bigger than their squabbles."

"They're gods," Talon said. "Do you think they'll recognize anything as bigger than them?"

Vola rubbed her brow, trying to smooth out the lines left by worry. Her friends weren't saying anything she hadn't already been over in her head a thousand times a night since the Broken had revealed herself. Why had she finally chosen a paladin? Why had she chosen an orc? Would Vola be strong enough to protect everyone from whatever came at them, whether that was a man who thought he could strip the whole world of magic, or a collection of gods too busy with their own troubles to notice the world they presumably ruled?

It would be nice if the Broken had explained anything to her when she'd decided she was done hiding. Anything at all.

Vola pushed through the door of the hotel. Outside, a walkway snaked up the mountains between the buildings made up of leftover wood lashed together with cords brought across the desert in caravans.

The harsh sun beat down on Vola's head, and she raised a hand to shade her face. Her green-tinted skin didn't burn as easily as Lillie or Talon's fair complexions, but she seemed to soak up the heat faster than the locals. Even without her plate armor.

There was an angry hiss, and Vola instinctively dodged as a squirt of greenish goo landed across the boards at her feet. The liquid sizzled and began to eat through the wood, throwing off a wisp of smoke.

Vola sighed. The swamp monster waited across the walkway, tied to a railing, but it had already chewed most of the way through the rope. It looked like the unhappy love child of a crocodile and a donkey. Slimy, scaled, and ugly enough that both parents had probably dropped dead at the sight of it. It oozed a bit at both ends and gave Vola a toothy glare.

"One day we will find a way to be rid of you," Vola said under her breath as she ducked the swamp monster's teeth and yanked what remained of the lead rope from the railing. She knew better than to assign the creature to one of her teammates. It was her turn, and she'd been the one who insisted they couldn't sell the thing to Lillie's mother at the field museum. "Don't make me regret saving you from dissection."

"I still think it would look ten times better inside out," another familiar voice said, and Vola turned to find a slim dark woman leaning against the wall of the hotel. Even in broad desert daylight, she looked like she was lounging in a shadow. The dark green jerkin she wore gleamed richly against her dark skin, and her black hair rose in a fluffy halo around her head.

One day Vola wanted to see Rilla actually wear the crown she was entitled to as the princess of Southglen's Dagger Throne.

"Have you been lurking—I mean, waiting long, Your Highness?" Vola said as Sorrel and Talon slung their packs over the swamp monster's back. She yanked its head around as it tried to lunge for one of them.

"Just getting some sun while I can," Rilla said, holding out a hand. Vola was surprised it didn't sizzle in this heat. "It's probably raining in Southglen. I hate soggy leather."

Vola waited till the others had strapped their bags to the swamp beast's back before slinging hers on and fastening the straps. "Oh, shut up," she murmured as it glared. "It's the only thing you're good for besides eating everything."

A huge shadow swooped over them, and they all glanced up instinctively. But the red shape swinging by wasn't familiar to any of them. Listrell and her lead guardian, Renvick, had already said their goodbyes and were presumably off collecting the rest of their dragon allies for the war ahead.

"Right," Rilla said, pushing off from the wall. "If you're ready, I'd like to get going before Anders wins this war by default." She didn't bother ducking into an alley or finding a more private spot to do this. She reached with fingers spread and ripped a burning shape in the air. The flames flickered, floating in midair for a second before spreading to form a large green doorway in the middle of the walkway. On the other side, there were a couple of intricately carved doors twice Vola's height. She couldn't see the rest of the palace that stretched above them because the portal was too close.

"You know it's hard to take your complaining seriously, Rilla, when you can open a portal directly to the front door of your castle," Sorrel said, grinning up at the princess.

"Don't take this away from me," Rilla said, her lip twitching. "Griping is my thing. It's part of my persona."

"Not taking it away," Talon said. "We like Your Grumpy Highness. Honest."

Rilla's eyes narrowed. "Just get through the portal. I can only hold it open for so long. And if we're going to war, then I have a lot of work to do to make sure Southglen stays safe before we leave."

As the princess of the Dagger Throne, Rilla was Southglen's spymaster. She kept the country safe from invasions and sabotage by being faster and cleverer than the threat. Or by throwing Vola and her team at the problem. Rilla might have first called them Mishap's Heroes as a joke, but they were really good at taking bad situations and turning them around.

All right, if Vola was being really honest, they usually made it worse before they made it better, but that was splitting hairs.

Talon gave Rilla a sarcastic salute before stepping through the fiery portal, hand on her dagger, Gruff on her heels. Knowing the ranger, she'd make sure their landing zone was clear before any of them stepped through into an ambush. The castle stood in the center of Glenhaven, and if it was under attack, then they had a lot more immediate problems than a war between gods. But Talon's paranoia kept them from making stupid mistakes, so Vola wasn't about to complain.

And there was that one time nobles had taken over the palace in a coup, so...

Sorrel trotted through next.

Lillie stopped on the threshold. "One day you really must show me how to make one of these."

"Later, Lillie," Vola said. "You literally don't have any more room for notes."

Lillie flushed and stepped through the portal.

And like a good leader, Vola brought up the rear, stepping from the hot desert afternoon into a muggy evening on the other side of the world.

TWO

THAT EVENING VOLA made her way to the All-Pantheon temple, down a couple of flights of stairs from the palace of Glenhaven. The entire city was built into the side of a cliff with terraces climbing higher and higher until it reached the palace at the very pinnacle of the whole thing.

Rilla was closeted in some meeting room with the other princesses, preparing the country for the coming war. As the kingdom's spymaster, it was up to her to work with the princess of the Shield Throne to create a good plan to protect Southglen while everyone else dealt with Anders.

Lillie was off trying to contact her father and brother who usually lived in the city but were currently away on some research assignment. Sorrel and Talon had promised to entertain themselves quietly. Vola just hoped they didn't burn down the city between them.

She stepped toward the temple entrance, but a figure coalesced out of the shadows beside the doorway. A door guard, dressed in the armor of the gods. It glowed slightly as he moved between Vola and the door.

"You may not enter here, black paladin," he said. His sharp elven features creased as he glared at her.

Vola's teeth clenched. She carried her shield with her always, the blackened surface declaring her status to anyone who saw her. But it had been long enough since she'd been in Glenhaven that she hadn't even thought twice about it. She could always ignore the whispers of the villagers they passed, and Firewatch had been inhabited by misplaced rogues and scholars who cared more for their studies than religion. She should have remembered it would be different here.

She tipped the shield so he could see the wing pattern spreading through the black of her shield. "I'm here to serve and to pray. Not to cause trouble."

He snorted. "Black paladins have forsaken their oaths. You serve no one but your own self now. Begone."

Vola lowered her chin. No law said she couldn't visit a temple. He had no right to keep anyone out, even a black paladin. And she would remind him of the fact if she had to. With steel.

An acolyte in white, face shadowed by the portico, stepped out of the doorway and put a hand on the door guard's arm.

No words were spoken, but the guard stiffened and glanced between the acolyte and Vola.

Finally, he growled under his breath and stepped back. "Watch yourself and don't touch anything. You'll sully it."

She could have spit at him, made her opinion obvious, but no. She was better than that. She raised her chin and followed the acolyte between carved columns into the All-Pantheon temple. The ceiling was open to the sky and stars winked above her.

Few people paid their respects to the gods this late at night, so the temple echoed with only the acolyte moving softly to light the candles around the edges. Little niches in the circular walls held altars to each of the Lesser Virtues and even a few of the Obstacles. There were still plenty of people who thought of the Obstacles as blessings and worshiped them as such.

Around the inside of the circle stood statues to the Greater Virtues, the upper echelon of gods, standing as pillars in the darkness.

Vola's eyes easily found the one imperfect figure among the bunch. This one balanced on one foot, the other leg missing from the knee down. She only had one arm, but she stood before a screen of flames that rose behind her like wings.

The Broken.

Vola could talk to her anywhere, just like she had with Cleavah. All she had to do was direct her thoughts toward the goddess and the goddess answered in her ear like a sister or mother standing close by to offer advice.

But it felt more official to call on her here, in a temple where Vola could see her standing with her fellow gods.

"Lady," she said in the darkness.

The air beside her remained still, but the acolyte finished lighting their candles and gently blew out the lit taper. She limped out of the shadows of the temple and into the moonlight spilling through the open roof, and Vola realized she was looking at Cleavah, Goddess of Vengeful Housewives, and a manifestation of the Broken.

The dark curling hair tumbled down her shoulders, and her skin glowed gold in the night. The simple linen shift she wore bared her shoulders and was belted at the waist. Every time Vola had seen her goddess appear as Cleavah, she'd always been dressed as a servant, working down where no one else wanted to be seen, serving those no one else wanted to serve.

"Vola," she said, her lips curling in that serene grin that made Vola feel understood and accepted.

"My lady." Vola shifted her feet. She'd spoken to Cleavah many times throughout her career. She'd spoken to her when she was just the Goddess of Vengeful Housewives; she'd spoken to her when they knew she was more than that, but not exactly how much more. And she'd spoken to her since as the Broken. But for some reason, even knowing the Broken was the same goddess she'd always called on, didn't make it any less awkward. Only more.

"Why the disguise?" Vola said, gesturing to Cleavah's form and then realizing that might be rude.

Cleavah just cocked her head to stare down at herself, but it made the goddess go cross-eyed. "I'm a little recognizable," she said, and glanced up at the statue looming above them. "The Greater Virtues don't appear to mortals often enough for them to be used to it. And..." She trailed off as she stared into the empty darkness. "People aren't as comfortable with how I actually look."

Vola's eyes flicked to the statue, taking in the missing limbs and the scars stretching across her face. "I'm the only one here, lady," she said quietly.

"Yes, I know." Cleavah cleared her throat and shifted her weight.

Vola's brows came down. Could a goddess feel awkward and self-conscious? That seemed contradictory. But Vola had known her for a few years. Maybe it was a little like Talon telling the rest of them she wasn't a boy; she was a girl. They'd known her for long enough to already have a picture in their minds. Changing that picture had taken persistence and willingness on their part and courage on Talon's.

"Why didn't you tell me who you were?" Vola said, eyes still on the statue. "From the beginning. Why appear as Cleavah at all?"

Cleavah followed her gaze, and the corner of her mouth drew up in something between a grimace and a smile. "You need to understand right now, I have always been the Broken. Cleavah is nothing more than a mask I slip on to hide the face others know. It doesn't change who I was this entire time."

"Okay," Vola said without hesitating.

Cleavah's eyes flicked to her in surprise, and Vola grinned.

"I've had practice," she said, thinking of Talon again. The ranger had always been a girl. The rest of them just hadn't known it at the time.

Cleavah hesitated before saying, "That makes things a little easier."

"I'd still like to know why. I know why Talon wore a hood—I think she still does sometimes when she's feeling vulnerable. I know why she called herself 'they' before she felt ready to claim what she really was." Vola turned to face the goddess squarely, ignoring the statue. "But why did you hide from me?"

Cleavah's eyes fastened on her face. "I have to be careful who I trust with the truth. Paladins who know who I am right off the bat tend to feel self-important. They take the prestige of working with the Broken, thinking I am the greatest of the gods, without remembering I was cast out for it. They think they are better than their compatriots who work with lesser gods. They don't realize that I am Broken. My power and my strength come because of my failures. Pride has no place in anyone working for me. And those who meet me as Cleavah? They don't want to work with a laughingstock. The ones who are willing to try it out usually find a better offer with another god before too long."

Cleavah held out her hand in a fist. "I needed a paladin who was strong." She flattened out her fingers. "But humble. Humility is as much a part of strength as courage is."

"And you never found any?" Everyone knew the Broken had never taken any mortal followers officially. She'd never given her divine blessing to anyone, healer or fighter.

"I was afraid. Anyone I chose would have to stand against the displeasure of the pantheon itself. I was afraid those prideful warriors would break before the gods. I need humility."

Vola winced. "My lady. You must know, I wasn't that paladin." She'd been as ashamed of Cleavah as all those other knights who must have rejected her through the ages.

"No, you weren't," Cleavah said with a smile. "But you accepted me, anyway. And you learned."

"So it was a test."

"Life is a test, Vola." Cleavah flung out her arms to indicate the entire world. "If you pass, you grow. Deceiving you was not supposed to be a trick. I am what I am, and I always will be. I need a paladin willing to fight for and represent those viewed as the least of the world."

A ripple of fire shook her from head to toe. And when it cleared, the Broken stood in the center of the temple under the night sky. Moonlight glinted from the puckered scars across her face. The greatest of the world. And the least.

Vola knelt.

The Broken rolled her eyes just like Cleavah. "You could have just said 'yes,' Vola."

Vola hid a smile. "Fine, it's cheesy. But I'm a paladin. If you didn't want a healthy dose of melodrama, along with my eternal loyalty, you should have gone for a cheeky monk. I know one you might like."

The Broken raised her hand to tap her lips. "There's an idea. I do like Sorrel a lot." She sighed. "But Maxim might object to my poaching on his territory. I guess we'll have to muddle through somehow."

Vola made sure to catch the Broken's black bottomless eyes and hold her gaze. "I don't know how to be your sole representative. I don't think any of this has prepared me for that. But I do know how to fight for the broken. I know how to protect the weak and the lost." Vola pulled her sword from its sheath and laid it across her palms. "Will you accept my sword in your service?"

The words weren't binding in any way. She'd already been chosen over and over. She couldn't escape the Broken now if she tried. But they had meaning nevertheless. The Broken had to know that she'd chosen this. Vola had chosen her, too.

A fierce light burned in the Broken's gaze for a moment before it was gone, hidden by that bemused smile she wore most often.

"This old thing? Certainly not." She spun to the statue of the Broken. She reached up to the stone hand that had to be at least twice as big as hers and yet seemed to shrink as she plucked the sword from the statue's grip.

It shrank as she brought her hand down until she held a long, gleaming sword. She turned her grip and moonlight flashed across the edge of the blade, bright enough to blind Vola for a moment.

She flung up her hand to shield her eyes. When she looked again, the goddess was holding the blade out to her, hilt first.

"I can't be seen with a champion with such an old weapon. Let's show them who you really are, shall we?"

The next morning, Mishap's Heroes were summoned to the Throne Room. The chamber was more than just symbolic. It held the Thrones of Southglen, yes, but those Thrones held enormous power in and of themselves. Anders had tried to siphon that power off for himself just months ago, inciting a coup by the nobles of the city to mask his actions.

Each of the fifteen Thrones embodied a specific aspect of the government and was ruled over by a princess chosen to serve that aspect. Vola and the others worked directly with Rilla, princess of the Dagger Throne and the kingdom's spymaster. But they'd also worked with War, Justice, and Shield. And the princess of Sewage Management.

Costa twiddled her fingers at them as they gathered in the center of the circle between the Thrones. She wore gaiters and a pair of goggles pushed to the top of her head.

"How's the swamp beast?" she asked, a gleam in her eye.

"Fine," Vola answered, hiding a wince. The others shifted their feet behind her.

"Not in the city, I hope?" she said. "Since there is a very specific law against creatures of unknown swamp origins roaming our streets—and our pipes."

"Um, no. Of course not."

"It's resting comfortably," Lillie added.

"Somewhere far, far away," Sorrel said.

"The prison doesn't count as within city limits, does it?" Talon muttered.

Vola elbowed her. "Yup. Not breaking any laws here."

The truth was, there'd been nowhere to stash the thing, and it wasn't like Firewatch had wanted them to leave it there either. So it was resting comfortably, as Lillie said, in the city prison just around the corner from the palace in a cell designed to hold the hardest of hardened criminals.

Hopefully, it would still be there when they got back.

The princess of Sewage Management's brows drew down in a knowing look, but she didn't pursue it.

The rest of the princesses trickled in one by one. This was only the second time they'd seen them all in one room together. Usually, they were split up, traveling around their kingdom, governing, putting out fires. Being figureheads.

Rilla sprawled on her Throne already, legs flung over the armrest. Her eyes locked on Vola standing in the middle.

Vola tilted her head in question. "What?"

"Is that new?" Rilla pointed to the hilt sticking up over Vola's shoulder.

Vola touched it self-consciously as Lillie, Talon, and Sorrel all turned, mouths open.

"The Broken gave it to me," she said. It was a greatsword, giant, and meant to be swung two-handed, but Vola was big enough that it worked more like a bastard sword. She could use two hands or one, depending on if she was using her shield or not.

Rilla flowed gracefully to her feet and held out a hand. "May I?"

Vola didn't see any reason not to let her examine the blade. She pulled it from her back and held it out to the princess.

Rilla took it and as her fingers closed around the hilt, there was a flash of light and fire limned Rilla's entire form, flickering around the edges. For just a moment, and then the flames sucked back into the sword.

"Geez," Vola said, rubbing her eyes.

Rilla remained in the center of the circle of Thrones, breathing heavily, blinking at the blade. "Well," she said as if she couldn't think of anything else to say.

"Are you all right?" Vola asked.

Rilla cleared her throat. "I'm not hurt. But let's just say it'd be better if you kept hold of it for oh, say forever."

The princess of the Religion Throne stepped closer to examine the sword as Rilla handed it back to Vola. "I had a message from an All-Pantheon priest this morning," she said, tucking her short straight hair behind her ears as she leaned toward the blade. "It seems they had a minor miracle in one of the temples last night. A statue of the Broken, which had been holding a sword yesterday, is no longer holding the sword."

"It was stolen?" the princess of Justice said sharply.

"No," the princess of Religion said, eyes on Vola. "The statue itself changed positions. It's now standing with its hand across its breast as if it never held a sword in the first place."

"You can all stop being so melodramatic about it," the princess of the War Throne said, waving a hand as if to shoo the subject away. She had her bright golden curls pinned on top of her head today. "We all know the Broken gave it to Vola, blah blah blah. I appreciate divine miracles as much as the next princess who was chosen by an esoteric throne, but can we sit down and talk about how we're actually going to use these miracles to get rid of this Anders fellow?"

Rilla muffled a snort as the princesses returned to their thrones and Vola sheathed her sword. "Yes, Your Highness," she said and plopped her butt on her throne. She didn't lounge this time, but sat forward, elbows planted on her knees and her hands clasped in front of her.

War glanced at her, unamused, but didn't say anything further.

The princess of the Shield Throne sat up straight, her long white hair cascading over the Throne behind her. "We have called up the army," she said. "They are on active duty and we are stepping up recruitment efforts as we speak."

The princess of the Health Throne raised her eyebrows. "That's a little aggressive, don't you think?"

"Anders has the power to strip the entire world of magic," Rilla said without preamble. "He already tried once, and we have no idea what else he's capable of. He needs to be dealt with. Now. Before he becomes even more of a threat."

"You defeated his lieutenant," the princess of the Education Throne said, head cocked. "That Nargilla character. Surely without her—"

"Without her, he'll have a harder time of it, yes," Rilla said. "But he has her plans. Our operatives confirmed he possesses the spell and the plans for the tanks that Nargilla was using." She nodded to the Mishap's Heroes. "It's only a matter of time before he starts up again. We need to hit him now, while he's still reeling from her loss."

War cleared her throat, and instantly the rest of the princesses shut up and listened. They might have been a group of equals, but they were all smart enough to recognize when one of them had more expertise than the others.

"We are not debating if we are going to war," she said. "That has already been decided." She glanced at Rilla, who gave her a grateful nod. "We are here to decide how we are going to war."

Shield nodded and took the floor with a graceful gesture, her long white hair trailing behind her. "Our army is well trained but small," she said. "And possibly rusty after so many years of peace."

War winced.

"We'll need help," Vola said and almost bit her tongue. She wasn't really sure why she and the rest of Mishap's Heroes were here. These women were perfectly capable of coming up with plans all by themselves. But every single one of them turned to focus on her when she spoke.

Vola cleared her throat. "This isn't just a problem for Southglen," she said. "It's a problem for the world. Firewatch recognized that already. They've promised to send a contingent. Fighters and researchers from the museum. And the dragons will come as soon as Listrell is done waking them up."

"Southglen has many allies to call on," Lillie said, stepping up beside Vola. Vola glanced at her in relief. Lillie didn't like drawing attention to herself, but she was much better spoken, and she was a citizen. The princesses might listen to her over Vola.

"We have a little time," Sorrel said from around Vola's hip. "Anders isn't preparing his attack yet. I'm sure Rilla would have told us by now if he was."

Rilla hid a smile with her hand. She probably had plenty of spies keeping an eye on Anders and his people.

"We will need the time to plan our defenses anyway," the princess of the Shield Throne said. "And they're right. Our offensive must include anyone else who is threatened by Anders's plan."

"Are you prepared for a diplomatic mission?" War asked Vola.

Vola blinked. "Us?" she blurted. Then she cleared her throat. "I mean, are you sure?"

"You're the ones with firsthand experience with Anders and the threat he represents. You've encountered his lieutenants and you've dealt with the areas where he's sucked the magic out of the world. You've even experienced it yourselves."

Vola grimaced. "Not something I want anyone to experience ever again."

"Which is why you are the best ones to convince our allies we need the help."

"They will need some diplomatic clout," the princess of Sewage Management murmured, scratching under the strap of her goggles.

War cocked her head. "So they will."

Rilla was already hoisting herself off her Throne.

"I suppose that's my cue."

Vola eyed her up and down. "You want to come with us?"

"Sure. If you'll have me. Can I be an honorary member or do I have to fill out an application?"

Vola glanced back at the others, who were trying not to laugh. "Well, we've had some pretty good examples of your skills," she said. "But I need to know you'll follow orders."

Rilla crossed her arms over her chest. "I know when to listen to my superiors. As long as they don't ask me to do anything stupid." She tipped her head and met Vola's eyes. "You guys get things done. I'm not about to mess with a system that works. I'll serve as your diplomatic liaison and a pair of daggers when you decide fighting is the way to go."

Vola grinned and held out her hand. "Welcome to Mishap's Heroes then, Rilla."

THREE

"So, how do you like the glamor and glory of being an adventurer, Rilla?" Sorrel asked over a week later as they climbed through the wettest forest Vola had ever seen. And they'd been through swamps before.

Rilla glared at Sorrel as the rain poured down on all sides. Her normally fluffy hair was looking a little flatter, and Vola knew from experience the wet leather of her jerkin had to be starting to itch.

To be fair, Vola wasn't doing much better in full plate armor. Water had a tendency to seep in through her neck and then drip down her spine and between her boobs. But she'd been caught once too often by an ambush while they were traveling to leave her armor strapped to the swamp beast.

Trees soared on either side of the road, their canopies lost in the near-constant mist that resulted from the rain. Vines that looked more monster than plant climbed the trunks nearest them and big ferns spread lacy leaves to collect as much of the moisture coming out of the sky as possible. Vola could make out the delicate fronds of purple and blue flowers clinging to the bark of the trees almost twenty feet over their heads.

It was probably very pretty in the one season it wasn't raining.

The swamp monster was in its element. Vola had never seen it do anything except glare and eat, but now it was frolicking. It pranced from one side of the wide cobbled road to the other, shaking its head to spray water on them.

"Well, I'm glad someone's happy," Talon grumbled. She reached as if to pull up her hood, but it had been torn to pieces back in the mountains known as the Firewall and she hadn't bothered to replace it. She paused when she realized there was nothing to pull up and wrinkled her nose. It was dripping. Gruff trudged along beside, his head and tail drooping.

The swamp monster danced ahead of them to the end of its long lead rope and turned its head up to the spray, long, slimy tongue lolling out of its mouth.

"Aw, maybe we've misjudged it all along," Lillie said. She had found a rain poncho somewhere and draped it over her head. She held up the edges like a tent.

They all looked at the swamp monster, wondering if maybe they'd been wrong about it. Maybe it wasn't as gross as it seemed. Maybe it was just misunderstood.

It lunged forward and snapped at something in the underbrush. When it straightened, a vivid purple centipede as long as Vola's arm hung from its mouth, hundreds of little legs wriggling. The swamp monster slurped, and the giant bug disappeared down its gullet.

"Nope," Vola said. "Pretty sure it's just nasty."

"How far is it to Mistvale?" Sorrel asked Rilla.

Vola hadn't thought it was possible, but the rain strengthened, pinging off her pauldrons.

"Several more miles to the edge of the forest. We'll reach the games by tomorrow, probably."

"I think what she meant to say was 'are we there yet?'" Vola said.

"What games?" Talon asked.

"The Friendship Games," Rilla said. "They're held every other year on a rotating schedule as to who gets to host them. Every nation on the continent is represented. So there should be leaders from all those Anders threatens."

"I've never heard of the Friendship Games," Talon said, Gruff trotting along at her heels.

"Yeah, but you literally lived under a rock until we met," Sorrel said.

"A cave," Talon said with a frown. "There's a difference."

"My parents competed," Vola said. "Years ago. Until they were banned because they kept winning."

"I remember. I watched Lydia Battlemane kill a minotaur with her bare hands when I was eight," Lillie said.

Sorrel gasped. "Aw, lucky. The monks don't believe in fighting for money or glory unless it's Maxim's glory. We weren't allowed to go."

"They probably knew you'd sneak off to enter and never be heard from again," Vola said.

Sorrel opened her mouth to comment and paused. "Okay, yeah. You're probably right."

"Sure, it's a good time, but it's also the best place to find allies." Rilla spoke under her breath, eyes on the woods.

"Why are you whispering?" Vola asked Rilla.

Rilla's gaze flicked to her. "There might be monsters in the rainforest. Were-gorillas and the like. Some are attracted to the magic the trees exude."

Vola glared at the trees. Rain, fog, and monsters. That seemed about right for what was supposed to be a diplomatic mission.

"As the newest member of the party, *we're* supposed to pull pranks on *you*," Sorrel said. "There is no way were-gorillas are a real thing."

"We never have to find out as long as we keep the noise down. They know better than to come too close to the road."

"Who thought it was a good idea to put a bloody great forest between Southglen and Mistvale, anyway? Especially one infested with monsters," Sorrel grumbled.

"The Graywood is far more ancient than either of the countries surrounding it," Lillie said. "It predates most forms of civilization and is home to more lifeforms than the rest of the world combined." She gestured to the canopy where even in the pouring rain they could hear hoots and howls from some of those lifeforms. Vola couldn't tell if it was a bird or a monkey or maybe some sort of plant that hunted its prey by luring it in with sound.

"Thank you, Encyclopedia Lillie," Sorrel said.

Lillie frowned. "Hey."

Talon's head went up.

Vola, instantly alert, gave them the signal to halt and hold position. They all obeyed, Rilla a split second behind the others.

"What is it?" Vola asked under her breath.

Talon gestured to Gruff, who took off between the trees without complaint, as silent as a shadow. "Listen," she said.

Vola strained her ears but couldn't hear anything. And then she realized that was because the only thing still making noise was that howler up in the canopy and a few insects that whirred through the ferns on either side of the road.

"Ambush?" Vola asked.

"Or another larger predator," Talon said. "The animals haven't minded us this whole time, but we've been sticking to the road."

"Monster?" Vola asked.

Lillie whispered under her breath, and a slight glow gathered under the ferns at the edge of the track, nothing too noticeable since it was mostly hidden under the curling fronds.

Sorrel casually strolled to the nearest tree and clambered up a vine to hang above them like a big, gray flower.

Vola drew her sword and settled her shield on her arm.

There was a growl and a short, sharp scream off to the left.

"Gruff found someone," Talon said.

"No duh," Sorrel said from above.

The wolf barked.

"They're going to go for it," Talon said. "Incoming."

Vola braced her feet. Now she could hear voices and the crunch of boots pushing through undergrowth.

The first enemy crashed through the ferns at the side of the road and a flash of light lit up the dim afternoon. A scream rang out, and the smell of burnt hair wafted toward them.

The figure staggered across the road, and Vola's gaze took in the fact that it was a human in sleek leather armor, carrying a pair of daggers. He dropped the weapons and flung his hands over his face, rubbing at his smoking eyebrows.

Vola took a firmer grip on her sword and stepped in front of Lillie as several more figures converged through the undergrowth.

Talon's bow twanged and there was a cry from their right.

Vola caught movement on the left and signaled Rilla. The Dagger Princess swept forward and knelt just as the enemy tried to clear the brush. Silent as a snake, she took his legs out from under him and he fell.

Sorrel cried out, "Death from above!" and fell on the one Lillie had blinded.

Lillie was already muttering another spell, and the area was clear enough that Vola felt all right stepping away from the vulnerable wizard. She charged for the only figure left, sword raised.

Her boots slid on the moss slick cobbles at the side of the road, and her feet went out from under her. She landed on her back, the air whooshing from her lungs.

She couldn't do more than sit there in stunned surprise for a moment or two.

Well, that didn't go well.

The enemy she'd been charging overshot her and stumbled past. She took a quick chance and grabbed his boot as it went by.

He hopped on one foot, struggling against her.

Whatever works.

She heaved and flipped him on his back.

Rilla ducked in and finished him.

Vola surged to her feet and surveyed the damage. Three attackers lay on the road, one riddled with arrows, one blackened and sizzling in the rain, and one cut into several little pieces.

Sorrel sat on top of the only attacker left alive. He lay face down, her staff pressed into his neck.

"Kept one alive for questioning," Sorrel said.

"Good work." Vola pressed her fist into the base of her spine and winced as she tried to straighten. "We'll—"

A low rumble threaded through the trees, starting low and ending as a shriek that shivered all the hairs along Vola's neck.

"Uh…Lillie, tell me that was your stomach."

"My body has never made a noise like that," Lillie hissed. "And if it did, I would seek medical help immediately."

A crack echoed across the road, like a very large tree breaking off at the roots.

"That's definitely not digestion," Sorrel said. The captured enemy beneath her heaved and tried to throw her off. Sorrel kept her feet like a sailor in a storm and shoved her staff harder into his neck. "None of that now."

Crashing footsteps raced for them, and Vola scrambled to place herself between the threat and her party.

Leaves and bits of vines exploded from the side of the road as a huge, dark shape smashed through the screening shrubbery.

Thick, fur-covered arms topped with massive shoulders supported the thing's torso and a small head featuring strong yellow teeth and beady eyes. Its narrow hindquarters were lost behind all of that muscle.

"Were-gorilla!" Rilla shouted.

"Oh my gods, you were serious about that?" Sorrel said. The massive beast tried to take a swing at her, and she leaped into the air to avoid it. The enemy she'd caught squeaked and covered his head.

Sorrel raced at the gorilla, staff whirling.

An arrow whizzed past Vola's ear to bury itself in the creature's thick pelt.

It roared its fury and beat both fists against the ground. The road rippled like water and the cobbles surged in a wave, spreading from the gorilla's fists.

Vola danced, trying to keep her feet as Rilla charged. The Dagger princess ducked under one of its massive elbows and thrust out a hand. Green light glowed at its feet and ropes swarmed up its legs to wrap around its narrow waist, trapping it in place.

The gorilla raised its fist in the air, and Lillie shouted a spell. The monster froze, its fist creaking and turning to stone before their eyes.

Its beady gaze fixed on its disobedient limb as if in confusion. Then its brow came down, and it flexed its forearm.

Shards of shattered rock pattered on the cobbles of the road, and Lillie's eyes widened.

"Uh oh," she said.

The gorilla roared, its hot breath steaming in the moist air, and it lunged for Lillie.

The wizard disappeared in pop of cool air and reappeared at the other edge of the road.

Vola skidded forward to take her place, meeting the gorilla's blow. Her raised sword connected with the beast's arm, and there was a flash of light. Flames burst along the edge of the blade and raced up the beast's fur.

White fire spread along its limbs, unhindered by the rain that still poured around them.

The gorilla roared again, and it lurched backward. It scrambled off the road, through the underbrush, and disappeared into the forest.

Sorrel flipped to her feet while Talon crept forward, bow still drawn and trained on the bushes where the monster had retreated.

Vola stared at her sword. Nothing differentiated it from any other sword. At least, not now that the monster had fled. Its blade was sharp and shining, but the flames were gone.

"Well, that's new," she said.

"Handy, too," Talon said, finally stowing her bow.

"Aw, man," Sorrel said, standing with her hands on her hips, staring down at a smear on the roadway. "The gorilla turned our prisoner into red goo."

"Ew," Lillie said.

"Guess we won't be interrogating him then," Talon said.

"Lillie, do you have a spell for that? You've made the dead talk before."

"I'm glad you think so highly of my skills. But even if I hadn't skipped most of Myron's lessons on how to be a necromancer, I would need a complete body to work with."

Sorrel grimaced as Vola turned to Rilla. "Do you have any tricks up your sleeves?"

"All my abilities are about sneaking and stabbing people in the back. I don't tend to speak with them after they're already dead."

Vola sighed and gestured to the other dead attackers. "Well, let's search them then and see if they have anything that could identify them."

No one tried to sift through the wreckage of the one the gorilla had stomped on. They may have been hardened adventurers, but there were limits.

"Empty pockets," Rilla said, rifling through one's clothes. "No badges or identifying markings. Not so much as a scar or a birthmark. This was a professional job. Assassins meant to fade into the background, even when dead."

"Their weapons aren't even unique enough to give any clues," Talon said, examining a dagger and tossing it aside. "Good quality but generic."

"Wait," Lillie said. She grimaced and used two fingers to pull a piece of paper from the breast pocket of one of the assassins.

Rilla's eyebrows drew down. "I swear I checked there."

"It was sticking out," Lillie said. "As if we were supposed to find it."

Rilla's jaw jutted out, and she opened her mouth.

"No, you're right," Talon said. "I checked that one, too. That wasn't there a minute ago."

Lillie passed it over to Vola and touched the band on her forehead. It had been a gift from Rilla, a long time ago. It allowed Lillie to see magic.

"Let me guess..." Vola said.

Lillie nodded. "A spell. Teleportation—a lot like mine."

Vola unfolded the paper, which was getting soggy under the rain.

"Do yourselves a favor," it read in strong, spiky handwriting. "Go find a beach and a quiet place to lie low, and maybe I won't take everything you love from you. Regards, Anders."

The ink began to run down the page, spreading as surely as the cold spread through Vola's gut.

"Geez, he really just signed his name to a threat," Rilla said. "Guy has some balls."

"He knows we're coming," Vola said. "More importantly, he knows where we are."

She glanced up and met their gazes. "Does this change anything?"

She asked it seriously. It was one thing to sneak up on an enemy. Another thing entirely to charge in head down when he knew you were coming.

Sorrel shrugged. "He still wants to suck all the magic out of the world, right? Well, then he still needs to be stopped."

Lillie nodded. "Yes, he cannot get away with this."

"I go where my pack goes," Talon said.

Vola's gaze went to Rilla. "What about you? Still want to come?"

Rilla's lip twitched. "Hell, yeah."

FOUR

MISTVALE TURNED out to be just as wet as the rainforest surrounding it. It really only rained in the afternoons, but while the mornings were bright and sunny, everything was still damp. It made for a humid city covered in green, some of which was intentional, but most of it was just mold.

Vola spent the evening they arrived polishing her armor, but she was pretty sure it would start to rust by morning no matter what she did.

She could have left it at the hotel when they left the next day, but she wanted to look as professional and serious as possible. They were asking for help to end a world-threatening bad guy after all.

Rilla led them past a market full of vendors hawking kabobs and fried cakes. Most of which were green, too. They smelled like greasy food everywhere, but Vola wasn't sure she trusted something that was the same color as swamp scum.

"Heading to the games, sir?" one called to Talon. "Don't go without your refreshments."

"Ma'am," Talon said with a growl and jerked her chin up.

"Is anyone not heading for the games?" Lillie said, shading her eyes so she could peer ahead at the massive coliseum built with light-colored stone and dark timber. Moss grew on at least half of it.

People streamed in and out of the mouth of the coliseum, which was carved to look like the head of a dragon, the low hum of their conversation echoing from the stone archway above them.

Rilla snagged the neck of Sorrel's tunic before she could join the throng.

"This way," she said. "We're not part of the common rabble today."

"Oh, fancy," Sorrel said as Rilla led them along the wall to a staircase festooned with flags. Purple and gold streamers fluttered in the heavy air.

Halfway up, a pair of knights in gold armor which contrasted directly with their dark skin and white turbans stopped them.

"Credentials," one of them said.

"Only country representatives and their retainers are allowed in the royal box," the other one said.

"Oh, for Ona's sake, Yarren. You know who I am. I spent months here getting that trade agreement hammered out."

"Nevertheless, I need your credentials," Yarren said, eyes flickering like he wanted to laugh but didn't dare.

Rilla gave a gusty sigh and dug in the front of her jerkin. Finally, she pulled out a gold circlet with rubies studded across the front. She settled it on her head.

"There, happy?"

"Enormously, Your Highness."

"You know, anyone can wear a crown." She pointed to Lillie's circlet. "See? It doesn't mean anything."

"Nevertheless, I enjoy hearing you go all growly."

Vola choked on a laugh and covered it up with a cough.

"Your retainers will have to leave their weapons behind, I'm afraid." Yarren's gaze flicked to Vola.

"Yeah, yeah. I know the drill. Hand them over, ladies. You'll get them back on the way out."

Vola reluctantly unsheathed her sword and hefted it in her hand for a second. She'd just gotten it and it already felt like a betrayal to just casually hand it over to some guard. Not to mention it might just as casually burn him up. Vola carefully placed it on the table beside the guards rather than risk it.

Lillie opened her hands to prove she had no weapons while Rand sat on her shoulder, puffing up his feathers harmlessly.

Talon unloaded her bow, her quiver, her daggers, another pair of daggers, a set of throwing knives, and a garrote Vola didn't even know she had.

"Are you sure that's everything?" Yarren said dryly.

"Her glare is certified as a weapon," Sorrel said. "But I don't think you can take that away from her."

"And what about you?"

Sorrel blinked at him innocently. Her staff had disappeared in the time it took the others to unload. Now she just had a pencil tucked behind one ear. "What about me?"

Yarren opened his mouth, but stopped and examined Sorrel again. "Very well," he said with a suspicious glance. "You may proceed."

"What happened to Maxim's Warhammer?" Rilla asked under her breath as they continued up the stairs.

Sorrel touched the pencil. "It's so much more convenient like this, don't you think?"

Rilla snorted.

At the top of the stairs, a broad box stretched at least thirty feet in both directions, situated on the first tier so the occupants had the best view.

There were a couple of wooden benches scattered through the box, but mostly big, throne-like chairs held richly dressed personages. Closest to them was a king, lounging across his throne, beckoning a server to bring a tray of fruit. Vola also noticed a bored-looking woman who read a book hidden on her lap, a boy no taller than Sorrel, accompanied by someone who was clearly his governess, and a young woman who sat uncomfortably on the edge of her seat as if she felt like she didn't belong there.

"Princess Allellarilla," the lounging king said. He was thin and gangly and had the most unhealthy-looking skin Vola had ever seen. Which was saying something, considering she'd grown up around orcs.

"We haven't seen anyone from Southglen, yet," he said. "Did you all decide your warriors weren't cut out for the games this year?"

"Oh, come now," the woman with the book said without looking up. "We all know Lydia Battlemane hailed from Southglen. And you've never managed to front a warrior that could have bested her, Hector."

The king—Hector the Third of Mistvale, Vola assumed—spluttered.

The woman shut her book and gestured Rilla to take a seat beside her. "*I'm* happy to see you, anyway. What took you so long?"

"We're not actually here to compete, Selene," Rilla said, straddling the bench beside the woman. "Southglen isn't sending a delegation because we're busy prepping for war."

Everyone in the box sat up or stiffened.

"War against whom?" the woman asked. She tucked long black hair behind her pointed ears.

Vola didn't recognize the name, but an educated guess told her Selene was probably a representative from Elfhome.

"None of you," Rilla said. "Don't worry. But this Anders is a threat to the entire continent. Maybe even the whole world. And war is an apt description when we're mustering troops and recruiting allies to help us beat him."

"Oh." The woman, Selene, relaxed and smoothed her dress over her knees. "Well, then."

"This isn't something that can be ignored," Rilla said, brow pulling down. "Or brushed off."

"No, but it sounds like a Southglen problem," Hector said. He spit a grape seed at the floor, making a servant dance back to avoid being hit.

"I beg your pardon, Your Majesty," Lillie said. "But it's everyone's problem. Anders has the ability to steal magic out of the world itself, as well as people and objects. Even the dead."

Hector cocked his head and pouted his lips. "You're too sweet to worry about such things, honey. There are people in your own country taking care of the problem, I'm sure."

Lillie's face flushed bright red, and Vola fought the urge to come to her rescue. Instead of stammering and fading back, Lillie raised her chin. "We are those people, Your Majesty. And luckily what's in my head is more important than what's on it."

Rilla cleared her throat violently, and Lillie shut her mouth with a snap.

Hector's brow furrowed, as if trying to see the insult.

"This is probably being blown out of proportion," Selene said, cocking her head. "I've found that adventurers who encounter these things aren't all reliable when it comes to reporting their successes and failures. They tend to inflate the former and downplay the latter."

"Considering we were the adventurers to discover the problem," Vola said. "And we nearly died in the process, we're not exaggerating anything."

"The spell that sucked the magic out of the land woke a dragon," Talon said. "Firewatch nearly burned down."

"Unfortunate," Hector said. "But again, that seems like a problem for Firewatch."

"Maybe we should at least form a hearing." The other young woman in the box spoke, shifting on the edge of her overlarge chair. "I know my queen would be interested in more details."

Hector made a rude noise and picked at a spot on his nose. "The Queen of Illthane has better things to do than entertain doomsayers."

Selene gave Rilla a sad little smile. "The truth is, there's always someone saying the world's about to end or claiming some evil is about to overtake the land." The elf waved an airy hand at Vola and her party. "The adventurers always manage to deal with it before it becomes a real problem, though. So it's hard to get excited about another prophecy of death and destruction. You know all this, though, so it's a wonder you don't have the sense to ignore it."

"Maybe that should tell you something," Rilla said between her teeth even though her lips were smiling. "I'm not ignoring it, so obviously there is something worth getting 'excited' over."

"Adventurers probably take care of the problems for you because they get fed up with trying to get you to listen to reason," Lillie said. "That won't work this time. One country's stupidity will doom the rest."

"I beg your pardon, young lady," Hector said with a huff. "But you are here as a guest. I will have you thrown out if you can't be civil."

"I'd like to see you try."

"Lillie," Vola said under her breath. "Is this helping?"

Lillie flushed bright red and ducked her chin. A muscle in her jaw jumped as she clenched her teeth. But the wizard didn't say anything else.

"Obviously you all are convinced of this threat," Selene said, spreading her hands in a placating gesture as Lillie stepped back, out of direct focus. "Perhaps the delegate from Illthane is right and we should have a hearing. If you have evidence of this threat and we believe you, we will send our own scouts to assess the situation and decide if we can send aid."

"That will take too long," Vola said, trying to keep her voice even. She had one eye on the leaders and one eye on Lillie who had pulled out her spell book and was flipping through it rapidly. Either a good sign or a bad sign, depending on who she was aiming for. "Anders knows we're coming. He sent assassins to waylay us on the road here."

Selene gave her a pitying look, and Vola knew what she was about to say. That sounds like your problem. Hector wasn't even listening anymore. He was leaning forward on his throne to watch the match below. A huge brawny swordsman with mismatched plate armor faced off against a lithe elf with a bow and a fistful of magic.

"Shh, shh," he said, flapping his hand at them. "Mistvale is up against Selene's man. This is my best warrior. The most powerful swordsman in Mistvale. No way is Selene walking away with the title this time."

Selene rolled her eyes, but she also sat forward, attention on the sands below. Mishap's Heroes and their warning were forgotten.

Rilla sat beside her, jaw clenched, looking foiled and angry about it.

Sorrel planted her hands on her hips. "I don't suppose beating someone over the head with a stick ever made them see reason."

"We could just leave them to their fate," Talon said. "Perhaps the university scholars will come up with a way to protect Southglen while leaving the rest of the continent vulnerable."

Vola shivered. "As satisfying as that would be..."

"I know, I know," Sorrel said. "We'd feel bad about it later."

A tingle at the back of Vola's neck made her head snap up. She knew that feeling. "What the...?"

Talon's breath hissed between her teeth. "That's—"

Down below, the fighters had ceased circling each other and were looking down at themselves in confusion. The brawny brute dropped his sword.

Vola gasped and pointed. "There," she said. In the center of the sands, dark shadows swirled, circling the two fighters, drawing more darkness into the middle.

Vola's gut went numb. They'd seen this before.

"What is that?" Hector said, staggering to his feet. Grapes and pieces of an orange fell away and rolled across the floor.

Rilla was already on her feet. "Oh my gods. This is the draining effect. This is what we were warning you about." She spun to Vola. "Could Anders be reaching us here?"

"I don't know how..." Vola shook her head and then her eyes fell on Lillie. The wizard stood with her eyes closed, her feet braced, and her hands out to either side.

"Lillie?" Vola said.

Rilla glanced at the spell book, open at her feet. "Are you doing this?"

"Yes," Lillie said, voice grating between her teeth. "At least as far as I'm able."

"You cannot perform spells in the presence of the monarchy," Hector said, rounding on her. Selene and the other delegates were on their feet, leaning over the railing to stare down at the swirling blackness. Screams sounded from the stands around the arena, and the entire structure vibrated with the tromp of panicked feet.

Below, the fighters turned to escape the spreading blackness, but they moved as if trying to push their way through sludge. The elf fell to his knees, and the swordsman bent at the waist to catch his breath.

"You wanted proof," Lillie said. "Here is proof that we know what we're talking about. Proof that we can't wait for you to decide this is a real threat."

"Holy crap, Lillie," Vola muttered. "Next time you want to get us arrested, give me a little warning first."

"No one's getting arrested if we can get them to listen to us." Lillie cracked her eyelids to glare at Hector. "This is the spell Anders had Nargilla Pipwattle design for him. He has the ability to do this only ten times larger."

"This is an attack!" Hector shouted. "An ambush on the leaders of the coalition!"

Boots pounded up the stairs, and the two armored guards burst into the box, swords drawn. Sorrel spun and suddenly she was holding Maxim's Warstaff trained on them while Rand mantled on Lillie's shoulder.

Rilla lunged forward, her hands up. "Not an attack," she said. "This is a demonstration. An exhibition." She jerked her chin at the arena, somehow including Hector in the gesture as well. "Lillie's right. This is the least of what the world faces. You've got your best warriors down there. See if they can handle it."

Hector and Selene exchanged a glance. "This is reversible?" Hector asked.

"So far," Vola said. "We've reversed it a couple of times."

He stepped forward and leaned over the railing. "You can beat this," he called down. "Make Mistvale proud."

Selene called something to the elf in a lyrical, fluid language.

The two fighters squinted up at the box and tried to climb to their feet. The elf made it, but the swordsman didn't.

Vola cast a look at Sorrel and Talon. Talon gave a little shrug that could have meant "better them than us." Sorrel leaned on her staff in a non-threatening way but watched the guards closely. They stood, waiting for orders, their eyes trained on Lillie.

The swordsman collapsed against the sand, his chest straining to rise and fall. The elf sobbed with effort and made it another two steps before tripping.

"What's wrong with them?" Selene asked sharply. "What is this spell?"

"I told you," Rilla said as the blackness crept through the sands, turning them dark as obsidian. "Anders has can suck the magic out of the world. The land itself has no more magic. Neither does anything trapped inside."

"I know Selene's champion wields magic," Hector said, his messy eyebrows lowering in thought. "But Mistvale's champion doesn't have any. Why is he affected?"

"Every creature in the world possesses some magic," Vola said, arms crossed. "It's inherent in our design. A gift from the gods. Spell casters have more, either as a connection to the land they were born with or as something they learned." Vola gestured to Lillie. Then she placed a hand on her chest. "And some are gifted with more by the gods."

"But even if you've never been able to use it, even if it's remained dormant within you, it can still be stolen," Talon said. "And it makes you feel like shit."

"Does it kill you?" Selene said.

"Eventually," Sorrel said.

"It's not the way I would choose to die," Vola said.

The elf landed on hands and knees. Tried to crawl forward and fell face-first into the sand.

"Enough of this," Selene said. "If even our strongest warriors cannot overcome this—"

Rilla held up her hand. But Vola was already moving. She gestured Sorrel and Talon with her and vaulted over the railing to land heavily on the sands below. Oof, she'd feel that in her knees tomorrow.

She steeled herself before stepping forward into the dead spot. She'd never, ever wanted to feel this again, but she trusted Lillie wouldn't actually kill them. And they had done this once before.

As her boots crossed the threshold between the normal sand and the black sand, a weight struck her between her shoulder blades and she staggered, falling to one knee.

There was a murmur from the royal box above them.

Vola steeled herself and fought to stand. It wasn't a feeling she'd ever get used to, like someone had taken all the strength from her limbs, a weight pressing down on her chest so she could barely breathe. But it was something she could learn to work around. And if she could stand up under full plate armor with all the strength stolen from her body, she could stand up under anything.

Vola grunted as she climbed to her feet. Sweat broke out on her brow and along her spine.

"Remind me to kill Lillie the moment we get back," Sorrel groaned from Vola's right. Vola's hypothesis was that Sorrel stood up under the draining effect much better than the rest of them because there was so much less of her to drain, but she knew in the back of her head that wasn't fair. Not that the front of her head cared right now when Sorrel was already limping across the sands using Maxim's Warhammer as a crutch.

"I thought we were fighting so we never had to feel like this again?" Talon said.

"Just once more," Vola gasped out. "Once more. Then we can rest and someone else will take over."

"You wish," Sorrel said. "You know that's not how this works."

"Just...find the anchor points," Vola said. "Lillie said this was Nargilla's spell and Nargilla's spell had anchor points. We destroy those, we destroy the spell."

"It won't destroy Lillie in the process, right?"

Vola shook her head. "Nargilla is still alive in the custody of the gods. And we didn't just destroy her anchor points, we exploded her entire system."

"You mean the Broken did," Sorrel said, but she was already trudging off, surveying the arena for Lillie's anchors to the spell.

Vola staggered to the two fighters and checked them.

"What's...what's happening to me?" the elf gasped. The swordsman was completely passed out, chest still rising and falling.

"Our royals are making an example of us," Vola said. It wasn't the whole truth, but it would work for the moment. "Just lie still. You'll be back to normal in a moment."

No healing would replace the magic he had lost, so Vola didn't even try. She just left him lying as comfortably as possible in the sand.

"Vola," Talon said. Her voice was weak, but Vola had been waiting for their signal. "The pillars...beside the combatant entrances."

Vola turned to look where she pointed. There were two entrances, one for each team or warrior competing. Pillars held up the archway and set into each pillar was a gem. Blue crystals for the north entrance. Red crystals for the south. They didn't glow, and Vola didn't have any magic to check them for spells, but little symbols crawled through them, making the back of Vola's neck prickle.

It was almost an exact replica of Nargilla's spell. Clever Lillie. She'd figured out how to set anchor points from a distance.

"Got it," Vola said. "I'll take the north, you two take the south."

Vola wanted to watch, to make sure they were good, but with her entire being drained, she could barely keep herself upright. She turned to the north entrance and trusted them to do their job.

Vola set her feet in the sand and trudged along. The distance felt doubled, tripled as if the entrance was getting further away with every step, not closer.

She took a deep breath and forced her legs to move faster. One last charge and this would be over and they could all kill Lillie together.

Using that little bit of anger helped her stir up the righteous rage in her gut. The rage that was a gift from one of the Obstacles but she used in service to the greatest Virtue.

She pounded across the sand, pulling her shield from her back, and when she reached the pillar, she swung it edge first into the crystal.

It shattered under her blow, pieces flying past her to sprinkle the arena. Vola used the last of her rage and strength to spin and smash the other crystal.

Then she let herself fall to her knees.

The first time they'd done this, they'd had the help of a goddess. And Vola had always assumed that feeling like the air had been sucked past her had come from the explosion when the Broken had shattered Nargilla's tanks.

But as Lillie's spell collapsed on itself, the air rushed past Vola again and it brought strength with it.

Vola blinked and found her limbs didn't tremble anymore. She reached deep inside and found that well of power that connected her to the Broken. A well that was cut off anytime she experienced the draining effect.

It was over. She climbed to her feet. Her strength might have been back, but she took it slowly, just in case.

Talon and Sorrel stood beside the other entrance, shaking out their limbs and stretching their necks. The crystals lay in pieces at their feet. Sorrel clearly had used Maxim's Warstaff, and Talon had managed to find another knife she'd "forgotten" somewhere on her person.

Vola glanced up to the box to see Lillie braced with her hands on her knees. She would have been ready for them to break the spell, but the backlash from all that magic pouring in and out of her had to be disorienting.

"Your Majesty," she said, as she pushed herself up straight, her voice ringing across the sands. "Delegates. This is what you face if Southglen fails to contain the threat. A very, very small piece of it."

Hector stared down at them as Vola stepped across the sand to help the two fighters to their feet. "What do you mean, a small piece?"

"I am not capable of everything Anders built with Nargilla. They have tanks that will hold much more power. Nargilla had the ability to drain entire cities. I can only manage a coliseum."

"But you're just a spell caster. We could have killed you and stopped the effect, correct?"

"You could have tried," Lillie said, eying the armored guards. "I'm a spell caster, but with this, I'm a spell caster with an infinite amount of power at my command."

Selene and Hector glanced at each other. The other delegates waited silently.

"And you were able to defeat this person once?" Selene asked, eyes on Vola.

"Nargilla?" Vola said. "Yes. But only with divine help. That's why we know how to handle the draining effect. We've had to fight past it before."

The two champions shook their heads in sympathy.

"Imagine this, but spread across the world," Rilla said quietly from between Hector and Selene. "And the more it spreads, the harder it is to fight back."

Vola and the others waited as the delegates pondered, their eyes on the sands that were still stained black.

"Very well," Hector said.

Rilla's chin jerked up.

"You will have our support," Selene said. "Perhaps together we can keep this from happening ever again."

FIVE

THE JOURNEY back through the rainforest wasn't as eventful as the first. This time they only had to fend off a pack of Changefoxes before they made it back to Southglen.

The Broken's intelligence had Anders setting up shop in an old volcano off on the edge of Southglen between the lush plains and the border to Mistvale.

"It's actually quite clever of him," Rilla commented when she'd first heard. "The area's been devastated for millions of years. It's all rock and scree. Not enough water to support plant life and not enough plant life to support game. Most people avoid it because it's just too difficult to traverse or cultivate. So he's had the place to himself for who knows how long."

"Oh great," Sorrel said. "Just what he needed. A head start."

They hurried on, racing to join the Southglen army camped on the plain just outside the desolated area.

The leaders of Southglen's allies had promised to send troops. In fact, Selene had left the Friendship games early to arrange for their march. But it took armies much longer to travel than a group of five, so they'd gone on ahead, hoping to reach the camp before Anders made his move.

They crested a hill at sundown and caught their first glimpse of the army camped below them. Tents spread across the plain and fires flickered to life as the sun went down.

It was the largest force they'd ever had to work with. But Vola couldn't help comparing it to the vast empty space beyond. The rock field lay flat and uninviting just past the last tent.

By the time they got down the hill, the sun had set and Rilla left them to get some sleep while she found the princess of the War Throne and let her know they'd returned.

In the dark, they just managed to squeeze their tent in between two others at the end of a row, and they secured the swamp beast outside, hoping it wouldn't get free to terrorize the camp before morning.

Vola slept fitfully that night, plagued by dreams of a faceless enemy that just kept running away. Whoever it was, they wouldn't stand and fight her.

She woke as dim light made its way through the flap of the tent, and she finally gave up on getting some rest. She slipped out of the tent, trying not to disturb her friends. Outside, she pulled on her boots and stood in the gray light just before dawn.

The camp was only just beginning to stir. They sat at the end of a row of tents, a trampled walkway between them and the next row. Down the way, toward the center of camp, a human in a stained apron rustled around a cookfire trying to get it lit. Across from them, someone stumbled out of their tent with a groan and shuffled off toward the latrines at the edge of camp.

Vola dug her hands into the small of her back and stretched. Her eyes still felt grainy and scratchy, but she knew closing them again wouldn't do any good.

Someone stepped up beside her, and Vola felt the air move before she even turned to see the Broken standing there. She was in her Greater Virtue shape, one leg, one arm, and covered in scars. But she'd dimmed the normal glow that seemed to emanate from her when she was being particularly godly. And Vola could barely make out the fiery wings behind her.

"Good morning," the Broken said amiably.

"Morning." Vola's voice came out rumbly, and she had to clear her throat.

"I don't sleep well before battle, either," the Broken said. "There were a lot of bad dreams in this place last night."

"And most of them don't even know what we're up against." Vola gestured to the man down the way who was returning from the latrine.

"No," the Broken said softly. "But they will soon find out. The dreams will get worse before they get better, I'm afraid." The Broken turned her head to look at Vola. "We are on the precipice. The edge before the storm."

"I kind of like storms, though," Vola said.

The Broken's lips twisted in a rueful smile. "Yes. But this one promises to be a downpour. Would you like an umbrella? Something to keep the rain off, maybe?"

Vola cocked her head. "What do you mean?"

"Come with me." The Broken beckoned and started off down the row of tents. She sort of floated, the fire at her back keeping her an inch or two above the ground.

Vola trotted to keep up.

Between one step and the next, Vola went from packed dirt and dead grass under her feet to smooth white tile. The air around her changed, the smell of musty canvas and hundreds of bodies packed together falling away and leaving fresh air that felt open and boundless.

Long white halls stretched on either side of her, opening into a chamber, echoing with soft whispers.

Vola scrubbed at her eyes, trying to rub away the grit. What the hell just happened?

"You know, I can hear when you think bad words, too," the Broken said. "Not just when you say them."

"Shi—I mean, crap."

The Broken grinned and led Vola to the center of the wide room. Vola got the impression there were no walls, just an eternal whiteness, and nothing bound them from above. No ceilings or balconies or anything.

Figures shifted and wavered around the room, indistinct shapes and colors with that endless whispering brushing against Vola's ears. She thought there might be chairs rising around her on tiers, but she couldn't exactly see them. When she tried to focus on one, she could make out edges and maybe the face of an occupant, but Vola had the distinct feeling that there was too much in that room for her to know or experience. Her mind could only grasp the barest edge of reality.

"Is everyone here?" a voice asked out of the air beside them. To Vola, it sounded obsequious, and nasally, like the speaker's nose was permanently stuffed. "Helleron? Yes, I'm afraid you must leave your party…Then bring the mutton with you, if you must."

The Broken cleared her throat.

"What?" the voice said. "Oh, all right."

An undulating figure solidified into a man, impossibly tall and slim with long limbs that had too many joints. Vola swallowed and decided not to look any closer. Besides, she recognized him from depictions in the temples and holy texts.

Vesteral, speaker of the gods. The man wasn't a god himself. He was a servant, immortal and implacable, dealing with every whim and fancy the gods could throw at him. His kind had lived many, many centuries ago, at the beginning of the world and had died out nearly a millennium before. He was the only one left.

"Sorry," he said to Vola. "We aren't used to having guests." He glared at the Broken, clearly not caring that she was one of the most powerful beings in the room.

Vesteral turned and an ebony staff appeared in his hand. He struck the foot of it against the tile floor with a clang that rang as if against walls, though there were still no walls. "Let's be official about this, shall we? I bring this summit to order."

Around the room the flashing colors of indistinct figures coalesced into individuals, men and women who sat or stood or lounged, exuding power in a way Vola couldn't quite explain to herself. They didn't glow, the way the Broken did in the real world, but something made Vola's stomach clench when she looked at them.

These were the Virtues and Obstacles that had thrown the Broken out of their ranks. These were the gods themselves, sitting on their thrones discussing mortal and immortal affairs as if they ordered breakfast.

The Broken touched Vola's shoulder and led her to an unoccupied side of the room. Vola stuck close to her.

It was one thing to serve the most powerful Virtue down in the real world. It was quite another to sit in the same room with the gods and see them as real people.

The Broken leaned toward her and gestured to a woman dressed in bright pink and orange. Her robes were cut wide and flowing but still managed to show off her graceful movements without tangling anything. Smile lines were etched around her mouth.

"Bierhel," the Broken murmured. "Greater Virtue of Joy. We can corner her later if you like. She does this joke of the day thing that really annoys some of the others but it always makes me laugh."

She pointed to a tall woman with straight white hair and a gray gown. "Ona, Greater Virtue of Honor. She's a popular one with the paladins." The Broken gave her a sidelong smile.

"And you know a little bit about Maxim from Sorrel, I expect." She jerked her chin at a man dressed in shining plate, standing as if at attention across from them. He'd removed his helmet to reveal artfully tousled black hair and a mouth pulled in a hard frown.

"Ah," Vola said. "Yes. He's, er, a bit hands-off when it comes to his followers."

The Broken sent a sad smile toward Maxim that he didn't notice. "Don't judge him too harshly," she said. "He cares...very deeply. And mortals are, well, mortal. You don't stick around very long compared to us. It can be very painful to care for someone who has such a short existence. Even knowing it is coming. We've all learned to live with the pain in different ways. Maxim has chosen to distance himself. He chooses many followers and allows many to choose him, but he doesn't allow himself to get close to any of them. It hurts him too much when they eventually leave."

Vola blinked. That wasn't something she'd ever considered before. To her, the years she'd spent with Cleavah and then the Broken had seemed long and fruitful, but her life was fleeting compared to the goddess.

"How do you live with the pain?" Vola asked quietly.

"I learned to make the most of every moment I have." She flashed a smile at Vola. "And I'm very picky about who I spend my time with."

Vola fought down a tingle of pride. "I'm honored, my lady, but...what exactly are we doing here?"

The Broken's smile thinned. "The same thing you were doing in the world. Gathering allies."

Vola's breath caught. "I thought...I thought they wouldn't listen to you."

"Not usually," the Broken said. "But this problem is anything but usual."

Before she could elaborate, the Greater Virtue of Honor stood.

"Right," Ona said, tilting her shoulder to let her fall of starlight-colored hair cascade behind her. "Shall we get on with it? I have some paladins that need looking after."

"What is this even about?" Maxim said. "I thought we all agreed the Broken could pursue this..." He waved a hand. "Quest with the mortals of this realm. Why must we concern ourselves with it as well?"

"You weren't at all concerned by the fact that this mortal enemy managed to strip me of my power?" the Broken asked into the silence. "Let's not pretend," she said sweetly as Maxim spluttered. "You all know who I am. You chose to cast me out because of it. And yet, this *mortal* managed to drain even me. He is a threat to all of us."

"Some of us recognize that, at least," Ona said and cast a glare at Maxim.

The Broken raised her chin. "I asked you here to this summit to establish what we intend to do about it. Practically."

"Fun," a voice said from the back. "I love strategy games. They're so much fun at parties."

Vola strained around the Broken to see who had spoken. A man lounged across his chair, skin slack as if he'd once been rotund but lost a lot of weight recently. He examined a leg of mutton in his hand before taking an enormous bite.

"Helleron," the Broken whispered. "Greater Obstacle of Debauchery."

Vola whipped around to stare at her. "The Obstacles are here?"

"This concerns them, too. Their power is as much at risk as ours. It's nice actually. I haven't seen us all together in one room in...quite some time."

Vola decided to take her word for it. Working with Obstacles had never really appealed to her, especially not as a paladin. She'd spent most of her adult life trying to get away from one in particular.

Her eyes searched the crowd for him, but she'd only ever heard his voice and fought his representatives. She didn't recognize him in the sea of faces.

"We could give the Broken over to this enemy," Helleron said, still munching his mutton. "While we all run and hide. That seems about right for us. Since we cast her out once already."

The gods chuckled, and the Broken flashed him a sharp smile. "I don't see that working for you this time around," she said. "Maybe if you'd taken the chance to flee when I was caught the first time."

"Now, he knows he can drain the gods," Vola said without thinking. "He'll be coming after you directly."

Vesteral's eyes narrowed at her.

Oof, had she just opened her mouth in front of the entire pantheon? She swallowed and tried to look like she wasn't completely freaked out.

"Ah yes," Maxim said. "Your mortal representative. How long has it been since you chose one?"

"Since my fall," the Broken said quietly. "I thought it was past time to choose another. This is a problem for all the world and therefore all the gods."

"You keep saying that," Maxim said, creases deepening around his mouth.

"I trust the Broken's judgment," Ona said. "In this and in all else."

The words fell like slabs across a stone floor, echoing with their own weight.

Vola swallowed. The gods hadn't wanted to risk being ruled by the Greater Virtue of Righteousness so they had cast her out. They'd only let her return when she promised not to try to rule them, to allow them to go their own ways. And she'd stood apart ever since. Was that changing?

Could it change? The pantheon was the pantheon. The war between gods was ancient history. Vola had never thought of it as something that was still happening.

"Very well," Maxim finally said. "Speak to us, representative. Tell us, what the mortals are doing."

"We're gathering our strength and our allies outside Anders's stronghold," Vola said. "We have other nations joining us for the assault and friends that we've gathered along the way who are lending their support." Or at least Vola hoped so. They'd sent all sorts of messages, but so far there'd been no replies.

We only just got to camp, she told herself. *Maybe there was a flood of people while we were gone.*

"That sounds promising," Maxim said.

Vola steeled herself to disagree with a god, but the Broken had brought her here for a reason. Clearly, she was supposed to help convince them. "Thanks, but I'm not sure it will be enough," she said.

Maxim tilted his head.

"Anders has the power of the world at his fingertips. Power to rival the gods."

Several of them shifted uncomfortably.

"We're going to need all the help we can get," she said. "More than mortals can provide." *Come on, take the hint.* They couldn't be dense enough to miss her meaning, could they?

Maxim frowned. "You have already taken care of his lieutenants, have you not? That seems plenty capable to me. Or are you saying that was a fluke?"

"Not a fluke," a familiar voice said from the back row. "Unless you doubt *my* power, Maxim."

A shudder went down Vola's spine. She'd heard that voice often enough this last year. And off and on before that. She still heard it occasionally, whispering in the back of her mind, urging her to lose her temper and destroy everything that stood in her way. She'd learned to work with it. She'd learned that losing her temper wasn't always bad. Righteous anger differed from straight up rage.

Vola lifted her chin and found Mulgash in the back row. Now that he'd spoken, she could match the voice with the face.

The man sprawled across a large chair looked nothing like an orc, which was disconcerting, since he was sort of their patron god. He was as pale as moonlight, with stark black hair and a straight nose. The only thing about him that indicated he was the Greater Obstacle of Rage was his round, bloodshot eyes.

Those eyes met Vola's, and his lips twitched in a tight little smile.

"Volagra and her team trounced my mortal representative. Spectacularly. If you'd like to dispute their might, you can talk to me. Convince me that I'm a weakling."

Maxim waved a hand. "We all know what you're capable of. I'm not disputing anything with you."

"Good." Mulgash crossed his arms and sat back. "Because if this threat has Mishap's Heroes worried, we should all be worried. Although, Volagra, I will expect a rematch when this is all over."

Vola glared up at the god of rage, trying to come up with a witty comeback, something scathing. And utterly failed. He'd just complimented her. In a room full of gods. And the Obstacles were here and ready to listen. She couldn't ruin that just because she'd fought with her rage her whole life and with Mulgash specifically.

But she'd also thrown his follower out a window, so she couldn't imagine his smile was entirely genuine.

As he said, they'd have to hash out their differences later.

The Broken didn't seem to have anything to say about this. She just watched them with amusement.

"Well, if that's the case," Maxim said, recalling their focus. "I suppose we can provide some backup."

Vola sucked in a breath. They'd won? After a divine war and millennia of ignoring the Broken, they were finally going to listen to her just like that?

"Some blessings here and there," he said. "Perhaps some holy weapons. That should do the trick."

The triumph drained from Vola's veins. "What? We're...the world is at stake and that's all you're going to give us?"

He was the god of Strength and Loyalty. You couldn't get much more warlike than him, and he was going to pass up the opportunity to actually go to war?

He gazed at her with sad eyes and spoke like he was explaining things to a recalcitrant puppy. "We are perfectly willing to help," he said. "But it sets a bad precedent to actually descend from on high and get involved personally. Obviously, there are some who do so anyway." He cast a look at the Broken. Her eyebrow twitched "But we will not bend the rules even for this."

"But…" Vola stood there, brow furrowed trying not to clench her fists. "We need more than that. A couple of blessings are not going to be enough here."

"Mortals do not grow if we don't allow them to solve their own problems. And there are…consequences even to us if we interfere."

He wouldn't meet her eyes.

Vola glanced at the Broken, seeking help.

The Broken's jaw clenched, and she stood. "Vola's right," she said quietly. "This is too big for them to handle. We need to do more."

"And are you forcing the issue, Broken?" Maxim's words snapped out.

The Broken glanced between him and Ona, who stiffened. There was a long pause where the Broken remained frozen, considering. "No," she finally said.

"Then we reserve the right to say no." Maxim turned with that final word and his image fuzzed and faded.

Many of the gods faded as well, following his example.

If the gods weren't led by anyone, then there should be some who were free to say yes as well, but it was clear to Vola who set the tone for the rest. They would follow where Maxim went.

Ona and Bierhel cast Vola and the Broken worried glances before they faded away as well.

Vola surveyed the pantheon as they disappeared into the air. There at the back of the pack, Mulgash remained, staring at her.

He tilted his head and gave her a sly smile. As if plotting something. Then he, too, faded and fuzzed away.

Vola turned to the Broken, who stood straight and tall. Unbowed by their opposition.

"It won't be enough," Vola said.

"I know."

"The consequences he was talking about," Vola said. "Did he mean caring? Is he worried about caring for mortals?"

"Sometimes the fear of pain can be greater than the fear of not doing anything."

"If they don't do anything, we could all die. Wouldn't that hurt more?"

The Broken's lips thinned. "Right now, he doesn't care enough about you for it to hurt. The gods will go on, even with all mortals gone. But if he intervenes…"

"Then he has to meet us on a personal level. He has to care about us and the fact that we might die."

"Yes," the Broken said, simply.

Someone cleared their throat, and Vola realized Vesteral was still there, looking at the ground at her feet. "I can show you out now, ladies," he said.

He walked off on his oddly long limbs. Vola caught a hint of regret in his eyes before he turned. Maybe he sympathized with a mortal species about to face extinction.

Maxim was their problem. The Broken was powerful, but even she'd admitted they needed the help of the rest of the gods. But Maxim and his fear stood in the way of that.

Then they would have to do something about that. They would have to make Maxim care. Care enough to help them and that would convince the rest of the gods.

And Vola had thought recruiting mortal allies was going to be the problem.

SIX

BETWEEN ONE STEP and the next Vola was back in camp, with the bare packed earth beneath her feet and the smell of burned porridge in her nose. She swayed, and a hand caught her elbow.

Vola blinked at Talon, the ranger's face drawn in concern.

"Are you back, now?" she said in her gravelly voice.

Lillie and Sorrel sat at their feet as if they'd been waiting for something. They stood when they saw Vola rub her face.

"What? What do you mean? Of course I'm back, I'm right here."

"Yeah, but you were right here this whole time without actually being here," Sorrel said, brushing off her backside. "You were just standing there staring off into space. It was a little creepy, to be honest."

"Oh," Vola said. "I didn't realize...the Broken took me somewhere. I didn't know it was only my mind that had gone. It felt real while I was there." She held out her hand, examining her greenish skin to see if it had changed somehow.

"That's the conclusion I drew when I couldn't find any sort of magic on you except for a sort of divine buzz," Lillie said. She picked up the towel she'd been sitting on. "We decided to guard you while we waited for you to return."

"Thanks," Vola said, cracking her neck. She might not remember it, but she felt stiff, like she'd been standing in one place for an hour. "I was probably safe enough; the Broken wouldn't have taken me otherwise. But it's nice to know someone's watching my back, anyway."

"Always," Talon said. She ducked into the tent and returned a moment later with her bow.

"First, tell us what was so important the Broken had to abduct you," Sorrel said. "No, wait. First, Rilla wanted to see us at the command tent. No, first the story."

Talon pushed her out into the lane between tents. "Walk and talk."

"We should also grab breakfast," Lillie said, following. "I have the feeling it will be a busy day."

Vola tried to describe the summit of the gods while they passed by the cook tent, but since she still wasn't sure how much her mortal brain had grasped, she had a hard time describing it.

"Ona seems to be on our side. Or at least she agrees that they need to do more than just sit up there and look pretty," she said, juggling a hot roll filled with cheese and sausage. "Maybe Bierhel, too. I get the impression they're my lady's friends in spite of everything that's happened between the gods. Mulgash even had some good things to say."

"Mulgash!" Sorrel yelped. "He was there?"

"All the Obstacles were. He…sort of defended us."

"Didn't we kick his ass?" Sorrel skipped out of the way of a soldier carrying a crate of weapons on his shoulder and hopped over a tent stake.

"That might be why," Vola said. "He saves face if a group of mighty heroes beat him, rather than…you know, us."

"Speak for yourself," Lillie said. "I am a mighty hero." Then she tripped over a guy wire and fell on her face.

"Very mighty," Vola said as she picked Lillie up. "My point is, this is going to be harder than I thought. Maxim…" She glanced at Sorrel, unsure of what exactly she should say about the halfling's god.

"Isn't exactly breaking down doors to come and help us," Sorrel said with a resigned shrug. "I'm aware."

"The Broken says it's because he cares too much. He doesn't want to get hurt. But we might need to get him to care more. At least enough to come down and do something."

"How do you get a god to notice what's going on?" Talon said. "They've been watching everything since the beginning. What can we do to get things to change?"

"I don't know," Vola said as they stepped between the last of the tents into the wide, open space at the center of camp where the princess of the War Throne had set herself up.

It might have been clearer here than in the ranks, but the open space bustled with soldiers visiting the quartermaster, boys running messages, and captains arguing at the edges of everything.

Vola skipped aside to let a runner through and found a large tent at the edge of the space with its front flap thrown open, either to welcome them in or to take advantage of the breeze.

A familiar figure in a dusty robe was bent over a table in the back with glassware and tubes stretching all over the interior.

"Myron?" Vola said.

The figure started, knocking over a rack of glass phials that poured their liquid contents into the dirt.

The tall, gangly elf blinked at the puddle, which rapidly turned the dirt into mud that smoked and steamed.

"Oh, that's probably not very good," he said.

"Should we, um, do something to clean it up?" Lillie asked.

The elf grabbed an empty bucket and flipped it over to cover the puddle. "No need," he said. "I've fixed it."

He finally looked up to see who had interrupted them. His straw blond hair had escaped its tie and fell in lank strands around his wan face. His eyes watered as he blinked.

"Oh, it's you," he said, brightening. "My first enemies. That was fun, wasn't it?"

Myron Vidal. Necromancer and researcher for Anders, providing him with power stolen from the dead. Vola was glad he didn't seem to have any hard feelings about the way they'd destroyed his lab or unleashed the army of undead that had turned on him to inflict their revenge.

"Hi, Myron," Vola said. "What are you doing here?"

"Trying to find a cheaper and more effective substitute for coffee," he said, gesturing to his glassware. "Something to keep the men alert without having to be brewed." He gazed ruefully at the bucket. Smoke drifted out from under the edges. "I have the alert part down. But I think most people will object to the way it eats their insides."

"Probably," Talon said, eyes on the smoke.

"I meant what are you doing in camp?" Vola said. "Last I heard you were still in a lab working for Rilla."

"Oh, I'm still working for her," Myron said. He pushed back his hair and leaned over to squint at the bubbling glassware. "She thought it would be good to have me along on the campaign. Anders is still using techniques he appropriated from me to store the power he steals."

"That makes sense." Sorrel crossed her arms and leaned against another table. Then she stepped back in alarm when something in a beaker hissed.

"Oh, yes. I don't generally do things that don't make sense. It's sort of a personal creed." He brightened. "Since you're here, would you like to try my coffee substitute? I still need test subjects—"

"Nope, nope, nope," Sorrel said as she disappeared out of the tent.

"Um, I think we'll pass, Myron," Lillie said. "Perhaps on a later version. When you have more data."

Vola shuffled backward, keeping herself between Myron and the rest of her party. "See you around, Myron. Be good."

"That's ambiguous," Myron muttered as they left. "I am good at many things. But which applies in this case?"

"Phew," Sorrel said as soon as they'd escaped. "That was close. He's as bad as he was when he was on Anders's side."

"I mean, he's not making zombies anymore," Talon said. "Or stealing their magic. That seems better, right?"

There was a crack and an echoing boom from behind them, and they jumped. Vola spun to see a column of smoke rising from Myron's tent.

"Yeah, better," she said weakly as soldiers and onlookers raced for the tent.

They hurried across the open space, ignoring the chaos behind them.

The command tent stood on a little hillock making it taller than the rest of the camp, and the flag of Southglen flew from its peak, two swords crossed over the crest to indicate that the Princess of the War Throne was in residence.

A group of gray-clad figures milled in front of the tent, sending nasty looks at another group of people dressed in armor and hoods.

Sorrel perked up. "Hazel," she cried.

The lead monk, a dwarf with thick brown hair and sharp blue eyes, turned at the sound of her name. Her face brightened when she saw Sorrel.

"Sorrel! We got your message calling for aid. Didn't bother sending a reply because we figured we'd beat it here."

Sorrel threw her arms around Hazel. The dwarf was only a foot taller than her, unlike most of the world.

"Good to see you, Hazel," Vola said.

The abbess of Sorrel's monastery nodded to Vola, Talon, and Lillie. "Likewise. We brought nearly everyone after Master Bao told us what happened in Firewatch. I hope we can help."

"Where is Master Bao?" Sorrel asked.

"Holding our place in camp," Hazel said with a glare at the group in armor and hoods. "Guarding our site against poachers."

"Poachers!" A man stepped up and pushed his hood from his head, revealing bright gold hair and a sour expression. "We need that space to be close to the command center. Battlemages are integral to the functioning of this army—"

"And we require a space close enough to the temple tent so we may continue our devotions." Hazel planted her hands on her hips. "Besides, we were there first."

The battlemage stepped forward, and Hazel dropped to sweep his legs out from under him.

"Whoa," Vola said as both sides of the argument surged forward. Monks and battlemages clashed as Vola thrust herself between Hazel and her target. She held the monk back by the collar and used her palm to keep the lead battlemage from advancing. She'd left her armor in the tent, but she was big enough to serve as a bulwark between the two factions.

"We're on the same side," Lillie said, hauling on a battlemage's arm.

"Ouch!" someone cried, and Talon danced away looking smug.

Vola exchanged a glance with Sorrel, and the monk gave her a grim nod. Vola let go of Hazel and let Sorrel drag her friend away while Vola concentrated on the battlemages. She put both hands on the leader's breastplate and shoved him back a step. He stumbled and crashed into his fellows. They went down like a faulty tower.

"Now," Vola said. "Maybe we can talk about this like adults and not like children."

"Causing trouble, Lightless?" a voice said behind Vola. "Why is it, every time there's a ruckus, a black paladin is involved?"

Vola stiffened as the voice reached deep past who she was now and pulled out the angry, helpless teenager she'd once been. She turned slowly, feeling like every joint and muscle had locked up in protest.

Lined up across from them, five men stood, armed and armored to the teeth. The one in the middle stared at Vola with light gray eyes.

Vola couldn't help noticing that Knight Commander Imralen still had a full head of thick white hair. If there'd been any justice in the world, he would have gone bald. Painfully.

Vola hadn't seen the paladin council or Knight Commander Imralen since they'd stood in the All-Pantheon temple in Glenhaven and stripped her of her rank, using holy fire to blacken her shield.

Something in her posture must have given her away. Lillie's breath caught in alarm, and Sorrel stepped up beside Vola to lay a hand on her forearm. Talon's leather creaked just over Vola's shoulder.

"You all right?" the ranger said.

Vola realized she wasn't breathing, and she forced air into her lungs. "Fine," she grated out between her teeth.

Knight Commander Imralen's gaze flicked over her shoulder, fastening on her shield. Even when she wasn't armored, she still carried it slung over her back. Not just because it was a rule—all black paladins had to declare themselves by carrying the sign of their disgrace—but because it was a significant part of who she was now. Her story was written in the blackened metal.

"Shouldn't you be curled up in a bar somewhere?" Imralen said, brushing imaginary dust from his arms. "That's all black paladins are usually good for."

"I decided to go the exterminator route," Vola said, crossing her arms. Her blood sang and the rage Mulgash was so fond of coursed just below her skin, but she'd had loads of practice holding it in check by now. This man had helped with that. "I take care of pests. If you decide to become a nuisance, I'll have to treat you like a pest, Imralen."

Imralen's face went a vivid red under his stark hair. "That's Knight Commander, if you please."

Vola raised her eyebrows. "Not to me," she said. And turned her back on him.

Holy Broken, that had felt good. She'd never brought herself to talk back to him before or to any of the masters. They'd held her career in their hands, and she hadn't dared jeopardize it. But with her shield blackened, she had nothing left for them to take away.

"Don't ignore me, black paladin," Imralen said, his voice ratcheting up a notch.

She smirked. "Now, where were we?" she asked the monks and battlemages. "I think we can settle this like professionals and not like squabbling children, can't we?"

Vola deliberately met Hazel's gaze first since she knew her personally.

Hazel sighed and removed her arm from Sorrel's grip, catching Vola's drift. "I can do that," she said. "Maxim applauds strength and courage, and he knows that negotiation requires both."

The head battlemage inclined his head after only a brief hesitation. "I'm willing to listen to anyone who's willing to insult the Knight Commander," he murmured.

The flap of the command tent flipped back with a slap of canvas, and the princess of the War Throne stepped through, Rilla close on her heels.

"Where are Mishap's Heroes? We need to get this—Oh, there you are," the princess of the War Throne said as she caught sight of them between the three factions.

When the War Princess was being official, she piled her gold curls on her head in an elaborate up-do that showed off the long graceful curve of her neck and downplayed the sharp angle of her nose. Today she'd pinned her tight braids back, ready for business, and her profile reminded Vola of a hawk eying its prey.

"Your Highness," Imralen said, taking a step forward. "We have brought the paladins you requested. The entire council and our troops are at your disposal."

"Great," War said without even a glance. "We'll see you on the battlefield."

Imralen spluttered. "Your Highness. We expected a more personalized welcome."

War's eyes narrowed. "What? You need a commendation for doing your jobs? No, sir. I'm not here to babysit you. What? What are the rest of you here for?" She glared at the monks and the battlemages.

"Er, there was a dispute over camping spaces, Your Highness," the battlemage said, quite bravely Vola thought.

"Like I have time to manage that. Lightless, you and your team are up. Let's go."

She spun and let the tent flap close behind her.

Vola glanced at the two factions.

Sorrel caught her look. "You go. I'll handle this." Her gaze slid to the paladin council. "And those."

"But the meeting…" Lillie said.

"You can fill me in later. I'm not much for decisions, anyway." She walked backwards still talking. "I'll go wherever you need me."

"Your Highness," Imralen said, voice going sharp.

"Come on, buddy," Sorrel said, taking his hand like he was a big child. "You had your chance. You blew it. Now retreat gracefully."

Vola bit her lips hard to keep from laughing as she turned her back on the council and led her party into the command tent.

Inside the central space, a large table held a map and strategic markers. A rumpled cot stood along the back wall, partially obscured by a curtain.

Rilla strode to the edge of the table and stared down at it with bleary eyes.

"Did you sleep at all?" Vola asked. The princess hadn't returned to the tent last night, and Vola hadn't been sure if it was because she didn't feel welcome or if it was because she hadn't found the time to go to bed.

Looked like the latter.

Rilla shook her head absent mindedly.

"You know, technically you're still under my command." Vola spoke while staring down at the map, too. "I could order you to rest."

Rilla snorted, then rubbed her eyes. "You sound ridiculous," she said. "But technically…you're right. And I will sleep as soon as this is done. I'll need the rest for what comes next."

Vola opened her mouth to ask for more details, but the War Princess stepped up to the table from the other side and cleared her throat.

Lillie and Talon stared down at the table, waiting patiently.

"Right, we're in as good a position as any," War said. "The Shield Princess is on alert back in Glenhaven. She will hold the line if anything gets past us. But it's our job to be sure nothing gets past us."

Vola nodded and surveyed the map and the tiny troops arrayed across it. The army camp rested on the very edge of the arable land surrounding an ocean of dark rock barrens. The volcano rose in the middle. Anders's stronghold.

"We haven't exactly been stealthy up to now," War said.

Rilla snorted.

"All right, not stealthy at all. But we also haven't been telegraphing our plans. Anders knows we're here. But hopefully that's about all he knows. And if we strike now, we may catch him scrambling to gather his own defenses."

"Are we ready for that?" Vola asked. "Do we have enough people?" She couldn't help thinking of the gods that should have been helping but weren't.

Rilla's lips twisted. "There are still some trickling in. But War is right. We need to make our move."

Vola took a deep breath and looked down at the map. "All right, then. Where do you need us?"

War took up a marker carved to look like an angular orc. "As front and center as anyone's gonna get. I hope you're ready for some action."

SEVEN

"I CAN'T DECIDE if this is a step up or a step down," Talon said, moving smoothly over the rough lava rock that blanketed the hills. Trees still stood, breaking the monotony of the burned plain. They were scraggly and twisted, burned long ago when the mountain had erupted and lava had flowed over the land. But their preserved corpses still marked the party's path.

"You were the one who seemed excited about scout duty," Vola said. "I just kept nodding my head and now here we are."

"Scouting for an army is pretty important," Sorrel said, clambering up a round outcropping of black stone. "And technically we're still working directly for a princess as well as directly *with* a princess." She grinned back at Rilla.

Rilla looked much better today. The six-hour nap she'd taken directly after their planning session had probably helped. Vola was rather proud the princess had trusted them to get the party's gear from the quarter-master and everything kitted out. She knew Rilla was particular about that sort of thing.

The princess had ditched her simple yet elegant jerkin for a leather cuirass, tight enough Vola couldn't see how she could actually move, and thigh-high boots lashed in place. She was lined with more buckles and straps than a packed-up tent, each one holding a knife or dart or vial of something deep and black.

Vola didn't ask the spymaster what she kept in her pockets. She was better off not knowing.

Scouting wasn't exactly glamorous. But it got them out of camp where people were starting to pick fights and step on each other's toes just for the fun of it. An army could only sit in one place for so long before it started to fall apart from the inside.

Gruff ranged out in front of them while Lillie's familiar, Rand, kept an eye on him from above.

The eerie cry of a gull a million miles from any body of water echoed across the rocky terrain and they angled themselves toward the spot where the War Princess wanted to stage the first assault.

"Hazel's team is keeping up well," Vola said. The abbess and her monks were out there supporting them from either side. Since no one knew what Anders was capable of with the power he'd already stolen, Vola hadn't wanted to advance alone. And both Rilla and the War Princess had agreed.

"Of course, they are," Sorrel said. "An abbey full of monks could take on an entire army." She paused at the top of a small rise and glanced back. "Er. They won't have to take on a whole army. Will they?"

Vola hesitated and shared a look with Rilla.

"There are reports of troops moving across the old lava field," Rilla said. "They aren't ours."

"So, Anders is gathering his own troops," Lillie said quietly.

"Who would be fighting for him?" Sorrel raised a hand to shield her eyes. The day was hazy. No fog, but with low-hanging clouds that reflected enough light to disorient them and still keep everything rather dim. "And why? He's the bad guy."

"Bad guys always have minions," Talon said. "Don't they?"

"Yeah, but what is he promising them?"

"Maybe some of the power he's been collecting," Lillie said. "That would be a temptation to a lot of people."

"Either way, it's a good thing we've got the monks along," Vola said. "I feel better with them around."

"Me, too," Sorrel said cheerfully and hopped off the rise. "Oh wait. You mean for combat. Yeah, that too."

Lillie smiled at her. "Have you been catching up, then?"

"Well, I mean, I did sort of send them all off with a slap on the wrist and an admonishment to be good for Hazel. It's nice to see that they're actually following her. I knew she'd make a good abbess."

"Did you get them to make nice with the battlemages?"

"That was easy. They all wanted the same spot, so I told them none of them could have it. I gave them spaces that were equidistant to everything, right next to each other. Now they have to learn to live with each other."

"What about the...the council?" Lillie asked, glancing at Vola.

"Well, I figured Vola didn't want to be running into them every other hour so they're on the other side of camp."

Vola winced. "It's fine. I don't actually resent them."

Talon gave her a look. "Yeah, right, try another one."

"I don't," Vola said. "I still think they're terrible old men with more power than is good for them, but they don't have any power over me anymore. And what's funny is they were the ones who made it that way. They freed me. I have all the support I need between you guys and the Broken."

Lillie gave her a sappy smile and Talon snorted.

"Aw, that's so sweet," Sorrel said. "But I still put them downwind of the latrines."

Vola choked on a laugh.

"Not only do they have to smell them constantly, they'll be awake all night as everyone and their dog traipses past to pee."

A short bark interrupted their laughter, and Gruff came bounding over the rough terrain and skidded to a stop beside Talon. He wound himself around her, whimpering.

Instantly, the rest of them circled up, keeping their backs to each other, surveying the terrain.

"What's wrong?" Vola said. "What did he find?"

"I'm not sure. He says it's a wall. But a regular wall wouldn't have spooked him this bad."

"Lillie, you want to check with Rand?"

Lillie's eyes were already closed, and Sorrel moved to cover her while she connected with the raven.

"Gruff's right," she murmured. "It's a wall. Of light. Right across the spot where War wanted to stage our assault."

"Is it an ambush?"

"I don't believe so." Lillie shook her head as she broke her connection.

"Then we should check it out," Rilla said. She glanced at Vola. "That is, if you want to. I'm still following your orders out here."

Vola's lip twitched. "And I take suggestions from my team. Move out."

The War Princess had designated a spot in the bend of an old river.

The meandering stream bed had been completely destroyed when the mountain erupted, but you could still see the edge of its course where the rest had been blown away.

"Geez," Sorrel said, prodding the lava rock, which had broken down into gravel-shaped pieces. "What happened here?"

"Steam," Lillie said shortly. "When the lava hit the river, it exploded in steam. It's quite spectacular, I'm told."

"As spectacular as that?" Rilla said and pointed ahead of them.

A shimmering barrier cut directly through their target area, straight, smooth, and slightly opaque. It glimmered like the surface of a pearl or those lights that floated in the sky far to the north. Mostly white but shot through with bits of blue, green, and purple.

It stretched higher than Vola was tall and disappeared somewhere in the low clouds above them.

"What is that?" Vola said.

"A wall?" Sorrel suggested.

"That's like no wall I've seen," Vola said.

"It reminds me of the wards around Glenhaven," Rilla said. "Only..."

"Only what?" Vola said.

She smiled ruefully. "Only I'm not keyed to these. I have no idea how to get past."

"Are we sure it's really blocking the way?" Sorrel said.

"How about you run at it and tell us?" Talon said.

Sorrel tilted her head. "Fair point."

"How far does this go?" Rilla asked. "Our previous scouts haven't seen it before. Gods, how many are trapped on the other side? I have to contact War." She stepped back and pulled a palm-sized mirror from one of her many pouches.

"Sorrel, can you signal the monks?" Vola asked, still staring. "Warn them if they haven't found it already, and if they have, ask if they've found the edges."

"Can do." Sorrel scrambled up a ridge parallel to them and cupped her hands around her mouth to cry like a gull.

Rand circled over them, angling his wings to keep an eye out on all sides.

Lillie shook her head. "Rand says this goes as far as he can see on either side. It circles the entire lava field with the volcano directly in the center."

Vola's lips thinned. "Seems likely to be Anders's work then."

Gruff crept forward a couple of steps, his nose snuffling toward the glowing wall.

"Stay back from it, Gruff," Talon said. "We don't know what it does."

"Lillie, do you have anything for that?" Vola gestured helplessly toward the wall. "Something that would tell us what it is, what it does. How to get rid of it."

"I'm not sure…" Lillie started. "Well, I guess there is one thing."

She whispered under her breath, and above them, Rand gave a sharp croak. He spun on his tail feathers and arrowed straight for the wall.

He struck the surface with a brief, blinding flash of light and a surprised squawk. Singed feathers fell around them.

"Holy shit," Vola said. Lightning cracked against the rock at her feet.

"Oh my gods, he's dead," Talon said. "Did you just kill Rand on purpose?"

"I didn't! I just asked him to test the solidity," Lillie said.

"And he couldn't think of a better way?"

"Well, I needed him to touch it in order to try something."

"Does it really count as murder if he's a familiar she can summon over and over again?" Vola said.

Talon's face screwed up. "That doesn't make me feel any better about it."

"I'll have him back as soon as I can sit down and cast the spell," Lillie said. "In the meantime, I learned several things."

"Like what?" Rilla said, stepping back over the rough ground.

"That barrier is stronger than anything I've ever seen," she said. "And it stretches at least two stories up which is where Rand was when he hit it."

"Is it even stronger than the wards Rilla was talking about?" Sorrel asked, sliding down a ridge to rejoin them.

"I think so," Lillie said. "I tried to dispel it through Rand as he struck." She shook her head. "I'm not a battlemage or anything but the way it just absorbed my power…Nothing got through. This is…I think this is what he's been doing with all the power he's collected so far."

"Hazel says the monks have found the same thing where they are. They're within calling distance, so not far, but no one's been dumb enough to touch it."

Talon glared at Lillie, who winced.

"So this is made up of all the magic Anders has managed to steal so far?" Rilla said, eying the barrier up and down.

"Yes," Lillie said. "I can do more tests to confirm but…if I had to guess from what we've encountered so far, it's made up of more than one kind of magic."

"The living, the dead, and the land," Talon said.

"And the Broken," Vola added. "The piece he got away with."

Lillie bit her lip and tilted her head back to examine the barrier. "Which will only make it stronger."

"And the only way to get to Anders," Vola said. "Is to break through."

EIGHT

As THE REST of them stood there staring at the barrier in dismay, Sorrel stooped to pick up a rock and bounced it off the rough ground so it flew at the ward.

The barrier crackled and then shimmered for a few seconds.

Sorrel shaded her eyes. "Could anyone see if that went through?"

Vola started to shake her head and then froze. The air around them wavered, and fog seeped up from the ground. Fog that hadn't been there two seconds ago.

"Form up," Vola said and drew her sword. The others centered on her, backs to each other as they watched the fog warily.

"Lillie, is this harmful?"

Lillie touched the circlet on her brow. "It's not elemental or poisonous, as far as I can tell. It's...an illusion?"

The fog drifted upward and clumped into large lumps, forming bulbous figures. The figures solidified, gaining weight and detail.

It was a little like watching the gods meld into reality, except way less colorful.

Vola blinked at the new terrain.

Instead of the endless black lava rock, there were now fields. Green grass and yellow wheat waved under a summer sun and a blue sky. Ahead of Vola, a barn stood beside a picturesque little farmhouse.

Nearby, a boy of about fourteen or fifteen raised a hoe over his head and brought it down, striking the ground in time to the off-key tune he was humming.

Vola felt a little pang. He looked a lot like Finn, although Finn had grown up in the city and picked pockets for his living rather than digging in the dirt.

Other forms worked out in the fields, a man and a woman and another girl at least.

"You're all seeing this, too, right?" Talon said.

"Idyllic farm, almost too perfect for words?" Rilla said. "Yup."

"What in Maxim's holy name is this?" Sorrel said.

"Lillie?"

"It's…definitely magic," Lillie said, touching her circlet.

Vola rolled her eyes.

"No, really? You think?" Sorrel said. She'd pulled the Warhammer from her back and held it out as if the farm boy was about to leap on them, teeth bared.

"Does anyone else feel like this is vaguely familiar?" Talon said.

"Yeah," Sorrel said. "Me."

"It's just like Lord Arthorel's manor," Vola said. "He had rooms full of immersive illusions just like this. Where you'd swear you were in a place." She glanced at Lillie. "Can you dispel it?"

"I can try. This might be above my pay grade."

"I guess you'll have to apply for a raise," Rilla said. She also watched the surroundings warily.

Lillie raised her hands to start a counterspell.

"Anders!" one of the distant figures called. "Time to come in for dinner."

Vola reached out to stop Lillie, but the wizard froze, her mouth hanging open.

"Anders?" Talon hissed. "As in our Anders?"

"Do we really want to claim him?" Sorrel asked.

"Shh," Vola said. "What's happening?"

The fifteen-year-old Anders propped his hoe on his shoulder and started for the house and the barn. But before he'd taken two steps, a scream rang out from the buildings.

Flames spread across the fields and licked up the sides of the farm-house, faster than was physically possible. Vola had the disorienting sensation of skimming through time.

"Mama!" the boy cried. "Pa!"

He raced across the fields, his hoe held like a weapon.

Dark figures swarmed the scene, faceless shadows wielding torches and grisly weapons.

Vola's heart leaped.

"What do we do?" Talon said. "This is…this is just a spell, right? A memory or…something."

Vola exchanged a glance with Sorrel as the dark figures cut through the door of the farmhouse. Sorrel's brow was set and her lips thin.

The boy lifted his face to the sky. "Please, help them!" he cried, as if praying. He swung his hoe at the nearest enemy and was struck down.

Vola's mouth twisted in a grimace. "In Lord Arthorel's manor, we dispelled the illusions by fighting them. Or confronting their realness."

"You want to do the same here?" Rilla asked.

Vola drew her sword. "Yes. And…and I can't just stand here."

"Me neither," Sorrel said. She sprang forward, staff swinging.

Vola signaled Rilla and Talon to flank as she followed Sorrel into the fray. Lillie stayed behind, weaving a spell through the air.

"Are we really helping the enemy?" Talon said, but she moved into position, anyway.

"He's a boy," Lillie called. "An illusory boy."

"Yeah, he's not tall enough to be our enemy, yet." Sorrel leaped at the first wave of faceless fighters and disappeared between their legs.

"That has nothing to do with it," Vola said. "Nargilla was shorter."

"I wasn't actually going to stop you," Talon said. "I was just pointing out the irony."

Vola smashed aside an attack with her shield and swung her sword around in an arc that cut one of the dark shadows from neck to knee. It dissolved in a swirl of smoke.

Definitely illusions.

Vola spun and dropped to one knee to avoid a blow to her head and brought her blade up to block another swing. She swung her shield around and bashed the shadow so it stumbled back. Straight into Talon's daggers.

Rilla ducked a blow and came up under the shadow's guard, twisting her blades into its neck. It dissolved into black smoke.

Vola winced. She'd never enjoyed staring at a man's face while he died on her blade, but faceless enemies were somehow worse. You couldn't look them in the eye. You couldn't look for clues about their actions or motivations. Even monsters were better than this. A wyvern defended its nest; an ogre needed to feed its family.

These were just shapes that fought and advanced like a thinking creature but wore the blank aspect of a shadow.

Vola whirled and chopped, surrounded by writhing bits of black fog both solid and not. Impossible to keep track of her people. It was her duty to protect them, but they were swallowed by the miasma, torn away from her as she fought.

Was this Anders's story? Had he really lived through this attack? Or was this the foggy recollection of a terrified boy? Blown out of proportion by fear and confusion.

Maybe it was both.

Vola shouldered her way through another shadow, throwing it to the ground and planting her blade so deep in its chest the point stuck in the soft earth underneath.

And the rest of the shadows faded away around her.

Sorrel stood nearby, leaning against the side of the burning farmhouse, panting. Blood trickled into her eyes from a cut at her hairline. Rilla crouched in the dirt, blades up and crossed, as if waiting for the next blow. Talon spun, looking wildly around the empty farmland, her daggers searching for more enemies.

Lillie stood where they'd left her, staring at the spell stretched thin and glowing between her hands.

In front of the house, Anders knelt, his face streaked with sweat and soot, his hands curled around a bloody hoe. Figures lay crumpled on the ground around him as tears streamed down his face.

"Why?" he croaked, voice hoarse from shouting or from the smoke. It billowed thick and black above them. "Why didn't you save them?"

Vola wasn't sure who he was talking to until he tilted his head and aimed a glare at the sky.

Boots crunched in the gravel of the narrow road that passed in front of the house.

Vola raised bleary eyes to see a man with midnight skin and dark eyes kneel beside Anders. He wore a set of mismatched armor, chainmail shirt under a leather cuirass with plate pauldrons, and rusted metal greaves. But he made it look good. Well-used by someone who knew what they were doing.

He reminded Vola strongly of Henri.

"The gods can't do everything," the man said, voice low and steady. "And you weren't strong enough to do it yourself. Not yet."

Anders stared up at him, the bodies of his family in the dirt around him.

The man extended a hand, and the boy took it.

Light flashed as their palms touched and the scene around them smeared and dissolved into the earth.

Vola was left kneeling on the rough lava rock, her sword piercing the stone as little fissures snaked away from the blade.

The others remained in their positions, just breathing the damp cool air, eyes still wide with shock and exhaustion.

Beside them the glowing barrier still rippled, flecks of green and blue and purple streaking its surface.

A rumble shook the earth at their feet, and the wall of light shimmered.

Then slowly, it pulled back, gliding over the rock away from them, shrinking towards the center where Anders's stronghold stood.

It slowed and stopped another seven hundred yards away. Just far enough that they could still see it standing there. Waiting.

"All right," Sorrel said, using the staff to push herself upright. "I'll say it again. What the hell was that?"

"Anders's memory?" Talon said.

"An illusion," Rilla said.

"Yes, but an illusion can still depict something real. Or remembered," Vola said. She picked herself up off the ground and yanked her sword free of the rock. Little flames licked through the fissures before dying out completely.

"But why..." Sorrel waved a hand at the distant barrier. Blood still trickled down her face. "Why did that move?"

"They're connected," Lillie said.

Rilla and Talon finally relaxed and gathered themselves. "What?" Rilla said.

"The illusion was connected to the barrier. That's what I was doing inside it. I was trying to see what it was anchored to. You were right. It is just like Lord Arthorel's manor. We broke the illusion, either by fighting the shadows with Anders or by completing the story he was trying to tell. And breaking the illusion broke its hold on the barrier."

Vola stared off at the glow on the horizon.

"But it's not gone completely."

"No."

Vola sighed. "So there are more illusions. More keys to break to get to the stronghold."

Lillie chewed her lip. "That does seem to be the case. I sensed at least four more anchor points while we were in there. We will have to break them all to get to the stronghold."

"Of course we do," Vola muttered. "You can never just walk up and storm the castle. There always has to be something, someone who thinks they're so clever."

"We're sure Lord Arthorel is put away, right?" Sorrel asked.

"He's serving his time in jail," Rilla said.

"Anders must have learned a trick or two from him before he was arrested," Talon said.

"I'll send word to put him under heavy guard, just to be sure," Rilla said.

"I take it we're going to have to see the rest of Anders's life story," Sorrel said. "In order to advance."

"Seems likely," Vola said. "There's obviously something he wants us to see."

"Typical," she said with a sniff. "Why are all bad guys narcissists?"

NINE

THEY RETURNED to camp by a straighter route this time, not having to be so careful to avoid Anders's attention. Clearly, he was prepared for them already.

The monks came, too, filing in beside them as if they'd just appeared out of the rocky landscape.

Around them, the army packed up, breaking down tents and camp furniture, loading everything onto the mules that would carry it or into the packs of individual soldiers. The War Princess must have assumed they'd either have good news, and they could advance, or bad news, and they'd have to retreat.

The cook had packed up his fire, wood, and all since there was little fuel to be had out on the lava field and a line of angry soldiers stretched away from his site. All of them had waited just a little too long to collect their lunches.

Myron puttered around, collecting his glassware and packing it carefully in sawdust-filled boxes. The sides of his tent were still a little blackened from his coffee-substitute explosion the day before, as were his robes, but on the bright side, the flames had given his hair a trim for him.

The command tent had already been struck by the time they got there. War stood by, dressed in gold-tooled leather, her hair pinned close to her head as she surveyed the packing of her maps and cot.

She caught sight of them and raised her chin. "Tell me," she said.

Vola wasn't sure how much she could read from their expressions, but she started at the beginning.

"We can advance to the location," she said. "But there's a complication. Anders erected a barrier miles and miles around the mountain. He's effectively penned himself in, and it won't be easy to get to him."

War rubbed her brow. "Always another thing."

"Hey, that's the same thing Vola said," Sorrel exclaimed.

"Why did you say we can advance?" War asked. "If that barrier is keeping us out?"

"We know how to take it down," Rilla said, crossing her arms. "Though it's annoying and circuitous, we can eventually get the army to the mountain. Or whatever is waiting for us in his lands. We still have those mystery troops to deal with."

"How?" War apparently wasn't one to waste words in a crisis.

"We found the anchor keys to the spell," Lillie said. "He's hidden them within illusions around the barrier. As long as we continue to break through them, we can push back the barrier, bit by bit."

"You were right," War said. "Tedious in the extreme. But I suppose we don't have a choice?"

"We can get someone in from the universities to study the barrier," Rilla said. "Maybe they'll have some better ideas for removing it. Sometimes a battering ram is better than a lockpick."

War placed her hand on her chest, as if surprised. "I never thought I'd hear you say that."

"Yeah, well, enjoy it while it lasts. If I get the chance to stab Anders in the back without warning, I'm taking it."

"You have my blessing," War said with a smirk. "It would save me a lot of trouble. Right, Mishap's Heroes. I guess this means you have a job to do. You'll ride out ahead of us and make sure we have somewhere to march to."

"A bad idea, to be sure," a voice said.

Vola's spine stiffened. Sorrel might have put them at the far end of camp, but of course, that didn't mean the man couldn't walk in order to make her life miserable.

"Excuse me?" she said, turning to glare at Knight Commander Imralen. "I wasn't aware you had a say."

"I should," he said. "I should have more of a say in the operations of this company than a black paladin with no rank. That's exactly why I requested a meeting with you, Your Highness."

"Which I couldn't duck out of," War muttered.

"The paladins have always been a cornerstone of Southglen's martial might. We are the ones people turn to, the ones people trust when there are bandits or robberies or anything requiring honor and strength. We are essential. Which means we should be a part of your war council. We should be making decisions alongside you as our monarch."

"When I need the opinion of a war council, I will ask for it," War said.

"And yet you continuously consult this black paladin, who was publicly stripped of her rank and thrown out of our sacred order for her actions."

War lowered her chin. "I am aware of the allegations against her. I'm also aware of how she's held herself, both before her demotion and after."

"You see the surface," Imralen said. "You see what she wants you to see."

"You know the best part about being a black paladin," Vola said, examining her fingernails. "Is that I don't actually have to stand here and take your hatred anymore. I can fight back."

"Is that a threat?" Imralen said, looking down his nose at her. He had to tilt his head back and squint to do it. "Do you see how your animal is threatening me?" he asked War.

"Watch your tone," Rilla said.

"I meant," Vola said with a glare of her own. "That if you don't like me, if you really have a problem with what I'm doing here, I'll meet you in fair combat. We'll let the gods decide."

War snorted. "That's hardly fair." She turned to Imralen and cocked her head. "You know, the gods chose her as their spokesperson. She represents the Broken. You really want to argue with the Greater Virtue of Righteousness?"

Imralen's mouth twisted and thinned.

"Or if you're afraid to go up against her," Sorrel said. "I'll happily fight you. I've served as a champion before. Come on. You wouldn't be afraid to fight me? Would you?" Her grin held far too many teeth as she tipped her head back to meet Imralen's gaze.

"Or me?" Lillie said.

"Do Rilla and I have to volunteer, too?" Talon said, exchanging a look with the Dagger Princess. "Or can we just assume you two will flatten him so he never gets up again?"

"Or I can just make it official and say no one is fighting anyone," War said, her hands planted on her hips. "Duels and honor fights have no place in a camp that's marching to war. In fact, I'll court-martial any party who pursues this conflict past today." She huffed and crossed her arms. "That's my official edict. My personal one is this..." She stepped up to Imralen, nose to nose. "Leave Volagra Lightless alone. You enacted your punishment upon her. And that's the end of her relationship with you. She is more essential to this war effort than you are, and if you go after my people again, I will kick your ass so hard you'll land back in Glenhaven. Do I make myself clear?"

Imralen's teeth crunched as he clenched his jaw. "Yes, Your Highness."

He spun and left the clear space which was rapidly transforming into trampled mud as soldiers and assistants packed out the last of the tents.

"Well, now that we're all friends again," War said, and Vola snorted.

War narrowed her eyes at her. "You and your team have a job to do. Do whatever you have to do to get us through that barrier. Take those illusions down. We'll be advancing behind you, so we're counting on you."

Vola straightened and gave her a sharp nod.

"Vola," War said as she started to turn with the others. "I don't blame you for wanting to bash his teeth in. But I meant what I said. God's representative or not, I'll kick you out of here if I find you've engaged with him in any way. Keep yourself out of his way and we won't have a problem."

"Understood, ma'am." There had been a brief moment where she'd thought she could finally pay the Knight Commander back for all the hurt he'd caused her during training. But even if she was a black paladin, she was still a paladin. And defending her reputation was not a good enough reason for violence.

She jerked her head at the others and they trotted back through the dissolving chaos of the camp. They still had to pull down their tent and load up the swamp monster. Then they'd have to find someone brave enough to wrestle with the creature while the army moved and Mishap's Heroes went on ahead.

On the other side of the quartermaster's tent, which was half packed away already, a hand shot out and gripped her elbow, hard enough to pinch the skin in the gap of her armor.

She reacted, twisting around and throwing her attacker over her hip.

Imralen landed on his feet with a glare.

Vola held up her hands. "I'm under strict orders not to kill you," she said. "Are you trying to get me kicked out?"

Imralen's face hardened. "Yes."

Vola rolled her eyes. Ask a stupid question...

Imralen stepped close, and Vola refused to retreat from him. She raised her chin, stretching to her full height. Imralen didn't seem to notice.

"You are a beast," he sneered. "A beast of burden. You don't fool me.

That veneer of civilization will crack, and then everyone will know you for what you are."

Vola rubbed her nose. "Your words don't mean anything to me anymore, Imralen. You lost your chance to earn my respect."

He shook his head. "An animal's bleating. Know this, I will defy the princesses to expose you. I will go up against the gods themselves to show everyone that you're not fit to carry that shield."

He spun on his heel and strode off through the camp.

"Well, that'll be fun," a voice said.

Vola cocked an eyebrow at Sorrel. "How long have you been standing there?"

"Does it matter? I think I could feel his hate from a mile away. You gonna watch out for him?"

Vola shrugged and started walking, catching up to the others. "I don't have much of a choice. War doesn't want me to play his game so I won't play."

"There are lots of other things he can do to hurt you other than fighting you directly."

"Then I'll have to deal with them when they come up, won't I? I can't engage."

"Maybe *you* can't," Sorrel muttered, hurrying to keep up.

Vola didn't blame the monk for wanting to fight back. Her skin crawled knowing Imralen was out there working against her somehow. And she knew nothing she said would keep Sorrel from watching her back, officially and unofficially. She just hoped her second in command was patient enough to keep it under wraps.

Mishap's Heroes led the army to the spot where they'd relived Anders's memory, and War declared they camp there until Vola and the others had pushed the barrier back some more.

Rilla insisted they set up their tent near the command tent this time. Maybe she suspected Imralen would try something less official, too. Or maybe she figured it would be easier to keep an eye on War from there. The Princesses of Southglen got along better than most siblings and War was perfectly capable of taking care of herself, but Rilla's nature made her suspicious and she tried to situate herself so she could protect her fellow royalty when she was able.

They had their tent up in ten minutes flat and Lillie hung her robe in the corner to give it a homier feel. Vola couldn't help remembering how long it took them in the beginning. How much cursing was involved and how many times they'd slipped and fallen into the swamp.

Not only did they work faster now, they could divvy up chores without even exchanging a word. Vola and Lillie pitched the tent while Talon took care of the swamp beast, making sure it was tethered as far away from the horse picket line as possible, and that there were enough turtles to satisfy it and keep it in one place for the night. Rilla had procured the beast's feast. And Sorrel had trotted off to the mess tent to look for some food for the rest of them.

On the lava field, the command tent sat on the same level as everything else, a little more understated than before. Probably a tactic to ensure that War didn't attract Anders's attention. Vola doubted an assassin could make it all the way through their camp *and* Rilla, but it paid to be careful.

Of course, that meant, she was harder to find in general.

"Excuse me," a soft-spoken voice said. "We're supposed to report to the Princess of the War Throne, but we seem to have gotten turned around. All these tents look the same."

The voice was familiar enough that Vola straightened with a frown and turned to find a short plump human wringing his hands behind her. He'd trimmed his graying hair since she'd last seen him, but the shape of his face still strongly reminded her of Lillie.

"Lord Ephyra," Vola said. "I wasn't expecting to see you here. What brings you?"

A young man poked his head out from behind Lord Ephyra. He was slim with reddish hair and Lillie's eyes. Her brother, Kellan.

"Volagra, correct?" Lord Ephyra said, his eyes lighting up with recognition. "Good to see you again, young paladin." He thrust his hand out to shake Vola's as if he were a common merchant. "We came with the university scholars." He gestured to the six or seven men and women behind him who stood shifting their feet, glancing around nervously.

"Hey, Lillie," Talon called through the tent flap. "Get out here."

"What is—Father!" Lillie cried, untangling herself from the tent. She lunged across the space and threw herself into her father's arms.

"Welcome, Lord Ephyra," Rilla said, with a smirk. "You'll forgive me for not throwing myself on you."

Lillie drew herself away with a flush and turned her attention on Kellan.

"You're forgiven, Your Highness," Lord Ephyra said with a chuckle. "We were on our way with the results of our research on Anders's spell when we received word that there was a new complication. A barrier of some sort? We decided to spend the resources to portal the rest of the way rather than waste the time traveling."

"I appreciate it," Rilla said. "War gets cranky when people tell her to wait. So the faster we can get her moving forward again, the better for all of us."

"I've known quite a few knights that fit that description."

Vola's breath caught at the familiar voice. It sent a little tingle down her spine and made her feel all awkward and proud and in awe at the same time. Henri had always had that effect on her, but it seemed like it was worse now she hadn't seen him in so long.

A stocky man with silver-colored hair, spiky from being under a helm all day, gazed at her from behind the scholars. The corner of his mouth rose, pulling at the long scar that stretched between the corner of his eye and his neck.

Lord Ephyra bobbed his head at the man. "Can I introduce you to Knight Henri? He's been keeping us safe along the road."

"Not a knight, my lord," Henri said. "Just a trainer."

"They know each other already," Talon said.

Vola wasn't the kind of person to fling herself at her old mentor, and neither was he. The feeling in her chest when he gave her a proud little smile was enough. It had always been enough.

There was a time when she would have turned her shoulder to hide the shield he'd given her and keep him from seeing everything she'd done to it. But she wouldn't do that now. Not with the Broken's wings spread across the black, telling their own story.

Henri stepped forward to clasp her shoulder, and Vola's breath hitched.

"I've missed you, Vola," he said quietly, while the others murmured their own greetings. "Glad I got the chance to see you in all this." His gesture indicated the camp, the war, everything that had happened since she'd rescued him from a slave ship and he'd gifted her with his own shield.

Vola cleared the lump from her throat. "It's good to see you, too." The words weren't nearly accurate enough, but what else could she say? Henri's simple presence, his acceptance, and pride wiped away every hateful word still lingering from Imralen's tirade.

"I brought someone else who'd like to see you."

Vola caught sight of the gangly youth behind him. The boy had filled out a bit, put more muscle on his limbs so he actually fit the leather armor he wore. But he still had a spray of freckles across his nose and carrot-colored hair.

"Finn," Vola said, the strange feeling in her chest twisting. The pride was still there, but instead of the awkwardness of youth, it was mixed with a little shame and regret. Shame for not protecting him better. Regret that she hadn't been able to finish his training herself.

This time she did want to reach out and bundle him into a hug. But he'd grown more than she'd thought possible, and she didn't want to embarrass him. Instead, she held out her hand.

He clasped it gratefully, his eyes shining.

"Gods, what has he been feeding you?" Vola said. "You're nearly as tall as me."

"Bacon," Henri said. "All the bacon, all the time. Kind of like you."

"No bacon anywhere in camp," Sorrel said, popping up between them, holding a tray full of bread and cheese and dried meat. "But there's some undefined jerky. Hiya, Henri. Finn."

"Sorrel," Henri said with an amused smile.

"Look, Vola. More people to watch your back."

Vola winced as Henri raised one eyebrow. "Yeah, I should probably warn you—"

"The paladin council is here," Finn said, rubbing the back of his neck. "Henri said they would come. We planned to steer clear of them."

"Probably a good idea. Hopefully, they'll be so distracted with me, they won't even notice you."

Finn licked his lips. "I, um. I know what you did for me, Vola. Back in Glenhaven. Shielding me from the council."

"Oh," Vola said, voice going flat. She glanced at Henri.

"He was ready," Henri said.

"I know what they did because of it," Finn said, his eyes going to her shield. "And I know why you didn't tell me, but...I kind of wish you had. So I could thank you. Before this."

"You don't have to—"

"I know I don't, but I want to."

Finn glared at her fiercely, and Vola blinked. Henri hid a smile.

"I'd say you taught him well," Henri said. "But I'm not sure you meant to teach him stubbornness."

Vola grinned ruefully. "Not intentionally."

"We should get to the War princess," Lord Ephyra said. "I'm worried that our information is of a time-sensitive nature."

"I can help you with that," Lillie said quickly. "And I need to look over your results from Anders's spell as well. I have what I gleaned from Nargilla, but I'm sure you've made some progress I haven't seen yet."

"I'd say you already have enough on your plate," Rilla said. "But you are the foremost expert on everything Anders is doing so far."

"If the barrier continues to give us trouble, we'll be back in camp a lot anyway," Vola said. "She can work with the scholars anytime we're here and not racing out to fight more things."

"And War will appreciate a representative from the scholars who can explain things to her using small words," Rilla said with a toothy grin.

TEN

WHEN THEY LEFT the next morning to find the next key to the barrier, Lord Ephyra and the scholars gave Lillie a list of conditions and parameters to check. Ephyra would have come with them himself, except War didn't want to risk civilians so close to the barrier. But Lillie knew plenty about the barrier and Anders's work already, and she had all of Mishap's Heroes to back her up.

They set out directly from the army camp and walked a straight line to the glowing, undulating barrier in the distance. War had commandeered Hazel and the monks to serve as scouts, looking for Anders's mystery troops.

"He can't have put the second illusion directly in line with the first," Talon argued as they trudged across the lava field. "He knows we're going to be working through them to break down the barrier, so he'll make them hard to find."

"That is, if his goal is to keep us from breaking through," Lillie said.

Talon's brow furrowed. "What do you mean? Of course he wants to keep us from getting to him. What else would he want?"

"Maybe he's just delaying us," Vola said. "Making sure we have to jump through his hoops so he has time to do...whatever it is he's doing in there."

Sorrel glared at the barrier suspiciously as they came up next to it. "He seems like the kind of narcissist to make us go through his story and use it to stage an ambush."

Vola glanced at Rilla, who had been quiet most of the morning. "What do you think?"

She gave them a sly grin. "A very wise mentor once told me, 'always assume ambush.'"

Sorrel whistled. "Catchy."

"Whatever Anders is planning," Rilla said. "We're following his rules, playing his game. He has the power. We have none. Unless we can find a way to surprise him, we're at a disadvantage. So…" She shrugged.

"Always assume ambush," Vola said. She stopped just feet from the barrier and glared up at it. "In that case…" She cupped her hands around her mouth. "We're here! What did you want to show us?"

Talon rolled her eyes. "We didn't even want to try for subtlety?"

"We don't have all day!" Sorrel called. "There's a war to fight, in case you didn't notice."

Vola tapped her foot and looked around at the bare lava rock.

Nothing. No wisps of fog or shadowy illusions. No ethereal figures ready to take them into the depths of Anders's mind.

Rilla raised an eyebrow. "I suppose it was worth a try," she said.

"So, what do we do?" Talon said. "Just wander around the edge until we find it?"

Vola noticed Lillie hadn't said anything in a bit, and she turned to find the wizard with one hand raised toward the barrier, the other holding a notebook.

"Lillie?"

She closed her fist. "Sorry, just taking some readings for the scholars." She jotted something down with her pencil. "What were we up to?"

"Do we just wander around until we find Anders's illusion? Or is there a way we can force his hand somehow?"

Lillie blinked and peered up and down the barrier. "I imagine we just wander. I don't have nearly enough information to force his hand yet. And I want to play by his rules a little longer to get more data we can use against him."

"Wander it is," Sorrel said, thrusting her fist in the air. "North or south?"

"I vote north," Rilla said. "That seems intuitive to me."

"North," Lillie said, absently.

Vola glanced at Talon.

"I literally don't care," Talon said. "Just so long as someone picks one."

"North then," Vola said.

They traveled along the edge of the barrier, taking care to keep far enough away that no one accidentally stumbled into it. Lillie had re-summoned Rand when they'd gotten to camp the night before, but he'd ruffled his feathers and shuddered as if he remembered what had happened when he'd disintegrated.

The wizard had had to bribe him with cheese and bits of sausage before he would hop back on her shoulder and clack his beak in her ear the way he did when he was feeling affectionate.

Now he flew above, monitoring their surroundings, but also steering well clear of the barrier.

"You know, if Anders is so into illusions, he could at least provide some more interesting scenery," Sorrel said as they trudged along. "I think I'm gonna die of boredom before anything else manages to kill me."

They had been walking for nearly an hour already with no sign of Anders's next illusion. And the barrier still encompassed a massive amount of space.

A shadow flickered beyond the shimmering opaque surface, and Vola hesitated. "What was that?"

"What was what?" Lillie said.

"I thought I saw something."

Sorrel reached for her staff, but Lillie looked blank.

"Was I the only one to see it?"

"You aren't the only one," Talon said. "Something's moving around back there. I'm just not sure what."

Vola stared hard at the surface, but everything seemed still now.

"Whatever it is, didn't seem very fast," Talon said. "Just very deliberate."

"I don't think that word is as reassuring as you meant it to be," Rilla said.

"Who says I meant to be reassuring?"

"Heads up," Sorrel said.

Wisps and bits of fog crawled out of the ground at their feet, gathering together into now-familiar figures.

"Well, I mean, this is what we wanted, isn't it?" Lillie said as the gray sky and black earth around them dissolved into an entirely new landscape.

Sawdust shifted under Vola's feet, cushioning them almost like the real thing, and light shone from mirrors set along the edges of a wide, open room. The late afternoon sun poured through high windows, illuminating racks of weapons lined up between mirrors.

Vola raised her eyebrows. She'd gone to one of the more prestigious paladin academies on the continent and their practice ring was only a little nicer than this.

Lillie immediately began muttering, her hands glowing with magic, and Vola assumed she was digging into the spell surrounding them.

Scarred fighters in worn leathers lounged around the room, watching the boy standing in the middle of the ring. His black hair had grown and now hung in his eyes. He'd shot up a few inches, the way teenagers often did, and he sported a fading black eye.

He faced the older mercenary they'd seen at the end of the last illusion, a dark man with short gray hair cropped close to his head.

"Pick up your sword," the mercenary said, gesturing to the blade on the ground at Anders's feet.

"No," Anders said, his brow lowering. "I wanted to learn magic, Master Johnson."

"You wanted to learn to defend yourself," Johnson said.

"Why can't I do it with magic? Everyone has magic. Everyone in the whole wide world. Rangers, and bards, and berserkers, and even paladins. They all get little spells here and there. Why do I just have a sword?"

The man met Anders's eyes squarely. "Everyone is born with a little magic, yes. Enough to connect us with the world. But it is one of life's greatest injustices that some are born with less than others."

"Can't I just learn more magic?"

"Some can," the man said.

Anders's shoulders drooped. "And some can't."

"You can spend years beating your head against that wall until you're bloody. Or you can pick up your sword."

Anders grimaced and knelt to grasp the blade.

"Why do you want magic so bad?" Johnson asked as he stood.

"It's closest to what the gods have. That divine power that can change the world. If I had that, I'd be able to do anything. No one would ever have to die again."

The man pointed his finger at Anders's face. "Magic is a tool, no more special than that blade. If you learn to use that, you'll be as powerful as any spell-caster. Now. Defend yourself."

The other fighters around the ring straightened up and closed in.

"Now?" Sorrel said, keeping her eyes on the fighters.

"Now," Lillie said, dropping her spell.

They sprang forward.

The boy, Anders, had clearly learned some things in his time with the mercenary already. He defended himself well enough to hold off two of the attackers, but Vola cut in and took down the closest one, who wielded a heavy mace.

Step and slash, shield up to block the blow, cut under, and step again.

Anders almost seemed to mirror her, as if echoing her earliest lessons. If this mercenary was half the teacher Henri was, Anders had been in good hands.

Sorrel hurtled by, staff swinging in an arc. Rilla ducked in behind Vola, guarding her back before reaching to slash another attacker.

Vola assumed this illusion was like the last one and they just had to finish the fight to break its hold on them and on the barrier. She counted as she fought.

"Six. Seven. Eight."

"Nine, ten!" Rilla said, taking down the last illusory fighter.

"Hmm," Sorrel said, gazing around as if disappointed. "These guys weren't very exciting."

"It was just a practice bout," Talon said. "I don't think it was supposed to be exciting. It was supposed to prove a point."

Sure enough, the man stepped up to Anders, where he stood panting. "Learn to use this," he said, lifting the tip of Anders's sword from the sawdust. "And you can defend anyone from anything."

"Aw, that's sweet," Sorrel said as the illusion dissolved around them. "But when you use it to become a bad guy, that's when you get people like us coming after you."

Vola blinked to clear her vision, but the world still blurred.

"Shh," Talon said. "I'll bet he'll make us watch that part next. Don't spoil the end—"

Vola gasped as a shape lunged from the shifting colors and latched onto Talon.

"Oh, shit," Sorrel said and whacked at the shape. But then a wall of bodies came at her, and she had to swing her staff around to defend herself.

Vola spun, sword ready, and caught a grayish figure on her shield. The edges of everything still fuzzed, but her reflexes saved her and she shoved the shape away.

A snarl ripped through the air, and Gruff flung himself on Talon's attacker to help her struggle free. She pushed the figure away and its arm came off in her hand. She stared at it for a moment.

"Zombies," she said and spat.

"They're everywhere," Vola said, using her shield to thrust the line of undead back. "They must have been waiting for us." Those were the shadows she'd been seeing through the barrier.

"I knew the arrogant pig would use his ego to trap us," Sorrel cried.

"Is this Anders's army?" Talon asked. She slashed with her daggers, cutting down the zombies ahead of her, forming a little wall the rest had to climb over. "You said he was moving troops around."

"I sure hope not," Rilla said, grimly. "Otherwise, we're screwed."

Army or not, they were pinned on all sides. The lava field was mostly an open plain, but Vola couldn't see past the wall of dead soldiers.

She concentrated on her sword, her grip creaking against the leather-wrapped hilt, and the blade burst into flames. Fire licked up the edge, reflecting in the zombie's eyes.

She swept it out in an arc, setting three undead on fire with one blow.

"Shield your eyes," Lillie said. She stepped back into the center of the circle they'd made and raised her hands.

"Oh, shi—" Vola flung her arm over her head just as Lillie's fist burst into flame and she punched the ground.

A wave of heat blasted out, and flames licked past Vola's ears.

The fireball swept around them, leaving them untouched but knocking over three ranks of zombies. The next wave fell over their brethren and writhed.

Sorrel straightened up and wiped her brow. "Hey look. Breathing room."

Rilla patted herself down and seemed surprised to find herself in one piece. "Angels, demons, and all the pantheon warn a body next time."

"I did warn you."

"I mean warn me that you can do something like that."

"Oh, yeah," Vola said. "Lillie can pocket some of her more explosive spells. By the way."

"Thanks, so much."

"Guys, this bought us time, but there's still a *horde of undead* between us and the rest of our army," Talon said. She still stood alert, Gruff beside her, ears pricked forward, his lip raised to reveal teeth.

She was right. The zombie horde was already picking itself up and climbing over the crisped corpses in their way.

"Lillie, can you port us out of here?"

She shook her head. "I have to be able to see where I'm going and all I can see is zombies. And the camp's too far. Rand, go for help," Lillie called to the familiar, who circled above them. The bird croaked and wheeled away toward camp.

"Looks like Anders learned a few tricks from Myron as well," Sorrel said. "He is still in custody, isn't he?"

"Last I checked," Rilla said.

"Okay, we need to pick a direction," Vola said. "Camp is that way. Theoretically, there should be fewer zombies between us and it, so we can try to punch through."

"Great," Sorrel said. "I always wanted to die fighting dead guys."

"We're not gonna die—"

"Less talking, more punching!"

And the horde was on them. Vola didn't have much of a choice except to protect herself and her team. But the enemy was endless, or at least what they could see of it, and she gave them about ten minutes before they were overwhelmed.

A screeching cry rang out across the sky, drawing their gazes up.

A giant shape blotted out the hazy sun and dove earthward. The great eagle fell on the undead, ripping and clawing a path through the horde before sweeping back up to the sky once more.

There in the space he'd created, a tall, slim figure in blue strummed a lute. The zombies in earshot went slack and fell to their knees. The simple little melody finally reached Vola's ears. A bawdy tavern song twisted into a soothing lullaby.

"I can only hold this for so long," the figure sang out in a melodious voice. "Shall we get the hell out? Or wait until I keel over from hoarseness."

The zombies lying at their feet began snoring.

"What the actual fuck?" Rilla said.

Vola just laughed.

ELEVEN

VOLA and the others surged forward to meet the bard while the eagle covered their retreat.

"The day you stop talking is the day I hang up my shield for good," Vola said with a relieved chuckle.

The bard kept up the soothing melody, plucking out the notes on his lute. He wore a blue-dyed leather tunic and black pants that left little to the imagination and he'd look like a complete fop if it weren't for the rapier hanging from his waist.

"Well, then," he said with a charming grin. "What a happy little reunion. But that's funny, I don't hear any gratitude."

"Thank you, Cyrano," Lillie said and darted in to give him a peck on his cheek.

Cyrano took a break from strumming to clutch his heart. "Oh, adoration from beautiful women is the best thanks I could hope for."

The eagle shrieked above them.

"But of course, I won't accept it because I have all the love I need," the bard said loud enough for the eagle to hear.

"Rilla, I don't think you ever met Cyrano and Raven," Vola said, gesturing between the bard and the eagle. "The friends who helped us defeat Inga."

"How do you do? And let's get the hell out of here," Rilla said. "How long will your sleep hold?"

"I like a woman who knows her own mind. About thirty more seconds and then we're on our own."

"Right," Vola said. "And how many more times can you do it?"

"Maybe once. It doesn't always work though. I got lucky this time."

"Then draw your blade. Lillie, I want as much fire as you can make in a line going that way." Vola pointed toward the army camp. "Sorrel and Raven, go in under cover of the flames and keep the area clear for the rest to advance. Rilla and Cyrano, protect our backs. Talon and I will keep Lillie moving forward. Go."

They weren't exactly an army. But they also weren't completely useless. Zombies didn't last long between Lillie's fire and the rest of them working in concert.

Even a horde of moaning undead was smart enough to recognize a formidable threat, and by the time they popped out of the mass of bodies, the undead army had begun shuffling back, disengaging from the fight.

Mishap's Heroes stood on a bare bit of lava rock and panted as the giant eagle swooped down and landed. His outline shifted and flowed until a young man stood before them, brown hair a bit long around his ears, all sharp elbows and knees, and a pointed chin. Not to mention he was completely naked.

Cyrano pulled a silk robe from the pack on his back and handed it to Raven. Then he stood between them and the shape-shifter to block their view.

"Eyes off," he said. "I'm the only one who gets to stare."

Vola rolled her eyes.

Raven held out his arm, draped in a blue and silver fabric that shimmered. "Silk?" he said. "On a battlefield? Really, Cyrano..."

"It was the only blue I could find, and silk packs down really small."

The gray clouds above seemed to press down on them and Vola squinted up, wondering if it would rain.

"Thanks for the rescue," she said. "It was timely. But what are you doing out here?"

"We came to join your army, of course," Cyrano said. "But when we got there, some princess pressed us into immediate service as scouts."

Rilla rubbed a smile from her lips, and Vola could imagine her telling War about the "some princess" comment later.

"She told us to find Mishap's Heroes and lend you support. Apparently, you're supposed to be dealing with this barrier thing."

Vola glanced over. She hadn't noticed it before while fighting zombies, but sure enough, the barrier had retreated after they'd dealt with the illusions.

Lillie's familiar drifted down from the clouds to land on Raven's outstretched arm. "Rand here led us to where you were," Cyrano said.

"I'm glad he's working out for you," Raven said as the familiar clacked his beak.

"Yeah, we've only killed him the once," Sorrel said.

Vola cleared her throat.

"Why did War think we needed support?" Rilla asked, eyes narrowing. "We hadn't discussed sending reinforcements before we left."

Cyrano and Raven exchanged a look. "There have been some...developments since you left apparently," Cyrano said.

"Spit it out," Vola said. The bard could dance his way around meaning for ages if they let him.

"Lord Arthorel escaped from prison," Raven said flatly. "She said that would mean something to you."

"Geez," Vola said and rubbed her forehead.

"Escaped?" Sorrel said. "That weasel? I would have expected him to stay put, considering they fed him and gave him clothes and a place to sleep. All he has to look forward to outside is being broke."

"Not to mention being an escaped convict," Talon said.

"That won't mean much," Lillie said, a stubborn set to her lips. "He's nobility. He believes he was entitled to sell those people. They were his tenants, and they belonged to him."

"And there will be plenty of others in Southglen who agree," Rilla said. "We didn't root out every malcontent in the coup last year."

"Still, Arthorel was an illusionist," Vola said. "How did he escape?"

Cyrano held a hand out, palm up. "He had help. They're not sure who or how, but he didn't break out alone. But who was this guy?"

"One of Anders's lackeys," Vola said, waving to the mountain barely visible past the undulating barrier. "You know how Inga was sending people to Anders?"

"Yeah. Brainwashed them so they'd be docile as he drained their magic, or so we assumed."

"Same thing. Lord Arthorel was broke and sold off the bandits and villagers on his lands."

Sorrel kicked a loose piece of lava rock so it went clattering away over the ruined plains.

"And now he's out," Lillie said, golden brows drawing down. "Free to do it all again."

"And that's not the last of the news," Raven said. "Someone went after Myron Vidal as well, right in the middle of the camp."

"What?" Rilla said, straightening.

"They tried to abduct him."

"Tried?" Vola said.

"Yeah, some knight named Henri and his student stopped them. Unfortunately, there wasn't a lot left to question after they were done, even for a necromancer. Myron himself doesn't know anything, at least as far as War can tell."

"Knowing Myron, he really doesn't," Vola said. "He was never that interested in being evil. Even if he is a necromancer."

"We are going to have a little chat about Anders and his undead army, though," Rilla said. "If I find out he's been moonlighting for Anders on the side…"

Lillie shook her head. "He's not."

"How do you know?"

"Who else would try to abduct him? It has to be Anders. He helped Lord Arthorel escape from prison, and he's trying to bring Myron back, but Myron chose our side. And luckily we have the people who can enforce his decision for him."

"Why would Anders be trying to bring them back?" Talon said. "He already has their illusion magic and the power to raise an undead army."

"Maybe he needs more," Lillie said quietly.

"Or maybe he just wants his old gang back together," Sorrel said.

"Whatever it is, he'll want the others back as well," Vola said. Then she exchanged a smile with Sorrel, Lillie, and Talon.

"What?" Cyrano said.

"Well, he'll have a hard time with that. Lillie's brothers are serving out their exile in another plane, Inga's dead, and Nargilla is being held by the gods."

"We were there for one of those," Cyrano said. "And I find myself perturbed by the fact that it sounds like the least exciting story in the bunch."

"Lesson one," Rilla said, holding up a finger. "Don't piss off Mishap's Heroes."

TWELVE

By the time they returned to the War Princess, she stood at the head of a column of warriors with her arms crossed and her toe tapping.

"About time," she said, as they finally came into view. "I assume the way is clear?"

"If by clear you mean there's an army of undead between you and your goal, then yeah, sure," Sorrel said with a shrug.

War's face froze before she finally glanced at the sky as if asking for patience. "Say again?"

"We cleared the illusion, and the barrier pulled back again as we expected," Vola reported. "But the risen dead ambushed us. There're hundreds of them, maybe thousands between us and the barrier now."

War set her mouth in a thin line and raised her hand to signal her commanders. "Move out, slow march. Let's make this slow and steady, people. Lancers ahead. Archers mid-ranks."

"You're just going in?" Lillie asked, brows raised. "Even with—"

"An army of undead?" War said and chuckled. "You forget. We're an army, too. Why do you think I bothered to bring them? Besides, I don't want to wait and give Anders another chance to steal back Myron. He's already got Lord Arthorel."

Vola winced and didn't argue.

They marched at the head of an army with a War Princess looking for a fight. Mishap's Heroes had already seen action this campaign. Now it was everyone else's turn.

Vola and the others led them across the lava field on a direct line to the barrier. The sun rode low in the sky behind the flat gray clouds, but they should have been able to reach it in a couple of hours of steady marching.

However, only an hour in, a rumbling under their feet interrupted them. The calvary's horses danced and bucked, and War reined her mount in with a firm hand.

Vola glanced at Sorrel and Talon and Lillie.

"Uh oh," Sorrel said.

Talon stepped forward and touched her fingertips to the ground.

"What is it?" War said, hand raised, ready to signal her commanders.

"Brace yourselves," Vola said. "Here come the dead."

Cyrano drew his rapier, and Raven morphed into his great eagle shape.

"Where?" War said, whipping around, trying to pinpoint the source and completely failing.

"Look down," Talon said. Just then the rock at her feet crumbled and mounded until a ragged head popped through the surface to look around.

Talon took the zombie's head off its shoulders before it had a chance to get its bearings.

"First division," War called. "Forward. Second division, hold the line." Then she leaped down from her horse and caught the next zombie to emerge with a kick to the head.

Undead erupted from the ground all around them. Long gangly figures held together by stringy tendons and half-rotted muscle moaned and lunged for the living that they could reach.

Raven dove from above, knocking a head off. Cyrano caught it on instinct.

"Whoa, ugly." He batted it away.

Vola caught it with the flat of her sword, and it burst into flames as it flew off into a line of undead. It exploded on impact, showering the advancing dead with bits of burning zombie.

"Vola wins that round," Sorrel called.

"It's not a competition," Vola said, blocking another zombie that lurched for Lillie. "Just stay alive."

"Stay alive and look as cool as possible," Talon said.

"Well, I can play that game," War said and uttered a blood-curdling war cry as she raced for a clump of zombies overwhelming Rilla. Her greatsword swung in an arc over her head and she spun, her blade a blur.

The zombies all froze, as if in surprise. Then, one by one, their torsos tumbled to the ground, leaving their legs standing free for a moment longer.

"Hey," Rilla said. "It's my job to protect you."

War raised her eyebrows. "You're welcome," she said.

"All right, the Princess of War is in the running," Sorrel said.

"What did you expect?" War said.

"It's. Not. A. Competition," Vola yelled. "Sorrel, watch your back."

"I can multitask." Sorrel knocked three zombies off their feet so she could bash their skulls in. They each popped with an alarming squish. "Ew."

Rilla glanced around the battlefield and heaved a huge sigh. Then she darted back through the ranks of the army.

"What the — Rilla?" Vola called.

Moments later the Princess of the Dagger Throne pushed through the lancers, keeping the horde at bay, dragging a figure in a long, stained robe.

"Fix this," Rilla said and shoved Myron forward. "Anders learned this from you."

Myron grumbled. "I was just in the middle of some very delicate experiments. I knew I should never have agreed to travel with an army."

"Experiments in the middle of battle?" Vola said. She spun to keep a zombie from creeping up on the necromancer.

"Of course." He surveyed the fight before him. "What an inefficient way to solve a problem."

"Do you have a better one?" Vola said.

"Probably." He tilted his head, eyes unfocused. "Sloppy work. Anders might have an awe-inspiring amount of power but he's only just learning how to use it."

Myron waved his hand over the field as if blessing it, and suddenly, all the dead fell, like puppets with their strings cut.

"You just had to ask. You didn't have to drag," he huffed at Rilla and then turned on his heel to push back through the ranks.

The fighters stopped, glancing around in confusion while the enemy went from undead to very dead.

"Of course," War said flatly. "We travel with a reformed necromancer. Why didn't I think of that?"

"Your strength is meeting an army head-on," Rilla told her. "Mine is avoiding direct confrontation."

War scowled and kicked the nearest corpse. "This was hardly an army. Barely even a division."

"That's probably why Myron was able to manage the whole field," Lillie said. "That and Anders's inexperience."

"You said there were thousands. So where are the rest of them?" War asked, swiping a hand across her brow. The sun hid behind clouds, but it made the light a flat featureless spike in their eyes.

"This must have been a graveyard once," Talon said, kicking at the crumbled lava rock. "Before the mountain exploded. And Anders used the dead to slow us down."

"We'll find the rest of the horde at the barrier, I expect," Vola said. "Or beyond it. They may be able to pass through freely while it kills those of us who try to get through."

"Hmm," War said. "Then we'd better leave this little distraction behind as quickly as possible."

She swung back on her horse, and ignoring the dead strewn in her way, she urged it forward.

Another rumble shook the ground underfoot.

"Now what?" War snapped.

Ahead of them, the lava rock fell away abruptly, like a vast canyon opening at their feet. War's horse reared and danced back in alarm. Corpses rolled over the edge and plummeted hundreds of feet before going splat.

Vola and Talon leaped back, dragging Rilla and Sorrel with them.

The rumble died away, leaving nothing but a jagged cliff of lava rock and empty air between them and the barrier.

"What. The. Hell?" Rilla said.

Vola crept forward again to examine the sudden cliff. The ground dropped off like a giant cook had taken a cleaver to it. Far, far below, Vola could make out the splattered remains of some of the undead they'd just fought. She raised her head and squinted, but couldn't make out the other side. Only the barrier shimmering in the distance.

"Lillie," Vola called. "He knows illusions now. Is this real? Or just a trick?"

Lillie pulled her hands apart and started delicately sifting through the air as if pulling a set of fine strings. "This is...definitely not an illusion." She blanched. "It's real."

"All right, so which of his lieutenants did he learn that from then?" Rilla said.

Vola shook her head. This wasn't illusions or necromancy. It wasn't the power of the Thrones of Southglen or mind control. What kind of magic could change the landscape itself?

"I think this is something from the gods," Vola said. "He still has some of the power he stole from the Broken."

War rubbed her face. "What does he think he's doing? You can't just rearrange the world any time you want. There will be consequences."

"Maybe he's not ready to fight us yet," Talon said. "This is another delay."

"Not ready—" War said, then looked like she bit her tongue. "This is war. Not a first date. He's had plenty of time to primp in front of the mirror if he wanted."

War reined her horse around. "Find a way over," she said, speaking to Vola and Rilla. "I don't care how. I have to go come up with contingency plans. And find a place to camp tonight if we can't make it across."

She withdrew to the front ranks of her army to consult with her commanders, leaving Mishap's Heroes at the edge of the canyon with Cyrano and Raven.

They all stared to the south. Then they all stared to the north. The canyon stretched as far as they could see in both directions.

"Well," Sorrel said, fists planted on her slim hips. "What now?"

Vola blew out her breath. "We find a way across."

"Can we climb down?" Lillie said.

Sorrel stepped up to the edge and frowned down. "Talon and I might be able to manage without breaking our necks, but it's very smooth. We'd have to use ropes. And even then, we'd have to get the whole army down the cliff. Mounts, pack animals, and wagons alike."

"And then, once down there, we'd be stuck," Rilla said. "No way up."

"I don't like it," Talon said. "If he can just rearrange the landscape anytime he likes, what's to stop him from swallowing us up into the ground."

Cyrano stared at her. "What a bright and cheerful thought," he said. "I'm so glad you shared with the rest of us."

"I figured if I had to suffer, the rest of you should, too," Talon said.

"Okay, so we're agreed. We don't want to go down," Vola said. "And there isn't going to be a bridge across, nor any way to make one that wide. So how do we get to the other side? Magic?"

Lillie shook her head. "Even if we get all the battlemages and university scholars on board, we wouldn't be able to do it. We have to be able to see where we're going to teleport. Or know the area well enough from memory."

Vola sighed. No physical way across. No magic. That really only left one option.

"My lady," Vola said quietly. The others heard her anyway and went silent.

The Broken coalesced out of the air at her shoulder, wearing her Cleavah aspect, all tumbling curls and dark golden skin.

"I see," the Broken said without preamble. She stared at the chasm, her lips pulled tight in thought. "Well, that's unsettling."

"Don't say that," Cyrano said. "Geez, she's as bad as you." He jerked a shoulder at Talon. Talon glared.

The Broken raised a dark eyebrow. "Because I feel the need to share my distress? Burdens are lighter when they're passed around." She winked at Talon.

Cyrano gulped as Raven morphed out of his giant eagle shape beside him. "You were listening."

"Rule number two," she said, gesturing to Rilla. "Always assume someone is listening."

"I like her," Rilla said. "Have I mentioned that I like her yet?"

"Yeah, Vola has the best goddess," Sorrel said.

"Careful," Lillie said. "That's the sort of comment that starts divine wars."

"Can you help?" Vola asked Cleavah, gesturing across the wide expanse.

She heaved a sigh. "I could…"

"But?"

The Broken gave her a rueful look.

"But the others wouldn't like it," Vola said for her. "They still don't think the gods should be involved."

Rilla glanced between them. "So this is political."

"It's political," the Broken said. "Imagine you knew something had to be done, but all your fellow princesses thought they were already doing enough. How would they feel if you went and promised another country troops and supplies and began feeding them inside information?"

"I'd be hung as a traitor," Rilla said flatly.

"Exactly," the Broken said.

"Then let me do it," a different voice said.

Vola wasn't the only one who jumped, even though they stood at the edge of a cliff. The deep, insidious voice was very familiar, but she'd only heard it outside of her head once before.

Vola whipped around to find another god standing between their little group and the rest of the army. Round, bloodshot eyes stared back at them.

"Who…?" Rilla said, obviously trying to figure out how this man had gotten behind her.

"Mulgash," Vola said. "Greater Obstacle of Rage."

"Thank you, my dear," Mulgash said, tilting his head.

"Ho, boy," Sorrel said.

Cyrano growled and took a deliberate step to place himself in front of Raven.

Mulgash's dark eyebrows twitched. "You needn't worry. I have no need for a familiar. And I have no need for Inga anymore, who was the one who wanted one."

"Great," Raven said over Cyrano's shoulder. "Then you won't mind if I stay over here, while you stay over there."

Mulgash's lips curled. "As if distance mattered."

Raven looked as if he might have flung himself off the cliff and changed on the way down if it weren't for the way Mulgash turned away from him, dismissing him as inconsequential.

"What are you offering?" the Broken asked.

"I'm not bound by our fellow gods' prejudices or strictures. I believe in your cause. I could help without the hindrances you experience personally."

Vola's eyes narrowed. "Why would you want to?"

He put a hand on his chest. "Just because we've been on opposite sides before doesn't mean we don't have the same interests at heart now."

"Do you even have a heart?" Talon muttered.

Vola cleared her throat over her. "Inga was working for Anders. And you were using her. Seems like you might still be wrapped up in all of it."

"Like you said. I was using Inga. What she did with my power was her business. But the moment this Anders started thinking he could take what belongs to me, that's when things changed."

Vola glanced at the Broken, but she didn't look angry or implacable. She looked calculating.

"I have no intentions of sharing my power with a mortal I didn't choose," Mulgash said, hand slashing through the air. "And since this is a problem for all of us—" he turned the gesture into a wave between himself and the Broken. "Then it seems like we should work together to get rid of it. Before we can't any longer."

Vola exchanged a look with the Broken.

"Do you trust him?" Rilla asked, not even bothering to lower her voice.

"No!" Cyrano said. "He helped Inga capture Raven and enslave him."

"Not to mention us and a whole bunch of innocent villagers," Sorrel said, eyes narrow and cold.

It was so similar to the look she'd had when Mulgash had taken over their minds. Vola had fought them in order to get her friends back to their normal selves. It wasn't something she ever wanted to see again, even in memory.

But...Mulgash was right. This was a problem for all the gods, not just the ones she liked. It was what she and the Broken had been trying to convince them of this whole time.

The Broken still looked at her. The goddess might have been the guiding wisdom for Vola, but Vola was the one who'd been hurt directly by the Obstacle in front of them.

Still, she was a paladin. She'd spent her whole life trying not to give in to the Greater Obstacle of Rage. What kind of holy warrior would she be if she gave that up now?

"Fine," she said.

There was a unified intake of breath behind her.

"You're going to trust him?" Talon said.

"No," Vola said, eyes locked with Mulgash. "I am going to use him, though."

Mulgash's lips stretched in a proud smile. "That's my girl."

"I don't belong to you," Vola said. "I'm spoken for already."

The Broken didn't say anything, just chuckled deep in her throat.

Mulgash shrugged. "Fair enough." And he stepped to the edge of the cliff.

The others moved to make room for him, giving him a wide berth, Cyrano and Raven especially. Rilla was the only one to remain a little closer, watching his movements carefully.

Sorrel and Talon looked between Vola and Mulgash, each with their own expression of confusion and doubt. Vola kept waiting for them to ask "what are you thinking?"

Instead, Lillie leveled a rueful smile at them. "I don't know why you're surprised," she said. "This is the same woman who forgave Ella for all those hurtful things she said when they were children. Even though Ella didn't deserve it."

Vola winced. That was different. Vola had needed to forgive the girl she'd grown up with. Without that hate, she was finally free to forget about all the hurt. It was more for Vola's sake than for Ella's.

"I'm not forgiving, Mulgash," she said, instead of arguing. "I'm just recognizing this is bigger than our differences. As soon as Anders is gone, we'll go back to hating each other, I'm sure."

Lillie stepped up to her and tucked her hand into the crook of Vola's elbow. "Sure you will."

Vola frowned at her. "Why do you say it like that?"

"Because I'm not sure you actually know how to hate. You've spent your whole life fighting against others who see you as violent and aggressive. You only know how to be gentle."

"I carry a sword and bash people in the face when they make me angry. Gentle is definitely the wrong word."

Lillie just smiled to herself and turned away.

Another rumble made them turn back to Mulgash, who knelt at the edge of the cliff. He had his hands buried in the lava rock as if it were thin mud and the muscles in his arms strained. Little bits of rock danced across the ground, their clatter completely lost in the all-encompassing grumble from the land itself.

War ran back to them at a dead sprint and skidded to a stop, sending a cascade of stones over the edge of the cliff.

Cyrano watched, his jaw set so hard his lips had gone white. Raven stared at the ground.

The chasm that had dropped out from under them now rose, like sea water pulled by the inevitable tide. Land surged back into place, lining up with the ridge where they stood.

The ground shuddered so badly, several of them staggered and fell to their hands and knees. Vola stumbled and planted her feet wider, putting a hand under Lillie's arm to keep her upright.

Behind them, the army murmured and clanked as soldiers tried to keep their feet.

The rumbling stopped, and the land fell still, though Vola could still feel a buzz under her boots.

The lava field stretched ahead of them exactly as it had been, and they had a clear shot to the barrier.

Mulgash stood and dusted his hands off. "There. If he wants to play with a god's power, he can play with some real gods as well." He shot a glance over his shoulder at Vola and War. "Do let me know if you need anything else, Vola dear. You have only to ask."

He disappeared into thin air in a shower of black and purple sparks.

"Do I want to know who that was?" War asked.

Vola winced. "Probably not."

THIRTEEN

THE ARMY CAMPED CLOSE ENOUGH to the barrier that its undulating light and colors lit up the canvas tents that night.

Talon was off, setting up their campsite and making sure the swamp monster didn't eat any more pack animals. The camp hostlers had threatened mutiny if it did. Rilla was closeted with War, planning the next day's push. And Lillie had disappeared to work the last few hours of the day with the scholars.

Vola and Sorrel had a rare moment to walk together and check on the different factions Sorrel had settled. The monks and the battlemages seemed resigned to living in peace with each other finally. Vola wondered if it had something to do with each group being close enough to see the others fight.

They definitely caught Hazel asking the leader of the battle mages for tips on avoiding magical attacks, and the leader responding politely to ask for some physical exercises that would increase his mages' speed in their heavy armor.

"Did you do that on purpose?" Vola asked under her breath as they left the two groups to their polite discussion.

"Do what?" Sorrel said with a grin.

Vola just shook her head.

Several more groups had joined the army as they marched through the lava field. Vola caught sight of a contingent camped under the Mistvale flag, and she suspected the large force of graceful elves in matching leather had been sent by Selene.

But there were also other smaller groups, villagers from towns and hamlets she recognized. Three spaces down the row, Cyrano helped a group of halflings from the village they'd saved from Inga. Sorrel trotted over to say hi to Sandry, who had grown much more proficient with the staff she carried. Sorrel had given her some preliminary lessons, but apparently the girl had taken them seriously and found another teacher to continue the lessons.

Vola half expected to turn a corner and find her parents, but so far she seemed to be the only orc in the camp.

She drifted toward the other side of the row and caught a familiar redhead with broad shoulders. He wore a set of practical leathers and carried a sword strapped to his back.

"Braydon?" Vola said.

The man looked up and gave her a friendly smile. "Volagra Light-bringer," he said. "It's been a while."

"It has," Vola said, not bothering to correct him on her name. She didn't really feel the need to get into it with a man she'd counted as a rival once. Though they'd managed to settle their differences. Really, they'd just had to save Braydon and his team over and over again until he'd finally admitted that maybe she wasn't a monster and was actually pretty good at what she did.

"I haven't seen you since Water's Edge," Vola said. It was the town where Vola had first met the others.

"Yeah. We got word that Mishap's Heroes was calling for help. After you saved most everybody in the village, it wasn't hard to convince some of them to come with me to fight. I even brought my old team. Had to drag Obron out of retirement."

All Vola remembered of Obron was a wizard swinging from a tree by his ankles, his robe around his ears. And it was more than she wanted to remember about the old man, if she was honest.

"That's great. Do you need anything?"

"He doesn't need anything from a black paladin," a voice said. Another figure joined Braydon, a tall, slim woman who carried two swords. Vola vaguely recognized her as one of Braydon's people. In fact, she'd gifted Vola with the hand axes that hung from her belt even now.

"Hey," Braydon said. "What are you talking about? That's our savior, remember?"

"You haven't heard? It's all over camp. This is Volagra Lightless. The black paladin."

Braydon opened his mouth as if to refute her claim, but his eyes flicked to Vola.

She steeled herself. "I don't make it a secret," she said and turned so her blackened shield caught the torch light.

"Oh," Braydon said, voice going low and flat.

"She lost her shield, Braydon," the woman said, turned so she could talk in his ear. "And they say she consorts with the Obstacles."

"Now where did you hear that?" Sorrel asked, coming up next to Vola.

"Does it matter?" the woman said. "It's true, isn't it? She's changed since she helped us."

"Yeah," Sorrel snapped. "She represents the Broken, now. That's why War trusts her."

Braydon blinked and his mouth fell open.

Sorrel yanked on Vola's arm and hauled her away down the row of tents and campsites before he could say whatever he was thinking.

Whispers followed them. Sideways looks and wards against evil. Vola tried to convince herself she was imagining it, but Sorrel's eyes flicked toward the looks, too. People she knew. Soldiers she'd talked to and joked with the day before stepped back and dropped their eyes as she passed. The cook's gaze locked on her blackened shield. And for the first time in a long time, Vola considered hiding it.

"This is Imralen's doing, isn't it?" Vola said. Even with her long legs, she had a hard time keeping up with Sorrel's determined pace. "Gods, why didn't I think of that before? He's doing exactly what he said he would do. He's making everyone see what I really am."

Sorrel stopped. "And what are you?" she said. "A paladin who was wrongly accused? A paladin who is doing everything she can to keep the world safe? A paladin who managed to convince a Greater Obstacle into helping people? Let them see all of that." She flung her arms out to encompass the entire camp. "Let them see who and what you really are, Vola. The things Imralen says about you behind your back aren't true." She poked Vola hard in the gut. It was as high as she could reach. "You know that. I know that. Lillie and Talon and Rilla and War know that. That's. All. That. Matters." She punctuated each word with a poke.

"Ow, your fingers are like little daggers."

"Let them see you, Vola," Sorrel said again. "And they'll be as proud of you as we are." The monk spun around on her heel and strode toward the center of camp where the command tent had been pitched.

Vola hesitated, feeling the looks burning into the back of her neck. It was the same. It felt exactly the same as it had her whole life. Walking down the street and hearing the whispers of "orc," "monster," and "obstacle-worshiper." Enduring the insults and the hazing while she'd been in training. Seeing the disbelief when anyone saw her shield and realized she wasn't just a paladin, she was an orc paladin.

She'd felt this her whole life, and she'd dealt with it for just as long.

What did she always do? She took a deep breath and kept going. She kept her shield up. She treated the people who insulted her with politeness —if not kindness—and she kept fighting for the weak and the oppressed. She kept doing what she'd been chosen to do, trusting that eventually it would pay off. Eventually, people would see her. The way she really was.

She trotted to catch up to Sorrel. "How is it I always forget that you're wiser than all of us combined?"

Sorrel rolled her eyes. "I work very hard to cover it up. Do you think it's easy to be this perky all the time?" She flapped her hands over her head.

Vola ignored her antics and leveled a gaze at her. "Thanks," she said.

Sorrel shrugged. "I'm your second, right? First job for a second in command is to support their leader. Whether that means doing what they say or making sure they're strong enough to give the orders."

They were close enough to the command tent now that Rilla must have heard their voices through the canvas. She poked her head through the flap.

"What's wrong now?"

"Nothing," Vola said as Sorrel slipped inside the tent.

"Imralen's just making Vola's life difficult," she said. "Which we knew he would. So we're not letting him get to us." She gave Vola a significant look.

"I don't know what that man's bitching about," War said, bent over her map table. "It's not like you're even in charge of anything. I decide when we move, where we go. And if I choose to do that based on your opinion, what does it matter to him?"

"He thinks I'll corrupt you," Vola said, willing to see the humor in it.

"Even if you do work with Obstacles, which isn't a bad thing in this war, they're not evil. They'll make us stronger."

Vola hadn't realized War was one of those who believed the Obstacles were a blessing, but then, she was the princess of the War Throne.

"You could just ask the Broken to manifest," Sorrel said, hopping up onto a pile of crates in the corner. "That would shut him right up."

"No," Vola said but didn't elaborate. She didn't know how to explain the surge of panic that thought brought her. The Broken had chosen her to be the one who fought for the weak and broken. So maybe it was as simple as she didn't want the goddess to feel like she'd chosen wrong. After all, in this instance, Vola was the one who was broken. And who would fight for her if she wasn't strong enough to fight for herself?

Her gaze went to Sorrel, who swiped an apple from one of the crates and examined its surface before she bit into it.

Vola smiled.

FOURTEEN

WHEN THEY LEFT camp the next morning, War had set up divisions around the perimeter to defend against the army of undead that must still be out there somewhere. Raven and Cyrano were trying to find the main body of the enemy supported by the monks while Mishap's Heroes slipped out the back and started trekking across the lava field around the edge of the barrier.

According to Lillie, there were still three key points anchoring the barrier that they had to get through and it seemed like the perfect time to strike since they'd messed with Anders's time-line the day before. Mulgash had enabled them to move ahead when Anders had wanted them to stay put. It made sense to push ahead now and catch him further off balance.

Lillie scanned the area carefully, using a couple of different spells Vola didn't entirely recognize. The whole point today was to not get ambushed.

Though Sorrel had pointed out that should be their goal every day. Mishap's Heroes. Purpose? Don't get ambushed.

Vola had the feeling they'd find this anchor point equidistant around the barrier as the first two. That seemed about right. If you wanted to anchor a circle, it made sense to do it from all sides.

"There," Lillie said and pointed.

"I don't see anything." Sorrel shaded her eyes, though the day was as foggy as the one before. It seemed like an ashy layer of clouds permanently covered the sun here.

"I can see the magic tied to the land. Almost like a knot. When we follow the illusions through to their conclusions, we untie the knot. This must be the next one."

"All right," Vola said. "But we're not getting caught the same way again. If he ambushed us once when we came out, he's probably just going to do it again."

"We should set a watch," Talon said. "We don't all have to go into the illusion. The fights haven't been that bad so far."

Vola nodded. "Three of us will go in. Two can stay here and keep anyone from creeping up on us. They can warn us if they see anyone setting up an ambush." She gestured to the flat plains. "That shouldn't be too hard."

"I'll stay," Rilla said. "The Dagger Throne is good at traps and defenses."

"Gruff and I can stay as well," Talon said. "We're used to standing watch."

"And you'll let us know if anything's trying to sneak up on us," Sorrel said.

"We can hold anything back until you return," Rilla said.

"Let's get it over with then," Vola said, drawing her sword. "The sooner we get in there, the sooner we can get back and deal with whatever Anders throws at us."

They slunk toward the area Lillie had indicated. Rilla and Talon stayed far enough back to remain clear of the illusion, watching for movement across the open lava field.

Between one step and the next, fog figures began rising from the ground. The bland, mostly gray and black surroundings blurred into the more vibrant colors of a temple yard in the fall. Several trees shaded them from the bright sunlight, their leaves a mosaic of yellow, orange, and red. Above them, the temple's stained-glass windows reflected little bits of blue and purple onto the vivid green grass.

Vola glanced around, immediately trying to get her bearings. Lillie and Sorrel flanked her. But Rilla and Talon hadn't come along. As planned.

Vola sent up a quick prayer to the Broken. *Watch over them while I can't.*

She recognized Anders's mentor, the dark man in the mismatched armor, lounging in the grass at the base of a tree. Anders, grown tall and muscular, stood beside him, watching their surroundings with wary eyes.

A stranger knelt beside them, flipping through a spellbook.

"Sit, boy," Johnson said. "You never know when you're going to get another chance to rest."

Anders shook his head, eyes still on their surroundings. "Brindle the

Butcher's men could be hunting us even now. An ambush is always a possibility. So if you're not watching, then I will." He said it without rancor, like they'd agreed to disagree long ago.

Johnson snorted. "That's why I hired you for this. You keep us safe."

Anders's lip twitched.

"Aw, Vola," Sorrel whispered. "He's just like you."

Vola didn't laugh. The comparison gave her a strange twinge in her chest. This was the man they were fighting? This strong intense fighter who just wanted to protect his party?

"Ah," Johnson said and pushed himself up off the tree roots. He stood and dusted himself off. "Here she is."

The temple door had slid open, and a woman stepped out. She wore a breastplate of solid steel over a lilac-colored gown that fell to her feet in delicate waves.

"Oh, I like her," Lillie breathed.

Anders seemed to agree. He stared at the dark-haired woman as she locked the temple door and walked toward them.

An arrow struck the tree behind Anders's shoulder.

"Shit. Ambush!" he cried. "It's the Butcher's men."

Vola spun to see a line of archers in matching uniforms taking aim at the edge of the temple yard.

Anders raced past her to engage.

"Is this our cue?" Sorrel asked.

"It seems likely," Lillie said. "We've had to fight in all of the others so far."

"Right, you two focus on the archers," Vola said. "I see a problem."

Four fighters were creeping up on the temple yard from the other direction. Vola charged them, shield down. She struck one with a thump, and he fell into his fellow.

These were faceless enemies, just like the first shadowy figures that had attacked Anders's home. Was that because he just hadn't bothered to create a more detailed illusion? Or was this how he remembered the altercation? Faceless shapes that threatened his people.

Vola managed to take out the first three fighters, but one got through her guard. But instead of attacking her, the figure darted forward to strike at Johnson, who had his back turned, dealing with the archers.

Anders turned in time to see the blow coming. He cried out, but he'd never reach the old mercenary in time.

Swirling light surrounded the enemy's feet and swept up his body, freezing the shadowy man's hand in place.

The woman from the temple stood halfway down the path to them, her hands raised and her eyes intent on the frozen enemy. Glowing lines snaked up her breastplate, illuminating the symbols etched into the metal.

The enemy's outline flared, and Vola had to fling her hand over her eyes. Then it fell into dust, a pile of pale ash gathering on the green grass.

Anders cut down the last archer and hurried across to Johnson. "Are you all right?"

The man raised an eyebrow. "Perfectly," he said.

The woman crossed the rest of the distance to them. "Well, that was an exciting beginning." Her smile fell just short of a grin.

"Mariel," Johnson said with a nod to the woman. "Thanks for joining us."

"Master Johnson." She returned his nod. "Of course. It will be a pleasure, I'm sure." Her gaze flickered over Anders.

Anders flushed a deep red.

The third man who'd sat under the tree snorted. His features were bland and generic. As ill-defined as the woman's were crisp and stunning. Clearly, Anders's memory was very focused when he set up this illusion.

"Mariel Stillwater is a cleric," Johnson said. "A spell caster and a healer. She'll be keeping us safe—"

"That's my responsibility," Anders said with a sharp glance between Johnson and the new woman.

"And I'm sure you do a wonderful job," Mariel said. "I'm not here to step on your toes. I'm here to provide more divine protection."

"Oh," Anders said. "The gods."

Her lips twitched at his tone of dismissal. "Yes, the gods. You don't believe you need their protection?"

"I...I've never had much luck in getting them to give it to me."

"Ah. Well, that's what I'm for." She used her toe to nudge the pile of white dust at their feet.

Anders blanched.

"Between the two of you, we should be well protected." Johnson glanced between them with a gleam in his eye. "I expect you to work well together."

"Yes, sir," Anders said automatically, as if used to obeying without question.

"We'll need it if we're going to take down Brindle the Butcher. There aren't enough curses in the world for that man."

Johnson and the third man started down the lane.

Anders hesitated for a moment while Mariel hid a soft smile. Then he extended his arm to her.

The scene dissolved as they followed the rest of their party.

"Aw, they're kind of cute," Lillie said.

Sorrel gasped. "Do you think that's what all this is for? To get us to feel sorry for him?"

"What else would it be?" Vola said, shaking her head to clear her vision. "Aside from sheer arrogance. Obviously, there's something in his story he wants us to see."

The lava field came into focus around them, the first few feet growing clearer as the illusion faded. Vola noticed Rilla immediately, crouched on the ground beside them, blades ready in her hands. Little creases around her eyes deepened as she sought Vola's gaze.

"Are you out now?" Rilla asked, voice tight and worried.

A bit of ice trickled down Vola's spine, and she searched for Talon. The ranger had her bow strung and an arrow notched, though she held it pointed at the ground.

"What is it?" Vola asked sharply. "What's wrong?"

Talon jerked her chin, and Vola squinted into the distance. Her vision wasn't entirely back to normal yet.

Her ears picked out what her eyes couldn't tell her yet. A low shuffling and moaning came from about twenty yards away.

She blinked and the blurry distance finally came into focus, as if the last of the illusion fell away.

The undead horde shifted just beyond a green line drawn in fire across the lava rock. Rilla's handiwork. They'd seen her lay traps before, even for the undead. Vola was impressed her magic could hold so many at once. Though maybe she shouldn't be. Rilla held all the power of the Dagger Throne, after all.

"Well, that's not unexpected," Sorrel said.

"Though I had hoped they would be more divided between us and the army," Lillie added.

"That's not the worst part," Talon growled, her voice as gravelly as it ever got.

Vola glanced between Talon and Rilla.

Rilla used two fingers to touch the rock at her feet. Ahead of them, the green fire broke in the middle and forced the horde apart, like a wave parting around a rock. The zombies shuffled and groaned, but Rilla cleared a path between them.

Smack in the middle of the horde, the lava rock rose in a hummock, and Rilla's fire cleared a path to the hill.

As the zombies roiled out of the way, Vola's breath caught.

On the small rise, a man stood dressed in full plate armor, a crimson cloak fluttering at his shoulders. He leaned on a greatsword, its tip scratched into the rock at his feet. His sleek honey-colored hair was tied back in a tail, revealing delicately pointed ears.

"Oh my gods, I thought he was exiled," Vola whispered.

His hair didn't have the same red tints, and he was a lot less soft around the edges, but the shape of his features still echoed Lillie's perfectly.

"Xavier," she whispered.

FIFTEEN

"HELLO, SISTER," Xavier said. He heaved his sword over his shoulder and started to pick his way down the rise between the zombies. Like a king descending to greet his subjects.

Lillie gulped so hard Vola heard it from six feet away. "What—How are you here? You were exiled. Banished."

He chuckled, though his smile didn't reach his eyes. "Yes, to a lovely little summer home in the Outer Plane. Thank you so much for that."

Lillie's jaw hardened. "I did what I had to do. You were going to destroy the Thrones. Topple our entire government."

"So you exiled your own flesh and blood without trial."

"Her decision still stands, Ephyra," Rilla said. "You're a traitor to Southglen. And now you're an escaped convict."

"Yes, funny how that works out."

"Where's Innis?" Lillie asked.

Xavier shrugged, making his plate clank. "Innis didn't have the stomach to do what needed to be done. He's not with me anymore."

"What did you do to him?" Lillie's voice went shrill.

"You ask as if you care."

She pressed her lips together. "I do care," she said quietly.

"Not enough, apparently," he said, just as softly. He raised his chin. "I thought you were soft. I thought you were the baby, coddled until you were useless. You ran away instead of facing the things you'd done. I thought the ruthlessness of our noble line had skipped you completely. I underestimated you." His eyes narrowed. "I won't make that mistake again."

He snapped his fingers and Rilla's spell holding back the undead horde broke in a shower of green sparks.

The dead surged forward just as Xavier charged his sister.

Lillie disappeared in a pop of empty air, and Vola lunged into the space where she'd been, catching Xavier's double-handed blow on her shield. The force of it rang down her arm and sent numbness zinging toward her elbow.

She heaved, making him stumble back. Vola swung her sword to take advantage of his unbalance.

Instead of trying to meet the blow, Xavier ducked, avoiding her altogether.

Lillie had reappeared behind Vola. She couldn't go very far with the undead pressing in on all sides.

Xavier sprang for her, completely ignoring Vola.

Three new figures coalesced, each one identical to the wizard, down to the blue-green eyes and the way they stood.

Xavier growled, eyes flicking from one image of Lillie to the other.

Talon, Rilla, and Sorrel held back the horde, cutting down the front ranks to form a barrier around them that the rest would have to climb over.

Vola struck Xavier from the side, long enough to distract him so the real Lillie could summon a wall of fire. It snaked between them and the undead horde, making the zombies hiss and moan and shuffle back.

"Get off me!" Xavier flung himself away from Vola, and he slashed at the nearest image of Lillie. It burst into a shower of light motes as his sword parted the illusion.

Well, those wouldn't last long. He'd cut through them like paper, and sure enough, he disintegrated the next one even while Vola was recovering her footing. There were only two figures left that could be Lillie, and even Vola wasn't sure which one was real.

She threw herself at Xavier, slashing at his face. He had to defend himself or be blinded.

Xavier stepped back to avoid the blow, but then immediately planted his feet and swung for an opening in Vola's defense. Vola raised her shield, deflecting the edge of his greatsword, which slid off the metal, slicing through the elbow joint of her armor.

She hissed and stepped back, her shield arm hanging limp at her side.

"Vola!" Lillie cried.

"I'm all right," Vola said, sweat standing out on her brow.

Xavier's eyes flicked between the last copy of Lillie and the one who had cried out, and Vola could see him make an educated guess.

He went for the real one. Lillie raised her hands, and a whirlwind sprang up between them, knocking Xavier flat on his back.

The others had their hands full keeping back the zombies that were brave enough to risk the flames. Heat made Vola's skin feel tight and stretched, and the air around them shimmered with it. The smoke sat heavy in her lungs, but she didn't dare cough. Xavier might have been focused on Lillie but he was too fast and too strong to give him any sort of opening.

He'd already rolled to his feet. He hesitated, and Vola thought he was glaring at Lillie, catching his breath. But she caught the movement of his lips and blue fire flickered across his blade, dripping onto the ground in little splatters of sparks.

Vola's eyes narrowed. What the hell? Xavier had never shown an aptitude for magic before. But then he was related to Lillie, Kellan, and Lord Ephyra, all accomplished spell casters.

A breeze touched her cheek, clearing the air around her head for a moment. "It's a wizard killing poison," the Broken whispered in her ear. "Don't let it touch Lillie. He's keyed it to her specifically."

"Great," Vola muttered. "Our enemies learn new tricks as fast as we do."

Lillie flickered and reappeared in another spot, but she was hampered by her own flames now, and the zombie horde beyond them.

Xavier anticipated her move and lunged in the opposite direction to catch her just as she was reappearing.

Vola lurched between them, but her arm ached and stayed limp, and she couldn't get her shield up in time. His blade sliced across her breastplate with an unholy shriek, spitting blue sparks everywhere. She stumbled and fell to her knees.

"Eyes." Lillie's voice came into Vola's head, calm and implacable, and Vola flung her arm over her face just as a brilliant orb of light sprang into existence above them.

Through the flames, the zombies shrieked in pain.

Vola waited for another blow from Xavier, but none came. She cautiously peeked around her arm and found him on the ground, rubbing at his face.

Vola climbed to her feet, her shield scraping against the lava rock.

Xavier cast around for his dropped sword, eyes streaming.

"Now, Vola," Lillie said, face hard and set.

Usually, Vola offered mercy when she could afford it. But there came a time when you'd used up all your chances, and Xavier had run out of mercy from all sides.

Vola stepped forward and raised her blade, ready to lop his head from his shoulders in one clean stroke. But he turned his torso at the last minute and the blow glanced to the side, leaving a long gash in his neck.

Xavier scrambled aside as Vola advanced, one hand dragging his sword, the other pressed to the blood spurting under his jaw.

Vola lunged for him and Xavier managed one more turn to take the blow on his back. Vola's blade left a gash as long as her arm in his plate and deep enough that blood seeped through the torn metal.

Xavier grunted and hesitated before he flung himself through the fire. He rolled across the rough rock on the other side, snuffing the flames that had caught his hair and cloak. Then he hauled himself to his feet.

He snapped an order at the remaining zombies. There weren't nearly as many as there had been before. Many had disintegrated from Lillie's sunburst or succumbed to the flames. Or piled high under Rilla, Talon, and Sorrel's attack.

Xavier glared through the fire, hand still pressed to his neck. He coughed like he was trying to say something scathing, but the smoke or his own blood choked him.

Vola wanted to leap after him, to finish what he'd started back in Glenhaven. But her legs trembled, and she still couldn't raise her left arm.

Finally, Xavier whirled and limped away, dragging his sword.

The undead horde shuffled and followed him, leaving the lava field clear except for the burned bodies of the fallen.

SIXTEEN

THEY WAITED in silence long after they couldn't see Xavier or his army before Lillie finally snapped her fingers and the walls of flame died down and smothered themselves, leaving plumes of smoke in the air.

Vola fell to her knees, clutching her arm.

Lillie knelt beside her, lips white and eyes tight with worry.

"Don't," Vola grated out, voice hoarse with strain and smoke. "Don't touch. I still have that poison all over me." The blue flames still flickered at the edges of the gash in her armor, threatening destruction to Lillie.

"What poison?" Lillie said. She ducked to get a good look at the gash, blue reflecting across her face. She went pale and gasped.

"It's keyed to you," Vola grated out. "I'll be fine once I catch my breath."

Lillie drew back, tucking her hands under her arms. Her expression closed off, as if her thoughts followed the brother who'd just done his best to kill her. Even during the coup, he hadn't really targeted her seriously.

Rilla and Sorrel knelt to help Vola instead, while Talon kept an eye on their surroundings. Xavier had pulled back, and Vola felt confident that he was hurt worse than they were, but that didn't mean he couldn't turn around and send more troops back their way.

"He's working with Anders," Vola said quietly.

"Makes sense," Rilla said as Sorrel gently slid Vola's shield from her arm. "He has combat experience. He was trained as a commander, though

I hear he wasn't a very good one. Anders is probably using him to lead his undead troops."

"That's not the worst bit though, is it?" Sorrel said, placing Vola's shield aside carefully. "Xavier and Innis were exiled. To another plane. They shouldn't have been able to escape."

"Not without help," Lillie said.

"Yeah," Sorrel said. "And Anders has already helped Lord Arthorel escape."

"If Anders has the power to reach across planes and free Lillie's brothers," Talon said, "then we know who he's going after next."

"Inga," Vola said. "And Nargilla."

"Isn't Inga dead?" Rilla said.

Sorrel gestured to the bodies littering the lava field. "So were all those guys. How dead do you have to be to avoid getting brought back as a zombie?"

Rilla and Sorrel helped Vola remove the damaged breastplate, keeping the sharp edges and the poison away from anyone who might accidentally touch them.

Vola breathed a sigh of relief when the weight left her shoulders. She rubbed her face with her good hand, and it came away streaked with sweat and soot. The others were covered in ash as well.

Vola reached deep inside to the well of magic that connected her with the Broken. Divine power swelled at her fingertips, waiting for her bidding.

"Lady bless," she said and pressed her palm to the wound on her arm.

White light flashed and sharp pain indicated that the skin was knitting a hundred times faster than it did naturally.

Vola coughed and Sorrel handed her a water skin. She took a swig to rinse her mouth out, then passed it around to the others while she examined the wound. A fresh scar stretched from the back of her elbow over the crook of her arm and down to the seam where her armor gaped a little to provide freedom of movement. She flexed her fingers to test the healing. Everything seemed in order.

"Anyone else?" Vola asked.

Sorrel shook her head. "Just some scrapes and burns. Nothing a little salve won't fix. I think we'd better save your healing for bigger things from now on. Who knows when we'll get jumped again?"

"I agree," Vola said. "Same with Lillie's spells." She glanced at the wizard. "Save them for battle."

"I don't exactly waste them as it is," Lillie said. She reached out to take Vola's arm and examine the fresh scar. "Thank you," she said quietly.

Vola shook her head. She'd barely done anything. "I know this isn't easy," she said. "We thought we were done with it. You weren't supposed to have to see them ever again."

"We don't get to choose what the world throws at us," she said. "Only how we will act when it happens. I'll be fine. Eventually. We should be preparing ourselves for what comes next."

Vola shook her head and pushed herself to stand. "I'm not worried about Inga."

"She had the power to control minds. She took us over, turned us against you. And…" Lillie ducked her head. "She knew you. Better than you knew yourself. Knew what you were going to do even before you did it."

"All right, so I'm a little worried about Inga." Vola gave her a rueful smile. "But she didn't know me well enough to keep me from getting you all back. And in the end, she's not the one who's the key to Anders's plans."

Lillie's mouth went round. "Nargilla."

"If Anders can help Xavier and Innis escape…"

"Then he might be able to steal Nargilla right out from under the gods' noses," Sorrel said.

Rilla's lips went thin while Talon and Lillie exchanged a look.

"I have to warn them," Vola said. "The gods need to know what they're up against."

They were gods. They should have been watching. They should have been all-knowing. The Broken certainly stuck her nose in often enough that Vola knew she had to be watching pretty much constantly. But the others hadn't proved themselves all that attentive. Maxim was revered for his strength and loyalty, but his followers all admitted he didn't really look in on them very often.

They would need a nudge to get them looking in the right direction. Even after the one she'd already given them about Anders.

So far, wrangling gods was more work than it was worth.

"You guys get back to camp and tell War to keep moving forward. The more we can drive forward while Anders is scrambling, the more we can keep him off balance," Vola told them. "Sorrel's in charge while I'm away."

Sorrel gave her a solemn nod.

"Get them back safely. I'll meet you there."

"You're going now?" Lillie asked, eyes wide. "Alone?"

"Not alone," Vola said as a little puff of displaced air told her someone had appeared at her shoulder.

"Never alone," the Broken said.

The others took her armor with them. Hopefully, the army blacksmiths could burn away the poison and repair the damage for her. Besides, she wouldn't need it where she was going.

She watched until her people disappeared into the distance, back toward camp. It hurt to watch them walk away. More than she'd thought it would.

They're heading for safety, she told herself. *And I have to do this now. If I wait, Anders could slip Nargilla right out from under their noses and we'd be fu—I mean, screwed.*

She glanced at the Broken out of the corner of her eye to see if she'd caught that slip.

"Ready?" the Broken said, catching her glance.

"As I'll ever be."

"Then walk with me."

Vola stepped alongside the Broken, the gravelly lava rock shifting a little under her feet until the next step she took landed on stable marble. The long bright hallway stretched ahead of them. A long gangly form was silhouetted against the white chamber at the end.

Vesteral, speaker of the gods, watched unblinkingly as they approached.

Vola glanced at the Broken, but she just gave a serene nod.

Vola cleared her throat. "Speaker," she said. "We need to speak with the gods that hold the mortal traitor Nargilla Pipwattle."

Vesteral arched one curved eyebrow.

The chamber echoed. No bits of color or whisper of voices indicated the presence of the gods this time.

"They aren't here," Vesteral said, correctly interpreting her glance. "The gods have many duties. They have their own lives which they spend ruling over mortals. They do not...hang around here waiting for a summons."

"Oh." Well, of course not. But it wasn't like she was familiar with the personal lives of the gods. Only what they showed to select mortals.

"I think what my representative means," the Broken said, with her own eyebrow tilt. "Is would you be so kind as to request Maxim's and Dierdre's presence? It's a matter of some urgency."

Vesteral sniffed. But he couldn't disobey a direct order from any of the gods. Much less the Broken, who stood apart from the others because of her power.

"Very well," he said. "Wait here."

"Where does he think we'll go?" Vola asked as his form faded and he disappeared. "It's a big empty room."

"You're in the realm of the gods here. This is a hub between every realm of the Greater Virtues and Obstacles. If you were determined enough, you could enter any of the realms you chose. Even without invitation."

Vola blinked at the vague outlines of the room around them, trying to figure out where the openings to these other realms were. Did the Broken have one? Did she live there when she wasn't hanging over Vola's shoulder? For some reason she couldn't imagine the goddess lounging on a couch eating grapes out of the hands of an attractive server.

A flicker of dark color and movement drew her eye, and she turned to find Mulgash coalescing on one of the tiers, his feet up on the bench beside him.

"What are you doing here?" she said, without stopping to think.

He shrugged, unperturbed. For a god of rage, Mulgash rarely showed any temper as far as Vola had experienced. He was always the calm voice in the back of your head, urging you to more and more violence.

"Keeping an eye on you," he said, examining his nails. "I did tell you I would be looking out for you, didn't I? Don't mind me. Keep doing what you're doing."

Vola's brows drew down, and she opened her mouth to protest, but Vesteral reappeared along with two other figures.

Maxim, in his golden armor, manifested first. With his deep ebony skin and even darker hair, he looked particularly statuesque in the sunlight that suffused the room. The woman with him had close-cropped steel gray hair and eyes a milky white that meant she should have been blind. But her gaze fixed on Vola without stuttering.

Dierdre, Greater Virtue of Justice. She had nearly an army of paladins who followed her as well as judges, lawyers, and the odd criminal who thought sucking up would improve their chances.

These two were the ones in charge of Nargilla and keeping the clever gnome imprisoned. At least until Anders was dealt with. Then she'd face her own trial before the gods whose power she'd tried to steal.

"Why do you call us, representative?" Dierdre said, her voice snapping like the strike of a gavel.

Maxim remained silent, staring.

Vola wanted to glance at the Broken again, let her take the lead. But the goddess was in an odd position politically. She couldn't give the others commands, and even suggestions would be met with disdain. It was up to Vola to ask and nudge.

Vola bowed her head. "Lady Justice," she said. "Lord Strength. I have a warning. The traitor Anders has more power and skill than we originally anticipated. He's collecting his former lieutenants from their various imprisonments, and he's even managed to help one escape from planar banishment. If he can do that, it's possible he could storm the realm of the gods and take Nargilla by force. And if he has her...he has the key to stealing the rest of your power."

Vola stopped to take a deep breath.

Maxim and Dierdre exchanged an indulgent look.

"It was good of you to come to us with this warning," Dierdre said. "Thank you."

Vola's mouth worked. "Then...you'll take precautions? Make sure he can't take Nargilla back? She's the key to all his plans. If he gets her, we'll have no chance."

"We are aware of all this. You warned us of her role when the Broken entrusted us with her imprisonment."

"Okay," Vola said. She still wasn't getting the response she'd wanted or expected. On the bright side, they hadn't dismissed her. But they didn't show the alarm she felt like the situation warranted.

"We appreciate the warning," Maxim finally said and placed his gauntleted hand on Vola's shoulder. It weighed her down and burned her shoulder through her shirt. "But you needn't worry, little one."

No one had called her 'little one' since she was ten and had grown taller than her father.

"There really is nothing Anders can do against us," Dierdre said. "Not while the Virtues and the Obstacles stand united."

There was a snort, and Vola glanced at Mulgash, still lounging on one of the tiers.

She wasn't the only one to notice him.

"You have something to add?" Maxim said, coldly.

"You're underestimating her again," Mulgash said in a singsong voice. "If Volagra Lightless is worried, you'd do better than to brush her off."

"Noted," Maxim said in a voice that told them he was just trying to shut Mulgash up.

Mulgash shrugged. "There's a part of me that just wants to say screw it and let you do what you want. It will be so much more fun when you see the truth. But if Anders gets Nargilla, he gets you. And if he gets you..." He spread his arms wide. "He gets the whole pantheon."

"That will not happen," Dierdre said with a cold glance. "Anders would have to get through both the goddess of Justice and the god of Strength and Loyalty in order to get to Nargilla. We're no mere Obstacles," she said with a sniff. "We're Virtues."

Mulgash surged to his feet, jaw tight. His knuckles went white, and Vola held her breath. Was she about to see an Obstacle actually strike a Virtue? It would certainly be interesting, but maybe she should find some cover.

Mulgash took a deep breath and visibly reined in his temper. Vola had to admit to a grudging respect. She knew first hand how hard that was and it had to be even worse for the god of rage.

He flashed a grim smile at Vola. "Now you see what you're up against. They'll discount anyone different from them, no matter their value or wisdom." He gave the Virtues a mocking little bow and sank into the floor, disappearing with a puff of warm air.

"Such dramatics," Dierdre said. She smiled at Vola and the Broken. "Hardly necessary and hurtfully untrue. We regard all with the same level of care. There's really nothing to worry you, my dear. Anders cannot move against us as long as we're united."

She turned, and Maxim went with her. Together, the two faded as if they walked through the wall.

"I trust the Broken can show you out?" Vesteral said, and bowed himself away as well.

Vola stood, clenching her fists. She had the distinct feeling she was standing behind a wall of glass shouting that a monster was coming while the people on the other side chuckled and pointed out her antics to their neighbors to share the joke.

She glanced at the Broken to ask if they were really overreacting. But the Broken stared at the wall where Maxim and Dierdre had disappeared, her eyes tight and sad, scarred mouth drawn down. The mixture of pain and longing and regret on her face was clear, and Vola looked away, embarrassed to be a witness.

If she were a mortal, Vola would have said the Broken missed her god siblings desperately. But there were far more layers here. The goddess missed them, yes. But she seemed proud and ashamed of them at the same time, and Vola knew there were deeper wounds there that she couldn't even begin to guess at.

The Broken was her goddess, not one of her teammates. But still, there was the pull to fix this. To say something that would fix what was broken. But how did you fix a broken goddess?

"It's good to see them working together at least," Vola said quietly. "Maybe one day, they'll be willing to work with you again, too."

The Broken cast her a rueful glance, and Vola felt like she'd missed the point.

"Don't let them fool you the way they've fooled themselves. They are not united. They might be working together, but they are not united."

The Broken turned and started down the hall. "And until they are, they are just as broken as I am."

Vola kept quiet. She didn't know how to fix what was wrong. She barely even knew what was wrong between the gods, other than a political rift. And patting the Broken's arm and saying "there, there, it will be okay" didn't seem fitting. Especially since she wasn't sure it would be okay.

She didn't expect the pantheon to follow a mortal. But what was she supposed to be representing if they didn't at least listen to the Broken sometimes?

Maxim didn't care about mortals. He'd forced himself to not care about them, to distance himself from the pain they caused every time they died.

His disinterest informed the rest of the gods, and it informed the way he interacted with Vola. He didn't listen to her because he didn't care.

So what would make him care?

Greater Virtue of Strength and Loyalty. Vola's lips curled. He had a follower who embodied both those virtues more than anyone else Vola had ever met.

Somehow, she had to get Sorrel into Maxim's path. The halfling was exactly what Maxim looked for in a follower. And she carried his Warhammer. If anyone could convince the Greater Virtue to care, it would be Sorrel Thornbough.

"I think we should introduce Maxim to a monk I know," Vola said.

The best part about working with a goddess was that the Broken followed her train of thought better than anyone, except for maybe her team.

A slow smile spread across the goddess's face. "That's not a bad idea."

"Think he'll go for it?"

"Coming along to the mortal realm? Oh, definitely not. He hasn't manifested to anyone in centuries. Every paladin thinks he'll be the next one Maxim speaks to directly, but they're all wrong."

Vola pursed her lips.

"But...I'll work on him," the Broken said. "There was a time he enjoyed swinging a sword alongside mortals. If he was ever going to get out of this rut of his, now would be it."

SEVENTEEN

VOLA REAPPEARED on the lava field in front of the mess tent, scaring the crap out of a boy carrying a pot full of stew.

He shrieked, and the stew went flying. Bits of meat and potatoes pelted the ground and the canvas of the tent.

"Shawn! You idiot, what's so frightening you're wasting good food like that? You know how difficult it will be to get more hauled out here?" One of the cooks came surging out of the tent, bearing a greasy ladle like a sword.

"It's the black paladin," the boy said, pointing. "She just-just appeared out of nowhere. I think she came up out of the ground after consorting with Mulgash."

"I did no—" Vola bit her tongue. The boy wasn't exactly wrong.

The cook seized the boy's shoulder and thrust him behind his wide bulk.

Vola sighed. "Mulgash doesn't live underground, anyway," she said. "He lives in his own realm." She strode off before Mulgash's rage could flicker in her eyes and prove his point.

Everyone had prejudices. It was nearly impossible to get to adulthood without having some ingrained opinion that hurt someone else. It was just bad luck that Vola seemed to embody most of the usual ones.

That and breeding but she'd pay to see someone confront her parents about that.

She turned a corner, putting more distance between herself and the mess tent. Where to find the others? They had to have gotten back by now. From the angle of the sun, she'd been gone for hours.

She paused for a second to get her bearings. Mishap's Heroes usually set up in any space that was left near the command tent, so she could start there.

She stopped as shouts wound through the canvas walls of the camp.

Or she could follow the sounds of arguing. Because if there was a mess around, she'd bet money her teammates would be in the middle of it somehow.

Sure enough, there was a knock-down, drag-out fight going on three rows over from the command tent, and several of the participants wore gray tunics.

At least it looked like Sorrel was trying to stop the fight. Not like she'd started it.

The monk held back two of her fellows, both of which stood several feet taller than her. But the halfling had her heels dug into the dirt and hauled on their tunics. The adversary seemed to be a small troop of Mistvalian foot soldiers.

Lillie stood to one side with her father, a couple of the scholars, shifting from foot to foot. Vola knew that look. She was trying to decide which spell to use.

Vola caught her eye and shook her head. *Save the spells*, she tried to say.

Lillie sighed and finally nodded. Then she gestured to the right where Talon stood, surveying the fight with crossed arms.

Vola signaled Talon to flank while she waded into the middle, yanking combatants off their feet.

"What the hell is going on?" she yelled. A little lightning bolt bounced from the tip of a spear on a nearby rack. "Do you want the War Princess over here to bring you all up on charges? 'Cause you're making enough racket to call her."

She hauled a soldier off his feet and set him back so the monks couldn't land a blow. Talon swept one's legs out from under him and made sure he stayed down.

Vola scanned the monks for the abbess and finally found the dwarf directly in the center of the fray. "Aren't you supposed to argue for non-violence most of the time? Save your energy. The enemy is out there, not in here."

"Believe me, we had good reason," Hazel said, her lips pulled back in a snarl. "Maxim would not thank us for backing down from an honorable fight."

From everything Vola had seen, Maxim wouldn't care. But since that was exactly what she was trying to fix, it seemed stupid to argue the point now.

Sorrel succeeded in hauling the other two monks back and now that the soldiers were mostly laid out on the ground, thanks to Vola, Hazel stepped back and adjusted her tunic.

"Now, explain this," Vola said.

Hazel and one of the soldiers started talking at once.

Vola held up her hands. "Never mind. Let's try again. First you." She pointed to Hazel.

The soldier snorted. "Of course, you'd hear out the orc lovers first," he muttered.

Vola turned on him. She could have snarled and shown off all the orc teeth since he seemed so interested in them. But she very deliberately kept her lips closed and raised a scathing eyebrow, the way the Broken always did.

The soldier fell silent.

"Now," Vola said. "What happened?"

Sorrel swept some loose hair from her brow. "Words were exchanged. There was some good-natured ribbing from what I could tell. But er, some of the remarks turned personal."

"He insulted Sorrel," Hazel said.

Vola glanced at Sorrel, who shrugged. "Must have been some insult," Vola said. "I've seen her keep her cool and her beer in the middle of an orc brawl."

"She didn't think there was cause for retaliation," Hazel said. "But I did."

"Someone might have implied that I was so short, there was no way you'd let me on your team. Unless sexual favors were exchanged."

Hazel's eyes narrowed.

"Hmm, and I thought simple skill would suffice," Vola said. "Maybe I should have held out for sexual favors."

Sorrel grinned. "Maybe. I'm probably not very good at them, though."

Vola caught sight of Imralen lurking at the edges. Her teeth creaked as her jaw clenched, but the Knight Commander remained silent and still.

"And what's your side?" Vola asked the soldier.

The soldier raised his chin. "We were just making conversation, and they jumped me. But I don't know what you expect from people who follow an orc. Violence is all they know."

There was a ripple through the crowd that had gathered, and many of the onlookers faded back as a whole division of orcs boiled out of the background and moved to surround them.

An older chieftain in his fur loincloth with leather bandoliers across his chest lowered his chin and glared at the soldier. "You'll want to be careful insulting our way of life, son," he said. "Since we're using that aggression to defend you and yours on the battlefield tomorrow." He glanced at Vola and cracked a grin. "Hiya, honey."

"Hey, Dad. Glad you could make it before we cleared everything out."

The soldier's eyes went wide, and Vola caught the little flick of movement where he checked with the Knight Commander.

Vola spun so she could pin the soldier with her gaze. And so Imralen lined up right behind him. She could talk to the one while glaring at the other.

"So, what's been going on here while I've been out there making sure this army has a place to advance to every day? Hmm?"

The soldier gulped and wouldn't meet her eyes.

"Picking fights with monks?" Vola asked. "And orcs?" She glanced at Lillie. "What about the scholars?"

The soldier didn't answer, but Lord Ephyra met her eyes. "There was some graffiti on our tent this morning. 'Go home, orc lovers.' Badly misspelled, too."

They were going after her friends now. Anyone who'd ever supported her. Imralen was waging a battle within the real war.

Vola checked on Talon, but the ranger kept her gaze lowered. If she'd been getting any harassment because of Vola, she wasn't saying.

Vola cursed inside her head. She was so busy running around trying to get through Anders's barrier, she hadn't had time to stop the spread of Imralen's poison back here. And now she was fighting from a weakened position.

"Go home," she said, suddenly weary. "Control yourselves. Or get out, because an army that's fighting amongst itself isn't any good to the War Princess or to the world. If you have so much of a problem with me that you have to attack anyone I've ever even had contact with, then you're too distracted to be a good soldier." She waved her hands as if she could magically be rid of them and stepped back, giving them all enough room to get out of her sight.

Talon helpfully reached down to lend a hand to the soldier on the ground.

"Get your hands away from me," he growled and staggered to his feet himself. He shuddered and spoke to one of his companions. "Did it touch me?"

Vola's hand shot out and wrapped around his throat. She lifted him with ease and slammed him onto his back against the lava rock. Then she placed her hand flat on his chest and held him there, making sure he could see how very little effort she expended in all of it.

"It's funny how no one notices when you're quiet and peaceful," she told him conversationally, ignoring the intake of breath around her. "They only notice when you get violent. So notice this and remember it. You want to attack me, you come after me. You go after one of them..." Her eyes flicked to her teammates one by one. "And I will show you the type of violence a black paladin is capable of. I'll show you what it's like to fight with all the fury of the Greater Virtue of Righteousness. Forget the Obstacle of Rage. He's a pushover compared to my lady."

She tapped his chest with her finger and pushed off of him to stand. She glanced around at the spectators still standing there, poised on the edge of something. Watching.

"I'm sorry. Did I say we were selling tickets? Move."

They scattered. Except for the orcs and the monks and the scholars. And Imralen, who just watched her with narrowed eyes.

She stared him down, daring him to say something, to attack her finally. To stop running around behind her back.

"How long before the princesses realize you're more of a problem than Anders is?" Imralen said. "You're taking us apart from the inside."

Heat beat in her chest. He was undermining her at every turn. He was the one whispering lies and discontent and blaming it on her.

And the moment she retaliated, she became the very thing he claimed she was. She held her breath until black threatened to overwhelm her. But she didn't move.

Imralen shook his head. "I hope you come to your senses and withdraw from the field before you get people killed."

He stalked off with an air of sad superiority that put a blazing target on his back Vola had to fight to ignore.

"Oh my gods, I want to kick his ass so bad," Sorrel said as Vola finally sucked in a breath.

"A dagger in the ribs," Talon said. "He wouldn't even have to know it was coming."

"A fireball so big it knocks him clear out of camp," Lillie said.

They all looked at her.

"What?" She blinked. "Too much?"

"I take it I missed something big if Lillie is talking about blasting people." Rilla stalked into the cleared area, hands on the hilts of her daggers.

Vola cracked her neck and rolled her shoulders. "We're fine," she said. "Everything's fine." Except she was losing to Imralen, and she had no idea how to stop it.

Rilla opened her mouth, then stopped and squinted at the people gathered. "Holy crap, when did we recruit all these orcs?"

"When you put my daughter in charge," the orc chieftan said, rubbing his head.

"Hi, honey." A lithe human woman in a fur-lined leather bikini stepped out from behind the big orc. Faint traces of silver streaked her bushy red-brown hair.

"Hey, Mom. Thanks for coming."

"We were trying to find the commander in order to present ourselves and followed the sounds of fighting," Vola's father said. "That's usually the fastest way to find someone in charge."

"Well, I can help there," Rilla said.

"Mom, Dad. I'm not sure you ever officially met my boss, Rilla. Princess of the Dagger Throne. Rilla, this is Gorgo, chieftain of our tribe, and his wife, Lydia Battlemane."

"Lydia Battlemane...Wow," Rilla said, reaching to shake their hands. "I grew up hearing about your adventures. I even caught your bout at the friendship games where you trounced that minotaur."

Lydia giggled. "Oh, that was such a long time ago. You're making me feel ancient."

"Oh no, ma'am," Rilla said, pumping Lydia's hand. "Not ancient. Fit and sprightly and most welcome." Rilla's eyes flicked down to what Lydia was wearing for a split second. "And maybe you'd like to visit our quartermaster for some fitting attire."

"It's armor," Lydia and Vola said in unison.

"Sorry," Vola told Rilla. "Long argument. You won't win. We've all tried."

"Well, I can at least introduce you to War," Rilla said after a moment's hesitation. "She'll be happy to see you. The more fighters she can move around her board the better."

Vola gave her parents what she hoped was an encouraging smile and sent them off with Rilla. Then she rubbed her eyes hard enough to hurt.

She felt more than saw the rest of her team come to stand with her.

"How bad is it?" she asked them quietly, expecting the truth, though she knew they'd want to shield her from it.

"It's not good," Sorrel said. "They're coming after the rest of us now."

"Little things that we can handle," Lillie said. "Like you saw. The graffiti and picking fights."

"But how much longer before it's such a problem that the princesses notice?" Vola asked. "How much longer before he really hurts one of you? Or Anders wins because Imralen managed to take us down before we even started fighting?"

They didn't speak for a long moment. "We don't know," Talon said. "But we wouldn't be doing anything differently if we did, would we?"

The others shook their heads.

"This is where we're supposed to be, Vola," Talon said. "All we can do is keep going. And maybe the rest of them will see the truth before it's too late."

EIGHTEEN

THE NEXT MORNING, War sent the new battalion of orcs to protect them while they searched for the next illusion.

After their last encounter and Xavier's ambush, Vola was glad her parents were along. But she couldn't help noticing that War had chosen the group most loyal to Vola. The least likely to turn their backs on her or get her party killed just because she was a black paladin.

War had to know what was going on in camp. She knew Imralen was complaining about Vola. She knew the fighters were at each other's throats over it. But did she know how bad it was?

Maybe War knew better than Vola and that's why they were out here again, not in camp where the problems were the worst.

Lillie limped along ahead of them on the rough lava field with her own little contingent of orcs, looking for the next illusion to break. A couple of them remembered Lillie from Inga's stronghold. They remembered the way she'd helped free them and they greeted her with hearty claps on the back and little bows they'd obviously practiced.

The ones that didn't remember her hung back, seeing only that she had the fair skin and pointed ears of the haughty elves and the regal bearing of a noble.

But their distrust melted as the wizard refused their help, scrambling over the rough terrain, even though it made her limp worse and Vola could see her wincing.

Orcs believed that pain made you strong. They believed that hardship wasn't something you hid from. And hiding your rage, your pain, and your suffering was unhealthy. So they respected Lillie's choice. And respected her more for making it.

Rilla, Talon, Sorrel, and Vola kept back a bit, giving Lillie room to work. The orcs ranged on either side of them in long lines, eyes alert for trouble. Gorgo led the left flank, Lydia the right.

Vola kept waiting for the undead to swarm or to rise up at their feet or come crawling over the horizon. But there was nothing for hours.

And then figures ambushed them from the low hills and hummocks of the lava field. But they didn't moan or shuffle. They screamed battle cries and rushed over the uneven ground.

Vola and her team drew their weapons, but there was hardly a need. Gorgo's fighters knelt and met the first wave with brutal efficiency, raising their weapons as the enemy charged. Lydia's group swept in behind to mop up the remaining survivors.

Vola and the others were left blinking, their weapons ready but no enemy to fight.

"Well," Rilla said, sheathing her daggers. "That was…anticlimactic."

"Anders must have sent a force for just the five us, not expecting any back-up," Talon said.

Vola stepped to join her father, who knelt beside one of the bodies.

"Did this seem strange to you, too?" he asked.

Vola crouched beside him. She turned the body over. "They're not dead," she said, looking down into the lifeless face of an elf.

Gorgo snorted.

Vola rolled her eyes. "I mean, they're not undead. They were alive. Until we killed them."

"Generally, that's how mercenary work goes," Lydia said, leaning on her battleax. "Things are alive until someone pays us enough to make them not alive anymore."

Talon and Sorrel joined them. "Maybe Anders's army isn't all zombies," Sorrel said.

"But who would fight for him?" Talon said. "Unless he's promising them something."

"Maybe part of the power he's stealing," Rilla said. "That's one of the big three. It's always money, sex, or power."

"Whatever it is, it's not enough," Vola said quietly. "These people weren't prepared to face us at all."

Gorgo sighed. "Bad press. There's always some well-meaning busybody ready to argue that mercenaries are vicious brutes because of this sort of thing."

"That's sort of funny coming from you, darling," Lydia said with a snort.

"I think before I swing my sword, thank you very much. I think 'gee, this guy's ax is headed for my head. I bet if I chop his head off first, I'll get to keep mine a little longer.'"

"We should move on," Lillie said. The circle of orcs around her hadn't broken during the attack. "We still have to break the illusion. And if Anders has more troops to throw at us, I think we'd rather be there than here."

"Good point," Vola said.

They moved on, leaving the mystery troops behind. It wasn't like they could bury them in the lava rock, even if they'd had the time.

For the first time in days, there was a break in the featureless expanse of rock besides the occasional skeletal tree. Half a house rose from the lava field, as if someone had attempted to settle the barren land and given up halfway through construction. Either driven away by the inhospitable terrain or by Anders himself.

"This is it," Lillie said as they approached the front door. It had been painted a bright cheerful blue, but the peeling plaster and bare wood created the opposite effect now and made Vola shiver.

"Of course it is," Sorrel said. "It looks like an ambush waiting to happen."

"Come inside, little mouse. I promise not to eat you," Talon muttered.

"Don't wolves normally eat herd animals?" Lillie asked as Vola pushed the door open and peered inside.

Warped floorboards creaked under her boots and a staircase led up to a second story open to the sky. The roof lay in collapsed timbers across the second floor.

"It's cozy," Gorgo said, poking his head over Vola's shoulder. "And it's backed up against the barrier." He gestured to the undulating magic that reflected through the empty windows at the back of the ruined house. "So it'll be easier to defend."

"Unless something comes through it you can't see," Vola said. "Keep that possibility in mind. If you stay far enough back, you won't get sucked into the illusion, too."

"Will do," Gorgo said, with a lazy salute. "Don't worry, Commander Lightless. We'll keep you safe while you're taunting bad guys."

"Thanks," Vola said, and just kept herself from calling him dad in front of his mercenaries.

She stepped across the rough gray floorboards, the rest of her team right behind her. The now familiar fog forms rolled up, obscuring the orcs around them as they moved toward the center of the house.

"You know, I'm starting to wonder if I'm ever going to get to hit Anders for real," Sorrel said as the peeling walls faded and the floorboards at their feet turned to cut stone.

Walls climbed up around them, opening onto a gray sky. Realistic wind blew sleet into their faces as they stood at the top of a tower open to the elements.

Johnson, Anders's mentor, stood in the center calling into the storm. Behind him stood the third man from the other illusion and Anders, who held Mariel's free hand. They all stared upward, faces pale and tight.

A crumpled form in crimson mage robes lay at their feet, as if they'd only just defeated Brindle the Butcher.

A scream echoed across the opening of the tower, and Vola threw up her hands to protect her aching ears.

Out of the gray clouds above fell a massive shape full of red and gold feathers and evil, curved claws. A giant raptor landed with a thump that shook the entire tower and opened its mouth to shriek again. Its talons dug gouges in the stones at its feet and its head darted back and forth, big black eyes fastening on the party before it.

"A roc," Lillie said behind them. Vola got the impression she'd meant to whisper, but the roar of the storm made her raise her voice to be heard. "A magical construct designed to—"

"Remember," Johnson yelled back at his team. "It will defend its master even in death. Either we die here, or it does."

The third man drew his hands together and whispered a spell. When he flung them out again, a purple glow settled around Anders and Johnson's weapons.

Johnson sprang forward with a cry. He swept the roc with his blade and dodged a buffet from its wing. He rolled up directly under it and slashed at the bird's wing, right where it attached to its body. The roc ducked its head, but it couldn't get to the swordsman underneath it.

Anders took the opportunity to lunge forward and slash at its eye. The roc screamed and threw him against the wall.

Vola tore her eyes away from the fight. What were they supposed to be doing here? Every other illusion had held something for them to fight. And those shadowy enemies seemed to be the key to breaking them from the memories.

A brilliant flash of light lit up the dark clouds and a column of white pierced through them, pinning the roc to the tower floor. Mariel stood with her hands raised and eyes closed as if she prayed the beam into existence.

"Anders, now!" the third man shouted. The spell caster kept his hand twisted, keeping the magic swirling around Anders's blade.

Anders thrust himself away from the wall and shook his head as if to drive off dizziness. He sprinted for the roc and vaulted from a broken table, his sword held above him for the strike.

The roc slithered and wriggled out from under the beam of light. But instead of meeting Anders's charge, it lashed out at the spell caster, alone at the back of the tower. In one mighty beat of its wings, it leaped across the tower and snapped the man in half.

"No!" Mariel screamed.

Anders landed badly and tumbled. His sword fell from his hand and lay naked on the floor, dull steel once again. He lay against the stone, his chest heaving as he stared at the remains of the spell caster.

The roc spun on its hind legs, beating its wings, creating a gale-force wind that threatened to sweep them off the tower.

Vola planted her feet and leaned into it. Could an illusion knock her from the top of the tower? What were their bodies doing back at the ruined house?

And where were the enemies they were supposed to be fighting?

She raised her arm to protect her eyes from the debris flung by the wind and glanced at the others. Sorrel and Talon squinted back at her while Lillie braced herself against the wall and stared aghast at the pitiful remains of the spell caster.

"Lillie," Vola called. "What are we supposed to be fighting?"

Lillie shook herself and met Vola's gaze with a bleak look. "I don't know." She peered into the empty corners of the tower. "I haven't seen anything, have you?"

Johnson was the first of Anders's team to recover from his shock. "Anders," the old mercenary called. "Cover Mariel. We've got to pull out all the stops now."

Anders scrambled for his sword and flung himself in front of Mariel while Johnson lunged to distract the roc.

Mariel flung her arms wide and threw back her head, her lips moving in time to a single word spoken over and over again.

Johnson cut at the roc's feathered breast, but his blade barely nicked the bird now. The roc beat at the man with its wings and he staggered back. A huge claw swiped at the mercenary and Johnson fell heavily, face down against the floor.

Anders screamed as the roc stood atop his mentor, claws cutting deep into his body.

Vola winced.

"What is the point of this again?" Sorrel said. "Are we really just supposed to sit here and watch this happening?"

"We're supposed to break the illusion," Vola said. "Whether that's by finishing it, or fighting, I don't know." There still weren't any other enemies for them to take care of. And the ones from the other illusions had all been faceless. Just figures to cut down. This roc seemed more real than some of the monsters they'd fought in their own travels.

Anders raced forward. He couldn't connect with the giant bird, but he ducked and dodged, making it chase after him instead of Mariel while she wove her spell.

She clasped her hands, whispering a name, and light filled the space between her palms. Then she threw it at the roc. The spell filled the fearsome creature, spilling from its mouth and eyes, and out from under its feathers.

It shrieked and thrashed, catching Anders across the chest and flinging him into the tower wall. Mariel raced forward and its claws tangled in her skirt, dragging her down under its convulsing beak and claws while it died.

"No!" Anders struggled to his feet, then collapsed. Finally, he crawled forward as the roc lay still amid a mess of feathers and blood.

He gathered Mariel's limp body into his arms.

Vola tried to breathe normally and found she couldn't around the lump in her throat. She'd held each member of her team, sometimes thinking they were dead, and it had nearly broken her. How much worse would it have been if she hadn't been able to heal them?

Anders's lips moved, and Vola realized she could hear him in the silence. The storm whistling above had died abruptly in the face of the roc's death.

"Please, please, please," he was saying.

Rilla watched, her face still as stone. Lillie held her hands over her mouth, eyes full.

Mariel didn't stir.

Anders threw back his head. "Maxim!" he cried, voice ragged. "She's one of yours." He pulled Mariel close and bent over her once again. "She's one of yours," he whispered. "Maxim. Please."

Finally, a single shadowy figure crept from the back of the tower, where a set of stairs led down. One, after all of that. It slunk toward the grieving Anders.

Vola ignored the ache in her throat and stepped to intercept the enemy. She didn't even try to sneak up on it. What was the point, anyway? This was just a memory. Nothing she did would affect the outcome.

As her sword cleaved the shadowy figure in two, a familiar shiver started at the top of Vola's head and swept down to her feet, and the tower faded around them, dissolving into a smear of black and white and gray.

"Well, that was uniquely horrible," Sorrel said.

"What is this for?" Lillie asked, scrubbing at her eyes. "What is he hoping to accomplish by making us watch all this?"

"To feel sorry for him, obviously," Talon said.

"Everyone's lost someone," Rilla said, sharply. "That doesn't excuse him from trying to drain the world of magic. My dad died when I was eight. You don't see me terrorizing entire countries."

Vola rubbed her forehead, trying to erase the after images of Anders's grief and failing.

Sounds came to them first as the rest of the world smeared into existence like watercolors running together.

The clash of weapons and calls of wounded soldiers slipped down Vola's spine, and she settled her shield more firmly.

"Heads up," she said. "We're coming out hot, apparently."

They circled up, keeping their backs to each other, and Vola kept her ears open as the colors shifted and gathered and finally solidified into the real world once again.

Orcs circled them, weapons drawn. They guarded the windows and doors of the ruined house as sounds of fighting drifted from outside. Vola found the familiar figure of Gorgo just outside the front door, and she raced to join him.

"We're out," she called as she stepped across the threshold. "What do you need?"

Gorgo glanced at her with a frown and kicked an enemy in the knee. He cut the man down as he staggered.

Then the world fell strangely still, and the orc chieftain wiped his brow. "Nothing, apparently?" he said. "It's just been little feints like that. Testing our defenses. I'm more worried about them."

Vola raised her gaze and her breath froze in her chest. Ranks of people stood in a solid wall just twenty yards from the ruined house. Just standing there, staring.

These weren't undead. These were fully fleshed humans, mostly. With a scattering of the other races represented.

"What are they doing?" Vola whispered.

"Exactly this," Gorgo said. "Every now and then a little group attacks, but it's more for show than anything. The rest are waiting for something. Before you went in, our backs were to the barrier at least. But now it's gone, we're too exposed."

Vola followed his gaze. The barrier had retreated once again, now that they'd broken the illusion. It shimmered quite a ways away, but it seemed much smaller now than before. Vola even fancied she could see the looming bulk of the volcano through the curtain.

"I don't like these," Gorgo said. "They're strange."

"I know our village is small," Vola said with a grin. "But surely you recognize humans."

"Smartass. That's not what I meant. These are acting odd. None of them want to talk."

Vola surveyed the enemy. Gorgo was onto something. For one, they looked nothing like soldiers. Where was the armor? And weapons? They carried rusted swords and pick axes. Like they'd picked up any old thing lying around. A blank-eyed woman nearby even wore a kilted-up gown covered in flour, as if she'd just walked away from her baking.

Something about her stare stirred in Vola's gut.

"Oh," Vola said. "Oh crap. Lillie!"

Lillie popped her head through a window.

"They're controlled."

Lillie's mouth dropped open, and she stared at the pressing enemy. "Oh." She said. "Oh crap." She wove her hands together and cast a shield around a group of them.

The subverted villagers blinked. Then one by one they toppled to the ground, eyes closed as their minds tried to recover from what had been done to them.

"Mind control?" Gorgo said. He whistled to Lillie. "Can you do that to all of them?"

Lillie stared around at the enemy army. "Not any time soon."

"Hey!" Lydia called from the left, where she stood with a line of orcs. "Hey!"

Vola spun to see a large man with raggedly cut hair and a beard that hadn't been trimmed in ages try to push past her mother. He wore the remnants of a knight's surcoat, but it had been so badly stained Vola couldn't even see what color it was anymore.

The man pushed again, and Lydia shoved him back. She roared in his face and launched herself at him, battle ax raised.

The man screamed and rolled away. The subverted villagers remained frozen, waiting. But this one had desperation in his eyes as he fought to get through Lydia.

"Lillie!" he called. "Lilliara!"

Lillie's head whipped around and her lips parted on a name. "Innis."

Vola charged forward and snatched the man away from her mother's ax blade. She hauled him to his feet and yanked him into the center of their circle, keeping her hand clenched on the back of his neck.

Lydia growled and followed.

"Just a second, Mom," Vola said. "I want to hear what he has to say."

"I can't kill him?"

"Depends on what it is he says next."

The man blinked wide blue-green eyes up at her. All four Ephyra children had inherited their mother's eyes, but Vola wasn't going to be swayed by how much Innis looked like his sister.

"You," he said, voice hoarse like he hadn't used it in a long while. Or like he'd spent a lot of time screaming. "You protected her."

Vola's eyes narrowed. True, the last time she'd seen this man, she'd done a pretty good job of keeping Lillie alive. But also, the last time she'd seen him, he'd been banished for treason.

Innis shook himself. He didn't try to pull away from her grip, but he did try to draw himself upright more, throw his shoulders back, and at least stand like a real knight.

"Lillie," he said again.

Lillie tumbled through the open window of the house and stopped short, keeping a good ten feet between herself and one of the brothers who'd betrayed her.

"Innis," she said, voice steady without inflection. "What are you doing here?"

"I came to warn you." He coughed and tried to clear his throat. "Anders. He helped us escape your prison, but...he's trying to take all the magic out of the world. He subverted all these people, just like he did to Kellan. And...and he's convinced Xavier this is all for the best."

"We know," Lillie said. "We saw Xavier already. He tried to kill us. Again."

Innis's shoulders slumped. "Lillie, I'm sorry."

"Might be a bit late for forgiveness, boyo," Sorrel said, leaning on her staff in the doorway.

Innis's eyes flashed. The first bit of defiance Vola'd seen since he'd disappeared through the portal to another plane. "I'm not saying it because I want forgiveness," he said. "I'm saying it because it needs to be said." He turned to Lillie. "I was wrong, and I'm sorry. I'm sorry about Xavier, I'm sorry I supported him for as long as I did. And I'm...I'm just sorry."

His eyes flicked to Vola, then Rilla, then Sorrel. "I'm not asking for forgiveness. I'm not asking for a pardon or exoneration. But I am trying to make up for my actions now. I left Xavier. I left Anders. And I came here to warn you."

"Warning would have been nice before we were surrounded," Gorgo said with a huff.

Innis shook his head. "This isn't the worst of it. Anders has a new commander on the field. She's out there right now. She holds the reins for these troops. They'll follow her mindlessly into the slaughter just because she tells them to."

Vola stiffened, eyes unfocused, while her lips thinned. "This commander. I take it she's a half-orc. Spell caster. Carries a staff and thinks she knows everything."

"Goes by the name Inga," Talon said.

Innis looked between them. "You're not surprised," he said.

Vola closed her eyes, drew a deep breath, and then released it with all the pent-up rage and exasperation she could carry. "Not even a little."

NINETEEN

A SHUDDER WENT through the ranks of subverted villagers, and Vola took an involuntary step back.

"To the house," she said as calmly as she could.

It didn't matter. The others picked up her urgency and turned to race for the ruined house. Its walls were crumbling, but it would be better than nothing.

Vola kept her grip on Innis and threw him through the open door as the sea of subverted villagers surged forward, covering the twenty yards between them in less time than it took to smash an egg.

Vola slammed the door shut behind them and leaned on it.

The entire house shook as the bodies hit the walls at the same time.

Several orcs rushed to take her place against the door, the rest guarding the windows, shoving bodies back through the openings.

"Um, so what's the difference between these guys and zombies again?" Sorrel asked as Vola raced to join her team upstairs. "Because these look about the same."

"We can get rid of these," Vola said. She leaned out a second-story window to stare down at the milling heads. "At least cut them off from Inga's spell. Lillie, we're gonna need a bigger shield."

Lillie bit her lip. "If I do that, Inga and Anders could learn how to counter what I'm doing. It will be that much harder to break their mind control the next time."

Talon joined Vola and Sorrel at the window, bow ready in her hand. On the floor below there was a violent crack, and they heard Gorgo call out to hold them back.

"I don't think we have another choice. Not if we want to get back to our own army. Are you ready to make your last stand here?"

Lillie's mouth firmed.

There was a ripple in the ranks below them, and Vola held up her hand to wait. The subverted villagers around the front door pulled back, leaving a clear path leading from the front step.

Vola followed it with her eyes and her gaze latched on the figure at the top of the bare hill beyond. She was tall and shapely, with gray-green skin almost a perfect match for Vola's, and she wore a blue gown split up her leg. Her hand curled around a gnarled staff.

Vola inhaled.

"I'll do it," Lillie said flatly, pulling her spellbook from her satchel. "Give me as much time as you can. And don't let her get in your head."

Vola set her jaw and signaled the rest. "Let's go."

"Right, racing down the path the bad guy has paved," Sorrel said, following Vola down the shaky stairs. "Throwing ourselves into her waiting arms."

"Do you have a better idea?" Vola asked.

"Nah, it sounds fun. Just because we know something is a trap doesn't mean we don't have to throw ourselves in feet first."

"It means exactly that," Talon said as they paused at the front door. "We could choose not to rise to her bait."

"Sneak out the back while she expects you to walk out the front," Rilla said.

"I don't think we could get everyone out before she noticed," Vola said. "It's not like there's a lot of cover out there to hide fifty orcs."

"There's not a lot of cover in here to hide fifty orcs," Gorgo said. "But we're making it work. You going out there?"

"I am," Vola said.

"I'm going with you," Lydia said.

"What?" Gorgo said.

"The last time Vola faced this monster, she nearly killed me," Lydia said, baring her teeth. "I would like to return the favor."

"You stay here and wait for our signal," Vola told Gorgo. "Guard Lillie and when the subverted villagers go down, you can join us."

She swept up to the door. The orcs holding it shut took one look at her face and stood back. Vola raised her boot and kicked the door open.

"You know it was unlocked, right?" Talon said.

Lydia cast Gorgo a concerned look, but Vola ignored it. Her rage was firmly in check, held on a tight leash, ready to be released when it would do the most good.

Talon and Sorrel's expressions were set. Rilla just looked determined.

Sorrel poked her head out the door, checked that the way was clear, and then waved them through.

Vola stalked through the door, between the ranks of subverted villagers, and up the lava rock that rose outside the ruined house. The figure at the top stood tall and straight with a little smirk that crawled up Vola's spine and lodged in the back of her head, making her seethe.

Vola stopped about fifteen feet away and planted her feet. "You look pretty good for a dead woman, Inga," she said.

The half-orc's skin was as firm and clear as it had been the last time they'd seen her. She didn't look particularly undead.

"I feel like you should be falling apart more," Sorrel said, tilting her head. "And hunched over. You need to work on your corpse shamble. Anders has a lot of undead that can give you some pointers if you like."

Inga's lips twitched wider. "That would only be helpful if you'd actually succeeded in killing me," she said.

"How did you survive, then?" Talon said. "I seem to remember you getting thrown out a window."

"I had friends in high places. Or don't you remember?"

"Mulgash," Vola growled. "Funny how he forgot to mention you were still alive when I talked to him two days ago." And she'd be bringing it up the next time she saw him, for sure.

"He definitely seems to have developed a thing for you." Inga examined her nails. "I don't really like people who come and steal my patron out from under me."

"I don't really like people undoing all the work I've done. I just cleaned up this mess."

Inga's eyes flashed. "Oh, don't get me started. You stole my patron. You stole my purpose. And you stole my magic. Without Mulgash..." She closed her eyes and took a deep breath before opening them again. "He saw something in you he liked. The Obstacle of Rage dumped me and chose a paladin. A white knight."

Vola lifted her shield. "Not so white, now, you might recall."

Inga rolled her eyes. "Oh please. You and I both know that means nothing with the Broken standing at your shoulder."

Vola stiffened. "The Broken?" she said carefully. Inga knew Cleavah's secret?

Inga snorted. "Yes, the Broken. How long did it take you to figure it out?"

Vola ground her teeth. If she'd doubted whether this was the real Inga or not, it was gone now. The woman had always had a way of getting right under Vola's skin, like a splinter. She wriggled and wormed her way into her mind, knew exactly what she was going to do before she did it, knew exactly what to say to make Vola doubt herself.

"How did you get your magic back?" Sorrel said, swinging her staff idly. "If Mulgash dumped you."

"What makes you think I did?"

Sorrel raised an eyebrow and indicated the subverted villagers around them as if to say "duh."

Inga sighed. "Point to you. The process is very similar, at least, even if the source is different."

Inga hadn't been born with magic. Like Anders, she'd been born with less than so many other people. She'd tried to go to the universities like Lillie. She'd tried to learn the magic she hadn't been born with. But her orc heritage had put her at a disadvantage. The authorities had kept her out, and Inga, full of bitterness and hate, had made a bargain with the Greater Obstacle of Rage.

Mulgash had given her magic and in return, she'd served him. Now without Mulgash, she'd be magicless once again.

Unless, of course, there was someone nearby with excess amounts of it who would be willing to lend her some. Someone who didn't have any scruples about stealing magic in the first place.

"So what did you promise Anders?" Vola asked. "What are you giving him in exchange for power?"

Inga grinned and gave Vola a look that said, "clever." "The usual," Inga said. "It's not complicated. He gives me the power he's collected, and I use it to further his cause. All the years with Mulgash gave me the skills to use it. Anders is ambitious, I'll give him that," she said. "But he's inexperienced. It would be like handing over all this power to you." She pointed to Lydia. "And wielding magic isn't like swinging a battle ax."

"I'd like to see you swing this," Lydia muttered.

Inga cocked her head. "But what are you trying to accomplish here?" she said. "Why all the questions?"

Vola exchanged a glance with Rilla while Sorrel raised her chin. "What do you mean, what are we trying to accomplish? You blocked us into that house. Then clearly you wanted to talk to us so we came out to oblige."

"But you haven't even tried to kill me yet," Inga said, folding her arms and tapping her chin. "And after trying so hard last time—and nearly succeeding—I just expected more from you. Unless…"

Vola's gaze wanted to crawl toward the second-story window where Lillie had to be working, but she didn't let it.

"Unless you're stalling for time," Inga concluded. Without even pausing for breath, she shot a ball of black fire at the window.

"Lillie!" Vola screamed.

A roar drowned out her cry as Innis surged from a hiding place among the subverted villagers. He leaped upwards and the ball of black fire burst against his chest. He fell with a heavy thump.

Vola sucked in a breath. She jerked her thumb over her shoulder, and Lydia scurried to check on him. The rest spread out around Inga without her having to say so.

Inga just shook her head. "You should know better by now, Vola. I'm always one step ahead of you."

Vola set her teeth and raised her shield. "Charge," she said.

She rushed for Inga, ready to bash the smirk from her face, but Inga disappeared with a wink.

Vola skidded to a stop on the top of the hill, narrowly avoiding a collision with Sorrel.

The half-orc reappeared on a distant hilltop. She cupped her hands around her mouth. "I learned a couple of things from Lilliara the last time I was in her head."

The crowd of subverted villagers who had stood silent and still turned in a circle to face Vola and the others.

"Charge," Inga called.

Vola whipped around, sword ready, as the villagers raised their makeshift weapons and rushed forward.

Light flared from the second floor of the ruined house, and it burst out across the sky, falling down to cover the army arrayed against them. As the light touched each villager, they fell into place. One by one they toppled, some falling over those in front until piles of villagers lay still, as if sleeping.

Sorrel and Talon turned to the window to give Lillie matching grins, but Vola was already sprinting in the opposite direction. Toward Inga.

Inga shrugged. "A setback," she said. "But nothing serious. I have no idea why Anders wants to meet you so badly, but he was very specific about not killing you. So…"

Vola brought her blade down and the edge whistled through empty air as Inga disappeared yet again.

Vola roared in frustration, but Inga didn't reappear to meet her challenge. There was nothing around them. Nothing but the house, fifty-some odd orcs, an unconscious army, and Innis.

Vola stood there for a moment, fists clenched around the hilt of her sword and the grip of her shield, fighting against the red that washed across her vision as the others raced for Innis. She was needed. She was the healer, but all she could do was stand there and try to breathe without screaming.

"Vola," Sorrel called.

Vola turned, fighting away the last bit of red, and sprinted back to the others.

Innis lay against the rough lava rock, his breath coming raggedly through his lips.

Lillie burst from the house and fell to her knees on the rock, gathering him into her arms. Vola knelt beside her, hands reaching for Innis.

The knight's chest was black and caved in. Vola couldn't even find the edge of his surcoat within the charred mess.

"Lady bless," she whispered, reaching for the well of healing within her that connected her to the Broken.

Light flared between her and Innis, and she poured the power into him, pulling flesh and blood and bone and organs back into place. An ache started in her own chest, mirroring Innis's wounds. But the harder she pulled, the more the healing resisted. The blackened bits of skin receded bit by bit, but not enough. Not nearly enough.

Vola continued to pour the power into Innis, but he soaked it up without getting any better.

What was wrong? This was bad, worse than anything she'd ever healed before, but she should at least be making it better.

Vola's mind raced over the last few minutes. Talking with Inga, the black fire racing toward the house.

Inga's power came from Anders. And Anders had stolen a piece of the Broken's power.

And she used the Broken's power to heal. But it wasn't enough, apparently. Perhaps a god's power couldn't counteract itself.

"I'm sorry," Vola whispered, shoulders sagging as the light faded between her fingertips.

"Lillie," Innis gasped out.

"I'm here." Lillie's voice was thick, and Vola could hear her swallow.

"S-sorry," he said, the word a bare puff of breath between his lips.

Lillie choked. She took Innis's hand and held it against her cheek. "Sorry."

In the next moment, he was gone.

TWENTY

THEY CARRIED Innis back to camp between four orcs who acted like they didn't even notice his weight. Lillie's face remained pale and stony as she limped beside them.

Vola nearly outpaced them several times, the seething anger under her skin driving her faster and faster. She couldn't fight this threat. Inga had run away instead of facing her. And Anders didn't seem to be hurt by the progress they were making breaking down his barrier. Which left Vola feeling penned in and useless. Like a sheep being herded against a fence. She couldn't fight back. She turned to bite and found nothing to hurt. All she could do was keep running forward.

Anders was taking everything she'd worked for, everything she'd accomplished in the last year, and stripping it away. All her work was being unraveled beneath her feet, and she felt like any second now she'd tear through that thin foundation and start falling.

And what could she grab onto?

The camp was packing up by the time they arrived. War must have an innate sense of when they were about to return with good news. Or she just had someone monitoring the barrier to send word when they could advance again.

Without saying anything, Lillie led them to the camp's temple, which was only two rows from the scholars. And without saying anything, the orcs followed her.

The acolyte manning the tent hadn't done more than break down the benches and altar inside. He didn't complain when they laid Innis's body inside out of the way with his hands crossed over his chest.

Vola sent Gorgo and Lydia off with the other orcs after a quiet word. Gorgo cast a worried glance at Lillie. But the wizard didn't notice, and Lydia drew him away gently.

Lillie found Ephyra and Kellan inside the scholars' tent, packing their things.

"Lillie?" Kellan said, stopping dead in the middle of the tent when he saw his sister. "What's wrong?"

"You two should come with me," Lillie said quietly. "There's something...someone you should see."

Ephyra and Kellan exchanged a glance before following Lillie.

One of the scholars looked up, brow drawn down. "Wait, we have all this to get done before—"

"Let them go," Vola growled. "It's a family matter."

The scholar looked like he would argue, but then he glanced at Vola's face and snapped his mouth shut. He stared down at his feet.

Vola instantly regretted her tone. "I know what you're working on is important. But it can wait a few minutes."

"What *are* you working on?" Sorrel asked.

"Plan B," the scholar said. "In case Plan A doesn't work out."

"Um, what's plan A, then?" Talon said.

"Break through the barrier and bash Anders's brains out?" Sorrel said.

"Sounds about right," said Vola. She stepped back to get out of the way as one of the scholars carried a box bursting with papers out of the tent. Vola couldn't imagine how annoying it had to be to haul all the books and papers with them every time the army moved, only to have to unpack and repack everything a day or two later. But they were still working to understand Anders's draining spell, and that seemed a lot more important than the inconvenience.

Normally Vola and the others should have gone to break down their own campsite, but they'd already done that this morning before they'd left. After the last few days, it seemed prudent to pack up their tent and belongings and load them on the swamp monster ahead of time. The hostlers kept begging them not to leave it with them, but they couldn't drag the thing out in the field with them. Rilla had finally put her royal foot down and convinced them to handle the swamp beast without complaining. Vola suspected bribery had been involved.

Raised voices drifted between the tents, and Vola was too weary to be surprised. Squabbling seemed more usual than it should be now.

Sorrel cast a glance at the rest of them, her eyes resting on Vola for a moment, before she said, "I'll go sort them out. I thought I made it clear last time…" She scampered off towards the bickering.

Vola took a breath and tried to clear the tension in her chest, but it stayed there, heavy and oppressive. She couldn't help feeling like she was responsible for all the fighting, even if she wasn't the one here to start things. Or end them.

A shadow blotted out the dreary late afternoon light, and a down draft ruffled her hair.

Vola threw up her hand to shield her eyes.

"Looks like the contingent from Firewatch finally got here," Rilla said with a grin.

A huge turquoise dragon circled lazily down from the clouds to land on the north end of camp where there was plenty of flat space. Several other massive shapes followed her, as well as a swarm of smaller horse-sized figures.

A bit of the tension bled from Vola's shoulders as she stared at the beautiful creatures. "Shall we go say hi to Listrell?"

It took longer than Vola anticipated to make their way through the frenetic packing. They had to reroute entirely around the mess tent, which had been brought down and laid across two different pathways. And someone had stacked about a million crates in the middle of a third.

Over all the chaos they could see flashes of colorful scales and broad heads big enough to swallow a cart, horse and all.

Finally, they broke out past the last line of tents and found the welcome sight of six dragons waiting on the field. Each had a small army of figures climbing down from their backs, little draconic shapes that they knew from experience would stand even taller than Vola. The dragons had brought their guardians with them. Fierce warriors bred to protect the dragons with their lives.

A whole herd of the smaller dragons, *draconis minimus*, swarmed around their landing site, each one about the size of a horse. Vola had often wondered if maybe the swamp beast was a mutant form of one of these, showing off only the awful bits of the species.

Vola hurried across the field, Talon and Rilla following. But as she moved, her heart sank. In the gray afternoon light, she made out a figure speaking to the big turquoise dragon. Listrell had her head bent low in order to hear Imralen and the poison he was surely pouring in her ear.

Talon must have heard her intake of breath.

"It's fine, Vola," she said. "Listrell knows you well enough to not listen to him."

It didn't stop her heart from racing and her steps to speed up.

They approached the dragons and more of them had their heads down, listening to Imralen now. Renvick, Listrell's lead guardian, stood beside her head, his rust-colored scales glinting with blue-green highlights.

Vola fought to keep her attention on Listrell and her friends, not the Knight Commander. But Imralen turned as she stepped up.

"Speak of the devil," Imralen said, a smirk breaking through his normal frown.

"Is it true there was trouble today, Vola?" Listrell asked, deep voice rumbling across the lava field. "Someone was killed?"

Vola felt something snap in the back of her head. These were her allies. These were her friends. People and creatures she'd fought to protect and earn their respect. Over and over again. From Water's Edge to Brisbene to Glenhaven to Deersford and Firewatch. She'd ignored the whispers. She'd ignored the flat-out insults and petty arguments. She'd trudged on and on, doing what she did best, helping people, hoping that one day it would pay off and people would look at her and see who and what she was.

And this man came along behind her and swept every deed, every calm word, every warm smile under the rug as if it had never happened.

She lunged forward and planted her fist in Imralen's face.

Imralen stumbled back, his hands going to his gushing nose as Rilla and Talon cried out. Several dragons reared up, and Renvick shot forward to hold Vola back.

He held Vola's shoulders as she surged against him, ready to finish Imralen. Finish him how she wasn't quite sure. She was angry enough to kill right now, ricocheting between protecting her allies and protecting herself.

Renvick's claws gripped her shoulders, leaving ten perfect scratches in her armor.

"Let me go," she growled.

"No, Vola. People such as us cannot react in anger the way others can. We are too big. Too threatening."

She hesitated and caught his glance. He stared down at her, slitted eyes hooded with sympathy.

"We cannot rage the way they can," he said quietly at her. "You know this. You have only forgotten it for this moment."

Her fingernails dug into her palms. "I'm tired of being the better person." Just once she wanted to hit the thing in her way. The prejudice and discrimination that had taken physical form in Imralen. She wanted to pummel him into the ground until he begged for mercy.

And that was made her step back. And realize that she wasn't thinking like herself.

Rilla and Talon dragged on her arms, hauling her back another step or two.

"What the hell are you doing, Lightless?" Rilla hissed.

Imralen glanced at his hands and saw the blood that had come from his nose. His lips curled in a snarl, but Vola thought she saw a glint of triumph in his narrowed eyes.

"This!" he cried. "This is what happens when you fail to contain your beast."

Vola surged forward again, but Rilla and Talon leaped to hold her back. Renvick stepped between them and placed a hand on Imralen's chest.

"Go, now," the big guardian said.

Imralen tried to straighten his clothes with a dignified yank, but the effect was ruined when he had to keep one hand up to stop the blood from spilling down his chin. "I've been telling you all this time, she's too close to Mulgash. A paladin connected to the god of Rage will ruin us all. Her violence will tear this army apart before we even get close to Anders."

Vola wanted to scream. He was the one tearing the army apart. He was going to ruin all their plans. But the others were all glancing at her, looking at her out of the corners of their eyes as if she'd explode all over everyone. Which maybe she already had.

Renvick crowded Imralen back, and finally the Knight Commander threw up his hands and stalked away.

Vola yanked herself out of Rilla and Talon's grip. Talon tried to step in front of her.

"Why are you listening to that bastard?" Talon said. "You've always ignored him before."

"Maybe I haven't been ignoring him," Vola said. "Maybe I've just been storing up every little thing he's said and realizing that ignoring him will never work. Maybe I'm tired of not fighting back. Letting him say anything he wants. Maybe it's time someone told him to hold *his* tongue."

"No one was accepting what he was saying," Listrell rumbled above them. She turned one golden eye on Vola, looking hurt. "We know you better than him. We would have defended you. If you had waited just one moment more."

Vola's lips thinned, and she looked away.

"Now you've just given him ammunition," Talon said, holding onto her arms as if Vola would rip away. Maybe she would. She felt like it. "He has all the proof he needs now."

Vola caught the quick look that passed between Rilla and Talon, but she couldn't interpret it past "what a mess."

Talon let go of Vola. "I'll handle the dragons," Talon told Rilla. "I've always been better with non-humans."

"I'm only half human," Vola grumbled.

Rilla shot her a sharp glance. "I'll handle Lightless," she said like she was taking charge of an unbroken horse.

Vola couldn't help swallowing. She didn't want to be the direct focus of the Dagger Princess's anger.

Rilla took her arm and dragged her away from the dragons. Vola got the impression that even if she dug in her feet and put all her strength into resisting, the rangy princess would win.

Rilla dragged her to a clear area outside camp, away from Talon and the dragons, away from the bustle of the packing camp, and Vola had enough presence of mind to think that at least this wasn't going to be a public dressing down.

"What. The. Fuck?" Rilla finally turned to face her. "What was that?"

Vola opened her mouth to answer, and Rilla waved a finger in her face. "No, wait. I'll tell you what that was. That was a tactical disaster. You're supposed to be smarter than that. I know you're smarter than that. But you just struck the Knight Commander, giving him everything he ever wanted."

Vola yanked her arm away from Rilla and paced exactly ten steps to the left, then spun and paced ten steps back.

"You know what he says isn't true," Rilla said. "You know the rest of us don't believe it."

"That doesn't mean he should get to say whatever he wants without consequence. I just gave him his consequences."

"I know this is stupid and hard but—and I can't believe I have to say this to you of all people—striking him in anger isn't the way to fix any of it."

Vola stopped and looked down at Rilla. The princess tipped her head back and stared back at her.

"How long am I supposed to stay quiet, Rilla?" Vola asked. "How long am I supposed to take the higher road? How long does it take to disprove the lies he spouts about me? Because none of that's working."

"Longer than four days."

"I've been rolling over for him for half my life!"

For once Rilla didn't answer. She just watched with calm, dark eyes.

Vola tried to run her hands through her hair, but her braid was tangled and thick with sweat and a little bit of Innis's blood.

"Knight Commander Imralen ran the academy," Vola said. "He made my life miserable. For years. The only thing that made it worth it was Henri. And the thought that as soon as I graduated, I could leave, and I'd never have to see his looks or bear his snide remarks again. And then..."

"And then?" Rilla said.

"Then I graduated and found out that Imralen was just a representative of the rest of the world. He wasn't the only one who saw me that way. He wasn't even the worst. And I realized that my entire life was going to be one long string of convincing people I'm not what they thought."

"What changed?" Rilla asked. "You've been doing this half your life, you said. So what changed today?"

Vola slumped. "It's easier to fight him when I know he's wrong."

Rilla's mouth went tight. She reached out and touched Vola's arm. "You're not responsible for Innis," she said.

Vola found an outcropping of lava rock and let her legs collapse. She buried her head in her hands. "Maybe not. But maybe I could have done better."

"Or you could have done a lot worse."

Vola huffed a laugh, but she didn't lift her face from her hands. "He's right about Mulgash. The Obstacles might not be evil. But they are obstacles. And Mulgash just won't leave me alone. Even after Cleavah and the Broken. Learning to work around him instead of against him. He just keeps cropping up. And it's like all that work I did is just...gone."

Rilla rubbed the back of her neck and sat next to Vola.

"Everything we've done against Anders so far, he's reversing. How do you fight against that? Just do the same thing over and over again? How long do you beat your head against the wall before you admit the wall has won?"

"If the alternative is letting him win?" Rilla said. "Forever I guess."

Vola shot a glance at her. "Thanks for the pep talk, boss."

Rilla snorted. "You don't fight alone, you moron. That's the trick, I guess. Every time you come back, you have more people on your side. All those people you think aren't listening to you or aren't getting convinced are gathering. Until one day you have enough to topple him."

Vola's eyes swept the camp, taking in the flags still flying. The different countries who'd come to their aid. The dragons, the scholars. The monks and the villagers. The paladins.

"You were right," Rilla said, startling Vola out of her reverie. "We haven't been defending you the right way."

Vola shook her head. "I didn't mean —"

"Shut up. It's my turn. You were right. Just because we know Imralen's a liar, doesn't mean he should get to spout lies all over the place. No one's called him on his bullshit. Your entire defense has fallen on you and how well you keep silent. And that's not right."

Vola blinked, then stared down at her hands clenched over her knee. She didn't trust herself to say anything right then. It could have come out as tears of relief and gratitude or a bitter diatribe about how too late it was. But neither of those things was right or true to the wash of confusing feelings she was actually experiencing.

"I'll try to do better," Rilla said. "And I'll bet you have plenty of people like Listrell." She nodded toward the dragons settling down outside camp. "Like Talon and Lillie and Sorrel who are already doing better than me."

It was hard to forget the rare fire in Lillie's eyes anytime someone tried to convince her Vola was a monster. Or the way Sorrel laughed and mocked those who spat poison words. Or Talon, who barely said anything but stayed standing beside the family she'd chosen even when her own fears were dragged out into the open.

And suddenly Vola felt warm and small and ungrateful all at once.

"Of course, that doesn't mean we haven't made an unholy mess of all this in the meantime. Between our silence and Imralen's bloody nose, things in camp are going to be worse than they were before."

Vola winced. "I'm sorry. For what it's worth."

"Thank you. You lie low out here with the dragons. If Lillie's right — and I've learned never to bet against her — we only have one more illusion to break before we get to Anders. After defeating him, no one will be able to question anything about you again."

TWENTY-ONE

VOLA WAS glad to step out onto the lava field with her team the next morning, leaving the turbulent camp behind her. She'd apologized privately to Talon the night before, and they'd spent the night under Listrell's shadow with Renvick and the rest of the guardians. Sorrel hadn't joined them, and they assumed she was busy managing disagreements back in camp, and Lillie had remained shut away with her family.

"Are you sure you want to come?" Vola asked her now. This was the first chance they'd had to talk since they'd left Lillie with the Ephyras the day before. "We've got Rilla and—"

"I'm coming, Vola," Lillie said, sharper than normal. "You can't convince me not to, so don't try."

"I was just..." Vola blew out her breath, knowing it was pointless to argue. Lillie was grieving. She was allowed to be irritable, and it didn't mean that she was actually angry with Vola. No matter how much Vola was angry with herself.

"She just means you seemed busy," Sorrel said. "With whatever the scholars are working on."

It was at least part of the truth. Lillie had been head down in her notes when they'd collected her that morning.

"Plan B," she said. "Yes. But...That's what my family does. When we're sad or anxious, we bury ourselves in research. This..." She gestured, taking in the five of them as well as the rippling barrier ahead of them.

"This is better. It feels more proactive. And…well, I'd really like to kill Anders or Inga or whoever gets in my way next."

Vola raised an eyebrow.

"Sounds good to me," Talon said. "Do you think when this is done, we can go back to regular adventuring?"

Vola swallowed away the lump in her throat. When this was over, would they even have a reason to stay together anymore? So much had happened…

"What is 'regular adventuring?'" Sorrel said. "I'm not sure I know anymore."

"It's…less than ideal quests pulled from a job board in a seedy tavern," Lillie said.

Vola shook off her melancholy and grinned. "It's getting paid in room and board because that's all the villagers can afford."

"It's thwarting kidnappers and bandits," Talon said.

"And rescuing princesses." Rilla cocked her head with a smirk.

"Huh," Sorrel said. "Sounds like we've had a pretty good run so far."

"Speaking of princesses," Talon said, and Vola turned to find War riding up the ridge behind them.

"What are you waiting for?" she said. "Get a move on. We're serving as your honor guard today." She jerked an elbow, indicating the ranks of elite Southglen guards behind her.

Vola's eyes narrowed.

War caught her look. "We're faster than we look. We'll escort you to the last illusion and watch your backs while you're in there. That'll give the rest of the army a chance to catch up so we're all in place for the final assault. Once that barrier goes down, I want our scouts in first. The rest will follow on their intelligence. I want Anders taken care of tonight."

Vola gave her a salute and signaled her team forward.

"That seems ambitious," Lillie said under her breath as they moved down the treacherous lava rock and started toward the barrier. "It's unlikely that Anders has just been sitting in his stronghold waiting for us to break through to him. He must have defenses in place."

"Like an undead army," Rilla said. "And anyone he managed to subvert into fighting for him."

"Inga did say he wanted to meet us personally," Sorrel said. "Maybe he'll make it easy."

"I don't trust easy," Talon said.

"Neither do I," Vola said. "Let's just get to the illusion and do our job.

I'm sure War is worrying about the details. And we'll let the scouts handle what's behind the barrier before we go charging in."

Lillie led them unerringly to the edge of the barrier. It now contained only the volcano and the space directly around it, and they could just make out the shadow of the jagged mountain behind the shimmering wall of light.

The gray clouds seemed to press down on them as they stood contemplating the clear area at the base of the mountain. Vola glanced up at the sky, but despite the clouds, they remained dry.

War and her elite guard arranged themselves around them.

"This is the last one, right?" Vola asked Lillie.

"It should be," she said. "I will be monitoring the spell from inside. To make sure. But yes. The barrier had five anchor points. We've done four. Ergo this should be the last one."

"Thanks for the math lesson," Talon muttered.

"Did you just use 'ergo' in a sentence?" Sorrel said.

Lillie gave her a baffled look. "Yes. Why?"

"Keep your eyes open as we come out of it," Vola said. "These have all been ambushes so far, and I imagine the last one will be the biggest trap of all."

Sorrel drew her staff. "Let's do this, then."

"Is it really a trap if you know about it before and walk into it, anyway?" Rilla said, fingering the hilt of one of her many daggers.

"Yes," Talon said "Yes, it is."

The lava field and the elite guard dissolved into smears of gray and black. Rough pocketed stone replaced the open air, forming a large cavern made up of more lava rock. It climbed far above their heads to a jagged opening that let in bright sunlight.

Vola couldn't help whistling. They must have been inside the mountain their physical bodies were currently standing before.

"This cave would have been formed by a lava pocket hundreds of thousands of years ago," Lillie said. "Back when the volcano was still active."

A couple of pickaxes and some shovels lay abandoned in the corner and some of the rock around them bore evidence of rudimentary excavation. Someone had been chipping away at the interior of the cave, expanding the walls.

A single rough wooden table stood in the center of the cavern, where the light was best. A figure stood over it, studying some sort of diagram. Vola craned her neck to see and caught sight of the man's face.

Anders. Now with pain lines etched in the corners of his mouth and a few strands of silver hair threading through the black, but still recognizable from all the memories he'd forced them to watch.

Vola glanced at Lillie to see if she had any clue yet what they were supposed to be doing this time. Lillie had the frown she always wore when she was analyzing something, but she didn't meet Vola's look, so Vola let her concentrate.

"Nice place you have here," a voice said from behind them. "You need some curtains or rugs to make it homier, though."

The familiar sing-song voice sent a shaft of heat through Vola's limbs, and she whipped around to find a gnome standing in the wide opening of the cave, her hip cocked nonchalantly. She wore a tattered robe that fell to about mid-calf and carried a staff tipped with a clump of black feathers.

"Please tell me we're supposed to be fighting Nargilla," Sorrel said. "I want to beat the crap out of her. Again."

"Shh," Vola said.

Nargilla's large eyes took in the cave and its sole occupant, and her seamed brown face creased in a smirk.

Anders pushed off the table. "Welcome, Miss Pipwattle," he said. "I hope you didn't have any trouble finding the place."

"The golems at the door didn't seem to want to let me in but we had a little chat. I assumed it was some sort of test to keep the rabble out."

"Hmm," Anders said noncommittally.

"Anyway. They were much friendlier as a pair of frogs. Impressive armature," she said. "But there's always a weakness to transformation. Golems aren't nearly as scary once you've turned them into something you can squish."

"I'll keep that in mind in the future," Anders said.

"So what does an abandoned volcano run for these days?" Nargilla said, digging at the solidified ash with her toe.

"Plenty," he said.

Nargilla cocked her head. "And you still have enough to pay that exorbitant fee you advertised?"

Anders's expression remained serene. "I do."

Nargilla tapped her chin. "Hey wait, I recognize your name now. You were part of the team that took down Brindle the Butcher and his roc. Weren't you?"

Anders's mouth went thin and hard. "The only survivor," he said, turning back to the table.

Nargilla whistled. "No wonder you can afford all this, if you got the dead guys' shares as well."

He glared at her.

She held up her hands. "Oh, sore spot? Sorry."

He went back to the paperwork on the table, and Nargilla checked him out from behind, her eyes traveling up and down his form.

"So about that exorbitant fee," she said when he'd been quiet for too long. "I'll knock a couple of zeros off the price if you want to just stand there and let me look."

Anders turned to stare, aghast, and Nargilla wiggled her eyebrows.

"The fee stays the same," he said. "It depends only on whether or not you can do the spell."

Nargilla snorted. "Trust me, that won't be a problem. I can suck the magic out of anything."

"Anything?"

Nargilla gave him a sidelong look. "That sounds like a challenge."

Anders pushed off from the table once again and took a piece of paper with him. "I have some very specific needs for this project. You'll have support from the rest of my contractors, but I need to know that you can handle your part of the work. It's essential."

He held out the paper.

"All right, sexy, I'm listening." She took the page and scanned it. Then her mouth dropped open. "You want all this?" The fun had gone out of her voice.

"I do."

"For what?"

"That's my business."

"Hey, if I'm going to be going up against the gods to steal their power, I deserve to know."

"Are you afraid of them?"

She rolled her eyes. "Hell no. They sit up there doing nothing. But this is serious." She waved the paper in her hand. "This is world-ending shit if we get even the slightest bit wrong. I should know what I'm getting myself into."

Anders hesitated for a moment. "You're right." He held up one hand, palm out. "The gods aren't fit to carry the responsibility that they do. Someone I love trusted him—them. And they let her down. They didn't even try." He glanced away. "They don't deserve the power they have."

"And you think you do," Nargilla finished for him. She rolled the paper up. "Welp, that will do, I guess."

"You don't have any objections?" Anders asked.

Nargilla shrugged. "I don't care enough to have objections. You're paying me buckets of gold. As long as your reason is better than 'I want to be more powerful than everyone else in the world.' And it only had to be like a smidge better." She caught his questioning look. "Hey, I'm not a complete monster. Oh, and I needed to be sure I get to keep my magic, which I see you've already made a provision for." She gestured with the paper. "So I don't really care. Unless you want me to be a god too and reign at your side?" She batted her eyelashes at him.

"No," he said shortly.

She shrugged. "Worth a shot. I know you're going for terse, but I really like a man who can hold his tongue and look sexy while doing it."

"If you continue with the sexual harassment, I can always dissolve our contract."

"Fine, but I get to do whatever I want with you in my head."

Anders made a face.

Vola lifted her lip. At least now they knew Nargilla had always been creepy. But what was the point of this illusion? No shadowy figures threatened the two conspirators. There was nothing for the barrier to be keyed to, as far as Vola could tell.

"Lillie?" she asked. "What's going on?"

"I'm not sure. I've found the anchor point in the spell," Lillie said. "But it's different from the others. Just completing this illusion will break it down. Except..." Lillie's eyes moved like she followed invisible lines through the world. "This one is connected to something."

"The barrier," Rilla said. "Weren't they all connected to the barrier? That's how we've been getting it to withdraw and shrink."

"This goes beyond that. I can't find where it ends." Her hands stopped moving, and her eyes went wide. "Oh. Oh gods."

"What?" A shaft of ice went down Vola's spine.

"Don't let it end! The illusion. Keep it going."

Vola lurched, but she didn't know what she was heading for. "How? Lillie, I don't know how to do that."

Around them, the illusion began to dissolve. The walls of the volcano faded and blurred to gray, and Vola reached out as if she could hold on to it, grip it between her fingers and keep it in place. Trusting Lillie, even though she had no idea what the wizard had seen.

But of course, it didn't work that way.

The scene fuzzed, but in front of them, the figure of Nargilla froze, her wide grin mocking them. Black and purple lights shot out from behind her, outlining her form in dark light until she seemed like a shadow within a shadow.

Then the dark light pulsed and a shock wave knocked Vola off her feet.

She hit the ground with a thud and the rough lava rock scraped her fingertips. She rolled over onto her elbows and shook her head, trying to clear it.

What the hell had just happened? Something bad. That was all she knew right now.

A musical tink tink tink echoed in her ear, and she realized rain pattered onto her armored back, matting her hair down.

The illusion was definitely gone now, replaced by reality. Vola blinked to bring the world back into focus and finally managed to lift her head.

Ahead of her, one of the elite guards of Southglen lay on his back, stunned. War sprawled just a little beyond, golden mail shining under a layer of rain.

Vola turned her head, her neck creaking from the strain. Her team lay around her, struggling to their feet. Talon, Sorrel, Lillie, and Rilla. All accounted for.

All arrayed around a single figure standing in the middle of their circle.

A gnome. Barely three feet tall and dressed in a tattered robe. Her coarse features were creased with a broad smile.

No illusion this time.

She stood there. Physically. On the field in front of Anders's mountain. Vola could see it now that the barrier had dropped, standing darker even than the clouds. A wide maw opened in the base, giving them a straight shot into Anders's stronghold.

But Nargilla Pipwattle stood in the way.

"Wow, you guys really do get into some trouble, don't you?" she said.

Vola scrambled to her feet, drawing her sword and shield. Sorrel pushed herself up using her staff.

"Oh my gods," Sorrel said. "Didn't we get rid of you once already?"

Nargilla put her hands on her hips. "What, you didn't want me here? That's your own fault, then."

"How?" Talon said.

"The illusion," Lillie said and coughed. Vola stepped across to help her up. "The illusion was tied to her."

"They all were," Nargilla said. "That Lord Arthorel really knows his business. And it's funny how you can attach just about anything to them when you have enough power."

"Your prison," Rilla started.

"Yup," Nargilla said. "Lord Arthorel's illusions, Anders's power, my prison. All connected so that every single time you broke one, it chipped away at my bonds just that much more. Until, poof. Here I am." She tilted her head. "I'm surprised you didn't see through the illusions. That was like, their sole purposed."

"Not their sole purpose," another voice said. "I might have linked up some other things as well."

A figure moved down the pale path that led to the maw in the base of the mountain, his feet crunching in the bleached lava rock. He stood tall with stark black hair. The rain stuck to it like little bits of starlight.

Anders looked much like his illusion self in real life, though a set of puckered red scars ran down his neck from the roc's claws. Like they'd never really healed properly.

"Oo, clever and sexy," Nargilla said. "I like it."

Anders's eyes locked on Nargilla. "Our arrangement has not changed, Pipwattle."

Nargilla shrugged. "It was worth a try."

"Well, now it's time to fulfill your contract. You'll find everything you need in the mountain. I trust I don't have to tell you to hurry."

"Nope. Army-leveling god power coming right up, Your Worshipfulness." Nargilla didn't even give the rest of them a second glance as she turned and trotted for the mountain.

Vola sucked in a breath. She was too far away, but they couldn't let Nargilla leave. They couldn't let Anders start draining the world. She signaled Sorrel.

Sorrel planted her staff against the ground and used it to launch herself at Nargilla, feet first, aiming a kick at her head.

Anders barely glanced at her.

An invisible hand struck Sorrel in mid-air and sent her flying back into Talon and Rilla.

"Oh, nice one," Nargilla said. "You must have been practicing."

Anders cracked his neck. "It doesn't take that much skill once you get the hang of it. Go. I will rid the world of these nuisances."

Vola's grip tightened on her sword. Anders was a fighter, not a spell caster. But he'd just swatted Sorrel out of the air like the most adept wizard. He must have been learning how to use all the power he'd stolen.

Nargilla trotted away, calling over her shoulder, "Tell the gods hi for me. I appreciate their hospitality but it was getting a little constricting."

Anders turned to face off against them.

Vola glanced back. War was only just picking herself up off the ground, shaking her head while her elite guard groaned and tried to climb to their feet.

How much power did Anders have? How much had he stolen already? And how much of that was from the Broken and the other gods? Gods who should have been able to hang onto Nargilla and failed.

Anders raised his hand, and Vola lunged. She brought her sword down to strike his arm from his body, but her blade struck something solid. A magical shield flared and threw Vola back.

Anders brought both hands down and lightning crackled from the sky. Vola threw up her shield and sparks crackled across the surface, undeterred by the rain.

Rilla and Talon righted themselves and rushed for Anders while he was distracted. Rilla went high and Talon went low. But his shield held, flaring.

Talon stumbled back, her hand over her eyes, and Rilla rolled away, holding her arm.

Vola's mind raced along several paths at once. How could they break the shield? It seemed similar to one Lord Arthorel had used, and that had just needed blunt force.

Vola signaled Sorrel again, and the halfling swung her staff. Maxim's Warhammer whistled through the air as she brought it down against Anders with a crack.

His shield flickered. But the moment it faltered, he flung up a hand.

Lightning hit Sorrel square in the chest, and she skidded along the ground to land at Vola's feet.

"Sorrel!"

The monk didn't stir.

Vola lunged for the halfling, her heart beating wildly in her throat, but power struck her between the shoulder blades and slammed her into the ground. The others fell to their knees, crying out in a chorus of pain and surprise.

Anders raised his arms over his head, and the clouds started to swirl. Flashes beyond the dark clouds made Vola's eyes go wide.

This was not good. Every avenue she followed in her head led to their destruction, or to a dead-end where Vola couldn't predict what Anders was capable of.

"Retreat," she tried to yell, but the crushing weight against her back turned it into a whisper. "We have to retreat."

Dust from smashed lava rock clogged her throat as she reached for Sorrel. But a flaming rock struck the ground between them, and she yanked her hand back. She twisted her neck to see meteors falling between them. If they stayed here, pinned to the ground, they'd be pummeled to death in seconds.

Across from Vola, Lillie managed to roll over, far enough to get her hands free. She whispered three words and a line of fire sprang up in front of Anders. He cried out and stumbled back a step.

The crushing weight left Vola's back, and she surged to her feet. Anders must only be able to concentrate on a spell or two at a time.

Meteors still fell around them, but Vola ducked her head and scooped Sorrel up to throw her over her shoulder.

"Go," she cried.

Talon went, walking backward to cover their retreat with her bow. Rilla stopped to help War, who turned and signaled her guard to get out.

Lillie took the chance to cast another spell and lobbed a fireball at Anders, who couldn't keep doing two things at once.

"Skill is more than just power," Lillie said. "It's knowledge and control. Concentration and—"

"You can lecture him later," Vola yelled. "Running now."

"I'm covering your retreat."

"Like hell you are."

Anders glared at them through the flames that flickered across the lava field, and the rock at their feet split. A meteor streaked in front of her nose, and Vola jumped back, stepping into a hole where a zombie was emerging. She cried out and kicked its head, her boot going right through its skull. But the creature kept climbing up, even without its head, and latched onto her leg.

Three more had hold of Lillie. The wizard set them on fire, but the undead didn't seem to care. These were more than just the normal zombies they'd fought so far. And they were cutting them off from their escape.

Lillie yelled in frustration and disappeared under the grasping limbs and rotting flesh.

Vola took a deep, bracing breath and let the rage rise in her chest. It felt a little too close to panic, but she'd learned how to control it, use it, focus it. The red seeped across her vision, narrowing what she could see, and she focused on the pile of undead that covered Lillie.

Vola roared and charged ahead. She flung bodies aside. Someone tried to clamp their teeth around her arm, and she shook free. A meteor sizzled past her ear, and she turned so it wouldn't strike Sorrel's limp form.

She kicked and dug at the undead until she found a pale arm with perfectly oval nails.

She yanked, pulling Lillie bodily from the pile. With one arm over Sorrel and the other around Lillie's waist, Vola glanced at the undead horde pulling themselves out of the ground. She glanced at the god-like being standing on the other side of the flames.

They were going to lose. They were going to die and the world would crumble with them. And there was nothing she could do.

"You have one more spell to get us out of here?" she asked Lillie. But Lillie's head lolled, her eyes unfocused, like she'd hit her head or used too much magic.

The rage sustaining Vola faltered. "Lady," she whispered, turning her head up toward the smoke-filled sky, letting the rain slide down her cheeks. "Lady, please."

Anders was right. There were so many gods who didn't care. Who thought that they could sit back and watch mortals in their conflicts and bet on the winner. So many like Maxim who thought that distance protected them.

But not all of them.

Not all. Right?

"Lady."

Arms closed around Vola, just as the first of the undead horde reached them.

"I have you," the Broken whispered in her ear.

And with a wash of clean, fresh air, they were away. Vola closed her eyes against the sudden vertigo and the bright light that threatened to blind her.

After a moment that lasted an eternity she felt rock beneath her feet. And she opened her eyes to find herself standing on the ridge with War, Rilla and Talon, Gruff at their feet. Lillie and Sorrel were still clasped close in her arms. The remains of the elite guard sat or lay around them, too beaten to stand.

The Broken stood beside her, staring back at the mountain.

Clouds ringed the distant volcano and meteors flared, bright against the underside of the haze as they rained down around the stronghold.

A tug on Vola's arm prompted her to let go of Lillie. The wizard rubbed her face and took a step forward before falling to her knees. The orange and red glare of the meteors lit up against her skin.

Anders already had power enough to rival one of the gods. And now he had Nargilla to give him more. She was there inside the mountain, beginning the spell that would strip the rest of the world of magic.

Vola cast a hopeless glance at the others around them. War's face was streaked with soot, and her eyes seemed glassy with shock.

Talon and Rilla both looked back at Vola as if waiting for orders or an idea, or anything. And Sorrel lay limp, looking singed around the edges.

The rage had left Vola completely, leaving a ringing hollowness in her chest as she stared out over the lava field. Most of which was on fire now.

"We are so fucked," she said.

There was no lightning bolt. The Broken didn't even pretend to be offended.

"Fucked indeed," the goddess said.

TWENTY-TWO

THEY DRAGGED themselves back through the deluge to meet the rest of the army. War gave the order to camp right there. They wouldn't be getting any closer to Anders's stronghold. Not with the meteor storm swirling over the place.

Besides, what exactly would be the point?

Anders had won. He had Nargilla. He had all his lieutenants. They were poised to drain the magic out of the world and set Anders up as a god to rival all the gods.

Lillie and Talon stood huddled together, watching as War and Rilla struggled to put up the command tent themselves. Soldiers and messengers scrambled around them, trying to organize the rest of the chaos. But in the rain and the dark with their leaders just as confused and frightened as they were, nothing was getting done properly. Everyone was just pitching their tents where they could and hunkering down to wait for orders.

Vola knelt beside Sorrel in a nook between the half-fallen command tent and the healers, who stood arguing over the ripped canvas of their tent.

The halfling still breathed, but it sounded ragged to Vola's ears and the skin across her chest and collarbone was streaked with black. As if some of Anders's lightning had crept through her veins.

Vola bent her head, ignoring the rain trickling down the back of her neck under her armor. She held her hands over Sorrel and spoke. "Lady bless."

Gods, what if this wound was just like Innis's? What if there was too much of the Broken's power in the lightning for Vola to heal it? She could only hope the magic Anders had used had come from somewhere else. One of his other thefts.

Light shone under Vola's palms and streaked into the halfling's skin, chasing away the darkness in her veins and leaving healing in their wake.

Sorrel took a deep, unfettered breath.

Vola sank back on her heels and rubbed her face as Sorrel stirred. The rain made the halfling flinch, and she finally opened her eyes.

"Welcome back," Vola said.

Sorrel blinked, her gaze flicking from Vola to the dark sky, to Lillie and Talon watching pale and silent from the shadows.

"All right," Sorrel said, rolling so she could get her elbows under her. "Tell me the bad news."

"We're screwed," Rilla said, coming up beside them and kneeling. The command tent sagged behind her. "That's the worst of it."

Vola glared at the ground as she slipped a hand under Sorrel's elbow and helped her sit. "Give her a second."

"No," Sorrel said. "I want to know. What happened after he hit me?"

"Lillie and Vola got us out of there," Talon said.

"But not without a lot of luck," Lillie added. "And some help from the Broken. Which I don't know if we're going to be able to count on again."

Vola's lips thinned as she stood and faced Anders's mountain. She could just about see the dim glow between the jumbled tents.

The Broken had ferried them to safety and then vanished. Again. The way she always did. Vola could feel her, just over her shoulder. That faint, comforting presence. But it wasn't the same as when she was here.

"So Anders just gets everything he wants?" Sorrel said, drawing her knees up with a wince. "He gets to be a god and there's nothing we can do about it?"

"What do you want to do about it?" Rilla said. "Go in there and get hit by lightning again? Or get pummeled by a flaming rock? That was just with the power he's already stolen. What happens when he starts to drain the rest of the world?"

"We all die," Talon said. "Then, as opposed to now."

"Well, I'm not going to just sit here and wait for it to happen," Sorrel said.

"You'd rather speed up the process?" Lillie asked.

Vola put her hands over her head to block them out and hunched down, folding her bulk into as small a package as possible. She felt like she was going to fly into a million pieces if she didn't hold on as tight as she could.

They'd thought Anders's illusions were narcissistic. An arrogant way to slow them down and funnel them into his traps.

But they'd been so much more than that. They'd been a clever way to get them to do his work. To free Nargilla.

And now to plant doubt. To wriggle that little worm of worry and question into a mind that had already seen too much of the gods.

Vola couldn't get the image of Mariel out of her head. Standing with her hands raised to the sky, calling on a god that couldn't be bothered to answer. Dying in Anders's arms while he prayed over and over to an empty sky.

The shadows overrunning Anders's family.

Maxim ignoring Sorrel.

All of them ignoring Vola. Ignoring her pleas, ignoring her warnings.

She knew what it was like to have a god who listened, one who stood next to her in battle and after. One who gave her strength and faith and hope.

But she also knew what it was like when that god disappeared. Leaving only the outline of her presence at Vola's shoulder.

How wrong was Anders?

And how much of what he'd become could have been prevented?

Vola's breath came faster. The rage rose inside of her and she let it. Held it simmering under the surface.

She'd learned to love Cleavah. And she'd learned to love the Broken just as much. But right now, she was angry. Angry at the pantheon for not listening to her. Angry at the pantheon for not listening to the Broken. And angry at the Broken for not pushing them and making them listen.

The time for politics was over. It had been over for a while; there were just some people too stupid to see it.

Vola unfolded herself and stood up straight to her full height. She didn't say anything, but the others fell silent, their bickering forgotten as they stared at her.

"Vola?" Lillie said. She stepped forward to place a hand on Vola's arm, fingers light. A reminder to anchor herself in the loyalty and strength of her team. "What is it?"

"It's the end," Vola said. She forced herself to focus and turned her gaze to Lillie's worried face. She put her hand over the wizard's fingers. "You guys want to come tell off some very important people?"

Lillie's eyes widened. Behind her, Talon cracked her neck.

Vola reached down and gave Sorrel a hand up. She handed the monk Maxim's Warhammer, which had come with them from the battlefield. Miraculously.

Vola met Rilla's eyes. "Coming?" she said.

"I didn't know I was invited," Rilla said quietly.

"I guess that's up to you. Are you a Mishap's Hero? Or not?"

Rilla raised an eyebrow. "Will I get to stab things?"

"Almost definitely," Talon said.

"Well, then, how can I refuse?"

Vola stepped away from the healer's tent, which they'd finally gotten off the ground. She hadn't done this by herself before, only with the Broken. But she carried a good bit of the Broken's power within herself, and she had a connection to the goddess that transcended most of the rules of the world.

Vola closed her eyes and found that power. Found the connection that drew her to the goddess just over her shoulder. She wrapped it around herself and her friends. And then she reached for a bright, featureless hallway and a plane that connected to countless divine realms.

She pulled, and something in her gut lurched. But the air around them still smelled like wet ash.

She yanked harder, but that only made her feel dizzy.

Vola stopped. Walking with the Broken had never felt like pulling before, had it? It was always like a stroll.

She took hold of the power one more time and stepped. And her boot connected with pure white marble. Smooth walls rose on either side, neither solid nor exactly ethereal.

"Holy hell," Rilla said.

"Actually, I believe this would be the opposite," Lillie said, peering at the marble under their feet.

Sorrel scuffed at it with the toe of her sandal. It squeaked. Vola herself was still dripping.

"All right," Talon said, glancing suspiciously from one side to the other. "Now what?"

"This way." Vola cocked her head and started down the hall. Really, she had no idea what she was doing, just a burning anger and the belief that anything was better than what the gods were already doing.

It's not like any of them had anything left to lose by getting this wrong.

The wide room at the end of the hall seemed empty at first, or at least as empty as it had been the first time Vola set foot in it.

But voices ricocheted around them, echoes of shouts and arguments that seemed a million miles away one moment and just beside her ear the next. Little flits of color flashed in the bright air, indicating agitation somewhere that wasn't quite here.

Vola planted herself in the doorway, her boots leaving wet streaks across the marble. Today, black streaks climbed through the white walls, fracturing the little bits of opalescent color in the marble.

She cleared her throat.

Beside her, the air shifted, a puff against the hair on her arms, and Vesteral shimmered into existence. His long face pulled into a scowl, and his gangly limbs twitched in agitation.

"What the—How did you get here?" he said.

"I walked," Vola said. "Oh. And I brought some friends. Hope you don't mind."

Vesteral spluttered until Lillie stepped up all sweet eyes and beaming smile. "Vesteral, isn't it?" she said. "I've read so much about you."

Even the immortal wasn't quite immune to Lillie's smile and while he sucked in a breath and decided what to do with a pretty face and flattery, Vola stepped across to the center of the room.

"Ahem," she said as loudly as she could manage.

Around the room the tiers filled with angry gods, appearing as if trickling in from another plane. Colorful robes and gowns and heavy scowls faded into existence until she was surrounded by outrage.

Several of them looked familiar from her time here before—she recognized Maxim and Mulgash, Ona and Bierhel—but none of them were the Broken.

And then one last figure formed, on the floor next to her, coalescing into a slim woman with dark curls cropped close to her head, one arm missing, balancing on her remaining leg. She stood in the center of the circle, arguing against the rest.

The Broken started and turned to find Vola beside her. And Vola felt a stab of shame for having resented her for even a moment.

Their eyes met, and the Broken's scarred lip tilted in a lopsided smile.

"What is this, Broken?" Maxim said, climbing to his feet to point at Vola. "How is she here? Did you bring her here?"

The Broken tilted her head. "The funny thing about choosing smart, capable mortals is that they think and act for themselves."

Vola felt the rest of her team coming up behind her, arraying themselves around the center circle.

Maxim stepped down from his tier, each stride eating several feet, although Vola had no idea how physical distance worked in this plane of gods.

He stopped before them. "You dare come here after you failed? I admire your courage mortal, but now it could be read as stupidity."

Vola raised her chin, counting on the rage under her skin to bolster her. Maxim towered over even her, his presence oppressive and judging.

"We failed, yes," Vola said. "We failed to see the trap even though we knew there had to be one."

Maxim scoffed and turned.

"But you failed us before that."

Maxim froze.

Vola half expected the Broken to leave them to their argument, to go sit among the other gods, or to whisper to Vola to stop, to be careful. But she stood beside her, silent, back straight.

"Excuse me?" Maxim said, voice quiet.

"You failed to heed my warning. I told you Anders was coming for Nargilla. And you did nothing. You rested, content in your own strength and superiority."

"He used you to get past that strength," Maxim said. "And you let him."

"You failed us long before that," Vola said.

"You dare —"

"Do you remember Mariel Stillwater?"

Maxim hesitated, his mouth hanging open as his eyes went deep and blank. "What?"

"Do you remember the ones who pray to you? The ones who serve and give their lives to you? Or do you forget them as easily as you ignore them?"

Without prompting, Lillie began whispering and an image of Mariel formed on their left, hands raised to the sky, skirt whipping around her. Another formed in front of them. Mariel lying broken and bleeding in Anders's arms as he screamed without sound. And a third formed to the right. Anders standing over a table, alone in a mountain, plotting his bid for power.

"Do you remember her?" Vola said. "Because she's the reason for all of this. *You're* the reason for all of this."

Maxim stared at the young woman's face. "I don't...understand."

"Mariel was one of yours," Lillie said. "Your indifference to her convinced Anders to take your power. He thinks he can be a better god than all of you."

"I'm not certain I disagree with him," Rilla said.

Maxim remained there, staring. "I do remember her," he said.

"Anders is angry," Vola said. "And I'm angry, too. I'm tired of gods who sit absent and indifferent. Who cast one of their number out for trying to actually do something." She cast a glance at the Broken who returned it with a mildly raised eyebrow.

"The thing is, you have a problem on your hands. A problem you made. Anders has the power to strip you of your godliness. And I can't stop him. Not without help. And...well, I'm not sure I want to."

She'd fight tusk and nail to keep Anders from hurting the Broken, but she couldn't see a single reason to raise a finger to help these indolent, indifferent bastards. If only the whole world wasn't going to suffer for her choice.

Lillie let the images dissolve away.

Maxim blinked at Vola and the others as if seeing them for the first time, and his eyes latched onto Sorrel.

Vola could hear her gulp and didn't blame her. Vola had had plenty of time to get used to Cleavah's presence. Sorrel had never actually seen Maxim in person.

"You carry my hammer," he said.

"Yessir. Or well, part of it. The other bit's where you left it."

"And it works for you?"

Sorrel spun the staff in demonstration. It morphed from a staff to a bow to a sword and back to a staff again.

"You must have shown great strength and loyalty to have found it, halfling."

"Her name is Sorrel," Talon said. "Sorrel Thornbough."

"We're still loyal to you," Sorrel said, but her voice was quiet and even Maxim couldn't mistake the doubt in her eyes.

A flurry of expressions passed over his face, too fast or too complex for Vola to fully grasp. She saw anger and shame, yes, along with a whole host of other things.

"Damn you," Maxim said, gaze latching onto the Broken. "You know this will hurt."

"It's supposed to hurt," the Broken said. "That's how you know you're doing it right."

"Would you rather the mortals dealt with pain?" another voice said, and Vola saw Mulgash sit forward. "Puny beings who are less equipped to handle it?" He winked at Vola.

Maxim cast him a glare, but then he shook his head. He looked out over the assembled Virtues and Obstacles.

A collective shiver went through them, nearly silent except for the ripple of colors.

And then the gods started to dissolve, disappearing once again from this plane.

Five of them remained. The Broken and Maxim still stood in the center of the circle. And Ona, Bierhel, and Mulgash stepped down from the tiers to join them below. Representatives for the entire pantheon.

Maxim gave them a bow. "I know I have done nothing to earn your trust. But will you work with me now? To see what can still be done?"

TWENTY-THREE

IT WAS STILL RAINING when Vola, Sorrel, Lillie, Talon, and Rilla appeared outside the command tent, trailing five gods behind them. The sun and the moon had long since set, leaving the camp in complete darkness. Here and there a few wizard lights sputtered valiantly, but it was clear no one had bothered to do more than fall into their bedrolls.

The only light nearby was the flicker through the canvas of the command tent.

Maxim squinted down as the rain pattered off his golden armor. "Ah. Precipitation. I'd forgotten this was a thing."

Vola exchanged a look with the other mortals and shook her head. Then she pushed into the command tent.

War stood over the table, her face still streaked with soot. The rain had made little runnels down her cheeks.

It looked like she'd convened everyone she could think of and squished them all in the tent together. Hazel sat shoved in with Lydia and Gorgo. Raven perched on a crate in the corner in his eagle form while Cyrano lounged below him. Renvick stood on the opposite side of the tent where the flaps had been pulled back far enough for Listrell to stick her nose in. Ephyra and Kellan stood along another wall, while Henri and Finn watched the openings. Knight Commander Imralen stood beside War at the table.

War shook her head when she saw them come in. "Shit, Rilla. Where have you been? We need to focus on damage control and you and your team go haring off after the battle?"

The Knight Commander looked up, eyes narrowed. Deep bruises still darkened the skin around his nose and under his eyes.

"Your Highness, I have to protest," he said. "You invited the traitor?"

"Blow it out your ass, Imralen," Rilla said, pushing through behind Vola. "No one is listening to your lies anymore."

"She's the entire reason we're in this mess now."

"No," Maxim said, crowding into the tent. "I am."

"I hope you don't mind," Ona said. "She brought friends."

Vola didn't know how to describe it since she'd been talking to gods in all their states for years now, but they did something when they were around other mortals which sort of hid their divine glory a bit. Probably so they didn't scare anyone right off the bat. They each had aspects they wore that glowed and pulsed with their power, but it was like they pulled a veil over that aspect. Keeping most of it hidden until they chose.

"Who are you?" War asked.

And Maxim chose to drop the veil.

The Greater Virtue of Strength and Loyalty's aspect was enough to take Vola's breath away, and she'd seen it before.

"Oh," War said, the word no more than a puff of air leaving her lips.

"This is…I don't—" Imralen started to say.

Rilla held up a hand. "Don't open your mouth again. We all know what you've been saying. And you're done." She turned to Vola. "Now, why don't you introduce your backup?"

"I don't think they really need an introduction," Vola said. "But this is War, princess of the Southglen War Throne. She's been spearheading our offense down here. Until—"

"Until you screwed it up," Imralen said.

Mulgash sidled up to the Knight Commander. "Hi," he said over his shoulder.

Imralen jumped and then glanced back at the Greater Obstacle of Rage, meeting his red eyes.

"Oh, I like you," Mulgash said. "You have so much more rage to overcome. And all of it so deeply ingrained. It's like you're holding onto it for dear life."

"Mulgash," the Broken said mildly. "Focus."

Imralen's eyes latched onto the Broken. She stood with Vola, still veiled, but she wore her Greater aspect underneath and there was no mistaking the scars and the missing limbs or the fire floating behind her.

The gods might have thrown her out, but there were statues, paintings, and tapestries of the Greater Virtue of Righteousness everywhere.

Strange how standing next to her made Imralen seem small and insignificant.

"My lady," Vola said, giving the Broken a little nod. "Would you take the lead?"

War stepped back, leaving plenty of room for the Broken to stand at the edge of the table with the other gods splayed around her.

They frowned down at the disaster depicted before them. The map showed Anders's mountain and someone had drawn a ragged line around it to depict the meteor storm.

"Anders had enough power and smarts to get past the gods and steal Nargilla right out from under our noses," the Broken said.

Imralen snorted.

The Broken sent him a narrow-eyed look, but he wasn't actually stupid enough to open his mouth.

"With her, he now has the power to drain the entire world of magic."

"He has started," Listrell said, her voice a deep rumble against the ground. "I can feel them setting up their spell just as they did in Firewatch."

The Broken nodded. "Yes. We feel the land as well."

"Couldn't you just…" Hazel started, and then flushed.

Maxim fixed her with a stare. "You are one of mine, yes?" he said. "Say what you will."

"Couldn't you just pop in there?" She gestured to the mountain on the map. "And destroy his setup? I mean, you're gods."

The Broken's mouth went flat and hard. "A portion of the power he has already stolen is mine. It locks us out."

"And we are not what we once were," Ona murmured.

Vola glanced at her in question, but the Greater Virtue of Honor didn't meet her gaze.

"Well, breaking through the barrier and facing him head-on didn't work," Sorrel said. "What's left?"

A burst of furious whispering drew their attention to the side of the tent where Ephyra and Kellan stood. Lillie had sidled up beside them and had her head bent toward her father and brother.

"This seems promising," the Broken said.

Lillie looked up, biting her lip.

The Broken smiled. "You have earned Vola's trust, Lilliara," she said. "And therefore mine. Speak."

"Well, there's always plan B," she said.

War's gaze sharpened. "Will it still work?"

"What is plan B?" the Broken asked.

"We steal the power first."

Everyone in the tent blinked at her. Lillie's cheeks burned a fierce red, but she raised her chin.

"If we don't want him to take the world's magic, then we take it first."

Vola couldn't do more than blink for several moments. That was… ridiculous, dangerous…and possibly brilliant.

Rilla's mouth hung open. "This is what you've been working on?"

"We have a solid understanding of Nargilla's spell now. And we have Myron who designed the original bits that held the excess magic. And with divine help, it would go even smoother." Lillie nodded to the Broken and Maxim.

Talon shook her head. "Draining the magic killed those spots in Firewatch. Permanently. How is this a good idea?"

"Nargilla didn't care about killing the world. We do," Lillie said.

"That's what we've spent all this time making sure wouldn't happen." Ephyra's gesture included Lillie and Kellan and all the scholars not present.

"The power would need a vessel," the Broken said.

"Yes." Lillie spread her hands. "We would have to choose someone to receive the power. Or several someones."

"Wouldn't that just create another Anders?" Gorgo said from his seat. "We'd be creating our own thieving demigod."

"One of the reasons to have more than one, I would think," Cyrano said. "In case one goes rogue."

"They would have to accept the power with the understanding that it would only be temporary," Lillie said. "Until Anders is defeated. And… well, I think our champions would be our best bet for taking him down. Anders has been going after the magic in people, the magic in the dead, and the land, and magical objects like the Thrones."

"And the gods," the Broken said.

Lillie nodded. "If we took these first, pooled them into our choice of champions, they would be formidable enough to face Anders head-on."

"Or we could lock them away and guard them," Ephyra said. "If all the power is locked away in one place, it will be easier to keep it out of Anders's hands."

Hazel's chin jerked up. "Only a coward would run from a fight that only they can win."

Ephyra shrugged, unfazed. "It is only one option."

"We would not run," Maxim said. "The gods will take on this burden and we will fight the threat and conquer it as gods should."

Mulgash snorted so hard he choked and spent the next few moments coughing.

Maxim frowned at him. "What?"

The Broken, Ona, and Bierhel gave the Greater Virtue of Strength and Loyalty pitying glances. Ona and Bierhel each then stepped aside and left the Broken to explain it to him.

"We fought an entire Divine War because you would not acknowledge my power over you," she said gently.

Maxim flushed, and Vola wondered if the Broken had ever actually had to say the words out loud before.

"Do you really think this fractured pantheon would look kindly on the five of us taking on even more power?"

"I'd like to think we learned our lesson the last time," Mulgash said, examining his fingernails. "But I'm not going to risk another Divine War on that gamble."

The Broken gave Maxim another sad smile. "I hate to say it but the power is safer in the hands of mortals."

"You're asking the entire pantheon to give up our power," Maxim said.

"I am." The Broken raised an eyebrow. "You're always going on about sacrifice. How you're willing to sacrifice yourself for the greater good. Are you willing to sacrifice everything in this way as well?"

"Damn you, again," Maxim said. "You know I can't say no."

The Broken spread her hands, a little smile playing on her lips.

"Then we must choose our champions," Listrell said.

"One for each," Ephyra said. "One to hold the magic of the living, one to hold the magic of the dead."

"The magic of the land," Listrell said.

"The Thrones," War said.

"And the gods." The Broken turned her head to look directly at Vola, where she stood with Talon and Sorrel. She cocked her head. "Funny how there are five of you."

Vola sucked in a breath. "Oh." She held up her hands. "Oh, no."

"I chose my champion a long time ago, Volagra. Are you going to refuse me now?"

Vola's mouth worked, trying to find an answer to that. But of course, there wasn't one. She'd decided to trust her goddess in a tight spot deep in Myron's laboratory. And she'd chosen the Broken again and again since then. She'd knelt before her in a temple in Southglen. She wouldn't back out now.

"No, my lady."

"Then you shall be my knight. As always."

"Now hang on," Imralen said. "Clearly the orc has tricked —"

The Broken's eyes flicked to Maxim, and she jerked her chin.

Maxim stepped to Imralen. "You were warned." The Greater Virtue of Strength and Loyalty picked Imralen up by the arms and carried him to the tent flap.

"You can't throw me out!" Imralen cried. "I'm the Knight Commander of the paladins. A holy warrior."

"Paladins must be kind as well as strong and just," Maxim said. "You are none of these. Learn better or do not bother returning."

He tossed Imralen into the rain and turned to dust off his hands.

"Any other objections?" the Broken said.

Hazel glanced around at the others gathered in the tent. "Nope. Honestly, we all like Vola. No one who knows her was really listening to him. But thanks for getting rid of him. He was really annoying."

Vola bit her lip and blinked rapidly. Apparently, she was the only one who'd been listening to him. The only one who mattered, at least.

"So Vola gets the power of the gods, obviously," Cyrano said, scratching his chin. "What about the rest?"

"Rilla will get the power of the Thrones," War said, casting a glance at her counterpart. "I know how much she hates being a princess so I'm not worried about her running off with the might of Southglen."

Rilla rolled her eyes.

"The magic of the land should go to Talon," Listrell said. "She is already in tune with the way it works."

"Same with the power of living spell casters," Ephyra said, face solemn. "Lilliara will handle it better than anyone."

"That leaves the power of the dead," Hazel said. "Which should go to Sorrel who will treat it with the respect it deserves."

Vola and the others looked at each other, and she noticed the same slightly glazed look in their eyes that said, "How did we get here again?"

"We shall have to do this quickly," the Broken said. "Anders already has a head start on us, and Nargilla has done this before."

"We have the gods on our side," Cyrano said. "How bad could it get?"

The Broken gave him a rueful smile. "You'd be surprised."

TWENTY-FOUR

By the time the sun rose, they had cleared a significant space in the center of camp. The rest of the army had packed up, and War stationed them around the ritual area, keeping watch in case Anders decided to interrupt.

This was their last chance. If Anders kept them from succeeding here, they would have lost the war. And the world.

After the council with the gods, War had ordered Vola and the others to sleep. They were the ones who would have to pull this off, and she wanted them at full strength. But Vola had spent most of the night staring at the canvas ceiling, and she knew for a fact Lillie had spent most of it rolling around. Ephyra and Kellan and the rest of the scholars knew what they were doing. And they had gods helping them out. But that wouldn't keep the wizard from feeling like she had to be there to keep an eye on everything.

They'd given up an hour before dawn and packed up the tent onto the swamp beast's back.

The camp was quiet, but definitely not still, filled with a frenetic sort of energy. Voices stayed hushed, but figures raced back and forth, following the whispered orders coming from the command tent.

There'd been a twitchy moment right after dawn when Myron had wailed that he couldn't make the tanks he needed out of thin air and why hadn't anyone told him he would need them.

Lillie calmed him down. "The tanks were only for storage, right?" she said. "To store the magic until it could be shipped to Anders? Well, we're not shipping anything anywhere. Your tanks are right here." She'd placed her hand on her chest. "We're the tanks."

After that he'd been perfectly happy puttering around, muttering about people doubling as tanks and possible uses in the future.

Vola hoped there would be a future where he could test his theory to his heart's content, though this might not be the sort of thing they'd want to attempt twice.

Vola, Talon, and Sorrel mostly tried to stay out of the way while Lillie flitted from the scholars to the gods to the princesses, trying to make sure everything was lined up just right. Vola didn't follow any of it. She just knew there were anchor points like Nargilla's original spell, which the gods had spent much of the night ferrying around to magically important places in the world. And there were representatives for each of the different types of magic that were needed for the ritual.

Rilla spent the time finalizing arrangements with War. Vola wasn't quite sure what those arrangements looked like. No one knew what would happen to the world if this failed.

"Blow up," Sorrel said when Vola asked the rest of them what they thought.

"The whole world?" Talon said.

"Figuratively or literally?" Vola asked.

"Both."

"You can't have both," Talon said. "You could look at any kind of trouble and say 'yep, I was right, the world 'blew up.'"

"Is this a competition now?" Sorrel asked.

"Maybe." Talon chewed her lip. "I want metaphorical. If this doesn't work, the world will metaphorically 'blow up.' That just leaves you with physical."

Vola buried her head in her hands. "You guys aren't making me feel any better."

"Were we supposed to?" Sorrel said.

The rain tapered off to an unpleasant drizzle around the same time Lillie finally came for them.

"We're ready," she said quietly. Anyone who didn't know her would think she was calm, but Vola noted the way her eyes shifted constantly and her bottom lip was raw from worrying at it with her teeth.

Vola decided not to call attention to it and just followed Lillie out of the tent into the gray dawn. The air was cool but heavy against their skin and the damp seemed to muffle what little noise came from the rest of the camp.

Around the cleared space, the scholars had arranged the different representatives, the channels that the spell would use to funnel all the different magics into their chosen champions. The Broken for the gods. Listrell for the land. War for the Thrones. Ephyra for the living spell-casters. And Myron had summoned a shambling zombie he named Fred to represent the rest of the dead.

Lillie nudged Vola into position beside the Broken and chewed her bottom lip some more. She tapped Vola's breastplate. "Maybe take this off. For now."

"Why?" Vola said even as she reached for the straps.

"Um. Just in case."

"Just in case of what?" Vola asked, but Lillie had stepped away to find her own spot in the center of the circle.

"Just in case we blow up," Sorrel said. "Don't want any shrapnel."

"No one is going to blow up," Lillie said from beside her father. She made a face. "I don't think. I just don't want the metal to serve as a conductor."

"And roast Vola alive inside her armor," Sorrel finished for her.

"We're all going to die," Talon muttered.

Sorrel sighed gustily. "But what a way to go."

Lillie gave the signal and there was no more time to worry.

There wasn't much to see here, but Vola knew that around the world the gods were activating their pieces of the spell. Beginning the process that would hopefully disrupt Anders's plan.

Vola blinked and squinted up at the gray drizzle. She could have sworn there was a change in the feel of the air on her skin. A shift in the state of the world itself. It crackled across her like little fizzles of lightning.

Pebbles danced across the ground as it rumbled. The land Nargilla had drained near Firewatch had turned black any time she cast her spell. The lava rock here was already black, so not much difference there, but Vola could make out lines of gray snaking out from the center of their circle.

And then a fist of power struck her in the chest, and she fell to her knees. The others thudded to the ground as well. But Vola's entire focus was pulled inward to the point where the Broken poured all the divine power of the gods through her skin, into her heart and mind, filling up every space in between.

Shit, Vola couldn't help thinking, even though she knew the Broken would be able to tell. Shit, shit, shit. They hadn't prepared for this. They'd done nothing, and Sorrel was right. They were going to explode. No one was built for this type of power. She was going to split down the middle and every drop of divine magic would go splashing out, spilling all over, and Vola would be dead. As dead as Fred.

She choked on a hysterical giggle and struggled to breathe, concentrating on her chest and the air moving in and out.

"Do not fear," she heard. A voice like the rushing of wind. "I'm still here with you."

The power sizzled along her veins, and she clenched her fists, worried it would spill out of her fingertips if she wasn't careful.

Slowly, she realized that the ground didn't tremble under her palms anymore. And the roaring in her ears hadn't gotten any louder. It remained constant, as did the hum in her chest.

She blinked, staring at the porous rock between her hands. Was it over? Or was this still the beginning? Fire filled her veins, burning from the inside. And maybe she'd be trapped in this sizzling state forever.

"Vola?" Lillie's voice sounded in her ear, louder than the roar. "Vola, are you all right?"

"Should it have hit her harder than the rest of us? Is that normal?" Sorrel said.

Talon snorted. "Is any of this normal?"

"The power she's holding is divine," Rilla said. "It makes sense it would hit her harder."

"Vola." Cool fingers under her jaw finally made her raise her head. Lillie's blue-green eyes met hers. "Are you all right?"

"Fine," Vola grated. Her voice sounded hoarse and used, like she'd been screaming, except she couldn't remember screaming. "I just feel like I got hit in the chest with a flaming battering ram."

Lillie's lips tipped in a relieved smile. "That appears to be a side effect, yes."

"You sort of get used to it," Sorrel said, rubbing her own chest.

"It worked, then?"

"Yeah," Rilla said, voice subdued. "Yeah, it worked."

She and Lillie gave Vola a hand to her feet, and Vola saw why she didn't sound terribly happy about that.

Every person around them, human, dwarf, elf, halfling, and dragon alike, had fallen to their knees or flat on their faces. Only a couple had enough energy to struggle upright again.

The land beneath their feet was already lava rock and made up of every shade of black and gray, but the air itself seemed to be dimmer, less vibrant. Just like the dead spots near Firewatch.

"Is it like this everywhere?" Vola whispered.

"Rand says yes," Lillie said. "As far as he can see. I think it's safe to assume it worked."

The Broken was on her hands and knees in front of Vola. They'd seen her like this once before, and it gave Vola an unpleasant wrench in her gut to realize she was the cause this time.

The goddess raised her head with obvious effort and gave them a wan smile.

"The rest is up to you now, Mishap's Heroes."

TWENTY-FIVE

THEY HAD TIME NOW. Not a lot, but enough to grow used to the power surging beneath their skin. Enough to establish a plan. And enough that the army could slowly drag themselves to their feet and grow accustomed to the way their limbs felt leaden and lifeless.

Vola remembered the feeling. She almost preferred it to this. Almost.

She touched the wall of the command tent by accident and it burst into flames under her fingertips.

Lillie put it out with a little cloudburst, making the canvas sizzle and smoke.

"Oops," Vola said.

"That would be a bit of my power," the Broken said wearily from the corner of the tent. War had handed it over to them after they'd talked tactics. She was next door, trying to stay upright without looking like a toddler learning to walk again.

"If you try to toss something across the room and it ends up halfway across the world, that's Maxim's strength. The trick is to keep it stuffed under your skin," the Broken said.

"Easier said than done," Vola muttered. Lessons from long ago kept flitting through her head. She'd had the entire pantheon and their different areas of interest memorized once. And if she concentrated, she could feel their heat and light tangling and unwinding beneath her skin. Ona's honor, Bierhel's joy, Erthand's determination. Every single one stuffed inside her.

With the entire pantheon at her beck and call maybe now she'd be able to counter that bit of the Broken's power that resided in Anders.

The others were having their own sorts of troubles. The ground tended to roll as Talon walked across it like it was rising to greet her. Rilla crackled with bits of lightning that twirled around her arms and legs. And Sorrel kept rubbing her ears like she could hear a million whispering voices at once.

Lillie was the only one who seemed to be taking this in stride. "I'm used to flinging fire when I'm angry or afraid," she said. "I guess I've already developed techniques for keeping it under wraps."

"Any suggestions?" Vola asked her.

"Think of your skin like a dam. Or a net, holding everything inside."

"I think my problem isn't about containment," Sorrel said, hitting the side of her head like she was trying to knock water out of her ear. "It's about distraction. Is this what necromancers feel all the time?"

"It's temporary," Vola said. She stripped out of the shirt she'd slept in and traded it for a padded surcoat she could wear under her armor. "We're giving it all back as soon as we get rid of Anders."

Lillie's lips thinned. "And what if we can't?"

"Way to instill us all with confidence right before battle," Talon said.

"I don't like this plan," Lillie said, lifting her chin. "The part where we all get to the mountain and kick Anders's ass, that's all right. That's normal. But I don't like Vola going down the middle with the army while we sneak in the sides."

"We don't have a ton of other options," Rilla said. She pulled a strap on her leather harness, checking all the little pockets and sheaths.

"She's making herself a target," Lillie said with a frown. "If we die, the power we carry is released back into the world. Anders has to know that if he kills any of us, he can scoop that power up. And Vola's just going to go striding out there with only the army to protect her."

"More like I'm protecting them," Vola said. "And that's the whole point. I'm going to make his life so miserable he won't even have time to wonder where you four are. The army is going to be way under-strength, yes, but so will Anders's undead horde and subverted forces. Hopefully," she added under her breath.

"You agree with this?" Lillie asked Sorrel. "Aren't you supposed to be her second in command?"

Sorrel regarded her solemnly. "It plays to all our strengths," she said.

"And she won't be alone," the Broken added. She seemed tired, but she was at least upright and didn't have a problem moving around like the mortals. Some of the other races were dealing with the draining better as well. The dwarves of the army were doing well, as were the dragons. The broken had said their magic might have been drained, but their natures remained the same.

"I don't want to talk about this anymore, Lillie," Vola said quietly. She knew the plan was solid. She knew this would give them the best chance against Anders. But she also knew just how fragile it was. They might hold the power of the world. But they were still mortals. And Anders just had to kill one of them to increase his power and make it that much harder for the rest of them.

Lillie's mouth snapped shut and her eyes went bleak. Like she knew what Vola was avoiding thinking about.

"I need to get ready," Vola said.

"I can help with that." Henri pushed through the tent flap and gave them all one of his radiant smiles. "It's been a while since I've been anyone's squire."

Lillie subsided back, giving him space.

Vola spared her a glance and opened her mouth, but she couldn't think of anything else to say. All her reassurances fell flat in the face of her own worry.

Henri stepped forward and took up her breastplate.

"You don't have to do that," Vola said. "I've been armoring myself since I graduated."

"What if I want to?"

Her lips twisted in a smile. "Then I guess it would be mean to not let you."

He helped fit her into the plate, tightening the straps expertly. And there was something soothing about his presence. He'd always had that calm air. When she'd been his student, she'd gotten the impression that he'd seen everything, so nothing surprised or worried him anymore.

He seemed subdued now, but his fingers were still steady. In fact he was the most normal-seeming human in camp so far.

"How's Finn?" Vola asked.

"You know teenagers. They're made of rubber," Henri said. "Finn's stronger than he looks. He'll serve as a full knight before too long."

"If he survives this," Vola said quietly.

Henri flicked one of her pauldrons so it rang in her ear. "None of that now."

Vola gave him a look. "How are you so cheerful? Does nothing frighten you?"

"Very little."

Her eyes narrowed. He moved a little slower than usual, she thought, but he didn't seem to be dragged down by the very air like everyone else. He was acting more like the dwarves and the dragons.

Her eyes flicked to the Broken.

And the gods.

"Thank you, Henri," Vola said as he tightened the last strap on her greaves and straightened.

"You're welcome."

"I don't just mean for this," she said, raising her arm. "I mean…for everything. All those years you taught me. Everything I know about being a paladin I learned from you. Not from Imralen and the others."

He cocked his head.

"And you've always been honest with me."

"I have."

"You're not…fully human, are you?"

He didn't seem surprised. Only amused. His gaze flicked to the Broken who shrugged.

"I told you she'd figure it out sooner or later," she said.

"I didn't doubt it," he said.

"I'm right, aren't I?" Vola said.

Henri shrugged. "If we're being completely honest, I'm not at all human. It's just a whole lot easier to serve my lady if I appear as one."

"What are you, then?"

"Let's just say I've been training knights for my lady since the beginning. And you are the first one she's chosen since her fall." He pulled her in close and kissed her on the forehead. "I'm very proud of you, Volagra."

He handed her her sword and shield, and then turned to leave. For a moment he stood silhouetted against the sunlight outside. It lined his shoulders and glowed like a pair of bright, iridescent wings.

Hazel brushed past him into the tent, and the moment was gone.

The stocky dwarf held a fabric-wrapped bundle under her arm, and she seemed tired but upright. "Is Maxim in here?" she said, glancing around.

"No," the Broken said. "But he can be."

A whisper of air and the Greater Virtue of Strength and Loyalty appeared under the peaked roof.

"How did you—" Talon said, jumping. "Your magic is gone."

"But not our nature," the Broken said. "We might not have magic, but we are still immortal with all the—let's call them perks—that come with it."

"Was I needed for something?" Maxim said. "I think the army is about ready for the charge."

"This won't take long, sir," Hazel said. She held out the wrapped package. "I sent for someone to bring this from the monastery. If we're ever going to use it, now would be the time." She flipped back the fabric to reveal a stone bigger than Maxim's two fists put together, carved all over with whorls and leaves. One side was flat and solid, the other came to a nasty point, sharp enough to pierce armor. There was a recess in the middle.

The air in the room grew brighter and sang, as if the stone called to something outside of itself.

The staff on Sorrel's back began to glow.

"Oh," Maxim said, soft and reverent. A million memories crowded his eyes as he reached out to touch the head of his Warhammer.

Then his smile tipped in a rueful grin. "That's funny. It's not looking for me."

He glanced at Sorrel, who waited with wide eyes.

"I guess you could just stand there, if you like," he said. "Or you can come take what's yours."

She skipped forward a step, but still didn't reach out for the stone. "I'm not really sure it's mine, sir."

"I left the two pieces here well protected, with Jodin Battlecalled. He established various tests to ensure only the right person bearing the qualities I honor would be able to get to them."

"She recovered both of them," Hazel said. "Even though we put her through a lot of pain denying that fact."

Sorrel held out the staff on both palms and offered it to Maxim. He took it and weighed it in one hand. Then fitted the end into the slot on the stone.

The Warhammer rang like a gong, complete at last. He held it out to Sorrel.

"Uh, I'm not really a warhammer sort of girl," Sorrel said.

Maxim grinned. "I know. But your friend there already has a weapon from her god. And I'd prefer to give this one to one of my own."

Sorrel blinked, then bit her lip before she reached out to take it from him. In her hands, the weapon rippled and morphed, and instead of holding a warhammer, she held a long polearm, tipped with wickedly curved blades at both ends.

A double-headed glaive.

"Oh, wonderful," Talon said. "Let's make Sorrel even more deadly."

Rilla elbowed her in the ribs. "Be nice."

"What? I meant it."

Sorrel gave it a spin and everyone in the tent ducked.

Rilla lunged in to catch the weapon's haft. "Save it for Anders."

"Does that mean you're ready?" War asked, stepping through the tent. "'Cause it's time."

Vola's stomach dropped, and she glanced at the others. "Give us another minute," she told War and the two gods. "And we'll be out."

Thankfully, they took her meaning without her having to explain fully, and War held the flap open so the Broken, Maxim, and Hazel could duck out.

Vola swallowed, tucking her hands under her armpits so she could ignore how they shook. They were out of time, and this was where they had to split up.

She wished she could wipe away the look of pain on Lillie's face, but she'd said everything she could say. Someone had to draw Anders's attention. And she'd spent the last year keeping these women safe. She couldn't do anything else now.

But they were more than friends. More even than family. Her soul knew them and loved them, and the thought of walking out of this tent and sending them off without her made something ache just below her left ribs. The thought that she might not see them on the other side…Anders had already proved to be smart and powerful. Even with the gods' power flowing through her, she was still mortal. And she was painting a target on her back as well as leaving them defenseless.

How did you say good luck without it meaning goodbye?

"I…I don't even know what to say." She tried meeting each of their eyes. "There isn't a word for…for how I feel about you guys. I'm not me without you. Not anymore."

And this could be the end of that. But she couldn't say that. Not to them, and definitely not to herself.

"We know, Vola," Sorrel said, her normally cheerful face solemn. "Believe me, we know."

Trust Sorrel to prop her up. Who knew a halfling would be so essential to the stability of a half-orc?

She nodded, clearing her throat. "Right. That's it, then." She had to leave. War was waiting, but also, she couldn't stand here just looking at them anymore without the knot in her throat turning into something ugly.

She turned to the tent flap.

"Vola!" Lillie cried.

Vola paused and looked back, keeping her eyes carefully on Lillie's soft boots and not on her face. She couldn't see her face right then and keep any semblance of calm. And she couldn't defend their plan one more time if Lillie decided to test it again.

"Don't you dare die before meeting us at the mountain," the wizard said.

Vola's eyes flashed up to hers involuntarily. Lillie stared back, gaze fierce and full of worry but also pride and wonder and hope.

Lillie surged forward before Vola could leave and wrapped her arms around the paladin, armor and all.

Vola closed her eyes. She could feel the power rippling under Lillie's surface, responding to her emotions, and the matching power under Vola's skin.

Another set of arms joined her, wrapping her below the waist. And another from behind. And another over all of them. Vola allowed herself this one moment, encircled by trust and care and fear.

Slowly they drew back, but Vola didn't feel like they left her alone. She felt like she carried them with her. Maybe they'd given her a little bit of their power in that embrace. Or maybe they'd been giving her little bits of themselves all along. Entrusting themselves to her the way she'd entrusted herself to them.

"Don't worry." She could say it now. Say it and mean it. She flashed them a real smile as she held back the tent flap. "I'll meet you at the mountain."

Outside the camp in front of the entire army, War waited on a white charger. The horse tossed its head and stamped. War reined him in with a firm hand. Dark circles ringed the princess's eyes, but she held her spine straight and kept her chin up.

The corners of War's mouth pulled down, and Vola stepped up to her, armor perfectly adjusted with her sword and shield crossed over her back.

War looked her up and down. "Are you planning on walking into battle?" she said.

Vola opened her mouth and then closed it. To be fair, she hadn't really thought that far.

"I usually do," she said.

"You usually fight skirmishes," War said. "This is different. You'll need the height. Especially if you're going to be a figurehead. The army needs to see you. As does Anders."

Good point. And she'd had plenty of training on horseback back at the academy.

There'd been a time when she'd dreamed of riding to the rescue on a white charger. That image of herself had been as much a part of her as her sword arm.

The dream had since faded. She liked to think she'd grown up since then and had a much healthier mental image of herself.

Still. Some dreams never quite died.

"I'll have to borrow one," Vola said.

War snapped her fingers and a weary-looking hostler stumbled away from the gathered army, back to camp.

The Broken stood beside War. For the first time since they'd been in the lava field, the clouds above had finally broken, leaving bright blue sky and glaring sunlight. The wet ground began to steam.

The bright sun hid the flames behind the Broken's shoulders, making the flickers look even more ethereal and wraith-like.

"You all right?" the Broken said quietly.

Vola felt a lot better. The shakes and the fear had dissolved from her limbs, and now she could stand there calm.

"I am," she said.

Vola took the chance to survey their troops. This was nearly everyone. Everyone besides Mishap's Heroes. Southglen's elite took up the middle with their allies from Mistvale and Elfhome flanking. Behind them ranged an assortment of others. The monks, the villagers who'd come to defend themselves, the battle mages.

Gorgo stood at the head of a phalanx of orcs. He might have been a little slower than normal, but he didn't show any exhaustion or struggle as he stood with his troops. Lydia paced beside him, swinging her arms to stretch. They each caught Vola's eye and gave her an encouraging smile.

Far, far to the right, Cyrano and Raven stood with the dragons, who waited for the signal to take flight.

And arrayed near the front, in full plate with the sun gleaming from all their shiny bits, were the paladins. Kinght Commander Imralen was nowhere to be seen, but ranging up and down the line of holy warriors was a bright figure in gold-washed armor. Maxim checked their weapons, their stances. He called out to hold the line steady. And when he saw her looking, he raised his sword in salute.

Henri stood with them, Finn safe and strong in his shadow.

A squeal made Vola frown and turn.

"Oh," she said flatly. "Oh, no."

The hostler had returned, dragging a long lithe shape covered in green and blue scales. Slime dripped in its wake. Far behind them a soldier slipped and fell and took his entire platoon with him.

"Sorry, ma'am," the hostler said as Vola glared at the swamp monster. "This is all we have left."

"What?" War said. "We brought an entire line of extra mounts to serve as pack animals."

"Yeah, it ate at least half of them and scared the rest away."

They all stared at the swamp monster, which chewed malevolently and glared back at them, its crest wobbling with fury.

"At least it's fitting," Vola said.

The Broken stepped up to take the lead rope from the hostler, who turned and sprinted in the opposite direction.

The Broken ran a hand down the thing's neck and murmured in its ear.

"Of course it likes you," Vola said.

"Oh, she's not that bad," the Broken said.

"She?"

"She's actually descended from dragons, you know." The Broken leaned back a little to eye the creature up and down. It spat, and the lava rock sizzled. "Although she's a little far from the family tree now."

"You think?"

The Broken closed her eyes and laid her forehead against the beast's neck, stroking down its slimy scales with her palm.

The swamp beast's scales shimmered, and Vola had to blink. The bright light made her eyes water and she winced away. When she could focus again, wide glistening wings extended out from the beast's flanks. Gossamer tissue stretched from each delicate rib, looking like bat wings in the sunlight.

"Holy shit," War said, her charger prancing back a pace.

The swamp beast shook its head, spraying slime in every direction and looking very smug about it all.

The Broken cocked her head at the swamp beast, looking almost as smug.

"Lady, Anders should be just as scared of you without magic as with."

"I only called to her nature, and she responded."

Vola sighed. She wasn't getting out of this no matter what, and War was tapping her knee in an annoyed little pattern.

Vola swung past the swamp beast's head, avoiding the teeth and climbed onto its back behind the wings. Her feet hung down, so they almost dragged on the ground. The creature wasn't really that tall.

War winced. "I was going to say that's better, but I'm not sure it is. I guess it'll have to do."

War turned to catch the attention of her commanders, her arm raised in readiness.

The swamp monster turned its—her—head and tried to nip Vola's boot. She yanked her foot out of the way and flicked the creature's ear. "Focus," she said. "There's plenty for you to eat out there."

Vola pointed the beast's nose at the battlefield. Ahead of them stretched the lava field. Undead swarmed the rock plain, shambling between the fiery impacts of meteors.

The Broken rested her hand on Vola's knee.

Vola swallowed. "Wish me luck, lady."

The Broken smiled up at her. "I don't have to. I will be with you the whole way."

She faded even as the feel of her presence grew stronger. Like a friend standing over her shoulder.

And War gave the signal to charge.

TWENTY-SIX

VOLA KICKED the swamp beast into motion. She squealed and reared up, wings flapping, sending a wave of fishy stench back at Vola. And then the beast launched herself forward, carrying Vola down the ridge-line, straight into the horde of zombies.

The army roared behind them and the ground shuddered with the sound of thousands of feet charging ahead. War's horse drew even with the swamp beast and neighed at the top of its lungs. The swamp beast shrieked in reply, and Vola would have sworn the creature grinned.

Well, if the intention was to draw Anders's attention, Vola couldn't think of a better way to do it. The swamp beast's wings glinted in the sunlight, and while she never really took off, she did carry Vola over the heads of the enemy in leaps and bounds no normal mount would have managed.

Their forces clashed with the undead, meeting in the center of the field with a roar Vola could feel in her chest.

She struck down a zombie who tried to pull her from the swamp beast's back and the swamp beast leaped six feet up to carry her to safety before falling on the next enemy with her teeth bared.

Vola caught a blow on her shield and heaved while another zombie landed at the swamp beast's feet where the creature could trample it to death. Or, well, more dead than before.

A wall of orcs marched beside her, pushing through the ranks of undead. Using their superior strength to keep the line moving forward.

Vola remembered what she was supposed to be doing and urged the swamp beast ahead. She was the figurehead. The shining object the rest of the army was trying to follow.

Their job was to engage Anders's forces. And Vola was supposed to draw his attention. All so the rest of Mishap's Heroes could get through without challenge. As long as they made it to the stronghold, nothing else mattered.

Vola kept an eye out for Listrell and the other dragons. They were supposed to give the signal when Sorrel and the others were off, but closer to the mountain, the dark clouds still circled, belching forth meteors that pummeled the lava rock.

A whistle made the hair on the back of Vola's neck stand up and the swamp beast twisted out of the way as a flaming rock struck the ground where they'd just been.

Vola breathed out a sigh of relief. She could get used to this unusual partnership, given enough time and evidence like that.

But also, the surrounding army was getting struck as well.

Normally this would be Lillie's job. Vola wasn't a spell caster, just a field healer. But Lillie wasn't here, and Vola was filled with so much power it crackled along the edge of her sword when she wasn't paying attention.

She tried to focus her concentration on the clouds above them, thinking "clear skies" really, really hard. But strangely enough, that didn't seem to work. How did Lillie do this?

"You're not Lillie," the Broken's voice said in her ear, sounding like the rush of wind through tree branches.

"Yeah, I noticed."

"Don't think how would Lillie do this. Think, how would Vola do this? We gave you our power for a reason."

That was less than helpful. Vola didn't do weather. She smashed things. She stood between her team and the bad guy.

She glanced down at her sword. It was worth a shot.

Vola urged the swamp monster up and the creature leaped into the air with a massive beat of her wings. She focused all her attention on her blade for those few seconds as they hung in the air, concentrating the Broken's fire along its edge and Maxim's strength into her sword arm.

Then she slashed along the bottom of the clouds, which split with a shriek of released air.

The spell protecting Anders's stronghold and sending meteors crashing to the ground shriveled up, the clouds twirling into a single point. That dark point exploded; bits of cloud scattered across the sky so the sunlight shone down unimpeded.

"Much better," the Broken whispered as the swamp beast landed again.

Now Vola could see the dragons twisting above in the complicated pattern that indicated Mishap's Heroes had left camp without incident and were making their way around the battle. According to the plan, Sorrel and Lillie would be striking out along the northern edge while Rilla and Talon took the southern.

Vola ignored the curl in her gut and waved her sword to tell Listrell and the other dragons that she'd seen the signal.

The bright, colorful figures broke up and circled to begin their diving runs. Listrell fell from the sky first, snapping her wings out at the last second and flaming an entire row of zombies.

Hurren, gleaming red and gold, led the smaller dragons to harry Anders's forces from the sides.

In that moment she was distracted, Vola's skin tightened and the hair along her arms tingled as the air grew close and hot. She flung up her shield just as a bolt of lightning gathered in the clear air above her and snaked down.

It cracked against the bright wings of her shield and she winced. But her shield held and the only effect she felt was her hair trying to stand on end.

Vola's lips peeled back as she bared her tusks. She'd pissed Anders off apparently.

Good thing she'd spent all that time around Lillie and her spells. Vola shook the feeling of lightning off as she drove the swamp beast forward.

The ground split and fire gouted ahead of them. Vola didn't even have to use the power of the gods this time. The swamp beast swerved around the flames, leaving the rest of the army to deal with it. Hopefully, none of them fell in.

As they ran, the lava rock rumbled beneath their feet, and even the swamp monster staggered in response. Vola gripped her sword and resettled her shield, glancing about to see what Anders threw at them next. At least she knew now that the plan was working. He wasn't throwing any of this at the rest of the army. Or off to their flanks, where Mishap's Heroes crept.

The rock ahead of them bulged into a massive hillock, and the swamp beast danced back a couple of steps. The black rock crumbled and rolled away from a mound of flesh that twisted and pushed until a giant bald head burst from the ground. A patchwork of skins, all different colors and textures, reared up out of the hole, tossing its head to fling bits of rock everywhere. Vola threw up her shield and let the gravel ping across it.

Flesh golem, Vola thought distantly. Too bad Myron wasn't here now.

The giant monster patched together from a motley selection of corpses lumbered forward.

Vola ducked and the swamp monster leaped forward under the clumsy swing of the giant. Vola slashed at the back of its bulbous leg, trying to find the knee.

Her sword flared with flame as it scored the flesh golem's hide, and the monster bellowed. But it didn't go down.

Listrell raced by overhead, blotting out the sun with her wings, and a shape jumped from her back.

Renvick landed on the golem's head with a roar and swung his warhammer. The golem reached over its shoulder to grab at the guardian. Renvick smashed its hand and leaped away, rolling across the broken ground as Vola moved in.

Flesh golem, flesh golem. How had they dealt with this the first time? Sorrel had smashed it over the head with a divine weapon, hadn't she?

But Renvick had already tried that, and the Broken had chosen her for a reason. So, what would Vola do?

She yanked the swamp monster in close to the golem's feet, keeping them behind the reach of its arm. Then she strengthened herself with Maxim's might and imbued her sword with Velvain's fury. The Goddess of Mourning hated undead.

Her next slash cut across the thing's back and fire sprang out of the wound. Each cut she made severed a piece of the spell holding it together. Blow by blow she slashed at the magic keeping it upright until it wobbled on its feet and then toppled, splitting apart as it did so until it lay in a pile of corpses.

"Bleh," Vola said.

The swamp monster spat a wad of slime onto the pile, which hissed and sent up a plume of foul-smelling smoke.

"You are the most disgusting dragon I've ever met," Vola said. "And I kind of love you for it."

Renvick gave Vola a salute with his warhammer and turned to join the rest of the fray.

"Watch yourself!" the Broken cried. And Vola had just enough time to bring up her shield before she was struck from above.

No spell this time. No meteors or fire or necromantic constructs.

Just pure, unadulterated power fell from the heavens and smashed Vola into the ground. The swamp beast squealed and struggled underneath her, wings stretched out on either side.

The pressure let up just long enough for Vola to draw in a breath, and then it slammed down on them again.

Vola cried out as the power ground against her, shoving her cheek into the rough lava rock and trapping her left leg under the swamp beast.

She tried to pull her sword arm free to slash at whatever was holding her down, but she couldn't move.

What good was all this divine power if she panicked and couldn't use it when she needed to?

She tried to pull Maxim's strength into her limbs again, but too much of her brain was preoccupied with not being able to breathe. She thought about using the Broken's fire to sear away Anders's attack, but would that smother her in the process?

The pressure let up again. And Vola acted as quickly as she could, bringing her sword up and around so that when it struck her again, she stabbed at it, point first.

But her sword twisted in her hand, wrenching her wrist and she was slammed into the ground and the sharp edges of the swamp beast one more time.

This time she was left staring at the sky. The dragons ducked and wove, turquoise over red, green around yellow.

It meant something. That pattern. They'd agreed on it for something.

A signal.

The rest of Mishap's Heroes had made it into the stronghold. And they were waiting for Vola to join them if she could. If she hadn't already perished on the battlefield.

She didn't have to beat Anders here on this battlefield. Alone. She just had to get away. To join the others and they could face him together.

She carried the power of the gods, and the gods were connected to the world. She just had to draw on that connection.

Vola closed her eyes and waited. One more second. Two more. Until Anders pulled back the pressure, ready to strike one more time.

And in that space of breath, Vola concentrated. She pulled the divine power out of her center and reached into the world, finding that connection. Then she leaped, aiming for Sorrel, Lillie, Talon, and Rilla.

Vola and the swamp monster winked out of existence.

TWENTY-SEVEN

ON THE OTHER side of a darkness that was both very short and infinitely long, Vola popped back into the world on top of a very angry, very flat swamp monster.

The world spun around them, and she tried to hang onto something while at the same time registering rock walls and the chance of threat.

No threat, but familiar faces stared down at her anxiously.

The swamp beast writhed underneath her, making her wince, and Vola struggled to roll off onto the floor.

The cavern echoed with the creature's fury, walls stretching above them. A chandelier of wizard's fire far overhead lit the whole room and high windows up near the ceiling let in the daylight.

The swamp monster finally managed to buck her off onto the floor and the ungrateful thing launched herself into the air and flapped once, twice. She reached the windows and with a scream of triumph, she crashed through the glass and winged away into the sun.

Vola shaded her eyes, but she couldn't see the swamp monster any longer.

"Thanks," she called. "You were really great...for like a half an hour."

Vola finally tilted her head back far enough to see Lillie, Talon, Sorrel, and Rilla. They all stared out the broken window. Gruff panted beside them, unfazed.

"Soo, I feel like we missed something," Rilla said.

"Was that the swamp monster?" Sorrel asked. "It looked like the swamp monster."

"Long story," Vola said. She tried to push herself to her feet, but her whole body ached and her wrist collapsed when she tried to put weight on it.

She pushed Maxim's strength into her limbs and stood. Rilla darted in to lend her a shoulder.

"You all right?" the princess said.

"Sure."

Lillie bit her lip.

"I'm fine," Vola tried again. "It's just, I did exactly what the plan said. Drew Anders's fire."

"And you're still alive," Sorrel cried, throwing her hands in the air. "Hooray."

"Celebrate later," Talon grated. "He knows we're coming."

Vola glanced around. The cavern seemed to be an antechamber carved out of the mountain. A wide opening under the windows led back out to the battlefield.

Heaps of metal lay in a circle around the cavern, and Vola squinted. Finally, she realized they were piles of armor, golems like the ones that protected the palace in Glenhaven. Sorrel and the others must have slipped inside and taken them by surprise while Vola kept Anders busy.

A part of her wanted to fling her arms around them, but Talon was right. This wasn't the time for celebration. And Vola wasn't the only one preoccupied with the tunnel opening up in front of them. Dim light bounced off the rough walls, and Vola thought she heard voices beyond.

She took a few seconds to pause and heal the bruises and strains Anders had left her with. She didn't want to go on at anything less than her best.

"Ready?" Sorrel asked her.

"Ready," Vola said.

"Are we going to be clever about this?" Talon said. "Or go straight through the front door?"

"We know what's in there," Sorrel said. "And they know who's out here. I say we kick down the door."

Vola checked the others. Rilla and Talon were nodding. Even Lillie's face was set as she met Vola's eyes.

"Time to end this," she said.

Vola settled her shield on her arm. "Sorrel, take point. Talon and Lillie be ready with ranged attacks. Rilla and I will cover you."

Sorrel disappeared down the tunnel, and the rest of them followed.

Twenty feet later, the passage opened onto the large central chamber of the mountain. The one they'd seen in Anders's last illusion. High above, a jagged hole opened in the ceiling, letting daylight stream down to the floor.

Clearly, Anders had been hard at work since that memory had taken place. The dimly lit rubble was gone, replaced by rows of tables along a wall cut out of the rock. In the middle of the room stood a group of tanks, just like the ones Myron had worked with back in Brisbene. Like the ones Nargilla had used in Firewatch.

These however were empty. Because the power that was supposed to be filling them was walking around inside Vola and the others. And the rest was inside Anders.

Five figures waited for them in various poses of forced relaxation around the room. Lord Arthorel, a skinny man with squinty eyes and chewed fingernails, fidgeted from the corner on the left. Xavier glared at Lillie, his arms crossed over his chest, the sunlight bringing out the deep honey highlights in his hair.

Inga lounged on a bench, her gown artfully arranged around her as she examined her fingernails. Nargilla sat on top of one of the tanks, rocking back and forth as if in rhythm to a tune only she could hear.

And Anders stood behind them all, his gaze trained on the passage.

They didn't look weighed down by the absence of magic.

Vola forced herself to breathe. She couldn't afford to pass out from lack of air here at the very end.

"Gah, finally," Nargilla said and rolled her eyes. "I was starting to think you didn't actually want to fight us." She swung her legs and jumped down from her position, landing with an "oof."

"I never doubted this moment would come," Xavier said. "They can do nothing else but be drawn inevitably to their foretold deaths."

Nargilla rolled her eyes toward the ceiling. "Lighten up, Mr. Doom and Gloom. Otherwise, this will be no fun."

"It's not supposed to be fun," Lord Arthorel said. Vola hadn't remembered how nasally his voice was, but now that she heard it again that seemed just right. "It is revenge. It is justice. They took my title. My lands, my power."

"Your god?" Inga said mildly.

Lord Arthorel frowned. "Well, no."

"Then let's not argue about who they've screwed over the worst," Inga said, smiling so her tusks glistened. "You would only lose."

"I'm just saying," Nargilla continued. "If you can't enjoy your work, then what's left?"

"Oh, don't worry, I will enjoy it immensely," Xavier said. He cracked his knuckles.

"Any requests, boss?" Nargilla said over her shoulder to Anders.

Anders's eyes narrowed a fraction. "Kill them."

"Well, yes. Obviously," Nargilla said, planting her hands on her hips. "Only way to get the power back. I was looking for something a little more original."

Vola was done waiting. Done bantering. This was the end and none of them were leaving until the other side was dead.

She flicked her hand so her sword tip flashed, and Lillie hit them with a fireball.

The smoke cleared, revealing Arthorel and Xavier coughing while Inga waved a lazy hand in front of her face.

Nargilla cracked her neck. "That's more like it."

Xavier threw himself forward.

Vola stepped to intercept him, hoping to throw him back with her shield. But he planted his feet and met her strength for strength.

He hooked a leg under her and tossed her on her back. She braced to take his next attack, but Xavier leaped over her, stabbing at Lillie.

Lillie disappeared between one breath and the next, reappearing halfway around the room.

Rilla slid in front of Talon, covering the ranger as she loosed an arrow, which arced above them. At the peak of its trajectory, it flared, splitting into a myriad of deadly projectiles which whistled as they fell on their enemies.

One struck Xavier, piercing the joint between his pauldrons and his breastplate. Nargilla dissolved into the rock at her feet to avoid the volley, and a shield flashed over Inga, protecting her.

So they still had their magic, Vola thought. Anders's power must have protected them when Mishap's Heroes drained the rest of the world.

Rilla and Sorrel converged on Xavier and Lord Arthorel, while Vola climbed back to her feet.

Fog figures unfolded from the ground, stretching up until they formed very familiar faces.

Illusory copies of Vola, Lillie, Sorrel, Talon, and Rilla stared back at them. Gorgo and Lydia readied their weapons. Cyrano and Raven and Hazel and Renvick and Listrell. So many they knew and loved.

Vola just sighed. They'd already seen this trick before.

"Don't you have anything new?" she asked Arthorel and lunged to stab her mother through the heart.

Arthorel frowned before Sorrel smacked him in the side of the head with her fist and followed it with a slash across his chest with Maxim's new and improved Warstaff.

Vola went after the illusions as Lord Arthorel defended himself against Sorrel. These were clearly here just to distract them. Rilla was engaged with Xavier while Lillie peppered Inga with spells, and Talon chased Nargilla about the room. But there were so many illusions in the way it would be easy to mix up friend and foe and accidentally try to stab the real Rilla or Sorrel instead. Gruff wove between them, teeth flashing at illusory ankles and hamstrings.

Vola lifted her shield to take an attack from the fake Talon and under its protection, she breathed out with forced calm.

She reached with the divine power still resting in her chest and found the point of magic within each illusion. The bright heart that held them together. And she tied them all together, linking each one to the next.

Then she surged to her feet, throwing back the fake Talon and slashing Cyrano. She took his head from his shoulders in one blow, and the chained illusions all fell to dust at their feet.

Vola glanced around to find Arthorel, but something tickled her ear and she ducked. A whisper and a giggle made her whirl, but she couldn't see anything. The cavern around her faded into splashes of bright colors that hurt her eyes, and she squinted against the pain, trying to see through to where the real world was trying to kill them.

Shit, shit, shit. She couldn't see. She couldn't even hear past the silky whispers in her ears. Anything could sneak up on her.

A hand grabbed her shoulder, and she cried out, spinning to strike with her blade.

"Vola!" Talon said. "It's me."

The air left Vola's lungs in a whoosh as the cavern faded back into view.

"What happened to you?" Talon growled.

"Arthorel's illusions."

Talon glanced across at Arthorel, who had pressed himself up against the wall. Sorrel stood in front of him, slack-jawed, her gaze focused on something that wasn't there.

"You go left, I'll go right," Vola said.

Talon didn't wait. She slipped off to the side. Vola made a show of growling and charging for Arthorel from the right, keeping his attention on her.

He managed to throw up a shield to deflect her blow, but he didn't see Talon coming from the other direction.

She stabbed him. As her blade sank into his neck, his form flickered sideways, and Vola realized he was an illusion himself.

Talon stumbled back and crashed into Sorrel, who fell with an oomph and blinked up at the ceiling.

"Snap out of it!" Vola said. "Where is he really?"

Lillie had a spell that showed her magic and could see through illusions, but she was busy keeping Inga and Nargilla occupied. Vola didn't want to distract her.

Wait, she was imbued with the power of the gods. And there were plenty of gods who dealt with magic.

Vola reached deep and called up the power of Gava, Greater Virtue of Perception, who hated deception and tricky illusions more than anything.

Vola scanned the cavern, ignoring the flashes and bangs of other magic, looking for Arthorel.

And found him looming over Sorrel, who was still reeling from whatever illusion he'd cast on her.

She gasped. "There!" she called to Talon.

Talon charged and leaped. And Sorrel being Sorrel rolled out of the way to let the ranger fly past.

Talon landed on Arthorel, daggers sinking into his chest. His real chest this time.

The illusionist hiccuped and stared down at himself as Talon yanked free and stepped back. Arthorel staggered. And fell, becoming nothing more than a heap of arrogance and magic and broken vows.

Vola looked up to find Anders staring at her from across the room. She raised her chin as if to say, yes, we're coming for you.

Rilla called out, and Vola spun in time to catch Xavier bearing down on her.

She blocked his swing badly and fell to one knee.

An enraged scream rang from the cavern walls, and suddenly Lillie was there behind her brother. She placed both palms on the back of his breastplate and sent lightning flashing across his body.

He cried out and dropped to his hands and knees.

Lille stumbled back, chest heaving.

Xavier pressed a hand to his face. "How many times do we have to go over this, Lillie? You're supposed to be the smart one."

Lillie's jaw clenched. "You don't have to do this, Xavier. You don't have to work with them. Anders is taking everything and turning it to ash. Magic, nobility, chivalry. Inga killed Innis. Don't you care?"

"Innis made his choice. He could have had protection. He chose something else."

"He chose what was right." Lillie swallowed. "I remember when I was small. When I was too little to play with Innis and Kellan, but you sat with me and showed me the stories in your books. The stories about knights who defended Southglen from evil. You always wanted to be one of those knights. You showed me their banners. Told me their stories."

"Boring," Nargilla said, head popping up from the rock where she'd been lurking. "When I was a kid, I dreamed of world domination."

Sorrel launched herself at the gnome, forcing her back into the rock.

"You can still be one of those knights, Xavier," Lillie said, holding out her hand. "You can still do the right thing. Father and Kellan miss you."

Xavier stared up at her, eyes so alike. "Really?"

Lillie smiled. "Yes."

Xavier reached for her hand and yanked her toward him, sword out.

Lillie whispered a quick word, and a blast of air threw Xavier off his feet.

"I guess I've always been more like Mother in that regard," Xavier said, climbing to his feet and brushing himself off. "You wouldn't remember but she chose to rise above messy things like emotions."

"I met her, Xavier. And she wasn't 'above' anything. She was just busy and selfish with no regard for anyone else," Lillie said. "And you can't pretend this isn't about emotion."

"Very well, I won't." He lunged for her again, having learned nothing.

Lillie blasted him with fire, and Vola ducked through the last of the flames to strike him with her shield. He grunted and staggered back a couple of steps.

Nargilla chose that moment to erupt from the stone behind them. Sorrel spun and slashed at her.

Vola was nothing more than a preoccupation for Xavier, who tried to lunge past her to get at Lillie.

Vola caught his blade on her cross guard and planted her boot in his crotch. He huffed in pain and turned his shoulder into her. She grimaced and slashed him across his arm.

Flames licked out from the slice, white-hot and flickering against his armor. The pale light cast shadows across his stubbled jaw and sharp nose.

Now that she'd met both Ephyra and Shereille, she could see the planes of Shereille's features poking through Ephyra's softness in Xavier's face.

Xavier stomped on her foot and backhanded her across the face.

Vola stumbled away.

Talon dropped her daggers and held her hands over the ground. Then she clenched her fists and yanked up.

The rock under Xavier's feet heaved and wrapped around his legs, trapping him in place.

Nargilla surged upward, standing half in and half out of the ground as she tsked. "Nice one," she said. "But we can't have our big, strong knight pinned down now."

She pulled at the ground, and the rock crumbled away from Xavier. She glanced at Inga. "You gonna help at all?"

"You seem to have it handled," Inga said, tilting her head. "I'll pick off what's left at the end."

"Right, well, it's not like I'm not used to doing all the work," Nargilla grumbled as she subsided back into the rock.

"Oh, fine," Inga said, and waved her hand in Xavier's direction.

The knight began to glow.

"Oh, for Maxim's sake," Sorrel said, and she leaped at him, Warstaff flashing. The light caught the curved blades, turning them into streaks of lightning through the air of the cavern. And then real lightning began to flash from the ends of the blades.

Vola realized the halfling was muttering to herself as she whirled. Things like, "Yeah, yeah, I'm trying" and "you could help me out, you know, since you know all about it." And with a jolt, she realized Sorrel was talking to the dead. She carried their power, and they were arguing with her about how best to use it.

With a series of slashes, Sorrel drove Xavier back, one step at a time. The knight raised his blade to block her, but her glaive slashed down and sheared his sword off at the hilt. She slashed across his chest, and his breastplate fell to pieces around him with a clatter.

Xavier held up his empty hands, his eyes wide and frightened, and Sorrel took the briefest moment to check with Lillie.

Lillie didn't hesitate. She spoke a word that made the air shiver and the ground rumble. Xavier screamed. Then he collapsed to the ground, eyes blank and lifeless.

Nothing had touched him at the end, save Lillie's voice.

"All right, so that just happened," Nargilla said. She pulled herself out from the ground and stood with her hands on her hips, staring at Xavier. "Did you know she could do that?" she asked Inga.

Inga shook her head. "She couldn't the last time I was in her head."

Vola signaled the others. Rilla and Talon on one side, Lillie and Sorrel on the other. And forward.

"Damn, I would not want to be a part of the Ephyra family." Nargilla eyed Lillie, who approached her side of the cavern.

"Well, I guess there's just one thing left to do," Inga said.

"Kill them? Yeah. Duh."

Vola gripped her sword. "You know we won't make it easy, right?"

"Good." Nargilla stepped forward, then stopped.

The gnome frowned and glanced down at her chest. Lines of light threaded through her veins, creeping down her arms and legs, illuminating her with a network of light.

The magic spread to Inga, whose mouth fell open.

Nargilla's eyes went wide. "Oh, no." She spun to point at Anders, who still lurked behind them all. "No, don't you dare!"

Vola shrank back, eyes narrowing. What was he doing? She followed the lines of light with her gaze, racing to interpret this new threat.

He was filling them with all of his stolen power. Stuffing them so full they wouldn't be able to hold it. And as soon as they reached the tipping point...

Oh gods.

For a brief second, Nargilla and Inga lit up so brightly, they left images flickering across Vola's sight. She had time to throw up her arm to protect her face. But not enough time to think about how to protect her party.

Nargilla and Inga exploded with a roar of wind and light, and Vola ducked as wave after wave of heat struck her with a physical force. Her sword vibrated in her hand.

Instead of receding, the explosion intensified, getting louder until it rang in Vola's ears.

Her sword shattered, and the force flung her back against the cavern wall.

Pain blazed along her spine and the back of her skull as she fell to the ground and lay there slumped. She tried to shake her head, but the movement sent a stab of white light behind her eyes.

She couldn't hear, couldn't see, could barely think or breathe.

But this was important. She couldn't just lay here. There were people to protect. And Anders was just standing over there.

Vola forced her eyes open. She blinked the water from them and squinted through the afterimages that flickered across her vision.

All she could see in front of her nose was rock. She rolled with a gasp and pushed up to her elbows.

A few feet away, Talon lay unmoving at the base of the wall, arm outstretched and empty.

Vola sucked in a breath and turned her head. Sorrel and Rilla lay on her other said, faces still and singed.

Lillie. Where was Lillie? Vola coughed and gasped and struggled until she could see the wizard crumpled and small against the wall.

Vola sobbed.

What had Anders done? He'd sacrificed Inga and Nargilla, and in the process, all the power he held had lashed out and reacted with the power the Mishap's Heroes held. There'd been no way to shield them because they were all the fuse to his bomb.

She tried to swallow around the ache in her throat. They couldn't be dead. They were just stunned. Knocked out. Dead would mean all the power they'd been holding would dissipate and flow back into the world.

Vola tried to crawl forward, dragging herself across the ground toward Lillie.

Just as she reached the wizard, a red glow gathered over her limp form. The same color as the fire she'd wielded so well in life. It grew stronger and stronger, just as the power from the Broken had when the goddess had destroyed the tanks in Firewatch.

Light flickered at the edge of Vola's vision, and she turned her head to see the glow above each of the others. Gray and blue and green. And it flowed upward and out over the cavern.

A world's worth of magic dissolving back where it came from.

TWENTY-EIGHT

"THERE," a voice said, and Vola recognized Anders as he stepped across the cavern. "That's better."

Everything seemed crystal clear, the edges of the tables and the rock walls sharp and crisp. But to Vola, it seemed like she was looking at it all through a pane of glass. She was over here and all that was...over there. At a distance.

Vola gathered Lillie into her arms, her throat thick and tight. Her eyes burned, but no tears fell. There was a hole in her chest that should have held grief and rage and pain, but there was nothing yet. And she embraced the nothing because she knew that what came next was going to hurt like nothing had hurt before.

"Bit of a waste, I guess," Anders said. He stared around at the destruction of the cavern. The tables and tanks remained intact since they'd been behind Anders, but everything else had been shattered, little shards of Vola's sword scattered across the rock floor. There was no trace of Nargilla or Inga. Not even a smear or a puddle. Everything had been burned away in that intense blast of light.

"You were pretty clever about it all. Shame to waste your talents. But you absorbed the power I was after. And the only way to separate you from it was to kill you. Now it's free to be gathered once again."

He waved a hand at the colors flowing and shifting above them.

A voice of rushing wind and the ring of blades spoke in Vola's ear.

"Don't worry, I've kept the power from dissipating completely. We can still keep him from stealing it all."

Don't worry? Vola thought. *Don't worry when the others all lay dead, and she'd failed to protect them, to keep them alive?* Her fingers tightened on Lillie's arm.

She was not looking at the wizard's face. She wasn't looking at any of them. Her gaze remained fixed on the rock walls.

"Now, I just need yours."

So he could be a god. So he could do a better job than them. And was that really so wrong? The gods hadn't been able to keep the others alive. They wouldn't even have been interested in what was happening here today if Vola hadn't forced them to be.

"Vola," the Broken said.

Anders drew a sword, movements sluggish as if time had slowed.

Vola bowed her head.

"Vola."

Anders was *right*. That though burned in her mind, a white-hot pain.

"Vola."

Except *he'd* killed the others. He'd destroyed them so he could have their power. Lillie, Talon, Rilla, and Sorrel. They were dead because of him. Not because of the gods.

And the Broken had helped her protect them. For months now, Vola had healed them and kept them safe using the Broken's power. And the goddess had never been stingy with it.

And in the end, she couldn't abandon hope just because she was alone. She'd been alone before, and she'd always found someone to help. Someone to hold on to.

She drew Maxim's strength into her arm and called to Sorrel's Warstaff. It answered, whether because it recognized her from the times she'd held it before or because she carried Maxim's power.

The double-headed glaive smacked into her palm and transformed into a sword the spitting image of the one the Broken had given her. A greatsword that she could wield in one hand.

She threw up her arm and blocked Anders's blow as it fell toward her neck. The sound of their blades rang against the walls of the cavern, and Vola pushed Anders back and surged to her feet, grabbing up her shield.

"You killed your people." Vola slashed at him.

He blocked and lunged. "Necessary," he said. "Just like killing you."

"You used them to destroy us."

"It should have destroyed you, too."

But her sword had absorbed the shock and shattered instead. The

Broken protecting her, even when she didn't have the power to protect anyone anymore.

Vola ducked and swiped at his legs. Anders spun back and countered the blow with a quick slash up her breastplate. The tip of his sword shrieked against the metal and nicked her cheek.

She pulled the Broken's power up, and the cut healed in a split second. Maxim's strength bolstered her sword arm and Mulgash's rage battered at the inside of her skull, turning her vision red. She didn't dare feel anything else right now. Not until this was over. Not until she'd destroyed Anders once and for all.

Mulgash's rage gave her strength and purpose when her strength and purpose had bled out along with her friends.

She feinted right and then kicked Anders in the knee when he followed. Instead of falling back in pain, he ducked his shoulder and shoved, sending her stumbling away.

Vola paused to catch her breath.

Anders was as good a fighter as she was. And this wasn't a time to push it to see who was better. If he won…if she died here, the world was lost.

But she carried the power of the gods.

She pulled the Broken's fire into her blade and lunged in for the attack.

She was fast enough to score a hit, the edge of her sword slashing across his chest. But instead of the feel of metal on flesh, there was a flash and a bang and the force of it blasted her back a few paces.

Vola resettled her grip as Anders checked himself. There was no wound. Only a line of thin pale fire that sputtered and went out as they watched.

Anders looked up with a grin. "That won't work, you know."

Vola huffed through her nose. Of course. He had some of the Broken's power as well. He'd used it to destroy his minions and her team. And now he was using it to protect himself against her.

Well, she had more than just the Broken.

She pulled Maxim's strength forward and attacked with that, driving him back and trying to smash him beneath the weight of a god's might.

He just laughed and thrust back with the Broken's power.

Vola gritted her teeth and tried something else. Tirza, goddess of Magic and Discipline, lent her the force of a gale. With every slice, she sent forth a wave of magic.

And Anders's power cut through it.

Vola staggered back, panting. She was imbued with the pantheon's power. But she could only use them individually. And each one was countered by the Broken. Who was the most powerful of them all even if they wouldn't recognize it.

The fractured pantheon wasn't nearly as strong as it needed to be.

She could hear the Broken's voice in her memory. "Don't let them fool you the way they've fooled themselves. They are not united. They might be working together, but they are not united."

"Lady," Vola whispered.

"I'm here."

"I can't beat him. Not when he holds a part of your power."

She could feel the Broken's regret and frustration ring through her and wished she'd phrased it differently.

"I need to unite the pantheon," she said.

The Broken was silent.

Anders eyed her across the way. "You can't win this."

He surged forward to attack. Vola countered with only half her attention. She was thinking. Concentrating on something else.

She blocked a blow, but he swept her feet out from under her and pressed her to the ground. She dropped her sword and gripped his blade with her bare hands to keep him from cutting her throat. Maxim's strength and the Broken's healing shielded her palms, but only just. Anders shoved against the power, making it bend and warp.

"This is why the gods have to go," he said, so close he spat on her face. "They're useless, powerless apart."

Apart, yes. They'd been apart ever since they'd kicked the Broken from their midst. Since they'd rejected her, they'd been fractured. The Virtues and the Obstacles. Maxim and Bierhel and Ona and Mulgash and Cleavah and so on across the board.

Together. Together they'd be a true pantheon. They'd be united under the Broken the way they were supposed to be. And maybe with all of their power resting in Vola right at this moment, Vola could do that.

But using the gods' power against one of their own, that's what fractured them in the first place. That's what sundered their bond and maimed the Broken and shattered the pantheon.

If she united their power and then used it to break the piece of the Broken that Anders carried, what would happen? Another fracturing? Another Divine War?

She gulped. Anders's sword pressed against her shield. Her strength was failing, and the blade crept closer and closer to her throat.

He was immune to her power the way it was now. The Broken's power in him made him immune to the divine power of the gods.

But not the magic of the world.

She turned her head a fraction so she could see Lillie's limp form out of the corner of her eye. Sorrel and Rilla lay beyond. And Talon on the other side.

"The magic hasn't dissipated," the Broken whispered, following her train of thought. "I hold it ready."

She could pull it into herself. If she united the gods' power, she'd be able to replicate Nargilla's spell without any of the casting or preparations. Without the circle or the representatives.

She could pull it into herself and cast him down.

But she would do it alone.

She closed her eyes. There was always a cost to healing. She had to pull wounds into herself and heal them from the other side. Sure, she carried divine power. But there were limits. And death was usually a pretty big limit.

But she carried the Broken's power. She knew the depth of it, even without the bit that Anders had stolen. And how much more could she do if the gods were united. Just enough?

Anders leaned on his blade. The shield protecting her cracked, and the edge of his sword cut into her palms.

She swallowed, gathered all the divine threads within her, all the Virtues, greater and lesser. And all the Obstacles, greater and lesser. And wove them together.

Light and dark, a mess of colors so bright it burned the inside of her eyelids as it roared through her. It swelled inside her mortal being and seared her from within.

Anders's eyes went wide. Maybe he saw something that warned him. Maybe he could see the colors behind her eyes.

He growled and shoved down, fighting to cut her head off. Vola's hands wouldn't grip anymore and her arms shook with fatigue.

Lady, I need a second. Just one second.

A shriek and a blur of murky green made Anders jerk.

The swamp monster dove through the opening in the roof and swiped claws across Anders's scalp.

Anders cried out and pulled away, slashing at his new opponent. The swamp beast ducked and dove, gossamer wings wafting a fishy stench into his face as he screamed at her.

Vola rolled and reached out her ruined hands toward her team.

"Lady bless," she croaked.

Divine power roared through her, scorching as it went. But she knew if she held it back even a little, this would never work. She blew out her breath and let it go, let it surge through her. It took the death, it took the damage the others had suffered and transferred it all to Vola, giving her their wounds, giving her their pain and their death.

Black crept across her vision. This was new. Usually, it was red and accompanied by a surge of strength. This came with bone-deep weariness. There was already pain. It seemed like she was made of pain. But now exhaustion numbed the rest, and all she wanted to do was close her eyes.

But she couldn't yet. There was one more thing she had to make sure of.

One. More. Thing.

The power swirled above her, hesitating.

The others lay still, unmoving. And the black flickered, threatening to take Vola with it.

Then Lillie stirred. Then Talon. Sorrel. Rilla. And above them, the magic of the world speared back down into them. The Broken had saved it for them. And now that they were back, it found a familiar home in their forms.

Shadows danced, and Vola fought to keep her eyes open to watch as Sorrel climbed to her feet, glanced around, and advanced on Anders.

Rilla and Talon joined her. Lillie pulled lightning and fire and little flickers of green and white into her hands.

Anders tried to duck away, seeing his fate in their faces, but Sorrel was far too fast to let him escape. She struck, and he fell.

Lillie called down a swirl of lightning and fire to pin him to the ground. And Talon and Rilla converged on him.

And Vola let herself go.

TWENTY-NINE

VOLA OPENED her eyes and found herself standing in a field of wildflowers, the bright sky stretching overhead and a playful breeze cooling her face.

She wasn't even lying down. Which was a bit of a surprise. When you died flat on the floor, you definitely didn't expect to wake up standing.

Vola felt like there was more than one thing wrong with that statement but wasn't quite sure she should poke at it hard enough to figure it out. There was a lingering ache in her body that she shied away from. An unpleasant memory best ignored until she had her feet under her again.

Feet. She glanced down. Her bare toes scrunched in the grass. Huh. Those weren't exactly how she'd left them, either. She was pretty sure she'd been wearing boots. Some sort of armor.

Nope, not thinking that hard.

Whatever she'd been wearing before, it was gone now. She wore a pair of dark trousers and a linen shirt. Simple. Comfortable. The type of clothing that said you have nowhere to be and no one to impress.

She held out her hands. The backs were criss-crossed with scars, and she shoved them behind her before she could think too hard about that as well.

"Everything is still there," a voice said. A voice like the rushing wind, though the breeze across Vola's face remained gentle. "You're not missing any pieces, I promise."

Vola looked up to find a woman standing beside her in the tall grass.

She wore her dark curly hair short, almost like it had been burned off at some point. Probably in the fire that had left all the scars on her face. She balanced on one leg because the other was missing from the knee down, and when she scratched her nose, Vola noticed she only had one arm as well.

Flames flickered behind her like massive wings, and when she spoke, Vola realized the rush of the wind was actually the sound of wings beating the air.

"Is this the afterlife?" Vola asked. That nagging sense that she was forgetting something was starting to get on her nerves.

The Broken laughed. "No. Can you imagine how boring it would be if it were? I just thought this would be more soothing for you after…"

After Vola had died. The pleasant fog of forgetfulness tried to take over again, to urge down the rotten memories, but Vola shook it away, choosing instead to remember everything. The good with the bad.

"They're alive?" she said, her face twisting as she remembered Sorrel leading the others in a final charge.

"They are," the Broken said gently.

Vola closed her eyes, cherishing that image in her head as she fought to breathe without choking. They were alive. There was no reason to cry, no reason to mourn.

When she could finally blink her eyes open again, the Broken was still there. Keeping her company, as always. But her image flickered a little.

Vola tilted her head. First, she focused on the Broken, with her scars and her strength. But the next thing she saw seemed to be Maxim's face with its sharp nose and broad jaw. His black hair and brooding features morphed until Mulgash stared back at her with his red eyes and pale skin.

"Are…are you all right?" Vola asked the figure she thought was the Broken.

"Better than all right," she said, and her voice was comforting in its familiarity. "We are whole. You united us."

"Then you really were broken," Vola said. "Fractured."

"They thought we would be better separate. That we would be more powerful with more autonomy." Her lip tilted in a rueful smile. "I disagreed. So they cast me out, and I fell in flames. They never realized they were tearing out a piece of themselves. And every time I tried to return to reunite the pieces, they turned away, choosing isolation and brokenness."

The Broken's mouth thinned, and she turned her face away for a second in pain. "So I took the flames of my fall and made them my own. I claimed their power for myself and kept going. I kept working. The gods had stepped back from the world, but that didn't mean I had to give up on either of them. I never actually thought we could be fixed. Not truly." She smiled ruefully at Vola. "I doubted. I guess there are many reasons I am called the Broken."

"What was your name before we called you that?" Vola hadn't even realized she was going to ask the question before it popped out.

The Broken stared up at the sky for a moment. "I don't know. I took that and made it my own as well."

Vola squinted up as well, but there was nothing up there but an endless expanse of blue. Not even a cloud.

She wanted to ask, "what now?" But she had the feeling that didn't really concern her anymore. Still, she wasn't used to not getting a say.

She took a deep breath and held out her arms to look at them. Scars covered her skin, turning her gray-green coloring into a patchwork of remembered pain. Every slice Anders had inflicted on the others, every bruise and cut and blow she'd taken onto herself, showed. The worst being the ones she couldn't see. The death blows that had taken their lives. She'd stolen those away as well, and now she stood here in a field of wildflowers instead of where she should be.

"I knew what I was sacrificing," she said, her voice thick. "I know the price of what I do, and I knew what it would do to me. I made that choice, and it should all be worth it as long as the others survived. Four lives for one seems like a pretty good trade."

"But?" the Broken said, staring at her.

Vola sucked in a breath. "But for once I want to be selfish. I wish it was five lives."

"Vola," the Broken said.

Vola winced.

"You are not stupid."

Vola glanced up in surprise.

"You know what you have done. For me and for the pantheon and for the world." She gave Vola a brilliant smile. "You have only to ask, my knight."

Vola fought hard to look at the choice logically. To give it a fair process.

Early retirement. Rest. No more sideways glances. No more blatant mistreatment because she was an orc. No more pain. No more worry.

Or...she could go back to all that. To the pain and all the rest. Except all the rest came with laughter and love and the wholeness of protecting the ones who meant the most to her.

She met the Broken's eyes. "Please?"

The Broken reached for her face and the scars that marred it, and Vola jerked back.

She touched the lines creeping up her cheeks. "I'd like to keep them. To remember," she said.

"You'll remember without them," the Broken said. "Trust me on that."

Vola felt herself flush. She would know. "Four, then," Vola said. "Let me keep four of them. I'd like to take the flames and make them my own."

The Broken didn't smile, but her eyes shone. "Very well."

The goddess reached for Vola, and this time, she didn't flinch away. The Broken folded Vola into her arms, hand pressing the back of her head. Her voice was the rushing of wings in Vola's ears as she said, "Lady bless."

Vola opened her eyes and found herself flat on the floor, her limbs leaden, her armor smoking and blackened, and she thought to herself, "This is more like it."

She tried to move and hissed in pain. The Broken might have fixed whatever it was that had sent her to that not-afterlife, but there was plenty left over to remind her she'd done some very stupid things before that. For instance, her hands were killing her.

Sorrel popped into her field of vision, which mostly consisted of the cavern roof with its hole. "She's not dead," Sorrel said, her voice an octave higher than usual. "Oh my gods, I was wrong. Vola's not dead."

Then she did something very un-Sorrel-like and dropped her head onto Vola's chest and burst into tears.

Vola struggled to lift a hand and patted the halfling's head.

Rilla came into view somewhere near Vola's feet, and Talon sat beside her head. Lillie took a position opposite Sorrel. It was a lot to take in right at the moment, but she needed to be able to see them and wouldn't have had it any other way.

"How are you feeling?" Lillie said.

Vola took stock. "Not dead," she said. That was about as good as it could get, all things considered.

"Um," Talon said, casting a glance at the sobbing Sorrel. "Were you? Or were we just imagining that?"

"No, you weren't."

"Don't you ever do that again," Sorrel said, lifting her head.

"Sure, as long as you don't ever make it necessary again."

Sorrel's mouth fell open, and she blinked.

"Deal," Lillie said. Her hand crept into Vola's, and Vola's fingers tightened on hers.

"Wait, we died?" Sorrel said.

"You don't remember that?" Rilla said, as Vola tried turning her head so she could peer between Lillie and Talon.

"I was really hoping that was a bad dream induced by head trauma when I hit the wall."

The swamp monster snuffled the ground across the cavern, her wings folded against her back.

"Where's Anders?" Vola croaked.

"There were too many pieces to find all of him," Talon said, grimly.

Vola winced.

The swamp monster caught sight of Vola and gave a little squeal. She galloped over to them, and Vola held up her free hand.

"Hey. You were actually really helpful," she said.

The swamp monster stopped and hawked a wad of toxic spit at Vola. It sizzled against her breastplate.

They all groaned.

"Its helpfulness does not exceed how gross it is," Rilla said.

THIRTY

Vola needed help standing and staggering out of the mountain. Everything seemed to be in working order, and Vola trusted the Broken to put her back together in one piece, but her limbs seemed to have trouble believing it for the first hour or two. Rilla supported her on one side and Talon on the other. They'd tried to drape her over the swamp monster's back, but the creature had tried to take a bite out of her, so they opted for something less fraught. Now the swamp beast followed them, ears pinned to her head as she glared at them.

The antechamber where they'd met was still scattered with broken glass, and they shuffled through to the entrance where they could see daylight shining through.

Had it really only been a few hours since they'd left the army? Vola felt like it should at least be dark or like a week later. Not the same day, with the same sunlight pouring down.

She winced away from the light after the dimness of the cavern and had to blink spots out of her eyes. Ahead of them stood War. She waited in the center of the battlefield, the point of her sword drooping to rest on the ground. Bodies, both undead and golems, littered the ground around her.

The rest of the army staggered behind her. Some were still on their feet, but many had fallen to hands and knees to rest among the dead. Vola caught sight of Cyrano supporting Raven off to one side. Monks were scattered among the soldiers and here and there an orc supported a human, keeping them on their feet.

The dragons flanked the army on either side, waiting.

War saw them and lifted her chin and her sword. She stepped forward, though from the way she wove, she was ready to collapse, too.

"Gods, I'm so glad it's you coming out of there," she said, wiping her brow. "These all finally fell, and no more rose to take their place so we assumed...well, we knew something had happened, just not what."

"Anders is dead," Rilla said, adjusting Vola's arm around her shoulders.

"You're sure?" War asked.

Sorrel raised her hand. "Witnessed."

"He wasn't immune to the magic they carry," Vola said, her arms tightening around Rilla and Talon involuntarily. "And the pantheon is whole now. I doubt they'd let him survive."

War blinked at her. The others all stared.

"The pantheon is what?" Lillie said.

Vola sighed.

The wind shifted across their faces, and Vola recognized the feel of a downdraft, like wing beats descending from the sky.

And the Broken appeared on the rock beside War. Figures stepped out of her form, like shadows detaching themselves from their progenitor, and Vola recognized faces. Hundreds of greater and lesser gods, Virtues and Obstacles alike, arraying themselves around the five of them and War. And standing at their head was the Broken, with Maxim on her right and Mulgash on her left.

The Broken placed her hand over her heart and bowed from the waist. The rest all followed her example.

And as they froze in their obeisance, Rilla and Talon both shuddered under Vola's arms. When Vola glanced at Lillie and Sorrel, they had gone rigid.

Power flowed out of them, streaming up into the air, dissipating back into the world.

It hung there for a few moments, glowing and catching all sorts of colors in the sun before it exploded out, streams and eddies of magic shooting away over the hills, down into the ground, and falling on the army in sparks and waves of colored dust.

Cries of awe and relief rang out across the exhausted army. Soldiers who had been prone on the ground leaped to their feet, laughing and staring at their hands as if they were made new.

Vibrancy came back into the world. The air itself felt wholesome and clear again instead of thin. Colors deepened, edges sharpened like coming out from underwater and seeing the world the way it was supposed to be seen.

War straightened, her eyes shining. Light crackled along her gold-washed mail and flashed over the army as the power of her Throne returned.

Raven morphed into a great eagle and winged out over the army, circling in tighter and tighter spirals, joined by the dragons as they trumpeted their joy to the sky.

Those who hadn't already leaped to their feet climbed upright and helped those around them. Spell casters all across the battlefield gathered sparks in their palms and fire gouted into the sky. Fireworks, bright splashes of lightning, and sparks of color decorated the battlefield as magic and life were celebrated by the survivors.

As the Broken straightened and the other gods faded back into her figure, she winked at Vola.

The party lasted the rest of the day and most of the night. War pitched their camp directly east of Anders's mountain where the field was flat and no one would fall into any crevices or gorges in a drunken stupor. Because Vola was pretty sure everyone was drunk that night. Except her, of course.

"I didn't even know we brought this much alcohol," she said, covering her mug as the cook and his assistants went through the hastily pitched tents with another round. They hadn't even bothered with tables. They'd just pitched their tents and sat on the ground like a massive picnic. It was kind of cozy.

Rilla gestured with her drink and ended up spilling at least half of it. "I think War built a portal special to bring in some celebrea—celebrit—celebratory supplies." She turned to Cyrano and leaned across to him, where he was wrapped around Raven. "Hey. Hey, say that five times fast."

The night sky lit up with more spell casters making sure their magic really was back, and Vola turned her face up.

Lillie gave her a really sappy grin and leaned her head on Vola's shoulder.

"I thought you only drank wine?" Vola asked her, nodding to the mug full of something too yeasty to be a good vintage.

Lillie made a face. "Hey, we died today. I'll drink whatever the hell I want." And to prove that point, she took a swig that knocked her over.

Vola chuckled and pulled the wizard's head onto her lap so she wouldn't wake up with a crick in her neck in the morning.

Across the way, Sorrel was still on her feet, with her arm slung around

Hazel's shoulders. They sang a hymn double the normal tempo, at the top of their lungs, and completely out of tune.

Vola glanced behind her to check on Talon, who sat in the shadows at the back of their tent, Gruff wrapped around her. "How are you managing?"

Talon raised her mug as if to toast Vola. "Do you think I could get a little umbrella for this?"

Vola laughed. She was still working through the half a mug she'd been given, just to be polite. The last time she'd had a drink, she'd passed out and woken up on a ship sailing to Glenhaven, so…

Although she might welcome oblivion this time, if only to avoid the sight of her parents making out in the opening of the tent next door.

Vola shifted Lillie to a more comfortable position, and while she was distracted, the cook came and refilled her mug before she could protest.

The swamp beast wandered through the party, dribbling acid saliva on anyone too drunk to get out of the way.

Vola held out her mug. "Here. You earned it."

The beast slurped it down and then turned to aim a burp right in Vola's face.

Vola coughed and when the tears finally cleared from her eyes, the swamp monster had wandered off, and Renvick hunkered down next to her. Bursts of light overhead splashed across his scales, making patterns that glowed in the night.

"Do guardians drink?" Vola asked.

"Not if they can help it," he rumbled.

Vola raised her mug, which was melting from the swamp beast's spit. "Hear, hear."

Sorrel stumbled over and tripped into Renvick's arms. He caught her and helped her upright.

"Hey, Renvick," she said. "We have a conversation we need to finish."

His claws played with the end of a tent cord. "I thought you'd forgotten about that."

Vola had thought Sorrel had forgotten as well. Or made her decision without him.

"I've been busy saving the world," Sorrel said.

"And now?"

"Now I'd like to figure out what we are."

Vola cleared her throat. "What happened to Hazel?"

"She couldn't handle the last verse of 'Maxim Be My Vision.'" She gestured across to where Hazel was staggering away with the help of her fellow monks. "They're putting her to bed."

Vola tucked her mug away where it wouldn't hurt anyone.

Sorrel yawned.

Renvick picked up the halfling and stood. "Let's talk. Then I can be your pillow. I do not have to sleep."

Sorrel narrowed her eyes and then shrugged. "Oh, why the hell not?"

Vola glanced in Sorrel's discarded mug. "I'm not sure I've ever seen you leave a drink half-finished."

Sorrel waved a hand as Renvick carried her to the next tent over. "I'm not leaving it. I'm just taking a break. I'll come back to it later."

And she snuggled down against his scales.

Vola closed her eyes only for a moment. But when she opened them again, light brightened the horizon and dew dampened the tents around them. Soldiers snored where they lay, oblivious to the rough rock beneath them.

Vola shifted Lillie over and stood up to stretch. Rilla lurked in the shadows just outside their tent, giving no indication that she'd spent the night celebrating.

"You look fresh," Vola said.

Rilla gestured to the rest of the camp. "I think you'll find there's not a hangover to be found this morning. Some sort of miracle I'd wager."

That proved true as the camp stirred and groups began pulling down their canvas and packing it away. The majority of Southglen's army would stick around to clean out Anders's mountain, but their allies had families and lives to return to.

Gorgo and Lydia stopped by to give Vola a hug.

"You're coming home for Yuletide, aren't you?" Lydia said, holding her daughter at arm's length. "All of you?"

Vola glanced back to see Renvick bidding farewell to a sleepy Sorrel, and Talon climbing out of the tent.

"Sure, Mom," she said.

"We'll see you around, Lightless," Cyrano said, his arm around Raven's waist as they passed on their way back to their tent. "I imagine there will be plenty of trouble to partake in wherever you're headed."

Vola gave him a mock frown. "What makes you say that?"

Raven gestured at the mountain in the distance. "You know. Evil kidnappers, tricky illusions, bad guys with god complexes. Just experience, Vola."

Soon after Renvick had taken his leave, the dragons lifted off from the edge of camp and swept low overhead, spouting fire in one last triumphant goodbye.

"You and Renvick?" Vola asked Sorrel, who stood beside her, shielding her eyes with her hand.

"Yeah," Sorrel said. "We'll see how it goes. He's got to stay with Listrell, but I'll see him around. And we each do love a little differently from the rest of the world. So at least it should be interesting."

Vola raised her arm to salute the dragons as they went by.

Sorrel moved to help Talon fold the tent, arguing softly about who did it better.

As Vola dropped her hand, Lillie slipped under her arm. Then she turned it over, her fingers tracing a scar across Vola's palm.

"This is new," Lillie said.

Vola ducked her head. The Broken had kept her promise. Vola had four new scars to go with all the others she'd earned over the years. The one on her right palm she liked to think of as Sorrel's. Fitting, since she'd never accomplished anything without the monk backing her up. The one on the back of her left hand was Talon's. There was one across her temple, stretching up into her hairline, that belonged to Rilla.

And the last one was stark and clear over her heart.

"For remembering," Vola said with a smile for Lillie.

War walked down the aisle between the tents as people took them down. She'd left the golden mail behind today, but there was a look in her eye that Vola recognized well.

She stopped beside them and raised her chin. "Did you get enough rest?"

Vola saluted.

Rilla wasn't nearly so polite. Or patient. "Spit it out," she said. "What's happened now?"

"A town on the coast," War said. "They've sent word to the Thrones in Glenhaven that they're being attacked by swarms of mechanical creatures. Started just yesterday."

Rilla pursed her lips. "Could be another baddy filling the void now that Anders is gone."

"That didn't take long," Sorrel said.

War met Rilla's gaze. "Falls under your jurisdiction as the Dagger princess," she said.

"I'll take care of it. Meet you back in Glenhaven to debrief."

War nodded and turned on her heel.

Vola waited, watching Rilla. The others watched Vola.

"Well," Rilla said. "Are you coming? Or are you taking early retirement?"

Vola scratched her nose and glanced at the others. Sorrel swung her Warstaff across her back and cocked her head, making her choice clear. Lillie beamed. Talon hoisted the packs without a word. And the swamp beast grazed nearby. There was no grass. Vola was pretty sure it was eating rocks.

"Retirement does sound nice," she said slowly.

"What?" Lillie cried.

"Peaceful. We could open a tavern. Sorrel would serve drinks, Talon could bounce."

"I'll bounce you," Talon muttered.

Vola bit her lip, then grinned. "Yeah, you're right. Might be a nice retirement plan. But we've got a lot more trouble to get into before then."

THANK YOU FOR READING

Thank you so much for choosing to spend time with Vola, Sorrel, Lillie, and Talon. The Mishap's Heroes might be done (for now...) but if you enjoyed the misadventures of a group of unlikely heroes, you might also enjoy the Mark of the Least books, a series of fairytales featuring epic adventure, a little romance, and characters with disabilities and a whole lot of attitude. Check out By Winged Chair!

If you loved this book, consider leaving a review so other readers can find more stories about heroes who don't look like heroes but save the day anyway. And if you do, be sure to share it with me!

Visit me:
https://www.kendramerritt.com/

ACKNOWLEDGMENTS

I started out thinking I was writing something fun and light and hopefully hilarious. But it turns out I can't just write fluff. Meaning creeps in from the sides and makes its home between the lines. And then someone likes it, and I have to write more, and more meaning forces its way in, and suddenly it's a whole "thing." I blame these people:

First, the Kickstarter backers, for making all this possible. And for believing in the series before I'd ever sold a copy.

Mom and Dad, for reading every book ever. And always asking where the next one is.

Arielle, Betsy, and Alison, for being the first inspiration for a group of inept heroes who have no idea what they're doing and manage to save the day anyway.

Miranda and Lacey, for sisterhood which looks a lot like party dynamics sometimes.

Kevin and Andrew, for inviting me to play this little game called Dungeons & Dragons.

Kyle, Mary, Amy, Clark, Tim, Greg, Lauren, and Dave, and a host of other party members, for providing endless opportunities for inspiration. These books are all your fault.

Lucy Lin, for all the amazing cover art. I don't think anyone else could have brought Vola and the others to life the same way you did.

Fiona McLaren, for copy edits and flexibility. And for enjoying my humorous fantasy as much as my slightly more serious stuff.

Kristin James, for giving the series a voice. And for nailing every punchline, making me giggle uncontrollably.

And Josh and Abby, for endless support. Especially when I decided to launch a series the same month I was supposed to have a baby.

ABOUT THE AUTHOR

Books have been Kendra's escape for as long as she can remember. She used to hide fantasy novels behind her government textbook in high school, and she wrote most of her first novel during a semester of college algebra.

Kendra writes familiar stories from unfamiliar points of view, highlighting heroes with disabilities. Her own experience with partial paraplegia has shown her you don't have to be able to swing a sword to save the day.

When she's not writing she's reading, and when she's not reading she's playing video games.

She lives in Denver with her very tall husband, their book loving progeny, and a lazy black monster masquerading as a service dog.

Visit Kendra at
www.kendramerritt.com

facebook.com/kendramerrittauthor

goodreads.com/kendramerritt

instagram.com/kendramerrittauthor

tiktok.com/@kendramerrittauthor

www.ingramcontent.com/pod-product-compliance
Lightning Source LLC
Chambersburg PA
CBHW031433200726
48289CB00001BA/7